L.A. ROCK SCENE COMPLETE SERIES

THREE STEAMY INTERCONNECTED ROMANCES

L.A. ROCK SCENE

MELANIE A. SMITH

WICKED DREAMS PUBLISHING

Published by
WICKED DREAMS PUBLISHING
info@wickeddreamspublishing.com
Boise, ID USA

Cover design, editing, and formatting by Wicked Dreams Publishing

eBook ISBN: 978-1-952121-98-2
Paperback ISBN: 978-1-952121-93-7
Hardback ISBN: 978-1-952121-99-9

CONTENTS

EVERYBODY LIES

Content Warning 3
Playlist 5
Prologue — Frankie 7
1. Frankie 11
2. Julian 24
3. Frankie 25
4. Julian 31
5. Frankie 37
6. Julian 48
7. Frankie 63
8. Julian 72
9. Frankie 75
10. Frankie 81
11. Julian 94
12. Frankie 106
13. Frankie 118
14. Frankie 129
15. Frankie 138
16. Frankie 143
17. Julian 148
18. Frankie 162
19. Julian 174
20. Frankie 187
21. Julian 202
22. Frankie 211
23. Julian 220
24. Frankie 230
25. Julian 247
26. Frankie 255
27. Epilogue 268

FINDING HIS REDEMPTION

Content Warning 287
Chapter 1 289
Chapter 2 296
Chapter 3 304
Chapter 4 311
Chapter 5 318
Chapter 6 323
Chapter 7 327
Chapter 8 332
Chapter 9 340
Chapter 10 348
Chapter 11 358
Chapter 12 368
Chapter 13 379
Chapter 14 388
Chapter 15 396
Chapter 16 409
Chapter 17 414
Chapter 18 420
Chapter 19 426
Chapter 20 432
Chapter 21 436
Chapter 22 441
Chapter 23 447
Chapter 24 453
Chapter 25 458
Chapter 26 462
Chapter 27 469
Chapter 28 481
Epilogue 484

SECRETS, LIES, AND TEMPTATION

Content Warning 491
Playlist 493
1. Nils 495
2. Alexsis 500
3. Nils 505
4. Alexsis 509

5. Nils   515

6. Alexsis   523

7. Nils   527

8. Alexsis   532

9. Alexsis   536

10. Nils   549

11. Alexsis   554

12. Nils   559

13. Alexsis   568

14. Nils   576

15. Alexsis   583

16. Alexsis   592

17. Nils   600

18. Alexsis   609

19. Nils   624

20. Alexsis   630

21. Alexsis   642

22. Nils   650

23. Alexsis   657

24. Nils   664

Epilogue   673

Bonus Epilogue   678

Acknowledgments   687

About the Author   691

Books by Melanie A. Smith   693

EVERYBODY LIES

CONTENT WARNING

Everybody Lies is a psychic suspense romance novel that includes elements that might not be suitable for some readers, including the use of profanity, open-door sex scenes, and other potentially sensitive topics. Visit https://melanieasmithauthor.com/elcw.html for a full list (warning: may include spoilers).

PLAYLIST

To listen along, check out the *Everybody Lies Spotify Playlist*

For Those About to Rock by AC/DC
The Pretender by Foo Fighters
Wicked Garden by Stone Temple Pilots
Inside You by Stabbing Westward
Black by Pearl Jam
Push It by Garbage
She by Green Day
I Won't Back Down by Tom Petty and the Heartbreakers
Just Like Heaven by The Cure
Down in a Hole by Alice in Chains
Zero by The Smashing Pumpkins
Fell on Black Days by Soundgarden
Sabotage by Beastie Boys
Ænema by Tool
Terrible Lie by Nine Inch Nails

Lake of Fire by Nirvana
In the End by Linkin Park

PROLOGUE — FRANKIE

Dolly sits on the floor next to Pandy. They drink tea while I wait for Momma and Jack. Jack is Momma's new friend. Momma says he is a nice man, but I don't like him. He smells like cigarettes. And he brings me peppermint candies. I hate peppermint candies. Momma says it's because he likes me. But I know she's lying.

"Francesca, dinner is ready, come to the table, *now*," Momma calls from the kitchen.

I watch Momma and Jack carry plates to the table, so I get up. I wait for Jack to go back in the kitchen, then I sit down in my chair. The plastic is squishy and sticky under my bottom.

Momma and Jack bring the rest of the food and it's finally time to eat. Tea parties always make me hungry. Momma gives me a big spoon of the beef and noodles. *Stro-guh-noff.* I say it slowly and quietly to myself. Jack gives me a funny look. He's always giving me funny looks that Momma doesn't notice. Just like the kids at school.

"How was school today?" Momma asks me.

"My teacher says I'm the best reader she's ever seen in first grade," I answer proudly, happy that she finally asked. "She gave me a book called *Little Women*."

Momma looks like she doesn't believe me. "I think you probably misunderstood her. That book is far too advanced for you. You're only six."

I frown, unhappy that she thinks I'm not a good enough reader for *Little Women*. "But I've already read some of it, and I like it," I protest.

"Don't lie," Jack snaps at me. He's been mean before, but I don't like being called a liar, and I can't stop myself from saying something back this time.

"I'm *not* lying," I insist. I jump down from the chair to get the book from my backpack, so I can prove it.

"Francesca Marie, I did not give you permission to leave the table," Momma yells. I stop, knowing I'll be in big trouble if I don't.

"But Momma, I can show you —"

"I said, *sit down*," she insists. "I'm going to have a talk with your teacher tomorrow about age-appropriate books. You'll bring it to me after dinner. I won't have you reading it anymore."

"Oh please, Sam, she's *not* reading that book. She's obviously lying," Jack says again.

"I'm not a liar, you're a liar." The words come out of my mouth before I can stop them.

Momma's eyes go wide. Jack's face turns red, but she puts her hand up and I know she wants to talk instead.

"You apologize right now, young lady. You know better than to speak to an adult that way." Momma's voice is too quiet.

I know that quiet. But I'm still mad because I'm not lying. And I know Jack lied to her. And even though she told me never to use my gift to hurt people, I don't care right now.

"But he lied to you last week when you asked why he was gone so long. He wasn't taking out the garbage. *He* is the liar," I scream back.

Jack isn't red anymore. Now he's white. And that makes me happy because I know that means he's scared. Momma is quiet now. Jack looks at her.

"She's just a kid. She doesn't know what she's talking about." *Lie.* "You gonna let her talk to me like that?" Jack's voice sounds scared too. Because I told on him.

"Francesca, go to your room, please," Momma says softly but firmly.

I swallow hard and nod. I'm quiet as a mouse as I unstick myself from the chair and stand up.

"She doesn't know what she's talking about," Jack says again. *Lie.*

I back slowly into the living room.

"I *was* takin' out the garbage, just like you told me to. I just got sidetracked talkin' to Jimmy." *Lies.*

The little voice inside me always knows. Now that they can't see me anymore, I turn around and run to my bedroom. I close myself in my room and hide in my closet, hoping Momma isn't mad at me.

I listen to their muffled voices. They get louder. They yell for a long time. Then the front door slams and the pictures on the wall shake.

Finally, Momma comes. The closet door slides open and she sits on the floor next to me. She looks really mad.

"I'm sorry, Momma," I whisper. "I didn't mean to, it just came out."

"I know, and I'm glad you told me," she says, sounding very tired. "But you have to keep it to yourself. The things you know can cause trouble."

I don't understand. "You really didn't want to know that Jack lied to you?"

"That's not the point. If people know what you can do, you won't be safe anymore," she says.

"Why not?" I ask.

My mother brushes a long strand of my dark hair behind my ear. "Because they'll think you're a freak, Francesca," she says impatiently. "And we don't need that kind of attention. Besides, most people really don't want to know the truth anyway."

"But I always want to know the truth. How do you know what you should and shouldn't do if you don't know the truth?"

"You can never know the whole truth, Francesca. People lie on purpose, but they also lie by accident. And people lie to themselves. There is no such thing as just the truth," she explains. "I think you're old enough now to learn the only real truth. That everybody lies."

1
____

FRANKIE

The room is dimly lit. I stand against the wall, my feet shoulder-width apart, both hands on the gun that hangs loosely in front of me. My eyes scan the other side of the room through my lightly tinted glasses, watching the shadowy figures come and go. Waiting.

Finally, I catch sight of my target. I exhale as I confidently lift the weapon, aim, and fire. And I nail the motherfucker right between the eyes.

The lights snap back to full brightness abruptly. I holster my gun and pull my ear protection off.

"Dammit, Frankie, you're supposed to get him in the chest," Mac grumbles, coming out from behind the safety glass.

I shoot him a grin. "That's hardly a challenge," I scoff.

Mac scratches at his flaming red beard and scowls at me. "Don't be thick," he chides. "You're not a goddamn sniper — you're supposed to be learning defensive shooting. If this was in your little club it wouldn't be so easy. It'd be dark, loud, an' a whole hell of a lot harder to hit your target. Aim for the torso. Harder to miss and shoot some drunk fecker instead."

I can tell he's really annoyed, because his Irish brogue is thicker than usual. And I can't argue that he has a point. "Fine, fine," I reply. "Reset?"

We've been at it nearly two hours, but I can't help enjoying something I'm so damn good at.

Mac shakes his head. "Another day. I'm starved," he insists, rubbing his round belly.

"I guess I could eat," I allow. With a sigh I remove my safety glasses and pull out my hair band, letting my bright pink waves cascade back over my shoulders. I work my fingers through the roots at the back of my head, rubbing the tension from the spot as we pack it out of the range.

"Tacos?" Mac asks, climbing into his junky old pickup truck that's probably as old as he is. And that's saying something. You'd think for being such a successful guy he'd have a nicer set of wheels. But it's part of his charm, I suppose.

"You know me, I'll never say no to tacos," I agree as the old engine rumbles to life. "So who is the meeting with this afternoon?"

Mac stares straight ahead, navigating traffic on the backstreets. "New money. He wants in on the casino buyout."

"Ah. So you're not looking for my skills in wooing moneybags out of his cash. You want me to tell you if he's dirty."

Mac is one of the few people who knows about my ability. And only because I know he can keep his mouth shut.

"Got it in one," Mac agrees with a smirk. "You still sure you don't want in on the deal?"

I laugh. Mac is a persistent old bastard.

"I've got my hands full at Baltia, but thanks," I reply drily. I'm not sure why he even asked. He knows I live and breathe that club these days.

"Awww, come on, for old time's sake?" he presses.

I can't decide if he's teasing or not. "All my cash is tied up right now," I insist. "And that'd be one hell of a favor for old time's sake. Even for the return."

Mac mentored me toward my goal of owning a nightclub. Having more than thirty years' experience in almost every type of adult entertainment business that exists, from casinos to bars and nightclubs to strip clubs, he took me on as his assistant and trained me. A little too well, perhaps. I got out from under his wing as soon as I felt confident that I knew what I needed to in order to go for it. And while he taught me a lot, he expected more. I was his work horse for the better part of a decade. Not that I'm complaining, but I've already got enough on my plate.

"How is the club? You gonna be in the red at the end of year one?" he asks curiously.

I laugh. "Of course I am," I reply. "But I'll be making money hand over fist by the end of year two. Don't you worry."

"There you go getting cocky again," he warns with a shake of his head.

I press my lips together to suppress a smile. He's not wrong — I'm probably being overly confident. But then, I was a good student and I've done my homework. And the club is finally taking off, as per plan. The plan that's been ten years in the making. I think I've earned a little confidence.

THE MEETING IS QUICK, AND MAC'S INVESTOR WAS CLEAN. JUST A YOUNG, enthusiastic tech millionaire looking to diversify. Don't get me wrong, he dropped plenty of lies in the meeting, just nothing unusual. The same bullshit everyone spouts.

I go home to shower, change, and eat before heading to the club. It's a Saturday night, always our biggest night of the week, so I opt for something "club dressy" but still comfortable enough. If I've learned anything these last eight months, it's that running a nightclub is practically a sport, but one you have to look good while doing.

I opt for black pants with enough cling to be sexy, but plenty of give in case I need to kick some ass. Metaphorical ass, of course. We have bouncers who handle the other stuff.

My shiny purple, halter-neck corset-top is also both alluring and still holds everything in properly without being sweltering. I roll my long, pink locks up into a simple twist and pin it in place. The halter and hair-up combo has the bonus of showing off the half-sleeve tattoos on both of my arms that connect over my upper-back. A pair of black, four-inch platform boots adds to the dangerously hot look but also puts me at an even six feet tall. Perfect for seeing eye-to-eye with most males who might think they can intimidate me.

And I'm not just talking about patrons. Being a female nightclub owner who looks considerably younger than my thirty-four years with tattoos, piercings, and crazy colored hair, well, just about everybody challenges me at one point or another. My employees. My suppliers. The deejays, band managers, agents, dancers, and other entertainers. Everybody. It's why my two biggest hobbies are boxing and shooting. You can't be too careful or too prepared, I say.

As soon as I'm inside, everything else falls away as it always does, and I've got my game face on. It's three hours until doors open at ten p.m., but most of the crew is already bustling around, getting everything ready for the night. Bartenders are checking stock, the cleaning team is working on the floors and bathrooms, and Ace, my stage manager, is talking to who I presume to be the band manager for tonight's act.

I watch everyone from next to the coat check for a minute, admiring the scene. This club was dying when I bought it, and I've worked my ass off to bring it back to life. It took forever to clean up all the old concert posters on the wall with fill-ins and a coat of lacquer, making it look less like a fading rock club and more like a purposely styled, modern tribute to the club's history. The old wood paneling was replaced with a sleek, gothic print wallpaper with dark, heavy curtains at the entrances to match. The old bar to the left of the entrance was completely ripped out, allowing us to fill the whole wall with a streamlined, steel designed bar-front onto which we could project any number of shapes, colors, and images throughout the night. The bar-height tables and chairs spanning the deck across the front of the club were all replaced with a similar design to the look of the bar itself.

But the sunken dance floor behind the seating area was simply refinished, its dark wood polished of scuffs, and it gleams with a new sheen. The stage at the back of the venue was also mostly just spruced up. I didn't want to kill what had made this club famous in the first place. The acts that have played here over the years are legendary. Every nick and dent on the stage are commemorations of their collective performances. Thankfully we've managed to keep the interest of some of the hottest bands around, blessedly smoothing the transition of ownership.

I spot my club manager, Nils, heading toward me from the hall on the other side of the bar that leads to the back offices. The tall, lanky Swede swaggers across the floor like he owns it. A former runway model, I think he just can't help it. But his good looks and charm are the shiny outside. Inside, he's a shrewd and precise club-managing machine. I wouldn't have survived this long without him.

"Mr. Larsson," I greet him in mock formality.

He does approving elevator eyes over me as he approaches. I return the favor. His fitted, designer black slacks and black button-front shirt are perfectly tailored. His shirt is unbuttoned just enough to show off his hairless, sculpted chest but doesn't give away *too* much. And his patterned dress shoes probably cost more than my entire outfit. He is, undoubtedly, ridiculously hot. Though far too much of a pretty boy to be my type. Which is yet another reason he was the best pick for the job.

"Ms. Greco," he retorts in a saucy tone, leaning in to kiss me on the cheek, and as usual I note that he smells better than most women I know. His shoulder-length blond hair tickles my collarbone as he pulls away.

I tip my head toward Ace, who is standing on stage with his hands in his pockets, looking at his shoes while the guy he's talking to gesticulates wildly. I can't tell from here if Ace is upset or not.

"What's going on there?" I ask curiously.

Nils gives the pair a glance and shakes his head. "That's Nick Pappas. He manages a bunch of acts we'll be hosting. I understand he used to do business with the previous owners as well. He's a real piece of work."

"Aren't they all?" I ask with a sigh. "Do I need to step in?"

Nils shrugs nonchalantly. "Couldn't hurt."

I give him a smirk, because his reserved, Swedish politeness always cracks me up. And I really know that's Nils-speak for, "Yes, please, go schmooze so I don't have to be the one to brown-nose this guy."

I check my makeup in the mirrored bar behind Nils's back and am pleased that I can see the smoky eye and bright red lip that are my go-to are still perfectly done. Heading down the stairs, I can feel Nils's eyes on my back. I assume he must have had it out with Mr. Pappas already, because he's clearly very interested in how I do with him.

Ace looks up as I approach, relief blossoming over his face. Since Mr. Pappas's back is to me, he doesn't notice as I hop the step up to the elevated platform. He is still gesturing wildly as he babbles.

"Gentlemen," I interrupt. "How are things going?"

Ace looks like he could kiss me, and I press my lips together, so I don't laugh. Mr. Pappas finally stops talking and spins around. Short and dark, his olive skin is greasy, and his suit is cheap.

"I think we have a misunderstanding about the —" Ace is cut off by Mr. Pappas whipping back around and glaring him into submission. But then, Ace is a go-with-the-flow guy, not really into confrontation. His grungy jeans, seventies band T-shirts, and hippie vibe certainly speak to that. He's great with the musicians. But stuck-up assholes like this guy don't really show him much respect, unfortunately.

"What junior over here isn't getting, is that I *specifically* requested separate restroom facilities for my guys. Now, you've done this before, and I don't understand what the goddamn problem is," Mr. Pappas spits. He looks me up and down. "Why don't you go get your boss? I'm sure he can straighten this out."

I take a subtle breath in through my nose and let all the things I can't say run through my head quickly before I respond. *He's about five minutes younger than you, asshole; no you didn't; and no, we haven't.* My next thought, however, I can say.

"You're looking at her," I respond with a sweet smile, extending my hand. "Francesca Greco."

Mr. Pappas's jaw drops momentarily as he stares hard at my chest, but he recovers quickly, roughly grabbing my hand. His shake is overly firm, and I suppress the urge to roll my eyes.

"Well, good," he grumbles. "Yeah. It's, uh, nice to meet you." He drops my hand and rolls his shoulders, eyes still fixated on my breasts. "So about the facilities."

My mouth twitches as I suppress an annoyed sneer. "I understand the previous owners may have been able to provide that; however, with bringing things up to code, unfortunately those restrooms are now shared between my employees and the performers, leaving the restrooms on the other side of the building dedicated to customers," I explain. "I apologize for the inconvenience, but I assure you my employees will not get in the way of your client's use of the facilities."

If I thought that was going to placate him, I was sorely mistaken. He turns as red as my lipstick, looking me in the eyes for the first time, and I know this is going to take every ounce of charm I possess.

"I was promised *dedicated facilities*," he all but yells in my face. *Lie.*

I fight the urge to roll my eyes at the inner voice. I didn't really need it to know he's full of shit.

"Do you remember who promised you that?" I ask, still sweet.

He blinks hard. "Well, no, but —"

"Okay, did you get it in writing then?" I press.

He scowls. "Well, no, but —"

"And you do understand that we're legally required to comply with health and safety codes that govern the purpose and use of facilities as allowed by our permitting and inspections," I continue.

"Well, yes, but —"

"And I know you wouldn't want us to risk getting shut down because we were caught violating those codes, since my club manager tells me you have other acts booked here in the future," I reply.

His shoulders slump, and if he had a tail, it would be between his legs. "Of course not," he grumbles.

"Good, then we're in agreement that your client will use the same facilities as per usual, and our employees will do their best to stay out of their way," I say with a smile. I lay a hand on his arm. "I appreciate it, Mr. Pappas. Not everyone understands the long list of rules we have to follow. You must be very good at what you do, knowing so much about clubs and all."

In my head it's said in a much more sarcastic tone. But out loud I manage to sound sincere, or a good impression of it anyway, and it has the desired effect. He perks up and puffs out his chest a little and Ace's eyes go wide with mirth.

"Yeah, I do," Mr. Pappas replies. "I'm glad I could help." His eyes drop back down south of my face, and I know he's calmed down and the storm has passed.

"Good," I reply brightly. "Well, it was a pleasure to meet you, Mr. Pappas. Please be sure to let me know if there's anything else I can do to help. But right now I should check in with my manager to make sure our VIP area is set up for the band."

"Uh, yeah, yeah, it was good meeting you too," Mr. Pappas replies, clearly a little confused as to what just happened. He looks between Ace and me for a few seconds before shaking his head and going backstage.

Ace bursts into giggles. "Thanks, boss," he says between snorts.

One of the roadies looks up from setting up the drum kit. "That guy's a dick," he says in a low voice. "I'm glad you didn't let him push you around."

I shrug. "I've seen worse," I assure him. I turn back to Ace. "And next time come get me or Nils sooner, okay? Between Nils's charm and these tits, we have all the weapons we need to distract asstwats like that."

The roadie snorts and Ace offers an apologetic smile. I shake my head and wander off to find Nils to talk promoters.

By midnight I can barely hear myself think. The band is in full swing and the whole club is packed wall to wall. It's actually my favorite part of the night. Being a human lie detector makes one-on-one conversations exhausting and irritating after a while. But being alone is a special kind of torture for me too. Being in a crowd, though, is strangely soothing. The energy, the excitement, the mass of bodies moving to the same beat, with the same purpose. It invigorates me. Always has. I let my hips sway as I lean against the railing, longing to lose myself in the crowd below me as they rage to the intensity of the music. Being boss has its downsides.

But it's been a good night overall so far for the club, so I really can't complain. Great take at the door and from ticket presales, and that's not even accounting for alcohol sales yet. Very few fake IDs, no fights, no drunk people passed out in corners. Well, maybe one or two. But Nils is pretty good at getting the bouncers on things like that before I even notice.

I'm perched in the corner of the VIP balcony, reveling in the atmosphere and scanning the crowd when I see Nils making his way past the velvet ropes and up the stairs. He's clearly headed for me. I give him a questioning look as he approaches.

When he gets to me he leans his mouth to my ear. "Johnny says there's a guy at the bar asking about you."

I look up into his ice blue eyes and raise an eyebrow as if to say, *So? A lot of guys ask about me.* There had been a few articles and news pieces when I bought the club and in the following months as we renovated. Great press, but they'd brought out some weirdos. Nils just shakes his head and motions for me to follow him. This one must be different.

At the bottom of the stairs, Nils pushes me toward the bar before returning to his rounds. Confused, I slip behind the bar and tap Johnny on the shoulder. He holds up a finger letting me know he's finishing the order he's working on.

I look down the length of the bar trying to spot whoever could be asking after me. In case it's someone I actually do know. But since the bar covers the whole wall of the club, it's hard to see everyone vying for a place at the counter, trying to get the attention of one of the four bartenders on duty. Not to mention it's dark, loud, and I'm starting to lose steam ahead of the second wind I usually get around this time.

Johnny finishes up and pulls me by the hand through the service door into the private storage area behind the bar we use for the security monitors. The doors are heavy enough to muffle the sound so we can hear each other. Johnny grabs a bottle of water and slumps into a high-backed chair at the bank of monitors on the far wall displaying feeds from the various security cameras around the club.

"Nils told you there's a guy looking for you?" he checks. He leans his broad shoulders into the soft backrest.

Johnny's short, dark hair is sweaty, his collared dark blue polo shirt also slightly damp. I resist the urge to chastise him for sweating all over the chair. We all sweat buckets every night. It comes with the territory. So instead, I nod and take the chair next to him.

His dark eyes flick up to the farthest monitor, showing the opposite end of the bar than we'd been on. He puts his finger under a large, hulking guy seated at a stool pulled into the corner. "That guy."

I squint at the image. He looks big. Dark hair. Dark shirt. Lots of tattoos. But his head is bowed, his face hidden from the camera.

"He asked for me? What did he say that made you have Nils come get me?"

Johnny is usually my first line of fending off the creepers, so I'm curious why he thinks this one is legit.

"He didn't ask for you. Mentioned you is more like it. But he called you Frankie, and he's been sitting there all night like he's waiting for something," Johnny replies, finishing his bottle of water. "I'm gonna hit the head before I go back out. Cover me and put eyes on him. Dave knows what's up, just let him know before you go over there." Johnny gets up and heads toward the door on the opposite wall leading to the staff restrooms that had been the subject of heated debate earlier this evening.

"I need exact words, Johnny," I call after him, staring at the screen and trying to discern more about the mystery man.

"He said, 'This is a cool club. It's Frankie Greco's place, right?' That's it." Johnny disappears to the bathrooms.

Now I understand why it raised a flag. There are precious few people who call me Frankie. Mac, my best friend Emma, and my family. That's it. Nobody at the club calls me Frankie. None of the news outlets had either, I'm sure of that. Not that it's a super uncommon nickname for Francesca. But it's just enough to be odd, without being threatening, exactly. Only one way to find out who this guy is and what he wants. With a shake of my head I get back up, throw an apron on, and tuck a few escaped pink strands back into place.

Heading back through the door, I poke Dave as I pass him to work the opposite end of the bar. He barely looks up, but I see him nod and send Jess back down toward Johnny's area to cover. I pass the fourth bartender, Peter, and he barely acknowledges my passing as he struggles to keep up with the throng.

I focus on paring down the line that's formed in Johnny's absence. After serving half a dozen drinks there's a small lull, so I lean against the back of the bar nonchalantly and grab a bottle of water. I scan the bar as if I'm just checking on everyone. The guy is so tucked into the corner, he's the last thing I see. But this time I'm only ten feet away from him, so I get a good look. Or I would have, had our gazes not locked as soon as mine settled on him. His eyes are dark and intense, and I get the sense he's been watching me the whole time.

Unexpectedly, my breath catches in my throat and it's like someone stuffed cotton in my ears. All the noise around me drops into the background. I struggle to breathe, telling myself it's an adrenaline response. He's not "mainstream" handsome, but he's attractive in a way that makes my insides tighten nonetheless. He has dark hair that is short on the sides, but long and wild on top. His jaw is a little too square and has a significant five-o-clock shadow, his nose is perfectly straight, but his full mouth is crooked under it. His thick eyebrows are set over his big, dark eyes in a way that makes him look like he's laughing. But the muscled and tattooed arms that extend out of his short-sleeved black T-shirt are no joke. And I wish I could say I'd seen him before, but there's not even a hint of recognition. Well, beyond my body recognizing that it would like to see more of that perfect physique hinted at under his tight-fitting shirt.

Before it can be classified as gawking, I stroll over to him, pretending to respond to his look as if he were asking for service. *Oh, I'd be glad to service him all right.* I can't help the thought, but I internally chastise myself for it anyway. I've never fucked a customer, and I don't plan to start with my dark, alluring, and potentially creepy stalker.

I lean in and use my carefully practiced bartender-in-a-loud-club voice. "Need anything?" I ask as casually as I can.

One of his eyebrows flicks up and he smirks, pointing at the empty beer bottle in his hand. The look is so ridiculously sexy that a flush creeps through me. I swallow hard and nod, taking the empty bottle from him. I reach behind me into the cooler and grab a new one, removing the cap as he watches before handing it to him.

He tosses a bill on the counter as he accepts the beer and takes a long pull. I pocket the cash and give him change. And before things pick up again, I decide to just go for it.

"I heard you're looking for Frankie Greco."

He sets his beer down and chuckles. "That's some grapevine you've got here."

His voice is deep and luscious and it sends shivers down my spine. God, why am I reacting to him this way? Down, girl. It's not like there aren't heaps of gorgeous men in here every night. Thankfully, I've had a lot of practice on my poker face, so I shrug in response, not wavering. He gives me an appraising look.

"You're her?" he asks skeptically, raising one of his thick brows.

I raise my eyebrow right back. "Maybe. You a friend of Mac's?"

He's the only one I can think of that might send this slab of a man into my club asking after Frankie Greco. But it's also bait.

"Yeah, Mac mentioned this was your place," he replies casually. *Lie.*

The familiar internal voice is like a punch in the gut, even though I was expecting it.

"Try again," I say tightly.

His eyes grow hard and he gives me a look somewhere between cautious and ravenous. But before he can respond I'm distracted by a wave of frat boys asking for shots. When I glance back at the corner, a lone twenty-dollar bill sits on the counter and the mystery man is gone.

2

———

JULIAN

Fuck. That round ass, come-fuck-me pink hair, and those gorgeous red lips that I can't stop thinking about having wrapped around my cock completely distracted me. And when those velvety blue eyes locked on me, I swear I almost came in my fucking pants. Control is practically my middle name, and I'm not some wet-behind-the-ears kid looking for a quick fuck in a dirty club bathroom. But fuck me if I couldn't breathe properly from that moment on.

Much less think and work the situation like I usually would. Because there was no guessing the most alluring woman I'd ever locked eyes on owned the fucking club. And it made me sloppy. I should've known not to show my hand. I'm normally much more subtle than that. I have to be. It's my job. She's just a job.

I'm totally fucked.

3

———————

FRANKIE

When I finally climb out of bed early the next afternoon, something about the encounter with the mystery man has me riled up far more than it probably should. My whole body feels restless in a way that the physical exertion of the night should've quashed. Unfortunately, Mac is unreachable on Sundays, rising early to hoof it out of the area to places that are beyond isolated so he can fish in peace. Meaning I can't even check in with him until tomorrow on the off chance he actually does know who this guy is.

I wander around my tiny Santa Monica apartment totally on edge. I contemplate going for a run, but while I'm mentally worked up, I'm not really in the mood for physical exertion. Suddenly, I have the urge to do something drastic.

I grab my phone off the counter and place the call before I can over-think it.

"Hey darlin', what's the haps?" Emma greets me.

"Hey babes," I reply hurriedly. "Got time for a chat this afternoon?"

"A chat and …" Emma trails off, knowing there's more.

"A dye?" I admit.

Emma laughs. "About time. You've been pink almost two months. What are we doing? Back to blue?"

"I was thinking my natural color," I respond.

"Wow, really? Do you even know what your natural color is anymore?" she jokes.

"Ha. Ha. Ha," I snip drily. "Can you take me to a four? That should be close enough."

"Sure can. Gimme an hour and be ready to pay me in pizza."

"Thanks, babes," I reply. "I wasn't kidding about the chat though."

"And I wasn't kidding about the pizza," Emma shoots back.

IN EMMA TIME AN HOUR MEANS TWO. SO IMAGINE MY SURPRISE WHEN AN hour and fifteen minutes later she appears.

"Whoa," I say, answering the door. "You're early."

Her hands are full of supplies, so she pushes me out of the way with a round hip. "Oh please, I'm not that bad," she gripes as she goes through the open bathroom door just off the living room and plops her stuff down.

I close the front door and head back to the living room to sink into my favorite squishy chair. "Yes, you are," I tease. "You were almost two hours late *to your own wedding*."

She emerges, hands on her hips, glaring at me. Her naturally pale-blond hair is pulled up in a tight bun and she is, as usual, wearing far too much makeup on top of an insanely gaudy pink, sequined romper. She's outrageous in every sense of the word, and it's one of my favorite things about her. We've been best friends since we were six and I love her to death.

"Doesn't count," she replies, folding her arms over her ample chest. "You can do whatever you want on your wedding day."

I raise my hands in defeat. "Peace," I say with a grin. "Now are we gonna do this or what?" I rise from the chair.

"Someone's in a hurry," she remarks. "What crawled up your butt today? Rough night at the club?"

I press my lips together. I may know when people are lying, but Emma Martin has the most finely honed intuition on the planet.

"I wouldn't say rough," I hedge. "It was a good night overall, actually."

She looks at me expectantly. "But?" She puts her hands back on her hips.

"Some guy came in asking for me," I respond, grabbing a dining room chair and hauling it into the bathroom.

She follows me in. "You're going to make me pull this out of you, aren't you?" she teases.

I sit in the chair with a sigh, knowing it'll trigger her to start on my hair. And I'm not disappointed as she starts brushing it out. "No," I finally reply. "I guess I just don't know what to make of it."

As she sections my hair and mixes the dye, I fill her in on everything surrounding the mystery man. She's started slathering my hair with the smelly cream by the time I'm done.

"So you're what, mad that the hottie got away?" she asks. "Or worried that he's a stalker ax murderer?"

I laugh. "Both, maybe?" I admit. "I don't know. Something about the whole thing really bothered me."

Emma's nostrils flare, a sure sign that she's trying not to laugh at me. "I bet."

"What's that mean?" I gripe.

She catches my eye in the mirror and grins. "It means you need to get laid, Frankie. How long has it been?"

I try to do the math in my head but can't even remember enough to recall specifically. At the very least the better part of a year. "A long time," I allow. "But that's not what this was."

"Mhm," she hums dismissively. "So what are you gonna do about it? Are we dyeing your hair so he doesn't recognize you while *you* turn stalker on *him*?"

"I don't think I could stalk him even if I wanted to. I don't even know the guy's name."

"Did he use a credit card?" she asks.

"Nope. Cash."

"Fuck. Well, that doesn't give you much to go on," she admits.

"I'll ask Mac about it tomorrow. But I'm pretty sure he wouldn't send some guy I've never met into my club without giving me the heads-up. He hasn't been shy about trying to get his friends VIP service in the past, anyway," I say.

"Well, I hope you find him one way or the other," she replies, tucking my last, soaked strand of hair under a cap. "Because at the very least I wouldn't mind the eye candy."

"You've only been married a year and a half. Ben not doing it for you anymore?" I tease her.

She pinches my arm as she goes around me to throw out her gloves and wash her hands. "I have no complaints in the bedroom, thank you very much," she replies haughtily. "But that doesn't mean I can't appreciate a big, fine man."

"You're incorrigible," I respond, removing the towel from around my shoulders.

She snaps the hand towel she was using at my ass as I exit the bathroom and it stings my cheeks through my thin leggings. "Less talking, more ordering pizza," she demands.

THE FOOD ARRIVES RIGHT AS MY HAIR IS READY TO BE RINSED, SO IT'S A few minutes before we can get our hands on the hot, cheesy slices. By the time we do, we chow down quickly, both of us clearly starved.

When we've finished eating, Emma catches me up on all the latest salon gossip as she dries and styles my hair into long, loose waves. Most of it is about minor celebrities I couldn't care less about, but I know she enjoys it so I just let her talk. She doesn't stay long after, excusing herself as she needs to get home to "make dinner." Said with a wink that I didn't need, considering we'd just eaten.

Trying not to think about all the action Emma's getting that I'm not, I spend a while looking in the mirror. I barely recognize myself without a crazy hair color. It's been years since I was anywhere near my natural dark brown shade. Even with the nose piercing, numerous ear piercings, and tattoos, it makes me look more businesslike. So, you know, there's that at least. But it's still going to take some getting used to. I'm still not sure why I did it, exactly. I just get impulses like that sometimes and completely switch directions.

I throw on a simple, tailored pair of black slacks and a shimmering, loose red halter with some red stilettos. And, of course, my signature red lip to match.

There's a charity function at the club tonight, so it won't be an extended affair, just a few hours, tops. Though it should be entertaining, with a burlesque show on stage and a silent auction, the proceeds of which will go to an Alzheimer's research fund. Nils has already told me he has it handled, but I figure it's best to put in an appearance anyway.

I ARRIVE AN HOUR AHEAD OF THE PRESHOW COCKTAIL HOUR, AND everything is pretty much ready to go, Nils being the miracle worker that he is. I steal one of the canapés and disappear back to my office. On the way, Jess flags me down from the bar.

"Ms. Greco?" she says as she approaches, staring openly at my lack of pink hair. "Someone stopped by for you this afternoon."

My heart pounds in my chest. *Could it be him?* I clear my throat. "Oh? Did they leave a message?" I ask evenly.

Jess shakes her head, her blond curls bouncing. "No, it was the guy from last night. He said he wanted to apologize for something? But he didn't leave a name or a number or anything."

My stomach fills with butterflies. He did come back. But why leave in the first place then?

"Did he say if he'd come back?" I press.

She shrugs. "He saw there was something going on tonight. I told him it was a private event and he left."

A frown creases my face. "That's all?"

Jess shrugs. "Yeah. I was a little, uh, surprised. He's um …" She trails off and blushes furiously.

"Yes, he's quite attractive, I'm aware," I reply drily. "Well, thank you for letting me know."

Jess nods and scurries off to continue prep. And I do my best to press on with my duties.

FOUR HOURS, A SAUCY BURLESQUE SHOW, AND A SMASHING SUCCESS OF AN auction later, I've seen the last employee out before I think about the mystery man again. I try not to feel disappointed at missing him stopping by as I lock up. Though knowing tracking him down will be nigh impossible leaves me feeling something I don't think I should be feeling. Especially not about a weird, overly familiar stranger that appears and disappears at the drop of a hat.

I climb into my cherry red convertible, a true American classic and one of the few luxuries I've allowed myself, and head home in the cool night air.

It takes me a while to get to sleep. And not just because I'm going to bed before four a.m. for once. My biggest problem is every time I close my eyes, I remember locking eyes with Mr. Mysterious and the shot of heat that ripped through me. Needless to say, it's not the kind of thing that's conducive to sleep.

4

<hr>

JULIAN

My fuck-up didn't go over well with the boss. So here I stand, again, in front of the bombshell's club, *nervous*. Again. I don't do nervous. It makes me fucking angry. I'm the one who makes people nervous, not the other way around. But I have only myself to blame. And she's just a woman. Mesmerizing, hot, and tough as nails. Gah. *Get your shit together, you fucking pussy.*

My eyes flick up to the black dome over the door. Fuck all. I'm being recorded. Realizing I'm only making it worse the longer I stand here, I man up and push the service bell. And I say a prayer that nobody is here. Then I can go back and say I tried without having to put my big dumb foot in my mouth again. Or better still, without having to do what I was sent here to do.

Just when I'm about to give up and leave, the speaker above the button crackles to life.

"Can I help you?" a woman asks, barely cutting through static. I can't tell if it's the same blond dingbat bartender I got before or Frankie herself.

"Yeah, is Frankie Greco around?" I shove my hands in my pockets self-consciously.

"Do you have an appointment?" she asks.

I scrunch my eyebrows together. Seriously? It's Monday fucking morning. What, did I interrupt this broad doing her nails or something? I seriously hope this isn't the goddess I'd laid eyes on before, or the illusion is ruined. Or, maybe I *should* hope for that. It would definitely make this easier if she was a bitch.

"No," I reply, trying not to sound irritated.

"Then I'm afraid Ms. Greco won't be able to see you today."

"This is ridiculous," I spit out before I can stop myself. "I just need a minute."

Seconds later I hear the door unlatch. It swings out just enough for a dark head to pop through. I do a double take, realizing it's Frankie, pink hair replaced by a deep brown that doesn't make me want to grip it by the base of her neck as I fuck her any less. I banish the thought and fix my face to a neutral expression.

Reluctantly, she steps out. She's got a hand behind her back and I instinctively stiffen before I realize why. I'm freaking her out. It might be the middle of the day, but she's a woman. Possibly alone in a club in a neighborhood that's sketchy at best. And while she's a tall chick who clearly has enough attitude to handle herself, I get it.

And even if she's got a gun, I'm not particularly worried. So I do my best to put her at ease, leaning casually against the doorframe and shooting her my best disarming smile.

"You changed your hair," I remark. "And you're tall for a girl."

Her dark blue eyes that clearly miss nothing sweep over me, sending chills down my spine.

"And you're just tall," she replies impatiently. "What are you doing here?"

There's that attitude. I like it. A little too much. I push myself up so I'm hovering over her. She freezes, so I hold back a little, eyeing her carefully to determine whether its fear or attraction that has her rooted to the spot.

My eyes trail down the shooting stars swirling down her shoulders, but I stop myself short of staring at her tits.

"I wanted to apologize for the other night," I reply with my carefully rehearsed line. "But maybe that was stupid. It just occurred to me that you probably see a million guys every night and you probably don't even remember me."

She glares at me shrewdly. "Then why would you bother coming back to apologize?" she challenges.

I can't help but laugh. This chick isn't about to fall for anything. I slide my hands into my pockets, feigning embarrassment. "I realized that night I might have been creeping you out, so I just left," I say honestly. "But then I felt like an asshole. I tried to just forget about it, but I couldn't. So yeah. I'm sorry if I creeped you out, and I'm sorry that I left so quickly. And now I'm rambling." I snap my mouth shut and she rewards me with a smile. Those full fucking lips turning up wake the sleeping beast between my legs.

"That still doesn't explain why you were looking for me in the first place," she points out.

I consider her carefully for a moment. "I knew of a Frankie Greco once. I thought you might be her."

She stares back like she's waiting for something. After a few beats, she narrows her eyes at me.

"Well?" she prompts.

Fuck, she's a tough nut. Time to give her back the upper hand. I shake my head and start backing away.

"This was a mistake," I mutter. "I should go."

I start to turn, definitely not wanting to go, but needing to play this just right. I'm rewarded when I feel a cool, silken hand slide over my forearm. I turn back, my eyes locking on hers as she grabs me, and I swear to the fucking Almighty my heart jumps in my chest. Like she felt it, Frankie sucks in a sharp breath and pulls her hand back. I try to shake it off, and hurry to regain composure so I can reel her back in.

"Apology accepted," she says, beating me to it. "But I don't even know your name."

My eyes sweep over her beautiful, guarded face, and something inside me wants to spill my guts, to really know her and let her know me. But that's the last thing I should do, for so many reasons. Instead, I extend my hand and offer the simplest answer possible.

"I'm Julian."

She slides her soft hand into mine and squeezes. It does things to me. Primal things.

"It's nice to meet you, Julian," she replies somewhat breathlessly. "But just so you know, I prefer to be called Francesca."

I cock my head to the side. "Really?" I ask skeptically. And not just because I was sent after *Frankie* Greco, but because the nickname suits her. Francesca seems too stuffy for a chick like her.

She gives me a funny look. "Look, I don't know you. *Frankie* is just a little too familiar for me. I'm weird like that," she replies defensively. She pulls her hand out of mine. Her eyes blaze a path down my face, over my chest and arms, to the hand she just dropped. Her face is red and she's breathing heavily.

She fucking wants me. Dammit. Unfortunately for her, that works to my advantage.

I give her a knowing smirk that makes her blush deepen. "It's not weird," I reply soothingly. "I'm the nutjob who can't stop showing up. It's not like you know me at all."

She starts to chew on her lip, and my eyes can't help watching. I clench my jaw, willing the thoughts forming back.

"Then maybe I should get to know you," she offers encouragingly, her stance loosening.

I flinch at the vulnerability in her voice and her eyes. I can't do this to her.

"As much as I'd like that, I don't think it's a good idea," I reply. Fuck,

fuck, fuck all. I'm going to be in trouble for this. What is it about this chick that makes me lose all sense? Fuck.

"Have it your way," she replies with a shrug that's so carefully indifferent it betrays her deep annoyance. "If we're done here, I'll be getting back to work. Thanks for the apology."

My mind scrambles, knowing I can't let her go that easily. But totally seeing how erratic my behavior is. Though I think it's obvious to both of us that I'm just as attracted to her as she is to me. I both want to stay and don't. Ultimately, I remember I don't have a choice.

She starts to open the heavy door, and I close the small gap between us and slam my hand against the door, blocking her retreat. She whirls around, and I stare down at her, her face so much closer to mine than I'd anticipated.

A primal heat passes between us. And she smells so fucking good. Like strawberries, and mint, and the salty ocean air. My fucking mouth is watering thinking about consuming every inch of her delectably curvy body.

"It's not a good idea," I repeat, "but I don't think I'm going to be able to stay away from you, either." As soon as I say it, I realize it's true. Fuck.

She takes a deep breath through her nose and looks down at her feet, and for a moment I think I've lost her.

"I'm surprisingly okay with that," she says softly. Her head tilts back up, her dark tresses tumbling back over her shoulders.

I. Am. So. Fucked.

I slip my free hand under her chin, looking deep into her eyes. I slide a thumb lightly across her luscious bottom lip.

"Okay." My voice is low and husky, betraying me. "Have dinner with me."

"That didn't sound like a question," she points out with a smile. "But all right. I'll meet you at the diner," she points to the one across the street, "at six."

I drop my arms back to my sides. "I'll see you soon, then," I promise, backing away slowly and keeping eye contact.

She makes a small noise of assent and slips back into the building quickly. I turn away to walk off whatever the fuck just happened. And I wonder how the fuck I'm going to handle what comes next.

5

FRANKIE

I'm back in my office, head in my hands, convinced I've made a huge mistake when Nils shows up. The moment he walks in the office and sees me, he turns around and leaves. He's only gone a minute, returning with two old-fashioned glasses and a chilled bottle of top-shelf vodka.

He sits across the desk from me and fills both glasses nearly halfway. He slides one across the desk to me.

"Drink," he commands. "And talk." Then he reclines his tall, lean frame in the chair, looking at me expectantly.

I look up at him for a moment before lifting the glass to my lips. The freezing liquid goes down with little sting. I would have preferred whiskey. There's nothing like its bold flavor and strong burn to remind you that you're alive. And then quickly dull that feeling.

Nils and I have shared a lot, but mostly only about work. That's not to say we don't get along personally — there just isn't usually a lot of time for it. I decide it's better to tell him what's going on, at least enough of it anyway so he doesn't think I'm hiding something about the business.

"It's not about the club," I assure him.

He leans forward, spinning his glass thoughtfully in his long, slender fingers. Finally, he looks up at me. "Francesca, I think you are an amazing woman. And I know you like to focus on things here, but we all have personal issues that we need to talk about sometimes," he says calmly. "And I'm here for you."

I roll my lips through my teeth. "Thanks, Nils," I reply. "I appreciate that. I feel the same way, you know."

He smiles vaguely and waves a hand, encouraging me to talk. And to my surprise, I don't just give him the high level. I completely spill my guts. I tell him about the first conversation with Julian after Nils had directed me to the bar. I tell him about the missed visit at the charity event. And finally about the conversation today. About the date I'm supposed to go on in just a couple of hours with the most confusing and alluring man I've ever met.

When I'm done Nils lets out a deep sigh. "Well, you're obviously into this guy, so you must have decided he's not crazy. And you have good judgement, Francesca. So why the deer-in-headlights look?" he asks bluntly.

"I just feel like he's not giving me the full story. And it's not like I have a lot of time for dating right now," I say with a sigh. I don't admit that I don't trust my assessment of this guy, as I'm far too distracted by him physically to think clearly. Even though he never out-and-out lied, he was all over the map, and I couldn't get a good read on why.

Nils laughs. "You're too hands-on here. You make my job too easy," he teases me. "Live a little. Go get laid. Nobody ever offers up their full story right away. Get to know him. See if you even care about his story. And even if you decide you don't, he's clearly got other things you need right now." He looks down into his drink momentarily before downing the remaining liquid and rising from his chair. The man can certainly hold his liquor. Another reason he makes an excellent nightclub manager.

"Thanks, Nils," I say to his retreating back. I'm flooded with grateful-ness. This is one of the things I like best about Nils. He doesn't mince words, and I can always count on him for an honest opinion.

He stops at the door and turns back to look at me. "You're welcome," he says. "Stop thinking so much."

I snort a laugh as he closes the door behind him. And I take another sip of my drink. If nothing else, a little more liquid courage won't hurt.

A FEW MINUTES AHEAD OF OUR DATE, I HEAD OUT OF THE CLUB AND TO THE diner. As I stride purposefully across the road, I decide Nils is right. I need to stop thinking so much. I work way too damn hard, and this could be good for me. Even if it's just a physical release.

I stride into the diner and spot Julian at a booth in the back. He is staring intently down at his menu and doesn't notice my approach. He's still wearing the fitted navy polo shirt he had on earlier. The one that I couldn't stop ogling him in. But he's switched into nicer jeans and his hair also looks like it has been more carefully styled. The click of my heels on the linoleum alerts him to my approach and his dark eyes snap up.

He slides out of the booth, standing to greet me. It makes me blush, and I stop at the table, feeling like an awkward teenager rather than an experienced woman in her thirties.

"You cleaned up," I remark with a teasing note in my voice. And I notice the shirt is unbuttoned at the top, revealing more tattoos on his chest. My eyes lift back to his and he's raised an eyebrow, that look of near-laughter playing around his eyes and mouth.

"Sure, yeah, I guess. I live close by," he offers as explanation, gesturing for me to have a seat.

I self-consciously adjust my green tank top and slide into the booth as he reseats himself across from me. "Well, that's convenient," I murmur. "Do you come here often then?"

He smirks unreservedly now. "Is that your best line?" he teases in a husky voice that sends a shiver down my spine.

"I don't do lines," I reply honestly.

He bites his bottom lip, but it doesn't keep the smile from pulling at his mouth. "That's refreshing. I don't, either."

"So what do you do?" I ask curiously. "Since you already know I run a nightclub, it seems only fair that I know what you do for a living."

Julian's eyes tighten and he looks like he might not respond for a moment. "I'm a headhunter," he finally replies, albeit somewhat reluctantly.

"So you lure people away from their jobs to go work somewhere else?" I ask. My tone is slightly teasing. I've got nothing against the practice, but it's not really the kind of job I pictured him doing. Maybe a mechanic. Or a construction worker. Anything that uses those big, strong hands and muscles of his.

He tilts his head to the side and narrows his eyes slightly. "Is there something wrong with that line of work?"

"Of course not," I backtrack. "What kind of businesses do you work with?"

"The kind that like discretion," he replies, leaning back in his seat and looking away.

I press my lips together to disguise my annoyance at his non-answer. "That's vague," I respond.

He looks back at me and laughs, and it lights up his whole face. And I melt just a little bit.

Just then Heather, the perky blond waitress who always works weekday evenings, stops by our table, eyeing Julian a little too openly.

"Hi, what can I get for you?" she asks, chewing on the end of her pen in an attempt at seduction.

Julian's eyebrows scrunch together, and he gives me a look. "Ladies first," he says to me with a gesture.

The pen slides out of her mouth and she turns to me with a heavy sigh. *Geez, dramatic much, lady?*

I give her the sweetest smile I can muster. "I'll have a club sandwich and fries," I say, batting my eyelashes at her.

"Anything else?" she asks dully.

And I just can't help it. "Yes, how about a verse of 'Killing Me Softly'?" I joke.

She stares at me like I've grown a second head and Julian busts up laughing.

"Just some iced tea, please," I tell her.

She turns to Julian as fast as she can manage and her whole demeanor changes, the pen finding its way back between her lips.

"I'll have what she's having," he says as he catches his breath from laughing.

She looks a little disappointed she didn't get to engage him more. She leans in ever so slightly and drops her voice. "Okay, is there anything *else* I can get for you?"

Christ, even I can see her cleavage from here. Julian catches my eye and holds it.

"No, thanks," he says firmly, keeping his eyes on me until she leaves.

"Wow," I mutter as she walks away, letting her hips sway in a far too exaggerated way.

"Yeah," he agrees. "I think she was a little young to get your reference. And a little oblivious to get that she was being disrespectful."

"Oh, I think she knew, she just didn't care," I reply, referring to the latter. "But you got the reference. Two points."

"Oh, really? And what are points worth?" he asks curiously, with a hungry glint in his eye.

"I'm afraid you don't get to hear about the points system until the third date," I tease him, finally relaxing into the conversation.

"Third date, huh?" he asks with a wink and a cheeky grin.

"Mhm," I murmur, blushing.

He leans back into the blue upholstered bench and slings his arm over the back of it, his muscles rippling distractingly. He runs the tip of his tongue over the inside of his top lip. Distraction turns into a lump in my throat, and suddenly I have a deep-seated need to run my tongue over his mouth, his perfect fucking chest, those arms. I take a deep breath and still myself.

"You're something else, Greco," he murmurs, his eyes dancing with amusement.

"Yeah? Why's that?" I ask.

"I never know what you're going to say," he replies seriously.

"Is that a good thing?"

He considers me for a moment, scrubbing a hand over the stubble on his chin. "It's fascinating," he finally replies with a small, crooked smile.

I shift uncomfortably in my seat, staring at him for a moment trying to figure out why I feel so awkward, when it hits me. I'm torn between my intense attraction to him and waiting for him to drop a lie. I realize how unfair that is and refocus on getting to know him. Because that doesn't mean I have to trust him. But I won't ever get there if I don't give him a chance.

Even so, there is still a question I want to ask him. I can't bring myself to form the words, though.

"You look like you just got caught with your hand in the cookie jar," Julian teases, leaning forward. "Care to tell me why?"

I decide to go for it and ask him about what he said outside the club earlier today. "Why isn't it a good idea for me to get to know you? Are you married or something? Gay? Escaped from a mental institution?" I try to keep my tone light.

He runs a hand through the long hair slicked back on the top of his head and it musses it back toward the wild, sexy mess it was when I first saw him.

"See, that right there is exactly what I meant. I wasn't expecting that," he replies, sighing heavily. His eyes flick back up to mine. "Not married. No girlfriend, either. And I think we both know I'm not gay." He gives me a long look full of promise and desire.

I look down, blushing, focusing on the tattoos winding around his wrist, words that I can't quite make out at this angle. It makes me wonder how much of his gorgeous body the tattoos cover.

"So mental institution escapee," I murmur, imagining tracing the lines on his arms with my fingertips. Or my tongue.

He huffs a laugh that snaps me back to reality and I look back up into his face. "No. It's just given my commitments, I shouldn't be trying to date you."

"And yet here we are," I reply softly.

Julian stares at me thoughtfully and I stare back unflinchingly. The attraction hums between us again. It's like nothing I've ever experienced. I just want to touch the man. And it's not like I can fault him for being too busy to date. I'd just voiced the same reasoning to Nils.

Waitress Heather chooses that moment to appear with our food, breaking the tension of the moment. She flirts with Julian the whole time, continuing to ignore me as she asks what else she can do for him, with heavy undertones that suggest she'd suck his dick under the table if that's what he wanted. It's all I can do to keep my mouth shut, and he brushes her off politely until we're alone once more.

"You know, I don't exactly have a lot of time for this sort of thing, either," I finally admit after we've both started in on our meals in silence. I look down into my plate, playing with a fry. "So maybe we just keep this casual."

Julian wipes his mouth with a napkin and sets it down on the table. "Really? Or is that just one of those things women say when they're afraid a guy is going to dick them around?" he asks matter-of-factly.

It makes me laugh loudly enough to catch the attention of the few people in the restaurant. "Yes, probably," I agree.

He stares at me unflinchingly. "I don't want to do that," he says.

I push my plate away and lean back. No internal voice clueing me in on a lie. So he doesn't *intend* to do that. But that doesn't mean he won't. I decide it doesn't matter, and I say so. It makes him laugh, and if I wasn't so confused I'd appreciate once again how gorgeous he is when he laughs.

Either way, it breaks the tension that had been building and I take the opportunity to change the subject. We spend a good, long while talking about other, less serious things, ignoring the dirty looks our waitress shoots us as dinner turns into dessert, which turns into coffee, until it's getting so late that I finally notice it's pitch black outside. I glance at my phone finally, noting it's after ten p.m.

"Holy shit," I gasp, showing Julian the time. "I didn't mean to keep you so long."

He laughs, his deep, rumbly laugh that shoots straight to my core and curls my toes. "I can't say I mind," he replies. "But I should get home. I do have to work tomorrow. You know, in the morning. We don't all run night-clubs." He winks at me and rises out of the booth, extending his hand to me. "I'll walk you to your car."

I suck my bottom lip between my teeth to suppress the huge grin threatening to break across my face. Despite my initial reservations, it was an amazing date. And we click on so much more than just a physical level. He's funny, in a dry, sarcastic way, and we have similar tastes. He almost seems too good to be true as I slip my hand in his and let him lead me out of the diner into the cool October night.

Walking alongside him quietly and comfortably feels so natural. I'm acutely aware of his huge, strong frame beside me. It's a short walk, though, and when we reach my car in the lot next to the club, I don't want to let go of his hand.

"That's your ride?" he asks in surprise.

I shrug. "Yep."

He lets out a long, low whistle and swings me around so I'm in front of him, my ass pressed against the driver's side door. My breathing acceler-ates as he steps into me, sliding his arms around my waist and dropping his mouth to my ear. His hot breath tickles me, sending shivers down my spine.

"It's almost as beautiful as you are," he murmurs into my ear. He pulls back to look into my eyes. "When can I see you again?"

This time I can't stop my smile. "Mondays and Wednesdays are technically my days off," I reply, realizing how that sounds as I'd worked today anyway. "Or most days in the early afternoon could work too."

"Wednesday then," he murmurs, looking down at me intently.

I can't say I'm sorry he picked the next time I'm available. The thought of waiting even two days seems too long.

I run my hands down his strong arms, relishing the feeling of being held. It's been far too long. He lets out a small sigh of contentment and, looking up into his face, I think he's going to kiss me. My whole body tenses in anticipation. But he takes his dear sweet time, lifting a hand to run down my cheek. I press my face into his palm, closing my eyes. His touch is electric, lighting up every nerve ending along its path.

"Open your eyes," he demands.

When I do I can see that his full lips are slightly parted, his massive chest heaving slightly under my hand. My eyes trail up his face. When our gazes meet, my breath stops for a moment.

"I'm not sure I want to kiss you." His words stop me cold, like a bucket of ice water on my libido.

"Excuse me?" I demand, slamming my hand into his chest to push him away. But it's like trying to move a brick wall.

He laughs, grabbing my wrists and spreading them apart easily like I'm a rag doll. I struggle anyway, trying to wrench myself from his grasp, but he tucks my arms behind my back, pulling me into his chest once more. I glare up at him, furious at his manhandling me.

"Easy there," he says soothingly. "Damn, you're feisty."

I scrunch my brow and pout at him defiantly. "And you're an ass," I retort.

The sexy smirk he's oh-so-fucking-good-at reappears. "Well, I can't deny that," he replies teasingly. "But I meant I'm not sure I want to kiss you, because I don't know that I'd trust myself to stop. And I really need to sleep tonight."

The fight drains out of me at his words, so he releases my wrists and I slump back against the car. "Oh," I say in a small voice.

He doesn't move. He just looks down at me, still smirking. "Are you always this spunky?" he teases.

"Only when someone provokes me," I grouse.

He brings out a lot of things I'm not used to feeling. I turn around, open the car door, and bend over to toss my purse into the passenger seat, forgetting for a moment that Julian's eyes are on me.

But I hear his sharp intake of breath. Then I feel his hands pulling at my hips, yanking me out of the doorframe, spinning me around.

His eyes are nearly black, his pupils dilated. "Fuck it," he huffs, and his lips are on mine.

He takes what he wants roughly, covering my lips with his, suckling at my bottom lip with his teeth before running his tongue across the seam of my lips, pressing for entry. Which I eagerly allow, meeting his tongue fiercely with my own, gliding my hands up his arms, across his chest, then wrapping them around his neck to pull myself into him.

The heat rises in my core as our bodies meld together, as I feel every inch of his hard body pressed against me. With his warmth, his smell, his body wrapped around me, I'm consumed by the intense explosion of our attraction. It overrides my senses, my logic, my whole body. His hands knead the soft flesh of my backside through my jeans, desperately trying to pull me closer. But there's no more space, and I can't tell where I end and Julian begins.

Until he pulls away abruptly, panting. The heat slowly fades to a simmer as he strokes his long fingers up and down my arms.

"You're something else," he murmurs, looking intently into my eyes. "But you'd better get out of here before I bend you over the back of this car and fuck you silly."

Holy shit. I gasp, my core tightening in response to his dirty, sexy threat. Part of me wants to call his bluff. But I'm not that easy. I press him away with one hand.

"You should get home," I respond, opening the car door and carefully sliding in on unsteady legs. I roll down the window and he leans his arms on the door, his face inches from mine.

"I'll see you Wednesday, Francesca," he says.

"Thanks for dinner," I reply, unable to keep the shit-eating grin off my face.

He leans in through the window and kisses me gently. "You're welcome," he whispers in my ear seductively.

We say our goodnights and I head home, knowing it'll be a long while before I sleep. And that even once I do, I'll probably dream about him fucking me over the back of my car.

6

———

JULIAN

"So you're seeing her tomorrow?" Sal asks again. The old man runs a hand back over the few greasy strands of hair he has left on his head.

I shift in his uncomfortable office chair, totally over this fucking conversation.

"For the third time, yes," I reiterate. "Want me to draw you a fucking picture?"

Sal's sharp eyes narrow, and he points a ringed finger at me.

"Watch your mouth, kid. Remember who you're talking to," he says ominously. He drops his hand to the ashtray in front of him, grabbing his cigarette and taking a drag like he's gearing up to rip me a new one.

I clench my jaw. Here comes the "I made you" and "you owe me everything" part of his speech. Old fucking news.

"Sorry, boss," I reply sarcastically.

And to my surprise, the bastard laughs. "You've always been a bold little shit," he scoffs, shaking his head and crushing the butt of his cigarette into the ashtray. "Whatever. This time, don't fuck it up, just get the goddamn information I'm sending you in there for."

I raise an eyebrow but don't fire back a snarky response. He's in a good mood. I don't know why, considering that his business is tanking and I don't fucking care, but I'll take it.

"I assume that means you still won't tell me what your plans are for this chick?" I ask, casually leaning back in the chair.

Sal snorts. "You ask a lot of questions. No, not yet. Just stick with her until you see how deep she's in."

"And if she's clean?" I ask. Because I'm pretty sure she is. I don't think Frankie would have accepted help to get where she is. At least, not the kind Sal is thinking. And I may not know exactly what he wants from her, but I don't think she's going to work for him, if that's what he's after. He may need her, but she sure as hell doesn't need this dirtbag. But, unfortunately, I do. At least for now.

Sal leans back in his chair, rocking dangerously far back in the piece of junk with a self-satisfied smirk.

"You like her," he accuses me in a taunting tone. If I didn't know him better, I'd say he was genuinely interested in my happiness. But thirteen years' experience tells me otherwise.

I don't break eye contact as I shrug. "She's cool," I allow. "But she's a job."

He allows his chair to settle back forward and leans toward me. "Good," he says with a manic glint in his eye. "Just remember to keep it in your fucking pants. We don't want this to blow up in our faces."

As if I needed the reminder that she's off limits. That it wasn't better for her if she never saw me again. That I shouldn't be having these endless thoughts of touching her, tasting her, making her mine in every fucking way possible.

So. Fucked.

As we arranged, I find myself at Frankie's door at five p.m. the next day. I tug at my black henley, smooth my dark jeans, and hope I don't look as fucking nervous as I feel. I tuck the surprise I have for her behind my back and knock.

When she opens the door, she looks good enough to make a guy forget just about everything else. Her high-waisted black pants fit her like they were spray painted on. The white top she wears bands over her gorgeous tits, a sliver of her soft, feminine stomach showing. Her lips are, as usual, as cherry red as her ride. Her hair is loose and wild, and I just want to wind my fingers into it.

But she's looking at me like I might be holding a murder weapon behind my back.

"Hi," she says cautiously. "Whatcha got there?"

"Hey," I reply. I let a mischievous smile creep across my face as I produce the pinwheel from behind my back and present it to her.

She takes it, not looking any less confused. "I'll just go put this in water?" she jokes.

I suppress a smile, instead leaning in and giving her a brief, but no less stimulating, kiss.

"It's a clue," I explain. "About our date."

"We're going to a kids birthday party?" she teases, stepping out and closing the door behind her.

"Something like that," I respond, trying to maintain the mystery.

She tries to wheedle it out of me the whole way to the car, but I won't budge. She'll see soon enough. When we get to my car, I open the passenger door and gesture for her to get in. But she's stopped on the side-walk, gaping at my ride.

"You drive a sedan?" she asks incredulously.

I raise an eyebrow, hoping she's not as judgmental as that sounded. It's no classic American convertible, but it's a pretty nice fucking car. "Is that a bad thing?"

"No, sorry, not at all," she responds. "I'm just a little surprised. It's so practical." She slides into the seat and I close the door behind her. As I walk around the car and climb into the driver seat, I weigh my response.

"What did you expect?" I ask curiously as I start the engine.

She ponders that for a moment. "A motorcycle maybe?" she finally replies as I ease into traffic.

I give a short, derisive laugh and shake my head. "Assumptions, assumptions," I scold her. "You look beautiful, by the way." I glance over at her gorgeous profile, trying not to salivate and reveal just how hot I find her.

"Thanks," she says. "You're not so bad yourself."

I wave a hand dismissively. "What, this old thing? Pshh."

She laughs and we banter back and forth for the few minutes it takes us to get to our destination. As we pull into a parking lot at the Santa Monica Pier, I see her head whipping around to take in her surroundings in shock.

"You're taking me to the amusement park?" she asks, laughing.

I flash her a grin. "Can't get anything past you," I reply with a wink. "It closes in a couple hours. I figured we could play a little before grabbing some dinner. Is that okay?" I look over at her as I park, suddenly worried that this was a bad idea.

To my relief, she shakes her head and laughs. "It's totally okay, I love this place," she replies. "I just wouldn't have guessed it was your sort of date."

There she goes again with the assumptions. Part of me is glad I can surprise her as much as she surprises me. Part of me doesn't want to enjoy this as much as I am. In any case, I can't help teasing her a little.

"Do you always stereotype so much?" I ask.

She opens her mouth, but closes it again quickly, seemingly thinking better of whatever snark she was about to lay down. Because she knows I'm right.

"Maybe? I don't know. I don't feel like I'm usually this judgmental," she replies, blushing.

I can't say I've ever seen a woman blush so much. I realize she must really be into me. And I could be a snarky ass in return. Or I could seize the opportunity.

I cock my head to the side, throwing some intensity at her.

"Just with guys who are interested in you, then?" I ask.

A sexy little smile blooms on her face. "So you're interested in me, huh?" she teases, dodging the question as she slides out of the car.

Fuck yes. I love a good chase. But I don't rush, taking my time getting out and following her to the park entrance. I catch up to her in a few long strides.

"I thought that was obvious after the other night," I remark, falling into step beside her, but staying a careful distance away.

She shrugs as we enter the park. "I didn't want to assume," she replies airily.

I laugh loudly. "Well, that's a first," I reply with a wink as we round the corner into the main stretch of the park. "Where to?"

She points to the mini-hoops booth to our right. "How's your game?" she asks.

I can't help letting an ironic smile slip over my features. "I guess we'll find out." I eye the plethora of stuffed critters lining the columns and eaves of the booth. "See something you like?"

I carefully turn my eyes to hers, letting the suggestiveness of my tone do its work.

She blushes furiously and turns toward the booth. Probably to hide. But she quickly points to a fluffy pink stuffed elephant hanging from the side of the booth. "I'm going to name her Juliana," she teases.

With a burst of laughter, I accept the challenge. "I'll see what I can do, but I make no promises," I respond. Again, with the double meaning. I swear I'm not even trying to.

I slap the requisite cash on the counter, and the teenager behind the counter gives me an I-don't-give-a-shit-about-my-job stare as he plops three tiny basketballs in front of me.

I line up for the first shot, trying to ignore Frankie's eyes on me. Fuck, that girl does things to my insides. Distracted, I let loose and it falls short, swiping the tiny net. Out of the corner of my eye I see Frankie cross her arms and lean into the pillar, her eyes flicking between me and the hoop. I notice that her tits are shoved together and peeking out the top of her shirt, unbalancing me even more. My second shot goes wide. I take a breath and try to shove the image of her out of my mind. It doesn't work, and my last shot misses as well, bouncing spectacularly off the backboard.

What-fucking-ever. It's not like I'm trying to impress her, anyway. I turn toward her and raise my arms in an exaggerated shrug. I did warn her.

Her face is a mask as she pushes up from her leaning position.

"Nice try, champ," she says, looking up at me.

Well, shit. She surprises me once again with her chill response.

"You want a try?" I challenge her.

"No, I suck at basketball," she admits. "That's why I asked you to do it."

The honesty makes me laugh. "Fair enough." I stare back at her for a minute. I can't get a read on her. Is she the tough chick or the sweetheart? She can't really seem to make up her mind. I kind of dig it.

"What do you like to do here?" she asks curiously.

Well, that's a huge fucking can of worms. I suppress a sigh and lead her down a couple of booths to the water gun race. "I used to play this for hours when I was a kid," I admit, taking a seat on one of the black stools that are cracked with age and use.

She slips onto the stool next to me, her eyes following my movements as I play absentmindedly with the long, metal tube affixing the toy to its pedestal. There's still one empty stool, so we're asked to wait a few minutes before they give up on having a full lineup.

"So you came here a lot growing up?" she asks shrewdly while we wait.

I turn to face her, unsure of how much to tell her. She slides her legs between mine unexpectedly and leans in, waiting for a reply. I look down into her eyes. Her long lashes frame her dark blue eyes, her bright red lips begging to be ravished. But being this close to her, I'm moved in a way that's so much more than the primal reaction I seem to have to her. She's looking at me like she wants to reach down inside and pull out all the good stuff. If only there were any of that to give her. But something about this moment makes me wish I had something to give.

"Yeah," I finally respond. "You're a local — you didn't come here when you were a kid?"

"Not really," she replies, the corners of her full lips dipping. "I grew up in East L.A. so it wasn't like a regular thing."

"So what was your thing? Were you a daddy's girl or a rebel?" I ask, keeping the attention on her.

"Can't a girl be both?" she asks with a sly grin.

I'm intrigued, but I'm not going to let her off the hook that easily. So, I just stare at her with a raised eyebrow, waiting for a real response.

She lets out a sigh. And I get it. I don't like getting serious either. "My dad died before I was born. So no, not a daddy's girl. And my mom worked all the time, so I was pretty much raised by my grandma. She's a fucking saint, and as much as I wanted to rebel, I couldn't bring myself to do anything to upset her."

Raised by her *grandmother?* Again, she surprises me. And I can see how uncomfortable she is sharing. "I'm sorry, I didn't know," I say softly, leaning forward and taking her hand, hoping the reassurance keeps her from bolting.

Her eyes are locked on our entwined fingers and she seems frozen in place. I disentangle a hand and tilt her face up to look me in the eyes. Her vulnerability is on full display. This is the moment I would usually bolt. And regardless of why I have to be here, right now, I just want her to look at me and know that she's not just beautiful because of the strength she tries to project, but also because of the things she thinks make her look weak. Of all people, I get how hard it is to share that part of yourself. It takes more guts than most people have. Including me.

Our intimate moment is broken by the attendant calling everyone to the ready. Simultaneously annoyed and thankful for the distraction, I turn to my ready position. Frankie does the same with a determination on her face that is adorable. I can tell she really wants to kick my ass.

Not even a minute later, the race is over, and Frankie wins. Coming in a close second doesn't matter. By an inch or a mile, I fucking lost. To a girl.

"Fuck. I *never* lose at that game. I think your gun worked better," I grouse jokingly as we step away from the booth.

She elbows me lightly in the side. "Mhm, that must've been it," she agrees, obviously humoring me.

I shoot her a mock dirty look as we get to the end of the row of games, still keeping a careful distance. Because I know if I don't, I'm going to lose control of this situation and what I need to be doing.

"So you grew up in Santa Monica?" she asks, playing with the edge of her blouse as I step up to do the ring toss. Her awkwardness tells me she notices the physical and emotional distance I'm trying to create.

I pay and take the stack of rings I'm given, weighing one in my right palm while I also weigh how to answer her. Silently, I gently lob the ring in a graceful arc toward the mass of glass bottles pressed together. It slides neatly around the neck of the bottle I'd aimed at. Frankie looks at me incredulously as the attendant congratulates me. I shut them both out and weigh up the next shot as I find my words. I decide she showed me hers, so I should show her mine.

"Not really," I reply, eyeing the remaining bottles and looking for my next target. "I was in the system until I was fourteen. I was all over the place before then." I can't remember the last time I told someone that. Because you tell someone you were a foster kid and they automatically label you: Reject. Troublemaker. Loser. I fling the second ring a little too hard and miss the toss. The ring goes bouncing around, pinging with the sound of failure.

Frankie's hand snakes over my forearm. Reluctantly, I turn to look at her. Just as I saw her, she sees me. Before I can stop her, she slides into me, her soft hands wrapping around the back of my neck to pull my lips to hers. It doesn't last long, but it feels like her telling me I'm wrong. That I do have the guts to share. The acceptance in her kiss is reassuring in a way it shouldn't be.

But as she moves away, I react without a thought. I fling my final ring aside and reach to pull her back in. To taste her again. Just for a moment I let everything out in that kiss, dipping my tongue into her mouth, sliding mine against hers as if the connection could save us both from haunted memories. Despite its depth, there's purity and innocence in the kiss that stirs something inside of me.

Someone clears their throat. I pull away to find the booth attendant holding a generously sized stuffed unicorn in offering. We both look at the last ring, nestled neatly around the neck of a small bottle, and burst out laughing. I accept the prize, offering the fluffy creature in Frankie's direction.

"You should keep it," she says. "You earned it, after all."

I scrunch my eyebrows together. What the fuck am I going to do with a stuffed unicorn? But I bite that back, opting not to completely ruin the moment. Instead, I shrug and tuck it under my arm, wandering to a bench across from the ring toss. We settle onto it without a word.

"What happened when you were fourteen?" she asks after a bit.

I pull at the unicorn's mane, separating the rainbow of colors, then smoothing them back together, over and over again. Order. Chaos. Order. Chaos. It's a good metaphor for life.

"I decided I was over it," I reply carefully, not making eye contact. "Over hopping houses. Shitty foster parents just looking to collect checks. My fucked up 'brothers and sisters' always looking for a fight. I just wanted to be left alone."

She takes a minute to absorb that, but thankfully doesn't offer any token expressions of pity. I fucking hate when people do that. Her atypical reaction makes me want to tell her more. Or maybe it's just her. Either way, I do. I try to start slowly, but before long the words are tumbling out of me as if they've been waiting years to come out. Which I guess they have.

I tell her about my years in the system, then living on the streets until I was nineteen, when I met Sal. I don't mention him by name, since he'd fucking kill me, but I do reminisce that he helped me clean up my act, gave me a job, and took me under his wing, ultimately helping me become the man I am today. If only she could really understand what that means. The things he asks me to do. And how, despite my gratitude for being saved from the streets, I'm finally old enough to know I need to get the fuck out. When I'm done talking, we sit in silence for a few moments before she says anything.

"Wow, I'm impressed," she says plainly.

I look up at her in shock. She looks like she means it. I shake my head morosely.

"You shouldn't be," I reply. "There's a lot you don't know about me."

She huffs a small laugh. "True," she allows. "But there's a lot I do know about you. You're considerate. Respectful. Oddly conservative in your vehicle choices. You love classic cars, hard rock, and cheap beer." That elicits a laugh from me, but she keeps going. "And despite a rough start, you let someone help you, you learned, and grew, and now it seems like you're doing pretty good for yourself. Oh, and you have excellent taste in women." She gives me a teasing poke in the side.

"You forgot my *other* skills," I reply suggestively, still smiling.

She raises an eyebrow at me. "Must have slipped my mind," she responds sarcastically. The fucking minx.

"Is that so?" I ask huskily, leaning toward her. "Maybe I need to remind you then."

Her pupils dilate and she sinks her upper teeth into her bottom lip, drawing my eyes back to her mouth. It flips that fucking primal switch, and I need to get her someplace. Fast. My eyes flick up to the photo booth behind us.

Her eyes follow mine, and as I grab her hand it clicks. She lets me pull her into the curtained alcove, closing it behind us. I don't waste time. I don't have a choice. I need a fix of those fucking lips. I press her into the wall, urgently claiming them with mine. The stuffed unicorn falls to the floor, forgotten as I taste her.

There's nothing innocent about this kiss. I wrap my hand around her neck, trying to plunder her as deeply as I can, our lips working fervently together. My other hand grabs at her, needing to feel her responding to me. It lands on her perfectly round ass, pulling her hips against mine in a grind that causes her to moan against me.

I feel her wrap her arms around my neck, pulling herself up to slip her leg behind my ass, pulling me in. My cock hardens at the thought of fucking her right here. And I know this has to stop. I slide my hands to her hips and gently keep her in place while I pull away.

She stares up at me, panting and bewildered.

I try to play off that I'm just as lost to this as she is. "Well?" I ask as calmly as I can, scooping up the unicorn from the floor and stuffing it in my back pocket.

She's clearly worked up, and it takes her a minute to understand.

"Yes, your *other* skills are amazing too," she allows with a roll of her eyes. Seemingly having gathered her wits, she straightens out her clothes and pushes me out of the booth until she can get by me. She's clearly annoyed, and I don't get it. It seemed like she wanted me to kiss her before, and by the way she was responding I know I didn't cross any lines she wasn't perfectly happy to blow to smithereens. So what the fuck?

"Fuck, what did I do now?" I let slip. And instantly regret it as she turns on her heel to face me, her nostrils flaring, her gorgeous lips pursed.

"Try groping me to prove a point," she snaps. She makes to move away, but I'm not going to let that go without setting her straight, so I grab her before she can get away and turn her around to face me.

She's already gone from angry to hurt, so I slide my hands around her heart-shaped face, willing her to understand.

"For fuck's sake Francesca, that's not why I did it," I try to explain. But

I can't think of any way to tell her why. So I show her, leaning down and capturing her lips with mine once more.

But different this time. Slower, more deliberately. I've always been better at show than tell, and I can feel her respond as her body softens into mine. I take the opportunity to slip my hands around her back, gently cradling her as I say with a kiss what I can't put into words.

The desire, the connection, the acceptance of each other is all spelled out mutely as we gently explore each other's mouths with our tongues. She tastes, and smells, like heaven. It's the silent primal bond that's between us made tangible in the perfect fit of our mouths and our bodies as she melts into me.

When we break apart, she puts her hands on my chest and looks up at me. The intensity of emotion is overwhelming, and I just can't deal with this right now. I'm all over the fucking map.

I lace my fingers through hers with one hand. "Come on," I say, pulling her to the ticket booth at the Ferris wheel. I'm hoping we can just enjoy the scenery and get a break from the intensity of the evening.

After we've climbed into one of the gondolas, spinning slowly to the top, I ask her more about her family, as nonchalantly as I can. I don't want to scare her off.

It's obviously a tough topic for her to discuss. She talks about her contentious relationship with her mother, that her grandmother always has to be their referee, but since the arrival of her younger brother twelve years ago they've managed to be more civil with each other for his sake. But that there's always an undercurrent of tension. I can tell there's a lot she's not telling me, but I know pushing the issue wouldn't help, so I just let her talk.

I try to put physical distance between us again, but I'm so wrapped up in what she's saying that every time I think to notice, I'm touching her. Holding her hand, stroking her thigh, wrapping my arm behind her shoulders. It's all too easy to fall into.

When she goes silent, finally, neither of us tries to fill the void. On our second circuit, as we flip oceanside we can see the sun setting in brilliant oranges and pinks reflecting off the dark ocean. It's always been one of my favorite sights.

"Did you plan this?" she asks, gesturing to the setting sun and nestling closer, leaning her head on my chest. It feels so fucking good to be close to her.

I let out a small laugh. "Maybe," I admit.

"You're smooth, I'll give you that," she replies.

If she only knew. A nagging feeling tugs at my gut. It takes me a minute to name it.

Guilt.

Here's this complex, smart, feisty, and gorgeous creature opening up to me. I'm such a fucking asshole.

I shake my head at my own thoughts, causing her to look up at me questioningly.

"Thank you," I say softly. I said it because I didn't know what to say, but I suddenly feel it, and more. "For opening up to me. And for not pitying me. The few people I've told did, or worse. It's why I don't usually say anything."

She nods. I can tell she understands, at least more than most people do. "I can't pity something that made you the man you are," she explains. "Because I like that man. A lot more than I want to admit."

There's that feeling again. Fuck. Sal was concerned about me fucking her. But now I'm concerned about something so much worse. "How much more?" I ask. Even though I think I know the answer, because I'm in the same fucking boat.

Her eyes rake over my face, and she's clearly unsure of what to say. But I'm not sure she needs to. I think we've both been hit harder by whatever this is than we expected. It takes a whole lot to scare me, but this might just do it. This situation is already too fraught with bullshit. I can't let this girl fall for me. She deserves so fucking much better.

"We've only been on two dates," she finally replies. "I don't know what to say."

I shake my head, withdrawing into myself, looking out over the water as the wind whips through our hair. As we descend to the bottom, the operator opens the gate and ushers us out, telling us the park is closing in a few minutes.

We wander silently to the exit, to my car. I open the door and turn to find Francesca looking at me with an expression between sad and scared.

"I freaked you out and now you're thinking this was a mistake." Her voice is low, but she's close enough for me to hear. And it's not a question.

We stare at each other in silence. What can I say to that? I do think this was a mistake, but not in the way she thinks. I want to punch something. I want to beat the ever-loving shit out of the forces of the universe that made us meet now. Under these circumstances. Because there's no way in hell I can be loyal to both Sal and Frankie. And I refuse to do that to her. Sal can get his intel some other way. But that doesn't mean I don't have to stay away from Frankie. There's no winning for me in this situation. And the why doesn't matter. No explanation is going to make this easier.

"I don't think we should see each other again," I reply sadly, avoiding admitting that I don't think she is a mistake at all. I'm the fucking mistake.

But if I've seen anything in my fucked-up life, it's the face of a woman determined not to cry. The face she's wearing right now.

"I'm not usually …" she trails off, clearly not sure what to say. "I didn't expect this."

I shut the car door and close the distance between us. I pull her face up so I can look her in the eyes.

"Me, neither," I respond. "I'm sorry, Francesca."

She blinks hard and nods. And her tough girl mask drops in, just like that. I'm almost thankful for it. Anything to make this easier.

She takes a step back. "Goodbye, Julian." She backs away.

"Let me drive you home," I plead. I want to reach out to her, but on some level, I know it's best to just let her leave.

She makes the choice, shaking her head and giving me a sad smile. "Take care," she says. And with a wave, she turns and walks away.

7

———————

FRANKIE

I don't walk all the way home. It may only be a couple of miles, but that would be murder in heels. Instead, I stop in a coffee shop a few blocks away on the Third Street Promenade and grab a latte, sitting at a table outside to people watch. Wondering how the hell things went so fast.

Before the water race, in that out-of-nowhere intimate moment we shared, I realized there was a sincerity about Julian that made me like him more than I'd let myself like anyone in a long time. Chalk it up to all the lying jerks I've encountered. But Julian seemed different. Or so I thought. Though I'm an intense person. I don't hide who I am. If he can't take it, best that he figures that out now.

Though the disappointment on his face as we parted is going to haunt me. But it's for the best. The man affects me in ways that are not normal. I can't even figure out why.

I need Emma. As I place the call, I know she's going to kill me for not calling her last night or earlier today.

"Three fucking days, Frankie. I can't leave you alone for three fucking days," Emma says, shaking her head and grabbing a breadstick from the center of the table.

"A little louder, babe, I don't think the chef quite heard you," Ben remarks drily, taking a huge gulp of his beer and shaking his head.

"If you wanted quiet you shouldn't have married her," I point out. I note that I sound as tired as I feel.

Ben, totally oblivious, laughs behind another sip of beer.

Emma points a finger at me. "Deflecting," she accuses me. "So that's it? It's just over?"

I shrug. What else is there to say? I've already relayed everything to her that's happened since she left my apartment on Sunday.

"You know if he hadn't ended it, I would've gone home, freaked out, and never called him again," I reply.

Emma snorts a laugh. "At least you know yourself," she allows. "Damn, I really wish I would've gotten a look at this guy."

Ben scoffs. "I'm sitting *right here*," he points out, annoyed, running a meaty hand over his short brown hair.

"So you didn't even get to …" Emma trails off, opening her mouth wide and gently inserting a breadstick into her mouth, sucking it suggestively.

Ben drops his head into his hands, groaning in embarrassment. They've cracked my pity party, and I laugh until I'm choking. I take a sip of water to calm down, then shake my head, wiping tears of laughter from my eyes.

"No!" I protest, still chuckling.

Emma grins widely, takes an enthusiastic bite of the breadstick and nudges Ben's arm, knocking his hand away from his face.

"You can look up, I'm done fellating the appetizers," she teases him. "And girl talk is over. For now anyway. Tell her about your promotion." Emma smiles encouragingly at Ben.

"Hey, you got a promotion? Congratulations," I offer with as much enthusiasm as I can muster. "What's the position?"

Ben shrugs his wide shoulders in a bad impression of modesty. "It's no big deal. They made me foreman." *Lie.*

Oh, boy. Here we go again. I suppress a sigh. I glance over at Emma. She looks extremely happy. I put on my practiced poker face.

"That's great," I reply, flicking my eyes back to Ben's sturdy frame. "Does that come with a raise?"

"Sure does," Ben says proudly. *Lie.*

"God, we'll *finally* be able to take a proper honeymoon," Emma gushes.

This is one of the things I hate most about my gift. Lying to people I love about the people they love who are lying to them. Because Emma specifically asked we never tell Ben about my ability for times like this. She thinks she wants to know. And while I've always known Ben is a compulsive liar, I learned long ago to keep my mouth shut about Emma's boyfriends. It just drives a wedge between us. And after all, everybody lies anyway. Though I just wish Ben didn't lie quite so much. Normally, I let it go. But this one is kind of big. And I know I'll have to say something next time I get her alone.

"That's exciting," I respond as sincerely as I can. But I don't ask questions, subtly discouraging continuing the conversation, saving Ben from digging himself deeper.

Thankfully, our meals arrive and there's silence as we tuck in. Well, as they tuck in. I pick at my food, realizing I don't have much of an appetite after all. I'm still yearning to really talk this out with Emma. Giving her an overview of what happened was fine with Ben around, but I left out a lot of the details. Especially the steamy ones, and we totally skipped a full dissection of the date. So now there are two things I need to talk to Emma about.

I DREAMT OF JULIAN THAT NIGHT. AND EVERY NIGHT THEREAFTER. HIS eyes. His body. His vulnerability. The terrifying realization that I was already falling for him after only two dates. By Sunday, the daily emotional dream rollercoaster on top of three crazy nights at the club in a row has me wiped and ready to take a couple of days off completely to regroup.

Unfortunately, life moves on, and I have to drag ass out of bed at ten-thirty to get showered and ready to go to my mom's for lunch at noon. Despite knowing I often need to work until six a.m. on Sundays, she insists on the monthly routine. At least it's not every week.

The drive takes thirty minutes, about the same as it usually takes me to get to and from the club. It reminds me of that saying that everywhere you go in L.A. takes only thirty minutes. If only. I'm lucky I rarely have to drive during rush hour.

Pulling into my mom's driveway, the modest rambler looks the same as it always does with its peeling yellow paint and white trim. Mom's tank of a classic German automobile, still solid despite its obvious age, sits in the spot closest to the front door. Tony's bicycle leans against the bushes under the front window. And as soon as I pull in I can smell melted cheese. It doesn't matter what meal it is at Mom's house, it always smells like melted cheese.

Before I've even made it halfway up the path, the front door springs open and Tony comes flying out, nearly knocking me over with his tall, gangly, twelve-year-old body.

"Frankie," he greets me with a squeeze.

"Geez, Tony, you're huge," I groan. "What'd you grow, like a foot since last month?"

He pulls back, shoving me playfully. "Yeah, and I bet I can kick your ass now too," he teases, balling his fists in front of his face.

"Hey, watch your language, kid," I tease back, slipping a punch in under his defenses.

He rolls his eyes and allows me to drag him inside. I drop my purse and keys on the coffee table in the living room, my hand instinctively reaching behind my back to put down the handgun that's usually nestled there. But I stop short, remembering where I am. I never wear it to Mom's. She hates guns, so I don't ever bring them here, much less discuss my affinity for them.

I go through to the kitchen, where I know I'll find the women and sure enough, they're busy stuffing pasta shells when I walk in. Tony bounds in behind me, sneaking a finger into the ricotta mix they're spooning from. Mom slaps his hand away and looks up.

"Frankie, you're early," she says, her eyes tight and unwelcoming.

"Nice to see you too, Mom," I reply sweetly, walking over to the older of the two women. "Hi, Nonna."

My grandmother turns her papery cheek toward me and I plant a kiss on it. "Hello, dear, how are you doing?" Nonna asks, her rhythm unbroken as she fills the casserole dish.

"Tired but good," I reply. "Need help?"

Mom nods at a cutting board piled with a loaf of bread, a stick of butter, a head of garlic, and a bunch of spices.

"You can make the garlic bread," she directs.

I huff a laugh. Mom is all business in the kitchen. Wait. Scratch that. Mom is just all business. Everywhere. At least around me.

I watch her for a moment, her greying head bent over, her slim, strong fingers deftly working. She's always been a little too serious and focused for her own good. Unlike Nonna. Watching Nonna is like watching a dance. She floats through the kitchen, spinning and preparing the food in a graceful rhythm, always with a smile on her ancient, wrinkled face.

With a chuckle, I turn to the bread and get to work.

"How's work, Ma?" I ask without looking up.

"Busy," she says crisply.

I snort. My mother runs the cleaning business her father started decades ago. She busted her ass to prove herself to Grandpa so she could take it over. I'd say it's the reason I barely saw her as a child, but I can't blame it entirely on that. Though I think it was a good excuse for her to avoid me, as she very purposely has never involved me in any of it, even as the business has seemingly grown and taken off.

"That's good?" I reply questioningly.

"It keeps food on the table," she replies in a curt tone.

Nonna looks askance at her and shakes her head.

"Hey, Tony," I call, over trying to make conversation with my mother.

He pops up on the other side of the counter I'm working on. "What's up, Sis?"

"How's school?" I prompt.

He grins and slides onto one of the bar stools and proceeds to catch me up on his last month. I don't miss that, for the first time, he mentions a *girl*. Twice. I give Nonna a look and she just smiles beatifically.

I've long since finished preparing the bread, but Tony keeps me captive, talking until the food is all in the oven. He's still quite possibly the sweetest kid on the planet with his enthusiastic positivity, and the fact that he's still not too cool to hang out with his big sister. I always forget how much I miss him until I'm here, away from the distractions of the club.

Mom leaves the kitchen once she's finished cleaning to go do God only knows what. Heaven forbid she actually have a conversation with her only daughter. But then, there hasn't been much mother-daughter bonding my whole life. Why start now?

In any case, Tony pulls me into the living room to show me his newest video games, and Nonna settles happily into her favorite armchair. She crochets quietly until Tony is contentedly playing his game solo. I take the opportunity to slide onto the couch next to her.

"How are you doing, Nonna?" I ask her loudly enough so she can hear me.

Her hearing has been declining for years, but she refuses to acknowledge it. I think she's just too vain to wear hearing aids. It drives everyone nuts.

"Oh, just peachy," she assures me without looking up from her work. "How are you, *really*? You look sad."

"I'm just tired," I respond.

Now she stops. And gives me The Look. "Frankie, I've raised you from a babe. I know the difference. Who is he?"

Dammit, how does she *do* that?

"Nobody, Nonna. Just a blip on the radar," I grumble.

Nonna cackles. "Anyone who can stir up the imperturbable Frankie Greco isn't a nobody. What did he lie about?"

I sigh and shake my head. "It's not that."

"Then what is it?" she asks simply.

"It was just going too fast. It wasn't right." It sounds lame even to me. I expect her to chastise me, to encourage me to give it a chance despite my reluctance to let people in, to get in a serious relationship.

But Nonna always surprises me.

"You know what's best for you," she replies with a shrug, returning to the blanket she's making.

I look at her skeptically. "Is this a trap?" I ask.

Nonna smiles widely. "Allow an old woman to plead the fifth when her lie detector of a granddaughter asks a question to which she already knows the answer."

Before I can respond, my mom walks in.

"What's the question?" she asks curiously.

Tony calls out in a singsong voice, "Frankie's got a boyfriend."

Fucking kids. They're always listening.

"Oh?" my mother asks, suddenly very interested as she sits next to me on the couch. "Why didn't you bring him?"

I reach over and slap Tony on the back of the head, but he just grins and keeps playing his game.

"I do *not* have a boyfriend," I grumble.

"Methinks the lady doth protest too much," Nonna teases.

I clench my jaw, knowing the more they get a rise, the more they'll keep going. So I just cross my arms and sullenly sink back into the couch cushions.

My mother stares at me for a minute before rising to head back to the kitchen. Probably to clean something that's already been cleaned six times. Any excuse to avoid direct conversation.

"I'm sure, like every man in her life, it'll pass," my mother says archly as she walks away.

"Geez, that was low, even for her," I snipe after she's disappeared.

Nonna finally puts her crocheting down. "Now, Frankie, darling, you know she's just projecting."

As if I needed the reminder that Mom has never been married, or even able to keep a man around for very long. But for very different reasons. She's unbearable and frigid. My relationships usually end over whoppers. Except with Julian who, ironically, only lied to me once, the first time we met, in an attempt not to seem like a stalker.

"I know," I respond. "But she's not wrong."

A weathered, frail hand slips over mine. "I love you, you know that," she says forcefully. "So I'm going to give it to you straight between the eyes. Learn to stop trying to make things go how you think they should, and go with what is. Even if it doesn't end up where you want, at least you let it run its course. But your expectations are stopping you from being happy, Frankie."

"Even if I wanted to go with it, I'm pretty sure I scared him off," I explain. "We hadn't even known each other a week and I was spilling my guts to him." I stop myself short of saying I was also ready to rip the man's clothes off in public and do naughty things to him. I shudder lightly at the memory of his lips and his hands on me in that photo booth. Some things you just don't discuss with your grandmother.

The old woman smiles knowingly. "That's how it *should* be, Francesca."

I open my mouth to protest, closing it again rapidly. The truth of her words is like a smack in the face. I was so scared of it because it was like nothing I'd ever experienced before. It was so fast. That is, compared to my previous relationships. But those didn't work out. So what if how I feel around Julian really *is* how it should be? The real deal? I suddenly feel nauseous.

"Mhm," Nonna mutters smugly, leaning back into her chair and picking up her crocheting again. "You let that man know you want to give it a go, and you'll see whether he's really too scared."

Needless to say I'm pretty quiet the rest of the visit as I process things. But by the time I'm passed around for hugs on my way out, my resolve is set.

As soon as I settle into the driver's seat of my car, I cradle my cell-phone in my lap, a blank text message to Julian waiting for my words.

I'm sorry about the other night. I just got freaked out. Can we talk?

And before I can chicken out, I hit "send."

8

JULIAN

Fuck. Fuck, fuck, fuck, fuck. I look at Frankie's text message again for the hundredth time and run a hand through my hair, tugging roughly as if that'll help me forget it. Right now, I need to focus on finding the words to tell Sal I've blown it.

No, no, no. That's not gonna cut it. I've got to spin it. After all, I learned most of what he wanted to know, right? I just have to hope it'll be enough.

I take a deep breath, fix the hair I mussed back into place, and smooth a hand down the black shirt and pants I'm wearing. Why the old man wants me to dress like the motherfucking grim reaper I'll never know. It's cliché and obnoxious in the still-way-too-fucking-warm Southern California autumn.

Focus. I have to focus. I lift a hand and rap my knuckles on Sal's solid wood office door. The dull thud reverberates through my tired brain.

"'Bout damn time, get your ass in here, son," he calls.

I get in one last eye roll and open the door. Sal sits behind his desk, his reading glasses low on his nose as he peruses a stack of ledgers on the desk.

"Christ, Sal, why don't you go digital already? Join the twenty-first fucking century," I say blandly as I drop into the chair across from him.

"Are you fucking kidding me?" Sal shoots back, tossing his reading glasses on the desk and leaning back in his chair. "I can burn all this shit and it's like it never happened. Put it on the computer, the FBI will be charging in here before the day is over." He looks at me sharply. "Now enough of that shit. Where are we with the Greco girl?"

"Like I told you she probably was, she's clean," I insist.

Sal shifts, looking deceptively patient. "I'll be the judge of that. Tell me what you've got," he directs thinly.

With a sigh, I relay everything she told me that was relevant. And just enough of what wasn't to make him happy. When I'm done, he leans forward onto his arms, tapping the sides of his face as he considers things.

After a few eerily silent minutes, he leans back once more and considers me thoughtfully. "You're even more into this chick than you were the last time you came in my office. I think you've done enough here," he states.

I clench my jaw, unsure of how not to rise to the bait.

"I'm a professional," I assure him. "And she's a job. But whatever the fuck you want, Sal."

Sal smirks knowingly. I forget sometimes that he's known me for so long. And I fucking hate that I didn't learn not to trust him until it was too late. I also hate not knowing what he's got planned for Frankie. It's one of the only things keeping me from walking away right now.

"Good. Because what I want is to make my move. So, stay the fuck out of it until further notice," he directs. "I'm serious, Julian. Deadly serious."

I shrug, feigning indifference to the sincerity of his threat. The exact opposite of what I'm feeling. Because I know Sal, and whatever he's going to do will hurt Frankie. If I thought I could get away with dealing with him myself, I would. But even in his downfall, he's still far too connected for that. And I'm just a little fly on a big fucking dung heap.

So instead of going straight to Frankie to spill my guts and warn her, like my instincts are telling me, I hit the gym to work out my frustration. Like a fucking coward. And I can't help thinking, again, Francesca Greco deserves so much more than I can offer her. So why can't I get her out of my fucking head?

9

FRANKIE

By Monday afternoon I still haven't heard anything from Julian. Instead, I'm sat at my desk in the club, with Nils and Jess sitting across from me, both awkwardly silent. I don't think I've ever seen Nils so uncomfortable.

"So is someone going to tell me why we're here?" I ask.

Jess shifts in her seat and shoots Nils a look.

"Ms. Wilson would like to lodge a sexual harassment complaint against Mr. Kelly," Nils relays calmly.

He goes to continue but I hold a hand up. "That's very concerning," I say, directly to Jess. "As you know we have a zero-tolerance policy for sexual harassment. Are you comfortable sharing the details with both Mr. Larssen and I?"

Jess tugs at one of her blond curls nervously. "I already told Nils," she says softly.

So he's Nils to her. Interesting. A little less formal than I like to be, but okay.

"All the same, I'd like you to tell me as well, so I can make notes," I explain. "We will, of course, keep what you say in confidence."

75

"Like, all of it?" Jess asks, clearly nervous.

I consider my response for a moment. "Well, as much as you want us to. Though if you want us to look into it, we may need to talk to Dave about it. But we won't share anything specific."

She shifts in her chair, weighing my words. "Fine," she sighs. "But like, he's totally going to deny it."

I shoot Nils a quick look and he shrugs imperceptibly. "Let us worry about that," I assure her. "Please, tell me what happened."

"It's just that we've been dating for a while," she starts. *Lie.* "But he changed, and I told him it was over, but he, like, clearly didn't get it." *Lie.* "He won't stop following me now, and he keeps trying to touch me even though I tell him to stay away from me." *Lie.*

I roll my lips through my teeth while I regroup on how to tease out some sort of truth that will help me figure out where this is coming from.

"So you and Dave dated?" I ask.

Jess's eyes widen. "That's not against the rules is it?"

"No," I reply, "I just want to make sure I have this straight."

She glances nervously at Nils. His expression is inscrutable.

"Yes," she finally replies to me.

After a beat, I conclude at least that much is true. "For how long, exactly?"

"I don't know," she hedges. "A month?" *Lie.*

Ooookay. "When did you tell him you wanted to stop seeing him?" I ask.

"Last weekend," she replies quickly. *Lie.*

I suppress a sigh. At least I got one truth. I continue to question her, but every detail after is a lie. That he's followed her home from work. That he's followed her around the bar, trying to touch her, kiss her, fondle her, to get her to get back together with him.

Fifteen minutes later I have a massive headache and only theories about why she's bald-faced lying. "Okay, I've documented it all," I say.

"We'll look into this as quickly and discreetly as we can. If we aren't able to resolve this by your next shifts, which are ..." I look at Nils.

"Thursday," he supplies.

"Thursday," I reiterate. "Then we'll adjust the schedule so you're working different shifts. Is there anything else you'd like us to do in the meantime?"

I look at Jess expectantly, and I haven't missed her growing frustration.

"So you can't, like, just fire him or whatever?" she asks, clearly irritated as she tugs on her curls again.

"No, but as I said we do take this very seriously, and we will look into it right away," I reaffirm. "If anything else happens, please let us know. I'll check in with you on Wednesday to let you know where we are." I stand, indicating I'm done. Mostly because my pounding head can't take anymore lies.

"Okay," she sighs. "Um. Thanks." She sounds anything but thankful. Irritated is more like it.

Jess stands reluctantly, followed by Nils. I suspect he realizes I'm feeling less than stellar by the softness of his manner as he quietly opens the door and gestures for Jess to precede him out.

"I'll walk Ms. Wilson to her car," he says softly.

I nod my thanks as he disappears behind her. Collapsing back into my chair, I dive into my stash of ibuprofen, downing a few with a full bottle of water.

I'm rubbing my temples firmly in circles, eyes closed, when I hear Nils's designer shoes tapping down the hall. The door clicks shut and a gentle swish of fabric tells me he's waiting patiently in the chair across from me to discuss this.

I take a deep breath and open my eyes. Nils is looking at me with deep concern. I'm not sure if it's for me, or the situation.

"Did you know they were dating?" I ask quietly.

Nils shakes his head. "No," he admits. "I've never even noticed them talking more with each other than they do with anyone else. If anything, I see Dave and Peter chatting together more."

"Did she give you any information she didn't share here today?" I ask.

Nils shrugs. "She was a little more graphic with her language, but it was more or less the same story," he replies.

I raise an eyebrow at him. "She calls you Nils and is comfortable telling you the sordid details of how someone has allegedly harassed her?"

His nostrils flare, which is the closest Nils ever gets to annoyed. "Is that the question you really want to ask?"

"Come on, Nils, give it to me straight," I insist.

He smiles grimly and leans forward. "She flirts. A lot. With everyone. Myself included," he admits. "But she's a bartender. It's how she makes the best tips, so I usually let it go."

"Seriously? That's bullshit, Nils, and you know it. You can't let our female employees flirt with you. It's totally unprofessional," I press.

Nils sighs and shrugs but doesn't offer any response. For all his talents, confrontation is not his thing. And I know that. I'm sure it's why he brought Jess to me rather than handling it himself if her flirtations make him uncomfortable. Though it suddenly occurs to me it could be the exact opposite.

"You don't have a thing for her, do you?" I blurt.

Nils barks out a sharp laugh. "Oh, Francesca, please," he scoffs. "She's only twenty-two."

I cross my arms over my chest. "And you're only thirty-one. You're not *that* much older than her. I don't have anything to worry about here, do I?"

The smile drops off his face as quickly as it came. "No, you don't," he replies firmly. "I may put up with her advances, but I don't encourage them. Nor do I have any interest in her that way."

"Good," I respond, leaning toward him. "Would you like to review the security camera files, or shall I?"

"I can take care of it," he assures me. "I'll let you know tomorrow what I find. I'll also call Mr. Kelly in so we can speak to him tomorrow."

"Thanks," I say. "Call Johnny, Peter, and Ace in too. We should talk to all of them. Not just to get as much insight as we can, but to make it seem like we're talking to everyone generally about the topic and anything they may have seen. It'll keep the heat off Jess."

Nils nods in agreement. "Good thinking," he replies. He pauses, considering me for a moment. "You think she's lying, don't you?"

I look at him, surprised. Given years of experience hiding my ability, I could swear my poker face is ironclad. "What makes you say that?"

"You said he 'allegedly' harassed her," he points out. "And you chewed on your lips while she was talking."

"You're observant, I'll give you that," I allow with a smile. "No. I don't believe her. But it's getting a full investigation regardless."

"Indeed. Our hands are rather tied, aren't they?" he muses. Shaking his head lightly, he switches gears, leaning back in his chair. "There's something else we need to discuss. That new Latin club two blocks away is opening this Friday."

I grimace, leaning back in my own chair. "I know. Their launch promos have been stellar." I heave a deep sigh. I've enjoyed making this club successful again, but in this business it's like balancing on the edge of a knife. During a knife fight. "I plan to go to the opening, of course."

"Of course. I'll go the following Thursday if that works for you," he offers.

I nod. "Sounds like a good plan."

Nils stands up to leave, turning back to me from the doorway. "Everything okay, Francesca?"

"Just super," I reply drily. "Why?" I cock my head to the side, taking in the tension in his tall, lean frame, the expression of concern on his face.

"You just seemed out of sorts this weekend. And you still are today," he replies vaguely.

I can tell he wants to ask more. I suspect about Julian. But I'm not ready to talk about it yet. "I've just been having headaches," I lie. Well, sort of lie. I still do have one at the moment. "I'll be fine, but thank you."

He huffs a breath through his nose, clearly not totally buying it. But I've got enough on my mind already without having to placate Nils. I turn back to the work on my desk in clear indication that I'm done.

He takes the hint and leaves. As soon as he does I pick up my phone, checking my texts for the millionth time today. This time Julian has responded. My heart leaps into my throat.

I meant it when I said I can't. I'm sorry.

At first, I don't feel anything. But slowly the numbness is replaced by anger, which is then replaced by pain. It was one thing for him to reject me when I'd rejected him first. But this? This just sucks.

Then I'm angry again that I care so much. I barely know this guy. And somehow he's managed to creep through my defenses. As scared as I was by the sudden onslaught of feeling, I'm just as upset that his rejection clearly wasn't because he found himself, like me, caring too much too fast. So here I am, out on a limb by myself, and it's just cracked under the weight of unrequited feelings. Fucking bullshit.

I go home that evening and I drink. A lot. Something I don't do much these days, as it's not conducive to running a successful club, ironically. But I make up for it in spades, finally passing out in the wee hours of the morning.

10

FRANKIE

I barely make it into the club on Tuesday afternoon, in large part thanks to about a gallon of water and a fistful of aspirin. But I still look like hell.

Thankfully, Nils doesn't say a word about my bedraggled appearance, he just takes me through his findings ahead of our staff interviews.

Unsurprisingly, his research demonstrated the exact opposite of Jess's claims. In several instances over the week, the footage clearly shows Jess aggressively pursuing conversation and contact with a retreating Dave. At least once, he's clearly forced to dodge her and disappear to avoid her advances.

Nils finds it baffling, which I find hilarious. I'm almost positive I know why, but I want to hear it from the staff.

We use the story that we're individually checking in with each employee to make sure they've read the employee handbook. So we go over the sexual harassment policy with each of them, along with every-thing else. And it's funny what people will tell you given the opportunity.

Johnny whines at length about how slow Peter is. Ace whines about what a hard-ass Johnny is because he sticks to the employee limit of two free drinks a night.

Peter is our first to say anything about inappropriate behavior. And it's specifically about Jess. He doesn't go on at length, but he basically says that Jess is crazy. That she doesn't have any boundaries. But after that he just keeps saying, "Ask Dave, dude, just ask Dave."

So Nils and I do just that. When we've finished going over the handbook and give Dave his chance, he doesn't complain about anyone. So we ask. Through some subtle coaxing we get him to finally admit that Jess pursued him for months, finally getting him to go out for coffee with her. When that went okay, they went out on a real date. After that Dave decided he really wasn't interested in her, and told her so. That was this past Sunday afternoon.

Then all evening Sunday, apparently, she went apeshit, calling him every five minutes. Texting him constantly. Showing up at his place, when he didn't even know she knew where he lived. And she didn't go away until he finally threatened to call the cops. Well, the second time he threatened and one of his neighbors echoed the sentiment, having been listening to the insanity all night.

Thankfully, Dave kept the texts. We assured him, of course, that he wasn't in any trouble, and that we'd deal with Jess. But once he was gone Nils and I were absolutely baffled why Jess thought she could get away with trying to report Dave.

I'd call her crazy, but the fact that she knew she was lying indicates something much worse. Something I don't encounter all that often. I try not to even think the word, because I hope I'm wrong. Because if Jess really is a sociopath, this could all go from bad to worse quickly.

⌒

I SEE JESS BY MYSELF ON WEDNESDAY. THOUGH THERE ARE CAMERAS IN my office, I leave the door open while Nils works down the hall. But as far as Jess is concerned, we are alone.

She sits confidently in the chair, clearly believing she's about to complete her revenge for Dave's rejecting her.

"So we talked to the staff yesterday," I open, pulling out the employee handbook and laying it so it faces her. "We simply went through this and gave everyone an opportunity to talk about how things are going here. It occurred to me that we should probably do the same."

Jess gives me a funny look, clearly unsure of where I'm going with this. But I know I'd best have this conversation equally with all employees, and I know as soon as we get to the next part, she's not going to like what happens.

She listens attentively and doesn't have any additional concerns or questions when I'm done.

"So you understood the parts on sexual harassment?" I ask clearly.

Jess nods, clearly still very confused. "Duh, obvs, that's what started this whole thing," she responds sarcastically, rolling her eyes.

"Yes, about that," I reply, steeling myself. "Unfortunately, video surveillance of the club contradicts statements you made when you reported your issue with Mr. Kelly on Monday."

I watch carefully as she goes from looking like a deer in headlights to looking like a woman scorned. And I brace myself for the fury of hell.

"I want to see the footage," she demands. "You must not have seen the right part. Or I bet you couldn't see it at all. Those cameras are at a bad angle, and it's so dark."

"They're state of the art, perfectly positioned, with night-vision capabilities," I assure her. "But unfortunately we have additional information that suggests you were, in fact, harassing Mr. Kelly."

I purposely keep it vague and as unaccusatory as I can, but she's obviously furious anyway.

"I don't know what he told you, but he's lying," she screeches, red faced and near tears. *Lie.*

I know whatever she says and does now is just to save face and will only dig her in deeper, so I attempt to cut that off at the pass. "It's not about what he said," I say as calmly as I can, "it's about the video feed *and* the text messages. They are irrefutable proof that you acted inappropriately."

Her mouth drops open, clearly flabbergasted. "You said you wouldn't tell him what I told you."

Yeah, that fixes it. I have to work not to roll my eyes. "And I didn't. The discussion came about as an extension of the same conversation we just had about the rules. I'm sorry, Jess, I know this situation is difficult for you. But unfortunately, we have to let you go."

"I didn't do anything wrong," she insists. *Lie.* "It's all his fault." *Lie.* "I've been a bartender for three years, in tons of different clubs and I've never had any problems before." *Lie.* "He's doing all of this to get back at me for dumping him." *Lie.*

I'm ridiculously troubled that she knows she's lying. Because if she didn't my internal lie detector wouldn't work. That she continues to blame it on him tells me that she's likely not capable of taking enough responsibility for her behavior to change it.

I decide against using logic with her any further. "I'm afraid it doesn't matter," I insist. "You've egregiously violated our policies and blatantly harassed a coworker both at work and at their home. You'll receive your final paycheck via direct deposit within the week."

I'm forced to repeat myself several times before I can get her to leave. But as she leaves my office angry and in tears, I know this isn't over.

THURSDAY NIGHT GOES WITHOUT INCIDENT, EVEN THOUGH WE'RE SHORT-staffed. Given that, however, on Friday I'm reluctant to go the opening of Los Jardines, the new Latin club down the road. After repeated reassurance that they'll call if they need me, I leave and I'm able to just make meeting Emma at the corner of Hollywood and Vine at ten-thirty.

Her pale blond hair is piled artfully on her head, her chest spilling out of a tight, red tube dress with chunky red heels to match.

"You look ready to salsa," I tease her as I approach.

She eyes my black halter dress with a cross-body ruffle. "And you look bo-ring," she sing-songs.

I hold up a finger, then twist my right leg to reveal a thigh-slit that would make a stripper blush. Okay, maybe not, but it's still sexy as hell.

Emma laughs appreciatively. "All right, you get a pass," she allows. "So we're checking this club out and going to find you some man-meat, right?"

I roll my eyes. "Because that's been working out so well for me lately," I grumble.

She tugs my hand, propelling me down the road for the few blocks to the club. I catch her up on my not-inconsiderably shitty week on the way, but I still can't quite bring myself to tell her about Ben's lying last weekend. Or exactly how much I was falling for Julian. I'm not sure why I hold that back. It would be like admitting what he and I had really could have been more than just an intense, physical attraction. And at this point I'd just rather forget about it.

As we approach our destination, all the usual stops have been pulled out, with spotlights and strobes visible practically the whole way. A huge line extends out from under the covered entrance, wrapping around the front of the building and down the block away from us.

We get to the red-roped side of the door and I pull us up to the massive bouncer holding the list. I give him my name and he opens the rope while making eyes at Emma. She winks and blows him a kiss on her way by. At that exact moment she is also unceremoniously shoved forward as someone pushes us from behind, causing Emma to press into my backside just as the door opens and a group starts to stream out. It sandwiches me behind the open door, Emma's generous curves keeping me from escaping back the way I came.

"Hey, watch it," Emma sneers, flinging her elbow back to dislodge the giant body pressing her into me.

"Ow, fuck, lady, what's your problem?" the guy she elbows cries out.

The bouncer presses him and his buddies backward, pointing at one of them in the back. "You gotta finish your cigarette out here, man," he says irritably.

The three huge men relent and take a step back, allowing me to squeeze out from behind the door as Emma steps up to tell off the asshole that pushed her.

But I'm distracted by the smoker, who now has his back turned to us. Because I'd know that ass anywhere.

Julian.

Panic grips me, and I turn to Emma to pull her away from the guy she's trading not-so-nice words with. It takes me a minute to get her attention.

"Emma, let it go," I hiss at her.

She finally turns and sees the look of sheer terror on my face. "Frankie, what the hell is wrong with you?"

She says it loud. And I groan, knowing I'm fucked.

"Francesca."

God. Fucking. Damn it. I glare daggers at Emma before turning around.

In fitted black jeans, with a tight black V-neck tee to match, and ridiculously sexy mussed hair, Julian looks as panty-droppingly gorgeous as ever. The shirt shows the hint of tattoos winding up his torso, the sleeves exposing the ones that cover both arms to his wrists. He'd be beyond ridiculously hot but for the cigarette hanging from his lip.

"Julian. I didn't know you smoked," I respond, trying to sound as bored as possible.

One of his buddies elbows him. "Who's your friend, *Julian*?"

Julian takes a drag of his cigarette, then grinds it into the ashtray of the trash can sitting on the curb.

"Just some chick," he responds with a shrug, looking as bored as I tried to sound. My heart drops into my stomach and it takes everything I have not to slap him. What the actual fuck?

Emma is frozen next to me, and I can see the realization dawn on her face. It's quickly replaced by anger.

"Fuck all of you losers," she spits, tugging my arm. She glares at Julian. And if looks could kill, he'd be six feet under. "Especially you, asshole."

Julian smirks, putting his hands up in mock surrender. His blasé attitude is beyond maddening.

And it gets worse as three of the most classless bimbos I've ever laid eyes on sidle up and latch on to Julian and his friends, eyeing us angrily.

It takes all my effort to close down my expression and walk away. Emma scrambles to follow me through the velvet rope, only catching up once we're inside. But Julian and his friends aren't far behind us.

I fume as we push through the crowd, making for the small, roped-off VIP section to the right of the massive dance floor. Once inside its confines, we collapse into a small, black leather sofa.

"Do you want to go?" Emma asks loudly into my ear.

I shake my head. "I'm working," I reply back into her ear. "Let's have a drink. I'll look around. Then we can go."

She nods her agreement, patting me reassuringly on the thigh. I lean into the sofa, allowing myself to recover before I think about anything else. I don't want to let this ruin my evening, but I don't see how I can just let it go.

One of the VIP area guards approaches us, leaning in to speak to me.

"Mr. Rivera has invited you to his private table," he says.

Carlos Rivera is the owner of Los Jardines and the reason I was on the VIP list in the first place. So I can hardly refuse him, though perhaps it'll be just the distraction I need.

I stand up and straighten my dress, swinging my hips so my leg slips through the slit as I strut out of the VIP area and across the dance floor to a set of tables just off the bar. In case Julian is watching, I might as well remind the bastard what he's missing out on.

Carlos turns out to be a pleasant, upbeat man in his mid-forties. He's energetic and charismatic, and he buys us margaritas, wishing us a pleasant time at his club.

After downing the drink, I feel distinctly calmer as I sit at the bar with Emma absorbing my surroundings. The club's design is basic, the Latin décor fairly subtle. But the music is high energy with Latin flair, and the packed dance floor pulses with the energy of the crowd. It's the multicolor strobe lights hung from the ceiling, however, that really give the place its atmosphere. All in all it looks like it's going to be pretty successful, but offers a different enough experience not to be direct competition, exactly.

I spot Julian and his crowd on the dance floor. One of the bimbos is wrapped around Julian, but he looks just as bored as he did outside. I huff a laugh and excuse myself to go to the bathroom.

As I'm coming out, however, Julian's bimbo is going in. I plan to ignore her, but she clearly has other ideas.

"Hey, you're one of the bitches that was messing with my boys," she snarks at me.

I don't even plan to respond. Her tiny tube top and barely there miniskirt are as cheap and trashy as she is, and I know no good will come of opening my mouth. Plus, it disgusts me to see what kind of woman Julian is really interested in.

But as I go to walk by, she throws an arm up to block me. I deftly duck under it without a word. It enrages her in a way that would make me laugh if I even cared that much.

Unfortunately she doesn't give up easily, and as I make to walk out of the bathroom hall back into the main area, she grabs my arm.

I whirl around and wrench my arm out of her grasp. "Don't. Fucking. Touch me," I say loudly and firmly.

And the dumb bitch finally seems to realize I've got a good six inches on her. This close to her I realize how tiny she is. I have to give her credit for being ballsy enough to start something.

"Whatever, bitch, stay away from J.C. — he's mine," she spits, turning back down the hall.

I blanch at her words, the memory of him telling me his last name at some point during one of our dates coming to the forefront. Charles. J.C. — Julian Charles. That's why his friends teased him when I called him Julian. I shouldn't feel offended that he clearly didn't even like me enough to have me call him what his friends do. Because I didn't let him call me Frankie either. Nonetheless, it stings a little.

And I'm not sure what to make of her claiming him either. He hadn't lied when he told me he didn't have a girlfriend. But maybe they don't use that label. My stomach turns at the realization that the little I thought I knew about him probably isn't even true.

Suddenly, the hair on the back of my neck stands up and my eyes involuntarily flick up to the dance floor to find Julian watching me. He towers over everyone around him, and his expression is dark with anger. I'm certain he saw the exchange. But I'm not going to give him the satisfaction of thinking I give a shit.

Disgusted, I turn and head back to the bar, sticking close to the wall to avoid the crowd, but I don't get far when a rough, warm hand closes over my forearm. I once again find myself ripping my arm away from unwanted contact and whipping around to face the person making it.

"Don't worry, I left your piece of ass alone."

My eyes lock on Julian's brooding face. I try to contain the anger seething from my pores, but I can tell by his expression, his body language, that he knows. And he's every bit as riled as I am.

"She's not my piece of ass."

I snort. "Whatever you call her then. You two deserve each other."

"Fine, have it your way. Gina and I are a thing." *Lie.* "That's why I can't keep seeing you." *Lie.*

"Liar," I gasp before I can stop myself, disgusted by the whole situation.

He arches an eyebrow. "I don't like being called a liar."

"Then don't fucking lie."

I try to step around him, but he locks his strong hands around my waist.

It pisses me off to no end and I move to execute a defensive maneuver with my arm, but with lightning reflexes he grabs it and uses it to pin me against the wall. I struggle uselessly against him as he presses me into the brick with his arms and torso.

"Still feisty, I see," he murmurs in my ear.

And I hate myself for the shivers it sends down my spine. "Still an asshole, I see," I retort hotly.

He chuckles and loosens his grip so he can back off. But he doesn't let me go.

"What's your damage *J.C.*?" I press mockingly.

He frowns. "Don't call me that."

"Sure thing. Of all people I get it. Only your actual friends call you that," I reply scathingly. "Clearly, I don't know you at all. And I'm not sure what you're doing right now, because I thought that's the way you wanted it. Do you just like making random women fall for you then going total dickhead on them? Does it get you hot so you can go back to that skank and fuck her cheap ass?"

"You've got a foul mouth, Greco," he replies calmly, still not letting me go.

"Go fuck yourself," I spit back. I can't remember the last time I was this angry. I thrash under his hold, but he still doesn't release me.

But he finally looks furious, his thick eyebrows drawing together in a scowl. And I'm sure I've crossed a line.

"I'd rather fuck you," he replies huskily, surprising me. And his mouth is on mine, his tongue angrily plunging into my mouth, his hands sliding to my hips and pulling me to him.

I was expecting anger, not lust, and the physical response I have to him is as strong as ever. I'm unable to resist, melting into him, lacing my fingers into his hair. I have enough of my wits left to hope his girlfriend sees and that it pisses her off.

And I also have regathered my wits enough so that when he lets me go, I slap him as hard as I can. "Keep dreaming, asshole." I turn on my heel and walk away.

When I get closer to the bar and spot Emma, I'm stopped short, totally thrown out of the anger from my conflict with Julian and his girlfriend. Emma is pale, with tears streaming down her face. She can't have seen or heard what happened, but I know instinctively it has nothing to do with me.

I close the distance between us nervously. "Emma, what's wrong?" I ask.

She looks up at me, fury written all over her face, and shows me her phone screen.

Text messages from Ben admitting he lied about his promotion. My heart drops into my stomach.

"You knew," she spits at me. "Didn't you?"

Fuuuuuuuuuuck.

"Yes," I admit. "I was going to tell you tonight, I swear."

Emma laughs. And I've known her long enough to know it's her "bitch, please" laugh. But she doesn't say anything. She just gets up and walks away from me.

Desperate to explain, I follow her across the dance floor, through the entryway, and out the front door.

"Emma, wait, please," I call after her uselessly. The club is way too loud for her to hear me from any distance, much less the twenty-foot lead she's got on me.

Damn, if she isn't fast when she's mad. She's already at the curb and is hailing a cab that's gliding up next to her. As she gets in, she pauses.

"No wonder Julian doesn't want you," she spits, tears streaming down her face. "You've got nothing to give, Frankie. You can't even be a good friend."

I'm too stunned to respond. And then she's gone.

I clench my fists and squeeze my eyes shut, fighting back the anger. The tears. The outrage. I dig deep and steady myself enough to walk back to Baltia.

But when I turn around, the three cheap bitches stand around me, closing in to pin me to the curb.

Julian's girl, Gina, is in the middle. "I told you not to mess with J.C. He's *mine*," she screeches, shoving me in the chest. And I understand suddenly why she was so bold. They outnumber me, even more than they did before Emma hightailed it out of here. While I'm decent in a fight, I don't like the odds. Especially with my back to traffic.

"I have no interest in messing with him," I reply calmly, trying to keep from getting pushed into the stream of vehicles that I can feel whipping by behind me. But I knew it wouldn't do much, and I was right.

She gets right up in my face. "Oh, yeah? Then why were you kissing him?" she spits.

"He kissed me." It's my own fucking fault. I *wished* for it to piss her off. Why am I so fucking stupid when it comes to this guy?

She laughs. "Please, why would he do that?"

I look down at her. "You really think I could force myself on him?"

That gives her pause. But not for long. Logic clearly isn't her strong suit. "Whatever, bitch, I told you not to touch him — now you're gonna pay."

"I'm really not interested in fighting over Julian," I say, putting my hands up.

The girls on my sides close in.

"Then you should have gone home when you had the chance," the one on the left says.

I don't look at her. I know it's a trap. And lo and behold, Gina swings at me, anticipating that I was going to look. But I see the blow coming a mile away and dodge it. She spins past me, and I'm no longer trapped against the curb. *Thank you, boxing lessons*, I think to myself.

I can feel the crowd watching behind us. Annoyed that the bouncers clearly don't give a shit, I back up slowly. But the bitches advance.

"Carmen, Gina, Tammy," an angry voice barks from behind me.

The brute that ran into Emma earlier comes around my right side. And that distracts me into looking. Rookie move.

Gina comes at me and *grabs my hair* like the bitch that she is.

Fighting the pain, I wrap my hands around her forearm and bring my right knee sharply up into her midsection. It knocks the breath out of her and she lets go. But I take no chances. As she gathers her wits, I land a right hook to the left side of her face. She falls back, landing flat on the pavement.

Her two friends scramble to her side as she pushes herself up on her elbows, holding her jaw, clearly in pain.

Julian and his other friend appear next to the brute.

I drop my guard, backing off. "He's all yours," I spit at the stupid bitch as she picks herself up from the ground. "For what that's worth."

The onlookers let out gasps and jeers, but I block it all out, spin on my heel, and walk away. Fuck them all.

11

JULIAN

I make it outside in time to see Frankie land a punch on Gina. What a fucking mess. I should've left as soon as I laid eyes on Frankie. Because before I know what I'm doing, I tell Paul to get the girls the fuck home before they get us arrested, and I'm down the sidewalk after her.

I don't stop to ask myself what I'm doing. I know what needs to be done. Thankfully, she's slow enough in heels that I catch up to her before she gets to Vine.

"Wait up," I call as I close in.

She walks faster and I have to try not to laugh. In a couple more steps, I put myself in front of her.

"What?" she snaps, crossing her arms over her chest and glaring up at me. And goddamn it if she isn't even more beautiful when she's angry. It softens me in a way that I'd take the piss out of my friends for.

"That's some right hook you've got there. You okay?" I ask softly, resisting the urge to take her hand in mine and check her over.

She tightens her arms around her body defensively. "Oh, so now you give a shit again?" she seethes.

I take a deep breath. My usual ability to keep up the careful pretense of indifference melts under her anger. And I just want to make it right. "Who said I stopped giving a shit?"

She laughs angrily. "I can't handle this."

She makes to step around me, but I mirror her, stopping her advance.

"Please, don't go yet," I beg. "I'm sorry. This is why I said I can't."

"You're not making any sense," she grouses.

I clench my jaw and stare at the sky, trying to figure out how to explain this to her without telling her anything that could put her in danger. Or me, for that matter.

When I look back at her, she's resolutely glaring into traffic, arms still crossed tightly over her chest. So fucking stubborn, but goddamn she's beautiful. And if she's as riled as I am, she feels this. It gives me hope and I can't help but smile.

I reach out and turn her face toward me so I can give her the only truth that matters right now. "I'm falling for you," I admit. "But those guys back there can't know that. That's why I can't do this."

She stares at me, like she's waiting again. "I still don't get it," she insists.

"It's complicated."

"I'm pretty smart."

I laugh. "Yeah, you are."

She looks at me expectantly.

"I'm sorry, Frankie, it would take a lot more of an explanation than I can give you right now. And when you got freaked out, it was a good reason to put a stop to whatever this is. But then you wanted to try anyway, and I knew I couldn't expect you to trust me if I couldn't tell you everything. And there's just a lot going on I can't even begin to …" I drop my hands to my sides, curling them into fists in my frustration. I'm fucking this all up. "Look, I'm sorry I was such an asshole tonight. I thought it would be easier that way, but I was wrong. I fucked up."

"You're right. I don't put up with secrets and lies," she replies, ignoring my apology.

Lies. That reminds me. "How'd you even know I was lying back there?"

Her eyes widen a fraction. "Good guess," she says. She uses the same fake I-don't-give-a-shit tone she tried to pull when we ran into each other outside the club earlier tonight. And my BS radar is going off.

"Bullshit," I say. "I don't lie often. And both times I've lied to you, you've called me out on it. So let's try that again. How did you know I was lying?"

"It's complicated," she returns with a sneer. "And like you said, it's not like I can trust you to tell me everything either."

Something in her words feels like a threat. And I wonder how much she knows. If she really is dirty, and she's just been playing me this whole time, knowing who I work for. But I'm pretty fucking good at what I do, and I almost always know a con when I see one. Could she really be that good? Or are her words just a coincidence? The part of me that wants to fight for her takes a step back.

"Fine, have it your way," I reply, stepping aside to let her pass.

"None of this is my way," I hear her mutter as she walks away.

I don't stop her.

With a sigh, I check my phone, and there's nothing. If anyone was suspicious of my disappearing act, it doesn't seem to have raised enough flags for them to say anything. I decide to head home, beyond over tonight.

But every step I take just feels fucking wrong. And I know deep in my gut that Frankie isn't really dirty. That everyone has their secrets. Especially me.

She's the first person in a very long time who hasn't treated me like a piece of shit. One little comment and I ignore all of my instincts about her. Fuck, I'm a head case. I have to remind myself that not everyone lives in my world. And even though I'm supposed to stay the fuck away from hers, I find my feet rounding the block, heading back to Baltia. Back to Frankie.

When I get to the front doors, I realize I have no fucking clue what I can say to her that will fix this. I was telling her the truth: I don't like lying, and I try to avoid it. Life is complicated enough. But there's just too much I can't tell her.

I keep going, rounding the corner to the parking lot next to the club. I spot her ride toward the back of the lot. I approach it, admiring the gorgeous machine. I sink down next to it, leaning against the side, hoping her vibes will give me something. I tilt my head back and close my eyes, waiting for inspiration to strike.

I MUST HAVE FALLEN ASLEEP, BECAUSE THE NEXT THING I KNOW, I'M BEING nudged awake.

"You're lucky someone didn't mistake you for a dead body and rob you blind." Frankie's voice cuts sharply into my fogged brain.

I open my eyes to find her staring down at me with her arms crossed again. "They'd be getting more than they bargained for," I reply, as the hand that was resting on my belt pulls out the short blade I have hidden there. I palm it, spinning it once before sliding it back in place. She doesn't look impressed.

"What are you doing here, Julian?" she asks, slumping against the side of the car, clearly exhausted.

I climb to my feet, subtly checking the time on my way up. Four fucking a.m. Goddamn, I was asleep in the open in this neighborhood for hours. She's not wrong that I was lucky to avoid trouble.

As I stretch and settle against the car next to her, I don't miss her checking me out. But I don't let it go to my head, instead focusing on looking as contrite as possible. Because I still don't know what the fuck I'm going to say. But here goes.

"I tried to stay away," I explain. "But I can't. And I don't know if this will work, but I want it to."

She shifts uncomfortably. "I can't do this right now," she sighs.

With a frown, I push myself up off the car. I can't say I blame her after how I behaved earlier. "Okay," I reply. "I understand." I kiss her on the forehead. Not where I'd like, but at least I get to be close to her one last time. "Bye, Francesca."

I start to walk away, kicking myself for how this all went down when she grabs me around the wrist, pulling me back. I look up in surprise, and she looks beyond annoyed.

"No, asstwat, I mean I am literally too tired to stand. Can we talk later today?" she clarifies.

"Fuck, I'm sorry," I say hastily, realizing she looks like she's about to collapse. "Do you want me to drive you home?"

She swoons a little against the side of the car, and I decide no matter what she says I'm getting her home safely.

"That might not be the worst idea. It's been a night." She unfolds her hand, revealing her car keys.

A knot in my chest I hadn't realized was there unravels at her invitation. And it might make me a little giddy, because the next thing I do is scoop her up in my arms and carry her around the car to the passenger side.

"Geez, Julian, I can walk to the other side of the car, you know," she protests. While she sounds annoyed, she looks impressed. But still tired.

I don't bother to respond, I simply jiggle the keys into the lock, open the door, and place her in the passenger seat as gently as I can. Then I walk back around to the other side, get in, and start the car.

"But that was so much more fun, wasn't it?" I finally reply with a teasing smirk.

Rolling her eyes, she buckles herself in and sinks into the seat, clearly too tired to banter. And it's a good thing I know where she lives, because she almost immediately falls asleep.

It makes getting her up to her apartment and into bed interesting. But I finally manage it, removing only her shoes and lying her on top of her covers. By the time it's done I realize I'm beyond tired too, and I'd have to call a car to get home. Staying it is.

I contemplate lying down next to her but decide to go back to the living room couch instead. And staying was a good decision, because as soon as I lie down, I'm out.

⌒

I ONLY GET A FEW HOURS OF SHUT-EYE BEFORE THE MORNING SUN streaming through the living room windows makes it impossible to sleep. I peek in at Frankie, and she's still out cold. And so fucking beautiful it hurts.

And I suddenly have an idea to win her over. I rush out the door, bringing her keys with me, and hope I have enough time before she wakes.

I get a car home, pick up a few things, change my shirt, and drive back to Frankie's, picking up coffee and donuts on the way.

When I quietly reenter her apartment, I'm relieved to find that she's still asleep. Producing the stuffed unicorn from our last date, I place it on the pillow next to her with a note, then return to the living room.

About fifteen minutes later, I'm about to have a second donut when I hear laughter. Rising, I cross the living room and the short hallway to stand in her door.

She's holding the unicorn in one hand, the note in the other. The smile on her face tells me my plan is working.

"Good morning, beautiful," I say, and her eyes meet mine. And I swear I lose my damn senses every time. "I hope it's okay that I crashed on the couch. I tired myself out getting you to bed." I wink at her suggestively. "I went home this morning, picked up some breakfast and brought it back, though."

"That's really thoughtful, thank you," she replies sincerely, climbing out of bed. "I have to get to the club soon so I need to rinse off and get changed." She stops in front of me and points nervously at the door to the left of where I'm standing.

Fuck, she did not say that. Now I'm picturing her naked and wet. I raise an eyebrow at her, but I say nothing. I don't trust myself, and I don't think that was an invitation. So I return to the living room without a word.

I try to concentrate on eating a donut. It takes all of my fucking focus. I'm already semi-hard from knowing she's in the shower mere feet away. I eat a glazed donut wondering if she tastes as good. Who am I kidding? Of course she fucking does. The next fifteen minutes creep by. Finally, Frankie emerges.

And if I thought that would help, well, it doesn't. She's wearing a spaghetti-strapped fitted black top and tight pink cropped pants. Her damp hair reminds me of the water that was just running down her huge tits, ample hips, and round ass. I shift forward to hide the bulge in my pants.

"Donuts? That's what you call breakfast?" she asks, grabbing the second cup from the coffee table and sitting down in the chair across from me. Too fucking far.

I level a look at her. "I don't bite," I tease patting the couch cushion next to me and thinking, *Well, not unless you want me to.* The thought does nothing to abate my erection.

She scoffs at me. "Says you. I'm still not convinced you're not a complete asshole," she replies honestly.

I cross my legs so I can lean back, and I laugh. "Fair enough," I admit. "So how do I make it up to you?"

She leans forward and grabs a cake donut with chocolate glaze out of the box on the table. "I don't know."

I realize what a bad idea the donuts were as I watch her eat. I swear I try not to fucking stare, but it's impossible not to with the delicate way she nibbles off a piece, her pink tongue darting out to lick the crumbs off her lips. Fuck me.

It also doesn't help that she seems to be just as aware of me watching her. And it doesn't stop her. By the time she's done eating, we're both squirming in our seats.

I stand up, round the coffee table, and drop to my knees in front of her. I focus on breathing, keeping control, as I take the hand she was eating with and raise her long, slender fingers to my lips. Then, without ceremony, I suck the fucking sugar crystals off of her fingers. She stares at me, transfixed, as my tongue caresses her fingertips. Her lips part and her pupils dilate, and I have all the invitation I need.

I smirk at her, pulling back and licking the last of the sugar off my lips. She stares just as hard as I stared at her eating that fucking donut like a saucy, sugary vixen.

She searches my face for something. I don't know what.

"How old are you?" she asks curiously.

I raise any eyebrow. Really? That's what she wants to ask right now? "Thirty-two. Why?"

She smiles. "You're a little young to have wrinkles," she teases me.

I narrow my eyes. She's stalling. I must be making her nervous. With a predatory grin, I lean toward her. But she throws her leg up between us before I can get too close, using it to push me back.

She's unsure. I get it. I haven't exactly been reassuring. But my primal brain is in the driver's seat right now, and I need to taste this woman. I look down at her shapely leg, sliding my hand under her pink pants, running my fingers up her smooth, soft calf.

"You think that's going to stop me?" I ask in a low, husky voice.

I can see the shiver roll through her body. She tries to hide it by taking a sip of coffee. It doesn't work.

"No, but a good kick to the head might," she replies.

"You're still mad. I get it," I reply, dropping my eyes to her leg as I continue to stroke it. "But if you can't think of a way I can make it up to you, I will."

I slide my hand to her ankle, gently holding her and lifting her foot away from my chest. I bring her toes to my mouth, placing gentle kisses as I rub circles into the sole of her foot with my hands. I look back up at her as I kiss further up her foot, to her leg. She's panting and I can see her hard nipples through her shirt. Fuck. Breathe in. Breathe out. Focus. Control.

I set her foot slowly and deliberately on the ground and run my hands up her legs, moving into her until I'm settled between them. When she doesn't protest, I slide my hands up her thighs, rubbing slow, firm circles into her hips.

"God-fucking-damn it, if I don't want to make it up to you right now," I breathe, struggling not to pounce. I lean in to kiss her, but she stops me with a hand this time. Fuck.

"Julian." She says my name as if in protest, but the sexy sigh to her voice, the tension in her curves says she wants me.

My lips part as I say her name with a sigh. "Frankie."

It's the first time I've called her that since the night we met. I can see the fire blazing in her eyes. She slowly sets her coffee cup down on the end table next to her.

And I can't tell if she's going to slap me or jump my bones. Fuck, at this point, either would send me over the edge.

She slowly takes my hand, brings it to her lips, and kisses it gently. And the need for her takes over. I pounce, our lips clashing fiercely, my teeth pulling at her lip, my tongue thrusting into her mouth. She presses away, gasping for air, and I know it's not a protest this time, it's catching her breath from the ferocity of my need. Of our need.

I move to her neck, trying not to bite too hard as my animal instincts take over. I slip my hands under her ass, pulling at her pants.

"Julian, I don't think we should —"

I step up my game for just a moment, closing my mouth on her nipple, over her shirt, pulling at it with my teeth and growling into her chest.

"You think too much," I say roughly. But I pull slightly away, waiting for permission once more. She whimpers at my words, arching her back and pulling me back to her breast.

With a wicked grin, I oblige, biting at her hard nipple while simultaneously dropping a hand between her legs, stroking her roughly through the fabric. Helping clear her mind. Because I can tell we both need this.

I know I'm right when she lifts her backside up. I let out a low, eager moan and relieve her of her bottoms until her dripping pussy is fully exposed to my hot, eager mouth.

Breathe in. Breathe out. Focus. Back in complete control, I run my thumb down the length of her, starting at her clit, over her slick lips, dipping slightly between her folds.

I sigh softly. "Beautiful," I murmur. I take a moment to appreciate the work of art before me. Then I use my tongue to trace back the path my thumb just made, ending at the hot, tight bundle of nerves with a flick. Frankie cries out, her hands gripping the arms of the chair, her legs trembling. So, I do it again. And again. Until her hips are grinding against my mouth, tilting her clit toward the rapid movements of my tongue. But I need to let it build if I'm going to take her over the edge like nobody ever has before.

That's my plan at least, until she slips her hands under her shirt, tweaking her nipples hard. It might just be the sexiest thing I've ever seen, and all I can do is stare up at her from between her thighs. Our eyes meet, and the lust and desperation in her gaze rips through me. It spurs me back to action as I'm overtaken by the need to watch her come apart. I run my thumb in circles over her clit, staring hungrily for her response. I'm not disappointed. She throws her head back, arching her back, pressing into my hand.

My fingers find their way into her, and she gasps, crying out with pleasure. This. This is the moment I wanted. Her, open to me, under my control, giving her the pleasure I get just from looking at her. Being with her.

I pump my fingers into her, changing up the angle I'm stroking her clit at as I go, watching for what pleases her most. When her breathing accelerates, I rotate my wrist, taking my fingers deep until I find her G-spot. And I press it toward her clit with my middle finger at the same time my thumb works her on the outside. In an instant she's screaming her impending release.

"Oh, fuck yes," she cries, closing her eyes as her body tightens. "Right there."

Sweet fucking lord, she's like my own personal porno. "Come for me, beautiful," I groan.

My words are like a match thrown on gasoline, igniting her. Her breath quickens, her body tightens hard around my fist. I keep going. When I think she can ascend no further, I flex both fingers deeply, sending her over the edge. She screams her release, her hands closing over her breasts hard as she pushes into my palm, prolonging the sensation.

As she slowly comes down the wave, I wipe my face with my other hand and slowly ease my hand out of her. I slide up to cover her mouth with mine, giving her back her delicious taste while getting a dose of the trembling intensity of her mouth.

She laughs, licking at my lips. "If that's how you're going to make it up to me, we might have a deal."

That makes me laugh. "Seriously?" I ask.

She uses her foot to push me away again, which I don't resist this time, and swipes her pants off the floor. "No," she laughs, pulling her clothes back on. "But it sure didn't hurt your chances."

I sink back into the couch, shaking my head and laughing. I'd do that every fucking day if she'd let me, even if it didn't fix anything between us. Her taste, the noises she makes, giving this amazing woman equally amazing orgasms. Fucking fantastic. I can't even begin to imagine what sex with her will be like. My already hard dick twitches in my pants at the thought.

She swipes another donut and sinks back into her chair, totally blissed out. She eyes me over the pastry in her hand. "Aren't you going to wash your hands?"

"Hell, no," I reply, bringing the hand I used to fuck her to my mouth and slowly licking my fingers. "At least not yet." Maybe not ever.

"You're a dirty boy, J.C.," she teases. She sets the rest of the donut she was eating down on the table.

"Had your fill?" I ask suggestively.

"Yep. You?" she shoots back, raising an eyebrow.

"Not even close," I reply, not breaking eye contact.

"You're confident, I'll give you that," she says, leaning back in the chair and crossing her legs.

"Not really. I've just made up my mind. I want you, Frankie, and I know you want me too." I smirk at her like the arrogant bastard I am. I can't help it if I'm used to getting my way.

"Oh really? And what about the things that are too *complicated* to talk about right now?" she presses.

"How did you know I was lying?" I counter.

She purses her lips. And I know I've got her on the ropes.

"We both have things we don't want to tell each other yet," I point out. "That doesn't mean this can't work."

I can tell she's trying to come up with a counterargument, but she stays silent.

"Mhm," I murmur. "That's what I thought." I rise from the sofa. "Think about it. I've gotta go."

I saunter over to her, plant my hands on the chair arms, and lean in so my face is inches from hers.

"I'll call you," I say lowly. My lips find hers in a brief but intense kiss before I pull away.

She looks completely dumbstruck as I walk to the door. And as it clicks shut behind me, I know I've won. Even though that opens a whole new world of complicated, right now, I don't fucking care. All I want, all I can think about right now, is Frankie.

12

FRANKIE

As mind blowing as my time with Julian was, unfortunately there's little time to parse through what happened and how I feel about it. I wasn't lying. I really did need to get into the club for an early event that's going to be a shit-ton of work.

When I get there, I find Nils helping Ace work with the lighting guys to get everything down for tonight's show. I take Nils aside and we check in. Everything has been quiet since I got here, though, so it's a struggle to stay on task. But once the club opens at ten, I don't have time to worry anymore even if I wanted to. The show sold out before the doors even opened, so we knew it was going to be insanity. With having let Jess go, I find myself behind the bar most of the night helping Dave, Peter, and Johnny keep up with the crowd.

I'm already pissed off for having to pick up the slack Jess's absence has created when it goes from bad to worse just after midnight as a huge fight breaks out at the bar. Some asshole comes crashing onto the counter, sending a row of pitchers waiting to go out flying everywhere and spraying everyone in the vicinity with beer.

Now I'm overworked, tired, *and* wet. So when Nils frantically flags me down it takes all my strength to keep from screaming. He pulls me into the security room, looking more panicked than I've ever seen him.

"We have a problem," he says, pacing behind the door to the bar. "I was on the balcony when I spotted Jess in the crowd. But by the time I got downstairs, I couldn't find her anymore."

"Are you serious?" I ask furiously. "What the fuck made her think coming here, especially while Dave is working, is in any way okay?"

Nils shrugs, agitated. "I should have warned Chris not to let her in," he mumbles.

I shake my head and sigh. "I didn't think of it, either. Let's just find her and get her out before it becomes a problem."

We exit, and Nils heads back into the crowd to alert the bouncers and search for Jess. As I scan the bar, two things become immediately apparent: Dave is no longer behind the counter. And Julian is standing there, looking around expectantly.

He looks so fucking good in his tight jeans and white T-shirt, his hair doing that sexy mussed thing, I want to go to him and run my hands through it and fold myself into him until everything else disappears. I'm a little surprised at the reaction, and part of me is still unsure if I really want to give in. Not to mention the Jess-sized problem wandering around the club, especially now with Dave MIA.

I stay there, frozen in my indecision long enough for Julian to spot me. And when he does his whole face lights up. A wave of mixed feelings washes over me. Happiness that he's here. Annoyance that he's here when things are so crazy between us. And at the club. Aggravation that things are so crazy. Anger at Jess. It's too much, and I think he sees the war of emotions on my face.

In two long strides, he's in front of me, wrapping me in his arms. It feels good to surrender for just a moment, but he pushes away when he feels the sticky wetness from the beer still on my black halter top.

"Looks like I missed something," he says in my ear.

I nod. "Sorry. I have to go look for someone," I say back in his. "Wait here?"

Julian agrees, so I flag down Johnny. It takes him a minute to work his way over to me.

"Where'd Dave go?" I ask loudly enough to be heard.

"Supply closet for napkins," Johnny yells back, pointing to the door on the opposite end of the bar.

I nod my thanks and point at Julian. "Give him whatever he wants, no charge."

Johnny raises an eyebrow but wisely doesn't respond. I head to the other end of the bar, toward our secondary supply closet, down the hallway marked "Employees Only."

The first door on the club side is just a buffer for the noise and in case anyone mistakes it for the public bathrooms. I step through that one and make sure it closes fully behind me before using my key to access the actual supply closet door to my right. It concerns me that it isn't open if Dave is supposed to be here.

And throwing the door open, I see the light is off, no Dave in sight. I close and lock the door again.

"Dave?" I call down the hall loudly.

A woman's scream echoes off the white tile walls. Panic rushing through my veins, I run toward the only other place it can be coming from. The employee bathrooms.

The first door is unlocked, the room empty. The other, however, is locked. I bang on the door with my fist.

I don't even have time to ask questions, or warn them that I'm going to come in if I don't get a response, before the door springs open and a half-dressed Jess tumbles out into my arms. She's sobbing hysterically, tears streaming down her face.

I look behind her to see Dave standing by the sink, his clothes disheveled, and a look of horror on his scratched and bloodied face.

IF NILS HADN'T FOUND ME IMMEDIATELY AFTER I FOUND JESS AND DAVE, all hell surely would have broken loose. As it was, we were able to deal with everything via the side door, which was closest anyway, without much disruption to the show happening inside the club.

With some terse instructions we were able to get one of the bouncers who'd previously bartended to help Johnny and Peter, and Julian unbelievably volunteered to pinch hit for security. With the adjustments, we managed to keep the front of the house running while Nils stayed with Dave and I with Jess until, at her request, an ambulance came for her. And, also at Jess's request, the police came for Dave.

Jess was too hysterical to say much besides he'd attacked her. And to call the police. So I hadn't much choice, even though the little voice told me she was lying. It killed me to say nothing, to watch them both taken away. To promise the police officers that I'd be down in the afternoon to provide all of our video footage, employee files, and other data pertaining to "the case."

Once they are all gone and everyone is back to their usual posts, I find myself standing in the employee hallway alone, listening as the stragglers are shown out, the after-party having been cancelled.

Knowing I can't hide any longer, I return to bar area to find the cleaning crew has already started. Nils sits at one of the bar tables looking as sad and tired as I feel.

Julian stands awkwardly by the stairs to the stage pit.

Sullenly shuffling around the tables, I approach him. "Thank you," I say. "I'm sure this wasn't what you came here for tonight."

He shakes his head, and reaches out to lace his fingers with mine. "I came here to see you," he replies. "But what you just went through … just tell me what you need, and I'll do it."

I chew on my lips, overwhelmed. "I need to talk to Nils," I reply. "But if you can wait a bit longer, I'd like it if you took me home."

He pulls my fingers to his mouth, kissing them sweetly. "Of course." He lets my hand go and I turn to head to Nils's table, but he's already making his way toward me.

"So you *did* go for it," he observes with a glance at Julian. "I wasn't sure there for a while."

I huff an ironic laugh. "Neither was I," I admit. I look around gloomily. "So that was a shit show."

Nils gives me a dim smile. "Never a dull moment. I'll meet you here tomorrow to go to the police station?"

I heave a sigh and nod. "I'll be in as soon as I'm up to get everything together. I'm too angry and tired to do it right now," I reply.

"God, of course, Francesca," Nils says with a wave of his long fingers. "Go home, get some rest. Text me tomorrow when you want me to meet you." He reaches out and squeezes my shoulder reassuringly. He gives another glance at Julian and leans in close. "Be careful."

I shoot Nils a sharp look and he backs up, raising his hands with a smirk.

When I turn back to Julian he's glaring daggers at Nils. I'm too tired to deal with a jealous Julian, so I choose to ignore it, instead gesturing for him to join me.

"Ready?" I ask tentatively as he approaches.

Julian's dark eyes flick to mine. "Yeah," he says shortly, winding his arm around my waist. "Let's get out of here."

But as soon as we're outside he lets me go, as if he no longer needs to mark his territory. Since I'm already worked up by the events of the evening it annoys me more than it probably should.

"You don't have to worry about Nils," I snap. "He's just my club manager."

Julian huffs. "Yeah, okay."

How two short words can be so laced with contempt and sarcasm is beyond me.

"Seriously, Julian," I say, grabbing his arm so he has to stop and look at me. "I don't deal well with possessive bullshit. And I've had a fucking awful night, so if you're going to have attitude, just go home."

He sighs and shakes his head. "I'm sorry," he replies, slipping his hands around my backside and pulling me into him. "I know. I'll drop it."

"There's nothing to drop," I insist angrily.

"If you pick a fight right now, nobody is gonna win," Julian murmurs, looking down at me, his dark eyes smoldering intensely.

I realize he likes it when I'm feisty. Even if it does make me into a total bitch at times. Either way, his words, his touch, and the small smile pulling at his full lips defuses the anger in me.

"You're right, I'm sorry. Take me home, please," I reply, going on my toes to bring my face to his.

Julian leans in to kiss me, softly and sensually, but he pulls away far sooner than I'd like. "You're sexy when you're giving in," he teases, unleashing his full panty-melting smile.

I disentangle myself from him and pull him toward the car. "Don't push your luck," I grouse back as seriously as I can.

He laughs as I hand him the keys. "I wouldn't dream of it," he promises with a devilish glint in his eyes.

When we get back to my place, I stand at the door, unsure of what I expected to do at this point as Julian looks at me like he's wondering the same thing.

"You should get some sleep," he tells me, his rough hand stroking down my face.

I consider him in the dark hall for a moment. He bears the usual signs of club work. Sweat, grime, and the smell of alcohol. Normally, I deal with a rough night by isolating myself and sleeping it off, but the thought of him leaving makes me feel miserably lonely.

"You look like you could use a shower and a nice, soft bed," I reply, opening the door and pulling him in behind me.

"So we're doing this, huh?" he teases as he drops the keys on the counter.

I set my purse next to it. "I don't know," I admit. "Do I really have to decide tonight? I really just want a hot shower and some sleep."

"Is that all you want?" he asks huskily, stepping into me.

"I want you to stay," I reply honestly, pressing my hands against the firm muscles of his chest. "That's all I know right now."

His thick eyebrows pull together as he studies my face, as if he's trying to figure me out through sheer willpower.

I tap him on the forehead, laughing. "Stop thinking. Start undressing." I point to the laundry closet on the other side of the living room. "You can put your clothes in the wash. I'm getting in the shower."

I turn on my heel and head into the bedroom, leaving a dumbfounded Julian in my wake.

I undress with a smile while the hot water of the shower starts to fog up the room. I wind my long hair up, tying it at the top of my head before getting in. I'm too tired to dry it after it's washed, and I can't sleep with wet hair, so it'll just have to wait until tomorrow.

As I slip under the stream of scalding water, I gasp at the sudden change. But I'm thankful for the heat, the cleansing of not just the physical evidence of the night — sweat, beer, and tears — but the emotional weight too. The heat wears at the tense muscles of my back from all the anger and frustration of the evening, until I feel myself mellowing out and winding down.

I hear the bathroom door open and I smile, glad Julian didn't wait until I was done. I don't know what I want with Julian, but I do know I want him with me tonight.

He taps on the glass. "Mind if I join you?" His voice is low and tired, but still sexy enough to stir me just a little. And that's saying something, given my level of exhaustion.

I open the door a crack in answer. As he steps into the not-quite-big-enough-for-two space, I only briefly register the satisfied smile before his massive chest fills the space in front of me. I realize I'm finally going to get a good look at his body, his tattoos, and … other things. The sudden thought perks me up considerably.

I scoot him around in a circle, so his back is under the water. The hot stream slips around his broad, muscled shoulders and he groans in relief.

"God, that feels good," he murmurs, closing his eyes and tipping his head back to let the water flow over the sharp angles of his face.

I slide my hands up his chest, tracing the designs on his pecs. He tilts his head back down and opens his eyes to watch me. Most of his ink is obviously religious. Hands clasped in prayer hold a rosary under my left hand. A large, ornate cross under my right. Dark angels adorn his arm on the side with the praying hands from the top of his shoulder to his wrist. The angel on top is inked darker than the rest, a look of wrath on his beautiful face. The others are surrounded by fire and crushed under his feet in apparent supplication.

"Lucifer," Julian supplies as my finger traces the angry features of the fallen angel. He watches intently as my fingers slip down the figures to trace the words at his wrist.

"Pride," I whisper.

"It was their sin," he explains. He shifts to expose his other arm to me, pointing at the top figure. "Michael," he names the angel on his other shoulder, "and his army of angels."

The angels on the other arm are surrounded by pristine, white clouds and heavenly light, have an air of serenity, and are breathtakingly beautiful. I tear my eyes away to look up into his face, to find him still and vulnerable as he awaits my reaction. I smile at him reassuringly, letting my fingers slide down his arms. The intense attraction that always thrums between us is a mellow hum tonight, in our tired state, but tugs at me nonetheless. Shaking myself back to the present, I switch my fingers to his other wrist to read the word written there.

"Humility." He smiles when I read it aloud, tracing his hand down my back.

His last set of tattoos are twins, seven in roman numerals, on each side of his ribcage. I run my fingers over them and he giggles. The sound makes me smile again, and I look up at him coyly from under my eyelashes.

"That tickles," he tells me, leaning down to rub his nose against mine before planting a soft kiss on my lips.

"What do they mean?" I ask curiously.

His eyes sparkle in the fog of the shower and he looks like a dream with his rugged, striking features.

"It's a reminder that there are seven deadly sins," he explains once more. "But there are also seven virtues. Every day I have to choose between them."

"Every day?" I ask, confused.

He runs his thumb over my lips. "Every day, beautiful. We all do, really."

"I didn't realize you were religious," I reply with a smile.

His answering smile is sad. "I'm not. But that doesn't mean I don't have faith. That there's a better way to do things in this world. And the next."

I'm silenced by the depth of emotion behind his words. Unsure of what to say, I grab the bar of soap behind him and carefully wash him instead. He allows me access, patiently watching me with those dark, intense eyes.

When the hot water has rinsed all the soap away, he takes the bar from my hands and runs it over my back with one hand, the other trailing down the tattoos on my upper arm.

"What about yours?" he murmurs.

I shrug, self-conscious. "They're all variations on the night sky," I reply. "Nothing particularly meaningful, just beautiful pictures I like."

He moves to soaping my front, his rough hands gently working around my breasts in a way that's more relaxing than stimulating.

"You like the stars?" he asks contemplatively.

"Love," I whisper. It's not a story I want to share right now, so I go on my toes to close the large gap between our mouths, still needing to pull him down to me because he's that damn tall.

He kisses me softly. "You're short without your high heels," he says with a smile.

"I'm still tall," I grouse back. "You're just a freak of nature. What are you, six-five?"

"Six-six," he says with a smirk.

"Freak," I mutter jokingly.

That gets a full smile and throaty laugh from him. Like everything else about him, his smile and his laugh do things to me that defy logic. I almost forget about the little voice inside when I'm with him. Somehow, he never triggers it, even though I know he's not completely honest with me. But like he's pointed out, it's not like I'm completely honest with him, either. Nils made a good point the day I decided to go out with Julian for the first time. Maybe I need to decide whether he's worth getting past whatever bullshit is holding us back to stop, well, holding back.

"Come on, I think we're clean enough now," Julian says, breaking into my reverie. "And I'm sure we could both use some sleep."

I raise an eyebrow at him. It's what I'd intended in the first place, but I'm a little surprised he's so willing to go along with it. Though admittedly I am tired enough that the intense heat I usually feel between us is still a low simmer. I'm more relaxed than anything in his presence at the moment. As he steps out of the shower, I get the full visual of his well-muscled frame and realize that considering how fucking amazing he looks naked, that's once again saying something about how exhausted I must be.

"You're right," I admit. "But ..." I trail my eyes over the perfect taut-ness of his chest, arms, and abs. And I finally let my gaze drop lower. *Good lord.* Now I know I'm tired because his semi-hard, generous package barely stirs the sleeping fire between my legs.

When my eyes move back up to his, he's tolerantly smirking at me. "Like what you see?"

I shrug nonchalantly. "Sure, I guess. What's not to like?"

His booming laugh echoes through the bathroom. "Damn, woman, you're stubborn."

I bite my lip, but it can't stop the smile and subsequent laugh that escapes me. "Come on, let's go to bed."

We finish drying off, stealing glances at each other all the while. Julian follows me into the bedroom, where I slip on a short, silky nightgown.

"Hmmm, I might have a pair of shorts or something around here you can wear," I murmur, flipping through my drawers. When I turn around Julian's already in bed.

"It's okay, I sleep naked anyway," he says, leaning against the cushioned headboard.

I take a deep breath. "Of course you do," I laugh, climbing into bed beside him.

"What does that mean?" he asks with an answering laugh as he slides down next to me.

I snuggle into my pillow with a yawn. "It means you're already practically irresistible and you know it," I murmur sleepily.

"Mmmm," he murmurs. "And you are much more relaxed than you were."

I look up at him from under my heavy eyelids. "Hm. You're right. I can go back to being in a foul mood, if you'd prefer."

Julian leans over me and turns off the light on my nightstand, plunging us into near darkness. I feel his large, warm frame slide back down next to me, followed by one strong arm sliding around my waist, pulling me against him in the dark.

I snuggle happily into his chest, his scent filling me, calming me, lulling me to sleep.

He brushes my hair away from my face gently. "No," he says softly.

"All I wanted was to make sure you were okay. I'm glad you're feeling better, beautiful. Now get some rest." His warm lips kiss my jawline under my ear.

A small happy noise escapes me as I drift off to sleep.

13

FRANKIE

The blackout shades in my room are drawn, so when I wake I have no idea what time it is. But I'm definitely alone in bed. I sit up sleepily, twisting to look at the clock and gain my bearings.

Before my eyes can even adjust, the bedroom door opens and a sliver of light expands across the bedspread as Julian comes back into the room. In the light I can see that he's still fully naked. And still fully gorgeous, his toned body flexing as he tries to quietly navigate in the darkness.

"Whatcha creeping around for?" I whisper.

"Gaaaahhhh," Julian shouts, jumping about a foot in the air.

I cackle delightfully.

"Geez, Frankie, don't do that," he grumbles. "I had to use the bathroom so I figured I'd switch my laundry. It's still early, you should go back to sleep." He slides back under the covers and his cool skin meets mine. "Mmm you're nice and warm."

"How early?" I ask.

Julian's hands skim over my backside as he wriggles into me. "Just after seven."

"Fuck, that is early," I mumble into his chest. "Wait, *I* should go back to sleep? Aren't you?"

He buries his face in my hair, inhaling deeply. "Not likely while I'm lying here naked next to you," he whispers seductively in my ear.

It has an immediate effect, and I can feel my body tightening in response. And so can he. His hand runs down my nightgown and over my hardened nipple appreciatively.

"Goddamn it, Frankie, you are so fucking sexy," he murmurs before pressing his lips to my neck as his hands continue to roam.

I push my hand against his chest, which I'd meant as a gesture of uncertainty, but when it hits the wall of muscle that is his body, it takes my breath away.

Honestly, what did I expect climbing into bed with him? That we'd wake up, shake hands, and go our separate ways? No. I have to admit to myself that this is exactly what I'd wanted.

If only I wasn't so damn worried about what he isn't telling me. But right now, as his lips stroke the sensitive skin on my neck and his hands work my breasts, my mind is blissfully blank.

Surrendering to the moment, I push on his chest again until he lets me roll him onto his back. As I rise to my knees I can just make out him watching me as I place myself between his legs. I stroke his thighs lightly with my palms, lowering my lips to him. He lets out a low moan, realizing what I'm about to do.

I capture him just with my mouth until he's expanded to fill its wet warmth before slipping my hand around the wide base of his cock. The noises he makes as I slowly and firmly work him have me just as ready as he is. I relent with my mouth, sitting back to take him in as I slide my hand up and down his length.

His hands are locked behind his head, his chin tipped up and eyes closed as he groans with pleasure. His body is so fucking perfect in every way that I can't take it anymore. I let him go long enough to get protection out of the nightstand, then roll it down his hard length as quickly as I can, my whole body trembling with the anticipation of having him inside of me.

"Oh, fuck, Frankie, yes," he gasps as I finish readying him. "Goddamn it, I want you on top of me so fucking bad." His husky rasp has me so wet it's all I can do to calmly slide up his body and meet his lips with mine.

His tongue plunges hungrily into my mouth, his hands closing around my face. I grab his wrists and free myself, slipping one hand between us to guide him into me. I then slide back mercilessly, and he fills me with an intensely pleasurable pain, our moans synchronized with the thrust.

"Shit, you're so tight," he groans. "And so wet. You feel so fucking good."

I don't tell him how amazing he feels, not trusting myself to speak. I'm already so turned on that anything could tip me over the edge. So I concentrate, pushing myself up to a sitting position and removing my nightgown as he watches, his eyes heavily lidded, his breathing heavy. And then I start to move. Slowly at first.

His hands find my hips, tugging at them. "Faster, Frankie," he urges. "Give me that pussy, please, God, it feels so good."

"If you keep talking like that, this isn't going to last much longer," I promise, stilling myself as a shiver rolls through me. Just looking at him hurts, much less hearing him talk dirty while I fuck him.

Julian looks up at me and laughs. "You don't like it?" he asks huskily, with a sly smirk playing around his deliciously full lips.

I raise his hands to my breasts, and his thumbs work my nipples in tantalizingly rough circles.

"I think I like it a little too much," I admit, biting my bottom lip.

Julian's eyes darken and he sits up, pulling me into his chest, ravenously consuming my mouth with his. He pulls back and looks into my eyes, his thumbs and forefingers now closing over my nipples and tugging at them.

"Lie down," he commands. "My turn to have my way with you."

My insides pulse and tighten, and he smirks, feeling it around his cock.

He raises an eyebrow and pushes me gently off him onto the bed. With one hand, he strokes himself firmly from root to tip and back down as he climbs to his knees between my legs.

His other hand slips over my dripping core. "Your problem," he says slowly, spreading my wetness, "is that you're always in charge." He leans forward, positioning himself to enter me. "I think you like having someone take control." He slides smoothly in, causing me to gasp at the sudden, insanely pleasurable sensation.

With one hand, he holds my leg against his shoulder. The other he uses to press against my clit as he starts to move.

"Tell me you like that, Frankie," he begs, his voice thick with need.

"Oh, yeah, I like that," I breathe.

"Good," he murmurs, his rhythm unbroken. "Now tell me you like it when I fuck your beautiful pussy."

My back arches off the bed, my core tightening as the eroticism of his words adds to the ache rolling through me. "Goddamn it, I love it when you fuck my pussy," I moan back as he continues to do exactly that, each thrust sending a new wave of ecstasy through me.

He lets loose a predatory grin and drops my leg back down, settling over me on his forearms. He glides mercilessly in and out, his breathing accelerating in my ear as he whispers a raunchy, explicit narrative about how good I feel, how much he's wanted to be inside of me, how hard he's going to make me come.

I've never had someone stimulate me this way during sex, and it has every part of my body clenching in anticipation. He doesn't even seem to mind that it has me so lust-fogged that I couldn't even form a sentence unless he told me what to say.

And rearing back while pulling me into his lap, he does exactly that.

"Tell me how to fuck you, Frankie," he instructs.

"Harder," I urge with a moan.

He thrusts harder, deeper. "You like it hard like that?"

"Yesss," I hiss as he pounds me just right. "Right there. Fuck, you're gonna make me come."

"Perfect," he says with a satisfied smile, "Now tell me how fast."

"Slower," I say, wanting to feel every inch as he pushes into my sensitive opening, then all the way deep down into the spot only the head of his long cock can reach. I want to climb to my orgasm as slowly as he brought me there with his hands and mouth, to feel that earth-shattering pleasure again.

He ratchets down accommodatingly until he's doing exactly that — hitting my G-spot with hard, slow thrusts. I feel the ache start to spread between my legs.

"Faster," I breathe.

He leans into me and picks up his speed just slightly. The ache builds and I throw my head back, unable to speak.

"Oh, damn, you just got so tight," he groans, closing his eyes.

I whimper at his words.

"I'm going to go faster. Hang on," he says breathlessly.

I nod mutely and grasp the sheets beneath me.

And he goes faster, asking over and over if I like the way he's fucking me. All I can do is writhe and moan in response.

And faster, now telling me how fucking good I feel. I have to grip the bed tightly to keep myself still enough to let the ache fill me as his words distract me to a whole new layered level of pleasure.

Sweat rolls off Julian's toned chest as he's finally silent, focusing on giving me all he's got. At the sight, I can feel my muscles contract, pulling him in deeper with each thrust. He shifts his weight to his left hand and slips his right one between my legs, stroking me in time with his rhythm, encouraging me with his sexy, dirty words once again. I throw my head back at the added stimulation, feeling the ache coil into a tight ball that threatens to explode through me at any moment.

"Come for me, beautiful," Julian says. It's his same plea as last time, but this time the tenderness in his voice undoes me completely.

"Ohhhhhh, yessss," I cry out as I tighten around him, riding up the wave, cresting, and still more until my body is shaking.

And just when I think I'm going to roll back down to earth he leans over me so he presses into my clit harder with every thrust and I'm riding even higher than before, screaming my release over and over.

Somewhere in the throes of passion I hear Julian loudly finding his own release. But I'm so racked by bliss that I don't come back down until he's slowed, then stopped completely.

He disentangles himself from my embrace and pulls out, leaning back on his haunches to catch his breath.

And now I'm the one who can't shut up, repeating "fuck" over and over as I try to catch my breath and wait for the shaking in my limbs to stop.

I watch Julian remove the condom and wrap it in a tissue before he lies down next to me, laughing.

"You okay?" he asks.

As the trembling of my arms and legs subsides, I lie, unmoving, on the bed next to him. "Beyond okay," I assure him when I can finally speak again.

Julian pulls the blanket back over us. "Good," he murmurs, curling up next to me and pulling me into a spooning position. "Now go back to sleep, beautiful."

I couldn't argue if I wanted to, as blissed out as I am, with his warm, strong body curled around mine, his abating erection pulsating on my backside, his lips resting against my hair. I drift peacefully to sleep, wrapped contentedly in Julian's ridiculously perfect arms.

When I wake again it's nearly noon and Julian isn't in bed. And a quick walk through the apartment tells me he's really gone. I check my phone and, lo and behold, he's texted me. *Figured I'd be a distraction, and you have things to do. I'll call you soon. x*

Shaking off the disappointment of waking up alone, I realize it was probably for the best. Because not only do I still not know if it's a good idea to agree to really give things with Julian the good old college try, he's also right — I have some serious shit to handle today.

IT TAKES THE AFTERNOON AND INTO THE EVENING TO PUT TOGETHER THE security footage and other data, go over it, and take it to the police station. To be fair, the time includes giving our own statements.

Jess isn't there, thankfully, and we aren't permitted to see Dave. Supposedly, he's in contact with an attorney, though, so we can only hope that everything will be okay. And guess at whatever details Jess provided to convince the police to hold Dave. Even without the advantage of knowing exactly when people are lying, Nils is absolutely in agreement with me that Jess set Dave up.

Disheartened and troubled, Nils and I are both famished, so we decide to head to the diner across the street from Baltia and talk things out.

As we finish our meal, I sit, picking at the last of my fries. I lean back in the booth, still trying to make sense of it all.

"So will there be any consequences for her when they prove she's lying?" Nils asks curiously, folding his long arms over his chest.

I huff a dry laugh. "How can they prove she's lying?" I point out. "At best we can hope they can't find enough evidence to support her story."

"Except we provided direct evidence that she lied to us," he counters.

I shake my head sadly and look up into his eyes. "That's not how it works, Nils, darling," I reply. "They weren't there. They won't take our word for it. For all they know we'd rather hush this all up to avoid bringing attention to the club." I shift in my seat, agitated. I hate when people get away with lying. Especially on something as damaging as this.

"Well, the video shows her following him into the bathroom," Nils says again for what feels like the thousandth time today. "She's going to be hard-pressed to prove she wasn't stalking him between that and the text messages he has."

I wave my hand dismissively. "There's nothing we can do about it, and I'm tired of talking in circles," I grouse, taking a sip of soda. "Can we talk about staffing? Because we were already short one bartender, and now there's no knowing when we'll get Dave back."

Nils leans forward on his arms. "I've thought about that," he admits. "And our situation in general. Even aside from this, business is a little too good for the coverage we've got all around. I think we need to make a few more additions as well."

I raise an eyebrow. I hadn't intended to increase staffing until after the first year, but I realize he's probably right. We've all been running ourselves ragged to keep up. And I, for one, could use a break.

"Okay," I agree.

Nils laughs. "I thought I'd have to fight a little harder," he replies with a smile.

"I've got no fight left," I reply, rubbing my temples.

Nils reaches across the table, uncharacteristically laying his hand over mine. "Hey, everything okay? It's not the brooder, is it?"

I laugh at his ridiculously accurate nickname for Julian. "I don't know," I admit. "I have reservations. But it's just everything. I think you're right, we need more help. It's all a bit overwhelming at the moment."

He studies my face carefully, still not withdrawing his hand. I turn my palm up and give him a reassuring squeeze.

"Really, let's do it," I reiterate.

He finally withdraws pensively with a nod. "I'll set up interviews as soon as I can manage. Two new bartenders and an assistant manager?"

"Sounds good. Thanks, Nils. For everything," I reply.

He runs a hand through his long blond hair, somehow seeming more bothered than before. "My pleasure, Francesca."

"Nils, is everything okay with you?"

He looks up warily, not responding right away. "Yes, no complaints here." *Lie*.

I suppress a sigh. "Come on, Nils, you can talk to me," I assure him. "You're important to me. To the club. If there's something going on, I want to know about it."

"I can't," he says, shaking his head. "Not after I encouraged you to go for it."

My eyebrows jump. "This is about Julian?"

He cringes and nods. "I don't trust him."

I smile widely and chuckle. "That makes two of us, Nils. But I appreciate your concern."

"Do you?" he asks, tilting his head to the side.

Suddenly, I'm not sure I like where this conversation is going. It feels too personal. Like there's something he's trying to tell me. Something I probably don't want to know.

"Yes," I say firmly. "As friends and coworkers, we should look out for each other."

He nods, and I hope he's read between the not-so-subtle lines. "Indeed," he says softly, holding my gaze. "Come on, let's get back to the club." He slides out of the booth.

But the walk back is silent and tense, and I wonder if I've heard the last of what's really on his mind.

On Monday afternoon Dave appears in my office door.

"Ms. Greco?"

"Dave," I reply, jumping out of my seat in surprise. "I'm glad to see you. Please come in and sit down."

He enters tentatively, and I note he looks exhausted and disheveled. I guess jail will do that to you.

"I was released this morning," he says by way of explanation as he settles into the chair across from me. "Everything happened so fast the other night. I wanted to come as soon as I could and tell you my side of the story."

I want to tell him there's no need, I know Jess set him up, but I know I shouldn't. "I'm all ears," I say instead, retaking my seat.

"I was going to the supply closet and decided to hit the head first," he says, nervously twisting his fingers in his lap. "But before I could lock the door, Jess came in and locked the door behind her."

He stops, shaking his head. I stay silent, not wanting to lead him one way or the other.

He looks up at me, brushing his shaggy brown hair out of his sad, grey-green eyes. He's a handsome kid, and it kills me to see him so miserable. He's usually so laid-back, happy-go-lucky even. What a shit lesson to learn at only twenty-two.

"She said she missed me. That it wasn't fair you were keeping us apart," he finally continues. "I tried to tell her again that it wasn't just you, that I didn't like her like that, just like I've told her before." He chews on his bottom lip. "She told me she'd give me one last chance to make the right decision, or else."

"Or else what?" I ask softly.

He snorts. "She didn't say, and I didn't ask," he responds. "I told her it wasn't gonna happen." He looks down and blushes a deep red. "She took off her shirt, and tried to touch me. I pushed her away, and she went nuts."

"Went nuts how?" I ask, leaning forward.

"She was like an animal," he says. It comes out a hoarse whisper, and he clears his throat and looks up, gesturing at the faint scabs adorning his cheeks. "She scratched the shit out of me, tore at my shirt, pulled her own fucking hair. Then she heard you call my name and she just screamed like a fucking banshee." He stops himself. "I'm sorry, it's just hard to talk about it without getting mad. It sounds crazy. The police looked at me like I was crazy. Like, why would she do that? They didn't get it. Honestly, I don't get it, either."

And I just can't take it anymore. "Dave," I say sharply, bringing his eyes back to mine. "There's definitely some crazy happening here, but I can pretty much guarantee it's not you."

He looks immensely relieved. "You believe me? You think it's her?" he asks.

"I believe you. She has already proven that she's capable of serious deception," I insist.

"I'm glad, but I don't know how the cops are going to know who to believe," he replies despondently.

"There was no question in my mind once we reviewed the evidence. And I'm confident the same will be true this time," I assure him.

"I hope so," he sighs. He scratches the back of his head. "So what happens now? With my job and everything, I mean."

I let out a heavy sigh. "Unfortunately, while the investigation is pending I have no choice but to suspend you," I reply.

The look on his face is one of the things I hate the most about being the boss. Because my hands are tied, and I'm unwillingly complicit in Jess's scheme to fuck him over for rejecting her.

"That's just fucking perfect," he spits venomously. Then immediately looks like he regrets it. "I'm sorry, I know you have to. This just sucks."

"I get that. And I can't pay you until this is resolved, but once it is — and it will be — you'll get backpay for the days you would've worked," I assure him. He looks slightly less unhappy at that news. "We'll keep in touch through this. Try not to worry too much. This will all be over soon."

Dave shakes his head sadly. "I have a feeling it's only just beginning."

14

FRANKIE

By Wednesday the list of people I haven't heard from has grown. The police. Emma. Julian. If I'm being honest with myself, the last one stings the most. I'm not sure what his definition of "soon" is, but not calling a woman you've slept with more than three days later isn't okay in my book.

I've resolved to call him this evening, but first I need to go see Emma. I haven't tried to call her since the club five days ago because I know how stubborn she is. I have to get in her face, beg her forgiveness. Even though it's not like I wasn't going to tell her about Ben's lies.

As I pull up in front of their building in Mar Vista, I try to drop the attitude. On my fourth deep breath, I realize I'm not annoyed at Emma for assuming I wasn't going to tell her. I'm mad at Julian for not calling. The realization makes me sad, which sucks, but at least I feel less angry and more prepared to face Emma without escalating the situation.

With a sigh I put up the ragtop and amble out of the car to face the music. I take my time climbing the stairs in her building, noting every crack in the wall on the way. *Geez, don't want to face the music much?* I should probably be giving myself a pep talk, but I'm not in a peppy mood, I guess.

I stand in front of Emma and Ben's peeling beige door and heave a sigh before biting the bullet and knocking.

As if she knew I was coming, and was standing there expectantly, I've barely dropped my arm when the door opens forcefully to a disheveled Emma.

Her blond hair is pulled back, but far messier than usual, and she's still wearing her pajamas. I guess if I didn't have to work in the middle of the week I'd be wearing mine too. I don't even have time to register her mood when she grabs my hand and pulls me into a big hug.

"Oh, Frankie," she murmurs. "I'm so sorry."

Surprised, it takes me a moment to return the hug. Her reaction is the opposite of what I was expecting.

"Well, this is already going better than I'd expected," I tease as she squeezes me roughly.

She pushes away, but grabs my hand once more and pulls me into their tiny one-bedroom apartment. She flops dramatically on their old, cracked brown leather couch and pats the cushion next to her. I sit reluctantly, still not believing she's magically over it.

"Seriously," Emma insists. "I was a complete bitch, and I feel like shit for it. Even if you weren't going to tell me, it wasn't your fault. It was Ben I was mad at. Can you forgive me?"

I laugh drily. I know the feeling. Same as how I'm not mad at her either, though I can't say the same for Julian.

I reach over and give her hand a squeeze. "I know how you feel," I commiserate. "And of course I can. I *was* going to tell you, I promise. There was just so much going on, and I wanted to work up to it. But I fucked up. And I'm sorry too."

Emma leans over and pulls me in for another hug.

"So what's with all the hugging?" I tease her gently. "Are you and Ben okay?"

She sighs, pulling at her stretchy pajama top. "We will be," she finally replies, fidgeting in her seat.

"Did he say *why* he lied?" I ask. I don't even want to know how she found out. I'm just glad she did before she went into vacation planning mode.

Emma's lips press together in a deep frown. "I've been getting on his case a lot about getting a nicer place," she admits. "But it's not like we can exactly afford it."

"That still doesn't make any sense," I press.

Emma shrugs. "I don't think he thought too hard about it — he just wanted me off his back," she responds. "Who the fuck knows what goes on in a man's brain?"

I huff a dry laugh, shaking my head. "Preach," I grumble, looking at my hands in my lap, fighting a wave of unexpected tears. It makes me angry, and I let out a growl as I press my palms into my eyes. I don't fucking cry for anyone, and I'm not about to start.

"Frankie, what's wrong?" Emma asks, clearly alarmed.

I drop my hands to find her staring at me bewildered. I can see it's just as jarring for her to see me like this as it is for me. And last she knew Julian was on my shit list. Not that he isn't right back there.

"Oh fuck, it's the asshole, isn't it?" she demands. She pushes me hard. "Dammit, Frankie, you let him back in and he fucked with you again, didn't he?"

"No," I protest. "Well, yes, but ..." I trail off, shaking my head in anger. But I'm less mad at Julian now. I'm starting to be angrier with myself. Emma is not wrong. I *knew*. I knew we were too similar. That it was going to be a fucking rollercoaster. I let myself be taken in by the attraction, by his promises, his words. I know I'm smarter than that.

In any case it's a burden I can't bear alone anymore, so I spill my guts to Emma. I tell her about what went down at the club while she was at the bar, and after she left, both with the fight with the bitches and with Julian following me. I tell her about our encounter the next day in my living room, and the mess at the club with Jess and Dave that night, and how Julian helped, cared for me, connected with me. How we fucked the next morning. And that when I woke up again, he was gone. And that I haven't heard from him since.

She's quiet for a moment, clearly incredulous. "Wow. You're really looking for trouble these days, aren't you?" she muses. She looks up at me suddenly with a wicked look on her face. "How was the sex?"

I laugh. "That's what you want to know?" I shake my head. "Fucking amazing."

"And everything else? I mean, do you really *like* this guy?"

I rub my thighs, irritated. "I guess? I mean, yes. Until we fucked and then he hasn't called for three days," I growl. "Part of me wants to write him off. But mostly I want to know why. Or maybe this is normal? Or am I supposed to call him?" I shake my head again, completely agitated and out of my element.

"Jesus H. Christ, Frankie, it hasn't been *that* long since you've dated," Emma replies, rolling her eyes. "You're totally right to be pissed. You guys fucked. He said he wants to be with you. He knows you're going through some shit. He said he'd call. He *should've* called."

I take a deep breath and lean back into the cushions. "You're right," I agree. "You're absolutely right. So what do I do now?"

"Say you call him, and he's an asshole. Do you really want to deal with that now?" she asks shrewdly.

I chew on my bottom lip, trying to be as objective as possible. I want to believe Julian isn't trying to be a dick, but let's face it, he's not doing himself any favors at the moment. And I've got enough on my plate.

"No," I admit.

Emma shrugs as if the answer should be obvious. And maybe it is. But she spells it out anyway. "Then don't call him. Deal with it when you're ready to."

"That's a strangely liberating way to look at it," I respond slowly. I roll the idea around in my head for a while. And the more I think about it, the better it sounds. He doesn't want to talk to me? Fine. I don't want to talk to him right now either. I sure as hell don't have the energy to get through that conversation.

I'M SITTING IN MY OFFICE AT BALTIA ON THURSDAY MORNING WHEN THE detective on Dave's case finally calls. He tells me they've dropped all charges. In combination with the pile of evidence against her story, apparently there have been two other restraining orders taken out against Jess in the last three years for stalking. He also shares that he's advised Dave to do the same, and for me to let him know if there are any further issues.

When I hang up, I'm relieved, but I still have an unsettled feeling. I sit, staring into the distance and stroking gentle circles into my desk while I try to pinpoint my disquiet.

It's how Nils finds me just before we're supposed to interview new bartending candidates. I fill him in on the latest and let him call Dave to confirm he can come back to work before we begin our interviews.

It takes the rest of the afternoon, pushing up into opening, before we've gotten through everyone, as I'd forgotten we were also interviewing for an assistant manager. We found the latter almost immediately, as Nils had a friend he'd worked with before whom he was itching to hire, so I just told him to go ahead. We also found one experienced bartender we hired on the spot — a stunning redhead in her mid-forties who didn't drop a single lie and whose no-nonsense attitude was immediately appealing — and had another few candidates to think on before we filled the second spot. All in all, not a bad place to be in.

But having been made to skip dinner, I'm in a pretty foul mood for the rest of the night. Though I can't blame it entirely on lack of food. Thankfully, one of the perks of the job is that it's hard to think about much else once the music starts.

~

Unfortunately, Friday does little to improve my mood. Nils and I make the decision on the second bartender and just as I have the phone in my hand to call, Jess walks into my office.

She beams at me as she enters, her blond curls bouncing innocently as she parks herself in the chair in front of my desk. "I'm here to ask for my job back. I realize what I did was wrong, and I think I deserve a second chance," she says cheerfully.

I'm completely dumbfounded. And just as quickly, extremely disturbed.

"Jess, you've been banned from being here. I'm not sure how you got in the door, but you need to leave, now, and not come back. Or I'm afraid I'll be forced to file an order of protection. You wouldn't want that, would you?" I prompt.

"But I'm a new Jess now," she replies, still chipper. "Dave got another chance. I should too."

It's not lost on me that she knows Dave has returned to work, and I wonder if she's been back to the club without our knowledge. The further this goes, the more disturbed I get.

"Yes, because the charges against him were dropped. I don't punish innocent people," I reply pointedly. "You were fired for provable misconduct."

Jess's mouth drops open stupidly, but the confusion on her face is rapidly replaced with rage. Red-faced and clearly beyond agitated, she springs from her chair and slams her hands on my desk.

"You can't do this," she seethes. "He got a second chance. If you don't give me one, I'll sue you for discrimination."

The absence of the voice tells me that it's not an empty threat. I take a deep breath through my nose and rise slowly from my chair, circling the desk to hold the door open in an obvious signal that I'm not interested in discussing this further. She folds her arms over her chest resolutely, glaring at me as she roots in place.

"In that case, I'm obligated to direct you to our attorney," I say firmly. "Now please leave or I will have you escorted from the building."

"Fine," she hisses. "But you're going to regret this."

And with that she stomps past me and out of the club. And I have an ugly feeling that she means to make good on her threat.

Nils slinks into my office.

"What the hell was that?" he asks.

I shake my head, not in the mood to discuss it.

"Can you call Rick, please? I didn't get the chance before Ms. Wilson's visit."

"Oh, I saw her coming, so I already called him. He'll start next Thursday. Really, Francesca, we should discuss this," he insists.

I sigh. He's right. But before I can, my phone buzzes distractingly on my desk.

"Fine, just let me check this," I grouse, circling my desk and grabbing my phone. It's Julian. The fucking bastard. I send it to voicemail without hesitation and shove my phone angrily into my back pocket. When I turn back to Nils, he's suppressing a smile. "What?"

He presses his lips together. "Sorry," he apologizes honestly. "I can guess who that was by the look on your face."

I narrow my eyes at him, and he puts his hands up, laughing. "I won't say a word against him," he promises. "I just hope you don't ever look like that when I call."

That throws me off and we stare at each other for a moment, tension hanging thick in the air. But before I can formulate a response, Ace appears and drags Nils away on some urgent sound-system-related business. Nils vows to return to discuss Jess, but I don't give a flying fuck either way right now. I bury myself in work to forget it all. Nils. Jess. Julian. Especially Julian.

Unfortunately, he doesn't take the hint, and over the next few hours until doors open, I feel my phone buzz several more times. I only glance at the screen long enough to confirm it's Julian and not some other, more urgent business, before going back to firmly ignoring him. But, if it's possible, it makes me even grouchier than I'd been the night before. Against my better judgment, I throw back a couple of drinks as I work the floor, trying to take the edge off the stress of the week. But the universe has the last laugh, as it's not enough to dull my internal turmoil, just enough to give me one big motherfucking headache.

FORTUNATELY, LATE THE NEXT MORNING I MEET MAC AT THE SHOOTING range. And every target is Julian. I nail each one in the head *and* the heart for good measure. It improves my mood considerably. That is, until Mac looks at me with his wise, old eyes that see everything. Thankfully, he doesn't say anything. He just lets me go at it until our two hours are up, then buys me tacos as we shoot the shit about everything else.

I haven't even mentioned Julian to him, and I'm not about to start now. That's not the kind of stuff Mac and I discuss. And the catharsis of killing dummy targets and eating Mexican food is short lived, as I realize I really do need to talk about it.

But I'm just not ready yet, so I head back to the club to keep busy until tonight. What I don't expect is the strange old man waiting for me at the front door.

"Doors don't open until ten," I call out as I approach.

He turns toward me and smiles. He looks to be in his late sixties but based on the cigarette hanging out of his mouth that looks like it fits nicely in its well-worn groove, he could also be younger. A few strands of thin, greasy hair are slicked back on his head. He'd be average height if he didn't stoop a bit, and he looks like he was attacked by a pawn shop jewelry counter.

"I know. I was looking for *you*," he greets me, extending a weathered hand.

I look down at it and cross my arms over my chest. "Yeah? What for?" I ask defensively.

He cackles happily. "You've got spunk, Frankie," he says fondly. "I knew you would."

If I didn't already immediately dislike him, I do now. "You've got two seconds to tell me who the fuck you are and how you know me before I kick your ass off my property," I warn him.

He huffs one last laugh. "My name is Salvatore Moretti," he replies. "And I'm your father, Frankie."

15

———

FRANKIE

I stand there, completely speechless, staring at this old man who claims to be my father. And the little voice inside me says not a word. It's a full minute before I find my voice again.

"You must be mistaken. My father died before I was born," I assure him. I don't know if this guy is crazy or misinformed, but the fact that he believes it tells me I need to be very careful.

"Ah," he says. "So that's what Sam told you."

I mash my lips together. Okay, he also knows my mother's name. That just means he's more well informed than the average nutjob.

"Look, I don't know who you really are, but I can assure you that I know without a doubt that my father did die before I was born."

He smiles patiently. "She lied to me about you, too," he says softly. "I understand that this must all be very shocking for you, and I debated just leaving you alone. But I've already missed out on thirty-four years of your life. Allow me to prove it to you?"

I want to tell him my mother can't lie to me. But I stop myself. I know better than anyone that there are so many ways to hide the truth. And I have to ask myself if I remember when my mother told me my father was dead, and how.

"How did you find me, then?" I ask.

He gestures to the door. "Perhaps we should sit down and discuss this?" he asks politely.

But the thought of letting this man into my club doesn't sit well. I tuck my arms closer around myself and shake my head. He sighs deeply, leaning into the building.

"Okay, then. I saw a news piece on you. And the club." He gestures to the building. "You looked just like my mother, and I knew Sam had lied to me. See, I knew she had a little girl, years ago. But she lied about your age, said you weren't mine. You looked different enough then that I didn't see it. As soon as I saw you now, though, I knew. And when I saw how old you really are, well, it was more confirmation of something I already knew."

I shake my head again, finding it impossible to absorb. "How did you know my mom? How did you not know she was pregnant?"

The old man sighs and runs a hand over his greasy head. "That's your mother's story to tell."

I laugh. I might as well go ask my mother to get a mani-pedi with me and have some girl talk. In other words, not gonna happen.

He eyes me shrewdly. "She's a tough nut, your mom. I know," he says.

I raise an eyebrow. "So how exactly did you plan on proving this to me?"

His thin lips stretch in a smile. "If you have some time, there's a hospital four blocks away. Same-day paternity tests." He checks his watch. "So long as we're there in the next forty-five minutes."

I mull on that. I have the time. I don't really need to be at the club for another few hours. And I realize I both have nothing to lose, and if I don't find out, it'll bug the shit out of me. At least this way, if he's crazy, I'll know now. And if he isn't, well, that's a whole other thing I'm not ready to unpack yet.

"Can you walk it, or do you need me to drive?" I ask him bluntly.

He straightens up, gesturing to the sidewalk in front of him.

"I ain't dead yet, doll. After you."

The next hour was quite possibly the most awkward hour of my life. But I did exactly as he'd suggested, and we parted ways at the hospital. Despite the shock and my initial reservations, I recognize he did his best not to freak me out. In that vein, he gave me his number when we parted so that I could call once the results were in. If I wanted to.

Feeling like I'm living in a surreal version of my own life, I blindly trek the four blocks back to the club and sit in my office until things pick up for the night. I try to keep busy, to keep my mind off Salvatore Moretti and, of course, Julian.

But by an hour before doors open, I find myself feeling pretty damn useless. With our new, more experienced bartender working seamlessly with Johnny, and Nils having an eager new assistant manager whom he already has a rapport with, there's really not much for me to do.

I should be happy. But instead I do something I haven't done in ages. I grab a beer and a pack of cigarettes and head out the side door to wallow. Slinking against the building, I take a long pull off the bottle before I nestle it between my legs, so it's less obvious. And then I light up a cigarette, taking a disgusting drag. And feeling like a fucking hypocrite. But as the nicotine soothes my nerves, I find myself caring less.

"Frankie. I didn't know you smoked."

I nearly jump out of my skin at the voice. And lo and behold, I look up to find Julian sauntering toward me.

"I guess ignoring your calls was too subtle. Fuck off, Julian," I snap, trying to look anywhere but at him. So I look up at the sky. But I'm disappointed again. You can never see stars in the city. Not even when you need them the most.

I finish my cigarette and take a long sip of beer. I feel, rather than see, Julian take a seat next to me.

"I'm sorry I didn't call sooner," he says softly. "My boss sent me out of town this week."

I snort. "I wasn't aware L.A. is the only place with phone service."

"It's complicated, Frankie. I couldn't call you. I wish I could've. I didn't stop thinking about you the whole time."

When the voice stays silent, I look at him in surprise. Usually, when guys say shit like that it's total bull. A line to get in your pants. But the asshole *means it*. And he looks so damn good, his five o'clock shadow rough on his strong jaw, his dark eyes pleading with me to forgive him. Goddamn it, this *is* going to be complicated.

"I don't know what you want me to say," I reply honestly.

A small smile tugs at the corner of his full lips. He slides a hand up my thigh and it sends shivers down my back.

"Say you missed me," he replies, his voice husky and inviting, his eyes dancing in the dark.

I want to. I really do. But I'd be lying. "I did at first," I allow. "But then I was too busy being pissed off that you didn't call. Or, apparently, didn't bother telling me you'd be going out of town and couldn't call."

Julian pulls his hand back and looks up into the sky, clearly at a loss for what to say.

"Don't bother looking for stars," I say, standing up and brushing off my pants. "You can't see them from here."

He looks up at me thoughtfully. "Yeah? Where can you see them from?"

I shrug, tossing my empty bottle into the trash can on the other side of the door. "Griffith Park. Or drive out to the desert." I turn away from him. "I've got to get back."

"Don't go," he pleads, standing up. "Not yet."

I turn back to him without meaning to and our eyes meet. Dammit, how I want to say no. But my body has its own ideas when it comes to him. And he knows it.

He advances a couple of steps until he's standing in front of me. He slips his hand under my chin, forcing me to keep eye contact. His thumb grazes my lower lip and it's all I can do to stay still, to not jump his gorgeous fucking bones, despite myself.

Thankfully, inside I hear sound checks, indicating we're close to opening. It clears my head enough that I take a step back, out of his arms, and gain control.

"I really have to go," I whisper.

Julian scrubs a hand over his stubble. "Let me make it up to you tomorrow night," he asks. "Please, Frankie."

His soft tone seeps under my defenses and I close my eyes. "You can try." I turn and go back inside before he or I can say, or do, anything else. I've already had enough for one evening, and it's only just begun.

16

FRANKIE

The paternity tests results don't actually come in until Sunday morning, when I'm still fast asleep after another crazy night at the club. But it was the contained kind of crazy. The kind that helped me forget everything going on. So it's to an unfortunate dose of reality that I wake, in the form of a voicemail confirming that there is a 99.9% chance that Salvatore Moretti is my father.

To say I'm dumbfounded is an understatement. I get dressed faster than I ever have, and I'm in the car on the way to my mom's house before I can even begin to process what this all means. I force myself not to think on the way. The more I think, the madder I'll get.

Though by the time I pull into her driveway, I'm still pretty fucking mad. Tony is on the porch, sorting collector cards. His face lights up when he sees me, and I do my best not to look like hell's fury incarnate.

"Hey, Big T," I tease him. "Mom home?"

"Frankie!" he exclaims, jumping to his feet. "Yeah, she's in the kitchen with Nonna. As usual." He starts to follow me inside, but I put a hand on his chest.

"You might want to sit this one out, little dude," I say firmly.

Tony's eyes widen, and he nods, stepping back to his cards as he watches me go inside.

Just as Tony said, they're both in the kitchen. They look up in surprise as I enter. My mother considers me dully for a moment.

"Your schedule's off, Frankie — it's only been two weeks," she says, turning to go back to whatever she was chopping.

But Nonna needs only one look at me to know that I'm well aware of the date. "Everything okay, dear?" she asks.

"No," I reply shortly. "Can we please be alone?"

Nonna looks like she wants to ask what's going on but wisely says nothing. She simply nods, planting a kiss on my cheek as she passes. I wait for the click of her bedroom door shutting before turning back to my mother.

"Frankie, I don't know what's bothering you, but if you're upset, we should really do this another time," my mother preempts me. I almost laugh. It's such a typical response. If I'm at all emotional, there's no discussion. Over the years I learned she sees it as weakness. So I try a different tack.

"Oh, I'm not upset," I say cheerfully. She looks up and raises an eyebrow. "Confused, maybe? See, this guy showed up at the club yesterday claiming to be my father. Said his name was Salvatore Moretti. I told him that just couldn't be possible, since my dad is dead. But then …" I hold up my cellphone and play the paternity results voicemail for my mother. In moments, she's white as a sheet. And I actually am less upset than I thought I'd be. The terrified look on her face makes me happy in a way I know it shouldn't. For once, I have power over my mother.

"Well," she says primly, trying to regain control. "Is there a question here? Because it sounds like you have all the information you need."

Not that I needed her confirmation, but that statement pretty much blows my whole childhood out of the water. Knowing about my ability, my mother agreed early on not to lie to me. Or I thought she had. But clearly the web of lies is much more subtle than I thought. And the thought of how far this could reach is staggering. I feel like the foundation of my whole life has been yanked out from under me.

"You played with my loopholes," I accuse her. "You've been playing with them my whole life."

My mother throws down her towel and rolls her eyes. "Of course, I did, silly girl. I'm your mother. It's my job to protect you from things that could hurt you," she snaps condescendingly.

"No, Mom," I correct her. "It was your job to prepare me to handle those things myself. If you can't trust your mother, who can you trust?"

"Exactly," she replies emphatically, slamming her hand on the counter. "I did what was best for you. Always. You should trust that that's true."

The voice is silent. I guess there's some comfort that she thought she was doing what was best for me.

"I've been an adult for a long time now," I press. "Why didn't you tell me? You knew he was still out there. You thought he'd just never find out about me?"

"That is a long and very personal story," she says tightly. "Suffice it to say that no, I didn't think he'd ever find out about you, and if he did, I didn't think he'd have the balls to come anywhere near this family again. Now. I'm done talking about this with you. You know as much as I'm willing to tell you, and I won't stand for you questioning my decisions when you have no idea what was going on."

And with that she waltzes out of the kitchen with her nose in the air. I hear the front door slam. And a moment later, the engine of the car roars to life, its puttering trailing off as my mother literally flees from the mess she created.

I sit down at the kitchen table and sink my head into my hands. It's not long before I feel Nonna's hand on my shoulder. She seats herself next to me, rubbing circles gently over my back.

"Salvatore Moretti was a very charming young man who worked for your grandfather," she starts quietly. I look up into her eyes. All the love I wanted to see in my mother's eyes is present there. "Your mother was only seventeen. We didn't even know they'd been seeing each other. Or whatever it was they were doing." Nonna sighs. "If you remember anything about your grandfather, surely it's his temper. But your mother didn't want your father to know about you, so he was simply fired. And told never to come near the family again. I'm sure it was very confusing for him at the time, and I believe he cared very much for your mother, but your grandfather's warning was enough. He was a very intimidating man."

I huff a laugh. Oh, I remember. He regularly lost his temper with me, at times becoming physical. I recall with a shudder one of the worst incidents, when he yelled at me for an hour straight the day I scratched his precious car. The same one Mom still drives to this day. When I refused to cry, he took a belt to me until I did. He was a sadistic hothead, and I can't say I miss him.

"But why? Why didn't she tell me once I was grown? Why keep up the lie?" I press. "And what else has she lied to me about?"

Nonna smiles indulgently. "Frankie, darling, surely you've learned by now that just because you know a lie when you hear one doesn't mean you know the truth," she says sagely. "Your mother has always been very self-contained. She doesn't explain herself to anyone, and she's not used to being questioned. You've always pushed her limits, and it's made her draw further away from you."

I blanch. "You're saying the way our relationship is is my fault?" I ask, insulted.

Her hand closes over mine. "No," she says emphatically. "It's just the way you both are. You push. She retreats. You quest for truth. She holds her secrets close. It's not your fault, it's fact. Don't ever forget that."

I examine my grandmother's face, grasping to understand something I can't quite pull from her words.

"If she'd just talk to me …" I trail off, not quite sure what I'm trying to say. "He's my father. But if she kept him from me, I want to know why. So I don't go into this blind."

"I can't tell you what you want to know," my grandmother says carefully. "But that's how life is, dear. Even when we think we know something, we're all really just flying blind. Things change. People change. You can never have all the facts. And even if you did, my darling granddaughter, you have always been stubborn, always had to learn things the hard way. I doubt anything your mother could tell you would change whatever it is you plan to do."

"You're wrong," I say with a twinkle in my eye. Nonna raises an eyebrow. "I don't *always* have to learn the hard way. Just most of the time." That gets a hearty laugh from her. "Thank you, Nonna."

She smiles brightly, and I lean in to hug her.

"You're welcome," she murmurs into my hair. Pressing me back at arm's length, she examines my face. "Now. How are things going with your young man?"

Picturing Julian, a smile creeps across my face. The joy of talking to Nonna is that her advice is almost always universal. And her words have not only helped me start to accept my new parental situation, but I also realize now that they apply to my feelings for Julian as well. I know he hasn't lied to me. I know he's got his secrets. But I don't need all the facts. I know how I feel about him.

"We're still getting to know each other," I admit. "But I think it's going somewhere. Somewhere really good."

17

JULIAN

"We're going somewhere really fucking good, that's all I'm going to say."

"Not even a little hint?" Frankie presses, twirling her dark hair around her perfectly manicured finger. Like that's going to sway me.

I fold my arms over my chest and smirk down at her. "Nope," I confirm. "And we're taking your car."

She levels a glare at me, but quickly thinks better of it as a devilish smile replaces it. "If you tell me where we're going, I'll let you drive."

I take a step forward, pressing her against the kitchen counter behind her. "Oh, I'm driving all right," I assure her. "But I'm still not telling." Her hands slip to the counter behind her for support, and her pupils dilate. And I know I've got the upper hand, which I fully intend to press.

In one swift movement, I lift her onto the counter and bury my face in her neck, running my tongue up the soft flesh. She groans beneath me, arching into my body. As I work her neck with my mouth, I slide a hand under her shirt, stroking and squeezing her gorgeous tits.

"You're driving me crazy is what you're doing," she says with a moan. The sound goes straight to my cock, and I swear if I hadn't just planned the perfect evening for her, I'd spend the rest of the night fucking her on this counter and any other surface she'd let me. It's been a full week since I've been inside her, and it's practically all I can fucking think about.

But I rein it in. That's not what tonight is about. It's about making it up to her. Again. Even if she is wearing a black skirt that floats around her in a way that's asking me to lift it and fuck her senseless.

With a sigh, I push back, letting her slide back down onto her feet.

After a few more unsuccessful attempts at not touching her, I finally manage to convince her to get into the car.

The whole hour-plus-long drive, she badgers me about where we're going, but I don't spill the beans.

As twilight descends and night sets in, we get farther out of the reach of civilization.

When we finally reach our destination, I pull into the small lot of a state park, lower the top and cut the engine.

"What are we doing here?" she asks, looking over at me, confused.

I simply smile and point up. She looks up, and watching her mouth drop open in awe at the unadulterated starry sky above us is just as rewarding as I thought it would be.

"Holy. Fucking. Shit," she whispers. She glances over at me, her eyes filled with tears. "This is amazing. Thank you, Julian." She reaches over and gives my hand a squeeze.

I tear my eyes from her to look up. And it is amazing. Beyond amazing, actually. The dark, velvety sky is dotted with all the stars you'd never see with the lights of the city drowning them out. Even the Milky Way is just visible, and the effect is un-fucking-believable.

I reach out and stroke her face. "I'm glad you like it," I reply. I lean my seat back as far as it'll go, and she does the same. Her hand slides back into mine and we lie watching the stars for a good long while without speaking. I glance over at her occasionally, watching her drink in the sight in blissful silence.

Eventually, I crack. I turn to her and trace a finger down the moon tattooed on her left shoulder. "So you gonna tell me why you like the night sky so much?"

"You'll make fun of me," she replies, keeping her eyes fixed stubbornly on the heavens.

I want to protest, but I can't make any promises. "Try me," I say.

She presses her lips together and finally looks over at me. She studies my face, so I study hers back. Her long, dark hair dangles over the headrest, putting her high cheekbones and full red lips on display. But it's her eyes that I can't stop looking at. Deeply, darkly sparkling blue, alive, and full of light, mystery, and emotion. If I could freeze a moment, it would be this one. To remember her like this forever.

Fuck. *Did I really just think of Frankie and forever in the same sentence? Am I that far gone?* I turn away from her and close my eyes. I realize I may just be getting carried away in the moment. Then again, maybe not.

"Okay," she says softly. My eyes open and snap back to hers. There's vulnerability there now. She props herself up on her elbow to look down at me. "When I was a kid, I didn't feel like I fit in with my family. My mom kept me at such a distance. My grandfather was a tyrant. And my grandmother spent most of her time buffering between my mom, my grandad, and me, that we didn't have the closeness we do now. I just felt alone." She breathes deeply in through her nose, then shakes her head. "I'm not explaining this very well. It's just complicated."

I sit up, popping my seat up, then climb into the back. I motion for her to follow suit, and she does. She settles onto the small bench seat in the back next to me, laying her head on my chest. I wrap my arms around her and plant a kiss on the top of her head. Her hair smells like strawberries, and she feels like fucking heaven in my arms. But I want her to open up to me, finally. I need her to. Even if I can't fully reciprocate.

"So uncomplicate it," I say simply. She strokes a hand over my chest, and fuck if it isn't the most relaxing thing I've ever felt.

"I used to run away. A lot. And nobody noticed," she admits with a sigh. "Eventually, I took to sleeping in the park near our house, trying to spot a star here or there in the darkness of the night while I told myself stories to make myself feel better. My favorite was that I was really an alien. And one of those stars was my real parents, trying to find me. To bring me home."

I can't help laughing. So much so, it shakes my whole body, and she sits up, glaring at me. I shake my head, wiping the tears from my eyes. "I'm sorry," I manage. "It's just too fucking cute."

"Cute?" she asks venomously. "My childhood trauma is cute?"

I shrug, trying to keep from laughing again. "No, baby, it's just that most kids would come up with something a hell of a lot more dangerous to get into than stargazing and making up stories about being an alien."

Her eyes glitter down at me, her face a mask suddenly. Self-consciously, I sit upright, worried I've seriously offended her. "I'm sorry, I —"

She puts her finger on my lips to shut me up. "You called me 'baby,'" she whispers.

I wrap my hand around hers, kissing her finger before drawing it away from my lips. "I did," I agree.

She sits up fully, drawing away. She looks nervous but determined. "Julian, the reason for my family trouble, the reason I had no friends growing up, that I didn't want any ..." she closes her eyes and takes a deep breath. "You asked me once how I knew when you were lying. That's why. Because I know. When people lie to me, I know."

Confusion and anxiety push away the extreme relaxation that had settled over me. My heart starts pounding in my chest. Maybe Sal was right about her after all. Fuck. If that's true, then she knows about me. And if *that's* true ... fuck. But I need her to tell me to my face. That she knows. That she's just been playing me.

"Like how? Someone gives you the dirt on anyone you ask about?" My voice comes out thin and scratchy. God-fucking-damn it, I need to pull it together.

"God, no," Frankie replies emphatically. She rubs her temples with both hands, frustrated. She looks up suddenly. "Have you ever played two truths and a lie?"

I give her a reticent look. While my initial panic has passed, I'm not sure I like where this is going. And all of my instincts are telling me to cut and run. "Yes," I say slowly, struggling to contain myself.

"Good," she replies, grabbing one of my hands with both of hers. "Tell me two truths and one lie. Things you wouldn't have ever told anyone. One at a time."

"I don't understand what this has to do with anything," I say shortly, quickly losing my patience. If she's fucking dirty we need to deal with this. Now. I'm already putting myself on the line even being here with her against Sal's direction. If she's just playing me, I'm the biggest fucking patsy ever. And like fucking hell I'm going to let that keep happening.

"Please, Julian," she begs, reaching for my face. I'm tempted to recoil, but instead, I stay as still as stone. Trying to wrap my heart in the same hardness. I'm usually so fucking good at it, but when she withdraws, sensing my aversion, the yearning on her face cuts through my resolve like a knife through warm butter.

I close my eyes. "I was born in a monastery." My chest tightens. "I love puppies." I bunch my hands into fists, struggling to keep my eyes closed. "And I've never been in love." As soon as the words are out of my mouth, my mind whispers, *Before now*. And I wonder if I just told two lies. But maybe not, if I didn't realize it until after I'd said it. After all, I never thought I'd find someone I could trust. Can't say I was wrong there. Or maybe I just never thought I had a heart to give someone. Much less one for someone to break. And because it feels like that's exactly what's happening...

I push the thought back and open my eyes. I stare at her, still stone-faced, waiting for whatever comes next.

Her hand slowly moves toward my face. I remain motionless while she wipes a tear from my cheek with her thumb, cupping my jaw when she's done.

"God, Julian, that's fucked up," she whispers. "Who doesn't love puppies?"

I blink. And despite myself, I start laughing. Hard. And the tears I didn't know were even there turn into tears of laughter. She sits back, biting her lip to restrain her smile, clearly unsure of what to make of my outburst.

"I'm sorry," I choke out, wiping my face with both hands. As I settle, I stare at her, still beyond confused.

"I know," she says. "It doesn't make sense. But I was being literal. Nobody's been giving me intel on you, Julian, if that's what you were worried about. Though don't think for a minute we're not going to unpack that one later." She raises an eyebrow sternly. "I just know when people lie. You can tell me another one if you don't believe me."

I give her a funny look. But okay. Let's fucking do this. It's as crazy as her claim, but I'll play along. "I put honey on pickles."

Her nose wrinkles. "Ewww."

"I cheat on my taxes."

"Lie."

Shit. "I cheat on my girlfriends."

"Pshh," she scoffs. "I don't even need the ability to know that's a lie."

I smirk at her, despite myself. "Fine," I allow. "I cheat at cards."

She smiles. "You're a dirty boy, Julian."

I lean back into the leather seat. Fuck. She *can* tell when I'm lying. Like, really. Like, really really. "How is this even possible?"

She shakes her head and splays out her hands. "I don't know," she says plainly. "I've been able to do it since I can remember."

I run a hand through my hair, still agitated, still finding it hard to absorb. "That's some fucked-up shit, Frankie."

A smile creeps across her lips. "Have I told you how much I love it when you call me that?" she asks, ignoring the mockery of my reply.

I huff a dry laugh. "Yeah, I caught that when you didn't bust my balls over it," I tease.

She shoves my shoulder. "Hey, I don't bust your balls," she protests. I raise an eyebrow at her pointedly. "Okay, okay, so I bust your balls a little. Sometimes."

I raise both eyebrows, giving her a skeptical look, and she blushes a deep crimson. It makes me laugh, melting the last of whatever negative emotions I'd been having.

"So how's it work?" I ask curiously.

"That's it? We're on to acceptance? You're not running for the hills?" she replies.

I run a hand over the budding beard on my jaw, considering that. "Guess not."

Frankie barks a laugh. "Loquacious as usual." She shakes her head.

"What's that supposed to mean?" I counter.

"You're a man of few words," she replies, then with a wicked grin, "except in bed."

"You're not going to distract me with sex," I deadpan.

Her grin widens. "Oh?" I shake my head and she laughs. "Maybe later then."

And I wasn't lying, but as we stare each other down, I have to admit, I'm a little distracted. Being in bed with her isn't something that's easy to forget. Being with her period wouldn't be easy to forget. And I find I'm not of a mind to, even in light of this new, bizarre revelation. It suddenly occurs to me that Sal would kill to know about this. As I stare back into her beautiful, blue eyes, I decide here and now that he's never going to hear about it from me, no matter what happens between us.

"You don't have to explain it if you don't want to," I allow, touching my finger to her knee. "It's part of you. Freaky. But part of you." Now it's my turn to grin. "Besides, I don't mind a little freaky from time to time."

She scrunches her nose and shakes her head at me. "Trust me, it's almost never the good kind of freaky to know what I know about people." She pauses. "Though it's not a magic bullet. I got a pretty big fucking reminder of that yesterday."

The tension in her voice worries me, and I know I'm still in this, because I care.

"What happened?" I prompt.

She looks up at me, seemingly unsure. She brushes her hair back and brings her knees up to her chest, wrapping her arms around them. Going into her little cocoon. I allow it, for now.

"I met my father," she says blandly.

And I'm confused again. "Didn't you say your father was dead?"

Frankie snorts. "That I did. But apparently that whopper got past me." She presses her lips together, barely hiding her anger.

"So, it's not infallible, this ability of yours?" I ask.

"No," she admits grimly. "There are loopholes."

"And you're upset because your mom used them."

She shakes her head. "No. She's been doing it my whole life. I think I knew that on some level."

"Then what's bothering you?" I ask, finally reaching for her.

When I take her hands, she looks relieved. "I'm used to not having a real relationship with my mother because of how I am," she says, playing with our entwined fingers. "And I've been fine without a father. If anything, her hiding him from me successfully tells me I have no way of knowing who to trust. So how can I trust him? How can I even begin to get to know him? But then, how can I not?" She heaves a big sigh.

I tug at her fingers, pulling her until she's between my legs, our faces inches apart. "Welcome to how the rest of us have to go into relationships. Blind. I don't trust anyone either. But you're right about one thing," I say, my eyes locked on hers, "you'd probably regret not checking the guy out."

She responds with a dim smile, moving in and rubbing her nose gently against mine. At this distance I can see every fleck in those beautiful blue eyes. "Thank you," she says quietly. "For not only sticking around, but actually being here for me."

I trace a finger down her cheek, sliding over her jaw and cupping her chin. "Still can't seem to stay away," I murmur with a smile.

She closes the gap between us, her soft lips grazing mine. Even that small touch is enough to rile me. I make to deepen the kiss, but she pulls back and considers me.

"Mmm. So what dirt were you worried I had on you?" she asks out of the blue.

Thank fucking God I'm good at keeping a straight face. I consider my reply carefully. "Nothing I won't tell you in time," I assure her. "But not right now. I think the better question is, what are you going to do about your father?"

Frankie shudders. "I don't know. I guess I'll call him and see what happens. But I gotta say, it's weird even hearing you call him my father. This is going to take some getting used to."

"I doubt he expects you to call him dad," I point out. "If I found my long-lost daughter, I'd be pretty weirded out too. Just call him whatever you're comfortable with. You guys will figure it all out."

"That reminds me, he called me Frankie right off the bat," she says. "I spent the first few minutes ready to punch him just for that."

I laugh. "I remember being quickly corrected on that," I recall teasingly. "Did you want to punch me too?"

She smiles mysteriously. "Yes," she admits. "But I couldn't decide what I wanted to do more — punch you or fuck you."

I raise an eyebrow. Damn. "Really?"

"Really," she confirms, running her hands up my arms in a way that toys with the edges of my control. But tonight was supposed to be me showing her I'm here. And even through some intense stuff, I still am, and I want this to be whatever she wants.

"Punching me would have been almost as much of a turn on," I tell her.

She gasps and slaps me playfully on the arm. "You're a dirty boy, Julian."

Her suggestive tone takes my semi to a full-on, but I sit still. "Only if you want me to be," I taunt her with a grin.

Her eyes flick down to my pants. "Either way, looks like you're ready to be one," she says. Her voice is husky and filled with desire. It takes all of my control not to have her on her back crying out my name.

I lean toward her slightly, and her body unconsciously sways toward me. I take a deep whiff of her scent. I can smell her arousal. It's fucking heady. "Smells like you're ready," I murmur into her ear. She gasps, her hand clenching my arm. With her other hand, she moves aside her skirt, then guides my hand between her legs.

I slip a finger under her black, lacy thong. Fuck me, she's so goddamn wet.

"Fuck, Julian," she gasps, her eyes closing and her back arching so her dripping pussy pushes into my palm. And I do just that, sliding two fingers in and fucking her tight little cunt. She writhes under me, one of her hands still clutching at me. She snakes it toward my zipper as I pump my fingers into her, running her hand over my cock as it strains against my jeans.

"You want that cock in you?" I ask her, unleashing control.

She bites down on her lip and nods, looking desperately into my eyes. She grabs my cock full on, squeezing. I suck a sharp breath through my teeth, telling her how good it feels when she touches me, but I don't let her stop my rhythm. In fact, I twist my wrist, flipping my thumb toward her clit so I can bring her to orgasm before I fuck her.

"Not yet, baby," I breathe. "First, I'm going to make you come so hard you forget your own goddamn name."

It doesn't take long. A few hard circles over the sensitive spot, along with a simultaneous massage of her G-spot and she comes completely undone, bucking and screaming her release. As I watch her red cheeks, peaked nipples, and trembling body, I can't remember ever being so turned on by a woman. Everything she does, she does to the fullest. She's fucking intoxicating.

"Fuck, Frankie, you're so damn beautiful," I tell her, covering her mouth with mine. She desperately nips at my lips and tongue as her orgasm recedes. As she finishes her descent, I withdraw my hand, unleashing my hard-on and fishing in my pocket for a condom. It's only a moment before she's recovered and removing it from my hands. But she doesn't put it on. Instead, her sweet, gorgeous red lips hover over my twitching, red cock.

"You want it?" she prompts.

I clench my jaw against the surge of desire that rips through me. "Fuck, yes, baby, suck my fucking cock with that beautiful mouth," I urge her.

There's no prelude, no teasing, she buries me deep in her hot, wet mouth, her tongue violently swirling around my dick as she sucks and pumps my shaft with her mouth and her hand.

"Fuck, Frankie, that's amazing," I moan. "But I'm not coming until I've fucked another orgasm out of you."

When she hears that her suction goes up a notch, her grip tightening. She fucking loves the dirty talk. And I can't say I've ever loved it quite this much. But damn if she isn't working me in a way that's going to make me explode any second, and I tell her as much. Thank God she only does it a few more times, because even with my self-control still mostly in place, it'd be practically impossible not to come.

She finally relents, and I hear the foil rip.

"Fuck, baby, that's the best fucking sound in the world," I groan. Her eager hands roll it down my length before lifting her skirt to give me a view of the little triangle of hair between her legs. "Damn, you have a gorgeous pussy." The sight makes me fucking hard as a rock, so when her tight folds slide over me, I feel every fucking inch of her warm wetness.

She grins like she's won a fucking prize as she buries me fully in her. Tilting back and forth, she sets a rhythm so much slower than her frenzied sucking, using the head of my cock to rub her G-spot. I watch her tits tighten, her back arch, as she pleasures herself on me.

"I love watching you fuck me," I breathe. "But it's my turn, baby." If I let her get herself off, it won't be nearly as rewarding. For either of us. So, I take over.

As she tilts me back into her, I slam upward. She gasps, her hands dropping to my chest so she can absorb the impact. I reach up and roll one of her nipples through my fingers. "You like it when I pound you? When I sink my dick deep and hard into your hot pussy?" Her body sways toward me. That's my sign that it feels so fucking good she can't even sit up anymore. I slam into her again, and her nipple slides out of my hand as her chest meets mine.

"Keep pounding me," she begs into my ear. I slam into her again. "Aah, yes, just like that. Harder, please, Julian, fuck me so much harder."

My head dips back as electric bolts shoot through my entire fucking body at her words. "God, baby, you're fucking perfect, in every way." I grab her ass with my hands, lifting her each time I swing my hips so I can drive into her harder, faster. Soon, she's clutching on to me, just along for the ride. "And you feel," *slam*, "so," *slam*, "fucking," *slam*, "good." *Slam, slam, slam.*

My breath hitches as my orgasm starts to churn below my cock. The way she's tightening, I know just what to do. I grip her hard, her soft flesh on fire in my palms, and I lift her ass in the air, holding her in place as I unleash. I fuck her so hard there's no breath for more dirty talk. I'm afraid I'm going to hurt her, but her continuous scream of pleasure eggs me on.

"Omigod," she screams only moments later. "I'm coming, I'm coming, I'm coming." She seizes tightly, her velvet pussy clenching around my cock, milking my orgasm out of me in bursts of hot gratification. It ends with me buried inside her, my cock pulsating, her still spasming around me.

As the tremors subside, Frankie's mouth finds mine. And the languid, deep kiss spreads the feeling of satisfaction through my whole body until I feel like I'm floating, with only Frankie to anchor me.

As I bliss out with her in my arms, I thank the universe for this moment. This amazing fucking woman in my arms. Feisty, unapologetically honest, and fiercely loyal, she's not just a good fuck. Scratch that, an amazing, off-the-charts fuck. She challenges me in every way. Makes me want to be this guy who's worth being hers. And fuck all if I don't want her to be mine.

As she breaks the kiss, I look deeply into her eyes and try to figure out how to say something I've never said before. The words stick in my throat long enough for her to pull away and get dressed. With the moment passed, I clean up too.

We drive back to her place in comfortable silence. I'm not worried. I'll find a time, a way to say what I need to. To stake my claim on her, if she'll let me.

As I kiss her goodnight at her door, it's all I can do to let her go. But I must.

"I'm traveling again this week," I tell her.

Her beautiful mouth droops. "Poop," she grumbles.

I laugh heartily. "Wow, watch the language there," I tease her. "But hey, I'm telling you ahead of time this time."

She smiles thinly. "True," she allows. "But I'll still miss you."

I look down at her, trying to bring the words, and failing once more. "I'll miss you too. But you'll have plenty to keep you busy. Especially if you plan to contact your …" I trail off, stopping short of calling him her father again. "What should I call him?"

Frankie wrinkles her adorable nose. "His name, I suppose," she sighs, looking up at me from under her dark lashes. "Salvatore Moretti. I wonder if he has a nickname, because that's a fucking mouthful."

My heart stops. "He probably goes by Sal," I say quietly.

"Huh," she says thoughtfully, chewing on that gorgeous bottom lip of hers. "That does fit his whole sleazy old guy vibe."

And if the name didn't confirm it, the description sure as hell does.

Fuck. Fuck, fuck, fuck, fuck, fuck, fuck, fuuuuuuuuuuck.

Sal is Frankie's fucking father. I've been fucking my boss's daughter.

After he told me to stay away from her. No — threatened me if I didn't stay away from her.

I'm illicitly fucking the daughter of one of the most dangerous crime bosses in Los Angeles. Not only is there now no way in hell I can tell Frankie what I've been trying to find the words for all night, if I don't stop seeing her it could unleash hell. For both of us.

But then, maybe it's too late for that anyway.

18

———

FRANKIE

I lie awake that night, unable to sleep. I mean, how could I? I just discovered my mother has been lying to me my whole life. Something I didn't think was even possible. Because what she usually resorts to is feeding me bits of truth, pulling the mom card, or just plain pretending I don't exist. But this time she let me believe a lie I'd apparently heard before I had the ability to hear the little voice inside or before it was even there. A new loophole that blows the lid off of my already fucked-up childhood.

My biological father is not, in fact, dead. Something that became quite obvious when he showed up at my club two days ago.

But let's shelve that, shall we? Why, you ask? I mean, that's a pretty big thing. Even for a girl who's supposed to know when she is being lied to. But there's another truth that hit me unexpectedly in the face tonight. I wanted to chalk it up to post-orgasmic bliss, but there's just no denying that what passed between Julian and me in the back seat of the car, after the most amazing fuck in the most amazing place ever, was more than just physical.

I'm falling hard for Julian. And that's a big deal. Not just because I can't remember ever being with a guy that didn't straight-up lie to me constantly. But also, because despite his seeming just as into me, I still can't get past there being things he's not ready to tell me.

I have to wonder if it's that they're so bad he knows they'd scare me off, or if he's just reserved. Which let's face it, he is. Well, most of the time.

A sly smile spreads across my face. It's hard to deny that the dirty talk might be playing a big factor in this. I'm pretty sure even without it the sex would still be insane, but damned if it doesn't take it to a whole other level of hot I didn't even know existed. But then, he turns me on in just about every way possible, inside the bedroom and out. Not that our fuck under the stars was in a bedroom.

A sigh escapes me thinking about what a perfect date he'd planned. No frills, just stars and orgasms. Not every girl's dream date, but it's pretty much mine. Both are a scarcity for me living in L.A., running my club, avoiding dating. But Julian is different. I hope.

Eventually I drift off to sleep, with visions of Julian's face dancing behind my eyelids, then in my dreams.

THE NEXT DAY I DECIDE TO TAKE MY FIRST REAL MONDAY OFF SINCE buying the club. I'm tempted to tell Nils I won't be in, but as I pick up the phone, I realize how silly that is. I'm not *supposed* to be in, and every time he finds me there on one of my "days off" he laughs at me and tells me to get out. He really is a gem.

Part of me also wants to visit Emma at her salon, to get her input on all of this. And I will, but maybe not right now. Right now, I still need to know more, and I don't want her swaying me one way or the other.

Before I can talk myself out of it, I call Salvatore Moretti. My father. Ugh. Weird.

"Frankie," he answers. "Great to hear from ya, doll."

I smile wryly to myself at his cheesiness. "Hey," I respond. "So yeah. This is me. Calling."

He chuckles. "Glad you did. I take it you talked to your ma?"

I huff a breath sharply through my nose. "That's one way to put it. I didn't get much out of her," I admit.

"Ah," he replies. "So you were hoping I could tell you more." He's not stupid.

"Or anything," I respond with a sigh.

"Like I said, some of it isn't my story to tell," he hedges. "But how's about I take you to lunch, and I'll tell you what I can?"

"That depends," I reply.

"On?"

"Do you like tacos?"

"OKAY, YOU KNOW HOW I SAID TACOS AREN'T MY FAVORITE? WELL, I WAS wrong." Sal — having confirmed that to be his preferred nickname — laughs and polishes off his fourth, and final, taco.

I brush crumbs off my lap and laugh, tossing my crumpled napkin on the picnic table.

"There's a reason there's always a huge line. Can't beat this place," I reply. With our appetites satisfied, I shift nervously. "So."

Sal wipes his face, puts his napkin down, and leans forward on his arms. "So."

"My mom said she didn't think you'd have the balls to ever contact me," I throw out.

Sal bursts out laughing. "Well, your mom would know a lot about balls," he chortles. "She's got a bigger pair than most guys I know."

"Even back then, huh?" I ask with a smile. I have always admired my mother's tenacity, one of the few things I was thankful to inherit from her.

Nonna may be right that our differences push us apart, but then, I think, so do our similarities. It's a no-win situation.

Sal shifts. "Yeah, even back then," he agrees. "But I didn't know about you back then, either, so tough to say if I woulda had the balls to fight for you." He immediately looks sorry for saying it. "Not to say you aren't worth it, doll. You're obviously a hell of a lady." Sal pauses, fishing a cigarette out of his pocket. "But things were complicated. Luca, your grandpa, he wasn't someone to cross. And that kept me from even trying to talk to your ma."

I look up into the bright sky behind him, squinting into the sun. The biggest, brightest star in the sky, casting its revealing light.

"Can't say I blame you," I admit. "One at a time, they were bad enough. But damned if when they teamed up it wasn't hell." I don't pull my poker face on fast enough, and I can tell Sal sees the pain etched there.

"I'm sorry I left you to that, kiddo," he says sadly, taking a puff off his cigarette.

I don't miss the nasty looks of those around us, though I doubt Sal cares about things like how many feet away from an establishment he is when he lights up. And I don't bother pointing it out. Given my mental state, it's all I can do not to ask for a drag. It's not a habit I want to get sucked back in to, despite my recent lapse.

"I had Nonna," I finally say. "She helped a bit. And Nonno died when I was a teenager. It got better after that."

"Maria is a wonderful woman," he replies with a sincere look of love in his eyes as he talks about my grandmother. "How is she these days?"

"Full of quiet wisdom, same as ever," I respond. "But now that Nonno's gone you actually get to hear it. Works out better for Tony than me."

"Tony?" Sal raises an eyebrow.

"My younger brother," I clarify. "He's twelve. Great kid. Probably all thanks to Nonna. Mom still works as much as ever."

"She was born like that, I think. She was only a teenager when we were together, and even then she was a serious, driven young woman," he replies with a grimace, folding his hands together.

"Yeah," I agree. Something in my gut twists, and I know I need to stop thinking about my mother for a bit. She's always best taken in measured amounts, even in conversations she's not present for. "So what about you? What is it you do again?"

Sal's lips twitch. "Well, I have a business that caters to a specific clientele," he hedges. "I mostly deal with imports. You know, whatever goods they need help bringing into the country. I also help manage their business affairs, logistics, that sort of thing. But I'm doing less and less of that these days, the older I get."

I raise an eyebrow. I've heard enough hedging and roundabout talk in my day to know what that might mean. "Mhm," I murmur. "Are we talking legal imports here?"

Sal looks up at me with a leering grin. "You're a sharp cookie," he compliments me. He spreads his hands out. "I do what I'm asked. I let my clients worry about the legal aspects."

I'm not loving this. "Uh-huh," I grunt. "What other services do you provide?"

"Whatever my clients require," he reiterates simply with another smile. "Don't you worry about your old man. I'm not about to get myself in trouble with the law." *Lie.*

Oh, geez. I fold my arms over my chest with a frown, purposely letting my displeasure show.

"Ah, come on Frankie, don't be like that," he urges. "Not all of us can run a successful night club. Seems like you're doing really well with that place."

So. Many. Red. Flags. "Yeah, my investors are pretty happy," I say pointedly. "I may even start recouping all the cash they put into it someday." It's a partial truth. Some of the cash did come from other investors. Though I'm the biggest investor in the club, having put in more than seventy percent of the capital. But in case he's looking for a new benefactor, or client, or whatever, I'm not going to make myself an easy mark.

He nods. "Been there," he says. "You seem real smart. I'm sure you'll do great."

"Thanks," I reply with a thin smile, wondering if this lunch was a huge mistake. The things I really want to know, the why, well, I realize only my mother knows. I heave a sigh, knowing I'll probably never have the answers I'm looking for.

"Tell me more about yourself," Sal presses. "I hope you don't spend all your time at the club. You got friends? Maybe even a boyfriend?"

I shrug lightly, my poker face back in place. "I have a few friends. Nobody I'd call a boyfriend," I reply. *Even if there is someone I want to call that.* "But the club takes most of my time. It's not a bad thing. I enjoy it."

"Good, good," he says with a nod. "Maybe once that's all settled down you can find yourself a nice boy and have a family." I don't stop the incredulous look that settles on my face. He quickly moves to cover his tracks. "You know, if that's what you want."

I press my lips together and try to consider where he's coming from. And I know in his time those were the life choices that went with security and happiness. So maybe that's all he's saying. The thought calms my independent streak considerably. Because after living through my fucked-up childhood, I'd honestly never planned to have kids of my own. Which is good, because with my ability, even getting married is a dicey proposition.

"Look, I appreciate that you want me to be happy," I finally say carefully. "But I am. Really. I'm finally in the place I've been working toward."

Sal nods apologetically. "That's great, Frankie," he says with relief. "That's all I want."

He sounds so genuine that despite my reservations, I can't help feeling like his approval fills some kind of hole in my life and my heart. I'm almost disappointed at myself at the realization. But then, I've lived my life bereft of a father.

When we make plans to have lunch again next Wednesday, I wonder if there will be enough good that comes of allowing Sal into my life. Or if I'm just setting myself up for more heartbreak. I make a mental note to ask him more direct questions next week. Before I get in too deep.

I'M SPARED HAVING TO CALL EMMA WHEN SHE TEXTS ME ON MONDAY night to remind me we're going to a Halloween party on Wednesday. It's one of those crazy ragers that, being on the actual holiday and on a week-night, mostly only people with nontraditional jobs will attend. So it's bound to be insane, and a shit-ton of fun. Plus, it's been a while since Emma and I cut loose like this, and I find I'm actually looking forward to it.

Unfortunately, with everything going on I'd forgotten to line up a costume, so as I stand in my closet on Wednesday evening, I find my choices are limited. Thankfully, club wear can easily double as a costume in a pinch. I grab a black leather minidress and some fishnet tights. Paired with raging sky-high lace-up boots, some heavy goth-looking makeup, and a red lipstick trail of "blood" out of the corner of my mouth, I make a decent looking vampire. The dark hair works well and, possibly for the first time, I'm glad I went back to my natural color. I don't worry about the fact that I don't have fake fangs. I'll just have to wear my sharp wit instead.

In the cab on the way to the party, I have some time to catch Emma up on my new-found father, Julian, and a few other happenings of the week. Her advice is predictable. *Check out Sal, what have you got to lose? Go for it with Julian, what have you got to lose?* If only the answer to both questions wasn't, well, everything. Emma has always been a goer, not a thinker. Thankfully, she recovers from hurt and rejection quickly. Me, not so much.

As we arrive at the venue, though, everything slips from my mind. It's a private residence in the hills of Malibu, and swank would be an understatement. The huge, imposing modern structure is decorated to the nines with realistic cobwebs strung across the building, backlit terrifying silhouettes in each window, and even a group of skeletons made to look like they're climbing up one of the walls and into the house. Partygoers surround the house inside and out, drinking, laughing, and dancing. Emma looks pumped and more than ready for Halloween revelry in her sexy fairy costume, her ample bosom barely contained by the shimmery pink fabric, with tiny gold wings dancing enticingly behind her.

As soon as we're inside, Emma goes straight for the booze. Our unspoken rule is she drinks, and I make sure she doesn't get in trouble. It's not hard, actually, as she usually ends up dragging me around with her, dancing with whatever hotties she can get her hands on. Either Ben doesn't know, or he doesn't care, and I'm not about to tell him.

And after she's had a couple of shots, she does pretty much exactly that. She finds the hottest, most scantily clad man in the place. Dressed like Lucifer, with small horns on his head and some face makeup, he's naked but for a tattered pair of jeans hugging his tight ass, purposely burnt in places. I'd say it's because he's supposed to be the ruler of hell and all that, but it might also be because he's that smoking hot. So, of course, Emma is all over him. Before I know it, they're grinding to the music, and one of Lucifer's friends is behind me, trying to keep rhythm as my body presses into the back of Emma's.

Emma snakes a hand behind her, pulling me in for a drunken dance, or hug, or God knows what. It makes me laugh, though, and I feel myself loosening up. I give myself over to the beat, letting Emma's infallible rhythm set the pace. Before long, we're out of breath and sweaty, and heading to the makeshift bar for some water. And then more booze for Emma. Lucifer trails behind her, clearly liking the taste he's gotten.

I shake my head, laughing. Emma, while not as tall as me, has always been a curvy girl too. The guys definitely seem to love it. Her confidence doesn't hurt, either.

I chug a bottle of water and make her drink some too. When I'm satisfied she won't be a drunken mess, I gesture to the hall with the bathrooms, then point at the floor. *Stay here*, I mouth. She nods, so I slip away to relieve myself as quickly as possible.

Thankfully, it only takes a couple of minutes and I'm back. Only to spot Lucifer and Emma, making out like teenagers. His hand is up the back of her dress, fondling her ass, and her hands are thrown wantonly around his neck as their faces are practically merged.

My heart drops into my stomach, and I push my way through the crowd as quickly as I can. I didn't think she was *that* drunk. I kick myself for not paying better attention.

As soon as I get to them, I use all my strength to shove Lucifer off of her.

"What the hell?" I barely hear him over the music. And I don't fucking care. I give him a death glare and cage Emma behind me. When it's clear I'm not going to let him get back to her, he finally stalks off into the crowd to find his next victim.

A tug on my arm makes me turn around to face Emma. She looks pissed. With a sigh, I grab her hands and lead her out the front door. We have to get a good thirty feet from the building before I can hear her.

"What the fuck, Frankie?" she demands, her hands on her hips, sounding perfectly sober.

"What the fuck, *Frankie*?" I echo in disbelief. "How about what the fuck, *Emma*?"

"I was just having a little fun," she spits. "You don't have to be such a fucking prude."

Whoa. She did not just.

"Are you serious right now?" I spit back. "You're *married*, in case you forgot. And I'm here to keep you from doing anything stupid."

Emma folds her arms over her chest defensively. "I'm also a grownup," she says heatedly, "and if I want to make out with a hot guy, I'm going to."

The anger drains right out of me. This isn't my best friend. Something is up.

"What's going on, Emma?" I ask calmly.

My change in attitude leeches the sass out of her. But she still clams up, and tears fill her eyes. "Let's just go home," she grinds out, heading back to the street, presumably to hail a car.

I grab her arm and stop her. "Really? You're not going to talk to me?" I ask, hurt.

She turns, her face laden with sadness. "No," she says, the tears spilling over her round cheeks. "I really don't need the judgment right now."

She may as well have slapped me in the face. My first reaction is feeling hurt. But the feeling is quickly replaced by anger. Of the two of us, Emma judges me far more than I judge her. The hypocrisy doesn't sit well with me. Thankfully, of the two of us, I'm also the one who is least likely to say something I'll regret later, and I'm able to keep cool enough to respond.

"I don't want to judge you, for fuck's sake. I want to help, Emma," I respond evenly.

"Fine," she shouts, throwing her hands in the air dramatically. "You want to know what's up? I'm getting divorced is what's up. I'm a fucking failure, and you knew it before I did. Happy?"

I want to say I'm not happy, because I know she's miserable. But she's not wrong: I've always known Ben was a liar. That he wasn't good enough for her.

"You are *not* a failure," I say, latching on to the one piece I disagree with.

She huffs and rolls her eyes.

I grab her by the shoulders and lean in to be on her level. That I'm already a good deal taller doesn't help, but the boots make it a challenge. Still, I hold my ground. "You're not a failure," I repeat softly.

Her lower lip trembles, her big, round eyes filling with tears once more. She only holds out for a moment before bursting into sobs and burying her face in my chest. I wrap my arms tightly around her, and she does the same. I stroke her hair gently until she stops crying.

"Why didn't you tell me sooner?" I ask. "You let me go on and on about my shit. I love you, darlin', and I'm here for you no matter what."

With a sniff, Emma straightens up, wiping her nose with the back of her hand. "I know," she admits with a nod. "I just wasn't ready to talk about it yet, and if we talked about me, I knew I'd have to lie to you, and then you'd know. It's like I can't win." She looks at me sadly.

It crushes my heart hearing that my ability stopped her from talking to me. Not for the first time, I wish it wasn't a part of me.

"I'm sorry," I say sincerely. "You shouldn't ever feel like you have to lie to me or not tell me things. If you don't want to tell me something, don't, but I'm here for you and I'll do my best not to be judgmental." I bite my lip, knowing that I can be. But it's only because I care.

"Deep down I wanted to tell you," she replies. "But I remembered all the times you tried to tell me about him while we were dating, and all I did was shut you down. I was just so *in love* I didn't want to hear it. And now look at me. I'm such a fucking idiot."

I shake my head, grasping her free hand in mine. "You're not an idiot," I insist. "There's a whole expression for it, even. 'Love is blind.' Right? It makes fools of us all." And I can't keep my thoughts from flitting to Julian. And if I was unsure before, I know now. I love him. Even though I know he's withholding. Even though I know better. Whatever magic that happens between two people that makes you fall in love has hit me hard. And I can't blame Emma for being its victim, either.

"Yeah," she finally admits begrudgingly. "But it still fucking sucks."

I laugh, and she laughs with me. "Yeah," I agree. "But it won't always be that way."

Emma shakes her head. "I hope not," she says quietly. "Come on, let's go get something to eat and talk."

I fall into step beside her, wrapping my arm around her shoulders. "Now that sounds like a smart plan."

For the rest of the night I let Emma spill her guts about the whole situation. And I do my best to just listen. She's obviously had a lot pent up, and I know I just need to put my own problems, my own judgments aside and be there for her. I even spend the night at her place, as Ben has packed up and gone to stay with friends. Despite the horrible circumstances, or maybe because of them, it feels good to really reconnect with her. Because through a full night of heart-to-hearts, I start to see why she felt the way she did.

I often let my ability dictate a conversation, rather than my heart, or even my head. I never thought much about how that feels for other people. The irony isn't lost on me that it causes just as much trouble for the people I care about as it does for me. Because everybody lies. It's a necessary coping mechanism. That's easy for me to forget with the constant voice in my head reminding me of every little transgression, like it's something unnatural, wrong, and harmful. And sometimes it is. But sometimes, it's just what we need to do to protect ourselves.

JULIAN

As I drive back into the city on Friday night, all I can think of is Frankie. Her gorgeous face, her tight little pussy, the verbal sparring that makes me want to not just fuck her but keep her. I'm so twisted up with need for her that it takes all of my willpower to check in with Sal first as he requested instead of heading straight for Baltia and ravaging the shit out of her.

Especially since Sal is getting on my last nerve these days. Everything that was good about our arrangement has long since died. And I know it's time to break away, but that's easier said than done.

His first words as I enter his office don't help.

"It's done?"

No hello, no making sure I'm okay, nothing. Didn't even look up from whatever file he's poring over. All he cares about is what he wants. Never mind that I nearly died in the process. But I never bore him with those details. I know he's long since stopped caring.

"Yeah," I say shortly, wiping the disgust from my face. "That all you wanted to see me for?"

Sal points to a chair across from him, still not looking up. I sink into it, looking affectedly disinterested.

"No. I know I told you to stay away from Frankie Greco, but I need you to do something for me." He finally looks up, leans back in his chair, and crosses his legs.

My heart races. Does he know something? I shrug as nonchalantly as I can, inviting him to continue. And he does. But what he asks strains my ability to stay cool. And I know the time has come to choose.

WITH A HEAVIER HEART THAN EARLIER THIS EVENING, I LEAVE SAL'S office and head to Baltia. I try to push it out of my mind, because I don't have to decide tonight. But by Monday … well, that's exactly what I don't need to think about right now. With no consequences now for going to do exactly what I would've done anyway, I go to the club. To Frankie.

As soon as I'm inside, I push through the noisy throng and spot her leaning over the balcony of the VIP section, scanning the crowd. Her long, dark hair is slicked back into a sexy-as-fuck ponytail, and she wears a pink halter top the same color as her hair used to be. Her tight leather pants look halfway between rocker and dominatrix. Both alternatives make me fucking hard for her.

As if she could hear my thoughts, her eyes lock on mine. Her expression doesn't change, but she straightens up and saunters casually down the stairs. My feet move before I'm even conscious of it, and I meet her as the gatekeeper opens the velvet rope for her.

Her black heels easily put her over six feet, evoking images of fucking her in nothing but those heels. She stops in front of me, still having to tilt her head up to look in my eyes. She's technically at work, so I refrain from pushing her up against the wall and showing her exactly how much I missed her. But the desire in her eyes matches the anticipation thrumming in my cock.

She slips her hand in mine and turns, leading me around the corner and down a hallway. At the end of the hall is a dark door that she leads me through and closes behind us. With a flick of the lights, I realize we're in her office.

She turns back around, leaning against her desk. "I missed you," she says evenly. Too calmly.

If I've learned anything about Frankie, it's that the calm is a mask for the ever-changing emotions underneath. I'm hoping the emotion she's suppressing is the same one I am.

I close the gap between us, stroking a finger down her cheek. "I missed you too."

She leans into the touch with a sigh, and in response my dick strains the limits of what my pants can take. She holds my hand in hers as it slides down to rest on her chin, lifting it to her lips and kissing it gently. She looks up at me from under her lashes.

"Show me how much," she says softly.

Desire shoots through me from head to toe, escalating the sensation between my legs. Calmly, I pull her up by her hands. I lean in, kissing her softly at first, letting everything I'm feeling flow through our lips as my tongue delicately plays with hers. She arches into me, her arms wrapping around my neck. I pull her into me as tightly as I can, deepening the kiss, letting it become more demanding.

I skim my hands down her sides, letting them rest on her gorgeous, plump ass. I knead her backside with increasing fervor, until she breaks away and moans into my chest.

"Say it, baby," I encourage her. "Say you like it when I touch you like that."

"Your hands feel amazing," she groans, tilting her chin up and offering her mouth to me.

I place a light kiss on her cherry red lips. "Tell me how you want to be fucked tonight," I whisper in her ear.

Her nails dig into my shoulders, and my cock twitches.

"From behind," she sighs.

I lick up her ear.

"Rough or gentle?"

She arches into me again. I love how turned on this makes her.

"However you want me," she whimpers.

"I want your skin against mine," I admit.

I'm happy to take her any way she wants, but I can't stop thinking of our naked bodies touching. I slide my hands under her shirt, peeling it upward. She lifts her arms like a good girl and lets me undress her. She starts to unzip her pants, but I grab her hands, lifting them above her head. I give her a stern look, and she bites into her lower lip and nods. She understands; I'm going to do it, and she'd better keep her hands over her head.

I slowly peel the leather over her gorgeous ass, trying to maintain control as the smell of her arousal fills my senses. She lifts her heels so I can slide each leg off, until she's fully naked, save the heels, just like I wanted her.

I continue to ignore my hard-as-rock dick as I stroke a hand back up her center, sampling her wetness, sliding over her round, feminine stomach, and pinching her nipples hard as my hands come to rest on her breasts. I give her a quick kiss, sweeping my tongue in her mouth possessively, and then I step back.

I hook my thumbs in the collar of my black T-shirt, pulling it over my head. She sighs happily, reaching out to run her hand down my pecs and stomach, fingering the tattoos, the grooves between my abs, and the trail of hair leading down to the top of my pants. I smooth my hair back, appreciating the desire on her face.

But when she goes to undo my belt, I stop her.

"Hands up," I command.

She complies readily, resting her arms on top of her head, panting for me. I undo my belt and kick off my pants. My long, hard cock stands to attention, dripping for her.

I make a motion with my finger for her to turn around. She complies, and I press down on her back, her extended arms draping over the desk as her chest comes to rest on the desktop.

I step back to admire the view. Her slightly spread legs display her damp, swollen pussy and her gorgeous ass. These are the moments I'm glad for my controlled nature. Otherwise, I'd come right here at the sight. Instead, I drop to my knees on the carpeted floor and lick her delicious pussy like a starving man.

"Fuck, Frankie, you taste like heaven," I moan into her.

She grips the desk beneath her, moaning her response, clearly unable to form words. I relent, only to let her catch her breath and say the words that will spur me on.

"Say it, baby."

"Fuck me," she pleads, looking back at me desperately.

I stand up, letting my erection graze her. Fire licks through me, and I clench my jaw against the pleasure. I slowly retrieve a condom from the pocket of my discarded pants and put it on.

"Mmmm," I mutter. "You sure you don't want me to lick you until you come in my mouth?"

She arches into the pleasure once more. Fuck, this woman is beyond beautiful.

"I need you inside me, Julian," she says with such intensity that I don't make her wait. I simply plunge into her fully, her tight, wet warmth pulling me in to the hilt.

"Fuuuuck," I moan, unable to form a full sentence. "Goddamn, I needed this pussy." I smack her right ass cheek. Hard. She cries out and clenches around me. "You like that?"

Looking back at me, she nods, all of her cheeks flushed. I pull back slightly, pumping while still deeply inside her, knowing it will stroke her into a dizzy heat. I'm not disappointed as she clutches hard at the desk, breathing heavily and moaning. I lean forward over her, gathering her ponytail in my hand. I give it a tug as I bury myself fully in her and she cries out.

"You want me to give it to you?" I prompt her, going back to gentle, deep thrusts.

She moans. "Fuck yes, please," she says.

I slam into her again as I pull her hair back, so she leans back toward me. Her breasts push out, taut and peaked. I reach around with my free hand, roughly grabbing one so her nipple presses between my fingers. I keep her pulled taut by her hair, roughly squeezing her nipple, and I unleash in a frenzy of thrusts, slamming deep and hard. My stomach muscles clench as I balance myself to make sure it's pleasurable for her. With less control it could end up doing the opposite of what I intend. But her body fits perfectly in my grasp, her hot nipple fully peaked under my touch, her beautiful body responding perfectly to the firm grasp I have on her hair, her tight pussy hungrily accepting my hard thrusts.

"You're fucking perfect, Frankie," I breathe as I fuck her. Her moans grow louder. "That's right, baby, let me hear you. I want to hear you when you come. Come for me now."

I slam into her with almost everything I've got, reserving only what I'll need for after. And like the sexy vixen that she is, one of her hands clamps over the one I have on her breast, while her other does the same job on her other nipple. With a jerk, she comes on my dick, screaming her release as she seizes around me. It's almost enough to make me explode inside her.

She slumps forward onto the desk, satisfied and panting. But I'm not done with her yet. I pull out gently, repositioning the rubber. I run a hand down her trembling legs, wrapping my other arm under her, and with one swift, gentle movement, I roll her onto her back, lifting her legs up. I slide her back onto the desk so her backside rests on the surface, with enough room to stand in front of her.

Rather than squat down, I lean in and mount her, wrapping her legs around me as I sink back into her delicious warmth. I lean all the way onto the desk, propping myself over her, so I can look into her eyes. Her hands come to rest on my face, and she pulls herself up to me for a kiss.

I give her a dangerous smile. "Starting to see how much I missed you?" I tease.

She feigns thinking about it, then smiles. "Maybe," she says. "But why don't you keep showing me, just in case?"

I flick an eyebrow up and smirk at her, tilting my pelvis so I slide out of her. And I gently slide back in. "Like that?"

She throws her head back and moans. "God, yes."

So I do it again, slowly, and ask again. She moans her agreement again. We do the same dance over and over, and the exchange speeds up. But before she crests, I back off to start over, to make the payoff that much more intense.

I focus on keeping rhythm, and telling her how good she feels, all the times I thought about fucking her this week, how much I missed her in every way possible. As I feel myself starting to build toward climax, I stand back up, lifting her ass with my hands and holding her in place. She rests her legs on my chest, her ankles on my shoulders.

Having her in this position, looking down on her wantonly splayed out on the desk, I know without question that I'll be true to her. Do anything for her. Do whatever it takes to be with her.

I slip my hand around the top of her thigh, using my thumb to circle her clit. Her eyes were closed, but snap open at my touch.

"Time to come again, beautiful," I groan.

Her hands fly to grip the desk's edge behind her, her eyes locked on mine and overflowing with desire. Still supporting her with one hand, I keep stroking her with the other, swinging my hips into her with increasing speed as I feel myself tighten, as she tightens around me. And in the last moments, as I watch her breath sharply speed up as her orgasm hits, I have to stop the words from tumbling out of me as I find my release.

I lie over her for longer than I probably should, unwilling to step out of this moment. But all good things must come to an end, and before I know it, we're getting dressed and slipping out of her office.

As if I fucked it out of her, Frankie's all-business demeanor is gone, and she keeps hold of my hand, leading me to the dance floor. The deejay is playing a sultry, heavy beat, and she steps into my arms. We move together just as flawlessly as we do naked, and I let myself sink into her smell, her warmth as she grinds against me. With the beast sated, it sleeps soundly for the moment, allowing me to enjoy being close to her without the need to fuck her silly.

She turns in my arms, her back against my chest, her hands on my thighs. I rock her in my arms to the beat, allowing the simple pleasure of touching her to fill me. But something causes me to look up at the balcony. And when I do, I lock eyes with her club manager, the Nordic bastard who clearly has a thing for her. He doesn't look happy. I offer no other challenge than returning his glare. I don't need to. Frankie is fucking mine.

FRANKIE ASKS TO STAY AT MY PLACE AFTER SHE CLOSES DOWN THE CLUB. It's nearby, after all, and we're both exhausted and sweaty. I don't even have to consider. I'm down with whatever will be the fastest way to get her naked again.

And not even fifteen minutes later, we're entering my apartment. The second we're in, I shove her up against the door. I get no protest. On the contrary, we help each other strip quickly so not even a minute after that, I'm entering her.

I fuck her hard against the door, and I couldn't give a shit about the noise or the hour. It's all over in minutes anyway, then she's screaming my name as I unleash an expletive-ridden orgasmic tirade in her ear. Completely exhausted from the volume of serious fucking, dancing that might as well have been fucking, and simply being awake for so long, it takes all my strength to make it through a quick shower with her before we collapse into bed, still slightly damp.

As I'm about to fall asleep, Frankie stirs next to me, clearly uncomfortable.

"Everything okay?" I ask sleepily. I turn to her to find her wide awake and looking terrified. It snaps me awake immediately. "What is it, baby?"

She looks askance at me and shakes her head. "It's nothing. I'm sorry, I don't want to keep you up," she replies softly.

I roll toward her, pulling her onto her side to face me, to look me in the eye. "Talk," I insist, kissing her collarbone along the line of small stars tattooed there.

She pulls a deep breath in. "I'm scared, Julian," she admits. I draw my face up to meet her gaze. "About the way I feel about you."

I prop my head up on my arm. "I'm not," I reply.

She gives me a confused look. "Yeah, well, I've already spilled my guts to you," she reminds me. "And that's what freaks me out. There are things you still won't tell me."

Ah. Fuck. And I may not be scared of what she's feeling for me, or I for her, but I am scared that telling her everything would ruin that. I just need time to disentangle myself from Sal. You know, without him killing me. And, as if that weren't enough, then I have to hope he never tells her he sent me after her in the first place. I realize that's hoping a lot, and that I may have to tell her someday. Fuck that, I know I *should* tell her. But there's something else I want to tell her more, and I know it's completely unfair.

"I get that," I admit. "Given the situation, things have been difficult for me too." I pause to take a deep breath. "But that hasn't stopped me from falling in love with you. I don't think there's anything that could've stopped that. You're fucking amazing, Frankie, and I want to be with you, even though we don't know everything about each other right now. Because I know we will, someday." As soon as the words are out of my mouth, I make a liar of myself. Because I've just laid it out there and I'm fucking scared shitless that she'll leave.

Tears spring to her eyes and she presses her lips together in a thin line. I go to reach for her, and she shakes her head, pulling back as the tears spill over her cheeks. Something inside me breaks. It's that fucking heart I didn't know I had.

I contemplate running. But the thought of leaving her is a fresh level of hell. So I decide to do something I've never done.

"Please, baby," I beg, imploring her with my eyes, my voice, not to pull away. "Of all people, I get how fucking hard this must be for you." And I realize right now truth is exactly what she needs. As much as I can give her. "You know how I grew up. Just like you, it made me not trust anyone, not even the man who saved me from the fucking streets." I shift to a sitting position and she mirrors me, almost unconsciously, hanging on every word. "I've had to do some horrible fucking shit to survive. You have no idea. But that's all I've done is just survive. I already told you I've never been in love before. I don't fucking trust anyone enough to get halfway there. Until you. I was lost, Frankie, from the moment I met you. I love you. I'd do anything for you. And I will tell you what you want to know, but I can't right now. I promise you, I will someday. Hopefully soon. Though I totally get if that's not enough for you." I drop my head in my hands, furiously rubbing away the tears forming at the thought of losing her now. It's the most I've ever told anyone about my feelings, and it's a level of raw I can barely stand.

Frankie sniffs deeply, and knowing she's crying nearly sends me over the edge. All of the control, all of the containment I've carefully placed on my emotions has been stripped away. This woman has broken me, and I'm laid bare at her feet.

"It's enough for now." Her quiet voice cuts through the silence, and I look up at her hopefully. She *is* crying. But there's something more in her eyes. "It has to be enough. Because, despite everything I don't know, I want to be with you. I want you in ways I never even knew were possible for me." She presses her lips together, clearly too emotional to continue.

With none of my usual confidence, I tentatively raise my hand to her face. When she allows me to touch her, I can almost feel the shattered pieces of my heart coming back together. But I need more. I also feel like I need her on a level I've never needed anyone. It's both exhilarating and terrifying.

I approach carefully, opening my legs and placing them on either side of her. She does the same, resting her legs over my hips. Still naked, her soft, warm center grazes me. But I'm more interested in getting her in my arms first, in feeling that she's really still here. I reach out and she settles into me, resting her head against my chest.

I cup her face with my hand, looking down into her eyes. But words have left me. So I kiss her softly, letting our mouths meld together. I stroke my hands gently over her back as our tongues dance, tasting deeply of each other. My body craves her in a way it hasn't before, wanting to be connected to her.

She pulls away and places a hand on my heart, as if desiring the same connection. She scoots forward and pulls herself into my lap. Her other hand slips between us, pulling my cock to her. The sudden movement stirs me, and I fully harden as she sinks onto me. Her eyes don't move from mine as she begins to ride me slowly, deliberately. I don't have words for how fucking amazing it feels.

Her arms encircle my neck, as mine encircle her, touching her everywhere I can reach. The slow rhythm we set lets me feel every inch of her inside and out. Her lips part, and her breathing accelerates. And I have to concentrate on not exploding from the mind-numbing pleasure she's giving me, because all I want is for her to feel this good. I pull her hips down as she slides onto me, deepening the reach of my cock as I reach down to gently stroke her clit. She clings to me, her mouth finding mine again as she moans her pleasure. The passion of it knocks me completely on my ass, and I'm speechless as she rides us both to climax.

It's only after, as I feel cum dripping down my shaft while I'm still inside her, that I realize I'd been bare. I look down at our joined, slippery center.

"Oh, fuck," I swear.

She smiles tolerantly. "It's okay," she assures me. "You know I'm safe. And I trust you."

Well, that gets my attention. I reach up and touch her face, unable to convey how much those words mean to me. How much I know they mean to her. "I trust you too."

The rest goes unspoken, but in the wee hours of the morning, Frankie slips into my arms and falls asleep. And it must be the forced connection to my emotions, but it makes me want to cry tears of joy. What the fuck is this woman doing to me?

WAKING UP NEXT TO HER IS JUST AS AMAZING. WE SPEND WHAT LITTLE remains of the morning making love. I feel like a pussy even thinking the phrase, but it has definitely crossed over from the fucking we'd been doing. And while it's not my usual mode, it's exactly what we both need right now. There is little said about any of it. Though I don't miss that she never said she loves me.

We go to the diner for a brief, quiet lunch before returning to my apartment to make love again. It's strangely silent, as if all my words were spent the night before, and none of them remain. Not even the dirty ones. Maybe especially not the dirty ones.

When it comes time for her to go to the club, I'm once again uncharacteristically nervous. The lack of discussing anything since last night is starting to unnerve me. But I have things to do, and I sense she needs some time to sort through everything.

I walk her to my door, pulling her by the hand into my arms. I stroke a hand down her cheek, looking into her eyes. Fuck, this woman owns me.

"Thank you," I say simply.

The contemplative look she'd had on her face disappears and she laughs. "For what?" she asks.

"I don't know," I admit with a laugh. "For a lot of things."

She goes on her toes to kiss me softly. "You're welcome, then," she says. "Am I going to see you tomorrow?"

I stare down at her, wondering how, even knowing I'm not lying, she doesn't seem to get how much I love her. That I can't be without her.

"If you want to," I assure her. "I'll be here."

She smiles dimly at me, and I wonder what's going on in her head. This is all so new to me, and it's unsettling.

"Okay, well, bye, then," she says meekly, unfolding herself from my arms.

I resist the urge to kiss her, still sensing that more closeness isn't going to resolve whatever doubts she obviously still has. So I let her go.

"Bye, Frankie."

I've done some hard shit in my life. But letting her leave, with a sense that she may not come back blows it all out of the water.

20

FRANKIE

fter getting to my office and changing clothes, I sit at my desk, staring impassively at the wall as the club bustles outside my door. Despite trying to sort through my feelings, I just feel numb. Unable to think past the fact that while Julian told me he loves me, he's still holding back.

As usual, he didn't lie to me. And while I love that about him, still knowing that he's keeping something obviously huge from me is terrifying in a way I just can't get past. At the same time, the thought of ending things makes me sick to my stomach. Two unreconcilable truths. Lies would be easier — then I could just write him off. I close my eyes.

A soft knock puts an end to my little pity party.

"Come in," I call, rising from my chair and moving toward the door.

It opens and Nils steps in, closing it behind him again. "Francesca," he greets me somberly.

"Nils," I reply warily, stopping in front of him. "What's up?"

He shifts uncomfortably from one foot to the other. "I wanted to check on you. Your behavior last night was … unusual," he replies delicately.

I raise an eyebrow and am about to put him in his place when I

187

consider he might be right. I was so glad to see Julian last night, and so turned on even after having him in my office, that I was uncharacteristically uninhibited with him on the dance floor. Thinking back to the moment, all I cared about was keeping my hands on him, and his on me. But now, in the light of a new day, it actually makes me blush thinking about my employees watching that.

"You're right," I admit, meeting his concerned gaze. "I apologize, it won't happen again."

Nils steps forward, closing the small gap between us. He runs his hand down my arm, grasping my hand firmly in his. His grip is strong and reassuring, but he looks imploringly into my eyes in a way that's more than a little unsettling. His amazing smell reinforces my discomfort.

"I'm worried about you," he says. "You've seemed distracted lately, and not in a good way."

I squeeze his hand, knowing he's just looking out for me. "Again, you're right," I agree with a sigh. "I've had a lot going on. I'm sorry if it's kept me from pulling my weight. But I'm here, totally. What can I do?"

He gives me a small, dangerous smile. And I know I'm going to regret asking.

BY THE END OF THE NIGHT, I'M BEYOND EXHAUSTED. WHILE I DON'T actually regret it, Nils really put me through my paces. But after going over all of the latest financials, reviewing our schedule for the rest of the year, restocking the bar, and seeing the band lineup through another packed night, I'm feeling back in the saddle. Reengaging fully in running the club gives me a sense of organized satisfaction that definitely bleeds over into the other areas of my life. And the deafening sound of hundreds of people enjoying the shit out of themselves is a welcome distraction.

As the night winds down and we start cleaning up, Johnny finds me.

"Hey, boss?"

I hop down from the stage to meet him at the stairs from the bar. "What's up, Johnny?"

He scratches the back of his head self-consciously. "You didn't by any chance go in the security room tonight, did you?"

"Nope, didn't need to, why?" I ask, crossing my arms over my chest with a frown.

Johnny takes a deep breath, his broad chest puffing up. "Fuck. Well, see, I went to reset it for the day, and it was down."

"Down?" I gasp. "Completely?"

He nods, looking sheepish. "I didn't see anyone go in," he hedges, looking everywhere but at me. "But it was nuts tonight. I'm so sorry."

With a heavy sigh, I shake my head. "It's not your fault," I assure him. "You're my head bartender, it's not your job."

Though I get why he feels responsible. Because the door to the security room is behind the bar, he's always kept an eye on it. And with me, Nils, five bartenders, a crew of security guards, and all the other employees milling around, it's not like it's exactly easy to sneak into restricted areas.

Nils walks by at that exact moment, and I gesture for him to join us. Johnny tells him what he just told me, and his response is nearly identical.

Nils's frown deepens the more he thinks about it. "I'll get someone from the company that installed the system to come have a look. Let's lock it up so nothing else goes awry," he says.

"Will do," Johnny agrees. "Seriously, I'm really sorry. I feel like an idiot letting someone just wander in and mess with it."

His words trigger something. "Not just anyone *can* mess with it," I recall. "It takes a code to shut it down, right?"

Johnny shrugs. "I've never done it, only saved the feeds and reset them for the next day."

"She's right," Nils interjects. "But only myself, Ms. Greco, and our security team have that code."

"Uhhh, I think that might not exactly be true," Johnny mumbles.

"Pardon?" I ask sharply.

Johnny pulls a face, then gestures for us to follow him. He leads us behind the bar, through the security door, and to the bank of monitors. He walks over to the mouse, setting it aside and flipping the mousepad underneath over. A yellow sticky note is affixed to the back of it. And on it is the security code.

Nils pinches the bridge of his nose and sighs. "Everybody out," he directs in an uncharacteristically harsh tone. "I'm resetting the code and locking up. After we close, nobody comes into the club until the security company has been in here tomorrow." His eyes snap up to Johnny's. "Am I clear?"

Johnny's eyes go wide. "Yes, sir," he agrees quickly.

"Good," Nils snaps. "Francesca, I trust you'll finish closing and tell everyone else while I take care of this?"

"Of course," I reply.

Johnny and I head out. I take a minute to reassure him first that it wasn't his fault. Then I let everyone else know to go home, and that doors are closed until further notice. That done, I return to my office, sinking into my chair.

My brain spins through the events of the evening, trying to narrow down the time window this would've happened in, besides the obvious of after doors open at ten and sometime before Johnny checked the feeds around three.

It occurs to me suddenly that if Johnny saved the files, I can simply look on our secure cloud server for the time stamp of the last video file. So I do.

The feeds are shut down a bit before one a.m. By that hour there aren't a lot of people coming in and out, as usually everyone who there's space for has been let in, but the club is always packed. Out of curiosity, I check to see when the last person was admitted through the door. I don't have to go back very far, but what I see makes my heart stop.

Julian, walking through the door on the tail end of a group of people I've never seen.

He couldn't. He wouldn't.

But if he did, why?

No.

He wouldn't.

I go back and forth for a good fifteen minutes before Nils finds me.

"It's done," he says wearily as he enters. He stops when he sees the look on my face. "What?"

I contemplate not showing him. I know he already dislikes Julian, considering him a distraction at best. But he has access to the footage too. So, with a sigh, I turn my laptop around to show the frozen image, time-stamp and all.

"He was the last one in the doors tonight before the video feed cuts out not but ten minutes later," I say as he stares wide-eyed at the screen. I snap the lid shut, frustrated.

"You think he had something to do with this?" Nils asks. The incredulity in his voice surprises me.

"I thought you didn't like the guy," I grouse.

"And I thought you did," he replies matter-of-factly, settling in the chair across from me looking anything but comfortable.

"I did," I agree. "I mean, I do."

"Do you trust him?"

I let out a deep sigh. "I thought I did."

"But now?"

I look up at Nils. "We haven't known each other that long. There are still things I don't know about him."

"Things that make you think he's interested in messing about in your business affairs?" Nils looks skeptical to say the least. He's right, really. It's a silly supposition and I'm totally jumping to conclusions. Having questions about what Julian is hiding is in all likelihood completely unconnected to what's happened.

"No, probably not," I finally reply. "But then, who?"

Nils shrugs. "It could've been anybody," he points out. "I'm reticent to make any assumptions until we have more to go on."

I huff a small, joyless laugh. "How mature of you," I tease. "I'm just jumpy right now. You're right. We should go home, get some sleep, and deal with this tomorrow."

A tired smile crosses his face. "I'll let you know as soon as I have something."

I lean back in my chair, willing my brain to shut the hell up. "Thanks." Suddenly a thought occurs to me. "Nils?"

"Hmmm?" He tilts his head to the side curiously.

"How come your personal drama never spills over into work? I feel like everyone else around here has been a hot mess at one point or another. But never you."

He rubs his lips together while he considers his answer.

"I'm on a personal drama hiatus," he finally cracks in response.

It does make me laugh. "Seriously? What does that mean?"

He shrugs. "It means you have to have a personal life to have drama."

"Oh," I say in a small voice. "I'm sorry, Nils. You do too much here. What can I do to help?"

He leans forward, looking me intently in the eyes. "While I appreciate the thought, I didn't mean to imply I'm dissatisfied." He pauses, his eyes searching mine. "Everything I need is right here."

I'm unsure of how to respond, so his words simply hang in the air. I decide against saying anything to discourage any unseemly affection he may have for me. Because I think I've made enough assumptions for the night, and I'm probably just being a bit too self-centered on all fronts right now.

Instead, I let him walk me to my car, then I use all of my remaining energy to get home safely. There's nothing left for my endless overanalysis, and when my head hits the pillow, I'm out.

⌁

AFTER I'VE WOKEN, SHOWERED, AND EATEN LUNCH, THE NAGGING FEELING that Julian might have something to do with this creeps back in. Sick of going back and forth, I decide to just ask him. And driving to his place will give me too much time to vacillate, so I simply call him.

"Hey, baby," he greets me. His deep voice gives me the same chills it always does. I push the feeling down.

"Why were you at the club last night?" I ask immediately, not up for dicking around.

The silence on the other end is unnerving.

"Fuck, you don't miss a trick, do you?"

"That wasn't an answer," I point out. I wonder if he's stalling, thinking he should've asked if my ability works over the phone. But then, maybe I'm not giving him enough credit. Though even feeling like an asshole for asking, I still need to hear his answer.

"I wanted to see you," he replies.

"But you didn't want me to see you?" I ask shrewdly.

"You were on my mind," he says. "But I didn't want to crowd you."

I pause, waiting for the voice. Nothing. He always sounds sincere, so there's nothing to contradict his answer. I've never consciously realized that before now, and I wonder if it's just with me, or if that's always how he is.

"That's the only reason you were there?" I press.

"I was only there because I wanted to see you. I saw you, had a drink, then I left," he says, clearly irritated. That's saying something. He's always unflappably calm and collected. Well, almost always. I recall the things he said to me Friday night, the emotion in his face, his voice, his touch. And I feel like a world-class ass.

"You should've said hi," I grumble, deflated. I'm mostly mad at myself. I've never been able to embrace good things in my life without a heaping side of suspicion.

Julian laughs, that deep, spine-tingling laugh that I know lights up his face. "Trust me, I was tempted," he replies silkily, his hungry tone causing my core to tighten.

"How about you come say hi now?" I ask.

There's a pause before he answers, and I wonder if he sensed and was offended by my previous unspoken accusation.

"You sure?"

"I'm sure," I say with a smile.

"Good," he replies. "Because I'm already on my way."

"You sneaky bastard," I accuse him incredulously. But I can't help the smile that splits across my face. "Did you leave before or after I called?"

"Before," he admits.

"And I called you while you were already on your way here. Damn."

"Yeah," he agrees. "Freaky, right?"

It is, and it isn't. It shows that he thinks about me as much as I think about him. But in his case, he was running toward me. And while I wasn't exactly running away, I was looking for a reason to.

And suddenly it hits me. That's why I suspected him, because I'm looking for a solid reason to run, because he told me he loves me. And even though I wanted to say it back, it's what really scared me. Not that I didn't know what he's holding back. I'm more afraid of what he's not. Because it means I have no reason to hold back anymore, either, not if I really want to be with him.

"When will you be here?" I ask, suddenly very nervous. But in a good way this time.

"Open your door," he instructs.

"Seriously?" I open my door and poke my head out, but he's not there.

"Well, fuck, I'm not *that* good," he laughs. And then he comes around the corner with a grin. "But pretty close."

I can't help it. I pocket my phone as quickly as I can and run to him. He catches me as I launch myself at him, lifting me up to meet his lips. I wrap my legs around his waist and kiss him hungrily. He walks us into my apartment, kicking the door closed behind him. Then he lies me down on the couch, not letting go.

Finally, I break away, panting, as he hovers over me.

"That was a pretty fucking nice way to say hi," he says with a smile.

I grab him through his jeans, and he's already hard for me. "No, *that's* a nice way to say hi," I tease.

He growls at me, burying his face in my neck, sucking hard. As usual, the lust that shoots through me causes me to bow into him.

"Julian," I plead breathlessly, pressing on his shoulders.

He relents, sitting up between my legs. For a moment, all I can do is stare. His hair and eyes are wild and dark, the black T-shirt and jeans he wears fitted around the bulging muscles of his chest and legs. And he's looking at me like he's won a prize. It takes my breath away again. He's good at doing that.

"What, baby?" he prompts me.

I take a shaky breath. "About what you said on Friday —"

He shakes his head. "You don't have to say anything, Frankie."

I shimmy up into a sitting position, and he rests back on his haunches. I put my hands on his taut chest, trying not to be distracted by his strength, his heat. There will be time enough for that.

"I know," I reply. "But I need to." I take a deep breath. "I do trust you. But for me, that's not a single decision. I've gone almost thirty years waiting for that voice in my head every time someone speaks. I know it's not fair, but it's made me used to constantly reevaluating my relationships. It's like a stream of new information that can shake even the deepest trust. So when I choose to trust you, I'm going to have to make that choice over and over again. Does that make any sense?"

Julian scrubs a large hand over his stubble. "Yeah, it does."

"Good," I say, letting out a sigh of relief. "Because I meant it when I said I can't imagine not being with you. I love you." Tears spring to my eyes. I blink them back, waiting for his response.

He just watches me, his eyes calmly roaming my face. When it gets to the point where I'm not sure whether he's going to answer, he leans forward onto his arms, crawling over me, pushing me back onto the couch. He answers with his kiss, pinning me into the cushions, his tongue delving forcefully between my lips.

When he breaks away, his mouth immediately wanders downward, cutting a blazing trail down my neck, to my nipple, grazing the soft sliver of stomach exposed between my shirt and shorts.

"You're not going to say anything?" I tease him.

He catches my eyes as his hands deftly slide my shorts and panties off in one swift movement.

"Oh, I will," he replies confidently. "But only after you tell me that while you come in my mouth."

I gasp as his lips descend on me, his tongue probing feverishly. When it hits my clit, I'm immediately feverish and twitching with pleasure.

"Fuck, Frankie, you taste like heaven," he growls into my core, quickly going back to sucking me senseless. His fingers join in, thrusting me toward the brink.

All I can do is moan and writhe under his skilled touch.

"Tell me, baby," he prompts, flicking my clit with his tongue.

"I love you," I gasp.

He twists his hand, replacing his tongue with his thumb as his other fingers continue to fuck me, making me cry out again. His mouth finds mine, and I lick my slick wetness from his lips. It's his turn to groan into me.

"I fucking love the way you taste," he groans. "And I fucking love the noises you make when I do this." He curls his fingers inside me and presses down on my clit, eliciting a scream of pleasure. "I love you, Frankie."

He pumps me faster, and I grip his shoulders as my orgasm builds.

"Tell me," he demands one last time.

I arch into him. "God-fucking-damn it," I gasp, all but screaming. "I love you."

And with a satisfied smile, his fingers twist and press me over the edge. I scream my release, clinging to him as I ride the wave. He doesn't let up, and it keeps going, and going, until I think I'll pass out from the pleasure. Finally, as he feels my body unclench, he relents, gently stroking me down the receding wave of bliss.

He leaves me to recover for a moment and I glare at him.

"What?" he asks with a laugh.

I give him an impatient look, swiping my foot over the hard lump in his pants.

"Take off your clothes," I demand.

He laughs at me, the bastard. "All in good time."

I raise an eyebrow, sit up, and take off my shirt and bra in one pull. The smile drops off his face as he stares at my chest, followed by the entirety of my completely naked body. A wicked grin of triumph settles on my lips.

While he's distracted, I undo his fly. And before he can stop me, I take him in my mouth. It's no small feat as he's already fully hard. But the gasp he lets out is worth it.

"Fuck, Frankie, be careful," he begs.

I suck hard off his tip, using my hand to continue working him. "No," I reply with just enough sass to make him laugh.

"Have it your way," he replies, resting his hand on the back of my head.

I make him lift his ass so I can completely free him from his boxers.

Cupping him with one hand, I continue to work him with the other hand and my mouth, sometimes together, sometimes one after the other.

He gently caresses my hair as I work, spurring me on to suck him to the edge, then bring him back, all to give him a taste of what he gives me every time he puts his hands on me. To show him that his pleasure gives me pleasure. To show him I love making him come just as much as he does me.

"God, I love watching you suck my cock," Julian groans.

I suck him harder.

"Fuck, Frankie," he moans. "I'm gonna come in your amazing fucking mouth if you keep that up."

I eye him with satisfaction as I twist my grip in time with my suction, and I can feel him clench under the slick pressure. Making him come in my mouth is exactly what I want, and I work him like I mean it.

His head lolls back and his hand slips down my hair, gripping it by the ends. Even when he's about to come, he's so careful. I clench inside, totally turned on as this gorgeous man trembles under my provocation.

I pop my mouth off his cock, continuing to ramp up with my hand as I rub my breasts along the back of his shaft to get his attention. He groans deeply but doesn't look at me.

"Watch me suck you off, baby," I demand. "I want you to watch yourself come in my mouth."

His eyes go wide, and I have to stifle a laugh. He obviously wasn't expecting me to throw the dirty talk back at him. What can I say? He has that effect on me.

His eyes lock on me, so I lower my mouth back over him, satisfied he's doing as I asked.

As my mouth settles back into the mix, he whimpers. I look up to make sure he's still watching. He looks hypnotized. So I go at it with everything I've got. Not moments later I feel the sticky, hot stream in my mouth as his whimpers turn to deep, low groans. He's still watching me, struggling to keep his eyes from rolling back in his head. I open my mouth to show him the last of his load squirting into my mouth, coating my tongue.

"Holy fucking shit," he swears. I gently roll my hand up his length and lick the last, pearly drop off the tip of his trembling cock. At the sight of it he throws his head back and clenches in pleasure under me. "Fuck." I feel him tighten under my hand and one final, huge gush erupts from him as he seemingly has a second orgasm. "Oh, my sweet fucking God. What the fuck was that?" He sinks back into the couch, breathless and truly spent this time.

I climb on him, straddling him carefully. "Say it, bitch," I demand.

Julian laughs, his head lolling tiredly. "I love you, woman," he replies, closing his eyes. "And I have no idea how you did that."

"Me, neither," I admit with a grin. "But it was fun."

He opens his eyes, laughing at me again. "You're crazy," he teases, pulling me into him and burying his face in my neck. "But I think I'll keep you anyway."

I smack him playfully on the arm, blushing at the implication. "If you think you can handle me."

Julian pulls back, looking into my eyes. "I'm serious," he says. "Be my girl, Frankie."

I smile, resisting the urge to point out that that wasn't a question. He already knows how much I dislike being ordered around. Well, when we're not fucking anyway. But this is different, and I know he's not demanding it. He's offering it.

"I'm already your girl," I admit. But I can't help busting his balls just a little. "What did you think, that I go around telling every gorgeous guy I meet at my club that I love him?"

"I'm gorgeous, huh?" He flicks an eyebrow up and leans in, nuzzling into my ear.

"Yeah, but probably not half as gorgeous as you think you are," I tease.

He nips playfully at my neck. "Probably not," he agrees, and it makes me laugh. I can't fault him for being cocky when he's got the cock to back it up.

"Have you always been overly confident?" I ask, sliding off of his lap and retrieving my clothing. I don't bother with the bra or panties, simply tossing them aside in favor of just a T-shirt and shorts. He watches, clearly approving of my choice, and I know he's going to have me naked again as soon as he can. It sends a shiver down my back.

He lifts his tight ass up, sliding himself back into his boxers and pants. "I wouldn't call it 'overly confident,'" he replies with a shit-eating grin.

I roll my eyes and disappear into the bathroom to clean up.

When I come back out, he's leaning against the living room windows, staring outside with a thoughtful expression. He looks up as I approach.

"What happened at the club?" he asks.

I purse my lips together. "What makes you think something happened?" I counter.

He levels a hard stare at me. "Don't treat me like I'm a fucking idiot, Frankie," he says in a quiet tone that's just as hard as his gaze.

I fold my arms over my chest, debating how much to tell him, and the lack of bra pushes my breasts dangerously close to spilling out of my shirt. He resolutely continues to stare at my face.

"Someone messed with the security cameras," I reply.

He stares at me blankly for a minute, running a hand through the tangled, dark mess of hair on top of his head. A muscle in his jaw ticks. "That all?"

I tighten my arms around me, not giving a shit if my tits spill out. Something about this conversation is making me very uneasy. "Yeah," I mumble, averting my eyes. "I didn't really think you did it. I think I was just looking for a way out."

Julian's face falls, his eyebrows tightening together as he frowns. I reach out to reassure him, but he steps back.

"I don't want out, not really," I clarify.

His beautiful, uneven lips settle into a small, sideways smile. "I know," he assures me. "I get you have reason to doubt me. I don't blame you, baby." He shakes his head and crosses his own tattooed, muscled arms over his chest, returning his gaze out the window.

It hits me. He thinks he doesn't deserve me. And my reminding him that I'm not happy about the things he isn't sharing isn't helping. That's a tough one for me. Because I both want to reassure him that I'm still here while wanting to shake his secrets out of him. I wish like fuck that he hadn't ever mentioned there were things he wasn't ready to tell me. But then, knowing about me, he probably thought it was safer to hide as little as possible.

"God, dating me must suck," I muse out loud.

Julian's on me in an instant, pulling my arms away from my chest and dragging me against his hard chest. His hand lifts my chin, then strokes my face. "No," he protests. "You're the most fucking amazing woman I've ever met. Don't doubt that." His lips reach down for mine, wrapping me in the warmth of his affection.

When he pulls away, I can't help laughing. "Thanks," I reply. "But I meant that you can't win. I push you to be honest, then I get impatient when you honestly tell me there are things you don't want to share yet." I shrug. "You've only known me a month. It's not like you owe me your full life story."

He continues to thoughtfully stroke my face, his eyes roaming over me. "Fuck, has it really only been a month?" he murmurs.

The intensity on his face is overwhelming. And I'm with him. It feels like so much longer. Part of me feels like I've always known him. When I'm not fighting falling for him, we just fit. Like he's a piece of me I didn't know I was missing. Because I've never been *that* girl. The one who needed a man to feel whole. But now that I'm his, well, I do. Despite my reservations, that's a difficult feeling to deny. And he looks at me like it's written all over my face, like I'm naked in front of him, not bodily, but my heart and soul.

"Yeah," I breathe. "Just a month."

His thumb finds my lower lip, and my mouth parts for him. His lips pull up in a small smile, and his eyes flick up to meet mine. "Feels longer," he whispers, his eyes darkening.

I nod mutely, unable to do much besides languish in the feeling of his hands on me. I want to remember this feeling for the next time I start doubting him. Determined to commit it to memory, I take in every detail of him as he stares back at me. But when his lips reach for mine once more, when I know he's about to take me in a way that goes beyond the intensely physical relationship we've had so far, I surrender, letting him in completely as I close my eyes.

JULIAN

I open my eyes, wishing away the headache forming in my temples. Fuck, I'm tired. I look around Sal's office, annoyed that he's once again late. I glance over his huge, old oak desk, scratched and scarred from years of use and piled with papers and cigarette butts. His ancient leather chair is peeling and practically falling apart. The standard issue office clock on the wall tick-tick-ticks away the minutes of my pitiful existence. My eyes start to slide closed again like they have a mind of their own.

Shaking myself, I stand up, choosing to pace instead. Anything to keep me awake. My mind wanders back to the reason for my exhaustion. Frankie. Giving herself to me in every fucking way possible. All fucking night. Tired as I am, the thought still stirs me. But I shake my head, knowing she's both my salvation and my damnation wrapped up into one. But I'll be dreaming of those red lips as I burn in hell.

The door flies open and Sal saunters in, a lit cigarette dangling from his crusty old lips. A chintzy pair of aviators sit on top of his greasy, balding head.

"Julian, what the fuck are you doing here so early?" he greets me, tossing the pile of folders in his arms onto the desk. Papers go flying fucking everywhere.

"I left you a message," I remind him.

He shrugs and sits in in his chair, searching the mess on his desk for something. "Yeah, so? I didn't think you meant this fuckin' early," he grouses.

"Well, I did," I say, putting my hands on the edge of his desk and leaning in to catch his eye.

He looks up at me, unimpressed. "So what the fuck do you want?" he asks sharply.

"Why did you send me in for retrieval if you already had someone else on the job?" I demand.

Sal leans back into his chair, folding his arms over his chest with a frown. "I didn't," he says, looking at me suspiciously. "But I take it that means you didn't do what I asked."

I stand back up, folding my arms over my chest. I stare him down, trying to decide whether he's playing me. Fuck, what I wouldn't give for Frankie's ability right now.

"It was too risky," I hedge. "And I don't have time for this shit."

Like lightning, Sal is up and fucking pissed.

"You have time for what I fucking tell you to have time for," he spits, pointing a crooked finger at me.

I don't move, blink, or give him any sign that I give two shits about his temper tantrum.

Breathing heavily, he seems to back down and reconsider.

Good.

"I'm actually glad you're here," he finally says. "There's something else related to this that I need to do this morning. Might make what I asked you to get unnecessary. You're gonna come with me, be my muscle."

Bad. And I know it's bad because I've got that feeling in the pit of my stomach. The one I get when he asks me to do something I know I'm going to fucking hate doing.

"Whatever," I reply with a shrug. "Let's get this over with."

Sal smirks at me. He opens his desk drawer and retrieves his gun. He holsters it behind his back.

"Good. You packing?"

I open my jacket to show him the gun under my left arm. What, does he think this is my first day on the job? Stupid motherfucker.

"All right then," he says. "I think it's finally time we go have a little chat with Samantha Greco."

He saunters past me, thankfully putting his back to me quickly, so he doesn't see the panic on my face. Pushing it down, I follow at a brisk pace. I can't let him know I care. And I sure as fuck can't let him know the last thing I want to do is go shake down Frankie's mother.

AS WE WALK UP THE PEELING STEPS OF FRANKIE'S CHILDHOOD HOME, I can't help wondering where the park is that Frankie used to go sleep in. Dream in. Think of being the child of aliens in. I suppress an ill-timed chuckle. Frankie is hands down the craziest, most captivating woman I've ever met. But everything she's told me about her mother, everything I know, says I'm about to walk into a bad fucking situation.

Sal knocks on the door. I hang back on the top step of the stairs to the porch, wishing I were anywhere but here. Or that I was here with Frankie. Meeting her mother under less fucked-up circumstances. But my life is a lesson in humility.

The door creaks open and an old woman peers out suspiciously. When her eyes land on Sal, her weathered lips pucker, and I get the sense she knows exactly who has come calling. Her eyes flick to me for a moment, then back to Sal.

"Mr. Moretti," she greets him. "I thought we'd be seeing you soon."

"Mrs. Greco," he replies curtly. "Samantha home?"

No greeting, no preamble. Boy, he must really hate this family to treat an old lady with such disrespect.

Frankie's grandmother considers him for a minute. Probably just to keep him on his toes, because she finally opens the door. "Yes, of course, please do come in," she says graciously.

As I step past her, she looks up at me with a glare. "How do you do, ma'am," I greet her with a dip of my head.

She sighs. "I'm well, young man, for now," she grumbles as she closes the door behind me. "But at least one of you has manners."

Sal shows himself into the tidy living room, taking a seat on the couch like he owns the fucking place. I stay standing in the entryway, crossing my arms over my chest.

"Please, have a seat," she says to me, her eyes jumping to Sal in distaste.

"Thank you, ma'am, but I'm fine here," I assure her politely.

She makes a small noise of indifference and disappears down the hallway. I eye Sal, who simply gives me a dangerous smile.

A moment later, a slim, short middle-aged woman appears. Her dark, graying hair is pulled back severely from her face, which has an expression that's as unforgiving as I imagined her to be. Out of habit, I scan her for possible weapons. Though I doubt she needs any. She could cut a man in half with just that nasty look on her face, which she immediately directs at Sal.

"You've got balls, I'll give you that," she snaps at Sal as she stops across from him. She glances at me, then back at him. "Coming here, armed? You always were a disrespectful asshole."

The fucker doesn't even get up, he simply smiles at her.

"Sam," he says. "You're looking good."

"Say what you came to say or get out." She's all business, just like Frankie said.

"Okay. Seems I have a daughter you forgot to mention," he says, a menacing tone creeping into his voice.

Samantha continues staring him down impassively, not rising to his bait. Knowing Frankie told her about the DNA test, I know she knows she's not in a position to argue. With that, at least.

Sal doesn't say anything else, seemingly waiting for her to say something. I fight the urge to shift uncomfortably, unwilling to show any weakness.

She considers him for a good long while. "I can only assume you've stayed away because my father threatened you. Even though he's dead, I think we both know that you're still not welcome here," she says carefully. "So I'm only going to say this once. Stay away from my family. Or else."

Sal, ever the suicidal motherfucker, laughs. "Or else what? I think we both know that I've got nothing to lose," he responds. "And since Frankie clearly hasn't joined your little family business," Samantha clenches at his taunt, "I fully intend to fold her into mine."

"You'll do no such thing," she says dangerously quietly. "I've worked too hard to keep her away from you, away from that world."

Sal snorts. "She's running a fucking night club in Hollywood," he chortles. "Did you think she'd be able to stay clean forever? If I don't bring her in, someone else will. You want that for our daughter?"

Samantha clenches her fists but shows no other signs of cracking. "Frankie is too smart to get wrapped up in any of that," she insists. "And she's too smart to fall for whatever line you plan on feeding her."

Before I can stop myself, a wry chuckle of agreement escapes me. Even without her ability, her mother is right. Frankie is way too smart. Samantha's icy glare flicks to me. And though I've faced down men twice her size who were armed to the teeth, the look she shoots me is enough to make me want to run for the hills. She has a terrifying command of the room, and my opinion of Sal's intelligence takes a hit. Why the fuck is he provoking her?

Thankfully, she seems to write me off a moment later, and she turns the heat back on Sal.

"Did you just come here to piss me off?" she asks evenly, voicing my exact thought.

Sal considers that for a moment. He finally stands up, sauntering to a stop right in front of her.

"No, doll," he says softly. "I came here out of respect. Not that you ever had any for me."

Samantha laughs, and it's just as scary as her steely expression. Harsh, and cold, and full of hatred and malice. "You have to earn respect, you piece of shit," she says to him. "Now take your goon and get out of my house."

He smiles. "I've gotten what I came here for," he replies. Then raising his voice, "Nice seeing you, Maria." Frankie's grandmother emerges too quickly to not have been listening around the corner.

"Fuck off, Sal," she replies nonchalantly.

I have to pull my lips into my mouth to keep from smiling. The old lady doesn't miss it and looks me up and down as Sal steams past me.

"You're too good for him, you know," she says boldly.

I clench my jaw, not wanting to agree within earshot of Sal.

"Sorry to have disturbed you, ladies," I say.

They exchange a look. Not wanting to make this worse, I turn and follow Sal out the door. Just in time to witness him crashing into some kid on a bike on the way to his car. The kid bites it on the sidewalk.

"Fuck, kid, watch where you're going," Sal yells at him.

I shoot down the steps, disentangling the boy from his bike and helping him up.

"You okay, kid?" I ask him.

He grips my forearms with wide eyes as he rights himself. I follow his gaze to my jacket, where it's shifted to expose the gun. Releasing him, I stand up quickly. His eyes shift to my face.

"I'm fine, mister," he says, reaching to cradle his left arm with his right hand.

"You sure?" I ask as he winces, clearly in pain.

"Julian, get your ass in the car," Sal calls impatiently from a few feet away.

"Sal, you hurt the kid," I return defensively. I look back to the boy. "Let me at least make sure you're okay."

He nods, sitting down on the curb. I carefully ease down next to him, making sure the holstered gun stays hidden in the folds of my jacket. He extends his arm so I can examine his elbow. It's scraped up and bleeding but doesn't look too bad. I pull a handkerchief from my pocket and press it gently against his elbow.

"It'll be all right," I tell him. "Do you need help getting your bike home?"

The kid blows his dark brown hair out of his eyes and gestures with his head. "Nah, I live here."

My eyes go wide. "You're Frankie's brother?" I say it without thinking. Of course, he is. He even matches Frankie's description of Tony perfectly. All awkward and gangly, every inch the twelve-year-old accident-prone kid he is.

I must say it a shade too loud, because it catches Sal's attention. Fuck, fuck, fuck.

"Yeah! You know my sister?" he asks.

"Sure do," Sal offers before I'm forced to explain. "In fact, I'm her dad. So we're kind of related."

I close my eyes and take a deep breath. He's doing exactly what Samantha just told him not to do. He's messing with her family. And I, for one, don't want to know what "or else" means.

"No way," Tony says with a frown. "Frankie's dad is dead." He glares defiantly up at Sal, who eases his old ass down on the curb next to him.

"Turns out I'm not," he says with a smile. "You can ask her yourself."

Tony eyes him critically. "I'll do that," he says. "Because she knows when people are lying." His words are full of indignant accusation, and if he hadn't just revealed Frankie's biggest secret to a man planning to use her, I'd find his fierce pride in his sister endearing.

As it is, my blood freezes in my veins. He's old enough to know how to keep secrets, but maybe he didn't know that this was one? Whatever the reason, it doesn't matter now. I hold my breath and look over at Sal, who thankfully doesn't seem to know what to make of his comment.

"Yeah?" he says, clearly humoring the kid. "That's cool. I had a grandpa who knew when people were bluffing at cards."

Tony's eyes go wide. "Then she got it from your family," he says excitedly.

Sal gives the kid a look. "Got what?"

"The voice that tells her when people are lying," he presses. "If your grandpa had it, maybe that's why she has it."

Sal looks up at me and catches my eye. I'm not sure there's any hiding the horror in my expression. And I can see the moment it dawns on him that the kid isn't joking. And that I've been hiding something from him.

"Yeah, that must be it," he says, his eyes still locked on mine. I wish I was someone else, so I could kick my own fucking ass. With one look, I've done exactly what I promised myself I wouldn't do. I've betrayed Frankie's secret to Sal.

Tony looks between me and Sal. "Hey, I gotta go," he says nervously, finally sensing the tension. "I only came home 'cause I forgot my math book." He rises and creeps toward the house. "See you around, though, okay?"

Sal snaps out of it and throws the kid a smile. "Sure thing, kid. See ya."

Tony smiles in relief, turns around, and heads toward the house.

Sal is completely silent as we get in the car and head back to his office. When we park, he taps the wheel with his thumbs.

"Anything else you're not telling me?" he asks, dangerously quietly.

"I don't know what you're talking about," I reply. In for a penny, in for a pound, I decide. May as well keep lying.

Sal turns to me. "You think I'm stupid?"

Yes, I think he's very stupid. Especially after the little trip we just went on.

"You think I'm stupid enough to keep things from you?" I counter.

"Why'd you look so guilty back there, then?" Sal asks pointedly.

I shrug, keeping the carefully controlled act in place. "Indigestion?" I offer sarcastically.

Sal pulls his piece out of its holster, laying it carefully on his lap.

"Julian," he says, "you've worked for me a long time. I'd hate for things to end badly."

The threat hangs in the air and I say nothing. What the fuck can I say?

Sal strokes the gun's grip thoughtfully for a moment. Eventually he reholsters it and turns to me.

"I've got what I need now," he says carefully. "Stay away from Frankie. I mean it this time."

I clench my jaw. The only thing I can do. What he means is, he'll be watching me. Or having someone watch me, anyway.

But even though there are other ways I could warn her, there is so much I'd have to tell her first. And I'm not ready to lose her. But if I say nothing, at best Sal will go full-court press to get her under his wing, which would leave her with little choice. And that's not a place I want her to be. Because that's exactly where I'm trapped, and it's ruined whatever life I could've had. At worst, well, we'd get to find out what "or else" means.

22

FRANKIE

As great as my week started, riding the high of being with Julian, by Wednesday morning it's come crashing down. I haven't heard a word from him since he left Sunday night. Not loving that this is the second time he's done this. Okay, that may be an understatement. I toggle between devastated and furious at any given moment.

To boot, Nils has called me into the office far earlier in the day than I'm used to rising. Needless to say, I'm not feeling terribly optimistic as I head into the club to meet him.

I find Nils in the security room, looking beyond troubled.

"I take it there's been a development?" I say by way of greeting.

Nils looks up from his pensive reverie at the bank of monitors. He flashes the smallest of smiles.

"Yes, there has," he replies simply, gesturing to the seat beside him. I oblige, and he begins to pull up a video file. "This was recovered by the security company."

He presses play, and it's immediately obvious it's the front door cam. The time stamp is *after* the uploaded feeds had cut out. "They erased their own entry," I exclaim. Nils, looking grim, nods and gestures to continue watching. And a moment later, I know why: Jess.

Nils stops the feed after she passes off camera. He shuffles through the files, beginning another clip. This one of the interior of the security room. It clearly shows Jess entering, spending a few minutes manipulating the security feeds, then shutting down the system with the code under the mousepad.

When he stops the feed, I turn to him. "Please tell me we've notified the authorities," I plead.

"Oh, yes," he assures me. "We're pressing charges. I've been assured that due to repeated trespassing offenses she'll at the very least do some community service. I doubt she'll darken our doorstep again. However, it's worth noting that she appeared to have done this so she could go into our computer system without being seen to take files relating to Dave. Depending on what her intentions were, it could dramatically add to her sentence. Unfortunately, it will take some time for them to build their case and prosecute, and they may never know exactly what she had planned."

I lean back with a sigh. "Does it matter? There's no explaining crazy," I mumble, crossing my arms over my chest. But strangely, I find myself relieved by this news. "At least now I know for sure it wasn't Julian."

Nils raises an eyebrow. "You still had doubts?"

I shrug. "Not really, I guess," I admit.

"If you're still unsure about him, maybe it's time to rethink things," he suggests in a tone that's a little too casual.

I shoot him a look. "I'm unsure about everyone, Nils," I reply honestly.

Nils considers that for a moment. "Are you unsure about me?" he asks curiously.

I smile wryly. "No," I admit. Then, with a wink, "Mostly."

Nils laughs, breaking the tension of the moment. "I'll take it."

"You should," I reply. "Anyway, thanks for letting me know. Alas, I need to get ready to have lunch with someone."

"Someone, as in Julian?" Nils asks, the smile dropping off his face.

"No," I reply. "Ugh. It's complicated."

The smile is back. "When is it not, Francesca?" he teases.

I'm a little surprised. Nils isn't much for teasing usually. He almost looks relaxed. I find it kind of strange, given the circumstances, but it works for him. I tell him so, eliciting another laugh from the usually reserved Swede.

Standing, he gestures for me to precede him out of the room. "Onward and upward," he murmurs.

I head to my office and finish some paperwork Nils has for me. That done, I debate for a few minutes whether I really want to have lunch with Sal. The whole situation is just weird, and it's not like I don't have enough other shit to deal with right now. But I'm not that asshole who cancels at the last minute, so I suck it up and head out to meet him.

I ENTER THE HOMEY LITTLE ITALIAN RESTAURANT SAL CHOSE, overwhelmed by the fantastic smell that instantly makes my mouth water. Before I even make it to the hostess stand, I see Sal rise from a table at the back of the restaurant, waving me over.

I admire my surroundings as I pick my way through the sea of checkered tablecloths. It's quaint in that it's totally predictable, with pictures of famous Italian landmarks on the walls, elaborate ceiling murals that hover somewhere between classic art and a cartoonish imitation of them, and customers digging into massive piles of pasta and huge plates of lasagna.

When I reach Sal, he gives me a hug, seeming much more upbeat than the last time I saw him. He smells like cigarettes and sweat, and I try not to wrinkle my nose as I pull back.

"Frankie," he greets me with a huge grin. He gestures to the small booth, inviting me to sit down.

"Sal," I return with a reserved smile. "Nice place."

"Yeah? You like it?" he asks, gesturing around him as he returns to his seat.

"So far, so good," I hedge. "How's the food?"

"Oh, it's fantastic," he assures me.

Having grown up in an Italian-American family, I decide I'll be the judge of that.

"So how you doin', doll?" Sal asks.

I shrug. "Same shit, different day," I mutter as I scan the menu. My eyes flick up to his, noting how overly interested he seems, looking at me intently, leaned forward like he is. "How are you?"

"Oh, I'm great," he effuses. "Just had a development that I think is going to bring some life back to my business." He smiles widely. "How's things at the club?"

Putting my menu aside, I fold my arms on the table. "Club's good," I reply vaguely.

"You sure?" he presses. "'Cause you seem a little on edge."

I huff an unamused laugh. "Just got a lot going on," I say honestly.

"That's owning a business," Sal replies with a shrug. "But hey, if you ever need anything, my services are at your disposal, you know."

I give him a look, unsure of why he'd think I'd use his "services" after making it clear I wasn't a fan of his obviously questionable business prac-tices. But the waiter comes and takes our order, so I have to wait a moment before saying anything.

"I mean it," Sal says as the waiter leaves, beating me to the punch. "We're family. Anything you need, just ask."

I drum my fingers on the tabletop while I contemplate my answer. "Thanks, but I like to keep things above board," I finally reply.

Sal laughs. "Hey, that's all good," he replies. "I go with whatever the client wants."

"I don't think there's anything I need that you can help me with," I say more plainly.

He smirks in response. "Not even security? Or personnel with fraternization issues?" he asks with a cunning glint in his beady eyes. "Because both of those could bring a lot of trouble to your doorstep. And I have plenty of experience with handling stuff like that."

The realization that he's somehow clearly gotten inside information on my business issues does three things. First, it freaks me the fuck out. I mean, who is this guy, really? Second, I'm instantly furious that he thinks it's in any way okay to involve himself in my life that way. Third, it convinces me more than ever that he's shady. And I'm about two seconds from walking out and never seeing him again.

But before I overreact, I calmly confirm whether he's as big of a sleazebag as he seems to be.

"There are two things you should know about me, Mr. Moretti," I say quietly. My formal address at least causes the insipid smile to melt off his face. "First, I can handle my own business, and I don't appreciate when people go behind my back to learn things that are none of theirs. Second, if you think for one second that I'm going to somehow give you access to my operations, you're sadly mistaken."

Sal laughs, leaning back in his seat, casually slinging an arm over the side of the booth. Clearly my outrage hasn't fazed him at all. "You got spunk, doll," he says with a chuckle. "But I think you got the wrong end of things. I'm not interested in your business. I'm interested in you." He continues to stare at me with a knowing smile and a sinister twinkle in his eye.

I give the voice a minute, surprised when it stays silent. He's not lying, and that is surprising.

"Why?"

"Besides the fact that you're my daughter?" he scoffs. I fold my arms over my chest. "All right, all right. You're a smart cookie, obviously. I could use someone like you on my side."

"I have absolutely no interest in being involved with your business. And I'm rapidly losing interest in anything having to do with you, period."

The waiter chooses that moment to return with steaming plates of pasta. And damn if the gnocchi he sets in front of me doesn't smell like heaven.

Sal gives me a knowing look. "At least eat your lunch," he encourages me. "Then I know you're not writing off your old man on an empty stomach."

It's such an Italian dad thing to say, I have to laugh. I decide he's right. At least about the empty stomach part. Shaking my head, I sample the food.

Unfortunately, I can't stop the moan that erupts when the tender, buttery dumplings simply melt in my mouth.

Sal laughs. "See? Your old man knows a thing or two."

Ignoring him, I focus on enjoying my meal. At least I'll have that to remember him by. Though I'm sure as hell coming back to this place without him. I try not to think about how much Julian would love this, because that's a fresh wave of shit I don't want to think about right now.

It doesn't take long before I've cleaned my plate. It's probably the best meal I've had, possibly ever.

"Okay, I'm full now," I respond. "So if I write you off, you'll know it wasn't hunger."

Sal gives a rueful laugh and shakes his head. "C'mon kid, it could be great for the both of us," he urges. "We both have things we could offer the other. Let me make up for all the time I couldn't be there and help make things better, easier for ya."

I go to protest again, but he holds up a hand. "You don't gotta say yes," he allows. "But at least don't say no. Just think about it for a while. I'll drop it, okay?"

He's a persistent old bastard, I'll give him that. But I know my answer isn't going to change. I also know, though, that fighting him on it isn't going to do any good. If I decide to, I can just never speak to him again.

"Fine, whatever," I reply, getting out my wallet.

Sal waves me off again. "Put that away, kid," he chastises me. I open my mouth to argue, but he waves at me dismissively. "Neither of our money is any good here. One of my clients owns the place." I can't help but raise an eyebrow, at which he smiles widely. "What? You didn't think there were upsides to getting into business with old Sal? Not everything is muddy, doll. I've got plenty of legitimate clients."

"If you say so," I reply evenly.

He stands up, still chuckling at me. At least my rejection amuses him.

"We'll talk soon?" he asks as he walks me out.

I shoot him some serious side-eye. "We'll see," I hedge. "Thanks for lunch."

"Anytime, Frankie. You take care, now."

I step out onto the sidewalk and try not to shudder as I feel his creepy gaze follow me until I'm out of sight. Yuck. I decide then and there that every instinct I had about the guy was dead-on. And I have no intention of wasting any more time being subjected to his sleazy attempts to fold me into his sketchy "business."

As I get in my car, I half want to go home and shower off the icky feeling. But I'm also still on edge over Julian. So I just text him. *Haven't heard from you. Everything ok?*

And if that isn't giving him the benefit of the doubt, I don't know what is. I sit there for a few minutes, fiddling with the radio, but there's no response. With a sigh, I start the car, lower the ragtop, and head home. I try to let the crisp November air blow away the heaviness in my heart. But it's only wind.

I END UP SULLENLY DRINKING A FAIR AMOUNT THAT NIGHT. TO THE POINT where I'm so indignant at not getting a response from Julian that I foolishly make the decision to go to his place and tell him off in person. But even in my tipsy state I'm not stupid enough to attempt to drive, so I call for a ride, ending up at Julian's door around midnight.

Not giving a shit about the late hour, I bang on his door as hard as I can. What I don't realize is that it's a bad idea to come over unannounced, making a ruckus at the door of a big, rather scary man. At least, not until he opens the door with a gun pointed at my face.

As soon as he sees it's me, he drops the weapon to his side. "Fuck, Frankie, what the fuck do you think you're doing?" His dark hair is in a tangle on top of his head, his stubble thickening toward a beard, and he's shirtless, displaying his muscled, tattooed chest and arms, and that gorgeous "V" pointing to the top of his low-slung sweatpants.

He shakes his head, turning away and depositing his piece on the counter, leaving the door open. I take it as an invitation and step inside, closing the door behind me.

"What the fuck am *I* doing?" I slur. "What the fuck are *you* doing? I don't hear from you for days, *again*. I text, you don't answer. That's not how you treat your *girlfriend*." I drunkenly spit the word at him with the malice born from three days of being ignored. Again.

Julian sinks into his couch, gesturing for me to sit with him. I fold my arms over my chest and stick my bottom lip out.

"Don't be like that, Frankie," Julian grumbles, running his hands roughly over his face. I finally take a good look at him. He looks worn out. And sad.

I walk over to him, standing to the side of his knees. He uses the opportunity to hook his leg around mine and pull me in. Toppling onto his lap, I throw my hands out and grab him to slow my fall. I end up in his arms, cradled in his lap with my hands on his shoulders.

He runs a thumb roughly down my cheek. "I'm sorry," he says simply, offering nothing further.

I push against him, trying to free myself. "Let me go, Julian," I insist.

His hands close around my wrists, pulling me even closer. "No," he replies with a smirk. "Now that you've woken me up, I get to make it up to you."

"Make it up to me? You think it's that easy?" I ask, wriggling in his hold. "How about an explanation first?"

Julian leans into me, and the smell of his skin is beyond enticing. "I'd rather just fuck you." I don't even have a chance to protest that that's his answer for everything before he pulls my arms behind his neck, dropping his hands to my chest as his mouth latches on to my neck. He works fast, squeezing and working my breasts as his tongue slides down my body.

I press my hands against his chest, but my protests grow feeble as my body responds to him. "We can't solve all of our problems with sex," I manage to breathe out. It's barely convincing, because there's a dripping wet part of me that obviously would rather just let him fuck me too.

Julian looks up at me. His dark eyes are stormy, tormented. "I know." His hands wrap around my back, and he lies me down on the couch, sliding down with me. His head rests on my chest and he squeezes my body to his. "I'm sorry, baby."

I'm not sure if he's sorry for not calling or for trying to distract me. But he sounds so sincerely miserable that all the fight leaves me. I wrap my arms around him and kiss the top of his head.

"I know," I whisper.

We lie, silently soaking each other in. I close my eyes, letting the feeling of his warm body against mine soothe me. I feel myself drifting off, and I try to fight it. But it's useless, and as I slip into unconsciousness, I vow not to let him off the hook this time.

23

JULIAN

I wake up around six fucking a.m., still wrapped around Frankie. Or at least, I'm guessing it's that early because the sky is just starting to lighten. I carefully slide an arm out from under her and use it to prop up my head so I can watch her. She's a fucking stunner. Even drunk and sloppy as she was last night.

I fucking hate that I let Sal bully me into staying away from her this week. As I watch her breathe lightly through her open lips, something inside me snaps. The timing couldn't be worse, but I'm done. I can't be Sal's bitch anymore. It's time to tell him exactly that, and where he can shove this job. And if I survive, I'll tell her everything. Then I just have to hope like fucking hell that she'll forgive me.

I've never been comfortable living in the shadows. The nastier aspects of my life are what they are. Violence, intimidation, doing whatever is necessary to survive, to come out on top, that's just how life is. But having to keep people at arm's length because of it hasn't ever cost me anything. Until now. And I'm fucking over it. I'm not letting this girl go. She's the kick in the ass I needed to set my life straight.

Even if that's easier said than done. But I'm sure as fuck gonna try.

First, though, I need to be inside the gorgeous creature in my arms. To hear her say my name as I fuck her. To get her off on my hand, my face, my dick. Just the thought makes me hard as a fucking rock. I free my other hand and trace her jaw, skimming down her neck, between her breasts, down the line of her jeans. My teeth find the nipple resting under her shirt as my hand rubs between her legs. She stirs under me. I let her nipple go, running my nose over it.

"Julian?" she murmurs.

"Hey, baby," I reply, sinking my mouth back over the fabric covering her breast.

She groans and bucks into me. Such a good girl.

"What time is it?" she asks, her beautiful eyes opening and searching the dim room for a clock.

I sit up, settling between her legs.

"Time for this," I reply, undoing her jeans and pulling them down. She gasps and starts to reach for me, so I leave them around her thighs, dipping my hand between her legs.

She's silky soft in my hand, but I waste no time enjoying the feel of her. I go straight for her clit, rubbing hard circles until her hand falls, and her back arches into it.

"That's it, baby," I sigh, slipping a finger inside her, feeling her juices rise to my touch. "Goddamn, I love how wet you get for me."

The heat rises in her cheeks at my words, and with a satisfied smile I plunge two fingers into her tight, wet little cunt. She cries out, and the sound goes straight to my dick. But I keep control, finger-fucking her as I watch her orgasm build. She grabs desperately at her tits, squeezing and pinching her nipples.

"Fuck, baby, if you keep touching yourself like that I'm going to have to join in," I growl at her.

She nods, panting, unable to speak but clearly silently begging me to do exactly that. I reach over and grab one of her tits, pressing into its tip with my thumb. I don't stop my assault on her pussy either, letting my other thumb push on and off her clit as I stimulate her inside and out. Finally, when I can tell she's ready, I clench down with all fingers, on her nipple, clit, and G-spot. She bucks wildly into my hand as I press hard circles. The screams that come out of her make me glad I'm wearing a pair of sweats I couldn't give a shit about. Because I'm so fucking hard for her, I'm about to rip through the fabric.

"I need you to fuck me. Now," she demands after she catches her breath.

Everything inside me tightens. "Don't have to ask me twice," I groan, ripping my sweats off. She kicks her pants off at the same time, and as soon as we're both naked, I grab her legs, roughly pulling her to the edge of the couch.

I run my hand up my shaft, mostly just so she can see how fucking turned on she makes me. She watches me with hungry eyes, and I can't help the smirk I give her. "You like that?" She nods, biting into her lip hard. "You want this big fucking cock in your pussy?" And I swear I see her nipples get harder.

"Yes," she begs.

I seat the tip at her entrance. I can feel her slick warmth waiting to suck me in, but I hold back. I rub her from clit to ass, spreading her juices all over us both.

"Please," she whimpers.

"You want it?"

Her head bucks backward. "God, yes."

"How do you want it, baby?"

"Deep and hard. Now. Please, now," she begs.

It almost undoes me, but hearing her beg is fucking next level. I slide in excruciatingly slowly, stopping short of fully immersing myself in her before I pull back out.

"I think I need to teach you a little patience," I mutter, continuing to go shallow and slow. She twitches beneath me.

"Just give it to me, Julian," she moans.

"Hmmm," I tease, trying to decide how best to drive her crazy. And I remember. It's face next. It takes everything I've got to pull out of her and see her look of despair. But I know she's going to like what comes next, and it'll make her last orgasm that much better if I wait to give her what she's asking for.

For now, I drop between her legs, plunging my tongue into her, hungrily sucking and lapping at her juices. The unexpected move has a string of curse words flying out of her mouth. I laugh, even though my mouth is full of her pussy.

Getting back to business, I focus on tongue fucking her this time, wrapping my hand around to thumb her clit as I do. As soon as she comes, I spring up and plunge into her, fucking her deep and hard just like she asked, as the last of her orgasm clenches her around me.

I tilt her ass up so I can reach every last sweet inch of her as I pound her into oblivion. Her tits bounce back and forth in a way that would make me come on the fucking spot if I didn't have such good control.

"That what you want, baby? Deep and fucking hard? You want my hard cock fucking your sweet little pussy?"

She arches off the couch, and a fresh gush meets my pounding cock. I clench my teeth, pull out, and flip her over. She turns her head, so she's not buried in the cushions as I plunge back into her relentlessly, continuing to lift her ass in the air so I'm drilling her so hard and deep the force is shaking the furniture with each thrust. Her low moan becomes one continuous sound that grows louder each time her gorgeous ass slaps against me.

"Fuck, Frankie, you feel so fucking good," I tell her. I start to feel the orgasm building behind my cock. I press deeply into her, using a tilt of my hips to slam the head of my cock over the spot inside her as I reach around and rub her on the outside.

"Fuck, fuck, fuck, fuck, fuck," she screams as she comes on my dick, her legs shaking, her pussy clenching harder than I'd dreamed possible. She milks me, and fire licks through my body as I empty into her.

I want to collapse. I want to wrap myself around her. Claim her. But I pull back. Some of the wetness between us drips onto the floor. I stare at her trembling backside, mesmerized as our combined juices drip down her red, swollen pussy.

"Shit, baby, now that's a view," I pant. She lets her ass fall onto the couch, turning her head to give me a teasing glare. But she's still clearly unable to form sentences, so I laugh, turning and going into the bathroom to clean up.

Since I'm already naked, I decide not to half-ass it, and jump in the shower. When I'm just about done, Frankie saunters in. Watching her through the glass as she prowls toward me, naked, has unbelievably given me a semi.

"You are too fucking gorgeous," I tell her as I wash myself.

She opens the door and climbs in. Without a word, she's on her toes, her mouth on mine, her tongue demanding a response. Never one to shrink from a challenge, I lick her tongue, then spin her under the hot stream of water.

I pull back, watching the hot water cascade over her perfect chest, her nipples clearly still hard.

"Still want more, do you?" I tease her, clamping down on both of her nipples between my fingers and thumbs.

She hisses in pleasure. "Apparently, I can't get enough of you," she agrees. "Even when I'm hungover and pissed off."

I raise my eyebrows. Well, good that I at least have a weapon to distract her with. And I don't fucking waste it. I drop to my knees in front of her, lifting one of her legs with my left hand, and using my right hand to both support her and finger-fuck her. My mouth latches on to her lips, her clit, and anything else my tongue can lap at as I bring her back up to climax.

She leans her back against the tile, and the water pours down her delicious curves. Her taste, her need for me, her hot, wet pussy in my mouth drives me fucking crazy. I've never worked this hard to please a woman before and loved every minute of it. As she comes apart for me once again,

I say a prayer that I get to do this to her always. That she'll let me do it to her always, even once she knows everything.

That thought sobers me considerably, and as I let her down, I don't respond as her hand finds my cock.

I stroke a hand down her face. "I think he needs a break," I say lightly.

Frankie's blue eyes, those deep, dark pools that fucking slay me, stare up at me, ripping away my defenses.

"You can't make me come four times and not expect a good blow job in return," she replies matter-of-factly.

Now that makes me laugh. I draw her to me, tucking her under my chin.

"Maybe later," I reply. "Some of us have to get to work."

Some of us for the last time.

Her bottom lip pops out. "Boo," she comments.

I smile, running my hands down her sides to grip her ass. "You're too fucking cute," I murmur, burying my lips in her neck.

It takes a few more minutes to stop touching long enough for us to get out and dry off. When we're dried and dressed, I walk her to the door.

"We'll talk later," I assure her.

She looks surprised. "Yeah?"

I hold back a sigh. "Yeah," I promise.

"Well, I'm at the club early tonight. Deejay competition. But I might be able to go in late tomorrow." She looks up at me, all fucking sweet and hopeful. And I hope I'm not about to make a promise I can't keep.

"Sounds good," I reply. "Tomorrow, then."

She gives me one last, sweet kiss before she leaves. I have to lean on the door after I close it behind her to catch my breath. And steel myself for what's next.

"What do you mean, you quit?" His voice is too calm. His eyes narrow as they hone in on me trying to look as blank as I can sitting across from him in his peeling leather chair. He even puts his half-finished cigarette out in his ashtray. All sure signs that he's dangerously pissed off.

I take a subtle deep breath in through my nose. "I mean, I'm done. I'm out."

Sal leans back, tapping his fingers on the arm of the chair. "You got another offer."

"Fuck, no," I protest quickly. "I mean I'm done, done. Out of the game."

Sal snorts. "There's no getting out of the game. So you've either turned on me, and I should kill ya right now, or you've lost your nerve, in which case I can't trust what you know to stay with you," he says, sizing me up. "Either way you cut it, there's out, and there's staying alive."

I shake my head. "Really? You think I'd turn on you after all this time? I've only stayed this long out of loyalty. I want a life," I respond, some of my anger finally seeping through as I gesture around. "This ain't no life, Sal."

Sal taps his chin in thought. "You're a good kid, Julian, or you were. But if you leave it'll spook everyone. We're already losing this war," Sal points out.

You've already lost, old man, I can't help thinking to myself. Though he's not wrong. I'd be like a rat leaving a sinking ship. And I'm almost sure others have already or would more than willingly turn on him.

"That's not my problem anymore," I say as evenly as I can.

That gets a laugh from him. "Says you," he chortles. "But you forget who the boss is here."

"C'mon, you've got Paul and Dino," I point out. "And even they're more muscle than you can afford right now."

"Good point," he says easily. Too easily. "Maybe I'll go cut one of them loose right now."

Now I know he's desperate. It's an empty threat. He can't cut them loose. Their families are one of the last pillars of support of what little is left of Sal's once vast empire. And it fully hits me that this is the best thing. The necessary thing. Because even without Frankie waking me up to what life could be like outside of this world, Sal is a sinking ship. I leave and maybe I die now, or I keep working for this cocksucker and maybe I die a few months from now instead. My odds fucking suck either way.

"I don't think you'll do that," I insist. "And I don't think, after everything you've done for me, you'd keep me from living my own life."

"And a year ago you would have been right," Sal admits. "But times are different now. If I go down, you go down with me."

Well, that fucking seals the deal. I rise, knowing I'm rolling the dice either way.

"Good luck, then," I say flippantly as I walk away. When I get to the door, I look at him one last time. "For what it's worth, I hope you survive this." I might even bet money that he does. He's a fucking cockroach. My only hope is that he has enough fatherly affection for me to just let me go. But I'm not stupid, and I don't turn my fucking back as I close the door.

When I leave, I sure as fuck don't go home in case Sal plans to immediately make good on his threats. Instead, I drive out to Santa Monica, hitting up the pier. The one place Sal's never thought to look for me. The place where I can feel free, remembering the short time of my life between escaping the hell that was foster home after foster home and getting caught up in the even worse hell that Sal rained down on me when I was too young, cocky, and stupid to know any better.

I sit on a bench all afternoon, watching tourists lose money at the carnival games, kids run amok everywhere, and couples making out on the Ferris wheel. I'd already been thinking of that early date with Frankie here only a few short weeks ago and watching them go at it makes me close my eyes and think about being with her. Touching her. Tasting her. Fuck, that woman's gotten under my skin fast. A month with her and I've found the courage to do what I've wanted to for years. I say a prayer that I survive this, so I can see what a lifetime with her would do.

By the time I head home, I realize it needs to not be home anymore. And fast. I should've thought of it before, but what can I say, I've had a lot on my mind. Either way, I need to evade Sal long enough for him to let me go.

I case my apartment building, going in only when I don't see anything out of place. But as I enter my apartment, I know I wasn't careful enough, and that I sure as fuck should've handled this *before* I quit, because Sal sits on my couch, with a gun pointed at me. My own is holstered under my left arm. I'd have no hopes of drawing it in time. Fuck. I'm losing my edge, being so careless. I let the door swing against the frame behind me, leery of even looking like I'm turning to close it.

"Couldn't find Paul or Dino?" I ask nonchalantly.

Sal smiles wryly. "Nah, I know they're your boys," he admits. "I doubt they'd have the balls to do what needs to be done."

He's not wrong.

"Is that you asking me to change my mind?" I ask.

Sal tips his head back and forth as if considering it. "If I asked, would you?"

"No."

"Didn't think so," he replies. "You made your peace with God, kid?"

Sal has always mocked my beliefs on sin, faith, and God. And it's always gotten under my skin, despite myself. He knows that. The fucker is kicking me when I'm down. I shouldn't be surprised. I always knew he was a piece of shit.

"No, but thankfully God's made his peace with me," I reply.

Sal's brows pull together. "Whatever, kid," he replies.

"I have a request," I spit out, stalling. If I can distract him, I might be able to get the drop on him.

His aim doesn't waver as he laughs. "You got some brass ones," he says. "Go ahead."

"Leave Frankie alone," I reply bluntly. "Whatever you have in mind for her, however you're planning to use her in this little game of yours, don't. She's your fucking daughter, Sal."

If I thought that would appeal to his emotional, fatherly side, I'd obviously forgotten that he's about to kill the closest thing to a son he's ever had.

"Answer one question, and I might consider it," he counters. And I know he won't either way. But I need to buy more time and hope to the fucking Almighty that he screws up.

"Go for it."

"Can Frankie really tell when someone is lying?"

I stare at him blankly, unwilling to confirm it, but unable to deny it believably. Sal stares back. Until comprehension dawns on his face.

"You're *protecting* her," he says incredulously. "Holy fucking shit, Julian, you *love* her."

I remain impassive. Again, I don't trust myself to deny it, knowing I wouldn't be able to keep the emotion out of my voice. Not when it comes to Frankie.

Sal shakes his head. "And here I sent you after her because you're the most coldhearted motherfucker I've ever met. Did you get her to fall in love with you too?" he asks.

He's getting the better of me, and I'm beyond furious. I'm sure it shows on my face.

"This is fucking perfect. I can work this to get her to use her little ability for me." He looks me up and down. "Maybe you haven't outlived your usefulness after all. I take it you haven't told her you work for me. That you only met because of me."

A loud thud in the hallways startles us both. On instinct, I take the opportunity to slip out the partially open door. I don't waste time, bolting around the corner to pass the elevators and take the stairs. As I whip by, I see the doors closing. I catch a glimpse of dark hair, a tear-streaked face, and gorgeous red lips.

24

FRANKIE

As I approach Julian's building, I look up to see him heading inside from the opposite direction. I run to catch up, but when I get inside, he's already disappeared. I push the elevator call button, in a hurry to get the wallet I didn't realize was missing until I got to the club. I just hope it's actually in Julian's apartment.

He's obviously faster than me, because the hall is completely clear when I get upstairs. Rounding the corner, though, I can see his door is cracked from afar. Curious, I approach, but I freeze when I hear voices coming from inside.

"…God's made his peace with me." Julian's voice is clear, and I realize he must be standing just on the other side of the door.

"Whatever, kid." The other voice is muffled, as if the speaker is across the room, though I can still make out the words. And there's something familiar about the voice.

"I have a request," Julian says. He sounds panicked. I freeze in place. Julian is unflappable. If he's unnerved, nothing good is going on behind that door.

The other man laughs. "You got some brass ones," he says. "Go ahead."

"Leave Frankie alone," Julian replies. My heart slams in my chest at the mention of my name. "Whatever you have in mind for her, however you're planning to use her in this little game of yours, don't. She's your fucking daughter, Sal."

The name and the voice click. My throat tightens and tears spring to my eyes. What the ever-loving fuck is going on? My head pounds as I struggle to comprehend how these two parts of my world could possibly be colliding. The truth hits me like a goddamn sledgehammer. This is what Julian has been hiding.

I reach out to grab the door handle when Sal's next words freeze me in place once again.

"Answer one question about her, and I might consider it."

Beyond confused, I search for something Julian might know about me that Sal would care about. I realize what just as Julian speaks again.

"Go for it."

"Can Frankie really tell when someone is lying?"

It feels so much like someone just punched me in the stomach that I nearly vomit. Julian told him my secret.

Or did he? I place a hand silently on the door frame, trying to hold down my dinner. Julian doesn't say a word.

"You're *protecting* her. Holy fucking shit, Julian, you *love* her." There's a pause, but I'm still reeling too much to process any of this. Not that I have time to, as Sal keeps going. "And here I sent you after her because you're the most coldhearted motherfucker I've ever met. Did you get her to fall in love with you too?"

And there it is. Confirmation of the truth that causes all the blood to drain from my face. Now I know this *is* what Julian was hiding, and why he's in there having a conversation with Sal. With my biological father.

Suddenly sure I'm going to be sick, I put my hand over my mouth and breath quietly and deeply through my nose.

But the hell continues. "This is fucking perfect. I can work this to get her to use her little ability for me. Maybe you haven't outlived your useful-ness after all. I take it you haven't told her you work for me. That you only met because of me."

It starts to sink in. Sal sent Julian in ahead to check me out. Julian has been playing me this whole time. Getting me to fall in love with him so he could what, soften me up to do Sal's bidding? I stagger backward mind-lessly, not even realizing I'm moving until I smack into the wall behind me and the voices inside stop abruptly.

In a panic, I run. I skid around the corner, ready to fly down the stairs when the elevator doors ping open ahead of me. I crash inside, mashing the button to close the doors. As they begin to slide together, the tears fall. And just as they close, I catch a pair of dark eyes look my way as they flash past.

I DON'T KNOW HOW I MAKE IT THROUGH THE NIGHT. I'M A ZOMBIE, mechanically pushing through my tasks for the evening. When it's all over, when the club is finally closed, I slump into my office chair, pulling a bottle of whiskey out of my bottom drawer.

But before I can open it, Nils walks through the open door without a word. I look up at him blankly, unable to form a sentence. He stays silent, rounding the desk and dropping to his knees, turning my chair so I'm facing him.

His hand reaches up to cup my face. "Do you want to talk about it?" he asks. There's a vulnerability in his eyes I've never seen before. It would scare me if I weren't so numb. If I didn't still feel like vomiting.

I shake my head wordlessly. His eyes roam over my face one more time before he stands, opening the bottle of whiskey and handing it to me. I take a giant slug, then hand it back. The burn reassures me that I'll be relieved of my ability to think about any of this very soon. Nils takes a more measured drink.

Somehow, a good number of drinks later, we end up on the leather sofa in the VIP lounge. He sits with me, matching me drink for drink, if not drinking as deeply as I do, until the words finally begin to pour out. When I've finished my story — well, as much of it as I can share without telling him anything I don't want him to know — he sets the whiskey down on the table in front of us, then turns to me.

"He's a fucking idiot," he seethes drunkenly. "If you were mine, there's nothing I would keep from you, nothing I wouldn't do for you."

I stare back at him, not comprehending those words from Nils's mouth. Somehow, he takes my confused silence as an invitation, and next thing I know his lips are on mine.

With my defenses down, I don't stop him. His mouth is warm, and skilled. So skilled. His tongue joins to mine, gently stroking me in sensual invitation. Part of me wants to let go, to fuck Nils on this couch, to use his body to erase Julian's hold on me. But a bigger part of me knows that would be a mistake on so many levels.

I disengage gently. "Neither of us is thinking clearly," I slur, offering him the out.

"No, Francesca," Nils breathes, his long, gentle fingers stroking my face. "I think I finally am. I've been in love with you all this time, but I didn't want to ruin things here. When the brooder came along, I realized I'd been playing it too safe. I don't want to do that anymore." His ice blue eyes search mine.

But there's nothing in me for him to find. Everything in me belongs to Julian. The realization triggers all the emotion I've been suppressing, and I start sobbing uncontrollably.

Nils sits patiently with me, stroking my back until it's over. I stand up to grab a fistful of tissue from my office. When I emerge, Nils is leaned against the bar looking considerably more sober.

"I've called a cab for you," he says softly as I approach him.

I sniffle, then hiccup loudly. His eyes go wide for a moment before we both burst into laughter.

"Thanks," I finally manage between giggles. I rest my hand on his arm. "Some night, huh?"

"Indeed," he murmurs, looking at me sorrowfully.

"Nils —" I start, but he holds up a hand.

"Let's just move on, shall we?" he suggests.

I press my lips together and nod. The service bell rings.

"That'll be your cab," he says, sliding his hand into mine and walking me out. Sure enough, it is, and he sees me into the back. "Forgive me if this is out of line," he pauses to smile ironically, "but you may want to stay with a friend for a day or two."

I hadn't even thought of it, but he's right. I could use the support, and it's better if Julian doesn't know where to find me. Or Sal, for that matter. I nod my thanks, and with another small, sad smile, Nils goes back into the club. I push everything that just happened between us down in my mind, in the same dark hole I've shoved everything else, completely unable to deal right now.

I give the driver Emma's address, texting ahead to make sure she's there.

OK if I come crash at yours for a couple days?

And even though it's an ungodly hour close to dawn, it takes only a minute for her to respond.

Yah, of course. U ok?

I blink back the tears that form at her question.

Eh.

Not sure what else to say, I pause, wondering how to prepare her for the hot mess that I am. But she beats me to it.

Get ur sweet ass over here, I bet ur tired. We'll talk later.

With a grateful sigh, I reply simply with *thx* and lean back into the headrest for the rest of the ride.

It goes by in a blink, though I may have dozed off for a few minutes on the freeway. When I get to her door, Emma pulls me inside and gives me a huge hug.

"Sorry if I woke you," I manage. As the booze wears off, I'm finding it harder to control my emotions. And as soon as the words are out of my mouth, I realize talking isn't the best idea. I just want to be unconscious, so I don't have to deal with the flood of emotion I no longer have the energy to hold back.

She shakes her head. "I was up. Not sleeping too well these days," she admits.

With a sigh, I look her over. She looks tired and sad. I realize she's probably missing Ben, even though we've talked and agreed over and over that it's for the best. Just like leaving Julian behind is for the best. Doesn't mean it doesn't suck.

I nod, pulling her in for another hug.

"C'mon," she says, pulling me into her bedroom. She points at the bed. "You. Sleep. Now. I'll be here when you wake up, okay?"

I look down at myself, realizing I'm sticky and smelly with dried sweat and all kinds of other crap that comes from a night of work. "I'm a mess. I'll shower first," I insist.

She looks me over. "Yeah, probably for the best," she agrees. She catches my eye and we both chuckle.

A quick, hot shower leaves me feeling considerably less of a mess, and I let the small amount of relaxation it gives me take over, so sleep finds me before anything else can.

I WAKE TO AFTERNOON SUNLIGHT AND THE SMELL OF COFFEE. TRUDGING out into the main room, I find Emma in the living room watching courtroom drama TV and eating donuts.

"This looks like my kind of party," I say drily.

She looks up and smiles half-heartedly. "Thought you'd be up soon, so I made you a fresh pot of the darkest roast I have," she offers.

"You're a saint, Emma," I breathe, following my nose into the kitchen.

I find the largest mug in the cabinet and fill it to the brim. No cream or sugar for this girl. Give it to me black. Like my heart right about now.

Ignoring the heat, I gulp it down and shuffle back to the living room, snagging a chocolate frosted cake donut.

We eat in companionable silence while the show's participants battle it out, screaming at each other over the judge.

"I love this shit," I say to Emma. "Makes my drama seem less drama-y."

Emma gives me a skeptical side glance. "Really? Because seems like there might be some seriously drama-y stuff going on about now."

With a sigh, I put my nearly empty mug down on the coffee table. "Touché."

"Ready to talk?"

"No." I shift uncomfortably in my seat.

"Maybe you should anyway," Emma urges. I look up at her. It's hard to argue with the voice of experience. So I tell her everything.

When I'm done, she looks into the empty donut box. "We're going to need another few dozen of these before we can even start dealing with that shit."

I shake my head and laugh. I stop myself before it turns into crying. "Yeah, that's about where I'm at."

"I'm sorry, babes," she says softly.

I look down into my hands. "I have no idea what to do next."

Emma rises from the armchair she's been occupying to plop down next to me on the couch.

"Oh, I do."

I give her a curious look.

She smiles tolerantly and tugs at the end of my hair. "Time for a change," she says with a glint in her eye.

"You know what? You're abso-fucking-lutely right," I agree.

Emma gets back up. "Then let's get this shit show on the road before you have to be back at the club."

Emma is a genius. Not just about the hair color, as that's really just her knowing how temperamental I am and that changing my hair is often part of my coping with changes in my life. But it also gives me something to do until I have to work. I've never been one to endlessly rehash what went wrong in my relationships, and Emma is respectful of that. I always feel like it makes me wallow longer. Actually doing something, distracting myself so I can just move on, works best for me.

When I show up at the club that night, it's with a new red ombré dye job that flows down from the close-to-natural chocolate color on top to a flaming, bright color at the ends that, in the shifting light, really does resemble flames. It completes my dangerously pissed-off look that matches my mood exactly.

However, I work hard to be as sweet as pie to my team because of it. It's not their fault half of my genetic makeup is from the biggest dirtbag I've ever met. Or that I fell for Dirtbag Junior.

The thought makes me physically ill. I can only assume everything he did from the moment we met was for his boss, to get me to fall for him for whatever advantage they think that gives them.

But then, he fell for me too. I doubt that was part of his plan. Surely being with me is getting in the way of being the coldhearted motherfucker Sal expects him to be, of him doing his job.

I decide it doesn't really matter. Fuck them both.

I physically force myself into the ebb and flow of managing the club to distract myself. Nils somehow manages to completely avoid me, communicating through Ace and Johnny when needed. I try not to pick at that hornet's nest, hoping it'll just fade back into the background. It's not like I hadn't suspected. But even without Julian around, I never would've let anything happen. Hopefully, now that he's professed his love he can realize and accept that it's not going to happen, and it's better for everyone if he just moves on. For now, I'm happy to give him distance, and tonight it doesn't seem to be interfering with anything.

When the band for the night is in full swing and the bar has died down a bit, I find myself with nothing to do but scan the crowd. It's not enough to distract me, and the anger starts to seep through my veins. Aggravated as hell, I go to my office and grab the pack of smokes I keep in my bottom drawer, slipping out of the side entrance. I sink down into my usual spot, lighting up as I look up at the sky, imagining the stars I can't see.

"I knew you'd come out here eventually." The voice cuts through my reverie. I tip my head against the building, holding back tears. Why did I not realize he'd be out here, waiting for me?

With one last, deep drag on the cigarette, I stomp it out under my boot and climb to my feet. I don't even look his way. I simply turn around to go back inside.

"Don't go," Julian pleads, his voice just behind me now. But he doesn't make any move to stop me. He doesn't have to. I'm completely frozen in place. My heart burns with anger, but the part of me that's still his responds to him, still wants to believe there's hope. It's the thing I love and hate most about love: Hope dies last.

"I've got nothing to say to you," I reply, turning to face him. It's as big of a mistake as I knew it'd be. He's right there, towering over me with his tight black T-shirt and jeans, his intensely dark eyes filled with sorrow and longing, smelling like cigarettes, alcohol, and *him*. It makes me clench, but not in the good way. My heart squeezes hard in my chest as the broken pieces work to tear me apart from the inside out.

"Yeah, well, not to sound like a fucking cliché, but I've got a lot to say to you," he pushes, his voice husky and tired.

I laugh, tilting my head up to the heavens. "That's just great," I say to no one in particular. I look back at him evenly. "Fine, talk." I remind myself that I don't give a shit about his explanation. I can tell he sees it in my eyes, but he presses on anyway.

"Yes, we only met because Sal sent me to you, to get information," he offers. "And I still don't know exactly what he wants with you," he pauses, letting me listen for the voice, or in this case, lack thereof, "but I've wanted out for a long time." He stares at me longingly. "Falling in love with you gave me the courage to do what I should've done a long time ago. Because I may have been a stupid kid who fell for his shit all those years ago, but I haven't been that kid for a long time." He looks down at his clenched fists. "So I quit. But I can't stick around, Frankie, or he'll find me. And in case it wasn't obvious, he's not exactly a kiss-and-make-up kinda guy. He's more of a bury-his-problems kinda guy." He lets that sink in before adding, "Literally."

Clearly, Sal is into even worse shit than I thought. But it still doesn't add up. "Why would he want you dead? As long as you're willing to stick around and keep softening me up for him, shouldn't he be happy?" My words are pure venom.

Julian shakes his head, stepping dangerously close despite my obvious anger. "I was never supposed to soften you up," he murmurs, looking down into my eyes. "You softened me up, baby, don't you see? I'm no good to him anymore. I don't want to be any good to him anymore. I just want my own life back. And I want you in it, even though I know I don't deserve you."

Believing him isn't a choice. I have no doubt he means it. He's spoken to me more plainly than he ever has to demonstrate his veracity. But truth and trust are two different things. And how can I possibly trust him when he kept something this big from me?

"No," I agree. "You don't. Goodbye, Julian."

And before the tears can fall, I close my eyes, purposely not subjecting myself to the look on his face as I turn around and go back inside.

Once I'm alone in the hallway, I don't crumble. If anything, seeing him, hearing what he had to say, has given me the closure I needed. I square my shoulders and stand tall as I walk back into the club, putting the whole thing behind me, literally and metaphorically.

⟳

"Yeah, but is it really behind you?" Emma points out the next day as we repeat our coffee and donuts ritual.

"Yes," I reiterate.

"Really?" she presses. "You're just gonna let Sal off Julian for sticking up for you?"

I look over at her skeptically. "If he does, it'll be because Julian refuses to work for him anymore, not because of me."

She shoots me back a cynical look. "Po-tay-to, po-tah-to," she replies. "To-may-to,   guy-who-loves-you-standing-up-to-a-killer-so-he-can-be-with-you."

I shoot her a dirty look. "What, you think I should go order around a guy who apparently kills people he doesn't like anymore?"

Emma waves her hand dismissively. "He's not gonna hurt you — you're his daughter. Plus, regardless, it sounds like he needs you, for what-ever reason. I mean, he's gone to a hell of a lot of trouble to learn about you, to get in with you."

I think about that. "You're right. I have the leverage to save Julian's ass," I realize.

"Exactly," she says firmly. "So what are you waiting for?" I shoot her a sharp look. "Okay, bad assumption that you actually want to help him. You obviously don't. Forget I said anything."

With a sigh, I shake my head. "You're not wrong. He did ask Sal to leave me alone. And I do want to tell Sal that I know what he's up to, and that he's not going to manipulate me into working for him. While I'm at it, I might as well ask him to leave Julian alone. You know, out of respect for whatever feelings we had for each other."

Emma rolls her eyes. "Oh, please, Frankie."

"Oh, please, what?" I snap.

"I want you to say these words out loud," she directs. I glare a warning at her but let her go on. "'I no longer have feelings for Julian.'" I open my mouth to protest. "Say it!"

I scrunch my face at her. "I no longer have feelings for Julian." *Lie.* "You're a bitch, Emma."

She cackles evilly. "I know. It's why you love me." She gets up and grabs my coffee mug, bringing it with her to the kitchen to refill. When she comes back and hands me the cup, she picks my phone up off the table in front of me and hands it to me as well. "You love him. You may not be willing to take him back, but you're gonna hate yourself if you don't do something."

Ugh. Well, lord knows I can't say she's wrong. After all, I know I'd be lying.

I MEET SAL THE NEXT AFTERNOON AT THE ITALIAN RESTAURANT. I PICKED it because it was in public, but if I'm being honest with myself, the thought of eating that gnocchi again is pretty appealing too. And definitely mitigates the steaming pile of shit I'm about to step into.

Like before, he's waiting for me at a table in the back. I dressed for the occasion, in fitted jeans and a black blazer over my red shirt to conceal the gun at my back. Just in case. After practicing with Mac all morning, I'm ready for anything. Thankfully, Mac didn't ask about my sudden, intense need to practice, and I sure as hell didn't offer anything up. In any case, as I approach Sal, I feel confident.

He stands to greet me, opening his arms for a hug. I stop and give him my best "you've got to be fucking kidding me" look. It's my opening salvo that all's not well.

"Or not," he says as I take a seat at the table. He slides back into his chair. "Everything all right? You seem a little out of sorts, doll."

His response answers the only question I had; whether he was aware I heard everything that day. Clearly, he's not. I don't waste time enlightening him.

"Well, when I found out my boyfriend's just some hired muscle sent by my dad in an elaborate ploy to get me to do God only knows what, I get a little tetchy," I snipe.

Whatever he was expecting to hear, it clearly wasn't that. He only raises his eyebrows for a moment, quickly working to wipe the surprise from his face.

"I knew that kid was a rat," he laughs, shaking his head.

"He's not," I counter. "Not that he's in my good graces, either. But for what it's worth, I overheard you at his apartment on Thursday."

"Ah," Sal responds curtly. "That."

"Yes," I reply hotly. "That."

Sal spreads his hands over the checkered tablecloth. "So you came here today to do what, exactly?" He looks at me, and it's the first time I notice that his eyes are the same shade of blue as mine. It makes me sad.

"If any harm comes to Julian, you'll never see me again, much less get me to work for you," I promise carefully. Not mentioning I have zero intention of ever doing either.

"That a fact?" Sal asks nonchalantly, leaning back. He pulls his hands back into his lap and looks up at me again. "What if I told you if you don't come work for me, he'll be the first to pay, but definitely not the last?"

I've been threatened before. I'm not easily intimidated, and I expected something of the sort from him. But the absolute casualness of his manner, how easily the words roll off his tongue disturbs me on a level that makes my blood run cold.

"You really think threatening me is going to help? Do I seem like the kind of person who bows to threats?" I reply.

"Don't make them if you can't take them," he replies with a smile, crossing his legs. "And sure as hell don't make threats you aren't capable of following through on."

I stare back at him impassively. "I don't think you'll risk it. You need me." I probably shouldn't be so sure of myself, but for some reason I am. Habit maybe? Whatever the reason, I somehow sense I'm running out of luck at getting away with being so cocky. Not that I've ever been very good at learning my lesson.

"What gives you that impression?" he asks, arching an eyebrow.

"Really? That's how you're gonna play this?" I ask with a laugh. "You've gone to lengths to dig up dirt on me. But I bet even you didn't realize how much you'd hit the jackpot until you found out about my ability. And the fact that you're willing to threaten to harm people I care about to get me to do what you want …" I let my words hang in the air.

Sal leans forward, dropping his voice. "You're a smart cookie, but there's something I know that you don't." I look at him quizzically and he gives me a leering grin. "There's nobody I care about more than me. You, on the other hand, well, there's lots of people you care about. People you don't want to see hurt. Your boyfriend. Your mother. Your grandmother." He pauses. "Your brother. He's a sweet kid, that Tony. You wouldn't want anything to happen to him, would you?"

"You bastard." The words slip out of my mouth before I can stop them. My heart pounds in my ears, and I'm practically seeing red. How *dare* he threaten my family.

Sal chuckles. "Technically, you're the bastard here," he points out. "But yes, I know I'm an asshole. Don't take it personally. I'm just doing what I've gotta do to survive, doll."

My eyes flick around the restaurant. We've been quiet enough to escape notice, but the place is packed. The urge to punch the fucker in his smug mug fades as the sea of faces around me come into focus. No need to make a scene.

I rise, trying to quell the shaking in my limbs to no avail. "Stay away from me. Stay away from my family."

"Not gonna happen, doll. You'll see. One way or the other, you'll see." He almost looks regretful. I shake my head and walk away. No. I don't know what the expression on his face was, but it wasn't that. He's a monster. And monsters don't feel regret.

⌒⌒

I SIT IN MY CAR, SHAKING WITH ANGER FOR A SOLID HOUR BEFORE I DECIDE that there's only one person I can talk to. One person who was there at the beginning, who will listen without judgment, and who might be able to tell me what to do.

I drive carefully to my mother's house, still unsure if I should be driving in my state. I can't shake the anger, but it's abating enough so I can feel what's under it: fear. When I park in the blessedly empty driveway, I realize I need to call Nils. It's already past the time I'd normally be at the club on a Saturday, and I'm not sure when, or if, I'll make it. He's more curt than usual, but thankfully he's still his generally composed self, assuring me that he'll take care of everything.

I take a deep breath, put my gun in the glove compartment, lock it, and get out of the car, thankful at least that my mother isn't here. It takes Nonna a minute to answer the door after I knock.

"Frankie," she greets me, clearly surprised. She steps back, gesturing for me to come in. "Everything okay, dear? Shouldn't you be at the club right now?"

I put my keys on the table by the door, taking the few steps into the living room. I stare at the couch, too nervous to sit down. Nonna comes up alongside me, laying her hand on my arm. I turn to face her, trying like hell to stay calm.

"No, Nonna, everything is not okay," I reply, struggling to keep control. "Mom was right about Sal."

Nonna's weathered face hardens. "What did he do, Francesca?"

I bury my face in my shaking hands. Nonna only calls me by my first name when things are serious. And it's exactly why I came to her. Because

I knew she'd take me seriously. But hearing her call me that drives home exactly how bad this situation really is.

"I don't know how to tell you this, Nonna, but Sal is beyond bad news," I hedge, realizing this may be harder to explain than I thought.

Nonna shakes her head. "There isn't anything you can tell me about Salvatore Moretti that I don't already know, dear. So out with it," she directs sternly.

"He's been trying to get me to work for him. He was threatening someone I care about. And tonight, I went to meet him, to get him to back off. And he threatened all of you," I say. "Mom. You. Even Tony. I don't know what to do, Nonna."

Nonna looks back at me in horror.

"What exactly did he say?" The controlled anger in my mother's quiet voice rips across the living room. I look up in surprise.

"But your car —"

"Is in the shop. What did the bastard say, Francesca?" my mother demands again, her eyes full of quiet fury.

I know it's pointless to keep the truth from her. Not that she's ever given me the same consideration. But I tell her anyway.

"That he has nothing to lose, but I do. And I'll lose all of you if I don't do what he wants from me," I admit.

My mother is terrifying under normal circumstances, but her small frame seems to swell with the rage that emanates from her. "And what, pray tell, does he want from *you*?"

I'm too shaken to be overly disturbed by the implication. "I don't know," I admit. Then, with a cringe, I tell her the worst of it. "But he knows about my ability."

"You *told* him?" she rages at me. All the years she lectured me to keep my gift hidden, all the times she tanned my hide when I let even the idea of it peep through around anyone who wasn't family comes rushing back to me.

It snaps me out of my fear. "Of course not," I return hotly. "I don't know how he knew."

"I know," a small voice says from behind my mother.

Mom whirls around to reveal Tony cowering in the hallway. "I saw him outside with the big man. He said he was your dad. That his dad knew things too. I thought that's where you got it."

My mother's jaw practically hits the floor. "He saw you? He *talked to you?* When?" she demands. Tony shrinks against the wall under her fury. In my concern for him, I still register that Julian was here with Sal, doing God knows what. So Sal clearly knows where they live and what Tony looks like. This is so much worse than I'd even imagined.

"On Monday, I came back for a book I forgot, and he was leaving," Tony squeaks. "I'm sorry, Ma, I didn't want you to get mad that I left school, so I didn't tell you."

Nonna looks between me and my mother. "Let's all try to calm down. That man has always had a big mouth and little to back it up," she says as soothingly as she can. But one look from my mother shuts her down.

My mother looks at me, and I can see the calculating malice behind her eyes. "Stay here," she directs to no one in particular. With that she heads to the door, snatching my car keys from the table.

"Hey!" I protest, bolting through the door after her. But she's too fast. In a flash, she's started my car and is pulling out of the driveway. I chase her halfway down the street before she's out of sight. Winded and out of my mind, I drop to the ground. Once again, I can think of only one person to turn to at this moment.

25

JULIAN

I sit in the dark, the soft clicking noises of the engine cooling breaking the quiet of evening suburbia. My eyes flick back and forth between the road and Frankie's mom's house as I consider the events of the day and how fucking messed up Frankie was after leaving that restaurant.

It's a place I've been a thousand times, so I know exactly who she was talking to. And what the motherfucker must've said to her to make her look as upset as she was. There's nothing Sal wouldn't do to have power over his enemies. And if you're not his friend, you're his enemy. He's got a lot of them these days.

I know I shouldn't be here. Still in L.A. I should've hit the fucking road after Frankie made it clear she wanted nothing to do with me. But the primal energy that has existed between us since day one, the underlying thread that binds us together, that led to us falling for each other, won't let me walk away from her. Even if I know some serious shit is about to hit the fan. Or, perhaps, especially because of it.

So I'm not surprised when shortly after Frankie goes into the house, her mother comes tearing out, hops in the convertible, and peels off with

Frankie herself hot on her heels. And when the convertible outruns her and Frankie drops to her knees in the middle of the street, I'm out of my car before I know what I'm doing.

As I get closer, I can hear her panicked breathing as she scrambles to type something on her phone. But she's shaking so fucking badly it drops out of her hands onto the asphalt.

I reach down and snatch it up, offering it to her. As she takes it from my hand, her eyes flick up to meet mine. Deep, sad pools of stormy blue stare at me, confused.

"How …?"

I shrug, offering her my other hand to help her up. "I knew this wasn't over," I say softly.

She brushes off my hand, hauling herself to her feet.

"No, I meant, how did you show up just as I was trying to text you?" she clarifies.

I raise an eyebrow. "Same answer," I reply.

She looks at me, clearly mystified before shaking her head. "Whatever. You have your car, right?"

I hook a thumb back over my shoulder, pointing out the sedan parked under the dark cover of a tree just down the road. The door is probably even still open.

"Good," she says grimly. "Because we're going after her."

She marches off toward the car and I haul ass to keep up with her.

"Where's your mom going in such a hurry?" I ask as I get ahead of her in time to open the passenger door.

"I have my suspicions, but I don't know how she plans to find him," she says sadly as she gets in.

Once I've gotten in on the driver's side, I grip the steering wheel as I absorb what's happening. "Your mother is going after Sal."

It's not a question.

"Pretty sure."

"He threatened you."

Still not a question.

"Yes. And everyone I love," she says softly, her eyes flicking to meet mine. And I know she's including me in that. Reminding me once again that I'm the biggest fucking asshole on the planet for hurting her.

"Heaven help him when she finds him," I mutter, starting the car. "I know his usual haunts, I'll start —"

"This will tell me where she is," she interrupts, holding up her phone.

"How's that?"

She opens it, selecting an app and punching in a code. "I set it up so I could track the car if it was stolen."

A smile tugs at my lips. This chick.

"You sure you want to do this?"

She looks at me apprehensively. "No. But it's my fault. I've got to stop her from getting hurt. He's dangerous."

I take a deep breath, not sure that putting ourselves between those two is a good idea. But it's past time this all ended, and it might turn into the exact opportunity I need. "Tell me where to go."

She gives me directions, not speaking otherwise. The tension is unbearable.

Finally, we pull up to a building I know all too fucking well. Frankie's car is parked just up the street.

"What is this place?" Frankie asks at the look of recognition on my face.

"Sal's apartment," I reply shortly, parking in a spot across the street.

I pull my 9mm out of the holster under my left arm and check the clip.

"You got another one of those?" she asks. "Mine was in the car, and I can't get it without the key."

I raise an eyebrow at her but say nothing. I reach down under my pantleg and grab the .38 Special that's concealed there. When I hand it to her, she frowns.

"Sure, give me the girl gun," she mumbles, checking the cylinder.

"If you don't want it, give it the fuck back," I tease.

She rolls her eyes and gets out of the car, shoving the gun in the back waistband of her jeans.

"That's a good way to shoot yourself in the ass," I murmur, following her out. But she's already jogging across the street. "Fuck, wait up."

She stops on the sidewalk, letting me catch up. "Look, I only needed you to bring me here and tell me what I should expect going in there. Beyond that, you should just wait out here. I only went to Sal in the first place to save your ass. If he shoots you now it was a complete waste."

I look her up and down. She's tough, but she's no match for what's probably going on up there.

"I know Sal. It was a complete fucking waste anyway."

She scrunches her face angrily, and I know she knows I'm right.

"Just tell me where to go," she demands.

I roll my eyes and hold the front door open for her.

"Fourth floor. Second door on the right. He's just as dangerous as you think he is, so I'm going in first," I insist as she waltzes past me.

She stands in the rundown lobby looking around. "We'll see. No elevator?"

I smirk as I stride by her toward the stairs. "No such luck, princess," I reply, taking the stairs two at a time as she struggles to keep up.

When we get to the fourth floor, I give her a minute to catch her breath. Putting my finger to my lips, I start down the hall, but she grabs my hand. I turn back and she's looking up at me. Her expression is raw and vulnerable. "Thank you," she whispers. "For being here with me."

It fucking guts me, and I can't help myself. I push her into the wall, lifting her up by her soft, beautiful ass as I bend down to kiss her. I don't have time for gentle, or long. It's rough and short, and she tastes like fucking heaven, as usual. I let her go before she has time to protest, taking her by the hand and leading her down the hall. But before we can get two steps, a muffled bang reverberates from behind the door just ahead.

"Mom!" Frankie shrieks, diving for the door. It springs open at her touch, and even though I clamber to catch her before she runs in there, she somehow slips through my fingers. Pulling out my gun, I barrel after her in time to tumble into Sal's empty living room.

She goes to scream again, and I wrap a hand around her mouth from behind. I bring the tip of the gun to my lips to tell her to keep fucking quiet. When she nods, I let her go and point with my free hand at the half-closed bedroom door.

It's been only seconds since the bang, but it feels like hours as we slowly approach and my heart hammers in my ears. Holding the gun up, I use my foot to swing the bedroom door open quietly as Frankie clings to my back.

The sight that greets me isn't pretty. Frankie's mom is looking down at her phone as she stands at the foot of the bed. The bed Sal is lying on, dead from what appears to be a gunshot wound straight through his mother-fucking heart. I can feel Frankie peeping around me. When she sees that her mother is okay, she rushes out from behind me.

"Mom," she cries again, heading toward her mother.

Samantha looks up in surprise, starting to reach for the gun lying on the bed in front of her when she realizes who it is. Frankie crashes into her, wrapping her arms around her, and I lower my gun.

"You're okay," she sobs.

Samantha pushes Frankie off of her. "I'm fine," she says shortly. But when her gaze slips over Frankie's shoulder and locks with mine, she dives for the gun. Instinctively, I raise mine.

In seconds flat, she's shoved Frankie aside and has her sights set on me. Frankie looks at her in horror.

"Drop your gun," Samantha demands.

"You first," I respond.

"Both of you, stop it, now," Frankie commands.

"Be quiet, you stupid girl," her mother seethes. "This brute works for the bastard that just tried to kill me."

"*Worked* for," I stress. "And looks to me like you came here looking for a fight. And won."

"Julian!" Frankie gasps.

Samantha sighs. "I'm not going to even ask how you know this thug, Francesca. But for once in your life, do as I say and stay out of this."

"Mom, come on, put your gun down. Julian is not going to shoot you," Frankie presses.

"That's right, Samantha," I agree. "Unless you try to shoot me first. Like you did with our old pal, Sal, there."

"It was self-defense," she hisses through her teeth.

"Tell that to the pillow with the bullet hole through it," I point out.

In my peripheral vision I see Frankie's mouth drop open in horror as she finally looks around at the evidence. Clearly there was a fight here. Things are knocked over, and the bed is a mess. But the bloodied lamp lying on the floor matches a lump on Sal's balding, greasy head. And the pillow was clearly used to muffle the sound of the shot that killed the poor, likely unconscious bastard.

"Aren't you happy he's dead? If you tried to quit, surely he was about to kill you anyway?" Samantha replies drily.

I shake my head ever so slightly, so as not to take my eyes off of her. "I'd be happy, except you plan to kill me anyway," I respond.

"No," Frankie pipes up, finally finding her voice again. "Nobody else has to die tonight. Mom, please."

"Shut up!" Samantha screams at her daughter, finally losing her cool. "You know *nothing*, Francesca. Nothing about what I've had to do to keep you and your brother safe. He has to die. He knows too much. You can't trust him. Our family isn't safe while he's still alive." Samantha's knuckles are turning white, and I want to caution Frankie to back off of her, to not push her too far in her current state. She's only beginning to see what her mother is capable of.

But Frankie always surprises me. She steps between us, backing up with her hand extended to me, silently begging me to stand down. I lower my gun. There's no fucking way I could ever keep it up with Frankie in my line of sight.

"You want to talk about family? About feeling safe?" Frankie asks. Though I know she's crying, she amazingly sounds perfectly calm. Her mother's aim falters ever so slightly, trying to find a way around her daughter. "I've never felt more loved, more accepted for who I am than he's made me feel. He's acted more like family to me than you ever have."

My heart twists in my chest. Because I feel the exact same way. I reach out for the hand Frankie is still offering and squeeze it tightly. Her return squeeze gives me the first ray of hope I've felt since we walked into this mess.

Samantha looks utterly fucking horrified. "You're making a huge mistake," she spits at her daughter. "And I'm going to fix it for you." She steps to the side to retrain her gun on me, but Frankie anticipates it.

She drops my hand, grabs the gun at her back, and steps in time with her mother all in one movement. And when she's done, I'm not the one pointing a gun at Samantha Greco anymore — Frankie is.

"Don't do this, Mom," Frankie begs.

Samantha lowers her gun, but it doesn't make me any fucking less alert. "Frankie," she says softly, almost lovingly.

Frankie starts to lower the .38. But it's all a trap. Sensing her weakness, Samantha quickly raises her arm, retraining her aim at me in an instant. Before I can even register what's happening, I hear the shot. I close my eyes, so I don't have to see the look on Frankie's gorgeous face when I die.

But the hot sting of a bullet entering me never comes. A low moan comes from across the room and my eyes fly open. Bright red blood blossoms over Samantha's crisp white shirt right over her heart. As the life leaves her, her face freezes in an expression of betrayal and anger. Her body slumps to the floor and the gun in Frankie's hands slips. I grab it from her before she can drop it, turning her to cradle her against my chest.

"Don't look, baby," I mutter into her hair. "Just don't look."

Frankie melts into me, her hands balling into fists over my shirt. She looks up at me, terrified.

"What have I done?" she asks as a sob rips out of her.

And even now, with almost all of the secrets I'd been keeping from her laid out on the table, I still don't have the heart to tell her the worst one of all. The one that wasn't my secret in the first place. That her mother stopped one crime boss tonight. But Frankie stopped the other.

26

FRANKIE

I hear sirens. They're coming for me. Good. I'm a monster, I should be put away. I murdered my mother. Strong hands hold me up, but everything else blinks in and out as I struggle to wrap my head around what just happened. She was going to kill Julian. I had to. I had to. I had to.

"Shhhh. Yes, you had to," Julian whispers.

I blink up at him. Was I saying it out loud?

Crashing. More loud noises. Police officers. Julian in handcuffs. Someone ushering me out of the room, telling me not to look at all the blood. Not to look at the bodies. *The bodies. Oh, God.* I fall to my knees and vomit. Cool hands hold back my hair, stroke my back.

I wipe my mouth and look up in time to see Julian being dragged away by two burly cops.

"No," I cry, reaching for him. I need him. Who else is strong enough to hold me together? I'm falling apart. Bring him back. But I can't make any more words come over the wretched sobs.

The female officer beside me motions for the men to stop. Julian drags himself across the room to me. Drops to his knees for me.

His warm lips press against my forehead. Yes. He's my glue. Please don't take him away.

"I promise everything will be okay," he whispers. "The worst part is over."

I look up at him, shaking my head, still unable to speak. *No. The worst has only just begun.* The fresh hell I'll live in forever. I killed my mother. What have I done?

Murmurs in the room. "Samantha Greco … her daughter …" Fear. Of me? I don't think so. I don't understand.

Blink, blink. I'm in the back of a police car. No handcuffs, just cold leather on my cheek.

Blink, blink. I'm in a room. All by myself. Yes, stay away from the murderer.

Blink, blink. Weathered hands hold mine. "Frankie," Nonna whispers lovingly. I shake violently. *No. I killed her. I killed your daughter. Don't love me.*

Blink, blink. I'm holding my knees against my chest. No more tears. Just pain. I hear Nonna ask me something. Just leave me alone. Lock me up. Go away. I put my hands over my ears.

Blink, blink. Warm, rough hands. Familiar. *Him.* "Frankie," he whispers. My fractured mind won't let me answer. "Take these." Cold, smooth. He puts the pills on my lips. "Please, for me." I open my mouth. *Only for you.*

A voice pulls me from unconsciousness. My mouth is dry, so I dart my tongue around, trying to moisten it. My eyelids are heavy, but I push against the weight. It's so bright.

A hand slides over mine, giving me a reassuring squeeze. "Slowly," someone whispers.

I blink until my eyes adjust, my tongue flicking again, this time to wet my lips. "Where am I?" My voice sounds like I ate sandpaper.

"You're still at the police station, dear," the voice says louder. I realize it's Nonna. And it all comes flooding back.

I snap upright. "Oh, God," I croak. "Mom."

Nonna snaps her fingers in front of me. "Look at me," she commands. I've never heard her so stern. It grabs my attention away from the panic that's starting to overwhelm me. "There's a lot you need to know, but not just yet. Suffice it to say that you've done *nothing* wrong, my dear. Do you understand me?" She looks down at me sharply.

Tears well in my eyes. How can I possibly believe that?

"I'm serious, young lady," she says in a slightly softer tone. "Don't shut down on us again. You're strong. You will get through this."

The truth of her words sinks in, and not just because of the absence of the voice. But because I know that. I am strong. I close my eyes and take a deep breath. When I open my eyes, I turn to her and nod to show her I understand.

"Where's Julian?" I rasp.

Nonna hands me a glass of water that I gulp gratefully. "He's skulking around here somewhere," she replies.

I want to laugh, but it hurts my throat. "How long have I been out?"

"Just the night," she says dismissively. "It's Sunday morning." She glances at her watch. "Quarter of seven."

"Then why do I feel like I haven't had a drink of water for a week?" I ask.

"They gave you something to calm you down. I'd wager it dried you out, too," she replies, offering the glass again. "Drink."

After I've done as she asked, I realize Julian must be free. "They let him go," I gasp.

"They did," she agrees. "Once they got his story, they had nothing to hold him on. He had no gunpowder residue on his hands. You, however ..."

I bury my face in my hands, but she tugs at my arms. "They'll want to speak with you, dear, but there's a good deal you don't know. They want me to wait to tell you until you've given your statement."

"Oh, so suddenly it's fill-in-Frankie time? Why now?" I snap.

Nonna gives me a disapproving look. "Well, I'm glad you seem to be doing better, at least." She sighs. "There were promises I made to your grandfather, and your mother after him, that I'm no longer bound by. But I'm an old fool for not having told you sooner anyway. I'm terribly sorry, Frankie. I hope someday you'll be able to forgive me."

I give her a long, hard look. "I'll let you know after you tell me whatever it is you've apparently conspired to hide from me my whole life."

Nonna presses her lips together, clearly trying not to smile. "Oh, dear. It sounds like my odds of forgiveness are rather low."

Her usual, graceful manner undoes my anger. I can't trust my emotions right now, and the last thing I want to do is make this worse. With a sigh, I swing my legs off the padded bench I'd been laid on. "Let's get this over with and we'll find out," I reply evenly. The motion makes me acutely uncomfortable. "But first, where's the bathroom?"

With a smile, Nonna points to a door in the corner of the room.

I do my business, and when I emerge a policewoman has joined Nonna. She looks at ease, but I don't miss her hand resting on her gun. Their silent stares are unnerving. I swallow hard and brace myself for what comes next.

I'M NOT ALLOWED TO SEE ANYONE ELSE UNTIL THEY'RE DONE WITH ME. It takes a full two hours of questions. Well, more like about ten questions, repeated in different ways. Like they're trying to catch me in a lie, or get me to contradict Julian, or even myself. It's exhausting, but, in a way, it's also liberating. As I relive the experience over and over again, I realize that my mother truly left me no choice. The guilt I felt at first has been replaced with extreme sadness, in large part over the relationship I never had with my mother. I find myself completely unable to understand why she did what she did because of it.

So when I'm done with questioning and am released, I'm eager to hear what it is Nonna has to say. When I meet her in the front lobby, I notice Julian hovering in a corner, clearly unsure of what to do.

As we leave, I approach him, taking his hand in mine and leading him out behind me.

Apparently, someone recovered my keys, as Nonna hands them to me as soon as we're out of the building. My convertible sits gleaming in the parking lot, my first visual reminder of the night before. With a deep breath, I head toward the car. But Julian's hand tugs against mine.

"You sure?" he asks. I look at him, bemused. "I mean, are you sure you want me to come with you?"

"Yes," I reply succinctly.

He gives me a sideways smile, but still throws a reluctant glance over at Nonna.

I turn around fully, placing myself in front of him.

"You're part of this whole thing," I explain, only touching him through our joined hands. "You have pieces of this story that only you know. And I need to know. I need to understand what's been going on. How long it's been going on. And what it all means. Do you think you can help me with that?"

Julian looks down at me intensely. "Of course," he murmurs. The scent of him washes over me, and I have to work to focus. "I'll tell you anything you want to know."

"Good." And with a determined pull, I drag him to the car. Nonna climbs in too, and we all head back to … well, I guess it's Nonna's house now.

When I pull into the driveway, I realize I haven't seen my brother. "Nonna, where's Tony?" I ask, suddenly anxious.

She lays her hand on my arm as Julian climbs over the side of the car to get out. "He's fine," she assures me. "He's staying with friends for a few days."

I breathe a sigh of relief, and we all head into the house.

Nonna tells me to go shower and change, not having been able to do so since yesterday. I see the wisdom, but I do it as quickly as possible. Unfortunately, the only clothes I have here are from years ago. I slip into the most fashionable thing I can find, a body-hugging blue sweater dress, hoping it's warm enough without leggings.

I emerge into the kitchen to find Julian sitting at the dining table while Nonna puts together some food and drinks. Julian eyes my dress appreciatively. Blushing, I sit down across from him, fidgeting with the hem of the dress as Nonna works. We all continue in the silence I suspect has ruled since I went to shower. After she's laid everything out on the table, she sits with us. We all eat mindlessly for a few minutes.

"Goodness, where should I start?" Nonna muses.

I shrug. "At the beginning."

Nonna shoots me an impatient look and shakes her head. "Have it your way, then." She takes a deep breath. "I suppose it started with your great grandfather. He and his wife immigrated here just before your grandfather was born. They opened a restaurant, but times were troubled then. They banded together with people they knew, other people who owned businesses in the community, to protect each other."

My eyebrows jump. "Protect each other? What does that mean?"

When Julian lays his hand over mine trying to soothe me, I realize it must have come out more shrilly than I intended. But seriously, does that mean what I think it means?

"It means they did what had to be done to make people leave them alone and to find the resources they needed to succeed. These days they call it an organized crime syndicate. And while they were less focused on crime back then, they were, nonetheless, still highly ruthless and ambitious," Nonna explains tightly. "When it was time, your grandfather took his father's place in the organization. Luca, God rest his soul, was an especially heartless man. He wasn't afraid to exploit others for his own gain. Under him, the organization grew in leaps and bounds. He became very powerful. And I'm afraid as your mother grew, she found it all very enticing. She and your grandfather had very similar dispositions." Nonna grimaces, clearly reliving her disappointment.

I wonder, not for the first time, how my gentle, kind grandmother was ever married to a man like that. Different times, I suppose. I stay silent as she goes on, still reeling from the revelation of my dirty family history.

"From a young age, and against my wishes, Luca involved Samantha in almost everything he did. He made sure she had around-the-clock protection because of it. Salvatore Moretti was one of her bodyguards."

Julian's face reflects the shock I'm sure is on my own. Sal didn't exactly seem like the strong protector type. And even the need for a bodyguard says Nonno was into some seriously bad shit. Like, it's-going-to-take-me-a-while-to-fully-wrap-my-head-around-it kind of shit. I shake my head, wondering if I'll ever believe that my mother had this whole other illicit life I knew absolutely nothing about.

"I know," Nonna agrees. "Sal was a little weasel of a man, even then. But he was ambitious. Unfortunately, he wasn't very smart. Before we even knew they were together, she was pregnant. Your grandfather, er, dismissed Sal." She shifts uncomfortably in her chair, and I sense there was a lot more violence in that act than she's comfortable discussing. And definitely more than I'm comfortable hearing about. This whole thing is just bizarre. "We decided it was best if Sal never even knew about you, which your mother was especially adamant about. What we didn't count on was your ability." She folds her hand over mine. "The very first time you asked about your father, your mother panicked. You were so little. Not even two. She wasn't expecting to have to answer questions that soon, so she said he was dead. When she explained what that meant, you wouldn't accept it. We thought you were simply stubborn. But looking back, it was the first sign. There were no others for a good long while, though."

"So I just went along with it after that?" I ask, puzzled.

Nonna shakes her head. "You never asked again, to my knowledge."

I lean back in my chair with a frown.

"Nonno and Mom didn't run a cleaning business." As the pieces start to come together in my mind, my stomach roils. "They were gangsters." Even saying it is beyond crazy. Though, thinking about it, it fits my mother to a T. Her commanding, stern manner that suffered no dissension. The strange men who would hover in our sphere for a short time only to disappear. Her strange "work" habits. Cleaning business, my ass.

"No, dear," Nonna admits. "Not as such."

Julian snickers. I throw him a sharp look and he snaps up in his chair.

"Sorry, I just ..." he laughs, then claps a hand over his mouth, getting ahold of himself before he continues, "I grew up hearing your mother's name spoken in fear. To think about her daughter being under the impression she cleaned houses or something ..." He struggles again to suppress an ironic laugh.

"Samantha worked very hard to keep that all away from her children," my grandmother replies waspishly. "She'd make an example of anyone who came anywhere near her family. I'm sure you know that."

Julian nods his agreement. "That I knew. But the rest, not really. It explains why Sal was always so determined to take over her territory. He hated her, and your grandfather. He had a fucking party when he died." His eyes snap up to my grandmother. "Sorry, ma'am."

Nonna rolls her eyes. "Don't be, I had my own party."

Julian's eyes go wide. I look at Nonna and we both start laughing. "Nonno was horrible," I explain to Julian. "Only mom was sad when he died." I don't feel the least bit bad saying it, though it's always been an unspoken understanding between my grandmother and me. The man was a complete terror, and it only got worse the older he got.

Though a lot of that makes more sense now. And I suddenly realize I don't feel much different about my mother's death than I did his. It makes me wonder how Nonna feels about it.

"How are you doing?" I ask her. "She was your daughter."

"And yet my relationship with her was no less complicated than yours," she sighs. "Perhaps even more so. I loved her dearly, of course. What mother doesn't love their child? But I prayed every night for her to step away from that life. Or for her to find someone who cared enough for her to help soften her edges." She looks meaningfully between Julian and me. A brief ache rolls through me, but I push it down. Whatever we are, or aren't, it can wait. "But she craved power. And that's a neverending cycle that only leads to self-destruction. I'm just sorry her end involved you like it did." Nonna's eyes fill with tears, but she quickly wipes them away.

I reach over and wrap my hand around hers. "I'm sorry for all of us," I agree. "But I'm glad I know now. It explains so much about our relationship, about my childhood. I just wish it hadn't ended like this."

"No, child," she assures me. "This is just another beginning." She rises from the table, clearly done with her story as she starts to tidy the empty plates. I'm sure I'll have more questions for her once I really start to absorb all of this, but for now I have other questions.

I glance over at Julian, who is leaned back in his chair with his arms crossed over his massive chest, quietly contemplating all that's been said.

"Walk with me?" I ask, standing up and offering a hand.

He takes it, rising to tower over me. "Sure." His voice is subdued, and he follows me quietly out the door.

We walk, hand in hand, in the cool November evening. I lead him to my park, and we sit down side by side on the bench I'd sleep on as a child.

"This is the place, isn't it?" he asks, running his hands over the weathered boards.

"Yep," I reply.

We're silent for a few minutes. I'm unsure of how to begin. Because this could be the end. Or not.

"Do you remember how hot and cold I was when we first started talking?" he finally asks.

I laugh sharply. "How could I forget?" I look over at him. "It wasn't that long ago, really." He's staring up at the sky, his arms splayed out on the back of the bench.

"I was only supposed to stake you out. Ask a few questions. Sniff around. See what your deal was. I wasn't supposed to get close," he explains. "But it was impossible to resist you. Even now, whenever I'm near you, you're like a star. You have gravity I can't seem to escape."

"But you wanted to?" I ask.

He shakes his head. "No," he replies flatly. "If we'd met under any other circumstances, I'd have tried to get you in bed that first night. But I was working. And Sal made it perfectly clear I wasn't to touch you."

"Except you did. A lot," I recall with a smile.

He turns his burning gaze on me. And despite the heaviness of the conversation, I can still feel it. The gravitational pull. That unshakable, deep-seated attraction I've never felt with anyone but him.

"Yeah. And it was fucking torture," he admits. "Knowing I shouldn't. Then being told not to. Then giving in anyway. Back and forth. It drove me nuts. I imagine it was even worse for you."

I give him an appraising look. "You're underestimating your appeal," I tease. "But yes, it was confusing, to say the least. And then awful, once I knew you were still holding something back." I heave a sigh. "I never imagined it was this huge."

Julian leans forward, staring at his fingers as he works them between his knees. "I'd say it was dangerous for me to tell you. To drag you into that world. But it was just selfishness. I didn't want to lose you," he admits. "And then I did anyway."

"You didn't," I correct him.

"Oh, yeah? What about that whole schtick where you told me to fuck off and agreed that I didn't deserve you?"

I shrug. "I'm an enigma."

Julian laughs. "That you are."

"What do you think Sal wanted with me?"

Julian doesn't seem surprised by the abrupt change. I'm sure he was expecting the question at some point.

"His organization was dying. You were the last play he had against your mother. Beyond that I'm not sure exactly *how* he planned on using you in that game. I'm not sure he even knew. He was just desperate, and like your grandma said, he just wasn't smart enough to pull it off. Not effectively going up against both you and your mother."

"So what happens to you now?"

"What do you mean?" he asks with a furrowed brow.

"Are you still in danger?" I ask, hoping some good may have come from all of this.

"No," he breathes out. "What little was left of Sal's organization will dissolve, or reorganize, or whatever. But my obligations died with him. Nobody will care what I do now. I'm a free man."

I try to understand the life he's lived. An abused foster child turned runaway turned lackey in a criminal organization. The things he's done. And I realize I can't. It's the world my mother shielded me from. Not that I ended up any less fucked up for it.

"What about you? What happens to you now?" he asks softly.

"The sad truth is, I don't know if this really changes my life much," I admit. "Learning that I had a father made me question everything. But at some point, I remembered I am who I am. My past may have shaped me, but I choose what my life is now. And as huge as this has all been, knowing what was really going on that whole time doesn't change what I want to do. I want to keep running my club. Maybe even expand someday. See where it all takes me."

"If I haven't lost you, does that mean I get to come along for the ride?" he teases with a smile.

I look at him analytically. "I don't know. Let me check one thing. Tell me you don't love me."

He looks at me like I'm nuts. "I don't love you."

Lie.

I grin widely. The voice is still there. And Julian still loves me. Despite everything we've been through, or perhaps because of it, the knowledge makes my heart soar. "I might keep you."

He turns toward me, hooking one of his legs behind my back and pulling me into his arms. He stares down into my eyes and strokes a thumb down my cheek.

"Good. Because I'm going to be your fucking shadow, baby." He leans in and kisses my earlobe. "I'm going to be with you as long as you'll have me." His mouth moves down, and he kisses my jaw. "I'm going to love you with everything I've got." His fingers tilt my chin up and he kisses my neck. "I'm going to pleasure you in ways you never even dreamed possible, then I'm going to wait on you hand and foot until you recover enough for me to do it all over again." He kisses my collarbone. "Every. Fucking. Day." He nuzzles into my neck, pulling me tight to his chest.

I close my eyes and breathe deeply of his scent. His words, his lips, his arms around me, it all penetrates the shield I've had around myself today. Oh, who am I kidding? I've always had that shield around me. I needed it to deal with my ability, and then to get through this ordeal.

But I have him now. And with everything we've been through, I can't imagine what could shake us. I love him. Body and soul. Despite his holding back the awful truth. Or maybe because he loved me so much, he couldn't bear to have it separate us. But it wasn't of his making, ultimately, and I can't say I'd have done anything differently in his shoes. So there's absolutely nothing left to hold me back.

I realize suddenly what my ability has been trying to show me all along. People lie for all kinds of reasons, but all those lies fall into one of two categories: selfish lies and unselfish lies. Julian's have all been the latter, the ones I don't need to worry about. He'll always be there for me, to protect me, to love me, to drive me fucking crazy for better or for worse.

"I think I can live with that," I reply casually. "I have just one condition."

Julian laughs. "Oh, yeah? What's that?"

"Lots of dirty talk," I reply with a grin.

Julian looks up at me with a predatory glint in his eye. "Are you trying to get me to fuck you on this bench?" he asks huskily.

A shiver rolls up my spine and I bite my bottom lip. His eyes zero in on it.

"No. I'm trying to get you to tell me *how* you'd fuck me on this bench," I tease.

Julian goes still and I don't even have to look to know he's hard as a rock. And I'm just as ready for him. And I know deep down, I'll always be this ready for him.

I'll always be his. And he'll always be mine.

27

———

EPILOGUE

One year later

FRANKIE

Oh. Fuck.

I look back up into the bathroom mirror, but my reflection is blurry, a blue halo of hair surrounding the tan blob of face. It takes me a minute to realize it's because I'm crying. I feel anesthetized, so I don't know if they're happy tears or … something else.

I look back down at the seemingly innocuous piece of plastic sitting on the counter. And the little plus sign that will forever change my world.

As the numbness fades, I start to panic. How did this even happen? I mean, I know *how* but … I shake my head. It doesn't matter now.

A million thoughts start clawing at the inside of my head, each begging to be heard, considered, freaked out over. I take a deep breath and wipe the tears away. I let one thought in: *How the fuck am I going to tell Julian?*

I snort a laugh. Who am I kidding? I can't hide this from him.

Before I can stop myself, I grab the clean end of the stick and march out into the kitchen, where I find Julian leaned back against the counter, sipping a mug of coffee.

His huge, muscled frame looks so fucking delicious in just boxers, his dark hair still sexily disheveled from sleep, and our usual morning sex. The sex that made me realize something felt … off.

He raises one thick, dark eyebrow as I approach. "Everything okay?"

It just goes to show how well he knows me now. Because my poker face is fucking good. It has to be, so people don't realize that I know when they're lying to me. Or maybe the bomb I'm about to drop has shaken me enough to change that.

"I think I'm going to have to rescind my offer on Los Jardines," I reply as evenly as I can.

Julian sets his coffee down, which I'm thankful for. I'm not exactly in the mood to be doused in hot liquid on top of everything else.

"Look, I know it's sooner than you wanted to be running another night-club, but I really think we can do this," he replies. Under any other circumstances, I'd find his faith and enthusiasm touching. But my breath catches in my throat and I can feel the tears threatening at the back of my eyes again.

"It's not that," I reply, my throat tightening with emotion.

He grabs my hips and pulls me into him, and the scent of him calms me just enough to keep it together. He slips a finger under my chin and tilts my head up.

"Then what? Talk to me, baby," he pleads, his dark eyes searching mine.

I press away just enough to hold up the stick. "I'm pregnant."

Julian freezes, his muscled body stiffening, his arms dropping to his sides, his eyes wide as saucers.

"Fuck," he whispers. But I can't tell if he's upset or happy at the news.

I hold my breath, trying not to let the circus of thoughts still battling in my head rule me as I wait for his reaction. Seconds tick by, each feeling like an eternity. We've never discussed having kids, save my occasional mention that I'd never really wanted to. He's been pretty quiet on the subject, which I hadn't realized until, well, he's now quiet on the subject.

"Please, say something," I whisper back finally, closing my eyes. But it doesn't stop the tears from rolling over my cheeks.

His hands find my face, his thumbs roughly brushing the tears away. "Look at me, Frankie," he commands.

I open my eyes, staring up at him, trying not to squirm under my vulnerability. His expression is still inscrutable.

"Are you mad?" I ask softly.

And the motherfucker bursts out laughing. I stare at him, bewildered.

When he gathers himself and looks back down at me, he leans down and presses his forehead against mine. "Fuck, of course not," he assures me. "You're having our fucking baby."

I sigh as the weight leaves my shoulders. "Oh thank God you're not angry," I breathe. "But are you sure? Is this what you want?"

Julian's eyes darken, his brows pulling together. "You're not thinking about getting rid of it, are you?"

"Fuck, no!" I protest. "I would never do that. But I know you didn't sign up for this. I don't even know if you wanted kids—"

He shuts me up with a firm kiss, that softens as I melt into him. His tongue slips between my lips, searching for mine. I wrap my arms around his neck and pull myself into him, into his comfort, his smell, his gorgeous fucking body that I don't think I'll ever get enough of. His hands slide down my back, over my ass, kneading and gripping me to him as I feel myself getting wet for him.

When he breaks the kiss, my whole body sighs in disappointment.

"I gotta be honest, I'm not sure what I wanted. But now that this is happening … fuck, Frankie, this is unreal."

I nod. "Yeah. I'm right there with you. But I'm glad you're not running for the hills," I admit.

He smirks down at me. "Like you could get rid of me." He drops a chaste kiss on my lips. "But I think we're gonna need a bigger place."

I laugh, tucking my head against his chest and sinking into him. "We're gonna need a lot of things."

He strokes my back gently. "Yeah? Like what?"

I shake my head and look up at him. "I don't want to think about it yet. I'm still wrapping my head around the idea of us being parents."

"Fuck, Frankie, how do you make that sounds so fucking sexy?" he murmurs, his dark eyes dancing.

My lips curl into a smile. "I don't, you're just a horn-dog," I tease him.

"You know you fucking love it," he growls, his lips crashing into mine. But he pulls back just as abruptly. "Is it safe? To you know…" He raises his eyebrows suggestively.

Now it's my turn to burst out laughing. "Of course," I reply. "As big as your dick is, it can't reach that far, I promise."

He shoots me a mock dirty look. "Good, because it's our day off, and if you don't want to think about it, I have ways of helping with that."

A light shiver travels down my spine. "Promise?"

He unleashes a feline grin as he scoops me up and carries me into the bedroom. "You bet your gorgeous fucking ass, I do."

He kicks the door open and lays me gently on the bed, stripping my nightie off and unceremoniously flinging it across the room. Then he rips his boxers off and climbs over me.

"I'm going to worship every fucking inch of you," he says, kissing down my chest and gently licking around a nipple. "I'm going to make you come so fucking hard." He keeps kissing down my stomach. His lips come to rest on my lower abdomen, his hands running gently along my hip bones. "God, Frankie, that's my fucking baby in there." He looks up at me, his eyes glassy.

I bite into my bottom lip, trying to focus on what's coming, instead of the intense emotions threatening to take over. Thankfully he resumes his oral explorations, and his head drops between my legs, followed by his hot tongue on my clit. My mind clears as pleasure courses through me and my hips tilt into his skilled mouth as he works me toward orgasm. He slips a finger in, more gently than usual, but no less stimulating as he strokes me.

"I love you, Frankie," he says. My eyes fly open to meet his. And the love there fucking kills me. Not just because normally he'd be talking dirty right now, but because of his complete acceptance of this huge fucking curveball. And I know together we can do this. I want to do this. I haven't not wanted him for a moment since I gave myself to him. And now I want this family with him.

"I love you too," I breathe back.

With a grin, his mouth clamps down on me, his tongue swirling in a way that makes any more speech, any more thought, completely impossible as my climax shoots through me.

As I descend, he climbs between my legs, and I can see how fucking hard he is for me.

"God, yes, give it to me," I beg.

He slides the tip around as he readies himself. And when he plunges in mercilessly, I'm thankful he's clearly not afraid. Because our physical connection is too important, too strong, to do anything but for the next nine months. As he fucks me into my next orgasm, tears leak from my eyes, finally feeling the joy of what's to come. Because I know with Julian it won't be anything short of perfect.

"WELL THIS IS JUST FUCKING PERFECT," I GRUMBLE, SETTING DOWN MY phone.

"What's that?" Julian asks from the couch across my office.

"I got a voicemail from our agent. We were outbid on Los Jardines."

Julian shifts. "Fuck. That sucks."

I shrug and let out a sigh. "Probably for the best." *Lie.* I pull a face. I can't even fucking lie to myself. Urgh.

Julian sets down the inventory reports he was reviewing and rises from the couch, coming to stand next to me.

"I know you wanted this. But there will be other opportunities," he assures me, stroking my hair.

"Other opportunities for what?"

Julian and I look up to find Nils standing in the doorway. Julian steps away and sinks back onto the couch, determined to ignore Nils, as usual. A favor Nils is always glad to repay.

"We lost the bid for Los Jardines," I explain.

Nils runs a hand over his now-short blond hair. "I see. I'm so sorry, Francesca."

I give him a thin smile. "Thanks. But Julian's right. Obviously it wasn't meant to be."

"I'll let Annika know," he says, referring to his assistant manager. "We've got a staff meeting in five ahead of setup tonight."

I nod my understanding and stand up to close the door behind him as he leaves.

"So when are we gonna tell him?" Julian murmurs, still pretending to look at his reports.

"The doctor says I'm only eleven weeks," I remind him. "I don't have to stop working for five months. We have time."

Julian finally looks up as I settle back into my chair. "Okay. But I want to be there when he finds out he'll be working for me," he replies with a smirk. He rises and clicks the lock shut. "Now. Five minutes sounds doable, don't you think?"

I shake my head and laugh.

"You're crazy."

He grins as he advances on me. "You know you fucking love it."

He's not wrong.

THE NEXT DAY, JULIAN AND I ARE LOUNGING IN BED BEFORE WE DRAG ASS into the shower to get ready to go back into the club for Saturday night insanity.

"So we going apartment hunting next week?" he asks, idly playing with my fingers in his.

"About that."

He looks down at me and arches an eyebrow.

"What about it?" he asks archly.

"Nonna wants to give us the house."

His brows scrunch together. "Where are she and Tony gonna live?"

"Yeah, about that…" I repeat.

Julian sits fully upright and faces me, looking at me expectantly.

"Don't freak out, okay?" I prompt. Julian's look darkens, but he doesn't say anything. "She wants to give us the house before she passes so there are no problems. But she's getting too old to deal with Tony by herself. He's a teenager now and gone is the happy kid he was before Mom …died." I choke on the word, burying the memories of that night. The night I killed my own mother to save Julian's life.

"Hey," Julian says, tugging at my hand. "I'm here."

I nod, brushing away tears I hadn't realized were there.

"She can help us with the baby, we can help her with Tony. You can't deny the kid loves you, and even growing like a weed, you're still twice his size."

Julian shifts uncomfortably. I realize suddenly how crazy it is to ask this man, who'd been alone for years, to not just accept that we're about to have a baby, but to also live with my grandmother and my thirteen-year-old brother. It's too much. I should've known better.

"I'm sorry, never mind, forget I said anything," I blurt. "Just because you've been so great about everything so far doesn't mean I have any right to ask this of you."

"No, it makes sense," he finally agrees, but I can see the weight of it in the tightness of his mouth, the tension in his shoulders.

"Just because it makes sense doesn't mean it's what's right for us. For our family," I point out.

Julian's head snaps up. "Our family." His voice is soft, and his face melts into a smile. "Your family *is* my family, baby, you know that. I just…" He shifts again.

"What? Tell me," I prompt.

He looks up at the ceiling. "How are we gonna fuck with an old lady and a teenage boy down the hall?"

I refrain from laughing, because I know how serious a concern this must be for him. But it's just too fucking cute.

"Valid concern," I say slowly, trying to keep the laughter from entering my voice. "But how are we gonna fuck with a baby around without help?"

He weighs that. "Okay, that's true," he finally admits.

"If you're worried we'll have sex less because of them living with us, I get that. But I think it's just going to be harder anyway with the baby, and you managing the club the last couple months of my pregnancy and until I can come back. And even after that, really."

Julian's expression darkens with every word, so I crawl into his lap, grinding my hips into his.

"You think I could do without having you inside me every fucking day? It's part of who we are together. Even if we have to have a quick, quiet fuck in the shower most of the time, then so-fucking-be it." I pause, realizing there's something else the doctor told me that I don't think I shared.

"What?" he asks at the sudden, pensive look on my face.

"On the subject of fucking…" I start, scrunching my nose. "We can't for six weeks after the baby anyway. Doctor's orders."

Julian groans and topples over backward on the bed, covering his eyes with his arm. "You've got to be fucking kidding me."

I can't help it, this time a giggle escapes me. "Let me show you what we'll be doing instead…" I kiss my way up his legs and he watches me as I take him into my mouth. As I convince him that it'll all work out just fine.

Six months later

JULIAN

I get home from the club at five a.m. on Sunday morning tired as a motherfucker. I don't know how Frankie fucking did this for so long. Especially while pregnant. Thank fuck she stopped working last month. I sneak into our bedroom and take a shower in our bathroom as quietly as possible, but when I emerge, she's awake, sitting up in bed.

"Hey, baby," I whisper, still not wanting to wake anyone else.

"Hey yourself. You should know better than to stand there naked and dripping. Get your fine ass over here and fuck me."

"What, you don't want to know how the night was?"

"You can tell me later."

Frankie rises to her knees, slipping her baby-doll nightie down over her breasts and my cock hardens in an instant. Fuck, her tits are so huge these days, and her dark nipples so large they're like fucking beacons beckoning me in. And who knew her pregnant belly wouldn't deter me at all — in fact seeing her carrying my son is the biggest fucking turn-on of my life. So I waste no time dropping my towel and climbing into bed.

I close my mouth over hers as I lower her to the bed, sliding behind her as I work her nipples with my fingers. Her ass rests against my cock, the bead on the end rubbing off on her gorgeous fucking thigh.

Her mouth breaks from mine with a gasp. "God, you're so fucking hard," she groans.

I fist my cock, slipping it under her nightie to rub against her dripping pussy. "You're so fucking gorgeous, baby, it makes me hard just looking at you."

She lifts her leg, and I don't waste time. With a tilt, I slide my cock in, groaning into her back in appreciation of her tight, wet walls around me. I pump slowly as I slip a hand under her leg to stroke her clit. With my other hand, I turn her head and bring my mouth to her ear.

"You like that, baby?" I ask, picking up speed. "Tell me you like it when I fuck your pussy, mama."

She arches her back, pushing her tits out, and my balls contract with the desire to erupt inside her. But I hold it together, slipping my hand around her shoulder, squeezing her breast up toward me.

"Tell me, Frankie," I beg.

"Julian," she moans. "I...oh, God..." She pants, her pussy tightening around me as she approaches orgasm. It must feel too good to say anything else, but it doesn't stop me.

"Yeah, I know you like that," I murmur into her ear. "God you feel so fucking good, baby. So fucking wet for me." I pump harder and I feel her contract around me. I press harder with my thumbs, circling until she's panting hard and struggling to hold in the screams. "Come on, baby, come on my dick like a good girl."

She turns her head into the pillow to muffle the screams of her orgasm as she tightens like a fist around my cock, and I come with her. Spots dance across my vision as I empty myself into my gorgeous fucking woman.

"Oh, shit," Frankie gasps. And a huge gush flows down my cock.

I pull out in surprise as the liquid mixes with my cum and rushes over us.

"What the fuck was that?"

"I think my water just broke." Frankie looks back at me, eyes wide.

My heart sinks. "But you're not due for two weeks."

She shoots me an impatient look. "It's a baby, Julian, not a band we scheduled. Babies don't fucking care about due dates."

"I just fucking came, I'm sorry I'm not all here at the moment," I snap. Then immediately regret it. "I'm sorry baby, it's just been a long night. Come on, let's get you cleaned up and to the hospital." I climb off the bed and make to grab the towel I'd been using.

"Julian?" Frankie looks up at me shakily.

I snap upright, looking back at her. "What? What do you need?"

"You," she replies, her bottom lip trembling.

Forgetting the fucking towel for the minute, I rush back to her, gathering her in my arms.

"It's gonna be just fine, baby. You'll see. I'm here, okay?"

She nods into my chest. "I love you so much."

I kiss the top of her head. "I love you too."

"We're gonna meet our baby," she says on a laugh.

I look down at her to see tears streaming down her face. "Yeah, we're gonna meet him. Focus on that." I smile down at her as her words really hit me. I'm about to be a fucking dad.

FRANKIE

"He's so *beautiful*," I whisper after they've handed me my baby. Twelve hours and a whole lot of pain, screaming, and pushing later. But looking down into his tiny face, it slams into me how much he looks like Julian, and I'm immediately in love. My tiny man. He was worth it, and so much more.

Julian comes back from washing up after helping cut the cord and wraps an arm around me.

"He's fucking perfect," Julian whispers. "And you did amazing, Frankie. I'm so fucking proud of you."

I look up at him and give him an exhausted smile. "You're gonna have to stop cursing so much now," I tease.

"Pfff, fuck that," he jokes. I scrunch my nose at him. "Come on, I've got a year or two before he starts talking. We'll figure it out."

"Yeah, we'll figure it out," I agree with a smile.

A BIT LATER, AFTER I'VE BEEN CLEANED UP AND HAD A CHANCE TO REST, we introduce our son to my grandmother, Tony, and Emma.

"Guys," I say as they all peer excitedly over my arm. "I'd like you to meet Nicholas Charles Greco."

Emma claps her hands together, tears slipping over her round cheeks. Nonna steps forward and reaches out questioningly.

I gladly slip her the baby, watching the utter joy on her face as she cradles and coos to him.

"Oh, Francesca, my dear, he's perfect," she says.

"Just like his momma," Julian says.

I look up at him to find him beaming at them both like the proud papa he is.

They all take turns holding him, even Tony, who forgets to be a cool teenager for a few minutes while he adores the tiny baby in his arms. When Nico starts to fuss, Julian gathers him back up in his strong arms, gently bouncing and soothing his cries nearly instantly.

Nonna's eyebrows rise knowingly. "You're a natural," she compliments Julian.

Julian grins widely. "I hope so. But I think this little guy is hungry," he says. Nonna and Emma nod knowingly and start heading for the door. Tony looks confused, but Nonna simply rolls her eyes and drags him along, and I can't help laughing.

Julian places Nico back in my arms and I get him latched on quickly. Looks like his dad isn't the only one taking to this new-baby business like a pro.

Julian settles onto the bed next to me, sliding an arm around my shoulders.

"I don't know that this is the best time, but…" He takes a deep breath, causing me to look up at him. There are tears in his eyes as he watches me nurse our son. "God, you're both so fucking beautiful."

I smile, tears coming to my eyes too. "And we both love you. What isn't it the best time for?"

"Marry me, Frankie."

My breath catches in my throat and I look up at him incredulously. It takes me a minute to find words again, but he waits patiently.

"We don't have to rush into anything just because of him," I say, looking down as Nico's little fist bunched over my breast.

"I'm not," Julian replies simply, shifting on the bed. I look over to see him fishing a black, velvet bag out of his pocket. He pulls open the tiny drawstrings and upends it, toppling a ring into his palm. He picks it up carefully between two fingers to show it to me. It's an emerald-cut sapphire surrounded by diamonds, on a diamond-encrusted band. "I bought this months ago. I just didn't know how to ask before now."

"I didn't actually hear you ask anything," I tease him.

He thinks about that for a minute. "You're right. I'm going to do this. Really do it." He rises, then sinks to one knee by the bed, clasping my hand in his. "Frankie, I never thought I'd find someone I could trust, much less love like I love you. I want to be with you until we're fucking old and senile. I want to raise our son to be a man we're both proud of. I want to spend the rest of my life with you. If you'll have me. Francesca Greco, will you marry me?"

I press my lips together and furrow my brow, pretending to really have to think about it. He rolls his eyes and huffs jokingly. I scrunch my nose one last time before breaking into a grin. "Fuck yes, I will," I reply.

Julian jumps up and kisses me so fiercely I have to cradle Nico to me to keep ahold of him. When he pulls away, I laugh.

"I love you," I tell him.

"I love you too, baby," he responds, settling back onto the bed next to me. "And I have one more surprise for you."

I look up at him, confused. "Yeah? What's that?"

"I bought Los Jardines."

"*What?*" I screech. Nico, who'd fallen asleep, startles awake and starts to cry. I silence him with my nipple and he happily starts sucking himself back to sleep.

Julian looks down with a frown. "Lucky little bastard," he grouses jokingly.

I roll my eyes and smack Julian on the chest as hard as I can without disturbing the baby. "What the fuck do you mean you bought Los Jardines? It was you who outbid me?"

Julian shrugs. "Technically it was Mac. We didn't want you to overtax yourself during the pregnancy, so he held onto it until you'd gone on maternity leave. Nils and Annika have been running it under my and Mac's supervision, and Johnny and I have been running Baltia."

There are so many parts to that, I can't even begin to process it. Much less how he did any of it without my knowing. But then, I have been a little … pregnant.

"When did Johnny learn to manage the club?" I ask.

"That's your first question?" Julian teases. I shoot him a dirty look. "Fine. Nils and I have been training him since I got the idea. Not that he was far off to start. He's been working there long enough to basically know how everything runs."

"Wow. I just … wow. Okay. So where'd you get the money to buy a fucking nightclub? Took me ten years to build up that kind of capital."

"Ah. That. Yeah, that's another thing. I kind of…" he blows out a breath, "…inherited Sal's financial holdings. The clean stuff anyway. Turns out he thought of me as more of a son than I thought. I knew you could contest as his only real heir if you wanted, but it was right after everything, and I didn't want to put that decision on you. So I put it in an account in both of our names. It's your money, really."

My mouth opens and closes like a fish for a minute before a wave of exhaustion has tears running down my face.

"Oh baby, I'm so sorry," he says, seeing my distress. "Fuck. I knew this was shitty timing."

I wipe at the tears. "It's overwhelming, but I think this is just hormones," I allow, gesturing to the tears. "How much money are we talking?"

"Enough to buy a few more clubs, a bigger house, and to put Nico through college."

"Fuck."

"Yeah."

"So I guess now's a good time to tell you my mom left behind a shit ton of cash too."

Julian doesn't look surprised. "I figured."

"I'm sorry I didn't tell you before."

He huffs a laugh. "I'm not exactly in a position to bust your chops for that. But I want us to agree to something right now."

"What's that?"

"I've been careful not to out-and-out lie to you. You know how I hate it anyway."

"One of the things I like most about you," I tease.

"But I've felt like I've been lying by omission this past year-and-a-half with Sal's money. And then with the new club. It fucking killed me, Frankie." His face is drawn in, and I don't need my ability to know he's telling the truth.

"I see why you did it. On both counts. It's okay, Julian. I'm sorry I didn't tell you about Mom's money either."

"That's the thing. I don't want us to hide things from each other. Even if we think it's for a good reason. It's been eating me fucking alive. I know it's weird, but—"

"It's not," I interrupt in agreement. "It was weird for me too. But you're completely right. The 'not really lies' are what messed with my whole childhood. I don't want that for Nico."

"Do you think he'll have your ability?" Julian asks, stroking Nico's back.

"I've wondered that. But even if he doesn't, I think you're right regardless."

Julian nods. "No more non-lies."

"No more non-lies," I agree.

"Now we get to see what happens next," he says. "Nervous?" His dark eyes sparkle mischievously. He takes my fucking breath away. And I know we're going to have a long and happy life together.

"Not even a little. Now my real life, the one after the lies, begins."

FINDING HIS REDEMPTION

AN ENEMIES TO LOVERS
ROCK STAR ROMANCE

CONTENT WARNING

Finding His Redemption is an enemies-to-lovers rock star romance novel that includes elements that might not be suitable for some readers, including the use of profanity, open-door sex scenes, and other potentially sensitive topics. Visit https://melanieasmithauthor.com/fhrcw.html for a full list (warning: may include spoilers).

1

Back in Black by AC/DC

West

"There is *nothing* more overrated than bacon, dude."

Andy, my driver, smirks at me in the rearview mirror. His light blue eyes are already mocking me. "Nope. I've got that beat: joining the mile high club. No contest."

"Are you serious? Look, everything is either wrapped in, flavored as, or made to look like bacon these days. It's ridiculous. But getting your rocks off at forty thousand feet? Well, that's just a good time, and in *no* way overrated. I don't know how you could even suggest that."

"Have you actually tried fucking someone in one of those tiny bathrooms? It isn't easy. Or fun. Or conducive to getting anyone off," he argues, one hand agitatedly running through his curly blond hair.

"Ever heard of private planes? Or the sin bin?" I counter. I watch with smug satisfaction as Andy's eyebrows jump in the mirror.

"First, private planes are some serious next-level celebrity shit, Mr. I'm

289

Flying Commercial These Days." He gives me a pointed look, and I flip him off for going for a sore spot. "Second: What's a sin bin? Is that slang for doing it in the place they have those tiny flight attendant chairs? Because that's not exactly private and definitely a good way to get banned from ever flying again."

I chuckle. "A sin bin is this little bedroom they have over the main cabin on some airplanes so flight attendants can rest on long flights where they change shifts. I'll let you figure out why they call it a sin bin." I waggle my eyebrows.

"Again: Fucking a flight attendant falls under 'next-level celebrity shit.' I'm sticking to my guns. For us everyday Joes, joining the mile high club is the most overrated thing I can think of. Fight me."

"Well, since I'm clearly not back to private plane status, I'll use this opportunity flying *commercial* to prove you wrong."

Andy laughs and smacks the steering wheel. "Video or it didn't happen."

I shake my head. "Are you trying to get me in trouble? I'm supposed to be a saint now, remember? The last thing I need is a video out there of me fucking some rando on an airplane."

"Yeah, yeah, yeah," Andy grumbles jokingly. "Ruin all my fun, why don't you."

"Uh-huh. This whole conversation was just to bait me into doing something stupid, wasn't it?"

I'm teasing, really. I've known Andy for years, since before rehab, even, so I know he wouldn't do me like that.

"West. Bro. You know nobody has to bait you into doing something stupid. You do that just fine on your own. So as much as I'd like to hear your take on airplane bathroom sex, maybe you're right and you should just focus on behaving for a while."

"Now you're ruining all *my* fun. I just said there couldn't be a video." I give him a wink just as he pulls to a stop.

He shakes his head at me while he radios the guards. A few moments later there's a knock on the tinted window.

"That's my cue. Thanks for the ride, man."

"Be good, West. For all our sakes."

"Oh, I will. I'll be very, *very* good," I promise with a sly smile.

He flips me off and laughs as I step out into the hazy California sunshine. Two guards quickly flank me, one on either side, and I hand my backpack off to one. The other reaches for my guitar case, but I give him a look that says exactly how dead he'll be if he touches my Rosie. *Nobody* touches my girl.

I slip on my aviators, look around, and realize that I'm in the best mood I've been in for a while. I'm sober. The band is back together. Our album is climbing the charts. And I can feel people's eyes on me. That is what I lived through rehab for. What I've climbed back out of the pit I dug for myself for. The attention. The adoration. The rock and roll life. Icing on the cake that is my resuscitated music career.

Before we can even make it three steps, one brave soul, a dude who looks just a few years younger than me, darts around one of my huge guards and thrusts out a pen and notebook.

"Holy shit, you're Kristoffer Westberg! Can I have your autograph?"

A lazy grin spreads over my face and I signal the guards to stand down. "Sure, man, anything for a fan." I lean in and grab the pen, scrawling messily one-handed over the page. As soon as I'm done, the guy holds his cellphone up and I barely have time to throw up a peace sign before he snaps a pic. He releases me, turning to giddily show the pic to his friend, and I shake my head and laugh as we walk away.

We manage to make it the next twenty steps to the terminal without incident, but as soon as we're inside, the familiar gasps of recognition and cries of "West!" follow me. I keep my cool, looking straight ahead like it's no big deal. Happens every day. But damn does it feel good. Like coming home.

The guards start spreading their arms and taking up space, presumably to keep people away, and I soon know why as I pick up flashes in my peripheral vision. I wasn't aware the paparazzi had infiltrated SFO, but hey, bring it on. I'm going to have to deal with it at LAX soon anyway. And the band's album dropped recently enough that we can use all the attention we can get. Enjoying it? That's just a bonus.

I take my time strolling toward security, letting them follow, take pictures, and shout questions my PR people would kill me if I answered as my guards continue to push them back. I can see the guys at the checkpoint exchanging nervous glances, but the small crowd of photographers and onlookers drops back — well, are pushed back by my guards — as I lift my guitar case and lay it lovingly on the conveyor belt, followed by a bin that I unceremoniously dump my wallet, keys, jacket, and shoes into.

As I make it through, followed quickly by my bodyguards, murmurs start back up, but nothing like what they were before. No more paps. And no one else approaches, even though I can hear the whispers. Like music to my ears after the quiet halls of the "wellness center" I spent far too long cooped up in to get back to this place. And by this place, I don't mean heading home to L.A. — I mean this place where I've gotten back my freedom, fans, and fame.

The rest of the walk to the gate and the boarding process are uneventful, save a flirty look from the chick at the boarding door. But the cute brunette flight attendant who greets me gives me a smile that says she knows exactly who I am. She manages to help me stow Rosie in the first-class closet and seat me without fangirling. Points for professionalism. But she won't be so professional later when I'm fucking her in the lavatory I passed on my way in. A shit-eating grin spreads over my face. I may or may not actually do it, but thinking about it is fun either way.

I don't make eye contact with the dude in the seat next to mine as I slump down and pop my earbuds in, sending the universal "fuck off" signal. He doesn't look like he'd be a fan with his pressed khakis and pristine polo shirt, and I'm certainly not looking to fuck him in a bathroom. The thought makes me chuckle.

The plane pushes back from the gate and gets into the air without event. When the same brunette flight attendant comes around to take our drink orders, I pause my music but leave the earbuds in.

"Mr. Marshall," she says to the dude next to me. "Nice to see you. I presume you'd like your usual vodka tonic?"

I can't help it, I raise an eyebrow and turn to look at the guy. Surprisingly, he looks sidelong at me and shakes his head. "Just a Sprite is fine, Mandy, thank you."

That gets my attention. Mostly because it's said in the exact tone I hear all the time. The one people use when they know they're within earshot of an alcoholic. Great.

"Oh," she says, sounding surprised. "Well, all right then." She turns to me, and I politely pop my earbuds out. "And what can I get for you?"

"Just ice water, thanks," I mumble self-consciously.

She moves on, but I can still feel Sprite guy's eyes on me. I pull off my aviators — that were clearly fooling no one — and run my fingers through my messy dark brown hair. I glance over at him and he smiles, offering a hand.

"I'm Morgan," he says pleasantly.

"Marshall, huh?" I reply, shaking his hand.

He chuckles. "Not *that* Marshall."

That gets a wry smile out of me. Maybe he does know who I am. Though I didn't really think he'd be related to the family that founded the amp manufacturing company. But you never know.

"Well, Morgan not-*that*-Marshall, I'm Kristoffer Westberg."

"So, what do I call you? Kristoffer? Kris? Or do you actually prefer West?" he muses.

I huff a short laugh. Yep. He knows.

"West is fine," I reply.

"Cool," he replies, nodding slowly. "You know, my sister is going to shit a brick when I tell her I met you."

That gets a chuckle out of me. "Well, if you have something I can sign, I'm always happy to autograph something for a fan."

Morgan considers me for a moment. "Thanks, but I wouldn't say she's a fan. Though she used to be your *biggest* fan. That was back in the day though."

Well fuck, that's got my attention.

"Used to be?"

Flight attendant Mandy returns with our drinks, and it just goes to show how distracted I am by Morgan's statement that I don't respond to the coy look she gives me. Instead, I watch Morgan pause to take a sip of his Sprite.

"Yep," he finally replies, smacking his lips on the "p" like a pompous ass. But he doesn't elaborate.

And I'm too fucking curious for my own good.

"So, what happened?"

The dude shrugs. "It's not my story to tell. But if you really want to know, she's a journalist at *Rock Scene Magazine* in L.A. now. You should go ask her." He reaches into the briefcase tucked against the wall of the plane at his feet and fishes out a business card.

I take the card, examining it curiously. *Max Marshall, Writer* is printed neatly over the magazine's logo, under which is an email address, phone number, and address downtown. It's a publication I've never heard of, but there are so many these days.

"Thanks," I murmur, still contemplating the little white rectangle. Wondering what turned Max Marshall off so much she went from my "biggest fan" to not one at all. Especially since she obviously hasn't lost her love of rock itself. The knowledge irks me more than I'd like to admit.

"Don't thank me yet," Morgan replies. I look up at the tone of his voice to find him smirking at me.

"Why not?" I ask warily.

Morgan tilts his head. "Because my sister brooks no bullshit. So don't ask if you don't want an honest answer. I mean, don't get me wrong, *I* think you guys are awesome. Max, on the other hand … anyway, just a fair warning."

I flip the card nervously as I think about his implication. She must really hate me. And I'm as annoyed by it as I am nervous. Sure, I fucked up, but that's in the past. I've paid my dues. The band's back and better than ever. So what's her damage? What can she possibly hold against me now?

I look back up at Morgan Marshall, who is now buried in his laptop screen with some serious "fuck off" vibes of his own going on. Obviously he's not in the mood for any further discussion on the topic. I'm so twisted up by the idea of Max Marshall and her story that I don't even try to fuck the hot flight attendant. Probably for the best since it's a short flight anyway.

I do try to chat up Morgan as we're waiting for the door to open, but he pointedly sticks to polite, superficial chatter. He's a software engineer who works in both the San Francisco Bay Area and Los Angeles, though he's based in L.A. He loves our new album and wants to know when the tour is. That's where I have to be vague and dodgy because it hasn't been announced yet. And after that we're disembarking, and I lose him as soon as I'm joined by my L.A. security and start pushing through the waiting crowd.

Probably best we didn't talk more about his sister. I want to hear it straight from the horse's mouth anyway. If there was ever a time to make sure every media outlet is on our side, right before announcing our comeback tour is it.

Guess it's time to pay a visit to *Rock Scene Magazine.*

2

Everybody Loves Me by OneRepublic

Max

"I'm sorry, can you repeat that?" I ask my assistant blankly.

"Kristoffer Westberg is here to see you," she whispers again, this time glancing over her shoulder.

"Did he say *why*?" I reply, looking into the main office area to make sure he didn't follow her from reception.

Rock stars like Kristoffer Westberg don't just drop by the office of a small, albeit well-established, industry magazine. Especially not specifically asking for a reporter who long ago stopped giving a shit about him and his band.

Alexsis screws her lips to the side and shakes her head. I refrain from getting on her case for not asking. But I can tell by the waves of nervous excitement coming off of her that the dark good looks and charisma that I'm all too familiar with have had their way with her tender, young heart. *Been there, sister.*

I rise with a sigh, putting my best polite face on. Alexsis fidgets nervously behind me as I step out from behind my high cubicle walls into the open-plan main office area.

And lo and behold, there he is, leaning casually against the wall next to the reception desk, somehow managing to look bored and above it all yet totally charming at the same time. The asshole.

He straightens up when he catches sight of us approaching, and my mind vaults back three years to the last time I saw him. Just as smoldering hot. Just as intimidating, even at only a couple inches over my five-foot-eight self. Same thick, dark eyebrows set over equally dark eyes. Same straight nose and defined jawline with just a bit of stubble. Same tight black T-shirt and dark-wash jeans. I guess when a look works for you, you stick with it. And I must admit — albeit begrudgingly —the look works for him at thirty-six just as much as it did at twenty-two. Possibly more.

What's different is that his dark eyes are much clearer this time as they rake over my Rolling Stones T-shirt and ripped black skinny jeans down to my black Doc Martens.

I stop in front of him and raise an eyebrow. "Mr. Westberg. What an unexpected surprise."

His eyes flick up to mine and his trademark too-cool-for-school grin slides onto his stupidly handsome face. And despite myself, more than a decade of being infatuated with this man can't be wiped away by a few years of disgust, as something deep in my chest twinges at his gaze. Christ.

"*You're* Max Marshall?" he asks with an incredulous note to his rough voice.

Both eyebrows rise to my hairline. "Expecting a man?" I taunt.

I take note of Alexsis slinking into the receptionist's chair and resting her chin on her hands to watch the show.

"Nope," he replies. "I met your brother on a flight last weekend." He holds up something I immediately recognize as my business card. "He said I should talk to you. But he didn't say you were…" He trails off, his eyes roaming intently over my body. "So young."

I fight back a scoff, knowing that is almost certainly *not* what he was thinking. And at thirty-one, I wouldn't exactly call myself young. Well, not compared to him at least.

"Yes, well, he also didn't bother mentioning to me that you were coming, so I apologize for the less-than-stellar welcome." I have to fight to keep the sarcasm and annoyance out of my voice both at my brother for sending this douche canoe my way knowing how I feel about him, and at West himself for living up to the creep he is in my head. "Is there something you wanted to discuss with me in particular, or is there something *Rock Scene* can do for the band? If the latter, I can have one of my colleagues —"

West shakes his head, his dark eyes glittering in a way that makes me more than a little uncomfortable. Like he knows a joke I'm not in on.

"No, I'm here for you. Is there someplace we can talk?"

That stupid traitor feeling in my chest twists again. Oh, how younger me would've once loved to hear those words come out of that mouth. I grind my teeth together in frustration as I mentally weigh how I want to deal with him.

"Yes, fine," I eventually say with exasperation. "Follow me."

I turn and catch Alexsis's expression of curiosity and shoot her a "don't even think about eavesdropping" look as I lead West through the office.

For good measure, I pass by my cubicle in favor of the conference room in the back corner. It almost never gets used, especially not at the end of a Friday afternoon.

He saunters by me into the small room, and when I turn back from closing the door, he's sprawled in the chair at the head of the six-person table. I take a seat pointedly on the other end.

With a grin, he leans forward on his elbows, his toned biceps flexing under the hem of his shirtsleeves. I look away, at the wall. Anywhere but at those arms.

"Morgan said you didn't like me. Clearly he wasn't exaggerating."

I drag my eyes back to him and lean forward on my elbows, giving him a challenging look. "My brother said that, did he?"

West's grin fades into a smirk. "Well, sort of. He said you 'used to be my biggest fan,'" he replies, using air quotes.

I can't help it; a wry laugh escapes me.

"Well, tell me how you really feel," he jokes with a smirk.

"Oh, you really don't want me to do that," I assure him.

He cocks an eyebrow.

"Maybe that's exactly what I want you to do."

I lift an eyebrow in return. "Maybe you should tell me what you wanted."

"This is what I wanted."

"You wanted to know why I'm not your biggest fan anymore?" I ask with undisguised incredulity.

West's chin dips in agreement, and I have to admit that I'm more than a little shocked.

"I'm not sure I'm comfortable having this discussion here." Read: *Are you trying to get me fired, asshole?* How can I sit in the office of the rock and roll magazine I've dedicated my career to and bad-mouth one of the biggest rock stars of my generation? As low as my brain-to-mouth filter usually is, even I know nothing good can come of it.

West's eyes capture mine and my palms start to sweat under the scrutiny, nerves seizing my whole body.

"Come on. Tell me why you don't like me anymore," he pleads with an affected pout.

I swallow hard against the lump in my throat. "Why does it matter?"

"It just does," he replies in a deceptively nonchalant tone.

But he wouldn't be asking if it didn't matter. A lot.

This is surreal.

I rub my lips together, deciding what answer won't jeopardize my job. But then I realize I don't owe Kristoffer Westberg a goddamn thing, including the truth. So I just stare at him for a minute, hoping he'll let it go.

After a few beats, he looks down, shaking his head, and says seemingly to himself, "She's lost that lovin' feelin'."

My eyes go wide as he stands and heads purposely toward me. And as he drops to one knee beside me, I realize exactly what he's about to do. He's about to go full *Top Gun* on my ass. Right here. Right now. Fuuuuuuckkkkk.

Just as he starts belting out *You've Lost That Lovin' Feelin'* by the Righteous Brothers, I lunge forward and slam my hand over his mouth before the whole office hears and comes running.

"Are you insane?!"

He grabs my hand and rises, pulling me with him all in one swift motion, and I abruptly notice the electric zap that crawls up my arm from where he's touching me and how *close* he is. How good he smells. Like cologne and cool night air and guitar strings. So much better than the last time we were this close, when he smelled like booze and weed and heartbreak. But smelling of it or not, West is a whole lot of heartbreak waiting to happen.

At the thought, I pull my hand back abruptly.

"Worked for Maverick," he says with a shrug, his eyes searching my face. "You really don't want to tell me what your deal is, do you?"

I lift my chin stubbornly in answer.

"Come on," he pleads winningly. "I'm all better now. Don't you want to jump back on the West train?"

I pull a face. "Don't you mean the Violent Mood Swings train?" And then I think silently to myself, *You know, your band, you self-centered ass hat?*

"Sure, yeah, that too," he agrees dismissively.

I sigh heavily. "Not for all the guitar picks in a Dunlop factory."

"Ouch, Maxi. Ouch."

I frown. "It's Max."

West grins. "Okay, Maxi. Whatever you say."

"You know, annoying the shit out of me isn't going to make me tell you," I snap at him. Even though I'm more mad that I actually find his bullshit kind of cute. His mischievous grin shows that dimple in his right cheek, and his behavior is a heady combination of endearing and playful. Dear god, help me. I take a step back, needing to distance myself in every way possible.

"Then forget why. I'm all better now. Don't you want to give me another chance?" he cajoles, leaning back against the wall and looking like a butt-hurt little kid.

"Yes, well, that's great, but just because you're magically all better doesn't change the way I feel. But really, good luck with the album and tour and stuff."

"Who said anything about a tour?" he asks slyly.

I narrow my eyes at him. "You guys aren't going to tour?"

"Yeah, of course we're going to tour. But nobody's said anything about one yet."

I throw my hands up. "Do you ever take anything seriously?"

"Absolutely. Music. Rosie. And why you're so mad at me."

I shake my head. "I can't believe you named your guitar after an AC/DC song," I grumble.

"How did you know that? I've never actually said that publicly," he says, squinting at me like he thinks I might be a stalker.

No need to tell him I flirted heavily with the line between groupie and just that once upon a time.

"It wasn't obvious?" I ask innocently, batting my eyelashes.

"Okay, fine. But don't think I don't know deflecting when I hear it. I'm the goddamn king of it, Maxi." He steps forward back into my space. "And maybe I need you back on board. Seriously." My brain goes numb for a minute as he stares down at me intently. And I *almost* forget everything he's done. Such is the magic of Kristoffer Westberg. "What's it going to take?"

I blink hard. "For me to forgive and forget?"

"Yes."

"You could try apologizing." I step back and frown. "But then, you owe that to a whole lot more people than me. More important people."

West's answering frown mimics my own. "Like who?"

He asks it like he's never even considered that he might need to apologize for the epic failure he was to his fans. Alcohol. Drugs. Arrests. More drugs. Breaking up the best goddamn band of my formative years. I'm the least of those he's hurt. And I know I'm not the only one who has no interest in his supposed reformation. In fact, judging by the album's weak sales, I'm in the majority.

All things I don't say. If he doesn't know, it's not my job to clue him in. And I don't think he'd listen anyway. He seems to think all should automatically be forgiven.

He continues to stare at me expectantly.

I take a deep breath. "Like your fans, for starters."

His expression darkens. "I went to rehab. Got the band back together. Put out a new album. That's not enough?"

I laugh ironically. Partly because he's just confirmed my exact thought about him. But mostly…

"What?" he asks in an uncharacteristically snappish tone, interrupting my train of thought.

"It's just funny. Because your comeback album is titled *Redemption*."

"So?"

I stare at him. He can't be serious. But I know he is. Poor, clueless fallen rock star.

"You don't get redemption without forgiveness. For which you need to both express regret *and* make up for it." I know I've lost him before he even replies.

"Meaning?"

"Meaning you think you've made it up to the fans, but you haven't expressed regret for the things you've done. Not publicly at least." His brows scrunch together, and I sigh knowing he just doesn't get it. "You need to apologize, West. And it needs to be big."

He scoffs. "And look like a pussy? I think my actions speak loudly enough. The album is doing just fine, after all. The fans are coming back."

I don't bother disagreeing with him.

"Then why are you here? You can't possibly expect everybody to love you. Why bother tracking down one silly little reporter who isn't a fan anymore?" I point out.

He steps back. "You know what? You're right. I don't know why I bothered coming here. All the people who matter are on my side. Have a nice life, Maxi."

He gives me a mocking salute. And then he leaves.

I'd laugh at his stubborn ass, but it's too sad. Because I know I'm going to be living rent-free in Kristoffer Westberg's self-absorbed brain as he struggles with the fact that not everybody loves him like he thinks they do. And as disappointed as I've been by him, I feel for the struggle he has coming. Because you can't fix something you don't think is broken.

3

Welcome to the Jungle by Guns N' Roses

West

"You're late, West."

"You're an asshole, Ward."

"Why don't you guys just fuck each other already?" Nik suggests.

I shoot her a comically lecherous look. "I think you mean, why don't I just fuck you already?"

I'm only half-joking. Nikka Jones, with her bright green hair, tiny mouthful titties, and tight ass, is definitely fuckable.

She snorts. "Even if I could stomach the thought of having a dick inside me, I'm pretty sure my girlfriend couldn't."

"Well, then you and Ward are both out of luck. Because if I haven't fucked him in the last eighteen years, I'm sure as hell not about to start now."

Ward smirks at me from across the rehearsal space and, all joking aside, I'm happy to let him bust my chops. Because Ward Pierce is the best, and oldest, friend I've got. We met and formed Violent Mood Swings when we were eighteen. Half our lives ago. But as good-looking as the dude is with his height, blond hair, and sweet tats, I just don't swing that way. Not even for one of the best lead singers of all time; seriously, dude's got a voice that has melted panties worldwide. Probably better for the band that I don't. We would've broken up even sooner and never gotten back together, given my relationship track record. And I use the term "relationship" loosely.

"All right, ladies," James, our only other remaining founding member, and the total dad of the group — seeing as how he's the only actual dad — chides us from behind the keyboards. "Can we rehearse or what? Some of us have families to get home to."

Michael holds up a drumstick in silent agreement. I snort. Because Michael lives with his parents. I can't give him shit for that though, even though he's twenty-eight, since he just came off a bad divorce.

"Yeah, yeah, whatever, bitches," I grumble, pulling Rosie out of her velvet-lined case. The vintage cherry Gibson SG Standard beauty was the first luxury I ever allowed myself once we hit it big all those years ago. And she's been my number one girl ever since. The only steady woman in my life. I tune up and watch Ward do his mic check.

Rehearsal goes fucking perfect, and even Ward, with his seemingly never-ending nit-picking is confident that we're ready to tour. But then, he should be: He wrote most of the songs and has made us rehearse more for this tour than all of our past ones combined.

He pulls me aside once James and Michael have headed out and Nik is packing up her bass.

"You were on today."

I finish locking my guitar case and look up at him. And if I couldn't tell by his tone of voice, the scrutinizing look pretty much says it all.

"Why don't you tell me what you really want to say?"

I plop down on the battered leather couch against the wall and pat the cushion next to me.

He sits down, folding a leg under him.

"You've been a little distracted lately. And you were late this morning."

"Still not a question," I point out with a tired smile.

"Don't bullshit me."

I roll my head toward him and look him in the eye.

"I can't stop thinking about that stupid fucking reporter."

"What does the reporter have to do with you being late?"

I grimace. "I couldn't sleep."

"Shit, dude, jerk off like the rest of us and get some shut-eye next time."

I roll my eyes at him. "I wasn't thinking about her like *that*." I shudder for effect. Trying to ignore the fact that she *is* objectively hot, with her long wavy brown hair, hazel eyes, cute button nose, pink bow lips, and tits and curves for days. But I still hate her. "It just gets me. Who the fuck is she to not forgive me? She obviously liked our music. Isn't the music what matters?"

"What's the Abraham Lincoln quote? You can please all of the people some of the time, some of the people all of the time —"

"Yeah, yeah, yeah. You can't please all of the people all of the time. I know. We've just worked so fucking hard, man. What if she's right? What if the fans don't show up like we think they will?"

Ward is one of the only people on the planet I'd admit my fears to. But even saying it out loud freaks me out on a level I'm not fully capable of dealing with. I went through hellfire to get here, and it can't be for nothing.

"I'm going to be honest with you, man." He scrubs a hand over the back of his neck. "I haven't paid attention to sales. Like at all. I'm not here for the fans. I'm here for the music. If the fans come back, great. If they don't, fine. We've come so far. You've come so far. I'm actually just really proud of our progress, and you should be too."

A sigh escapes me. Because I wish I were as confident as Ward. Deep down though, I'm just not. I need the validation. But like fuck I'm going to admit *that* out loud. Even to Ward. Just admitting it to myself just shows how much good all the damn head-shrinking I had in rehab did. But baby steps. Admitting it to myself is hard enough. Let's not go too crazy and start talking about this shit out loud like we're a couple of chicks or something.

"You know I'm all about the fans," I reply. "I'm just worried that we're doing all of this for nothing."

Ward waves a hand. "Do what you do best, man. Be happy with your effort, with how far you've come. That's what matters most," he reiterates.

"You're very zen today." I pull my head back and look at him. "You're not smoking weed again, are you?"

He laughs. "Hell no, dude. Los Angeles may be the same old jungle, but you're not the only one who's changed. I'm high on life. You should be too. We're getting paid to do what we love again. The rest will come in time, I promise."

I stomp my feet dramatically. "But I want it noooooooow." It's my best Veruca Salt impression — the Willy Wonka movie one, not the alternative rock band — whining and all.

It gets a laugh out of Ward, which is what I was going for.

"Well, to be fair we have been playing it kind of safe. Since Nik and Michael are new and all. But I know the fans are important to you." Ward considers me for a moment. "We could up the stakes. Get some more attention."

I sit up, suddenly very interested. "Like how?"

"You could sing that song you wrote."

My face falls. "You know I can't do that."

"And you know it would be a game changer. You're good. Plus it's something new. Something different."

I shake my head emphatically. "Not gonna happen."

"But West —"

"Drop it."

Ward grimaces. "Fine. Guess you'll just have to humble yourself to the fans then."

"Just because some reporter at some nothing magazine says I need to apologize —"

Ward holds up his hands in surrender. "Fine, okay. Forget I said anything."

"Oh, I wi—"

"Reporter?" A sharp voice cuts in from the door.

We glance up to find our stout band manager filling the doorway, fixing us with a stern look. Or maybe that's just his face. Burke McKinley is one of the best in the business for a reason: He's a no-nonsense hard-ass, but he also gets shit done for his acts.

"Shit," I exclaim. "Sorry, Burke, didn't know you were here."

"Clearly," he says curtly. "What's this about a reporter?"

I roll my eyes and groan, sinking deeper into the couch like the rebellious teenager who still very much lives in my brain.

Ward shakes his head at me. "Some chick who writes for a rag called *Rock Scene*. She used to be West's 'biggest fan'" — Ward uses a cutesy voice that makes me glare at him — "but apparently thinks he needs to formally apologize for his piss-poor behavior."

Burke's eyebrows jump so high they nearly hit his receding hairline. He steps inside and shuts the door, grabbing a black metal folding chair from the stack against the wall and setting it backward in front of the couch. He sits down, straddling it to face us.

"I know that magazine. Small but well-respected." He taps his chin thoughtfully. "You know, she may be on to something."

I give him a disbelieving look, but he holds up a hand.

"Hear me out. It's been a while since you've interacted with the fans directly, at least publicly. And if we're going to tour, it can't hurt to get all the good press we can. So how about an apology tour? You go around apologizing, kissing babies, holding puppies, that sort of shit?"

I lean forward on my arms to respond, but Ward beats me to the punch.

"He's a musician, not a politician. That's ridiculous."

Burke narrows his eyes at Ward. "You think they don't do that for good reason? Image, son. It's all about image."

"We're a *hard rock band*," I cut in. "Isn't that kind of the exact opposite of the image we're going for? I mean, rock stars bite the heads off bats and kill chickens on stage —"

"Dude, that last one wasn't the band, that was the audience," Ward points out.

I roll my eyes. "You get my point though. We're not all babies and puppies and 'I'm so sorry for succumbing to the rampant sex, drugs, and alcohol that pervade the industry.'"

"Kristoffer," Burke starts in his best dad voice, "if there's a reporter out there willing to say it to your face, there are a hundred who aren't. I think it's the conservative approach to take this seriously."

Ward and I exchange unimpressed looks. I turn back to Burke.

"If I took everything reporters have said about me seriously, I would've offed myself by now," I reply. "But look. I get what you're saying. Image. Press opportunities. We can do that. How about 'Win a Date With West?' Or something like that. Something the fans really *want.*"

Ward groans and rolls his eyes so hard I whack him on the back of the head.

"Come on, man," he laughs. "You have to admit that was a pretty douchey suggestion."

"And backwards," Burke adds. "You have to create desire before you fulfill it."

"Fine. What do you propose, then?" Ward counters.

"I'm hearing you," Burke assures us. "No babies. No puppies. But I think this apology idea could work. It plays on people's sympathies." He glances at me. "And you can be charismatic when you want to. Work that to your advantage. Make *sure* the fans are back on board ahead of the tour announcement. It can't hurt album sales either, and we've got to start hyping any way we can ahead of the tour."

I purse my lips, trying not to give in just because he's using his best attempt at flattery. I do love some good flattery.

"Would it really be that bad?" Ward asks me directly.

I shoot an annoyed sidelong glance at him. "Not for you," I point out.

"One way or the other, I'm talking to PR about this. So what's it gonna take to get you on board, kid?" Burke asks flatly.

I throw up my hands. Burke is like a dog with a bone when he latches onto something. Goddamn Maxi Marshall and her stupid grudge.

Maxi Marshall. That's it.

"I want the reporter who suggested the idea to be there the whole time."

I ask knowing she'll never agree to it. There's my out.

Burke looks impressed. "That's fucking brilliant. I love it." I didn't mean it to be brilliant, but hey, two birds, one stone. "I'll get with Ford and we'll make it happen." He rises. "Oh, and I heard you guys practicing from my office. Sounding good. We're going to nail this tour, guys, you'll see."

He absently waves over his shoulder as he leaves, and I'm still silently absorbing what the fuck just happened. After a couple of minutes of silence, I look over at Ward.

"What the hell did I just sign up for?" I lament.

Ward snorts. "A public flogging led by a reporter who hates you?"

I groan and slump backward into the cushions.

"I'm so fucked."

Ward laughs and sinks next to me, patting me on the leg.

"Yes. Yes, you are. And not in the good way, either."

4

Don't Make Me Do It by Huey Lewis and the News

Max

"No."

"No?"

"I'm sorry, did I stutter? N. O. No."

"I'm sorry, did you forget that I'm your boss?"

I glare across the messy blue metal desk at Jason. "Did you forget how much I hate Kristoffer Westberg?"

"Can't you just get over it? At least enough to do this project?" he presses.

I smush my lips together. I haven't told him about West's visit. I didn't think he needed to know. But now …

"I … there's something you should know." Jason looks at me expectantly. "He came here last week." I give him the quick rundown on why he came and what was said. The highlights, anyway.

"Shit." Jason leans back in his chair.

"Yeah."

His dark eyes flick back up to meet mine. "I still need you to do this."

"Even though he's basically stalking me now?" I retort hotly.

He glances nervously at his office door. "You know they're going to be here any minute. I already told his manager you'd do it."

My jaw drops. "You did *not*," I gasp.

Jason levels a look at me. "I did. Because I'm. Your. Boss. This is *huge*, Max. Just what we need to raise our profile and attract new readers. We couldn't say no."

"But why meeeeeee?" I whine.

Jason runs a hand through his inky hair, his eyes soft and apologetic.

"The deal was contingent on your involvement." I start to protest but he holds up a hand "Don't worry. They are hiring you for a professional project, as a representative of *Rock Scene*. I'll make sure everything is on the up and up. You're not going to be stalked by a rock star on my watch." He smirks playfully.

I fold my arms over my chest and try my hardest not to pout. "Yeah, we'll see about that. So exactly what kind of professional project are we talking here?"

"We'll find out in —" he checks his watch. "Well, anytime now. They're late."

Figures. I groan and let my head slump down onto the close edge of his desk. I take a deep breath and sit back up. Then I take a moment to mentally put my big girl panties on.

"I'll hear what they have to say. That's all I can promise right now." Wow, that even sounded convincing to me.

Jason's relief is obvious. "Good. Let's go get set up then."

He rises and opens the door, gesturing for me to precede him out with an encouraging look. I roll my eyes and walk, huffing all the way down the hall to the conference room. Pointedly *not* stopping at my cubicle for something to take notes with. I know I'm being childish, but I find myself unable to stop.

Jason says nothing about my lack of preparedness, but before we can make it to the room, Ashley, our receptionist, intercepts us.

"They're here," she whispers to Jason like West and his posse are going to hear us all the way across the building. I refrain from rolling my eyes at the reverent wonder in her voice. I've already rolled them about a thousand times in the last ten minutes. Wouldn't want them to pop out. Jason, on the other hand, responds by following her back to her desk.

I head into the conference room to give myself another minute to prepare. I choose the same seat as last time, at the foot of the table. I've barely begun to contemplate all the ways this could go wrong when I hear multiple voices, including Jason's, approaching.

My insides tumble as four men file into the room. Jason, West, Burke McKinley — a broad, short man with little hair and lots of presence whom I've never met but would have to live under a rock not to recognize — and a fourth guy who looks way too young to be invited to this party.

I rise from my chair and slap on the least-fake smile I can muster.

Until my eyes connect with West's as Jason and the other two men talk. He winks at me nonchalantly, and my smile melts into surprise as a jolt runs through my body like he just threw a live wire at me. He holds my gaze until I hear Jason introducing me.

"And this is my best and brightest, Max Marshall," Jason says, gesturing toward me as he steps around West to allow everyone comfortably into the room.

I catch a small smirk on West's lips as I force myself to look away.

"Gentlemen," I greet them.

The younger one who I don't know steps forward and offers a hand. Up close he looks not a day over twenty-five, is around West's height, and has light brown hair and blue eyes. He's not bad looking.

"Ms. Marshall, I'm Ford Nelson, West's public relations manager," he greets me importantly.

I watch West roll his eyes as he slumps into the chair behind Ford. My eyes flick back to Ford, mentally banking the fact that West clearly does not like Ford. Suddenly I find Mr. Nelson quite intriguing.

"A pleasure," I reply sweetly. My eyes move to Burke McKinley, who is settling into the chair across the table from West. "And Mr. McKinley, it's an honor to meet you."

"Call me Burke," he responds gruffly, sliding a piece of paper each to Jason, at the head of the table, and me. "And sign these while you're at it."

I glance down at the page. It's a nondisclosure agreement. My eyes flick up to Mr. McKinley's — Burke's — but it's Ford who pipes up.

"Standard NDAs. The lawyers won't even let us talk until you sign, I'm afraid."

Jason signs without hesitation. I, however, actually read it. Thankfully, it's not long. And Ford wasn't lying, it is all pretty standard. No disclosing anything we're not permitted to for the rest of our lives or they take everything we own and make us pariahs in the industry, blah blah blah. The usual. The ink hasn't even dried on my signature when Burke reaches out and whisks it away.

"So," he puffs. "It's actually thanks to your idea, Ms. Marshall, that we're here today."

I cock an eyebrow. "It's Max. And I'm sorry, did you say *my* idea?"

West is tracing circles on the table with a finger, but I don't miss the small smile at my question.

"I did," Burke affirms. "You suggested it would be prudent for West to apologize publicly. And that's exactly what we plan to do. A series of apologies, actually. An apology tour, as it were."

Whatever I was expecting to hear, it sure as shit wasn't that. They're turning his repentance into a fucking PR opportunity. Awesome. I don't know how they think this will work, but real remorse can't be choreographed.

"I'm still not quite sure I understand," I admit. "A tour? Like he's going to go to cities around the world and apologize to the fans? Like, that's it? And I, what, document it all?"

"We were thinking something more focused. Pre-chosen people or groups of people. We haven't nailed that part down yet, but the vision is to format it something like a reality TV program."

"We don't do extended video pieces. A few minutes here or there for interviews, but we're no production company," Jason interjects.

"We have a production company in mind for that part. What we need is someone to host, after a fashion," Burke explains. "Someone to go with West on a series of prearranged visits, to ask him questions before and after, then to document it in a multipage spread and online article that will go live at the same time as the finished video piece." He holds his hands up like he's writing a billboard. "West's Road to Redemption."

A snort escapes before I can stop it.

West sighs and looks up at the ceiling.

Ford raises a brow. "You don't like it?"

I press my lips together and shrug. "I just … I don't think I'm your girl."

"You're our girl because West says you are," Burke says flatly. "You're a reporter, aren't you? That's all this is. Reporting on a tour."

I shouldn't be surprised in the least that it was West particularly who brought me into this. Payback for not bowing and scraping, I suppose. And I don't bother correcting him that I'm not a reporter, I'm a journalist. I doubt he cares about the difference, even if I do.

I lean forward, knitting my fingers together as I choose my words. Finally, I look up, between Burke and Ford. "I presume you want everything done in a light favorable to West. Which is why I'm telling you: I'm not your girl."

A sly smile unfurls on Ford's face. "Ah, but that's the catch. We want honesty. Well, to a point. On the tour especially, we *want* someone who will ask the difficult, real questions. We're looking for raw moments that will capture the fans. Mind, they'll be edited later to ensure the desired effect, of course. And the article … well, maybe a little softer there, but no less honest. Though not *un*favorable. The idea is to show enough of the man he is in the fans' eyes trying to become the man they want him to be. And by the end, we really want to get the fans feeling that he's changed. Do you think you can work within those terms?"

Do I think I can contribute to deceiving fans into thinking any of the bullshit they orchestrate is reality? That West has really changed when I'm not convinced he has? My eyes land on West, who has returned to messing with the table. But like he feels my gaze, his eyes snap up to meet mine.

"I can't control what you edit to make things appear the way you want, but I also can't participate in something that's all for show," I say to Ford while keeping my eyes on West. Then I tip my head to West. "Are you going to really do this?"

West tilts his head to the side and his brows pinch together.

"Why else would I be here?" His first words since he showed up.

Despite their surface meaning, his words don't sit right with me. I give him a long, hard look and he smirks back at me. It just underscores my sense that West still has a long way to go before he's ready to earn that redemption he thinks he's entitled to.

"I'm not sure that I can," I admit, tearing my gaze from West to meet Ford's eyes. The disapproval there is obvious.

I glance over at Jason, who has been suspiciously quiet this whole time. All he does is shrug. Great. Guess I'm on my own.

"Let's reframe," Ford offers. "The current plan is to announce the album tour at the end of next month. How successful do you think ticket sales will be, Max?"

I give him a funny look. "What the hell do I know about ticket sales?"

"I think you know what I'm really asking," Ford insists.

I purse my lips. Ah. Yes. Yes, I guess I do know what he's really asking. The same thing West was asking the first time he showed up here.

With a heavy sigh, I decide not to shy away from the truth this time. "I'd noticed album sales were weak, and I wasn't surprised. Not because the album isn't good. It is, actually. But because, like me, I think a lot of people aren't willing to overlook the past. West burned a lot of fans with his actions. The cancelled concerts. Showing up so stoned off his ass he could barely play. The end was rough enough, even without the little public incident that landed him in rehab and broke up the band. He pretty much obliterated their trust. And if he doesn't earn it back, I wouldn't be surprised if the tour bombs even harder than the album."

I keep my eyes on Ford, who is nodding like he knew I was going to say exactly what I did. But I don't look at West. I can't. As much as I'm disappointed in him for what he's done, I still don't want to hurt him. Because I've been on the other end of that hurt, and it sucks.

"And there's the real issue at hand," Ford says firmly. "Critic reviews have been just okay. The fan response hasn't been a fraction of what was expected. The album is not proving out, on social media in particular, which, as you know, is everything these days. We couldn't figure out exactly why, much less come up with a solution until you provided one."

"Why didn't you tell me?" West's angry words are directed at Burke.

"Sorry, kid, I didn't know how. I knew what it would mean to you."

West's eyes flick between Jason and me. "Can we have a moment, please?"

Jason practically shoots out of his chair, and I realize just how superfluous he must have been feeling during this discussion. "Yes, of course. Max?" He tilts his head toward the door.

I nod and rise, leaving before I can give in to the urge to mouth to West, "I'm sorry." Because despite my own feelings toward him, I am. I never wanted to be the one to deliver such a harsh truth. Thanks to me, West has just been clued in to exactly how broken his life still is.

5

Hooker With a Penis by Tool

West

"So, anything else you've been hiding from me that I should know about?" It comes out with heaps of sarcastic anger, and I'm okay with that.

This is bullshit. How can the album possibly be doing so badly without me knowing? Except, I should've known. At the very least when Max tried to tell me. It annoys me almost more than I can stand that she was right.

Ford, the pretentious little fucker, glances nervously at Burke.

"We weren't trying to hide it, exactly," Burke grumbles. "You just had enough on your plate. But now you know. And now you also know why it's so important that we do this little apology project."

"Since when did the social media response to music become more important than what's actually good?" I muse out loud. Neither of them answers, not that I expected them to. "Whatever, man. I'm not happy about it, but I can't think of a better answer on the fly. Can't we regroup and go a different direction?"

I hate feeling trapped. And right now I feel like a baby bear in a cave that's just been woken by a hunter looking for a nice new throw rug. I'm not sure who's the hunter in this situation, Ford or Max. Regardless, Max may end up being the one to skin me alive publicly.

"Why not this?" Burke insists.

"Haven't we had this discussion?" I say with a sigh. "It's pandering, man. And so not rock and roll."

Ford fixes me with a disdainful look. "Worried about selling out?"

Now that makes me laugh. "Son, I sold out when you were about four years old. You can't not in this industry. But I'm also not about to do something that's contrary to the image we've worked hard to create."

"Even if that image isn't working for you anymore?" Ford asks pointedly.

I glare at him. I'm never so sullen as I am around Ford. Dude's a dick, and it's all I can do not to punch him in his shiny face.

But unfortunately, the dick has a point. I guess that's his job, after all: maintaining our image. But I still don't get when and why social media became such a big deal. I bet it pisses Ford off too, come to think of it, not being able to completely control the message. Being subject to the ever-changing whims of the masses.

Welcome to my world, fucker. Once upon a time it was cool to be the troubled rock star. But when the consequences of living up to expectations go bad, they all turn on you in a flash, leaving you to pick up the pieces of your shattered life. I shake my head, pushing the bitter thoughts back into the shadows.

"So, what happens if I say I'm fine with things the way they are? That I don't want to play along with this game of Humiliate West?" I challenge.

"First," Ford replies arrogantly, "making you look human is not humiliating you. Only you can humiliate yourself if you continue to behave like a spoiled, entitled brat. Second, if you don't heed our recommendations, I'm afraid Nelson Public Relations will be unable to continue working in an advisory capacity to the band."

I fight back a snort at his pompous declaration, wondering if he passed that little change of strategy by his daddy before deciding on a course that could fuck over the family business.

"And I didn't want to have to play this card, but if you don't give the sponsors something to placate them ahead of the tour, your label is threatening to drop you too," Burke pipes up.

The label is ready to bolt? My head swings between them both. You've got to be fucking kidding me. Didn't I *just* ask if there was anything else they'd been keeping from me? I'm so pissed off I can practically feel the veins popping in my forehead.

But exploding will get me nowhere. I knew I was on thin ice. I guess I just didn't see the cracks had already started to form. And even I'm not stupid enough to keep pushing my limits.

"Fine. Get them back in here and let's get this over with."

With a smug grin, Ford rises and pops open the door just in time to hear Max's boss say, "We're not going to be the magazine that said no to Kristoffer Westberg. It would bury us."

"Sorry to interrupt," Ford says, not sounding sorry at all. "But we're ready for you." And with that he heads back to his seat, leaving the door open.

Max's boss comes back in, looking sheepish. Max follows looking downright pissed off. For some reason that pleases me.

"So, are we a go?" Jason asks, steepling his fingers under his chin.

"Absolutely," Ford insists. "The tour announcement is only six weeks away, so we need to get moving on this like yesterday."

"*Six weeks?*" Max blurts out. "That's insanity."

Jason gives her a sharp look.

"It's what we've got," Burke replies gruffly. "If that doesn't work for you we can go somewhere else —"

"No," Jason interrupts. "We'll make it work." He shoots another look at Max. "If Alexsis assists, that shouldn't be a problem, right, Max?" The tense undertone of "don't you dare fucking disagree with me in front of them" almost makes me laugh. I'm an asshole, but there it is.

Max takes a noticeable breath in through her nose, then responds tightly, "Of course. We'll make it work."

I fight a smile as I watch her, waiting for the obvious tension coiling her body to explode all over every damn one of us. And even with all the heavyweights in the room, I'm willing to bet Maxi Marshall's wrath is something to behold.

"Good," Ford all but purrs. "Now, Ms. Marshall. Since you were the one who came up with the idea, tell me: Who should West apologize to?"

Max gives him a bewildered look. "Aside from the fans, that's on West. How am I supposed to know everyone he's pissed off?"

"You know, that's a good point," Ford responds cryptically. "I think the fans may be the least of our agenda, actually. If we made this more personal, the fans would come just for the spectacle. And in a way, he'd be humbling himself to them *and* the people that they never even knew mattered to him."

Suddenly my humor at Max's discomfort evaporates and I shoot daggers toward Ford. Because I know exactly where he's going with this.

"We're not bringing my family into this," I interject tightly.

Ford turns toward me with a wolfish grin. "Is that who matters to you? Because if so, that's exactly what we need to do. I know humbling yourself isn't in your repertoire, West, but like it or not, that's exactly what you're going to do. And apologizing to your family, your friends, or whoever you actually *care* about … well, that's so much more impactful. Don't you think?"

I cross my arms over my chest and sink back into my chair, unwilling to rise to his bait. But that doesn't stop him.

"If you really care about the tour, the *fans*, I think that's exactly what needs to happen," he concludes, exuding smug-bastard vibes like it's going out of style.

Still, I keep my mouth shut, shaking my head slowly.

Burke's phone starts vibrating on the table. He silences it and looks up at me. "I have to get back to the office. You stay here and work with Ms. Marshall on the list. We'll get the contracts in place ASAP and start moving. Got that?"

He doesn't even wait for an answer, rising and shaking Jason's hand, doling out pleasantries before he leaves, dragging Ford with him.

"Well," Jason says awkwardly. "I guess I'll just leave you two to get on the same page."

Max looks pleadingly at Jason, but much to my amusement, he avoids her gaze and ducks out, closing the door behind him.

And she looks so perturbed, I can't help poking her just a little. "Well, Maxi. Here we are again. Alone at last."

6

———————

Under Pressure by Queen & David Bowie

Max

The temptation to leave is strong. Anything not to have to look at West's stupid smirking face.

"Are you really going to make me do this?" I blurt out.

A wicked smile curls West's lips and he leans forward, getting dangerously close. "Seems like your boss is the one making you, based on the bit of hallway conversation we caught earlier."

"He's only making me because you asked. So un-ask," I push.

"Now, why would I do that? We have so much fun together, don't we, Maxi? Don't you wanna be my friend and help me out?" I don't answer, which makes him chuckle. "I'm a little disappointed, honestly. I'd counted on you getting us both out of this. But don't worry, if I have my way, neither of us will have to do this."

He's disappointed in *me*? Well, that's rich.

"Yeah, and exactly how do you plan to do that?" I snap.

323

"There's always another option, Maxi. Always."

My hackles rise, but I refrain from telling him to stop calling me "Maxi" because I'm pretty sure the more I do, the more he calls me that just to get a reaction.

"Another option? There isn't another option, West."

"Sure there is. Matter of fact I suggested one, but Burke wasn't having it."

"Well, it was probably some asinine self-serving suggestion like 'Party with West,'" I joke.

"It was 'Win a Date With West' actually," he corrects me.

There's no stopping the tide of uproarious laughter that bursts out of me. What. An. Arrogant. Bastard.

"It's not *that* funny," he grumbles, the butt-hurt-kid look back.

I wipe the tears of laughter from my eyes. "Oh, but it is. Really, though, I hate to be the only one to tell you the truth — again — but their solution is perfect. You're not going to convince them out of it."

"Perfect? How's that?"

I take a deep breath to calm the last remnants of laughter out of my system. So out of touch, this one. "Because this is going to be massively uncomfortable for you. And it's going to be a spectacle. People are going to gobble it up. Love you or hate you, *everyone* is going to want to watch a huge former rock star debase himself and, in all likelihood, get yelled at by a bunch of people who say all the things everyone's thinking. And then they get to watch you react to it. It's viral gold."

"*Former* rock star?" he asks acerbically.

I snort. "That's what you got from what I just said? Figures." I shake my head. "Look. You may as well just accept that this is going to happen." As soon as I say it, I realize that applies to me too. Fuck.

West smirks at me like he knows exactly what I'm thinking. And exactly how fucked I am by this too.

"Guess we're in for a ride, then."

"Yeah, well, we'll see about that," I grumble. Maybe I can convince

Alexsis to step into a bigger role on this. Wouldn't be a hard sell, especially if it means more time with West.

"Oh, if I have to do this, you have to do this."

I purse my lips at him, considering that. "Are you at least going to apologize honestly?"

"I don't know, depends on who I have to apologize to."

"Right. So, the bare minimum."

"That about sums it up."

"This. This is why you've disappointed so many people," I say with exasperation.

"Now you sound like my old man, which isn't surprising, since I like him about as much as I like you." He pauses. "Okay, that might not be fair considering how much I loathe him."

I resist rolling my eyes at his declaration of dislike for me. I also resist saying it's very much mutual. Instead, I focus on what we have to do.

"Sounds like he might be a good place to start, then," I reply.

West's brows jump. "Oh no. Not gonna happen."

I raise an eyebrow in return. "You still think you can get out of this, don't you?" He doesn't respond, just smirks at me. The bastard. I rise, already so over arguing with him. "All right, I can see we aren't going to get anywhere with the list today. But you might want to start seriously considering stepping up for once in your life. Because if you don't … well, it's sure as hell going to hurt you more than it hurts me."

His face pulls together in confusion. Knowing I'm getting nowhere, I turn to leave.

"What if I told you going through this might be worse?"

I turn back and he's risen and is now standing just a couple of feet away.

"For you," I point out, returning one of his many smirks.

"I guess you're used to train wrecks," he replies, staring at me intently and radiating some seriously tormented vibes. "But I'm pretty over them at this point, Maxi. I want to get off this ride. I'm done being the bad guy."

My heart twinges in my chest at the reminder that he's just human. Not an untouchable rock star. He's a man. One who made some very bad choices and has suffered for them. Who doesn't realize or won't accept that he can't simply stop suffering for them whenever he chooses.

"Then start being the good guy," I reply.

The angst on his face is too much. I turn and walk out the door, leaving West alone with his demons.

7

Crucify by Tori Amos

West

"Stop, stop, stop!" Ward cries over the music, popping the mic back onto its stand. He whirls on me as the music dies off. "West, man, what the fuck?"

I jut my chin out, glaring at him. I know I'm fucking it up. But I also don't know how to not bite his head off right now.

He continues to stare at me expectantly. "Out with it. Your chords are harsh and out of tune. Which means you're in danger of snapping a string, or possibly even your beloved Rosie's beautiful little neck. If you need to burn off some anger, don't take it out on her, man."

I blow out a breath and slip the black leather strap over my head, gently seating Rosie on her stand.

I open my mouth. Then shake my head and close it. I prop my hands on my hips, digging deep to find a way to not be a whiny, aggressive little bitch.

"Reporter?" Michael asks from behind his set while twirling a drumstick.

I huff a laugh. "Not this time." I pause, my annoyance at Maxi Marshall simmering too close to the surface, even if she's not my biggest problem right now. But really, why does she have to be so irritating? I bet a good fuck would do her wonders … by someone other than me. Of course. I think. God, what's wrong with me? "Well, not exactly, anyway." I heave a sigh. Fine. Here goes. "I've been trying to come up with something to give the label and the sponsors that doesn't require heaping doses of public humiliation."

"Good luck with that," Nik says with a snort. "Ford told us what they want you to do. The public's going to lap that shit up, man. It'll be over in a few weeks. Just go with it."

My eyes meet hers, and I remember that she's the youngest of us all at twenty-six. And she's all over social media. If anyone in this room knows what they really want, it's her.

"Okay, fine. Maybe I get it, in theory. It's like a car wreck. You can't not look. But is that really going to translate to sales?" I ask. "I'm not convinced."

"Well, look at it this way," Michael says with a note of irritation in his voice. "If you *don't* do it, we're done. And some of us didn't have a huge rock career back in the day. For some of us this is our shot. You really gonna fuck that up for us?"

Nik shoots him a nervous glance. "Come on, man, give West a break. This is heavy shit. Would you wanna do it?"

"In a goddamn heartbeat," he replies without hesitation. "No apology tour, no shot. Even if it doesn't boost ticket sales, without it there are *no* ticket sales. It's a no-brainer." He's looking at and responding to Nik, but I'm hyperaware that every syllable is directed at me, and I can't help the rage it brings to the surface.

"That's easy to say when it's not you that's going to be served up as the media sacrifice of the summer in the name of entertaining the masses. I signed up to make music, not be a scapegoat for society's frustrations with famous people."

"How about just their frustrations with you, then?" James asks quietly. He looks up, his kind brown eyes meeting mine, and I can see the ache in them before he even continues. "Because that's the crux here, dude. It's time to stop being selfish. So you've got to decide, what's more important: your ego or the band?"

Pain lances through my heart. Is it really selfish not to want to be forced into this? Is this whole band against me? I look to Ward, who can barely meet my eyes.

He gives a half-hearted shrug. "I know it's difficult, but you have everything to lose if you don't do this, West. Stop wasting time trying to find a way out of it. There isn't. Their minds are made up. Own it and you have a shot at everything you want. Keep fighting it and, well, we're all going to lose."

I blink hard at the sting in my eyes, anger bubbling up from inside of me.

"I'd fight for you guys if you were in my shoes," I snap. "But sure. It's not like I haven't worked my ass off to get here. I'll just keep carrying everyone's burdens."

"Don't be such a fucking martyr," Michael snaps. "It's not like you didn't make this problem."

I clench my jaw so hard to keep from punching him in his stupid ginger face that I can hear my teeth straining under the pressure. The thought of cracking a tooth pisses me off even more. Wouldn't that just be the shit icing on this turd cake?

"Over the line," Ward barks at him. "If you're lucky enough to get a taste of success you may understand someday how easy it is to fall into the sex-drugs-and-rock-and-roll trap."

"And what it costs you to climb back out," James agrees. "We're here for you, West. But it would seem you're not done climbing yet."

The threat of tears gets even more real, so I roughly grab Rosie and turn, done with this fucking conversation.

"Whatever. I'm out of here."

Because I can't stay. I can't break down here. I can't process this in front of these guys. Not even Ward.

I have a sudden need to self-medicate that is stronger than it has been since I started rehab. I need to get out of here. Now. I need to be alone so I can wrestle with the demons inside me.

THE OCEAN IS A PRETTY GOOD SUBSTITUTE FOR BOOZE, AS IT TURNS OUT. Its calming, endless undulation soothes the mind, body, and soul. Even though the sun has long since set over the horizon and the evening has cooled to the point that I have goose bumps, here I sit, on my balcony overlooking the Pacific Ocean, with Rosie in my lap, absentmindedly strumming. Having made no real progress. Or anything even resembling a decision.

That's what they all want me to do. Decide. Only, there's really no decision to be made. Or is there?

The strumming turns into a melody and I hum along. Never quite singing. He beat that out of me a long time ago.

"You're going to make my ears bleed with that god-awful voice of yours!"

"What are you, killing a cat in there?"

"Shut up, kid, you couldn't carry a note in a bucket!"

I stop humming, heat creeping up my neck. Anger? Embarrassment? Who knows. But I keep strumming, the music a balm for every horrible thing he ever said or did to me to take my joy away. But there are some things that can't be taken from you, and love is one of them.

It's only been my love of music, of making something beautiful come out of the old, beat-up acoustic I'd inherited from a guy who was too embarrassed by it to take it to college with him, that pulled me through the abuse that was hurled at me.

He never criticized my playing, funnily enough, which is why I knew: I was good. I am good. But he had to direct his attentions somewhere, and Erik, my older brother, was a pro at making himself scarce. So it all landed on me. Better me than Annika, my younger sister. She had enough to carry. She was, after all, the one who killed mom. At least, according to my asshole father. Personally, I don't think dying in childbirth constitutes homicide, but then, I'm a good-for-nothing piece of shit — his words — so what do I know?

But twenty years and not enough miles later, he still can't take this from me.

It's that thought that breaks me. I'm taking this from myself if I can't swallow my pride. If I can't give them what they want by making it through a few stupid apologies.

My fingers scrape the strings, and I pull back when I feel the moisture. Shit. I'm crying all over my fucking guitar. I use my T-shirt to wipe Rosie off before lovingly setting her down next to me.

I furiously wipe the tears away, unwilling to surrender my composure to memories of the man who once broke me when I was just a boy. But now I'm the man, and if I do nothing else with my life, I need to be a better one than him.

"Then start being the good guy."

Maxi's words ring through my ears. As usual, she's right. And she's wrong. Because it's just not that simple. It's not like I haven't tried to be. But apparently doing it my way hasn't been enough. So I guess it's time to do it their way.

8

The Hand That Feeds by Nine Inch Nails

Max

A few days later, I find myself back in the conference room discussing the apology tour project with Alexsis while we wait for West and the production company guy to show.

"So, like, what's your deal with West?" Alexsis asks, veering abruptly off the topic of who will research what.

"We don't have a deal," I reply defensively.

She tilts an eyebrow. "You *so* have a deal."

I shrug. "I was just a fan of the band for a long time, and then he broke them up. Kinda pissed me off and I don't pay attention to them anymore. End of story."

"Cute. But I meant now, not then."

"I don't know what you're talking about."

"I'm talking about the sexual tension I could practically smell across the office both times he was here."

I wrinkle my nose in disgust. "Then sexual tension must smell a lot like hostility because there's a lot of that going in both directions," I reply firmly.

"Oh please," Alexsis scoffs. "It's schoolyard basics. Boys only tease you when they like you."

I look her straight in the eye. "That's bullshit. Boys tease you to get a reaction out of you so they can fulfill their own need to feel in control. West is angry because I'm a female who doesn't want to jump his bones. So he teases me to feel like he has some control over me. Same reason he wants me to do this whole 'apology tour' crap."

"Well, that's an interesting theory," comes a voice from the door.

I look up to find West smirking at us.

For a moment, I'm tempted to be embarrassed. But you know what? Fuck that.

"Ah. There you are. Perfect timing," I say sweetly, with the most saccharine smile I can muster.

"Perfect to join in the West bashing? Because that's the party I'm here for," he says, sauntering in and plopping down at the head of the table.

I'm taken aback by his response, but before I can reply, Jason, Ford, and a third man with sandy hair and round glasses enter the room.

"All right," Ford begins, taking a seat next to Alexsis. "West. What's our lineup?"

Jason sits next to me, while the stranger settles at the end of the table.

"Oh, this is Carter Lonnergan, head of the production team for this project," Ford adds as an afterthought. "Carter, this is Max Marshall and …" Ford turns, realizing for the first time that Alexsis is next to him. And clearly he likes what he sees. He's checking her out so hard that Alexsis blushes as we all watch.

"This is Alexsis Monaghan," I offer.

"Alexsis," Ford says. "So nice to meet you."

Alexsis smiles demurely, and I can't tell if she's into him or not.

"So, the lineup?" West prompts Ford.

"Yes, of course. The lineup. What have you got?" Ford responds.

West leans back in his chair, his gaze shifting to Carter. "How many stops do I get?"

Carter shrugs. "Depends on where they are."

"Mostly around L.A.," he responds. "One in San Francisco."

"That's not much travel, so probably as many as you've got," Carter replies. "We've got a few weeks to shoot, then we'll need a few weeks in post."

West nods. "Okay, here's what I'm thinking." He leans forward and raises a fist, putting up a thumb. "The band. I don't know if you want that as a group or individually."

"Hmmm. Let me think about that. Keep going," Carter says.

West throws up a finger. "My older brother. He's out in Corona."

"Why your older brother?" Ford asks, finally fully engaged.

West shoots him a wary look. "We haven't spoken in fifteen years. He was the first to walk away when he found out I was using."

Ford nods his approval, so West throws up another finger and sighs. "Sadie Sullivan. The groupie who introduced me to cocaine. We were together when the band went down."

Carter lets out a low whistle. "Well, that ought to make for good TV."

West ignores him, throwing up another finger. "My little sister. She's in San Francisco," he says to Carter.

"And why her?"

West inhales slowly, clearly reluctant to answer. "I introduced her to a guy. She followed him there. It wasn't a good thing."

My throat tightens as I read between the lines, but I make a mental note to ask him about it privately. Nobody else says a word, so West continues, throwing up the last finger on that hand.

"My dad." The last word comes out broken and hoarse. West clears his throat. "Also in Corona."

"We could do the dad and the brother at the same time," Carter offers in Ford's direction.

West shakes his head. "You can't. Take my word for it."

Carter's eyes widen a fraction. "All right. That all?"

"The fans. But …"

"What?" I prompt, my curiosity forming the word before I can stop myself.

"I think we should do something more than a meet and greet."

"What are you thinking?" Ford ask, clearly also curious.

"I'm thinking a small private concert," West explains quietly. "We let the fans know what it's for and have them submit something on why they should be chosen. One of you can decide how that all goes down. But at least it would help us find the ones who need that reconciliation the most."

The room is dead silent when he's finished. Finally, Ford speaks up.

"I'm impressed. That's a fantastic idea, West."

I would never say it out loud, but I actually agree. And for the first time, I feel like maybe this whole thing has a chance.

"Thanks," West replies, lifting a finger and beginning to trace circles into the tabletop.

"That's all a great jumping off point," Ford continues. "Our team has also discussed and agreed that there needs to be strong social media involvement throughout. TikToks of before each apology appeal. Reaction Instagram Reels of after — without spoilers, of course. Both are to give tidbits without giving too much away. We're also planning an airing party where the official tour is announced. It'll be aired on IGTV, Facebook, and YouTube." He pauses, tapping his fingers on the table. "Given your idea, I think maybe we should hold the private concert after the apologies so we can include it in the airing. Though we could also livestream the event itself on Facebook for full exposure and impact."

"That sounds like a lot," West says apprehensively.

"And that doesn't include the magazine," I pipe up. West gives me a look that's almost desperate. "But I'll have Alexsis push all that material we'll already be doing to our website. I may just need additional time around each visit to ask questions that are for the article."

"Great. It's settled then. West, Max, and Alexsis will work on preparing for the apologies and social media posts. I'll contact Burke to arrange the private concert. Carter and I will contact your family and the band to schedule shoots."

"I'm sorry, you'll what now?" West asks sharply.

"Would you rather blindside them?" Ford returns just as cuttingly.

The two men stare at each other so fiercely I swear the temperature in the room rises.

"No. I guess not," West finally agrees. "But I'm not sure they'll all agree."

Ford's mouth lifts on one side. "Oh, I think they'll all want to hear you grovel. But if they don't, I'm prepared to persuade them."

I'm immediately disgusted by his implication, but West beats me to speaking.

"You are *not* paying anyone off to do this, Nelson," he says angrily.

Ford smiles. "I'll do what it takes to save your career." He pauses, tilting his head. "Won't you?"

I've never seen someone look as much like a trapped animal as West does at that question. I'm pretty sure if West had claws, Ford would be lying on the floor right now trying to keep his insides from falling out.

"Of course," West replies in the least convincing tone I've ever heard.

"Good." Ford makes to leave, patting West condescendingly on the shoulder as he passes. "Play nice now, kids. Carter?"

"Yes, sir." Carter leaps up and follows, leaving the rest of us in the room.

"Kids?" Jason scoffs. "What is that guy, like twelve?"

"He's twenty-four. So yeah, pretty much twelve," West replies.

Jason shakes his head, rising. "Well, once again, I think I've proved I'm pretty much useless here. I'll be in my office if you need me," he says to me.

I smile up at him gratefully. But once he's gone, and it's just me, Alexsis, and West …

"Alexsis, can you give West and I some time alone?" I ask quietly.

"Of course," Alexsis replies, jumping up and darting out of the room before I can even blink. Okay. Maybe she is interested in Ford. Because I get the feeling she only agreed so quickly so she could try to catch him before he leaves.

As soon as she's gone, I shake my head. "I sure hope Ford and Alexsis don't start something or Alexsis is going to be useless to me."

West fixes me with a smirk. "Seems like you may think she's already useless to you. Because I know you really don't want to be alone with me."

"Now, that's where you're wrong," I say. "I thought it might be easier to do what's next with just us."

"Mhm, you keep telling yourself that," he murmurs. "But I know you're starting to come around."

I roll my eyes. "You wish."

West leans forward, rubbing his bottom lip with his thumb as if in thought. "I'm starting to wonder if maybe I do," he replies.

Something inside my chest catches, and I clamber to keep the conversation moving forward. "So. The apologies. We're starting with the band?" I prompt, hoping my desperate attempt to turn the attention away from what he said isn't obvious. Then again, I don't care if it is, as long as we move on.

West's dark eyes search mine for a moment. And for that moment all I can do is hope he doesn't keep teasing me. Or I may really start coming around. He does seem to suddenly be awfully cooperative, and some of his ideas were really thoughtful.

"Yes." He says, then he blinks and leans back. "The band. Well, mostly Ward and James. But Nik and Michael have put up with an awful lot of my shit for the last year and a half too."

"Hmmm. But surely you'll have more to say to Ward and James?"

West lifts a shoulder. "James is too laid back to care about apologies, really. I think he forgave me *while* I was fucking everything up. But Ward? He's different. He acts like he doesn't care, so I acted like I didn't either."

"But he does."

West nods slowly. "I think of anyone, I owe him an apology the most."

"Maybe we should save him until last then?"

West huffs a laugh. "I may owe him the most, but he will be the absolute least drama."

"Ah," I say, realizing what he's done. "You ordered them in what you think will be the least to the most difficult."

He dips his head in confirmation. "Yes, ma'am."

"Now I'm 'ma'am'?" I ask dryly. "I think I prefer Maxi." I almost face-palm as soon as the words are out of my mouth. He shoots me a mischievous grin, and I suspect I'm going to be ma'amed constantly for the next six weeks. Christ.

"Moving on," I continue swiftly. "The older brother. Not going to be much drama?"

"I'd bet no. He's a runner, not a fighter. He spent most of our childhood out of the house just to avoid, well, everything. Anyway, I think he might have some harsh things to say, but that's about it."

"Do you think he'll forgive you?" I ask curiously.

West spreads his arms. "I'm clean and sober. He never had an issue with the rock star bit. Just the drugs."

"Who had a problem with the rock star bit?"

West's face falls. "Don't worry, we'll get there."

I squint at him for a minute, debating whether I want to press the issue. But I guess if we'll get there…

"The ex?" I prompt.

West grins. "That is going to be big drama. Sadie never disappoints."

"So again, why not put her last?"

"I may be dreading that one, but I'd rather face her before I face my dad."

"And your sister?"

"You're a little too good at your job, you know that?" he asks, scratching the back of his head.

"Am I making you uncomfortable?" I tease. Kind of hoping I am. It's a small payback for all his bullshit, but I'll take it.

"I don't know. Why don't you try asking what you really want to know?" he pushes back.

Well, shit. He's more perceptive than I gave him credit for. But fine. He wants it direct? That's certainly something I'm good at.

"You introduced your sister to drugs, didn't you?"

"Damn, Maxi, you don't fuck around," he teases, though the heavy sigh following belies his distress. "Yes. I did. And to my drug *dealer* while I was at it; he's the fucker she left with."

I nod lightly, studying him. He looks tired.

"Why are you suddenly being so cooperative?" I ask curiously.

He cocks an eyebrow. "I'm not stupid enough to bite the hand that feeds me," he replies carefully.

"I see." Though I feel like there's more to this. But I'm sure I'll have plenty of time with him over the coming weeks to figure it out. "And your dad?"

"That's going to take more time to explain than you've got right now."

I lean back in my chair and cross my legs like I'm just getting settled in. "I've got all the time in the world."

"Yeah, well, I don't. I've got places to be, Maxi. How about we talk about that another day? Since he's last and all, there should be plenty of time. Wouldn't want you to get sick of me too quick." He winks, but I see no cuteness in his eyes. He's just done.

"Fine. This is your shit show," I concede, rising to show him out.

"You don't know the half of it," he mutters as he follows.

His tone makes me wonder if I really want to know the other half. But like it or not, I'm pretty sure all of West's dirty secrets are going to be bared for everyone to see, with me in the front row seat. While I can't feel too sorry for him, seeing as he mostly brought it on himself, I also can't say I envy him. Because the shit show has only just begun.

9

All Apologies by Nirvana

West

"So, we're gonna like, just start? I don't get a list of questions ahead of time or something?" I ask, shifting nervously on the rehearsal room couch.

Maxi rolls her eyes. Cute.

"That wouldn't be very spontaneous," she points out, twisting around to shuffle in her bag.

"Yeah, that's kinda the idea," I mumble.

"What was that?" she asks, whipping back around.

"Nothing." I smirk and shove my hands in my pockets. We haven't even started apology number one and I'm already over it.

Carter and one of his minions walk in hauling yet another load of camera and lighting equipment. They go back to adjusting the setup pointed at the couch.

"Do I at least get to know who's up first?" I poke.

Maxi finally emerges from her giant bag holding a moleskin notebook and pen.

"You are," she says with a sly smile.

I narrow my eyes at her briefly but remember my resolution to play along. Well, as much as I'm capable of. I have my own internal bet on when I'm going to hit my limit, but that's neither here nor there right now. Maxi wants to play just us? I'm definitely down with that.

"All right," I agree. "What do you want to know?"

Maxi looks back at Carter. "We ready?" He gives her the thumbs up, the makeup chick darts in to powder our faces for the seventeenth time, and then the countdown begins.

And then we're rolling.

Goddamn, I forgot how it feels to be in front of a camera. It's like the first time you stick your hand down a girl's panties. You feel like you have no idea what you're doing, but you're excited. And one wrong move and your night is toast.

"So, West, with this interview, you've officially begun your apology tour. How are you feeling right now?"

I wasn't expecting her to dive in like that, and I gotta admit it throws me a little. It begins indeed. I do not, thankfully, spit out what was just going through my head. At least I have that much presence of mind.

"Gotta say, Maxi, I'm nervous," I reply with a grin that's contrary to the truth I spoke. But the way her mouth tightens when I call her Maxi makes me smile wider. Maybe this will be fun after all.

"I don't blame you. You're about to apologize to your bandmates, new and original." She pauses, presumably for effect. "Who are you *most* nervous to apologize to today?"

I take a deep breath and puff it out. Also for effect.

"I think you all probably know," I reply, donning a humble look for the camera. "While all my bandmates deserve an apology, no one deserves one more than Ward."

"You and Ward Pierce have been friends for a long time. But then, the same could be said of James Kennedy, couldn't it?"

I dip my head in agreement. "Yes. We're all like brothers. But James was smart enough to stay away from the temptations that came with the gig. Ward was always right there next to me, yet somehow stayed on the right side of the line." I chuckle dryly. "Well, the less worse side of the line."

"Not your side of the line, you mean?" Maxi asks, looking from me to the camera.

The question makes me feel more defensive than I know I have any right to.

"The non-addict side of the line."

Maxi has no cute retort for that. They never do when you drop the A-bomb.

"Anyway," I continue as if it's no big deal — even though it's a very big fucking deal — "because he was closer to it all, he suffered more of the consequences of my behavior than James did." Not that they didn't both suffer. We all did.

"Ah, like the time you both got arrested after the Vegas concert in 2017?"

Just the mention of that night has my eyes dropping in embarrassment. And the booze-deprived monster deep within wakes up. I'm not sure if it's the mention of that epically embarrassing night, or because of the nerves that expand beyond my ability to rein them in. My finger finds my knee, drawing soothing circles. Calming it back to sleep.

"Yes, like that," I agree, looking back up and holding Maxi's curious gaze.

She swallows hard, and I know she gets how low of a blow that question was. But then, that's what this whole charade is about, right? A bunch of low blows I'm expected to take because I had a problem I couldn't handle on my own, borne of equal parts my own bullshit and the temptations I couldn't avoid.

"I see. It sounds like he's definitely the most deserving of an apology." She pauses. "I guess we'd better get started then," she replies blithely.

As if on cue — wait, of course it was a cue — Ward walks through the door and around Maxi to sit next to me on the couch. Exactly how we've sat so many times recently, Ward as ever acting as my moral compass, reality check, and shoulder to whine on all in one. Because I don't cry on anyone's shoulder, least of all Ward's. In front of the TV, watching *Moana*? Like a little girl. But never in front of Ward.

And yet, for some reason, as he sits down, smiling in that reassuring way he does, I feel tears prick the back of my eyes. Fuck.

Happy thoughts. Rosie. Guitar Center. Tits.

There, that did it. Tears gone.

"Hey, man," he greets me with a grin.

I reach out and we fist bump. "'Sup, dude."

We both laugh and I look back at Maxi, who begins asking Ward a bunch of dumbass questions about when we met, moments that "defined our friendship," and a bunch of other touchy-feely bullshit. None of his answers are unexpected, but then before I'm ready, Maxi turns to me.

"So, you guys have been through thick and thin, and here you are now," she sums up. "West, do you have anything you'd like to say to Ward?" She cocks an eyebrow, clearly signaling me to do my thing.

Well, all right then. I take a deep breath and turn to Ward.

"You don't have to say it," Ward offers, his smile slipping to the side.

"Oh, I'm gonna say the shit out of it," I assure him. I look back at Maxi again. "Can I say shit on TV?" I look at the camera. "Probably not. I probably shouldn't say fuck either then, right?"

Maxi face-palms. "We'll edit it later," she mumbles.

"Just keep going," Carter says from behind the camera.

I turn back to Ward and my smile hitches. "I'm sorry, Ward." The words feel better than I thought. And suddenly they start pouring out. "I'm sorry I've never said I'm sorry. I'm sorry for all the times you had to follow my drunk, stoned ass around trying to keep me from epically fucking up." I glance up at the camera. Pretty sure that was two things I shouldn't say on TV. Oops. I give a mildly apologetic look before turning back. "But most of all I'm sorry it wasn't enough. That I wasn't strong enough to —"

"You had me at 'sup dude," he says jokingly. But I know what he means. I'm already forgiven.

There are those damn tears again. I blink hard and nobody is more shocked than me when I practically tackle Ward in a hug. A bro hug, of course. I pat him on the back and pull away as soon as I realize what I'm doing.

I look over at Maxi, and she's looking at me like I just kicked her puppy.

"Carter, can we pause or cut or whatever?" she asks.

Carter, now seated to the left of the camera, looks up from behind his computer and nods.

Maxi turns back, her eyes narrowed sharply. "That was too easy."

I cock an eyebrow. "I'm … sorry?" I reply. I didn't even mean to mock her. It's just a gift.

She rolls her eyes. "Come on, West. If we're going to do this, you actually have to do it. None of this over-the-top fake apologizing stuff." She turns to Ward. "Did you guys practice this, or do you just naturally BS for the camera?"

Ward stares back impassively. "Define 'practice,'" he replies slowly.

Maxi throws her hands up and makes a disgusted noise. It's too fucking funny watching her lose her shit, but I also don't want to be here all damn day.

"Keep your panties on, we didn't practice. That was all classic West and Ward," I assure her.

"Really? Because it sounded extremely rehearsed. On your end at least." Her eyes flick back to Ward. "And 'you had me at 'sup dude'? Really?"

Ward finally cracks a grin. "I thought it was funny."

I thought it was funny too, but I don't say that out loud. Instead I hold up a fist and he bumps his against mine.

"So not taking things seriously is going to be a theme here," Maxi grumbles. "All right then. I take it back. If this is authentic, then I guess that's what we've got to work with."

"As authentic as J. Lo's booty," I assure her.

"Or Tyra Banks' tits," Ward offers.

"Can we stop talking about famous women's body parts, please?" Maxi begs, clearly sorry she ever stopped to question us.

I don't even try to contain the smirk because I know how much it gets under her skin. And sure enough, her eyes angrily dart to my mouth.

"Are we ready then?" Carter asks dryly, causing all of our heads to turn toward him.

He's so quiet I'd kinda forgotten he was there.

"Let's do this. Rest of the band, then?" I prompt.

Carter nods and whirls a finger high in the air.

One of his assistants counts us down and we're back to business.

"And just like that, all's forgiven," Maxi says sweetly, tipping her head to the side. Then her eyes go comically wide. "Oh, but what about the rest of the band?"

Another cue, clearly, as James, Nik, and Michael file in.

A couple of assistants pop into the room, adding chairs for Nik and Michael as James sits on my other side on the couch.

The process repeats on a much lower-key level, with each member of the band talking about our history, me offering a token apology, and them accepting.

Then Carter has each individual band member sit on the couch alone and talk to Maxi about how they feel about me, where the band's at, and our future. Again, nothing surprising. Or rather, the only surprise is how nobody seems to have anything really bad to say about me. Disappointments here and there, sure, but nothing as bad as stuff I've thought about myself in my own head. Or about what they must have thought at some point. So, either they're playing nice for the cameras or they really are just that awesome.

As cynical as I can be sometimes, I kind of hope it's the latter.

In any case, this was meant to be the easy one. Because it's only going to get harder from here.

Finally, what feels like hours later, they have us "rehearse" while they take some filler footage, and then we're done.

As I'm packing away Rosie, Maxi approaches me.

"What are you still doing here?" I ask, zipping up the gig bag.

"They wanted me for some additional post footage," she grumbles.

"Aww, so you didn't get to hear us rehearse? Bet you're really sorry you missed that," I tease.

"Oh I caught the end of it," she assures me. "It's not like I haven't heard you play before."

"Ah, but up close and personal is different."

"I've heard you play up close and personal," she retorts, hands flying to her hips.

"Oh *really?* When was that?" I ask, actually curious.

"A long time ago," she says, her expression abruptly closing down. "Anyway. Carter asked me to remind you to *not* prepare for talking to your brother. They want it as —"

"Spontaneous as possible, I know, Christ," I swear. "Any idea when that little party's going to happen, or do I just get called in morning-of like today?"

Maxi shrugs. "Next week sometime. We'll all have to get there at the same time, so I imagine there will be a bit of a heads up."

I suppress a sigh, unwilling to show any emotion around this woman. She'd probably eat me alive at the first sign of weakness. Normally I'm fine flying by the seat of my pants. But this … this is like waiting for a bunch of surprise ass-whoopings. As if I didn't already have enough anxiety on a daily basis.

Maxi watches me curiously as I process.

"Stop shrinking me right now," I tell her.

She blushes bright red. "You just looked, I dunno, upset. I wasn't 'shrinking' you. But …"

"What?" I press.

One of her shoulders lifts. "As much as this is the last thing I want to be doing, I know it's probably the same for you. Harder, even. I know you're getting the worse end of the deal here, so I'm trying make this go as smoothly as possible, and that includes making sure you're okay."

I scoff. "Even though you hate me?"

She returns my scoff with interest. "I don't *hate* you. That would require feeling something for you. And that's not a road I ever plan to travel down again."

Oh, well, now she's got my attention. "You saying you used to feel something for me, Maxi?" I ask with a sly grin, leaning toward her. Joke's on me, though, because she smells like lilacs and rain. Damn.

She stiffens at my proximity. "I was young and stupid. You can't possibly hold that against me."

I immediately think to myself, *I've got plenty of things I'd like to hold against you.* And then I internally bitch-slap myself. What the hell, West?

"I don't," I reply abruptly. "And you don't need to feel for me. I'm fine." And with that, I haul Rosie off the table and get the fuck out of there. Away from everything that conversation stirred. Revulsion at being pitied. Attraction toward someone who has made my life into this hell. My own anxieties.

I spend the whole drive home thinking about all those things and more. But as I fall asleep that night, it's just Maxi on my mind, and I want to kick my own ass.

I don't get off on chasing girls who don't want to "feel something for me." I like my women willing and into it.

So why can't I stop thinking about Maxi Marshall?

10

Swallow My Pride by The Ramones

Max

Almost a full week goes by before the next stop on the tour. I stand in the parking lot of the location just north of Corona, hands on hips, while Carter and his crew scramble around between two vans and the building, getting everything set up.

"So, what genius picked a bowling alley?" I ask Alexsis with more than a hint of sarcasm in my tone.

She laughs. "That would be Erik Westberg, West's older brother."

I look at her in surprise. "Really? Because this seems like something Ford would insist on. You know, to make West look like just a normal kind of guy."

Alexsis purses her lips. "You said that like you think Ford is —"

"A little full of himself? Yes, yes I do think that."

"He's actually a really nice guy," she returns with a frown.

"Oh *really*?" I ask with interest. "And how do we know this?" Though I'm pretty sure I know.

She grins, twirling a lock of blond hair around a finger. "Because he may have taken me to dinner last weekend."

I slap her playfully on the shoulder. "And you didn't tell me this until now?" I gasp accusingly. "For shame, Alexsis, for shame."

"I didn't know if it was okay, but I couldn't hold it in any longer," she admits.

I smile, remembering the elated feeling that comes with the start of something new. Not that I've felt it in a long time. But it's hard to contain, equal parts hope and delicious tension.

But before I can ask for more details, a car with tinted windows rolls up. "Yeah, well, you may want to hold on to the rest until later. Looks like Ford's least biggest fan just arrived."

And proving my point, West climbs out of the back. His hair looks damp and instead of his usual plain-black tee, he's wearing a Ramones T-shirt. Black, of course, with the band name and logo on it.

"The entertainment has arrived," he says grandly, stretching his arms out. Then he looks up and frowns. He catches my eye and points at the building. "Maxi, what the fuck are we doing at a bowling alley?"

I can't help it, his confused, indignant tone makes me burst out laughing.

"Hope you brought your bowling shoes," I tease, pulling Alexsis toward the building.

West trails behind us, his long legs quickly eating up the ground between us. "No, seriously, are we really doing this here?" he asks.

"Apparently," I confirm.

And to my surprise, West laughs. "Erik."

It wasn't a question, so I just look at him, waiting for an explanation. But he doesn't provide one, following us into the building.

As we approach the desk, I can see Carter and crew setting up at one of the lanes. Oh boy. We're really doing this.

"I hope nobody expects me to bowl," Alexsis pipes up.

I huff a laugh. "Don't worry, I think West gets that honor."

West smirks at us both. "Yes, well, let's get this show on the road then, shall we?"

"Your brother's not here yet," I return. "At least, not as far as I know."

"Perfect," West says, rubbing his hands together. "That'll give me time to warm up. Do we have the place to ourselves?"

I give him a bewildered look. Does he really bowl? He cocks an eyebrow, waiting for an answer.

"Um. Yes. I think we do," I respond, still completely baffled by this turn of events.

"Excellent," he hums, turning toward the desk and engaging the attendant to get his shoes.

"Alexsis," I mumble.

"Yeah?"

"Are we really about to watch Kristoffer Westberg bowl?"

"Weird, right?" she replies. I glance over at her, and she's looking at West with the exact expression I feel right now. It's just too unreal.

"I have to admit," I say slowly. "I've interviewed a lot of musicians. But I've never done an interview while they're bowling. I have no clue how we're going to pull this off."

She shrugs. "I say we go with it. What's the worst that could happen?"

Famous last words.

Who knew West could bowl? Who knew West even liked bowling? Not this former superfan, that's for damn sure. And yet, as we finished setting up, that's exactly what he did, and he did it pretty damn well, all while answering questions about his brother.

He was, once again, more forthcoming than I'd expected, explaining how his brother had always been about doing the "right thing" — aka what their dad wanted — all while somehow avoiding the man himself as much as possible.

He did skirt around the issues with his dad again, but openly talked about how much he hated his brother as a kid and that now, as an adult, he can see more where he was coming from.

It's the first time Kristoffer Westberg has surprised me in a good way in a very long time, and it gives me hope that this will be another successful apology. Ford and Burke seemed happy with the first one, anyway, so I figured if this went the same way, then we'd be in good shape.

Luckily, once his brother did show, things seemed to take off on their own between the two of them and they didn't even need me. Like, at all. West and his brother had a very natural conversation about West's time in rehab and how he's been clean more than two years now.

His brother not only forgave without being asked but also asked for West's forgiveness for the disappearing acts he apparently used to pull on the regular. It was almost touching. There wasn't any hugging like with West and Ward, rather a friendly handshake.

And now, Alexsis is interviewing Erik in another part of the building while I get ready to do West's post interview.

As I sit down to West taking off his bowling shoes, he looks up at me and my heart trips in my chest. He looks *happy*. If I hadn't gotten to know him better, I wouldn't be able to tell. But his smirk is more a smile, and there's a light in his eyes I don't often see. It takes me a moment to place what it makes me feel: pleased. I'm pleased that he's happy.

I sink into the closest orange plastic chair, unsure why that weirds me out so much.

"You know, I know you're here to do my post-apology interview thing. But I realized there's something very important we haven't addressed," he says.

"Oh? What's that?"

"We haven't talked about your taste in music. I think I need to find out what kind of rock expert you really are before I answer any more questions," he says, leaning back in his chair.

"And how, exactly, do you plan to do that?" I ask suspiciously.

"Just a few harmless questions of my own." But the mischievous glint in his eye betrays him. He's feeling peppy and looking to test me. But two can play at that game.

"Hm. How about this. You get to ask me one, then I get to ask you one?"

He cocks an eyebrow. "Fine," he agrees.

"All right, you go first," I tell him.

His answering grin is feline. "Fender or Gibson?"

I level a look at him. He knows that I know how much he loves his precious Gibson guitar. His pride and joy. His *Rosie*. "Fender."

He laughs. "I knew you were going to say that."

"Mhm," I murmur. "Jimmy Page or Eric Clapton?"

"Jimmy Page," he returns with no hesitation. Good man. "Rolling Stones or The Beatles?"

I scoff. "The day we met I was wearing a Stones shirt, dude."

"Still a valid and very fundamental question," he defends.

I roll my eyes. "Rolling Stones, obviously. Bohemian Rhapsody or Stairway to Heaven?"

He's actually quiet for a minute. "Bohemian Rhapsody."

That surprises me, given how iconic Stairway to Heaven is, especially with guitarists.

"Don't tell anyone I said that, though," he follows up.

"Your secret's safe with me," I promise.

"All right, all right. Now. A very important question." He turns his head and gives me a serious look. "Who would win in a fight between Billy Corgan and Courtney Love?"

I bark a sharp laugh. "Courtney Love, hands down. For reasons I assume are obvious."

He chuckles and nods.

"Bon Scott or Brian Johnson?" I ask.

"Damn, you're not pulling punches, are you, Maxi?" he says with a teasing tone. "Bon Scott."

"Really? It's not just because he's the original, is it?"

West shrugs. "Sometimes you can't forget the one who made you fall in love." His eyes meet mine.

I swallow hard. He just said a mouthful. "So did I pass?"

He narrows his eyes at me. "Yeah, I guess you're okay."

My eyebrows jump of their own accord. Well, that's a shift. Here I was thinking I was the biggest, or at least most recent, thorn in his side. Now I'm *okay*. Interesting. Guess we'll see how long *that* lasts.

"Glad we got that out of the way," I reply. "So can I do my job now?"

He slings an arm over the chairs, staring at me with a glint in his eyes. "Yeah, Maxi. Go for it."

I fight the urge to roll my eyes because I get it. He wants to feel like something about this is on his terms. Under his control. All things considered, his test was actually pretty enjoyable.

Oh god, did I really just think of West and "enjoyable" in the same sentence? I must be getting soft.

As soon as Carter's assistant is ready and we're rolling again, I purposely don't go easy on West, grilling him on his conversation with his brother. I even get him to squirm at one point. I'm a bit sadistically happier about that than I should be.

But whatever little measure of control he took, I needed back. Because when it comes to West, I can't trust myself; there's too much of my past that was spent adoring him, and I've had to shake myself out of those patterns. So I need to stay in the driver's seat here.

We finally get everything we need, and Alexsis and I compare notes before we pack up and head home for the evening.

I check in with Carter before leaving, and he gives me the news: The next apology is this Sunday. West's ex. I don't know whether to dread whatever drama is bound to unfold or plan on bringing popcorn.

As I head out to my car, ruminating over that, I don't even see West leaning against exterior of the building just outside the entrance.

"Hey, Maxi."

I look up, startled. "What are you still doing here?"

"I'm waiting for my driver."

"Can't you call an Uber or something? Or is that not safe for formerly famous rock stars?"

"Ouch, Maxi, ouch," he sighs. "I prefer my guy. At least, for another year anyway, until I can get my license back."

I shrug, finding it hard to feel sorry for someone who had multiple DUIs within a couple of years. "Did you need something?"

"I heard Carter talking about Sadie."

"Sadie? Oh, your ex?"

"That's the one. Sunday?"

"Sunday," I confirm. "You ready?"

He shakes his head and laughs. "Never."

A drop hits my nose, causing me to look up. "Oh shit, it's —"

"Raining," West finishes as the small drops promptly turn into a deluge. Well, for Southern California anyway. "Fuck."

"Come on," I call, running toward my car. "Get in."

He doesn't hesitate, running the short distance and practically diving into the passenger seat as I get in the driver's side of my tiny coupe.

A glance in the rearview mirror tells me I look like a drowned rat, though thankfully my makeup isn't visibly running. But I look over at him, and his T-shirt is soaked through, sticking to the lean muscles of his chest. Drops of water run over his sharp cheekbones. In short, he looks like a wet fucking dream. The bastard.

"Where's your driver?" I ask.

"Downtown. I can wait for him inside."

I shake my head, resigned. "In this weather? It'll take him hours to get here. I'm in Culver City, I'll drop you off on my way home."

"I don't *live* downtown, that's just where he is. But I can get a ride from Culver City."

"So where do you *live*?" I poke back.

"The Palisades."

I snort. "Figures." Shaking my head, I buckle in and start the car. Why on earth did I just sign up for an hour or two stuck in a car with this guy?

Because I'm not an asshole, that's why. If I were, this would be so much easier. Well, this wouldn't *be* at all, as I'd have refused to see him the first time he showed up at *Rock Scene*. But that's not who I am, so here we are. Dripping wet and fogging up the windows of my car while I drive the former rock god who shaped my younger years across Los Angeles. Life is weird.

"Thank you," West says, breaking through my thoughts as I pull onto the main road.

I glance over at him. Still looking like he just won a wet T-shirt contest. If they even have those for dudes.

"You're welcome," I reply begrudgingly.

He beams. "That was really hard for you to say, wasn't it?"

An unbidden laugh chokes its way out of me. "Yes!"

"What'd I do, Maxi? To make you not want to feel anything for me anymore?"

"Why do you care?" I deflect. "You don't like me either."

"That's what I thought too. But I'm starting to think I may have been a bit hasty on that front."

I shoot him a skeptical look.

"No, really. You didn't have to drive me home. You didn't have to do *any* of this, really. But you are. You're obviously a good person, Maxi. So if there's a problem here, it must be me."

His words hit me right in the heart. "You're not a bad person, West."

"Thanks," he murmurs. But from his tone I can tell he doesn't agree.

I glance over to see him rubbing circles into his knee with one finger.

"Why do you do that?" I ask, nodding toward his hand.

"You ask a lot of questions but won't answer any?"

I laugh. "That's literally my job description," I remind him.

"Fair enough," he allows. "Off the record?"

I debate that. But if we're going to be in this for another, what, three or four apologies? Anyway, we're going to need to build some sort of trust here.

"Off the record," I agree.

"It's a soothing mechanism." He pauses. "For when I feel like drinking."

I look over at him in shock. Because he does it *so* much.

"Yeah. I feel like drinking a lot," he says, as if replying to my thoughts.

"Wow. I had no idea you still struggled so much."

He shrugs. "It's not as bad as it was at first."

"But at least you're not an addict anymore," I offer. "You've got your life back. You'll get there."

A small smile graces his still-damp lips, and he looks at me with those dark, soulful eyes of his. "I'll always be an addict, Maxi. But I'm still me. Always have been, always will be. Even addiction can't take that away. Nothing can, really."

I swallow hard against the emotions his words stir in me. Pity. Compassion. Confusion.

"Why are you telling me this?" I ask, my throat dry as I try my hardest to concentrate on driving. But now that we're on the freeway, slowed to a crawl, it doesn't require enough of my focus to ignore the gnawing feeling in my stomach. *Guilt.* Even though I know that particular emotion should be all him.

"So you know I'm still that guy you felt for once. In here." He thumps his fist to his heart.

I blink hard against the tears. Lord, no. Remember, Max, remember.

"The last time we met," I say, my voice thick with emotion, "you know, before you showed up at my magazine, you almost got me arrested for prostitution."

West pulls back. "I'm sorry, I did what now?"

I huff out an unamused laugh. "Three years ago. You guys did a concert at the Forum. Afterward, some friends and I were looking for our car and we found you guys outside a back entrance. You called us over. Started to flirt. God, I was so stupidly flattered. I'd worshipped you for more than ten years. Then some cops came by. And I think …" I blink hard, fighting back tears of anger this time, all of the guilt evaporating as the memories pour back in, "in hindsight I think you were just trying to keep them from realizing you were high or had drugs on you or whatever, but you told them I was a prostitute trying to get you to hire me. I got handcuffed and shoved into the back of a police car while you guys high-tailed it out of there with your security team. I cried and begged and pleaded, trying to explain that I wasn't a hooker. I think they finally figured out what had happened, because they let me go with a warning. Or they didn't want to make a scene since my friends were freaking out the whole time. Either way, it was one of the most traumatic experiences of my life. And that's the night I lost all respect for you. Oh, and your band, who didn't bother correcting your wildly harmful and false accusation."

I grip the steering wheel, purposely not looking at him. Expecting him to say something. Anything. A denial. An explanation. An apology. But the exact thing he's been begging me to tell him got no response. Nothing.

The whole drive. He stayed silent. I kept looking ahead.

I broke the silence eventually, asking him where he lived. Quietly, he told me. And nothing more even as I dropped him off. Not even a goodbye.

11

So What by Pink

West

I'm an asshole. Wait, what's worse than being an asshole? Because that's what I am. A lowlife piece-of-shit addict with a knack for destruction. My own life. My band. Other people's lives. I don't discriminate. I'll burn them all to the ground.

It doesn't matter that I care now. It doesn't matter that I'm not using anymore. It doesn't matter that the band is back together or that I've made a couple of stupid apologies. It doesn't change anything. My regret changes nothing. How do you unburn a bridge?

Obviously, my thoughts have spiraled since Maxi's revelation. In light of the horrifically awful way I behaved toward someone who revered me ... well, it all feels futile. Some misdeeds are too heinous to be forgiven. So why bother apologizing? What's it fixing, really?

Oh yeah. My career. That.

It's the last thing I have. The only thing. If I can salvage it, maybe the rest won't matter. At least, that's what I tell myself. I have to. I have to have *something* I can focus on that *can* be fixed. And as much as I hate it, I've been given a road to follow to make that happen. So I'm going to fucking follow it and take what's coming to get at least that back.

Addiction may have completely changed the course of my life, but I won't let it take music from me. Or any fans still willing to see past a bunch of drug-and-alcohol-fueled bad decisions. I have to believe there are enough of them left to make this worth it.

I heave a sigh as my driver speeds down the freeway toward my next life implosion. Toward Sadie. Another woman who hates me for good reason.

But when we pull up at a strip club, all I can do is laugh. Looks like not much has changed, because this is exactly where we met.

As soon as I step out of the car, as if I'm searching for her, my eyes land on Maxi. I can tell by the tension in her body, the hard set of her jaw, and how hard she's gripping her takeaway coffee cup that she is not a happy camper. And while I would usually immediately think of all the ways I could tease her for it, today I feel *bad.* Jesus Christ.

In this moment, I know everything has changed. I saw her as the enemy before, the driving force behind this public lesson in humiliation and groveling. But knowing why she carries such hatred toward me? I can only accept the blame. I can't make it right. She doesn't want me to. But I can stop baiting her at every turn. Stop trying to get a rise out of her.

It's going to be hard. Because damned if it isn't fun watching her react.

As if she hears me thinking about torturing her, her head turns, and we lock eyes. And something lurches inside of me in a way that makes me wonder for the first time if I feel something more for her than dislike or regret.

Fuck. I think I respect Maxi Marshall.

Christ, I do. The woman is here. Though snarky, she's doing this. How could I not respect that?

I approach carefully, given our epically awful last conversation.

"Hey," I offer.

One of her dark, slender eyebrows raises. "Hi?"

I open my mouth to apologize, but snap it shut. How stupid would an apology be? *I'm sorry I almost got you arrested for prostitution, but I understand now why you'll always hate me?*

"So, your ex is a stripper, huh?" she asks, saving me from pulling together an apology I don't have the first clue how to make and sound sincere.

I shove my hands in my pocket and nod. "This is where we met, actually."

She rolls her eyes and I smile a little. And for some reason, my body relaxes.

"I guess I shouldn't be surprised by that," she murmurs, taking a sip of coffee.

"A little late in the day for caffeine, isn't it?" I offer lamely. *Christ, West.*

She snorts. "Thanks, Dad."

I shake my head, not wanting to banter back like I usually would. "Whatever. So, what's the plan? You guys aren't leaving me alone with her like you did with Erik, are you?"

A wicked smile spreads over Maxi's full, red lips. "Are you *afraid* of your ex, West?"

I shrug. "You would be too if you knew her."

That gets a full laugh out of her. "I met her a few minutes ago. She's gotta be a hundred pounds soaking wet." She eyes me up and down. "Pretty sure you could take her."

I scoff. "How little you know me. I'd never fight a woman, Maxi. Not even one as pretty as you." And with a wink, I decide to leave it there and find someplace else to be.

I make to head into the club, but one of Carter's assistants stops me at the door. "Sorry, Mr. Westberg, we're not ready for you yet."

I frown at him but raise my hands and back up. But when I turn around, Maxi's close behind, smirking at me.

"Hoping to get a lap dance while you're here?" she asks dryly.

I cock an eyebrow. "Why, are you offering?" I want to take the words back as soon as they're out, but verbally sparring with Maxi is second nature now.

She pulls a face. "Um. No." Then she takes a too-quick sip of coffee. But it doesn't stop me from seeing how red her face turns. Interesting.

"Don't worry, I'm not into chicks who'd be happier if I spontaneously combusted," I assure her.

Maxi throws up a hand. "For the last time, I don't hate you," she responds, sounding exasperated. "That would require —"

"Feeling something. Yeah, I've heard that song and dance before, Maxi. I'm starting to think you're saying it to convince *yourself*."

She props her free hand on her hip. "And what exactly does that mean?"

I sigh heavily, mostly frustrated with myself as I close the gap between us, so we're not overheard.

I stop directly in front of her, leaning in and catching her eye. The intensity between us skyrockets as soon as her hazel eyes meet mine.

"It means you have every right to *feel* something toward me, Maxi. Hate. Dislike. Anger. Whatever. But please, stop pretending I didn't completely shatter your trust. I deserve it. I deserve whatever you've got to throw at me. And you deserve to let it out. Whenever you want to do that, I'll listen. And afterward I'll still be as fucking sorry about what happened as I am right now. You have no fucking clue how sorry I am. I wish I could take it back, but I can't. But please, for the love of Christ, stop pretending like I didn't hurt you."

Maxi stares back at me in shock, her mouth hanging open.

"Mr. Westberg, Ms. Marshall, we're ready for you now," Carter's assistant calls from behind me.

And when I turn back to Maxi, she's already skirted around me to head into the club, leaving me to wonder if she really heard me or if she's going to continue avoiding her very real feelings toward me forever.

With a shake of my head, I head in after her. Carter is just inside.

"I hope you're already rolling because shit's going to get real, fast," I tell him.

Carter's brows hop up and he turns and nods to his assistant. Maxi pops up on my other side just as they indicate they're recording.

They have us sit in the club's waiting area on sticky baby blue vinyl couches.

"So, West, we're here today to see Sadie Sullivan, the woman you were dating right before rehab. How are you feeling?"

I try hard not to reply with a snarky comment. But I'm getting pretty sick of being asked how I'm feeling about everything all the time. Because trust me, they don't want the truth.

"Well, Sadie's a firecracker, so I've gotta admit that I'm a little nervous."

"Did you two not leave things on a good note?" she presses.

I can't help the skeptical look I give her. She must know. Everyone knows.

"Seeing as the last time we were together we were arrested for fucking on a theme park ride, in full view of the public, I'm going to go with no, we didn't leave things on a good note."

"That was the day you were busted for possession with intent to distribute, wasn't it?"

I huff an unamused laugh. "I still don't get why they think one couple couldn't do all that coke," I reply jokingly.

Maxi frowns. Oof. Not winning any awards for cute here.

"Yes," I follow up. "It was the last straw, as far as the legal system was concerned. That was when I was given the choice between jail and rehab."

"Was it part of the court order for you to stay away from Sadie?"

I shake my head. "That just happened. I wasn't allowed visitors in rehab for the first month, and by the time I was … I dunno. I guess I thought it was best to just let her go." Best for my sobriety, that is, but I don't voice that part.

"But you were in a relationship for two years, correct?"

I nod my confirmation, though I wouldn't exactly call it a relationship. Intoxicated fucking is more like it. Sadie loved to fuck. She loved the drugs. And she really loved being with someone famous. But she didn't love me. And I didn't love her either, for that matter.

"Wow. So you pretty much left her hanging," Maxi says.

I fight the glare I want to shoot her. But I guess I deserve her judgment, more so than anyone's.

I spread my hands in surrender. "That's why we're here today, right?"

"Right," Maxi says softly. "Are you ready?"

I rise. "As I'll ever be."

Carter's assistant scrambles forward to show me into the club proper as the camera follows. Since they just opened, thankfully only a few people are at tables, mostly up against the stage. But the assistant, whose name I clearly never remember, veers to the right almost immediately, and I know exactly where he's taking us.

A private room. One that normally entertains every manner of debauchery, much of which Sadie and I engaged in here ourselves. And my suspicion that they brought us here for the mere spectacle of flesh and sex is pretty much confirmed. These places never let people bring cameras in, yet here we are, about to film in one of the most private locations they offer.

At least there's a camera rolling to keep Sadie from actually murdering me.

"I'll be here the whole time," he assures me, making me wonder if Maxi managed to say something to him.

Or maybe the management here required we not be left alone in a room together with just a camera. That makes me laugh.

The assistant knocks and I'm suddenly wishing I'd worn a cup. Or anything that'll protect my balls when Sadie decides to try ripping them off.

"Come in," a female voice calls.

The assistant opens the door and gestures for me to enter. I walk in and they follow. And there she is. All five-feet-six-inches of Sadie in all her platform-heeled, curled-blond hair, shiny pink-lipped, barely-there cowgirl outfit glory.

"West," she cries, throwing herself into my arms.

I'm so caught off guard, I let her, and the camera moves around us to capture the reunion.

"Nice to see you too, Sadie." Well. Maybe this won't be as bad as I thought.

I pry her off me as subtly as I can. And as soon as she's away, she reels back one arm and smacks me so hard my head twists to the side.

"Holy shit," I cry. "What the hell?"

"That's for never breaking up with me, asshole," she yells. Then she *pushes* me.

But just as Maxi pointed out, she's tiny, so it barely registers. Once she realizes that, she swings out with a leg. I attempt to dodge it, but she gets me in the shin with the sharp tip of her heel and I lean to the side, pulling the weight off my leg in reaction to the pain.

"And that's for getting me arrested," she spits.

"Okay, I get it, I'm sorry, Sadie. Really. Jesus. You can stop now," I cry, throwing up a hand when I see her coming back at me.

"Oh, I'm just getting started," she says, making to knee me in the groin.

But I push her knee aside with one hand before she can connect. She topples backward into me, but not content to be thwarted, she reaches up with her clawlike nails as she falls, grabbing at my face.

I hear the assistant calling for security as I dart into a corner and she rights herself.

"I'm not here to fight," I assure her, holding my hand up and hobbling from the injury to my shin.

"Then you shouldn't have come," Sadie hisses.

She lashes out with a fist that I grab, spinning her around and holding her back against my front, her arms locked in mine, rendering her helpless. Unfortunately, my starved dick likes it more than I do, and she knows it, grinding against me. With a hiss, I release her and she spins away, facing me and looking like she's trying to figure out where to strike next.

"You were there too," I remind her. "Nobody forced drugs on you. That's what we did, Sadie, it's who we were together. But I'm not that guy anymore. And I'm sorry if I hurt you, but you have to stop now."

She screams like an animal and launches herself at me just as a huge security guard catches her by the waist. She wriggles and screams against him.

"Fuck you, West. FUCK! YOU!" she screams. "You ruined my life that day. I will never forgive you. *Never!*"

The security guard hauls her out, only to be replaced by an older man. "I think you guys should leave," he huffs. "Hope you got what you came for."

ABOUT HALF AN HOUR LATER, AFTER CARTER'S CREW HAS PULLED OUT OF the strip club, I find myself sitting on a bench with the club in the background, waiting for Maxi to do the post interview. I've already checked myself for damage — there's just one scratch along my jawline to go with the painful bruise on my shin — now I just need to calm myself down.

"I watched the footage. You weren't wrong about her." Maxi's voice suddenly behind me startles me so much I jump a little. She settles on the bench next to me. "Sorry, didn't mean to scare you."

I give her a small smile. "Not your fault. I'm a little on edge right now."

She nods understandingly. "I don't blame you. God, what a vindictive bitch to use an opportunity where you were going to apologize to physically attack you. I won't even ask why. She's clearly got issues. But I think the real question is, are you okay?"

"You're concerned about me?" I ask, shaking my head in disbelief.

"I'm … yes. I'm concerned. And I'm angry. And disappointed. And hurt," she admits, twisting her fingers together. "But I also feel guilty. I don't want to be any of those things at you. Maybe because deep down I know what addiction does to a person, and that I'm blaming you when I should be blaming the disease."

"I made the choices that led me there," I reply. "But thank you for saying that."

"Are you sure you're okay?" she asks skeptically.

I look at her. Really look at her. Her luscious, wavy hair. Her rocker chick band T-shirt style — today it's The Who. But mostly I look at her and think about the things you can't see. Just like you can't see addiction, Maxi doesn't show her pain either. But I know it's there. And knowing I caused it sucks balls.

"Yeah, I'm fine, thanks. Are we fine, Maxi?"

She huffs a sigh out of her nose. "Look, I know I've become some kind of metaphor for you earning forgiveness. But you don't need me to forgive you, West. I'm nobody to you. There is no 'we.' Yes, what you did hurt me, but I'm a big girl. I've been dealing with it for years, and I'll continue to."

"Is that a fancy way of saying you won't forgive me?"

She twists her fingers faster. "I hear your apology. And I appreciate it. I don't know. I *want* to forgive you. I'm just not there yet."

"That's fair," I admit.

She looks up at me. "Did Sadie knock the sass out of you? You're being so calm and mature."

I laugh. "Maybe." I shrug.

"Dude, seriously. You haven't made fun of me once this whole conversation. This is weird."

"It is a little weird, isn't it?"

Now it's her turn to laugh. "Glad it's not just me."

Carter and crew show up, starting to set up their equipment for the post-apology interview. But before we get there, I can't let one thing she said go unchallenged.

"Maxi?"

"Hm?"

"You're not nobody to me. Not even close."

12

In Between by Linkin Park

Max

After our strange conversation outside of the strip club, my biggest concern was that when we flew to San Francisco, I'd have to sit with West. I have no idea what to say to him right now. I don't even know what I think about everything he said yet.

Thankfully, I ended up taking an earlier flight to do some legwork with Alexsis. Giving me time to unpack what his words made me feel.

He said everything I'd ever wanted to hear from him and more. But instead of feeling vindicated, I'm more confused than ever. So here I am, sitting in coach, talking to Alexsis about it.

"Maybe it's because you spent the last three years pretending you didn't hate him," she offers. "That's a hard switch to just turn off."

"I didn't hate him," I protest. "Why does everyone think that? There's so much more wrapped up in what happened. I don't hate him, not at all.

But I was angry. Am angry? I don't know. *That* is a hard switch to turn off."

"And you don't have to. Just because he's got a sudden pathological need to be forgiven doesn't mean you're expected to magically get over it."

"Thank you," I tell her. "I definitely feel that pressure. But you're right. I don't have to. Let's talk about something else. How are things going with Ford?"

Alexsis pulls a face. "Eh. After the first date magic wore off — okay, maybe second or third date — I realized you were right. He's a pompous asshole."

I heave a comical sigh of relief. "Well thank god you figured that out on your own."

"I guess. I just don't get it. There were sparks! And he had so much promise. Why does it have to be so hard to find a decent guy?" she groans. "I mean, how many frogs do I have to kiss for fuck's sake?"

I chuckle. "You're asking the wrong girl. There's a reason I don't date more. At some point it becomes a chore, and you just have to back off and realize your life is pretty fucking awesome as it is."

Alexsis tilts her head. "You know what? You're right. I graduated college. I'm a journalist at a rock magazine. I'm traveling to — er, not-so-exotic but still cool locations."

"San Francisco *is* cool. And maybe after we get this apology shoot we can go out and see some sights before we head home."

"I'm down with that," she agrees. "Speaking of the shoot. We should start spitballing locations since the owner of the café the sister wants to meet at isn't on board."

"Okay, what have you got?"

She opens her laptop and pulls up a marked map. "Café is here," she says, pointing. Then shifting her finger a bit to the right. "There's a public park nearby."

I shake my head. "You don't know the full story behind this apology," I realize.

"I guess not. But why does that affect the shoot location?" she asks, puzzled.

"Trust me. We don't want this one public. Can we just get a suite at the hotel? Something with a living room?" I muse.

"That could work. I'll get on it when we check in."

"Perfect. Thanks, Alexsis. You know. For listening."

She gives me a funny half-smile. "Anytime. When you realize you still have the hots for West, I want to listen to that too."

I roll my eyes. "Ha! Don't hold your breath."

Despite what I said to Alexsis, her comment triggered something in me. Something I didn't realize until we met up with West in the living room of his suite, which we've decided to use for the shoot. But as soon as we walked in for our pre-apology prep and interviewing, I knew. I knew she was right.

The sight of him pacing. Running his hands through his thick, dark hair. The intensity. It's exactly what he does on stage. What I've personally watched him do on stage more times than I can count, granted usually with Rosie hanging from a strap around his neck. But it's that intensity that always drew me to him. The dark, pulsing energy that rolls off him in waves. It's like a magnet.

I should hate this guy for all eternity. But I don't. What is wrong with me? Do I have a savior complex? Perhaps, though I don't think that's the appeal for me. While part of West's draw has always been the tortured bad-boy angle, I've seen firsthand now that he's not bad. But he is troubled. And while I don't think for a minute anything I could do would fix him, it's hard not to want to go wrap my arms around him.

But I don't do that. Instead, I stand frozen just inside the door, a realization hitting me like a ton of bricks: Forgiving him is like giving myself permission to remember the rock star I fell in love with from afar. Except now I know him up close. And he riles me in good and bad ways. But it's the good ways that worry me. Because I don't think I'd survive another Kristoffer Westberg heartbreak. And the bad ways? I have to admit, it's kind of exciting to spar with him verbally. I know he enjoys it. Maybe I do too.

He looks up and catches my eye. I suddenly feel naked, like he can see every thought that was passing through my mind. As he continues to hold my gaze, the feeling intensifies, until Carter grabs his attention to discuss logistics.

Before I'm prepared, I'm pulled in for the pre-interview. West and I take a seat on the couch while they finalize lighting.

"Hey," I offer lamely. "So this is going to be a tough one. You ready?"

"More than you know. I'm just so fucking relieved they got her to agree to come here. I don't even care if they paid her to do it," he admits.

My brows bunch together. "You didn't think she would?"

He gives me a look. "I already told you where she's at. She knows what I want. I've been trying to get her to talk to me for more than a year, but she's refused all contact."

"I don't think they paid her," I offer. "Maybe she was just ready this time."

He shakes his head. "I'd like to believe that, but I was here a month ago and nothing had changed. I'm just bracing myself for the possibility that she's not coming for the reasons I hope she is."

The anguish on his face gets to me, and before I can think about it, I reach out and squeeze his hand reassuringly. I have no words to offer. What do I know about his sister or their relationship? The least I can do is offer comfort.

He gives me a smile I haven't seen before. His eyes are warm, his mouth tilted up on one side. He squeezes back and my heart flutters. I'm so screwed.

"Okay, we're ready," Carter calls.

I pull back self-consciously and give thoughts of West's smile a giant shove out of my brain. Time to focus on the task at hand.

We finish the pre-interview and the wait begins. But the time his sister was supposed to arrive has come and gone. As time passes, whatever small bursts of conversation were happening cease. Carter regularly checks with the driver who was supposed to pick her up. He's there, she's just not answering the door, or her phone.

Just when we're about to give up nearly two hours later, there's a knock on the door. Carter's assistant answers and we hear a strangled cry.

"Kris?" a woman's voice calls.

West, who'd been sitting on the couch, head in hands, looks up in surprise and quickly bolts to the door.

"Annika?" he returns. And then a broken sob rips out of him as he draws the tiny female at the door into his arms.

Carter has his assistant swing the camera toward them, but something inside me protests.

"Carter?" I call softly. He looks at me. I point to the camera and shake my head. He pulls a face. "Turn it off."

With a small sigh, he complies.

West leads his sister into the room and one look at her tells me my instincts were dead-on. A massive bruise covers her right eye and part of her face. She has scratches on her neck. And she looks deflated. Like she's hit rock bottom.

West settles her on the couch and I get his attention. He steps to the side where she can't hear.

"We don't have to film this," I tell him. "Say the word and I'll get everyone out of here."

West closes his eyes for a moment, his shoulders dropping with relief. He reopens them, his eyes now glistening, and simply says, "Thank you."

I swallow hard and nod, quickly working to usher everyone out. "Call me when you're ready."

He nods, and I leave with the last of the crew. The last thing I see as I close the door behind me is him crouched in front of his shaking, beaten little sister.

Nearly six hours later, just after ten, there's a soft knock on my hotel room door. I keep the bolt closed and open the door a crack to find West leaning against the doorframe.

"Can I come in?" he asks, his voice hoarse.

I close the door, unlatch the bolt, and reopen it. "Of course," I reply, gesturing for him to enter. Trying not to be self-conscious of my sweats and "Peace, Love, & Music" Snoopy T-shirt.

He tugs on the hem of my shirt as he passes. "Cute," he murmurs with a small, tired smile.

"Thanks," I reply, closing the door.

He settles on the small, utilitarian navy couch across from the bed. No private living room here. The only other furniture is a dresser on the wall between them. I take a seat next to him, which is as far away as the loveseat will allow.

"How'd it go?" I ask.

He scrubs his hands over his face. "You were right. She was ready. The bastard beat her when she told him she was going to see me today. She had to wait until he was gone to leave. She won't be going back."

"Is she still using?" I ask.

West shakes his head. "No, thank god. Apparently she got pregnant a year or so ago and stopped. She still lost the baby, but she hasn't gone back. At least, not to the hard stuff."

"Well, that's a relief. So she finally wanted to leave?"

He tips his head back and forth. "She wasn't sure how she could, so I told her to take my room. For as long as she needs, I'll make sure she has a place to stay away from him. I tried to get her to come home, but she's afraid of everything right now, especially our dad."

"Sounds like there's a lot of that going around. But I guess I'll get to see firsthand why that is soon."

"I'm sorry I threw us off today. Is Carter pissed?"

I look up at him in shock. "Fuck Carter," I reply vehemently. "If he couldn't look at your sister and see that doing a fucking interview was the last thing she needed, then he's a fucking waste of space."

"Wow, Maxi, that was more cursing in one breath than I've ever heard out of your mouth," he teases. Then he leans in. "I like it."

I snort. "You would appreciate a foul mouth."

"No. Well, yes, but that's not what I meant. I like that you get what's important. It's something I'm still learning. I think you're a good influence, though, Maxi. I may keep you around a while."

I scrunch my nose. "You get me for …" I quickly calculate how many days between now and the airing party. "About three weeks. Though I doubt we'll need to see each other much during post."

"Well, that's a shame."

I shrug. "So you dropped by to let me know your sister is okay?"

He sinks into the couch a little, clearly exhausted, leaning his head back and stretching out his legs. "Yep. And to ask what my penance will be. Then I'll go get another room."

"Carter plans to do post in the morning before we leave." I pause. "And we also planned to do the shoot in your suite because we couldn't get another room; the hotel's fully booked. So you can just stay here."

He opens his eyes and looks up at me. "Well, fuck, Maxi. A pretty girl asks you to sleep over, you can't say no. But I don't have to. I can go crash with Carter or something."

I roll my eyes. "I have a king-sized bed, there's plenty of room, and we're both adults. Besides, you don't even like Carter and you look like you're about to fall asleep right there." As if to prove my point, his eyes had drifted close in the middle of my rant, and they now pop back open.

"You're a saint, Maxi."

I snort, rising and heading to my side of the bed. "Hardly." I point at the side I wasn't planning on sleeping on. "You can take that side. Consider it your reward for doing right by your sister today."

With a sleepy smile, he rises, kicks off his shoes, then falls face-first on top of the covers. And I'm pretty sure he falls right to sleep.

Me? I lay on my side of the bed wondering what form of temporary insanity caused me to invite West into my bed. Even if it's not like *that*. Sometimes I'm too nice for my own good. Or, as Alexsis would probably say, it's just a sign of all the "secret" feelings I have for West. Well, news flash, Alexsis, they're not secret. I've just learned to ignore them for a very long time.

I WAKE IN THE MIDDLE OF THE NIGHT FOR ABSOLUTELY NO REASON AT ALL. The room is eerily quiet, but now that I'm awake, I realize … I really need to use the bathroom. I debate for a good few minutes, not wanting to chance waking West.

I glance over my shoulder to find him lying on his back, though still on top of the covers, but he's perfectly still. The longer I wait, the stronger the need becomes, so I finally give in.

I do my business as quietly as I can manage before creeping back to the bed as slowly and stealthily as possible.

"You can stop acting like a cat burglar. I'm awake," West says dryly.

"Shit, sorry," I mumble as I climb back into bed.

In the dim moonlight peeking around the drapes, I see him tilt his head toward me.

"It's not your fault. I never went to sleep."

I glance at the clock. It's almost two.

"Makes sense you'd be a night owl," I reply, wiggling to get comfortable.

"I'm actually fucking exhausted, but every time I close my eyes I see that bruise on Annika's face and I get pissed off all over again," he admits.

My heart twists. "I'd be angry at the fucker who did that to her too."

West rolls toward me, and I pull my head back in surprise. He's still not super close, but the move makes me nervous for reasons I'm not willing to examine too closely.

"I'm the fucker who did that to her," he says ardently. "Or I might as well have. I introduced them. I introduced her to heroin, Maxi. Nobody else. This is on me."

I scoot up on my pillow. "How old was she then?"

His brows scrunch together. "Twenty-five. Why?"

"Because that means she was a grown woman, perfectly capable of making her own choices. That's not to say you didn't play a part; I'm just pointing out that it's not all on you."

He huffs a breath out of his nose in clear disbelief. "Annika's worshipped me since we were kids. She even wanted her own guitar when she was ten so she could be just like me. She's always wanted to be like me. This isn't on her. It was reckless, thoughtless, and totally fucking insane to bring her into that world." He shakes his head and flops backward onto his pillow.

I blink hard against tears as my heart bleeds for him. For Annika. For their family, and what both of their addictions have done to all of their lives.

"Did she forgive you?"

West shakes his head, and I'm surprised, until he says, "Yes. But I don't fucking deserve it."

"Nobody *deserves* forgiveness, West. They earn it. And I think you earned it today."

"Thanks," he murmurs, surprising me. I expected snark. Or at least more protest. He must really be twisted up over this. "Let's just hope Carter, Ford, and the rest of those fuckers think so too."

"Don't worry about that. I have some ideas for what we can shoot to cover our asses."

"Good. Because I'm all out of fucks to give." Every word is laced with exhaustion. The soul-deep, heartrending kind, and it's all I can do not to reach out and comfort him.

But touching him would be a very bad idea. So instead, I offer the only comfort I can think of.

"West?"

"Yeah?"

"For what it's worth? You've earned my forgiveness too."

I swallow hard against the conflicted emotions saying those words out loud brings. Because I really do forgive him. But I haven't forgotten yet. I'm not sure if I ever will.

West's head slowly rolls toward me. And though I can't see his eyes in the dark, I can feel them searching for mine. I close my eyes, the vulnerability of this moment too much to bear.

Really, though, how could I not forgive him? He's crawled out of the pit of addiction and, despite understandable protests, is laying his life out in front of the masses while he attempts to make amends for the things he's done. That takes a strength of character I'm not sure many people have, myself included.

So as wary as I am of him, it's a truth I can't withhold. And one I'm pretty sure he needed to hear right now.

But the silence stretches on.

"You still awake?" I ask self-consciously.

A deep chuckle rumbles out of West. "I'm awake. I heard you. I just … I'm kinda shocked, to be honest, Maxi. Thought you'd take that grudge to the grave. Not that I'd blame you."

"Is that your way of saying thank you?" I ask wryly.

"Yeah. I guess it is."

I snort. "You're welcome, then. Get some sleep, West. You're going to need it."

He doesn't respond. But a few minutes later, I hear his breathing even out. I sit up delicately and carefully lean toward him. He's finally asleep.

I watch him for a moment, fighting that feeling that keeps grabbing me. The one that says this is all too unreal; that I'm the one sleeping, my subconscious creating this fantastical dream to resolve all the feelings I've had about this man over the years.

Except I know if it were me dreaming this, it would've been without all the snarky banter that makes me want to slap him. And there would have been a lot less clothing.

With a quiet chuckle, I roll over and allow myself to drift off, equal parts wanting and fearing to have those particular types of dreams about West again. But they're just dreams, right?

Father of Mine by Everclear

Max

Two days after San Francisco, we're back in Corona for West's apology to his father. And while I'm looking forward to finally understanding this piece of West's puzzle, I'm not looking forward to another awkward-as-ass encounter.

Because from the moment we woke up Friday morning, we had no clue how to behave around each other after the momentarily peaceful connection we'd shared in the wee hours of the night.

Those moments shook the foundations of our whole dynamic. And now what? Now awkwardness with a side of tongue-tied idiocy.

Because of which the first half of Friday was spent avoiding conversation during down moments while we recreated what happened between West and his sister with interviews — not including his sister, of course. The second half was travel, which none of us did together. Alexsis went back first thing, then me after interviews, then the crew after taking some scenic footage to cut in, with West staying behind another day to look after his sister. So I didn't even get to tell Alexsis what had happened, and she's not here today to act as a buffer. But thankfully I didn't have to travel with West. Half a day of trying to reestablish our rapport was more than enough.

But today will be a full day of just me, West, and Carter and crew. Oh, and Bill Westberg.

In an effort to find something to talk about, I tried asking West a bit about his relationship with his father on Friday morning, but he continued to stubbornly deflect talking about it. So I'm pretty much flying blind here. This ought to be fun.

I pull up outside of West's childhood home to find the production van already there, with Carter sifting through equipment in the back.

"Hey, Carter," I greet him.

His sandy blond head pops up and he adjusts his glasses. "Afternoon, Max. I'm glad you're here early." He sets some recording equipment down and takes a seat on the tailgate. "Ford and I had a meeting yesterday. He's happy with what he's seeing, but since we couldn't get the actual apology with the sister on camera, he wants to make sure this one packs an extra emotional punch. Plus it's the last before the private concert."

I frown, instantly knowing what he's asking. "You want me to push West's buttons before the interview."

Carter nods slowly. "Something like that. You seem to have a knack for it anyway."

I shake my head. "Except West has purposely kept me at arm's length on this one. I have nothing to go on. I wouldn't even know where to start."

Carter removes his glasses and starts cleaning them on his shirt. "Ah. Yes. Well. I may have had a bit of a chat with Erik Westberg that went beyond what we technically needed for the shoot."

I quirk an eyebrow. "About?"

"His sister and father. I wanted to be prepared."

"You know something," I accuse.

Carter nods grimly. "I know everything."

WEST BREEZES IN MINUTES BEFORE WE'D PLANNED TO START SHOOTING. I know it's part of his attempt to keep me in the dark, but he's unknowingly already lost that advantage, courtesy of Erik and Carter.

"Maxi," West greets me with a curt nod. Not awkwardly, but definitely more reserved than usual.

It takes me a moment to realize his energy is *nervous*. And if I was unsure before, I'm dead certain now. I can't do what Carter and Ford want me to do.

"We need to talk," I respond, pulling at his arm and leading him to my car. "Get in."

He gives me a quizzical look but does as I ask. As soon as the doors are closed, I realize I don't even know how to begin.

"Are we going somewhere?" West asks.

I shake my head. "No." I take a deep breath. Here goes nothing. "They want me to push your buttons before you go in to talk to your dad."

West snorts. "What else is new? This whole charade is about pushing my buttons, isn't it?"

I press my lips together in frustration.

"This is worse. So much worse."

"Worse how?"

I pause, not wanting to reveal his brother's role in this. No sense shaking that tree. Might as well let him assume it came from his father. Lord knows West kept them well away from his sister, so he'll know she wasn't the one to spill the beans.

"They know everything, West," I say carefully. "And they want me to tell you in the pre-interview that your father has had professional help and is — their words — a different man now. They want to see you break down. They want you two to reconcile on camera. And they want you both crying."

West pales. "Do *you* know everything?" he asks somberly.

And the anxiety written all over his face, in his voice, makes my heart shatter.

But before I can respond, someone knocks on the window behind West's head, startling us both.

He pops the door open to reveal Carter.

"We're ready," Carter says abruptly before walking away.

With the door still propped open, West looks back at me.

"You don't have to do this," I tell him.

His jaw clenches. "Let's go, Maxi."

"Wait," I call.

But he's already out of the car.

So, with seemingly no other choice, I join him.

Carter has cameras set up on the front walkway, clearly intending to shoot with the house behind us. His assistant lines us up on our marks.

And then we're rolling. For the first time, I may be just as uneasy as West is.

"We're here outside of the Westberg family home, getting ready to talk to your dad," I say, looking toward West. "How are you feeling right now, West?"

"Just peachy, Maxi, thanks for asking," he replies drolly.

"Really?" I press. "Because from what I understand, your dad wasn't the nicest guy to you as a teenager."

"Nope," he confirms brightly.

And his perky yet sarcastic responses are unnerving me even more.

"You left home at sixteen because of his abuse, didn't you?" I continue, trying to get us to the end of this line of questioning with my sanity intact.

"Sure did," he agrees just as peppily as before.

"But," I start, swallowing hard against the lump forming in my throat at what I have to say next, "your mom died giving birth to your sister. So he went it alone as a parent. That must have made it hard for him. Hard for everyone, really."

It's a softer version of what they wanted me to say, but right now all I want is real emotion from West. Not the bullshit face he's putting on to get through this, even though I don't blame him for it.

"It was hard. But you know, what's done is done." He shrugs.

I suppress a sigh. This is going nowhere. "So, for your part, what are you apologizing for today, West?"

"Well, I sure didn't make it easy on him," West replies, appearing thoughtful, but I know him better now. And right now I can completely smell the bullshit. "I was rebellious from a young age. He wanted me to go into a 'serious' career, not music. I started drinking and smoking at twelve. So, you know, any parent would be upset about that."

I have to give him credit. To someone who didn't know him, it would sound genuine.

"Sure. But he's admitted to having behaved … poorly," I say, stumbling for the right word. "He's even had therapy and is supposedly a changed man. Kind of like you."

West's gaze lands on mine sharply, a muscle in his jaw ticking. And I know instantly that the comparison gets to him.

"I guess we'll see," is his only response.

And I'm honestly impressed by his self-control.

I nod in agreement. "I guess so. Because it's time for a father-son reunion."

As soon as the cameras stop, West walks away from me.

I watch his back retreat helplessly as Carter approaches.

"That was not exactly what we were looking for," Carter admonishes me.

"I can't out him on television, Carter."

"You mean you *won't*," Carter clarifies.

I roll my eyes. "Fine, I won't. But it's West's past. If it's coming from anyone, it has to come from him."

Carter considers me for a moment. "Fine. As long as we get the waterworks, I can't say I care. But it would make for great ratings."

It's all I can do not to punch him, but thankfully West rejoins us and

I'm distracted out of my anger as one of the assistants explains how the next shot will go.

And then, once more, it's showtime.

For the first time since the beginning, I can't help feeling like it really is all just for show.

With cameras trained on us, I reach up and knock.

The door swings open too quickly for West's dad to not have been standing there, waiting.

"Kristoffer," his dad gasps. And I can see real emotion on his face, at least.

"Hi, Dad," West offers dully.

Bill Westberg launches forward, pulling West into a hug. My eyes go wide and I hold my breath, waiting for West to shove his father off of him.

But while he's stiff, I have to give West credit for allowing it much more than I'd expected. He does somewhat awkwardly pat his father on the back until he lets go.

"Come in," Bill offers, stepping back and allowing us over the threshold.

The exterior cameras stop as they get us set up quickly in the living room, just inside the door past a small entryway. The house is sparsely decorated, with barely more than utilitarian furniture. In a word, it's depressing. And maybe it's just what I know, but being in the house gives me the heebie-jeebies.

Thankfully with just a few minutes, a little makeup, and some lighting adjustments later have us rolling again. That much closer to getting the hell out of here.

"So, you know why we're here, Mr. Westberg," I offer from the lone armchair.

West sits on one end of the three-person couch, his father on the other.

"Yes, but please, call me Bill," he says warmly.

I take him in fully for the first time. He looks so much like West, except his eyes are blue. And, of course, he's a good twenty-five years older, with gray sprinkling through the dark brown of his hair, and fine lines at the edges of his eyes and lips when he smiles.

I try my best to shove my own judgments aside and simply do my job.

"Bill," I respond. "How long has it been since you've seen your son?"

"Twenty years," he responds. "Twenty long years."

"And though it may go without saying, you two didn't part on the best of terms," I prompt.

"No," his dad agrees. "I was hard on Kris. I knew he was talented, but I wanted more for him than being a struggling artist."

"Except he wasn't," I point out before I can stop myself. "Not for long, anyway."

Bill shrugs lightly. "The odds weren't in his favor. Surely you can understand that, as a parent, I had to be honest with him about that."

"That's fair," I agree. "But that wasn't all the blowup was about, was it?"

It's as close as I'm willing to skate to the issue.

Bill clears his throat. "No. I had ... other issues. But I've gotten help," he says, now turning to West, his eyes glistening. "Without your mom here, I lost my way. And I'm sorry, son. I hope you can forgive me."

My eyes flick to West, and I'm surprised to see the similar sheen of unshed tears in his eyes. West shakes his head, something I'm realizing is a habit, and not necessarily indicative of what he's about to say.

"I don't know. Can you forgive me for being such a disappointment?" There's a bitterness to his words that rings with truth.

"Oh, Kris." His dad says, a sob catching in his throat. "You were never a disappointment to me."

West blows out a breath and simply nods, wiping at his face as a tear starts to fall. Bill leans forward and offers a hug to West, who reluctantly allows it. Bill's head is turned toward the camera, and there's no mistaking the tears streaming down his cheeks.

I glance back at Carter to find his eyes fixed on the pair, smiling happily. It makes me angry, but at least he's getting what he wants. Hopefully that means this farce can come to a quick end.

And it does. With a few more platitudes from me, a bit more fatherly blubbering from Bill, and the barest of responses from West, we wrap.

West rises, visibly shaking, while the crew starts to move back outside for post.

He makes to walk by me, out of the living room, but I reach a hand out and touch his arm. He pauses, looking down at me.

"You okay?" I ask quietly.

He shakes his head tightly. "Get everyone out. Now."

My eyes go wide, but I get Carter to hurry and within a couple of minutes, we're headed out the door.

"I'll be out in a minute," West says, following me to the door. His expression brooks no questions, so I simply leave.

The sound of the door closing behind me sends shivers down my spine. As much as I don't want to leave West alone, I know that's what he wants right now. So I join the production crew at the edge of the property again, standing in for camera adjustments. Thankfully, based on Carter's comments, he's as pleased as he seemed inside. The whole situation just makes me sick.

When I hear the front door open and close behind me, I whirl toward it. West is walking down the steps, flexing his hand.

My heart drops, knowing what he most likely just did. Not that I can blame him. If my father had done what his had, I'd have left home too. And if I'd been forced to "apologize" to him twenty years later? I'd punch him too. Probably more.

Even more surprising, West makes it through the post interview perfectly, showing no hint how upset I know he must be.

I'm left in awe of West. And of his father's audacity. Because what kind of father — nay, *human being* — abuses their own children and then thinks he can just move on? Because it was not just the occasional kind of verbal abuse we all endure growing up. It was physically, beating his children to the point of broken bones. Mentally, gaslighting them on all their forms of abuse to convince them it was all in their minds. Emotionally, by making them feel worthless. And, most horrifically, from ages too young to even fathom, abusing them sexually at length, often in front of each other as punishment.

I don't care what bullshit Bill Westberg spouted in that house. People that depraved don't magically change. And I also don't care what West said; I know he hasn't forgiven his father. His years of drug abuse make sense now. Who wouldn't want to forget all of that?

But moreover, who could ever truly forgive someone who did that to them?

Another concern follows me home: Will West forgive *me* for playing a part in today? Because I feel disgusted with myself.

I also feel angry on West's behalf. Not just at his father, but at Carter, Ford, Burke, and everyone else who wants to drag him through this travesty for the sake of entertainment and ticket sales. I don't know why West is tolerating it, but the fact that he is doesn't absolve me of my role in it.

My only small comfort is that today's shoot with his father was the last personal apology. The private fan event will be a cakewalk in comparison. I can only hope that, in the end, the apology tour is really worth it. But that's West's call, not mine. And based on his participation today, I can only assume he thinks it is.

But then, he's had his dignity stripped from him his whole life. Maybe he's too used to it. Maybe I'm the odd one out for thinking he deserves better. Because he does. Underneath all of the drug use, the mistakes, there was someone hurting. Someone who is now trying to atone for ... well, being human.

I, like so many others, thought more about how he'd disappointed me rather than how life had disappointed him. And hopefully, like me, everyone else will see how very wrong they were.

14

With or Without You by U2

West

"Let the insanity begin," Ward declares magnanimously, spreading his arms wide. "I'll just be backstage."

He winks and ducks offstage, not waiting for a response. I shake my head and walk out of the stage pit, up to the greeting area we've set up by the bar.

Nils, the manager for the club, Baltia, meets me at the main table. Dude could be Ward's long-lost twin brother with his tall, thin frame and blond hair. Minus Ward's tattoos, though.

"Need anything else?" he asks.

"Nope. Frankie's not gonna be here tonight?" I ask.

Nils shakes his head. "Her and her husband are having a birthday party for their one-year-old first thing in the morning."

I laugh. Frankie Greco married with a kid. Stranger things have happened, I guess. "Well, say hi to her for me."

Nils nods. "Will do. It's good to see you healthy, man."

I slug him playfully on the arm. "Thanks. It feels good to be healthy. And thanks for hosting this on such short notice."

He shrugs. "You know we've always got your back. Besides, you were one of Baltia's first acts back when Frankie redid the place. It's the least we can do."

I make to respond when I notice Maxi walk in, her assistant in tow. It's been five days since I saw her at my dad's house. And I'm no less conscious of what she knows about me. But somehow, I'm still glad to see her. Maybe it has something to do with the fact that she's more dressed up than I've ever seen her in a tight black strapless number and red heels, her hair still tumbling in waves over her shoulder, her lips painted red to match her shoes. Jesus fucking Christ, she's hot.

"Hey, Maxi," I greet her as she approaches, shamelessly staring at her. I gesture to Nils. "This is Nils, Baltia's manager."

Maxi's assistant, Alexsis claps a hand over her mouth. "Oh my god, Nils Larssen?!"

I smirk, knowing Nils was once a runway model. So he's probably just as used to the groupies as the acts he books are.

She waves her hands in excitement. "You don't remember me, do you?" she asks him.

Maxi and I exchange a bewildered look.

"I'm sorry, I don't," Nils says. "You are …?"

"Alexsis Monaghan," she squeals, then turns to Maxi. "Nils was an exchange student who stayed with us … oh my gosh, what was it? Fifteen years ago?"

"Holy shit," Nils gasps, his eyes now trailing over Alexsis. "Seventeen years ago. You were a baby. What, five years old? I'm surprised you even remember me. Now look at you." And boy does he look at her.

Not that I blame him. I hadn't paid much attention because Maxi was there, but Alexsis is wearing a red halter dress that looks painted on her ample curves. She's a little short for my taste. And a little blonde. But then,

I guess I'm just a sucker for a brunette. My eyes flick to Maxi at the thought to find her staring at me, which makes me smirk. Which, in turn, makes her roll her eyes.

I chuckle, coming back to reality.

"Are you kidding? You were my first crush," she tells him, batting her eyelashes.

And now *I* roll my eyes. I catch Maxi's eye and cock my head to the side, inviting her to step away with me. She nods and we slip away. Nils and Alexsis don't even notice.

"Well, that was cute," Maxi says.

I huff a laugh. "Small world, I guess."

"So, you ready for tonight?"

I lift a shoulder. "As I'll ever be. Ford's sending a photographer. You'll be documenting the awesomeness. Club's providing muscle in case any of the fans get crazy."

"Or handsy," Maxi mutters.

I grin. "Not jealous, are you?"

She rolls her eyes. "Oh, please," she scoffs.

The normality of sparring with her calms me somehow.

"Well, if you want an autograph too, all you have to do is say so," I tease, stopping at the table and gesturing at the stack of photos waiting to be signed.

"I'll keep that in mind," she replies dryly.

"You do that," I reply with a wink. "You're sticking around for the concert, right?"

"Of course. Part of the job." She shifts feet. "West?"

"Maxi?"

"Are you … upset with me? For Sunday?" She blushes bright red, and I don't think I've ever seen my feisty little journalist so self-conscious.

"No, Maxi. We were all just playing our parts. I appreciate that you tried not to blindside me, actually."

She nods but still looks unconvinced. "Okay. I just … I felt bad. It was just all … badness."

I snort. "Truer words never spoken. And water under the bridge. Let's get a drink, shall we?"

Maxi goes for the hard stuff, though for obvious reason I stick with seltzer water.

Before I know it, it's time for the meet and greet with the approximately five hundred fans selected. It sounds like a lot, but considering this place could comfortably hold twice that, it still feels intimate.

And it feels fucking good to be signing autographs, taking pictures, and making the fans happy. None of them are even angry, mostly expressing their concern for me and that they're glad the band is back together. Still, I do my best to play along and make apologies wherever they seem natural. It actually feels good.

But what feels fucking phenomenal is getting on that stage and playing the shit out of our classics, plus a few of the new songs, and watching the crowd go nuts.

And what feels way better than it probably should is spotting Maxi in that crowd, front and center. Smiling, despite herself. I may play to her a little more than I want to admit.

When we play the last song of the night, my eyes flick up to find Ford, of all people, standing on the VIP balcony. I didn't know he was going to be here tonight, but it sends tension rippling through me. Until I see him give me a distinct thumbs up.

Fuck.

Well, all right then.

That ends the set on a fucking fantastic note, and when we head backstage, even though it's almost one o'clock, I'm feeling wide awake, riding the natural high of performing for a crowd.

Nils, Alexsis, and Maxi appear as the roadies start breaking things down.

"Great show, West," Nils says, slapping me on the back. "Can't wait for the tour."

"You and me both, dude," I assure him.

He and Alexsis slip away and Maxi steps up.

"You can tell me you thought we were awesome," I tease her with a wink.

She huffs and crosses her arms. "You were okay."

I laugh. Damn, she's stubborn. "I saw you out there. You were having fun, Maxi Marshall."

"Fine," she admits. "I might have enjoyed it … a little."

"Have it your way," I reply. A sudden thought sends a pang shooting through my chest. "Maxi?"

"What, West?"

"I'm going to miss you."

"I'm right here."

"No, when this is over, I mean."

Her eyes search my face. "But I'm so mean to you."

I smile at her. "I don't think you're mean. You just don't take my shit. I like that."

She rolls her eyes.

"And I like how much you roll your eyes at me."

Maxi scoffs. "You're so weird."

I chuckle. "Maybe. Or maybe I just need someone to keep me on my toes. To tell me the truth when I need to hear it."

"Are you trying to get in my pants or something?" she asks accusatorily.

Now I full-on laugh, holding my stomach and everything.

"It's not that funny," she murmurs after a minute.

I finally settle back down. "It is. Because there's so much more to you than your pants, Maxi. So much more."

"Oh god, Alexsis was right."

I look at her curiously. "About what?"

"It's like boys on the playground. They tease you because they like you. You like me!" she gasps incredulously.

I cock an eyebrow. Hm. There's a thought. "And if I do?"

"You can't like me. You hate me!"

"I don't."

"Oh, you so do."

"I really don't."

"I don't believe you," she insists.

The problem is, she's not entirely wrong. When this all started, I didn't like her. And sometimes she still gets under my skin. But I respect her. And fuck it if she's not right. I think I like her. No, I know I like her. She's feisty and funny and caring. And gorgeous. Especially right now, looking like the goddess queen of groupies, even aside from her outfit. Her eyes are lit up, her energy hypnotic. She's every rock star's wet dream.

"Shall I prove it?"

Before she can protest, I take a step to close the gap between us and lean in, lightly placing my lips to hers. I give her a second to stop me, but when she doesn't, I lift my hand to her face, slipping it behind her neck, and threading my fingers through her silky hair to hold her in place while I really kiss her.

It takes a minute, but she starts to respond, her lips working against mine. And like a trigger's been pulled, my whole body responds, molding against her, my other arm slipping behind her to pull her even closer. I swipe my tongue into her mouth and she groans. The sound wakes my whole body in a way it hasn't been in far too long. And then we're all lips and heat and gasping for breath … that is, until I let her go.

She stares up at me, panting and confused.

"We may drive each other crazy," I murmur. "But I kind of dig it. Tell me you dig it too, Maxi."

"I do," she admits softly. Then her brows bunch together and she whispers, "Fuck."

That gets another laugh out of me. "Know what day it is?" I ask her.

"Tax day?" she snarks.

"Well, technically that was yesterday. Which makes today —"

"April sixteenth. Crap, West, it's your goddamn birthday."

My eyebrows shoot up. "You know when my birthday is?"

She levels a look at me. "I was your biggest fan for a long time, remember? Of course I know when your birthday is." She holds up a hand at the look on my face. "And before you get any ideas, there will be no sexual birthday presents just because I had a mental lapse and let you kiss me."

"You kissed me back," I protest.

She purses her lips. "Okay, I kissed you back."

"I wasn't going to ask for sex."

"I said sexual."

"Well, I wouldn't say no to a blow job," I tease.

And she *punches* me. Though I kind of deserved it.

"Ouch," I say, feigning injury as I rub my arm. "I was kidding."

"No, you weren't."

"Okay, I wasn't. But really, this is weird for me too. I didn't plan to kiss you."

"Then why did you?" she asks, her eyes going soft.

I step into her, reaching up to palm her cheek. I try to find an explanation, but I don't fully understand it myself.

"I don't know," I admit. "When we first met, I thought I couldn't stand you. But something changed. And now … maybe I can't stand to be without you."

She closes her eyes and sighs. I lean down and kiss her again, this time going slowly. I realize something about holding her just feels right. Like all the other bullshit just goes away. In a way, it's a little like being high. Mind-numbing, but in a good way.

This is why they warn you against relationships right when you get out of rehab. Thankfully, rehab was a long time ago.

Because as I taste her, as her tongue meets mine and every neuron in my brain says "more," well, I'm pretty sure Maxi Marshall is my new drug of choice.

15

Sharp Dressed Man by ZZ Top

Max

"And you haven't seen him since after the private concert?" Alexsis asks, stunned.

"Nope."

"Wow," she mouths. "He didn't even call?"

"Oh, he did."

"And you didn't answer," she surmises.

"No."

"And … why not? You admitted you like him. What's your hang-up?"

I take a deep breath. "I do like him. More than like him. That's what scares me."

"You think he's going to break your heart again," she offers.

"Bingo."

"Always a risk," she agrees.

I give her a look. "Thanks. That makes me feel so much better," I tell her sarcastically.

She chuckles. "Well, if it helps, you look like a million bucks," she offers.

I look down at my pale pink lace and tulle gown, my brown waves sleeked over one shoulder. And I know my makeup is subtle but on point.

"I do, don't I?" I reply airily. "You look pretty fantastic yourself."

She twirls in her silver sequined mermaid dress. "Why, thank you."

"Any chance you invited a certain club manager to attend the airing party tonight?" I ask.

"Nils? Why would I invite him?" she asks, confused.

I laugh. "Oh, Alexsis. My dear, sweet, Alexsis. You like him, right?"

She blushes bright pink. "He's way too old for me."

"He's what, thirty?"

"Thirty-four."

"That's only twelve years," I say, though admittedly that's no small deal. "Besides, he obviously likes you too."

She brushes me away. "Oh, he does not."

"Mhm," I murmur. "Whatever you say." Then I mouth "he totally does" and she bursts out laughing.

"Whatever. Is our ride here yet or what?"

I check the app on my phone. "Just about. We can probably head out."

We catch our ride and head to the theater where the airing party is being held. We're arriving early, so I'm not particularly self-conscious about our ride. A limo would just be too weird for me.

I have to admit, I'm extremely curious to watch the fully edited show. Though seeing myself on screen will be a trip. Why does everyone always hate their own voice? Being a journalist, I should probably get over that.

In any case, we head in and meet Carter, Ford, and Burke. Jason, our boss, was going to come too but got sick. So we're left to hold our own. Thankfully, it's literally just the viewing plus an optional after-party.

Apparently, Ford and Burke have seen the finished product, but the tour sponsors will be watching it right alongside the public, so they'll see the reaction play out on social media in real time. All of the lead-up posts had great responses, though, so I'm not too worried.

But if I were West, I probably would be.

Speaking of West, I'm obviously nervously waiting for him to arrive. While trying to pretend I don't care at all. Fooling absolutely nobody, not even myself.

I guess I shouldn't be surprised when the lights blink, signaling that showtime is imminent, and he still hasn't appeared. That's a rock star for you. They arrive when they're damn good and ready.

The show starts, and it's just as jarring watching myself as I thought it would be. But West … goddamn he looks good on camera. None of his magnetism is lost.

The band interview plays well, coming across as funnier than I remember it being. But then, I was so nervous. And irritated.

Erik's apology is interesting to watch, since I wasn't close enough to hear everything while they were bowling. It's likewise equally funny and touching. Still light.

Then comes the ex. Dear god. It's even crazier on screen, with close-up camera work on Sadie's surprise freak-out attack. The audience gasps and oohs appropriately, lapping it up.

Annika's segment, however, brings the mood down considerably, but with just enough tenderness, particularly in West's very emotional post interview, it's bound to melt hearts across the world.

But the second it transitions to the apology with his father, I realize I can't watch this part. I don't want to watch this part. Alexsis's mouth pops open as I quietly and quickly bustle out of the theater.

As soon as I've closed the door behind me, the anxiety about that encounter begins to mellow.

"Well, that took you longer than I expected."

I whirl around at West's voice to find him standing in the foyer. In a black-on-black-on-black three piece suit and tie that's perfectly tailored to his slim, fit frame, he's more handsome than he has any right to be.

"What?" I ask blankly.

He chuckles, walking slowly toward me with his hands in his pockets.

"I guessed that you wouldn't last fifteen minutes. So kudos to you for lasting almost a whole hour."

He stops right in front of me. The smell of his expensive cologne fills my senses.

"You didn't go in at all, did you?" I ask, trying to ignore how close he is.

He shakes his head. "I lived it. That was enough."

I nod, unsure of what to say in response. His eyes rake over my lips, and I have to stop myself from shivering.

"You never called me back," he eventually points out.

"I'm sorry," I reply honestly. "This has all just been really overwhelming."

He laughs, and there's that smile. His real one. Not the snarky one. Not the teasing one. The genuine one. My favorite one.

"I have an idea what that's like," he replies. He tips his head toward double doors on the opposite side of the foyer. "I'm pretty sure they've already got the appetizers out in there. Hungry?" He offers a hand.

I reach out and take it. "Starved."

He leads me across the intricately patterned carpet at a leisurely pace. "By the way, you look absolutely stunning," he says casually.

"Thanks. You look pretty sharp in that suit."

"Aw, this old thing?" he replies with a wink.

He leads me through the double doors and into the after-party space. Against the wall to our right is a long banquet table that is, in fact, laden with appetizers and flutes of sparkling champagne. All ready for a celebration.

As I load up a plate, I can't help chuckling to myself.

"What?" West asks.

"I just think it's funny that you showed up late to the airing that you didn't even end up watching, but you're early for the party. That sounds about right."

He smirks at me. "Hardy-har. West likes to party."

"Oh no, I didn't mean it like that," I say, giving him a concerned look.

He smiles and pops a mini quiche in his mouth. "I know. Champagne?"

I wave it away.

"You don't have to abstain just because I'm not drinking," he says with a frown.

"Oh, that's not why. It just feels premature to celebrate."

He raises an eyebrow. "Worried for me, are you?"

I pop a grape in my mouth. "Of course. Aren't you?"

The door bursts open before he can respond and Alexsis runs in, brandishing her phone. "There you are," she exclaims, stopping in front of us and thrusting the phone under West's nose. "You're a trending hashtag." She beams, pointing.

And sure enough, her social media tracker has #forgiveWest trending high on all major social media platforms. With exponential increase over the last hour that's continuing.

"Uh, I don't speak social media," West says. "Someone care to explain?"

Burke saunters up just as others begin to file into the room, the rest of the band foremost. "It means you just saved all your asses," Burke explains. "Actually, mine too, come to think of it." He claps West on the back. "Good job, kid."

"Seriously?" West asks, jaw dropping. "The tour is on?"

Burke tips his head side to side. "Well, that'll officially be up to the sponsors. But I think it's pretty safe to say … yes. The tour is on. And our contact at the label texted me the thumbs up."

Everyone whoops and hollers. And now it feels like a celebration. Champagne is handed out, save West, who gets cider, and everyone cheers and toasts to West's victory. To not only saving the tour and contract, but to bringing the band back to relevancy, if the continued social media trend throughout the night is any indicator.

Well, at least for as long as they can ride this momentum. And with the tour promo ramping up, I have no doubt they will.

After about an hour of celebrating and networking, I'm a little peopled out. I try to say goodbye to West, but he's absolutely surrounded and grinning like he just won the lottery. So instead I say goodbye to Alexsis, who is also clearly enjoying herself, and head out to get a ride home.

I've only been home long enough to trade the beautiful but uncomfortable gown for sweats and a T-shirt when there's a knock on the door.

A quick glance out the peephole drops my jaw. I swing the door open.

"Why aren't you at your party?" I demand.

West smirks at me. "I had more important places to be."

I step back in shock, letting him in. "West, you just got your goddamn career back. My apartment cannot possibly be the most important place right now."

I close the door behind him and stare at him, hands on hips.

He steps into my space, reaching up to hold my chin.

"See, now, that's where you'd be wrong. Sure, it felt good to know that I did it. That the tour is on. That everything is going to be okay. But when I realized you were gone … I felt like I was missing something. Because without you, none of this would've been possible. So it would seem that wherever you are … well, that's the most important place."

I pull his hand down. "Don't say things like that."

"Why not? It's true."

"Maybe. But you can't just say things like that."

"Things like what?"

"Things that make me feel for you," I shout. So loud that I clap my hand over my mouth. "I'm sorry."

He chuckles and steps back into my space. "You're not alone, Maxi. I feel it too. Even when you yell." He lifts his hand and strokes it down my cheek, and it chips at the wall around my heart. "And I feel it when I touch you." He leans in, grazing his lips ever-so-softly against mine. The wall cracks. "And I definitely feel it when I kiss you."

His mouth presses harder into mine, and the wall comes tumbling down. I wrap my arms around his neck just as he pulls me into him. Our mouths quickly become hungry, tongues tangling, lips taking, as my hands wind into his thick, dark hair and he pulls me by my ass against him. I can feel his arousal between us and I groan, twisting my hips with need.

His head drops to my neck, licking and sucking at the sensitive spot just under my ear.

"I need you, Maxi," he says huskily into my ear.

I sigh happily. Because as much as I've fought it, I think I need him too.

"Are we really doing this?" I ask, dazed.

West pulls back, bringing things to a screeching halt. My body hums for him to keep doing what he'd been doing, but my brain is glad for the breather.

"Obviously I want to." His hand cups the back of my neck. "But we're only doing this if it's what you want too."

Laughter bubbles out of me. "I've wanted this since I was seventeen years old," I admit.

His brows shoot up. "Damn, you sure know how to make a guy feel special."

I grab him by the lapels of his suit jacket, marveling at the silkiness of the expensive material. "You are special, West. More than I think you know. More than even I knew."

I stare up into his eyes. And even if he doesn't fully appreciate the truth in those words, in this moment, I do. West has remade himself. He's done everything asked of him and more to reclaim what he'd lost, at no small cost.

And though I was deeply disappointed in him for a time, he's shown me that he's not the person that addiction made him into anymore. The enigmatic, talented, and impassioned musician I fell for from afar has returned in the form of this man whom I've come to respect and admire, despite our preferred method of communication being sass. Or maybe a little bit because of it.

When he doesn't respond to my assertion, I decide I don't need him to. I'm ready to stop holding back. To take a chance on West. He's earned it. And it's time for me to stop lying to myself about how I really feel.

"Touch me, West," I beg.

"Fuck, Maxi," he breathes. "Anything for you."

His fingers skate down my neck, to the collar of my shirt. His fingertips lightly feather over my breast as his hand comes to rest at my waist, slipping under the back of my shirt.

His warm hand slides up my back, pinching the clasp of my bra until it pops open. He grins down at me.

"Time to take this off," he commands.

I bite into my bottom lip, gripping the hem of my shirt. And I slowly start walking backward, leading him to my bedroom. Unsurprisingly, he follows.

Once we're inside, I raise the hem of the shirt inch by inch, finally slipping it over my head. I shimmy my bra off and let it fall to the floor with the shirt. I put my hands on my hips.

"Your turn," I tell him.

West just stands in the doorway, hands in his pockets, staring at my chest. His eyes are dark, his body uncannily still.

"West?" I prompt.

"I'm sorry, I just ... look at you, Maxi. Wow."

"Oh, you haven't seen anything yet," I promise with a sultry smile.

I hook my thumbs in my sweats, inching them down. He licks his lips. So I inch them down farther. His hands pop out of his pockets, opening and closing. I let the sweats fall to the floor with my panties before stepping out of them. He stands there, staring for a moment longer before taking three long, purposeful strides and stopping in front of me.

I look up at him. His eyes are practically obsidian and he's radiating heat. A shiver runs down the length of my body. And he hasn't even touched me yet.

Instead, he uses his body to walk me backward until I hit the bed. Then in one swift move he lifts my legs and has me on my back. I cry out in surprise, but I'm abruptly interrupted by his mouth connecting with my core, causing me to cry out for other reasons.

Still, he uses only his mouth, his tongue tasting every inch between my legs. Swirling over my most sensitive spot. Dipping into me teasingly. Setting a mad pace between the two.

He pulls away. "Maxi, look at me."

I lift my head and our eyes meet. His eyes don't leave mine as he slides two fingers into me. As he begins to pump them. As he reaches up with his other hand to apply pressure to my clit just so …

And I'm coming. I throw my head back as my orgasm explodes through my center, the energy spreading quickly through my entire body. I hit my peak and let out a sigh, cresting back down languidly as he withdraws.

As he pulls off his tie and shucks the rest of his clothing, I scoot back to the head of the bed and watch. I've seen pictures of West with his shirt off before, but I've never seen it in person. So when he removes the jacket, vest, and shirt, I'm treated to a pleasant surprise. He's more cut than he ever was in his younger years, though not bulky. His biceps, though … I didn't realize how huge they were. I'm definitely staring at him as hard as he was at me.

"Careful or you might set me on fire with that look," he says with a teasing note in his voice.

My eyes flick up to meet his. "I'm not sorry. You're fucking hot, West."

He laughs and crawls over the bed to me, capturing my lips with his. I pull at his unlatched belt, freeing it from his pants. As I work at the button on his slacks, he pulls back.

"I'm going to say this now, because I'm pretty sure once you get these off I'm not going to be up for talking," he teases.

I raise an eyebrow. "Oh?" I don't admit how much the implied promise makes my toes curl.

He smirks down at me, balancing over me in a way that makes his biceps that much more defined. God, I just want to lick them.

"I haven't had sex with anyone in over two years," he admits. "And STDs were, thankfully, one of the few things I managed to avoid. You?"

I pull a surprised face that he doesn't miss but also doesn't comment on.

"It's been a year. And I'm clean," I reply.

He grins. "Good." He leans in and kisses me chastely. "Are you on birth control?"

"Yep. Shots. But I'd still prefer to use condoms. You okay with that?"

West leans in, running his nose down my neck. "I just basically heard you say you're ready for me to fuck you," he murmurs in my ear. "So I don't care if you want me to wear a fruit roll-up, there's no way I'm saying no."

I laugh and lean toward the nightstand, fishing out the box of condoms that's probably gotten dusty, it's been in there so long. I check the date, hoping that they aren't expired.

"Oh thank god, there's a good month left on these," I say with relief.

"Are you sure? Because I can always go get more," he teases, pretending like he's about to leave.

"Just get over here and fuck me," I reply impatiently.

He grins and climbs onto the bed. "Yes, ma'am."

And as promised, he stops talking and removes his pants in earnest.

When he turns back to me, I get a full view of exactly how ready he is for this. But after more than two years, that's not exactly surprising. Still. The sight of him hard for me is just … mind-blowing.

He reaches over me to grab a condom while I'm busy staring at his cock, then lets me keep watching as he rolls it down his length.

As he settles between my legs, I continue to watch him in disbelief. He stares down at where our bodies meet, carefully rubbing himself over me. I throw my head back. It feels so damn good. And as he presses at my entrance, easing himself in slowly, I almost lose it.

"God, Maxi, you're so tight," he says.

And then he moves and holy shit.

I gasp and open my eyes to find him watching me. I bite into my bottom lip and he goes harder. I nod and he tips his head back, clearly enjoying this as much as I am as he goes even faster.

Watching him fuck me is the sexiest thing I have ever or will ever see. The tight muscles of his stomach contract, his dark eyes are hooded, the low rumbling in his chest beyond turning me on.

I move with him, encouraging him to keep building. And as he does, the beginnings of an orgasm start to swirl in me again.

"Maxi."

My eyes pop open, though I hadn't realized they were closed. His dark eyes meet mine, and I can see in their depths why he brought me back. He's close to the edge.

I pull him down to meet me, kissing him sweetly before wrapping my legs around him. I tilt with him, hard and purposefully, and moments later he's groaning out his orgasm, his face buried in my hair. My orgasm sputters, hanging in the balance as he slows.

I whimper, and his head snaps up, his eyes meeting mine. I see the realization there.

And he picks up the pace again.

"Oh," I exclaim, surprised at how hard he still is.

"You like that?" he murmurs in my ear, pumping again.

"Yes," I admit on a groan.

He keeps going, somehow still hard. The tightening in my low belly intensifies, my orgasm regaining speed. Knowing he can't do this forever, I slip my hand between us, swirling a finger over my clit in time to his thrusts.

He leans up on his arms and watches me as he continues to fuck me. I nod my encouragement. He goes harder. My free hand grips the pillow behind my head and I wordlessly nod, swirling faster.

He starts slamming so hard it hurts, but it's exactly what I needed to tip me over the edge. My back bows against the force of the climax that unfurls in my veins. His hand reaches down to grip my hip, joining us as deeply as he can, and it sends pleasure ricocheting through my entire body once more.

As I relax, I slump back down. I feel totally boneless as I stare up at him. He's sweaty and panting and a complete surprise. What kind of man comes then keeps going just to get you off?

I shake my head in disbelief. And gratitude. God, that was hot.

And then another thought flits through my mind. I just got thoroughly fucked by Kristoffer Westberg. I bite my lip, but it doesn't stop the shit-eating grin that spreads over my face.

"Well, you look happy," he remarks as he pulls out and makes to dispose of the condom.

"After that? How could I not be?" I murmur happily.

He slides back into bed next to me. "Good," he says, placing a kiss on my neck. "Because after we've rested, we are going to do that again."

"Promise?" I ask with another grin.

God, I can't stop smiling. It was beyond good. And the thought of doing it again … well, I don't dare to hope he enjoyed it as much as I did. Because giving in and believing he really wants me are two different things.

He rolls on top of me, caging me under him. I slide my arms around his neck. "Promise. I'm just sad we waited so long to figure this out."

"Figure what out?" I ask, puzzled.

"How good we are together."

I worry at my bottom lip. He can't mean what my heart wants to hope he means. No. He surely must mean all the bickering we've done could've been avoided if we'd simply just hopped in the sack together in the first place.

"Cute. But I don't think sex would've magically fixed all of our problems."

West grins and leans in, kissing me gently. "I'm not just talking about sex."

My heart melts. And with those six words, I'm a goner.

16

Bad Case of Loving You by Robert Palmer

West

As I enter band rehearsal on Monday, I'm greeted by a slow clap. And it's not just the band. There's actual crew today, which means tour prep has officially begun.

I grin like a fool, spreading just one arm out since I'm carrying Rosie with the other, welcoming the attention. The recognition that I pulled it off, from the people who really count. It probably doesn't hurt that I just spent the last two days buried in Maxi either, which was its own kind of reward. Yep. Right now, life is pretty fucking good.

"Thank you, thank you," I call magnanimously. "You may all bow and scrape now."

Nik approaches and punches me playfully in the gut. "You wish," she taunts.

I double over, feigning injury. "Not the thanks I was hoping for."

She smirks and picks up her bass, hopping up onto the small stage.

James walks by and claps me on the back. "Punching is Nik-speak for 'I'm proud of you,'" he jokes.

I shoot him a smirk knowing that's James-speak for "I'm proud of you too." But nothing is less rock and roll than hugging and sharing your emotions. So I know that's the most I'm going to get from any of them. Except maybe Ward when we're alone. Dude's scarily in touch with his feelings these days.

With a chuckle, I unzip the gig bag and get Rosie ready for rehearsal. "Yeah, yeah," I grumble teasingly. "West took one for the team, whatever."

"Hey, we played our parts," Michael protests. "I mean, I can't say it wasn't fun hearing you grovel, though."

I snort. "Too bad it was all for the cameras then, huh?"

I'm looking down as I tune Rosie, but when eerie silence falls after my words, I look back up.

Everyone is staring at me.

"What?" I ask innocently.

"Are you fucking kidding me?" Ward pipes up.

My head swings toward him standing at the mixing boards with one of the techs.

"Uh. No. You all knew it was just for show." A bunch of shocked faces stare back at me and my heart drops. "You didn't know?"

"Uh. No," James mocks. "Seriously, West?"

I set Rosie down carefully, because I just went from zero to pissed in two seconds flat, and I don't want to hurt her. "Seriously. I signed up to do what was asked of me. Nobody ever said it had to be real."

"That was kind of the whole fucking point, though, wasn't it?" Nik says. "I mean, why even do it if you didn't mean it?" She shakes her head in disgust.

"You guys can't be serious," I insist. I gesture at Nik. "You're the one who said, 'Just go with it.'" Then I fling an arm Michael's direction. "And you were the one who told me if I didn't do it, we were done. So I fucking did what I had to. Nobody ever said it had to be real."

"And I said not to be selfish," James points out. "That you weren't done making this up to people."

"I *humiliated* myself on a worldwide broadcast seen by hundreds of millions of people," I seethe. "A broadcast, that I might add, once it was edited and narrated bore little resemblance to what actually happened anyway. It was all a PR opportunity mashed up with placating the masses. Even if there had been any truth in there, it would've been lost in editing."

Ward shakes his head as the techs skitter out the door, clearly realizing this shit isn't going to get better and not wanting to get caught in the middle.

"What about your own conscience, man?" Ward nudges.

"My demons are my own. The only people whose opinions I care about are in this room," I insist.

"Yeah, and what about us?" Ward presses, now the clear voice for the group as everyone else has fallen silent. "Was your apology to us bullshit too?"

I press my lips together, and if looks could kill, Ward would be six feet under.

"Don't go there." I shoot glares at each of them. "Look, you guys may be pissed off at me, but I really thought you knew. Either way, this absolutely does not leave this fucking room unless you want to undo everything I worked for. Because whether the apologies themselves were real or not, I just went through a whole ration of shit to get us back on track. I swear I thought I was doing what you guys wanted me to. So please, don't throw me under the bus now. You'd just be fucking yourselves over."

Nik snorts. "We're not stupid. Of course we're not going to say anything."

James stares at me sadly. Then, after a minute offers, "I'll talk to the techs too."

My gaze flips back to Ward.

"All right. What about Max, then, West? Don't think I don't know where you slipped off to on Friday night. Where you've been all weekend."

"Oh, so you're stalking me now, are you?" I throw at him accusingly.

Ward shakes his head. "I'm just looking out for you, bro. Things have clearly changed between you two. How's Max going to feel when she finds out?"

"She's not in this room, is she?" I snap back.

By his expression I can tell he gets exactly what I mean. I hadn't planned on telling her, even though I'm pretty sure she already knows.

But then, I thought the band knew too.

And clearly Nik gets my meaning too, because she can't keep herself from jumping in and offering, "This is the chick who hated you? You're with her now?" She snorts. "Yeah. Lying to her seems like a great idea."

"What is this, thank-West-by-making-him-feel-like-shit day?" I snap. But deep down I'm irritated because I know they have a point. About Max, at least.

If she doesn't already know like I thought she did, how will she take it? Will she be furious? Or will she understand that I was doing what I had to?

"No," Michael mutters, going back to adjusting his kit. "Apparently this is bitch-smack-West-with-reality day."

"Great. Consider me bitch-smacked," I reply sarcastically. "Can we just rehearse already?"

Michael shrugs noncommittally. Everyone else stays silent but goes back to setting up, except for James, who I can only assume is going to talk to the techs before bringing them back in.

Great. Just fucking great. A few minutes ago I was high on life. And now I'm debating whether I should play it safe and keep my mouth shut or risk it all so see if I've started something with Max on a foundation of lies.

As I finish tuning Rosie, I let out a heavy sigh. Because I know what I have to do. It's what I should do. It's what the me of a few years ago would've never done. I've got to talk to her.

God, I hope I was right in the first place. I hope she already knows.

But my decision just proves how bad I've got it for Maxi Marshall. Because the last thing I want to do is break her heart by lying. But to be the guy she deserves, if I'm wrong, I may end up breaking her heart with the truth.

17

You Give Love a Bad Name by Bon Jovi

Max

What's the best way to cap off one of the best weeks of your career as a rock music journalist? Sex. Definitely sex. With a rock star. Which I'm very much looking forward to when West gets here … oh, any minute now.

I imagine most people would want to go slow. I mean, we just got together a week ago. Or maybe have dinner first. And sure, I'm hungry. But all week, I was sent messages about the show. Fans wanting to know if we're going to share more content online. Band managers asking me to feature their acts. The owners of the magazine personally gushing about what a great job I did.

Sure, I'm proud of myself. But every bit of praise made me think of West. How none of it would've been possible without his stubborn ass tracking me down. And how far he's come since then. How far *we've* come.

It didn't hurt that he spent most of last weekend showing me all the ways he knew how to use those talented fingers of his. Plus, you know, the rest of him.

And the pillow talk. Good lord. I forgot what the beginning felt like. Fresh and exciting and … well, pretty much a lust fest.

And I'm ready for Lust Fest Part Deux.

Dressed in skintight black jeans and a low-cut Sex Pistols tee, I definitely look groupie-level hot. So I'm pretty confident he's not going to care about skipping straight to the good stuff.

He's only fifteen minutes late when there's a knock on the door. I'd call that progress.

I swing the door open with a grin, ready for seduction … only to find, in place of the smoking hot sex god musician, there's a broody tired-as-fuck-looking hot mess of a man leaning against my doorframe.

"West?" I say, bemused.

His eyes search mine. All of the warmth and playfulness they usually hold is absent. A pit forms in my stomach.

"Can I come in?" he finally says.

I step back. "Sure, of course."

As I close the door, he walks in, kicking off his shoes and settling onto my old, tan leather couch. Well, sitting. He's not particularly settled as I take a seat next to him. More like perched on the edge of the cushion. And one finger is drawing circles on his knee. Shit.

"Rough week?" I ask tentatively.

His eyes flick up to meet mine.

"I have to ask you a difficult question," he hedges.

Something about his tone makes the pit in my stomach grow. "Okay," I reply slowly.

He looks down and his finger continues to work clockwise on his dark jeans.

"The apology tour," he starts. "Did you …" He looks up at me "…did you believe it?"

My brows scrunch together.

"Are you worried that it seemed fake?" I ask.

He shakes his head. "No. I know the public ate it up. I'm asking if *you* believed it."

I lean back, unsure quite how to answer that. "Um. Yeah? I guess. I mean, you probably remember that I gave you shit at the beginning because your apology with Ward seemed too easy. And, you know, we both know the one with your dad was fake as fuck. That's not to say I blame you in the least. But other than that … of course." I pause, trying to work out what's bothering him. "Did someone else call bullshit? Is that what's upsetting you? Because I'll totally kick their ass."

He huffs a small laugh at the joke. "So if the other apologies *were* fake … would you blame me?"

I open my mouth to respond as the words sink in. And then I close it. Is he saying what I think he is? Part of me wants time to think about this before I speak, but unfortunately my brain-to-mouth filter just isn't that good.

"Were they?" I ask bluntly as I feel heat creeping up the back of my neck. A dangerous mix of anger and embarrassment churns under my skin, making me feel itchy all over.

West closes his eyes and sighs. "Yes."

And suddenly I want to vomit.

I was right. My first instinct was right and he …

"You *lied* to me." The irate words tumble from my mouth.

West opens his eyes and looks at me. His gaze is full of sorrow, regret, and exhaustion.

"Not on purpose. It may sound ridiculous, but I thought you knew."

I bark a sharp laugh. "You're right, that is ridiculous. I explicitly said I didn't want to participate if it was all for show. If it was all bullshit and didn't mean anything to you. Why even bother if it didn't?"

I rise as I speak, pacing in front of the couch.

"That's pretty much what Nik said," he mumbles. Then he catches my hand, forcing me to turn toward him. "I'm sorry, Maxi."

It takes all of my strength not to scoff at his apology. Because I can see that he's sorry, and I know firsthand how difficult it is for him to apologize. But sometimes sorry just isn't enough.

"You're *sorry*," I say sarcastically. "Well, that just fixes everything." I glare at him. "Your sister? Was that a lie?"

West shoots up in front of me. "God, no," he protests, grabbing my other hand and holding both in his. "At least, not all of it. I really did apologize to her."

I grind my teeth as I consider that. "Your band?"

West looks at me warily but doesn't respond. So yeah. That one was a lie.

"Holy shit, West. Your brother? Sadie?"

He nods. Both lies.

"Me? Your apology about the night at the Forum? The one just now? Are those lies too?" I ask, my voice strained with emotion.

"Absolutely not," he responds vehemently. "How could you even think that?"

My eyebrows fly up. How could I think that? Is he joking?

"Because now I have no idea what's truth and what's a lie. Why should I believe you? You could be lying that you weren't lying."

West pulls a face. "What?"

I wave my hands in frustration. "I can't do this. You should go."

"Wait, Maxi, please, I —"

"No, West. No. Whatever you're going to ask. No. I can't. I already gave you another chance and you blew it. But even if you hadn't already screwed me over once, I can't trust someone who lies to me. And I can't be with someone I don't trust."

West's face caves and despite myself, it hits me right in the gut. I want to reach out and comfort him, but how do you comfort someone who has deceived you after having been forgiven for something even worse?

"Come on, Maxi, there has to be a way through this. Please," he begs.

He reaches his hand toward my face, but I take a step back. Knowing if he touches me I'll be that much more likely to give in.

I shake my head. "Maybe. But not right now. Right now I need some time to process the truth. I think you should leave," I reiterate.

West goes to reach for me again but stops himself, his hand clenching into a fist and dropping to his side. "I'd rather stay and talk."

"Why? What else could you possibly have to say to me that would make any difference? What could be more important than the fact that you —"

"Because I love you," he all but shouts over me. Whatever words I had die on my lips at his confession. "I love you." His tone is softer and his eyes search mine softly. "I know, it doesn't make any sense. But I do. Please. Don't shut me out."

I blink hard against the tears. He means it. I can see that. Or at least, he thinks he does. But how could he possibly love me?

"You don't lie to someone you truly love, West. If you really want to be with me, you should go figure your shit out. For real this time," I persist.

"I thought I had," he says, sorrow dripping from every word. "But maybe I don't even know what that looks like."

"It looks like doing what's right when nobody else is looking. It looks like telling the truth when there's nobody who cares whether you're lying. But mostly, it's figuring out what's stopping you from doing those things."

"What happens if I never figure it out?" he challenges. "I just found you. I can't lose you now."

"You lost me before you ever knew what you had," I reply. "Because of your choices. And while I understand now more than ever how your choices have been shaped by … things out of your control … well, at the end of the day, they're your choices. And the consequences of them are also yours to deal with."

"So that's it?" he asks. And a tear skates down his cheek.

My heart cracks in half. Again.

But I don't let him see me cry. I simply nod.

"You can show yourself out," I say quietly.

And then I turn and head into my bedroom, closing the door behind me.

I put my back to the door, sliding to the floor. And then I let the tears go. Quietly, though, in case he lingers. But as soon as I hear the front door close, I don't hold back anymore.

If it's possible, this time hurts worse than the first. Or maybe it's the compounded betrayals. Or maybe it's because this time I wasn't the only one in love. This time it was real. Or at least, I thought it was.

18

King Nothing by Metallica

West

"Well, I hope you're happy," I grumble at Ward after everyone else has left rehearsal on the following Monday. A fucking shitty rehearsal, as it were. I was barely mentally present, focusing more on how pissed I am at all of their ungrateful asses.

Ward cocks an eyebrow at me. "Ah. Talking to me again, are you?" he asks dryly, plunking down on the couch by the door. The same one we used for the first apology interview. The irony isn't lost on me. "So what am I supposed to be happy about?"

I stay standing where I am at the equipment table. "Max didn't know I was being less than truthful on the apology tour either," I grumble.

"Lying," Ward offers. "It's called lying, West. So how'd the truth go over?"

I look up and shoot him a glare. "About as well as you'd expect. She dumped me."

He nods slowly, the glint in his eye telling me he thinks I deserved it, but he doesn't say anything.

"Can I ask you a question?"

Ward smirks. "I have a feeling you're going to no matter what I say."

My nostrils flare. He's in full douchebag lead singer mode. His arms splayed over the back of the couch. One ankle resting on the other knee. His arrogance shining through that pretty face of his. One I'd love to punch right about now.

"If you thought my apology was honest, was your forgiveness?"

His response is automatic. "If the apology was bullshit, de facto so was the forgiveness. Whether I intended it to be or not." He pauses. "I think the better question is, why wouldn't the apology be real?"

His hard veneer slips a little and I can see the hurt behind the question. But if he thinks his wounded feelings compare to the reality of our history, he's got another thing coming.

"Oh, gee, I don't know, maybe because you're the one who got me into heroin in the first place?"

Ward snorts. I know he doesn't get it. He's not an addict. It's not how he's wired. Unless an addiction to being a know-it-all asshole is a thing.

"Yeah, and you got Annika addicted. You're no angel either, West."

"And I apologized," I point out. "The only apology that was real, might I add, because she's the only person who deserved an apology from me. The rest of you assholes did everything you could to encourage my behavior. You" — I jerk my chin at Ward — "so someone in the band was partying too. So it wasn't just you. Erik so he could feel superior in looking down his sanctimonious nose at me. Sadie because she needed the high from the drugs and from fucking a rock star. And my dad …" I trail off, shaking my head.

I can't say it. But I know it's because it made him feel secure that nobody would ever take me seriously. That I wasn't a threat to him because I couldn't keep my head straight long enough to function, much less bring to light everything he did.

"So why'd you pick us for your apologies then? Why do it at all, for that matter?"

"Because I had no other choice," I roar at him. "But I'm sick of pretending I'm the only one who fucked up here."

Ward rises. "Look. I've tried to be supportive. I've tried to be patient. But the truth hurts, West. And the truth is, you're pointing your finger, but there's no one around to blame but you. Nobody forced you to take drugs. You could've said no. Nobody forced you to be a dick to Sadie, to abuse your little sister's trust, to be a complete asshole to your family. To your fans. To Max." He stops in front of me, his expression frustrated. "I'm glad you got clean, man. But if you're going to really get your life back, you need to start taking responsibility for your choices."

"You're a fucking hypocrite," I scoff, grabbing my gig bag and moving around him.

"Never said I was perfect," he calls to my back. "But at least I don't play the victim card."

And I've never seen red like I do in that moment. My brain disconnects from my body and I whirl, flying toward him, fist raising of its own accord.

The only mental clarity I have is noting the surprise on his face as I punch him.

I WENT TO EXACTLY ONE NARCOTICS ANONYMOUS MEETING BEFORE I decided they weren't for me, along with AA, sponsors, therapists, and everything else that I thought was for weak-ass pussies who couldn't keep their shit together.

Except, as I down my fourth double shot of Jack Daniels, I'm starting to think maybe it was less for pussies and more … well, to avoid exactly where I am right now. Thankfully, I'm already too drunk to care. Which is hilarious, because way back when, I'd just be getting started. And now I'm practically a lightweight. Well, by comparison. It's almost funny.

Or it would be if I wasn't still furious. At Ward. The band. Max. Myself. I'm also sober enough to know I should drag ass the few blocks home and sleep this shit off, rather than let it turn into what it would've back then too. Harder drugs. Preferably heroin, yes, but I'd never say no to cocaine either. And a good, high-as-a-kite fuck-fest, usually with Sadie and at least one of her stripper friends.

While I can't say I have easy access to those kinds of drugs anymore, it wouldn't be difficult either. And getting women … well, even before the apology tour, there were clearly enough of them who didn't care about my fall from grace and gladly would've fucked me. Not that I fucked any of them. Not since before rehab, anyway.

I was trying to be good. Trying to put my life back together and focus on the band. And until Maxi, I didn't have the first clue how to be with someone while I was sober. Hell, I didn't have the desire to.

But I've lost her, just like I've lost Ward. And probably the rest of the band.

Boy, this tour is going to be fun.

I throw way too much money on the bar and stumble out onto the street.

The sun has just set, with the dimmest of deep pink and purple glows still visible over the darkening ocean waves across Pacific Coast Highway. It'd be beautiful if I wasn't in the middle of throwing myself a pity party.

Fucking ocean.

"Holy shit, guys, it's West!" I hear someone say behind me.

I realize as I look up that I'd been teetering on the edge of the sidewalk. I glance back at the group of dudebros behind me. There are three of them, and they look like a bunch of preppy-ass college punks looking to do some Jägerbombs, or whatever the kids are into these days.

One of them starts pulling out his phone as they rush at me. The one who I think spoke claps me on the shoulder.

"Dude, I can't believe it's you! You're awesome," he says.

One corner of my mouth tips up. Hey, at least the fans still love me. That's what I wanted … right?

"Thanks, man," I reply.

"Take a picture with us," the dudebro to his left says as the guy with the phone positions himself slightly in front of us with his camera front-facing to get us all in the shot.

I shrug. "Okay, sure, why not."

They get the picture, then dudebro number one, the one who spoke first, says, "Come drink with us."

I wave him off. "Nah, I gotta get home, man. Rehearsal tomorrow and everything."

Dudebro number two jumps in. "Come on. It's on us. Whatever you want man, just hang with us. Our friends would be so jealous if we bought you a drink."

And I'm just drunk enough that the appeal to my ego works. "Yeah, okay, just one drink," I agree.

⌒○

I WAKE UP THE NEXT MORNING TO A CLANGING NOISE THAT SOUNDS LIKE A rhythmically challenged kid banging on a steel drum kit. What the fuck?

My surroundings start to come into focus. I'm on a hard surface. It smells bad. And as my blurry eyes adjust I realize … I'm in a mother-fucking jail cell.

I bolt upright and my eyes land on a young police officer leering at me through the bars, holding a nightstick up against the metal. That must have been what was causing the clanging.

"Rise and shine, pretty boy," he taunts. "Your manager is here to bail you out."

My head pounds and my stomach churns, and not just at the thought that I did something bad enough to land me here. Bad enough to need to be bailed out. But also because I'm pretty sure I drank the whole fucking bar last night.

At least, that's how it feels based on the level of hungover I am right now and how little I remember of the evening. I check myself before rising, mentally noting that at least I didn't vomit or piss all over myself. So I've certainly had worse nights.

As I'm led into the main office, I catch sight of Burke's expression. And if I didn't know better, I'd say someone died. I only hope it's not about to be me.

19

Under the Bridge by Red Hot Chili Peppers

Max

I'm woken early Tuesday morning by my phone ringing shrilly from the nightstand. I grope for it sleepily, fumbling as I attempt to slide to answer. I barely register that it's Jason.

"This better be good," I say, half joking, half serious. Because I also notice it's not even six a.m. Even if he is technically my boss, it still annoys me.

"I woke you up." It's not a question.

"So early, yet so observant," I grumble, sitting up in bed and rubbing my eyes. "What's up, Jason?"

There's silence from his end for a few moments. "Christ, I thought you'd already be up. That you'd already know."

"Know *what*?" I ask, annoyed.

An incoming text pings in my ear. "I just sent you the link. Get in here once you've watched it. We're going to have a full day on our hands," he replies cryptically.

"O…kay?" I respond. But he's already hung up. Great.

With a tired sigh, I kiss my last hour of sleep goodbye and click the link Jason sent.

A YouTube video pops up and loads. The time stamp is almost one a.m. this morning. The only object I can make out as it loads is a wood surface of some kind.

"Duuuuude, you're *West*," says some surfer-dude-sounding guy from behind the shaky cellphone camera. The view lifts to focus on West, flanked by two other guys who appear college-aged. And they're clearly in a bar, drinks in front of all of them. The wood surface was the table.

I suck in a sharp breath and my heart starts pounding. No. No, no, no.

"I'm Weeeeest," he slurs in response lifting a glass of amber-colored liquid and downing it. "Fuck yeah, man!"

Exactly what I feared. West has fallen spectacularly — and very publicly — off the wagon.

The guy to West's left downs his drink and cheers. The guy to West's right holds up his glass.

"This one's for you, West. You're my fucking *hero*, man! You took it on the fucking chin with that apology tour, bro." Then the kid downs his drink.

West starts laughing.

"Did I say something funny?" The guy on the right asks blankly.

"No. I just hate to burst your bubble," West says, giggling. "But it was all fake."

Well, shit. He's fallen off the wagon and spilled the beans. I suddenly get exactly what Jason meant. This is officially a complete and utter disaster.

The guy on the left bursts out laughing just as the guy on the right sets down his glass, looking in shock at West.

"No, no way, dude," he says. "Come on. Really?"

"Yup. It was all total bullshit. Sorry." He shrugs. "In my defense, they made me do it."

I want to cover my eyes. I want to stop watching the train wreck. But I can't seem to make myself turn it off.

The kid on the right continues to look devastated. "That's just … that's just wrong," he says, his cheeks reddening in apparent anger.

West shrugs, then looks over at the guy holding the camera for the first time. "Dude, no more pictures," he slurs.

"It's not a picture," the guy holding the camera says in a taunting tone. "It's a video."

West's face goes from annoyed to angry in two seconds flat. "I didn't say you could record me, dude. Turn that shit off. Delete it."

Camera guy laughs. "Hell no, man, this shit is gonna blow up. Posting in three, two —"

West lunges for the camera and the remaining few seconds of video are a blur of fists and glass and wood.

I watch it again. And again. And again. Every viewing nauseates me more.

When I can't handle any more, I check the view count. It's already in the hundreds of thousands in the five or so hours it's been up.

Holy. Shit.

I drop my phone and put my hands over my face. West, what the fuck have you done?

just after seven.

He stops typing and closes his laptop, gesturing for me to take a seat. As I do, he gets up and closes his door, then returns to his chair.

He folds his hands on his desk and gives me a serious look.

"They arrested West last night for assaulting the kid making the video.

West's manager is bailing him out as we speak. That's all I know right now, but I expect a number of things to happen today."

I nod, feeling sick at his words, even though I'd assumed as much.

"Let me guess," I hazard. "The video will continue to go viral. They'll call off the tour. They'll hold press conferences disavowing all knowledge that West's apologies weren't truthful."

Jason nods grimly. "At the very least. They're trying to get it taken down, as it's technically evidence in an active police case," he replies. "But it's a video of a major rock star breaking his sobriety, assaulting someone, and admitting he duped his fans. Now that it's out there, it's going to be practically impossible to stop."

I close my eyes for a moment, trying not to think about what this will mean. Determined to keep it together, I open them again and look back at Jason, whose face is filled with concern. Despite not knowing of my brief lapse in judgment in the sleeping-with-West department, he clearly understands that this will be tough for me. Because, oh yeah, my career and the magazine's reputation are on the line too. Goddamn West.

"What do you need from me?" I ask.

"I've already got PR working on a press release to go out this afternoon. They're going to want your input. And start working on an article detailing our involvement in the apology project to make it clear that we were explicit in participating only under the condition that this was a genuine endeavor. We were assured it was, and thus we had no knowledge to the contrary. Use examples from the tour — the sister would be a good one — that show you truly believed him to be sincere." He hesitates, then looks at me warily. "You didn't know he was faking it, did you?"

My chest tightens with anxiety. Because even though West lied to me, fell off the wagon, and utterly destroyed everything we worked for ... I can't find it in me to betray him. Even if he's betrayed himself.

"I had suspicions at first, which West denied. So no, while we were filming I was under the impression that he wasn't faking it," I reply truthfully.

Jason examines my face for a few moments. And I know he's not stupid. He can clearly read between the lines. But I know he's also smart enough to realize there's no point in pushing the issue.

So he lets me go, finally free to be alone with my thoughts while I try to figure out how on earth I'm going to write this article.

I haven't gotten far when I receive word that the tour has officially been cancelled. And Violent Mood Swings has been dropped by their label. The band, save West, has scheduled a press conference for early this afternoon that, thankfully, Alexsis will cover while I try to gather my thoughts on all of this.

I spend the day trying to distill a dangerous mix of emotions and facts into something that can salvage the magazine's reputation. While I manage it adequately, it's not without constant flipping between revisiting my anger at West's charade of an apology tour and concern knowing how devastated he must be. Because now he's truly lost everything.

It's underscored when Alexsis returns from the band's press conference. She tells me that every single one of them more or less threw West under the bus by blaming him and only him for the lies. I suspect they think they're doing it for his own good, trying to help him learn the lesson I also want him to learn: that at some point he needs to stop half-assing it and really fix things. But I know he'll only see it as a betrayal, a loss. And it is both of those things.

But the loss of his band, his *friends*, the fans, the tour, his record contract … and I guess you can toss me on that list too. Oh god, and his family. Now that this is out there they'll know he was lying. It's so much all at once.

It's going to crush West. And he's already slipped, as evidenced by his drunken toppling of everything left that he held dear.

My deepest fear is that this is going to achieve the exact opposite of showing him how much harder he needs to try. I'm terrified that it's only going to send him spiraling farther down, back into the abyss he only just climbed out of. Possibly even deeper.

Despite everything he's done to me, I don't want that for him. And it's with that thought I realize that I'd never stopped having feelings for Kristoffer Westberg. Not through any of this. Not since the very beginning. Even the negative feelings were fueled by knowing I still cared.

As much as I hurt for West, I don't even consider contacting him. He needs to feel this pain. To live with the weight of it. Because there's a slim chance that I'm wrong, that it will be exactly the wakeup call he needs to get his life back together, for real this time.

At least, that's what I'm hoping for. And you know what they say: Hope dies last.

20

Hurt by Johnny Cash

West

One minute, I'm floating. The next, a sharp jab in the ribs snaps me out of a light, drug-induced sleep.

It takes me a while to come to. Minutes? Hours? Who knows. Time has lost all meaning. Everything has lost all meaning. A pressing need to take a piss forces me to wake up enough so I can stumble to the bathroom sooner rather than later.

But opening my eyes, I'm not where I thought I'd be. Thankfully, I'm not in a jail cell this time, but being in a bed I don't recognize isn't exactly great either.

I lift my head and peer through the dim early morning light to find Sadie passed out next to me, her elbow lodged in my side.

Fucking awesome. I check myself over only to find I'm still fully dressed, though that could mean I'd gotten dressed afterward with the intention of leaving and just passed out before I could. The odds of being in Sadie's bed and not having fucked her are pretty low, unfortunately. At least, if our history is anything to go by.

As I climb out of bed and find her bathroom, I try to bring back my memories from last night. But all I can remember is yesterday morning, waking up in jail. Everything after that is gone. The kind of gone alcohol alone can't account for.

Given my still-detached senses and general calmness, I'm going with heroin, and not a small amount of it. A sniff of my shirt as I use the bathroom tells me there was also plenty of booze. And Sadie's signature jasmine scent clings to me.

I know I'm sobering up though, because I start feeling disgusted with myself on every level. I have no doubt I crawled back into Sadie's good graces just by having drugs. It doesn't matter how pissed she is, if I've got what she wants, she always takes me back. That's probably why I went to her; I know what a doormat she is. And some habits are hard to break. Many habits, apparently.

I head back to the bedroom but hesitate on the threshold. Just the sight of her sleeping there throws me back. It's my life before rehab all over again.

Except worse.

I start to remember everything that preceded this little bender, and I turn around, headed for the living room. I can't lose it within earshot of that crazy bitch. So instead, I swipe my cellphone, a pack of smokes, and a lighter from the bedroom and head for the door, intending to smoke outside before going back to find the wallet and keys I was unable to locate right away.

But on the way past the dining room, I spot a glass door that leads to a small balcony. That'll do.

I slip out, the cool morning air waking me quickly. I light up a cigarette, something else I haven't done in years. Christ, I really am on a roll, aren't I?

Well, if I'm going to completely blow my second chance, might as well do it properly. I take a deep drag and practically groan in relief at how fast the nicotine buzz hits.

My phone vibrates in my pocket, distracting me. I pull it out and see a text from Ward, among other notifications.

Seriously? Drunk dialing me? After everything you've lost in the last 24 hours because of drinking? DO BETTER.

I swallow hard as tears spring to my eyes. As the memories of yesterday land. Of finding out I'd been arrested for assault. Also known as punching some kid who made a video of me admitting the whole apology tour was a sham. And then said video exploding, outing my lapse in sobriety and the calculated duping of my fans. Which unsurprisingly led to the tour being cancelled and losing our record contract.

As if that wasn't bad enough, my band then completely turned on me for absolutely no reason. They didn't even have anything to gain from pointing the finger solely at me; we'd already lost everything. No, they just couldn't pass up the opportunity to kick me while I was down.

As I process Ward's text, it suddenly occurs to me that he may not be the only one I drunk-dialed. My stomach drops as I scramble to go through my calls and missed notifications.

Yep. I called Maxi. And she texted me back. Fuck fuck fuck fuck fuck.

I open her text and my breath leaves me.

If you care about me at all, you'll leave me alone and focus on yourself. Figure out what forgiveness really means and then maybe you can stop faking it. All of it.

I stare down at the phone, heart ripped in two. Wet spots appear on the glass and I realize I'm crying.

I've lost the band. I've lost my oldest friends in the world. I've lost Maxi. My family has probably seen the video. I couldn't give two fucks about my brother and father, but god, if Annika sees it … I close my eyes and fat tears slip under my lids and down my cheeks.

My world has been burned to the ground. And here I stand on the balcony of the succubus bitch who rode me for fame and drugs. Who would gladly continue to suck the life out of me.

I sink onto the concrete base of the balcony, pressing my head against the metal bars.

Figure out what forgiveness really means.

That's what Maxi said. But that's the rub — I have no idea what forgiveness means. I am sure of one thing though: This time I'm beyond forgiveness. I'm not going to get a third chance at this life.

I put out the cigarette butt and rise, leaning over the balcony. And if I thought I was crying before, it's nothing to the tears that fall stories and stories down to the pavement below.

Maybe I should just ... lean farther. Let myself go. Stop fighting so fucking hard for a life that doesn't want me. The thought makes the tears fall faster, and a sob rips out of my chest. The metal rail cuts into my abdomen.

The pain snaps me out of it a little. That I can feel pain. That I'm alive. And knowing my fuck-up self, if I tried to jump, I probably wouldn't die. I'd probably end up paralyzed or in a coma or something, trapped in a body that no longer obeys me, just like my life doesn't.

For some reason the thought makes me laugh. I've really lost it now, and I should probably get my shit together and go home. At least fall apart in private. With a sad shake of my head, I go back inside.

21

Darkest Days by Stabbing Westward

West

"Y ou better not have finished my smokes," Sadie greets me from the kitchen as I step back inside the dingy little apartment.

I roll my eyes and chuck the pack at her. "I only had one, keep your panties on," I grumble. My eyes scan the kitchen and dining room, not finding what I'm looking for. "Where's my wallet and keys?"

She laughs. "Oh don't worry, my panties were firmly on all night, no thanks to your limp dick," she shoots back venomously, then points toward the front door. "Your shit's on the floor over there."

Insanely relieved that I did not, in fact, fuck Sadie, I stride over to the door and find my things exactly where she said, just inside on the floor. Clearly carelessly dropped there as we came in.

I snatch the items up and tuck them into my pockets.

"Well, it's been real," I call to her. "Have a nice life."

She snorts as she pours herself a cup of coffee. I mean, don't bother offering me any, bitch.

"Yeah, sure," she says dismissively. "Next time you come back, at least bring some vitamin V with you. It's a waste of heroin not to get a good fuck with it."

"I'm not coming back," I assure her. *And I'm definitely not touching you ever again*, I think to myself.

She leans against the counter, sipping her coffee. "If that's what you want to believe," she mutters.

"That's reality, Sadie. Last night was a huge mistake."

"So you're not going to get high again? Really?" she taunts.

I run a hand through my hair, agitated. I hadn't actually thought that far. Do I want to? Yes. And no. But she has a point — now that I've slipped, there's a very real chance I could slip again. And again. Until it's not slipping anymore. Until it's just my life.

Feelings stir in my chest. Fear. Guilt. Despair. And I realize … I don't want that. This time I really, truly don't. Yesterday was … well, one of the worst days of my life. I was in a bad place. One I don't want to be in again.

"No," I reply resolutely. "I'm not."

She snorts. "Okay then. But when you do, we both know you're coming back for some ass," she says with a shrug, taking another drink.

I shake my head. "Don't you get tired of living like this, Sadie?"

"Don't you?" she shoots back caustically.

"I *am* sick of it. I fucked up last night."

She sets her mug down, coming around the counter between us and stopping in front of me.

"You did fuck up last night. But I know how you can make it up to me," she says sultrily, staring up at me from under her eyelashes.

I look down at her. Her makeup is smeared. And even though she's only twenty-six, the bags under her eyes, the sag of her skin from drugs, partying, and god knows what else, make her look twice her age.

With a feline grin, she presses against me, rubbing her hand over my cock.

A couple of years ago, I would've instantly grabbed her and fucked her up against the door. Now? Junior doesn't even stir. Not even a twitch. I'm well and truly repulsed by the situation.

How was I ever attracted to her? To this lifestyle?

I wasn't, is the answer.

So why did I let it consume me? That's the real question.

"Damn, West, there's something really wrong with you," she says, dropping her hand after getting no reaction. "I've fucked sixty-year-olds with harder dicks than yours."

I step back in disgust. This is all wrong. All of it.

"Well, then I'll leave you to go find a sixty-year-old to fuck," I tell her. "Bye, Sadie."

I walk out the door and down the stairs, stopping in front of her apartment building to text my driver for a ride home.

It doesn't take him long, and he doesn't ask questions. And I'm glad for it, because I already feel shitty enough.

As soon as I get home, I don't even shower. I head into my music room and grab my first guitar. I could have grabbed any of the dozen I own, but that one called to me.

As I settle onto my balcony, the late-morning May air finally starting to warm, everything still feels *wrong*. I know it shouldn't feel right, given how epically awful the last couple of days have been.

But this is the place I go so all of that can fade away. So I can let the music, the waves, the fresh air take it all away. Except it doesn't. I strum mindlessly, trying to find a song, any song, that will help me connect with what I'm feeling.

Problem is, I'm feeling way too damn much. Anger. Sadness. Defeat. Helplessness. No … I don't feel helpless, I decide after a few moments of turning the word over on my tongue.

I feel powerless.

I have no idea how to fix any of this. How to fix myself.

The last time I felt this wasn't before rehab. No, rehab was a court-ordered solution. It wasn't something I sought, though eventually it turned into something I chose to continue. No, the last time I was this low, I was sixteen and seemingly trapped in the hell that was my life. I was never smart like Erik. My music wasn't good enough for my pedophile father. Even I was almost too old for him to abuse anymore. But Annika … I can't even think of what he did to us. And when I'd try to use music to escape, he'd try to take that away too.

There was nothing right about my life. Everything felt wrong, *was* wrong. But I had no clue where to begin to make it right. Fuck, I was just a kid. What did I know about anything?

So I ran. Like a coward, though not before making Erik promise to take care of Annika. Since he was so adept at avoiding Dad, I thought he could help her. And I couldn't take it anymore. It was too heavy a burden to carry.

So I vanished and did my best to forget about it all. I lived on the streets for two years, playing my beat-up guitar for change and picking through garbage cans for food. Fighting with other runaways for territory. Stealing to survive. And when the opportunity presented itself, doing drugs to feel something besides the well of pain inside. In some ways it was better. But I never really forgot.

It wasn't until a month after my eighteenth birthday that I met Ward in front of a bulletin board outside of Guitar Center. And the rest, as they say, is history.

The tears start again at that thought. Because now it really *is* history. All of it. Because of me.

I know this has to stop. Because nothing has really changed since the darkest days of my life at age sixteen. I'm right back there now, at thirty-six.

Except now I'm not a helpless teenager with more scars and guilt than brains. And even if I don't know how to fix this any more than I did then, I know I can't keep burying those feelings. If I'm going to break this cycle, I need to dig them up and bring them into the light. Something I didn't even do in rehab. I've avoided it, putting band-aids on the problem, hoping it'll just go away.

But the demons inside are clawing their way out. They're ruining my life. And clearly I'm not going to slay them on my own.

I need help.

The guitar slides from my lap. I lean forward, not fighting the tears for the first time. Letting them go.

Letting it all go.

22

Shout by Tears for Fears

West

Two months later…

"So. Kristoffer. How was your week?" Dr. Marks asks, tilting her head in that way only a therapist can.

"Well, Sherry," I tease her with a wink. "It wasn't bad, actually."

She smiles tolerantly, her amber eyes crinkling under her silver-rimmed glasses.

"Your energy does seem calm today," she remarks knowingly. "You went to your meetings?"

I nod slowly. "I'm down to one NA meeting a week," I respond.

"Still two AA meetings, then?" she asks, concern tinging her voice.

"Yep."

She makes a note, then looks back up at me. "I'm a little surprised. It's been two months. Do you still feel like you might relapse?"

"Not really," I admit. "It's just become a habit I enjoy. Is that weird?"

"No," she allows. "But you'll eventually need to learn to cope without so many."

I hesitate on whether I want to share why I really didn't scale down this week. Why I felt like I needed the extra support. Not because I felt like drinking, just in general.

That is, until I remember my promise to myself to stop feeling powerless and accept help.

"I saw Annika last weekend."

Dr. Marks' eyebrows fly up because she knows it's been something I've been avoiding. "And how did that go?"

"She's doing great. She's got a job at a lawyer's office, of all places," I tell her with a chuckle. "We talked about our dad."

She nods, leaning forward, clearly eager to hear more. "And?"

I uncross and recross my legs nervously. Talking about my feelings never gets easier, no matter how necessary it is. But Sherry Marks has helped me more than anyone ever has. She's got that concerned grandma vibe that never makes me feel judged. Something about her makes me feel safe letting it all out.

"I told her I felt guilty for leaving her there with just Erik. Especially since I know now how little he did to protect her."

"And you felt like that was your job."

I nod, a lump catching in my throat. "Yes."

"Even though you were only a child yourself?" There's that head tilt again.

The lump thickens and my eyes burn. "Yes."

"What did she say?"

I blink hard, staring down at my finger, which is now tracing circles into my thigh. "She said there's nothing to forgive, that what he did to us wasn't my fault. And even if I was there it wouldn't have stopped anything. But that if I needed her forgiveness, I had it."

A tear slips out and I wipe it away self-consciously.

Dr. Marks leans over and puts her hand over mine. "Did her forgiveness help?"

I look up, a little surprised at the question, though I don't know why. She has a way of asking things I don't expect. Things that cut right to the issue.

"No," I admit. "Not even a little. Though I am glad she seems okay now."

Dr. Marks inhales slowly. "Because you've come so far in understanding the role the abuse played in your addiction and your relationships, I'm going to tell you something I think you're finally ready to hear."

I look at her warily, but I don't stop her like she says I always can if I need to. So she continues.

"Maybe it's not her forgiveness you really need," she offers softly with a squeeze of my hand. Then she withdraws, allowing me to hear that. To process that.

I rub circles into my jeans as I do. As I really absorb what she's suggesting.

"How can I forgive myself? Even if it wouldn't have made a difference, if I'd stayed …" I look up at the ceiling, blinking hard against the tears, swallowing against the lump in my throat. "At least she wouldn't have been alone."

"Like you would have felt alone?"

I look at Dr. Marks abruptly then. Because I know exactly what she's suggesting, the word she's used for that kind of thought process in the past — *projecting*. I'm projecting my trauma, the way I'd feel, onto Annika.

"Yes, that's exactly right," I reply.

"Did Annika say she felt alone?" Dr. Marks asks.

I shake my head. "No, she didn't. She always had a million friends. Even if she didn't tell them. Or couldn't tell them. She always had a place to go, people who liked her for her. I was the one who didn't have many friends. I was the one who missed Erik when he stopped hanging around the house so much. I was the one who always felt alone."

"So when you, a mere child yourself, ran away from the physical, mental, emotional, and sexual abuse your own father committed against you, you felt guilty for leaving her. Because if she'd left you, you would have felt abandoned and alone."

"Yes," I admit. This time I don't wipe the tears away. What's the point?

"You feel like you failed your family."

I nod. "So as punishment, I failed myself?" It's not really a question. Because as I utter the words, I know without a doubt they're true.

Dr. Marks simply folds her hands in her lap and looks at me with equal parts compassion and encouragement.

She doesn't have to confirm the truth. That that's exactly what I did. I punished myself by behaving so recklessly that I pushed away everyone close to me while the drugs took me away from the deep chasm of hurt I was trying to escape. That I sought validation from people who couldn't know me, and therefore couldn't hurt me: the fans. They became everything while I subconsciously sabotaged my life.

And in doing that I also hurt my friends, my band. Maybe even because I *wanted* to hurt them. Maybe I wanted them to abandon me because I thought I deserved it for abandoning Annika. And this is all probably why I lied to Max too. Maybe deep down I wanted her to have a new reason to hate me, so she didn't get too close. Because god knows shit got real the moment I realized I'd fallen for her.

I really don't want to be this fucked up anymore. I want to know what it's like to be happy. To not run from my demons all the time.

"How do I just … change?" I ask, my mind still reeling. "How do I stop ruining everything I touch as penance for all the things I've done?"

"You've done the hardest part in recognizing the root of the problem."

"And the other part?"

"It's as simple and as hard as forgiving yourself."

And we're back here again. To something I have no clue how to do.

"How?" I say, a pleading note in the word.

She contemplates that for a moment. "Imagine Ward had been in this situation as a teen instead of you. Imagine he'd been abused by his father, as had his sister. Imagine if he'd left, then flagellated himself for it for years to the point of imploding his life spectacularly, until as an older adult he was finally able to start dealing with what had happened to him. Would you tell him to forgive himself in this situation?"

Oh, now she's just *trying* to make me cry. I sniff hard. As mad as I was at Ward a couple of months ago, I still consider him a brother. More so than my actual brother.

"I'd tell him he'd suffered enough. That he is good. That he is loved. That if he needs someone's forgiveness, he can have mine." I swallow hard, hanging my head, suddenly acutely aware of both why Annika said what she said as well as the point Dr. Marks is trying to make.

"And I'd tell you to take that big heart of yours and turn it toward yourself. You are good, Kristoffer. You are loved. But just like in the example with Ward, the person whose forgiveness you need before you can believe or accept anyone else's is your own."

I stare down into my hands, the occasional tear wetting my palms.

"When you're able to do that," Dr. Marks continues after a few minutes of silence, "you'll know how to move forward. You'll know who and what is really important to you, and you'll do what you can to make amends."

I clench my hands into fists and use them to rub at my eyes. "And if they don't want to hear it?"

Dr. Marks breathes a sigh out of her nose. "All you can do is try. You cannot control another's reactions. And if you truly accept that, you'll have peace no matter the outcome."

I continue to look down, realizing my right index finger has started tracing circles again. It's almost automatic now when I'm thinking, having long ago stopped being about the need to drink. That small thought makes me realize how far I've come. And how far I have yet to go.

Dr. Marks' words follow me home and haunt me into the evening.

As I'm getting ready for bed, I look up into the mirror. I look tired, but healthier than I have in a long time. And I'm ready to do this.

"I forgive you," I say to my reflection. With those words that are as true as the heart I'm about to lay on the line, tears blur my eyes. "I forgive you."

23

Eye of the Tiger by Survivor

West

When James opens his door, I have to admit, I panic a little. What if he's angry? What if he only let me come over to tell me off? What if, what if, what if.

Dr. Marks warned me not to do this and to remind myself that all I can do is try.

So when, without a word, James steps over his threshold and wraps his arms around me, I gotta admit, I wasn't expecting it.

"Hey, man," I joke, hugging him back.

He steps back and holds me at arm's length. "Fuck, it's good to see you, dude."

"*Daddy*," a tiny, chastising voice gasps from inside. James' four-year-old daughter, Zoe, appears in a purple tutu dress, wagging a finger and clutching a naked doll that has only half its hair. "That's a bad word."

James chuckles and tips his head, inviting me in. He leads me into the kitchen where his wife, Jeudi, is stirring something that smells incredible with one hand while propping their son, Zed, on her hip with the other.

"West," she greets me with a smile. "I was so glad to hear you called a meeting with the band." She leans forward and kisses me on the cheek. "You look good."

"And you look like a domestic goddess," I reply. "What is that amazing smell?"

She grins. "It's nothing fancy. Just pasta sauce," she says dismissively.

James shakes his head. "She's too modest. It's braised beef ragù," he says. "It's pretty much why I married her." He gives her a wink … which I'm hoping means he's joking.

The doorbell rings, interrupting any possible explanation, and James points down the hall.

"I'll get that. You can go hang in the studio, you know where it is," he tells me.

Nerves twist in my stomach, but all I do is smile and nod, waving at Jeudi as I head to James' studio.

It's a decently sized room with an upright piano in one corner and a couple of keyboards lined against the opposite wall. A few folding chairs sit around the couch on the back wall, ready for our little meeting.

It doesn't take long for James to appear, Nik and Michael in tow. Nik gives me a wary "hi" and Michael gives me a look. That's it. I guess I shouldn't be surprised. We've always been little more than bandmates, and he's usually the first to challenge me when I say or do something he doesn't like. He'll definitely be the hardest sell. They both settle onto the couch.

James starts to say something but is interrupt by Ward entering the room. His eyes meet mine solemnly, and I can see the battle on his face. Hug me or hit me? It's weird, but it makes me even happier to see him for some reason.

"Hey, man," I greet him quietly.

"Hey, West."

We stare at each other for a moment and I realize so much hinges on how he takes this. He's really the unspoken leader here.

I watch him as he sits down on the closest folding chair, draping a hand over his crossed legs. "So what did you call us here for?"

I puff out a sigh and take a seat in the folding chair across from him. James takes a seat next to Nik on the couch.

I look around at the faces of my band. My friends.

This is it. The moment of truth.

"I called you guys here to apologize. For real this time. And to prove it, there are some things I have to tell you first. Things that aren't easy for me to share."

My eyes flick up to Ward, who is now leaning his chin on his knotted fingers, his elbows propped on his knees. He and James both know about my childhood, but only Ward knows any details. But I know even Ward considered it the past, not understanding how much it still affected me. Not that I did until recently either.

So I tell them everything, sparing them the most explicit parts of the abuse I endured, but still giving them enough to leave them horrified and hanging on every word. Even, or perhaps especially, Ward.

I explain that all of my behavior since the moment I left home has been a result of it all, but I didn't realize it until I hit true rock bottom just over two months ago. That part they pretty much knew, of course.

"So my therapist, along with my meetings, have helped me understand why I've been self-sabotaging. And how to stop."

"And you think you can?" Ward asks.

"Yes," I say plainly, leaning back in my chair.

"Man," Michael says, his voice laced with awe. "I had no idea, dude." He shakes his head.

And it's the first time I think he's ever expressed any sort of empathy toward me.

"Well, it's not exactly something I just throw out there at dinner parties," I joke, trying to ease the tension of what I just laid on them. I look around at each of them in turn. "I didn't tell you guys for pity, though. I wanted you to understand what I've come to. That I felt guilt for all of that, and that's why I've been such a self-destructive asshole. I think I felt like someone should feel guilty, and fuck knows my dad clearly doesn't. But I realized it's not my cross to bear. It wasn't my fault. And now I can stop punishing myself for it and, by extension, everyone around me."

"You're like, all emotionally connected and shit now," Nik murmurs, watching me through narrowed eyes. "It's freaking me out a little."

I laugh, loud and honest. "It freaks me out a little too. But I feel so much better it's not even funny." I sigh, not sure this conversation is headed where I'd hoped but still feeling good about being honest with them. "So now you know. And I hope you also know that when I say I'm sorry this time, I mean it in a way I never could've before. I'm so fucking sorry for screwing this up for you guys. I know that doesn't undo anything, but I hope someday you can forgive me."

Michael looks at me. Really looks at me, in a way he never has before. "I had no fucking clue about any of this. I just thought you were an entitled asshole," he admits, and Ward snorts, presumably agreeing with the me-being-an-entitled-asshole part. Because, fair. "I mean, I can't say I'm not pretty fucking disappointed … but for what it's worth, I forgive you."

Nik nods slowly. "Same," she says nonchalantly. Michael gives her a sharp look, and she rolls her eyes. "All right, all right. I forgive you."

I smirk, knowing she probably considers it very un-rock-and-roll to get so mushy. Fuck knows I used to. But I'll take it.

I look to James next, who has had his hand over his mouth ever since I dropped the sexual-abuse bomb. He drops his hand, shaking his head.

"I had a clue, but even I didn't know how bad it was," he admits. His brown eyes soften as he meets mine. "It took a lot of strength for you to come here today. To tell us all that. Thank you."

"Don't thank me yet," I caution. "I'm just getting started."

James chuckles. "Well, you're doing a pretty good job of it, from where I'm sitting."

Ward raises an eyebrow at him and James shrugs.

"You guys are all a bunch of softies," Ward grumbles at them. But I can already tell by his tone that he's right there with them. He sighs heavily and swings his head to look at me. "Fine. I forgive you. But don't think I'm not going to make you show me you mean it after what you've put us through."

I grin widely, not blaming him in the slightest. "I'm glad you said that. Because I meant it when I said I'm just getting started. I hoped you'd all be ready to give me another chance, even though I know I don't deserve it. Because I've been working on something that you might be interested in."

Ward looks unimpressed, and I can tell he's a long way from forgetting my behavior. "We're listening."

"A concert. One so epic that it might just get us back in with everyone we've — *I've* burned."

James frowns. "And how are we going to do that when the label still holds the rights to all of our material?"

"I may have written new material," I respond. "Like, a whole album's worth of it."

Nik snorts. "You can write songs?"

"He's actually extremely talented," Ward breaks in, looking at me curiously. "Whose vocals did you write them for?"

I suppress a smile, his question outing that I've got him hooked. "Yours, of course," I assure him. "Except one song."

"You're going to sing?" Ward asks hopefully.

"I'm going to sing." And even with all the progress I've made, something about saying those words unravels the last bit of fear coiled in my chest.

"Well, color me shocked. This could work," Ward murmurs.

"Why the one song?" Michael asks curiously.

I take a deep breath. "Because the rest of the songs are to get the fans and, hopefully, the label back on board. But my song? That one's for a girl.

The girl. The one who started all of this. And she needs to know I haven't stopped thinking about her this whole damn time."

"You're in love with the reporter," Nik accuses me with a gasp.

I huff a laugh and nod. "Sure am."

Nik grins in response. "That's so fucking cute. I'm in."

"You've had a busy couple of months, haven't you?" James asks contemplatively.

I chuckle. "That I have."

A slow smile spreads over his face. "All right, kid. Let's hear this album of yours."

24

We Will Rock You by Queen

West

"No, you're still going early," I tell James. I replay the bridge, pausing at his cue. "Then you come in here."

James nods, so I keep going as he picks up on the cue, finally. At least, I hope he does. Ward watches on while trying to look like he isn't. I flick him a look and he grins, holding up his hands.

"Just keeping an eye on things," he says defensively. "We hit the recording studio Monday, after all."

"This is nothing," I assure him. "We're ready."

And we are. Still, I heave a sigh and set Rosie aside. It's been an exhilarating — but exhausting — few weeks.

James continues to practice as I pack up for the day, and Ward sidles up to me.

"So. Recording next week at the good graces of our friendly L.A. indie rock network. Concert the Thursday after that, venue by the good graces of the stunning Frankie Greco and her towering intimidator of a husband. And Nik's girlfriend is on promo, sticking flyers to anything in L.A. that's not moving. Everything's falling into place. How about you? Got all your ducks in a row, West?" he asks. Except that's not what he's really asking.

"Nothing fell anywhere, we've been busting our asses 24/7," I point out. "And no, to answer the question you're really asking, I haven't talked to Jason about the article yet, you passive-aggressive jackass." I say it with a laugh, because I'm mostly teasing him. "But I'm meeting him for a drink tomorrow night."

Ward tries to look cool, but I can tell he's relieved. He's so tightly wound sometimes, I wish he'd find a girl he cares about as much as I care about Maxi. Because there's nothing like a woman who makes you want to be a better version of yourself.

And that makes me remember … fuck, I miss Maxi. I've tried not to think too hard about it these past few months, but this is all because of her. Don't get me wrong, getting my shit together was for me. But this concert? This apology? It's for her. I mean, if it gets the fans and the label back, great. At this point, though, I honestly couldn't give a shit.

Because, shockingly enough, my self-worth no longer hinges on the whims of the masses. And thank fucking god for that.

But a life without Maxi Marshall? That's like Simon without Garfunkel. Hall without Oates. Jimmy Page without Robert Plant. In other words, unthinkable.

Still, I put off the meeting with Jason because this is the part I'm most nervous about. What if he won't go along with what I have in mind? What if he tells her?

I shake my head as I zip Rosie back into her case. Dr. Marks is right. If I'm not careful, I'm going to what-if myself into an early grave.

With a chuckle, I head home with the hope that I'll find something to distract me until tomorrow evening.

DISTRACTIONS OR NO, TIME MARCHES ON, AND SATURDAY EVENING FINDS me entering a café near *Rock Scene*'s office, looking for Jason.

I spot him at a table near the back, and I glance around nervously at the packed room. I should've thought this through a little better. The whole point was to keep this on the down-low. Not just from Maxi, either.

I slide into the seat across from Jason, his eyes landing on me in surprise.

"You showed," he remarks.

I smirk. "Yep. I did."

He nods. "All right then. I'm going to guess this little meeting has something to do with the buzz that Violent Mood Swings is putting on a concert in a couple weeks?"

I'm secretly pleased that he knows. That means our grassroots marketing plan is working.

"Sort of," I admit. "But it's also sort of about the fact that I created a shitstorm for you guys a couple months back. And I'd like to make amends for that."

Jason arches an eyebrow, disbelief written all over his face.

"Is this another 'apology'?" he asks, with air quotes and all.

I laugh, despite myself. "Cute. I'm pretty sure saying 'I'm sorry' would go over like a lead balloon at this point," I reply. "So I'm here to offer you an exclusive."

Jason snorts. "Well, I have to admit everyone's curious how and why you guys might be getting back together. What exactly will you give us?"

I smile, spreading my hands out. "Everything, Jason. The whole story, from cradle to grave to rising again."

"Still think you're God, do you?" There's no humor in his voice.

I realize it did come out sounding like that, especially since the version of me he knows is pre-rock-bottom.

"I like to think of it more like a phoenix rising from the ashes," I offer. "Don't you want to be the magazine that reveals why I burned it all to the ground?"

Despite himself, I can tell he's intrigued. And I know he can't afford to pass up this opportunity.

"When do you want it to run?"

"As soon as possible."

He considers. "I can get it online within a few days of you sitting down with Max. But print doesn't go out until the day before the concert."

"I'm not looking for publicity," I tell him. "And I don't want Maxi on this particular article. Hell, I'm pretty sure she'd tell you exactly where you could stick this interview if you even asked her."

Jason snorts a laugh. "Yep, that sounds about right," he agrees. "Though I don't blame her for being pissed at you."

"You don't know the half of it," I reply. "Which is where my only condition comes in."

He folds his arms over his chest with a dubious expression, one that says he was waiting for the catch.

"I want to do the article for two reasons: First, to give you guys the edge back and hopefully put to rest any doubts about your involvement with the lies I told. Second, to show a certain feisty-as-hell reporter that I'm not fucking around this time," I explain. "That's why someone else needs to do the article. So it gets printed. So she sees me laying it all out there."

"And the condition?"

"I want her to cover the concert."

Jason narrows his eyes. "Why?"

I frown. "Does it matter?"

"She's like a little sister to me so, yes, it matters. I'm not sending her there so you can publicly humiliate her."

"You've got the wrong end of this, man," I respond with a grin. "Because it's all about publicly humiliating myself. And then making sure she damn well knows how I feel about her."

Jason leans forward on the table, looking at me intently. And he does have that big brother "I'm going to beat your ass if you fuck with her" vibe going.

"And how do you feel about her?"

I rub my lips together. If she hasn't told him anything, I'm not sure whether it's a betrayal of her trust to. But then, as far as I know, she doesn't reciprocate my feelings anyway. And I've probably got a snowball's chance in hell with this woman. But for Maxi, I'll take those odds.

"I'm in love with her," I admit quietly. "Even if she doesn't love me back. I need her to know. I need to show her how fucking sorry I am."

"You sure about this? Because from where I'm standing, I'm pretty sure she's hated your guts for years."

I smile sadly, still hoping that's not true. Still willing to take the chance.

"What do I have to lose that I haven't already lost?"

25

———————

Missing You by John Waite

Max

"Max?" Alexsis's voice draws my gaze to the door. "Do you have a minute to look over an article for the website before it goes to Jason?"

I pull a face. "That'll take more than a minute." I throw my pen down with a sigh and gesture for her to hand it to me. "But for you, of course."

She hands me the small sheaf of papers nervously, settling down in the extra chair in my cubicle.

"You're going to watch me read it?" I ask dryly.

She shrugs. "I just … thought you might want to discuss it with me while you go."

I furrow my brow. "You know if I have to ask you questions, it's not ready for Jason, right?"

"I know." Alexsis bobs her head, and her nervous energy is weirding me out.

I fight the urge to pull a face, unsure what's up with her today but assuming she just needs reassurance. "Well, you're a talented writer, I'm sure it's fine," I mumble as my eyes start to scan the page.

But I only take in the headline before my eyes snap back up to hers, suddenly understanding her nerves.

"What the fuck is this?" I ask plainly, dropping the pages on my desk like they're on fire.

"Just read it. Please?"

"This is an interview with Kristoffer fucking Westberg, Alexsis. When did you do this?" I demand. "*Why* did you do this?" Even I can hear the hurt in my voice. She knows this subject is off-limits.

"You'll understand when you read it. And you need to read it," she urges. "Trust me."

I snort. "Trust you. Like I trusted West?"

"It's okay to be mad at him. But this is going live, and it's going to be a big deal. I figured it was better if you read it before everyone else. So you weren't unprepared."

I furrow my brow and frown. I hate to admit it, but she has a point. The last thing I need is to be blindsided by West again.

"Fine," I snap, snatching the pages back. "But I don't have to like it."

Alexsis presses her lips together and her nostrils flare. She's clearly trying not to laugh at my petulant attitude. Because I know I'm being a little over the top, it almost snaps me out of my funk. Almost.

But as soon as I start reading, the funk is back in full force.

Until it's replaced by my stomach dropping into my shoes. And maybe a tear or two. And a hand over my mouth.

When I finish, I gently place the pages down and lean back in my chair.

"He really told you all of that?" I ask in a whisper. But I already know the answer. Of course he did. How else would she know?

She nods. "Yep. I think it was harder on me, actually. He seemed surprisingly okay talking about the whole thing."

I shake my head. "It seems like an odd publicity stunt and totally not like West to share all that. But then, I guess they need all the help they can get ahead of whatever farce of a concert they intend to put on next week."

"So you know it's all the truth?"

My eyes meet hers. "Why? Do you not believe him?" I ask curiously.

"That's not what I meant, but yes, I believe him. He's … different."

I snort. "If I didn't know this" — I pick up the article — "was all true, that statement alone would make me think this whole thing is an act. Then again, the publicity stunt angle still fits, even if it is true. Why else would he do this?" I drop the article back on the desk, disgusted.

"Oh, Max. Isn't it obvious?"

I level a don't-go-there look at her. "No. It's not. Not to me at least. But I also don't give a shit."

Alexsis gives me a look filled with pity. She hesitates. "It's okay to miss him, Max. Even though he hurt you."

Indignation tingles over every inch of my skin. "I do *not* miss him," I scoff.

Alexsis's expression turns to exasperation. "Oh really? Then why have you been sulking around for the last three months doing google searches and scanning social media for news about him when you think nobody's looking?"

My eyes go wide at being called out and my face flushes. "I'm not sulking! And that was just … morbid curiosity," I stammer defensively.

God, I'm so lame.

I've totally been sulking.

I totally miss him.

I'm a stupid, stupid woman who is obviously a glutton for punishment. What he did … it went beyond potentially trashing my career, which thankfully has mostly recovered. He trashed my trust. Again.

And I shouldn't worry about him. I shouldn't look for him in every headline. I shouldn't want to know what the band's doing back together and what's going on with this concert. I shouldn't love him.

Because that leads to only one place: more heartbreak.

But … what if everything he was quoted as saying in the article is true? I rifle through to the last page, trying to remember exactly how he worded his response to Alexsis asking why he was sharing all of this. When I find it, I realize I'd merely skimmed it the first time.

"Because this time, it's real. And to prove that, I need to set right what I did wrong. At least, as much as people will let me. But I also get I may not deserve that in some people's eyes. And that's okay too."

On a second, closer read, I wonder … he couldn't have been talking about me … could he? Tears prickle at the backs of my eyes, and I blink rapidly to contain them. On some level I want to believe it's the truth. But even if it's his truth, does it change anything? Trust isn't so easily rebuilt. Even he gets that.

I look up to find Alexsis watching me. "I'm not supposed to tell you this, but Jason's going to ask you to cover the concert. You don't have to interview the band or anything, just go. I thought you might like a chance to think about that *not* in front of your boss."

She rises, making to leave.

"Alexsis, wait," I call after her.

She turns back to me and I offer her the printed article. "Here."

"I meant for you to keep that one," she says softly.

I sigh heavily. "Thank you," I murmur.

And she knows I don't mean for the printout, because she gives me a sad smile, then leaves.

After she's gone, I contemplate reading the article again, now that I've calmed down a little. And maybe I should. Maybe I should take off the bitter filter I've been viewing the world through lately.

But then again, maybe I need to look at it that way because the truth is so much scarier. Risks always are. And West is a risk I can't imagine myself taking ever again.

26

I Won't Back Down by Tom Petty & The Heartbreakers

West

Preshow jitters rarely used to be an issue for me. Maybe it was the drugs and alcohol. Or maybe I was high on the energy of the crowd, the adoration of the fans.

Or maybe no show has ever mattered quite like this one.

Six days ago, I exposed myself to the world. Digitally, as it were, not in the perverted way. Though I have been known to do that in the past.

But no, this time it wasn't physically. This time everyone knows my story. Facts and happenings I tried hard to ignore for most of my adult life. It's all out there now, and the show sold out not long after. So clearly people are curious. Hopefully some even show up for the actual music.

Either way, today I expose the only part of me I didn't in that article: my heart. Today is my grand gesture. My *Say Anything* moment. Except instead of a boombox, I've got Rosie, a kickass sound system courtesy of

Baltia, and an epic ballad written expressly for one Maxi Marshall to end what I hope will be an equally epic evening.

But first, I've gotta get there. And fuck if today didn't make me miss having our own crew. Fortunately, the backbreaking work of lugging all our gear into the club, setting up, and doing soundchecks kept me from thinking too hard most of the day. But we're minutes to doors open now, and there's nothing to distract me from the swirling pit of nerves in my stomach. I should've gone with the rest of the band to get something to eat ahead of the show, but I have zero appetite. And I don't want to have something in my stomach to throw up if the nerves win. God, the nerves.

They've been made worse by not knowing how Maxi took the article, or if she even read it at all. And while Jason said he'd "do his best" to get her here … well, not knowing if she'll show is another level of torture I was unprepared for.

I feel the equipment crate I'm sitting on shift and a voice to my right says, "So I hear tell from Ward this show isn't just about getting your career back."

I huff a breath out of my nose and turn. "It's still a trip seeing you without crazy-colored hair," I say.

Frankie grins over at me, tugging at her now-dark-brown locks, though at least she's still wearing the bright red lipstick she's famous for. A few years ago I was a falling rock star when she was a new, unknown face on the rock scene. She'd just bought Baltia, but now she's a legend in her own right for what she's done with it and several other clubs since.

"It's a trip seeing you sober," she shoots back with a teasing note to her voice. "So is it true? Is this really about a girl?"

"Yep," I admit, not knowing what to add that won't make me even more nervous than I already am.

"And you love her?" she pushes.

"Yep." I inhale deeply to calm myself. I'm not sure I've admitted that out loud to anyone but Maxi before, but Frankie has a way of eliciting honesty. Doesn't hurt that she's intimidating as hell.

Frankie is silent for a beat, assessing me.

"Is she why you cleaned up your act?"

I smile. "In a way," I respond truthfully. "She was the kick in the ass. Getting sober? Owning my shit? That was for me."

Another beat of silence passes. "Damn, West, that's some deep shit right there. Never thought I'd see the day. But I'm happy for you."

"Thanks. How's it looking out there?"

"Line's not just around the damn block — I'm pretty sure it stretches all the way to Hollywood and Highland," she replies with a grin. "One way or another, you're making rock history tonight."

I laugh. "No pressure, though, right?"

"Fuck yes, there's pressure," she responds matter-of-factly, rising. "But you're wicked talented." She looks down at me. "And you've got a true heart. You have no idea how rare that is. Trust me." She claps me on the shoulder. "You'll be fine. Now put on your big girl panties and let's do this fucking thing."

I shake my head and laugh. Trust Frankie to light a fire under my ass. I rise, retrieving Rosie from her stand backstage. I never leave her onstage because I always need to kiss her for luck before a show, which I do. Been a long time. And even though it's not the tour I thought I'd get, I'm happy to play music for a crowd again. I test a few chords, and her gentle hum soothes the raging inferno in my gut. Let's do this fucking thing, indeed.

Distantly, I hear the doors open and the crowd pour in. Drink orders start to be called so loudly I can hear them from backstage. Chairs scrape. Feet thunder down the stairs to the stage pit. This is fucking happening.

A few minutes before showtime, the band regroups backstage, and at Ward's direction we huddle, arms slung over each other's shoulders in a circle. There's no opening act, so we're going to be up very soon. As we silently embrace, we listen to the volume in the club ramp up as people cram in.

With a squeeze of Ward's hand on my shoulder, he breaks the huddle.

"All right, fuckers. What are we gonna do tonight?" he asks, first pointing at James.

"Play like no one is watching," James replies with a grin. Ward rolls his eyes and points to Nik, next in the circle.

"Go balls to the wall," Nik says.

Now Michael rolls his eyes. "Girls don't even have balls," he groans.

Nik points at her tits. "I believe it was Joan Jett who said it best — 'Girls have got balls. They're just a little higher up, that's all.'"

I chuckle as Ward shakes his head and points to Michael.

"Make mama proud," he says.

He's such a mama's boy, so I'm thoroughly unsurprised. Ward smirks at Michael but doesn't say anything, he just moves his hand to point at me.

"I gotta see about a girl," I say.

Ward stares at me and slaps a hand on my shoulder. "You are one sappy motherfucker, West."

Nik looks confused. James laughs at the expression on her face.

"Give her a break," I tell him. "I'm pretty sure she was like two when that movie came out."

"What movie?" Nik asks blankly. James, Ward, and I all crack up.

But before we can fill her in, out on the stage, Frankie takes the mic and starts hyping up the crowd. A hush falls over the band, and not just to hear her talk. That Frankie herself is introducing us … well, it drives it home how epic this is.

When she cues us to take the stage, my adrenaline starts pumping. We enter side stage and the crowd goes fucking apeshit. Cheers, calls, hands reaching, bodies pressing toward the stage, the whole nine yards. From what I can see under the bright lights, the place is crammed wall to wall.

I grin over at Ward as I plug Rosie into her amp and he takes the mic. And without preamble, Michael cues us in and the music explodes through the club.

We picked a fast, hard song to start, and it was hands down the right choice. The energy level in the place is palpable, and I give everything up to the music. I'm home. All of my worries, gone, surrendered to the melody.

We finish the first song and go straight into our second, taking the tempo back a bit. The crowd is loving it, and I gotta admit, I'm relieved. While my songs aren't *totally* different, it's definitely not our usual sound either. I don't know how Ward constantly puts himself out there writing songs that people may very well shit all over. I'm just glad that doesn't seem to be happening tonight.

As we start a third song, though, the tenor of the crowd changes in a way I didn't expect as a surge of bodies presses people closer to the stage. I look over at Ward, who looks back at me with a shake of the head. Neither of us may know why, but something just shifted.

We keep going, but the masses are now making some very different noises. A movement side stage catches my eye. Nils has come onto the fucking stage and is yelling in Ward's ear.

My stomach drops and Ward motions for us to stop, which we do immediately, plunging the club into rumbles of confusion. Bodies press more frantically at the base of the stage. With the light up I can see people crammed into every nook and cranny, and things are starting to get … shovey. I look back nervously at Nils, and it's then that I notice a cop and a fireman behind him as he takes the mic.

"Everyone please, stay calm," Nils urges. I pale as the crowd starts booing. He waves his hands, but they don't quiet down. "Unfortunately, the police and fire marshal are shutting the concert down." At that, the crowd goes insane, and not in the good way. There's jeering and loud booing and a few people throwing things as the shoving starts to get more violent.

For a split second I wonder if I should be afraid. But then Frankie strides quickly up to the mic, her husband not far behind. She's got presence, but this guy … he's a wall of dark, muscled terror if I've ever seen one. And the sight of the two of them looking like hell's fury is enough to quiet the place.

"Look, we're sorry, but you can thank the horde of gatecrashers who thought it would be cute to rush security, who then had to call the cops to contain it. Please, for the love of fucking Christ, cooperate and you'll receive a flyer at the door that'll tell you how to get your money back."

Frankie steps back, but her husband stays in place, glaring at the crowd. There's plenty of grumbling as everyone turns back toward the stairs, pushing toward the exit, but no challenges to the enforcer watching them go. They're distinctly more orderly. And if I weren't so freaked out right now, it might almost be funny.

"What the fuck just happened?" I ask, joining Ward, Frankie, and Nils at center stage, Nik and Michael following close behind.

Nils frowns. "We were already oversold when a group of assholes without tickets decided to just push their way in. It was only about a dozen people, but then *everyone* in line behind them decided to jump in on the action," he replies, disgust lacing his tone. "We had extra security, but there was no way we could've stopped them. I'm pretty sure half the fucking city was still waiting outside hoping to see the show. So even after the police got here, it took a few minutes for them to even be able to get in. I had to bring them in the goddamn side door. Then the fire marshal showed up and didn't even give us the option to thin the crowd. He just declared it over."

Frankie throws us all an apologetic look. "Sorry, guys. If I'd have known the line was that bad, I would've dealt with it before we got started."

I shake my head. "It's not your fault a bunch of assholes ruined it, but thanks anyway." As the implications of the show being shut down sink in, I remember the only part of this that mattered in the first place. "Oh fuck." I look up at Ward. "Maxi."

Ward purses his lips. "We don't even know if she was here, dude."

"Maxi … you mean Max Marshall?" Nils asks.

"Yeah, you know her?"

"Of course. You introduced us, remember? At the private fan concert?"

I want to smack myself in the forehead. Duh. "Did you see her tonight?"

"Sure did."

A warm feeling spreads through my chest. She came. That's something. A new plan starts forming in my head. But then I look at my bandmates.

Ward snorts. "Don't worry about us. This shit happens. Bright side? This is going to be big news. And with the crowd that was here tonight? We're going to have zero problems rescheduling. At a bigger venue though, maybe." He shrugs apologetically Frankie's way. She waves a hand dismissively back.

"Are you sure? Because you guys are important to me too, and I don't want you to think —"

"Fuck, would you just go get the girl already?" Michael cuts in, exasperated.

A wide grin breaks over my face. "Thanks, guys." And then my face falls. "Shit, my driver is busy until later because I thought I'd be here."

"Where do you need to go?" The deep voice rumbles out of Frankie's husband, and the hairs on my arms stand up. I give Frankie a look and she smiles slyly.

"Culver City," I respond.

"You bringing that?" he asks in return, pointing at Rosie.

"Shit, no." I slide the strap over my head and hand her to Ward.

"You're leaving your guitar behind?" he asks, his eyebrows shooting up.

"I don't have time to argue, just take her," I insist.

"How are you going to play her song without your guitar?" James asks.

"I don't need the guitar," I assure them.

Ward takes Rosie, holding her delicately. So delicately I almost laugh. But I don't have time for that shit.

"Can you drive fast?" I ask Frankie's husband.

He raises one, thick eyebrow, but it's Frankie who answers. "Don't worry, West. Julian's got you covered."

27

In Your Eyes by Peter Gabriel

Max

"Well, that was insane," Alexsis says as we take a seat in a pie shop just down the block from Baltia.

"I assume you're referring to the concert and not your choice of cereal on pie," I reply, gesturing at the Froot Loops-laden concoction sitting in front of her.

She grins. "You clearly haven't tried it," she replies, then points at my chocolate brownie pie slice. "Chocolate is boring and predictable. This is surprising and exciting."

I grimace. "I'll stick with my chocolatey silky deliciousness, thanks."

She shrugs. "Suit yourself." She takes a bite of pie, looking so sublimely happy I have to chuckle. "So, of the little we saw, what did you think?"

I shrug back. "It was all right." Such a lie. It was many things, but just "all right" wasn't one of them. "Thanks for coming with me. Even if I didn't end up having to talk to him, I'm glad you were there."

"Of course. I'm glad I went. I love their new sound. Shame it was such a freaking circus it got shut down early."

"Yes, well, clearly they underestimated what a circus it would be. And they do seem to have gone a new direction," I reply.

Alexsis rolls her eyes. "All right, Max. Can we drop the polite chatter? I can tell you're totally shook right now."

I raise an eyebrow and shoot her a smirk that could rival West's. Because even though she's considerably younger than me at twenty-two, I'm pretty sure "shook" isn't a thing anymore. She sticks her tongue out at me in response and I laugh.

"Fine, yes, I'm 'shook.' Are you happy?" I reply.

"Are you?" she returns. "Happy, I mean?"

"Not really."

"Then me neither."

I snort. "While I appreciate the solidarity, I really don't want to talk about it." I take a large bite of pie so I can avoid doing exactly that.

"If you say so. But I think you'd feel better if you got it off your chest." She takes a bite of her own pie, clearly thinking while she chews. "You can't tell me seeing him up there wasn't …" She shudders theatrically for effect.

I suck in a sharp breath and close my eyes against the memory. The image of him up there on stage.

"Yes, fine, it was fucking hot," I allow. I'm not sure how I could forget what it feels like to watch him up there. It's a mix of awe and lust that's hard to ignore.

"And you're sure you can never forgive him?"

"I don't remember him asking since he's decided he's all fixed up this time around."

"I don't remember you giving him a chance to."

I tap my fork on the plate. "Fine, all right? Seeing him made me realize that if he asked I probably would. Because it was one thing to be mad at him when I didn't have to see him. But I'm not totally oblivious to the fact that Kristoffer Westberg is one-hundred-percent my kryptonite. As soon as I saw him tonight, I remembered that. So I'm just thanking god that shit all got shut down before he had a chance to invite me backstage or something."

"You say that like it's a bad thing," she points out.

"He's a ticking time bomb of emotional wreckage," I snap back.

"I dunno. Seems like he might really have his shit together this time."

"No, that's just the West effect working on you too. One interview and bam," I slam my hand down on the table between us. "Off melt the panties. Then you're groupie putty in his capable smoking-hot-guitarist hands."

"Well, you'd know firsthand how capable they are," she points out with a grin.

I scrunch my face up. "That part I do miss," I admit. "The crazy West-coaster? Not so much."

"Even if he has —"

"Changed? Come on, Alexsis. You're not *that* young. You don't get with a guy expecting him to change. Besides, even if he has, he's still a rock star."

She finishes eating her last bite of pie in silence, then carefully sets down her fork.

"Even if he is, it's all in how you choose to see it. And what I see is a guy trying to make things right with his band and the woman he —"

"So help me god, do not say 'loves.'"

"I don't have to — he already did, remember?"

"Oh I remember," I reply with a hard edge to my voice. "That's the problem. Letting him love me would be —"

"Dangerous? Crazy? Just what you need?" Alexsis interrupts.

I frown. "I wasn't going to say any of those things," I respond defensively. Except I *was* going to say something pretty similar to the first two.

"Yeah, it's annoying when people interrupt you, isn't it?" she points out blithely, taking a sip of water. "And do you know why you keep interrupting me?"

I roll my eyes. "Why?" I ask dryly.

"Because you're *afraid*." She shakes her head slowly. "To think, the woman who I look up to. My role model. Afraid of taking a chance on love."

"I've already taken too many chances on West," I point out.

She tilts her head to the side and scrutinizes me. "But isn't that what loving someone is? Taking a chance every single day that they'll stick around? That the rug won't get pulled out from under you? Because I'm just not buying the 'he's a rock star' angle. You're a goddamn rock journalist for Christ's sake. Lame excuse, if you ask me."

And my eyebrows are so high I'm pretty sure they're about to pop off my forehead. "Well, tell me what you really think, why don't you?" She grins at me. And then I add softly, "I'm your role model?"

Her smile relaxes into something sweeter. "Yes. Even though you're kind of being a hypocrite right now. What, you want to get close to the rock life but never be affected by it? Not gonna happen, sister. Give in. You want him. He wants you. Everything else is just … stuff. You'll figure it out. I know you can. Because you're a badass, and you're not my role model for nothing."

My heart aches at her words. She's actually completely right. And hearing it that way makes me realize, I'm not just afraid of West because I love him.

"But what if you're wrong?" I ask, swallowing hard against the lump in my throat. Preparing to voice a fear I didn't even realize I had until now. Until she pushed me to look closer. "What if now that he's got his life back he realizes his feelings for me weren't real? That they were just a part of all the fucked up emotions he was working through?"

"Why would you think that?" she asks, her voice filled with exasperation.

That ache in my heart swells. "He hasn't talked to me in more than three months. He asked *you* to write the article. And he didn't even invite me to the concert, Jason had to tell me to go. If he wanted to see me, if he wanted *me* … well, this is West we're talking about. The man's not exactly shy about going after what he wants."

I look down, blushing hard. God, I had no clue what really lay under all my anger and fear was plain old insecurity.

"So you're saying you would take him back, you just don't think he wants you?" Alexsis asks.

I look up, tears now swimming in my eyes. "Yeah, I guess that's what I'm saying. Is that messed up? To want someone you thought you were pissed off at — and for good reason — but turns out you were just afraid they didn't really want you back?"

"Yeah, actually, that's pretty messed up," she admits.

I laugh, and a tear slips out.

"Well, if he doesn't realize how fucking awesome you are, then it's his loss," she says, lifting her chin.

"Exactly," I agree. "I say good riddance West, and bring on more pie."

"If you can actually eat another piece of pie after that, you really are my role model," Alexsis jokes.

I look down at the crumbs left on my plate and glance at my watch. I'm pretty sure they're closing soon, not that I think I could actually eat another piece right this second anyway.

"Eh. Maybe a piece to go," I agree.

Alexsis laughs. "Sounds good to me."

We rise, heading for the counter, but I stop her with a hand on her arm.

"Thanks, Alexsis."

She smiles back at me and puts her hand on mine to give it a squeeze. "Anytime."

"And you know I've got your back the next time you need to moan over some idiot who doesn't know what he's got," I assure her as we wait for the counter girl.

"Well, here's hoping I find that idiot soon. Pie can only keep a girl happy for so long," she teases airily.

AS MY RIDE DROPS ME OFF AT MY APARTMENT BUILDING WAY EARLIER AND way more sober than I'd planned on being, I'm somehow thankful for my life right now. As crappy as the last few months have felt, I truly have a lot of good things going. My career. My family. My friendships. Love lost isn't the end; it can always be found again if you're open to it.

It's a thought that brings a sad smile to my face as I walk through the open wrought iron gate into the courtyard, the August night air warm and dry. And even though I know I shouldn't wonder, I do. What's West doing right now? Is he upset about the concert being shut down? Is he burying his disappointment in some groupie?

Ugh. That last thought makes me shudder in disgust. I look up as I approach the arched entry door to the building itself.

And the answer to my question sits on the top step. My breath catches in my throat as West rises, slowly descending the steps to stand in front of me. He looks exactly as he did onstage in his uniform tight black tee and dark wash jeans. Except his dark eyes look tired and a five o'clock shadow is starting to bud on his strong jaw. Everything about him, perfect and imperfect, makes my heart pound in my chest.

"Hey, Maxi."

I want to close my eyes against the swell of emotion his voice brings in me. I can feel the tears in my eyes. And everything I knew I'd feel around him floods me at once. Loss so deep it tears me open. Love so strong it heals. Hope that grates too sharply on the jagged edges of my heart.

"What are you doing here, West?"

His eyes search mine, dark and intense. He smells like sweat and guitar strings, heaven and hell, salvation and damnation.

"You went to the concert," he says.

My brows pull together at his non-answer. "Yes …?"

"I didn't know if you would. But I figured it was more likely if it wasn't me who asked."

My mouth pops open. "Jason … but … that was really you?" As soon as the stuttered accusation is out of my mouth I realize it may not make much sense.

But he nods anyway. "I didn't think you wanted to talk to me. So I had this whole plan."

"To get me to cover your comeback concert?" I ask.

"Yes," he admits, shoving his hands in his pockets. "But mostly to play the song I wrote for you."

My eyebrows jump. "You wrote me a song?"

"Yep. And I came here to sing it to you. But now that I'm here, that feels all wrong."

My heart lurches at the thought that I may not get to hear this song, one I didn't even know about until a minute ago.

"You wrote me a song," I say again, softer, breathier.

One of his hands pops out of his pockets, starting to reach … until he stops it, clenching it into a fist and letting it drop to his side.

"I did. Actually, I wrote a whole album because of you. Went to therapy for the first time since rehab because of you. I'm standing here, the closest to whole I've ever been … because of you, Maxi. And I could sing you a song. But I think just telling you is better. No flash. No theatrics. Just the truth."

My breathing stutters. "And what's that?" I whisper.

"That I'm not going to be completely whole without you." He loses the battle with his hand, and he reaches up to cup my face. His fingers send warmth skating over my skin and running down my spine. "You speak truth. You don't back down from a challenge. You don't hide behind lies under the guise of doing what you think you have to. You're beautiful, and strong, and you don't take shit from anyone, especially not me. And I think I've loved you from the moment you told me there were more important people than you who needed my apology. It's just took me a while to realize that wasn't true. There's nobody more important than you. Not to me."

"You can't possibly mean that." My voice wavers as I fight a losing battle against the tears in my eyes.

He smiles softly, stroking his thumb over my cheek.

"But I do. You showed me what I'd let myself become. And that I couldn't stop hiding from it anymore. You were the only one who knew every awful thing about me. And you still chose me. I thought I'd never forgive myself for lying to you, for ruining what we might have had."

I tilt my head into his palm, and he runs his fingers down my jaw.

"But you did?" I prompt.

"I did," he confirms. "Turns out I needed to learn to forgive myself to give myself permission to be loved. And, you know, to not be a complete asshole."

A laugh escapes me. "You're not a complete asshole."

He scrunches his nose and tips his head back and forth. "I really was, though."

We both laugh, and the tears finally find their way out. I brush them away self-consciously.

"And the other part?" I ask, not wanting to use the word "love." It all feels like too much right now.

"It's why I'm here," he says plainly.

I press my lips together and look up into his eyes, fighting against thinking too hard about all of the broken pieces inside of me.

"Why don't you come up and we'll talk," I offer, taking a step back.

His hand falls and he shoves it back in his pocket, nodding slowly. "Cool."

He follows me inside and up the stairs.

The minute it takes me to fumble for my keys and get the door open makes me feel like a teenager sneaking her boyfriend into her room. Except I'm far from the teenager who mooned over him. Now I'm the woman whose heart and mind are still more at odds than I'd like them to be.

Once we're inside, I gesture to the beat-up tan leather couch dominating the small living room.

"Want a drink?" I offer as I kick off my shoes.

But West is having none of it. He slides his hand over mine, tugging me toward him. I allow him to draw me in front of him but not too close. I stare up at him warily.

"Am I too late? Are you seeing someone else?" he murmurs.

"No," I say, my mouth going dry. "And no."

The left side of his lips tip up. "You know, the last time I said this, it didn't go over well."

Nerves tumble in my tummy. "Lies and love don't tend to work together in the same conversation," I reply delicately.

His brows pinch together. "I'm sorry for lying to you. For disappointing you, again. I promise you, I am doing everything in my power to be the man you deserve."

The war between me and my brokenness ceases. Because the truth in his words is undeniable. But more so is how I feel about him. The chance I can't not take. And maybe he's exactly what I need to heal my heart.

"I believe you. That article, West … that was unbelievable."

His gaze softens. "I'm glad you read it. After everything I did, it was the only thing I could think of to even begin to explain — much less expect — forgiveness."

"But that's why you did it, isn't it?"

He shakes his head adamantly. "I don't need the forgiveness of strangers. I need the forgiveness of the people I love." He pauses, his eyes tightening with worry. "Will you forgive me?"

"I forgive you," I reply, almost automatically. Because I realize I already had. I've always known who he is deep down. And this time it really does feel like he's on the right path, finally. "But you're going to have to keep showing me."

He smirks. "I have a few ways in mind," he replies huskily.

My breath hitches at the glint in his eye. "Oh yeah?" I ask, barely above a whisper. "Like what?"

He draws me into his arms, dipping his forehead to meet mine. "Like telling you the truth. Always," he promises. He pulls back and stares deeply into my eyes. "I love you, Max Marshall."

A slow smile spreads over my face. He called me *Max*. I don't point it out, but the gravity of it underscores his declaration like his subconscious is making promises to take this seriously too. If I'd had any doubts left whether he was worth the risk, they'd be gone. But I don't.

"And then what?" I ask teasingly, running my hands down his chest.

He cocks an eyebrow. "Well, I was going to save fucking you for later, but if you insist." And without hesitation, he leans forward and flips me over his shoulder, carrying me toward the bedroom.

I squeal with surprised laughter. "Holy shit, West!"

He walks into the bedroom and drops me on the bed, climbing over me. Before I can even catch my breath, his mouth lands on mine, his lips pushing my mouth open, his tongue invading my senses. Heat and desire pool between my thighs and I moan into his mouth.

He makes to pull away, but I put my hands on his face.

"I love you too, Kristoffer Westberg," I breathe.

His face draws together in an expression somewhere between relief and delight before his mouth is on mine again, his hands pulling at my clothing. And I'm right there with him, until we're both naked, until he's worshipping every inch of my body.

His mouth trails down my chest, leaving a blazing trail of kisses that spread heat across my skin. His thumbs circle my nipples as his mouth goes lower, his teeth against the sensitive plane of my lower stomach creating a sharp contrast to his hot, silky tongue that sends jolts of pleasure shooting through my core.

And when his lips land on my inner thighs, I whimper with anticipation. His hands leave my breasts to join his mouth and as his tongue works my clit while he slides two fingers deep inside me, I arch off the bed.

"Oh my god," I groan. "Yes."

He pumps with his fingers. "I love hearing you, Maxi."

He speeds up and I lose my words. With a grin I can feel rather than see, his tongue returns to the mix, lapping in circles and sending me into a frenzy. I come hard and fast, pushing into his mouth as I grip the bedspread under me.

When the white hot fire of my orgasm starts to recede from my limbs, I push up. First to my elbows, watching him rise between my legs. And when his hard, ready cock comes into view, I push up to fully sitting, taking him in my mouth with the fervor that only post-orgasmic bliss can induce.

I spare him nothing, shoving his silky length deep into my throat as I suck hard, using one hand to follow my mouth up and down as the other massages him lower. His hands fist into my hair as he groans and pushes through my lips to the rhythm I've set. I relax, silently begging him to fuck my mouth. And he does.

God, the noises he makes. Deep groans that reverberate through him. I'm so wet and worked up I can barely stand it. I feel him tighten in my palm an instant before he pulls out of my mouth.

I look up at him, licking my lips as he sucks in a breath through his teeth.

"You are so fucking sexy," he tells me. Then he pushes me back on the bed and runs a hand between my legs. "Shit."

He leans forward to where he knows the condoms are in the nightstand. A rip of foil later and he's on me, his eyes boring into mine as he positions himself between my legs. And then mercilessly slides in hard to the hilt. I don't break eye contact. I can't not watch him.

He fucks me with a desperation I feel deep in my soul. A need to be joined to him like this, to surrender to him, to us. He works my clit, clearly approaching his own peak quickly and not wanting to leave me behind. His other hand touches me everywhere. My face. My neck. My breasts. My stomach.

His touch has a reverence, a depth it's never had. And when we come together, it's forgiveness in flesh, repentance from fear, redemption by love.

28

Open Arms by Journey

West

I wake up in the middle of the night, lying beside Maxi in the dark. And she's snoring so loud that I'm pretty sure it woke me up. Instead of being irritated, it brings a ridiculous grin to my face.

Because I'll fucking take it in a heartbeat. Getting her back is everything. I'll surrender some sleep to her chainsaw-like snores.

I get up and use the bathroom, then stop in the kitchen for a drink of water before heading back to bed. As I climb back in, I realize there's no snoring.

"West?" Maxi's sleepy voice cuts through the dark.

I slide all the way back under the blankets, settling in next to her. "I'm here," I assure her, stroking her hair and wrapping an arm around her.

She wiggles into me and my dick approves, pulsing against what I think is her stomach.

"I dreamed you were singing my song," she mumbles into my chest.

I chuckle. "Really? Or are you just trying to get me to sing it to you now?" I tease.

I feel her smile against my skin. "Will you?"

I run a hand down her hair and take a breath. I was so scared of this moment just yesterday. But now? Not even a little bit.

So I sing to her, losing myself in the story behind the song. It starts off with my life before her, thinking I had it all figured out. Until it moves on to the struggle and frustration of realizing I'm not the man she needs. Finally finishing with the gratitude for learning to forgive, to love both myself and her. Whether she ever loves me again or not.

As I float back to reality, I feel her tears on my chest. I lean in to wipe them away.

"Good tears or bad tears?" I ask after a moment when she doesn't say anything.

"Good," she assures me with a sniff. "You have an incredible voice. Why have I never heard you sing? You know, for real."

She gives me a glare, and I instantly remember what she's referring to: my attempted Maverick moment all those months ago. God, I almost forgot about that. But now's not the time to tease her about it. Now's the time to pony up some of that honesty I promised her.

"Truthfully? My old man relentlessly beat me down anytime I opened my mouth to sing. Kind of takes the fun out of it."

She shakes her head against my arm. "I'm sorry to hear that. You really do have a gift. I had no idea."

"You're just saying that because you love me," I tease. Partially to deflect the praise, having a hard time believing it after all the negative programming. Partially to remind myself that she loves me. Guess I'm not the arrogant bastard I once was, because I feel a little cracked open by all this emotional crap.

She leans up, and I can see the outline of her face above me. "I'm saying that because you have the huskiest, sexiest singing voice I've ever heard. I was touched by your song, West. More than I can even put to words. Nobody has ever written me a song, much less one that beautiful. But your voice?" she takes my hand and brings it between her legs. And she's soaked. "That's what it did to me."

"Fuck," I groan, my lips finding hers in the dark. Then, between kisses, "You sure know how to compliment a guy."

"And you've sure learned what a woman needs to hear," she replies against my lips. She slips on top of me, her wet core grinding over my dick. And if I thought I was hard before, I'm like granite now.

"Careful," I caution her, not sure how much skin-on-skin I can take before junior explodes.

"I'm done being careful," she murmurs, tilting her hips so I slide into her.

I throw my head back as we groan together. Because holy shit. As her breasts settle on my chest, her lips meet mine, and her hips work me in and out of her … I'm so fucking hers.

I can practically feel the love and trust radiating out of her, and I want to cry like a fucking baby. I never thought I could let someone love me like this. I never thought someone like her could love me like this.

But it's a brand new day. And me? Well, I may not be a brand new West, but I'm sure as fuck going to keep trying. There's no going back, really. Because this woman owns me, body and soul, and fuck if I'm ever going to let her go again.

EPILOGUE

I Melt With You by Modern English

West

Two years later…

"You know, I never thought I'd get to go to a concert without being recognized," I murmur as we take our center seats, a few rows back from the stage. It's not a huge venue but big enough for a sizable crowd.

Maxi smirks up at me. "Don't lie. You miss it," she teases me.

I try not to grin. I swear. But the woman knows me. I don't even need to respond. I simply lean over and kiss her, unwilling to admit it out loud.

But that's not why we're here.

A few minutes later we're joined by James and Jeudi. The women sit next to each other on one side of me, already chatting away as James settles on my other side. We fist bump and exchange greetings.

"So the first concert of our bright new hope," he says, jerking his head toward the stage. "Pretty exciting."

I bob my head. "Sure is." My eyes fall on the row of guitars to one side of the stage.

"You miss it, don't you?" James asks shrewdly.

I throw my hands up and laugh. "Why does everyone keep asking me that?" I tease. And then I sigh. "Yeah. I guess I do. But not as much as you people seem to think. It's nice, helping rising artists the way nobody helped us."

"You mean, not screwing them like we were screwed," James says with a snort.

"Yep, pretty much," I agree. "But you know. It's hard to regret a past that brought you somewhere pretty fucking awesome."

James slaps me on the shoulder. "Aw, look at West, all grown up."

I smirk. "You have no idea."

I'm saved saying any more as the concert starts. And I have to give it to them: Our little rising stars nail that shit. I feel like a proud papa. It's pretty weird.

I mean, don't get me wrong, even though it wasn't my first choice, I still love this gig. But when you go to put out the album you wrote, produced, and recorded all on your own, then your former record label threatens to sue you for using the band name you thought was yours but they had trademarked? That not only puts an end to ever making music with said band again, but it also leaves you severely disillusioned against the music industry.

Who even knew that was a thing? Obviously, not us as kids when we signed the contracts. The knowledge of how much they owned us left me with more than a bad taste in my mouth. It was the straw that broke the camel's back of my music career.

Could I have formed a new band? Possibly. But it seemed like as good a reason as any to retire. It certainly helped me continue my journey toward being a better version of myself. And James had apparently been toying with the idea of going into production and distribution for a while, so it all kind of fell into place and voilà. Instant rock label.

We go out for drinks with James and Jeudi after, then head back to my place, where we pretty much cohabitate anyway, getting home just after midnight. Perfect.

Maxi makes for the bedroom, but I shake my head, grabbing her hand and leading her through the living room, out onto the balcony. It's too dark to see much, but the ocean laps quietly at the shore below us and the hot summer night has barely cooled.

As I turn to face her, she's giving me her "What the fuck are you doing?" look and I have to laugh.

"It's after midnight," I say by way of explanation.

She looks at me blankly. "And?"

"And … it's your birthday?" I prompt.

"Ugh. Don't remind me."

"I still don't get why you hate your birthday so much."

She shrugs. "I just never saw the reason for celebrating. I mean … yay, you managed to stay alive another year? Kinda lame."

I smile. "Then how about we find a way make it special?" I offer, waggling my eyebrows.

She raises one of her own eyebrows at me. "I still don't want to fuck on the balcony, West. Too uncomfortable. Too much potential for witnesses."

I grin and chuckle at her. I'll wear her down on that one someday. "That's not actually what I meant."

Her brows furrow. "Then what?"

"Then this. I tell you how much I love our life together. That I don't miss being a rock star. I don't miss being a fuckup. I don't miss not knowing what I was missing out on. Every day, Maxi. Every fucking day, you make me so goddamn happy. Even when you're busting my chops. Maybe especially then." I wink at her and she rolls her eyes. And god, I fucking love her sass. I draw closer and take her hands in mine. "You're the one who made me want to do better. To be honest. And now, honestly?"

I reach into my pocket, fishing out the ring I've been holding onto for weeks. I hold it up between us, pressing my forehead against hers. She gasps when she sees it and looks up at me. "I want to spend the rest of my days with you. There's nothing we can't do together. You're my future, baby. So I just have one question." I stop and look deep into her beautiful hazel eyes. "Max Marshall, will you marry me?"

Maxi's eyes sparkle with tears. "You're so getting fucked on this balcony," she responds, her voice thick.

I laugh. "Is that a yes?"

She nods, throwing her hands over her mouth. "Yes," she cries between her fingers.

I bite into my bottom lip to hold back my own tears, scooping her up and swinging her in a circle. Her arms slip around my neck to hold on, and I cover her mouth with mine. Mine. That's what she is: all mine.

And I thought I'd understood forgiveness and everything after before. But this? This is my redemption. A life with Maxi. Fuck the fame. All that matters is loving her and being loved by her. Forever.

SECRETS, LIES, AND TEMPTATION

CONTENT WARNING

Secrets, Lies, and Temptation is a forbidden age gap romance novel that includes elements that might not be suitable for some readers, including the use of profanity, open-door sex scenes, and other potentially sensitive topics. For a full list visit:
https://melanieasmithauthor.com/sltcw.html

PLAYLIST

To listen along, check out the *Secrets, Lies, and Temptation Playlist on Spotify*

The Steam

Do I Wanna Know by Arctic Monkeys
Need You Tonight by INXS
Closer by Nine Inch Nails
Wicked Game by Chris Isaak

The Romance

Glycerine by Bush
Help Me Be Good to You by Heather Nova
I'd Do Anything for Love (But I Won't Do That) by Meatloaf
It's Only Love by Heather Nova
Everlong by Foo Fighters

The Journey

Girls Just Wanna Have Fun by Cyndi Lauper

Criminal by Fiona Apple
Little Earthquakes by Tori Amos
Losing My Religion by R.E.M.
Shake it Out by Florence + The Machine

1

NILS

"You sure you've got this handled?" Frankie asks me for the tenth time this afternoon.

I smirk at her from the leather chair across her giant desk. "Of course I do. Now go home already."

She lifts a dark eyebrow and purses her bright red lips. "I think you've taken a little too well to running the joint."

I shrug, fighting a smile. "Maybe."

She nods slowly. "You're good at it, you know."

My eyebrows jump. It's rare that a compliment falls from those luscious lips of hers. "Thank you," I reply with quiet surprise.

"In fact, I was hoping ..." She trails off, then shakes her head. "Nah, never mind. You're probably not up for the challenge."

That gets a chuckle out of me. "I'm not your two-year-old, Francesca. Reverse psychology won't work on me."

"Clearly, since you used my full name, you cheeky bastard," she teases with a wink.

"What is it you need?" I ask pointedly.

Frankie taps a red fingernail on the desk. "You know we're closing on Allure next month."

I nod. There's no way I could forget Frankie and Julian's third acquisition, a nightclub about a half mile from Frankie's first club, Baltia — this club — and a bit more than that from her second, Los Jardines. I've been wondering when she'd ask me to handle the takeover, just as I did with Los Jardines.

"And?" I prompt, bemused. I don't usually have to pull things out of her like this. Frankie never has a problem saying exactly what she wants. One of the many things I admire about her.

"And ... I'd like you to train Emma before the transition."

I can't help the confused look I give her. "Emma? As in, your best friend, Emma?" She nods in confirmation. "To do what?" I ask baldly. Emma is all curves and sass, and usually only around for the free drinks Frankie allows her. I never knew her to have any ambition beyond being a hairdresser.

"To manage it," she replies. I open my mouth to protest but Frankie throws up a hand. "I know she won't be ready to take full responsibility for running a club after a month. But that's the end goal, down the road."

"*Far* down the road," I grumble under my breath.

Frankie smiles tolerantly. "She's smarter than you think, and she's used to working her ass off. Give her a shot. Please. If you don't see potential in her to at least be an assistant manager in three months ... well, we'll go from there. But I promise I won't stick you with her forever if it's not working for you."

I study Frankie shrewdly for a moment. "Did she ask for this?" I finally respond.

Frankie examines her fingernails, avoiding eye contact. "No. I asked her." Her dark eyes flick back up to meet mine and I see anxiety there. "I need more people in this that I trust if we're going to keep expanding. It hit us hard when Annika left, and Johnny's got his hands full with Los

Jardines, even with your help. I don't want to bring in someone new right now. Someone I won't be sure will stick around."

I process that for a moment. "Fair enough." I don't voice that with two kids, one right after the other, I know how hard this must all be for her to balance. She's barely taken any steps back, save the occasional night off like tonight so she can be with her husband and children. "I'll do my best to bring Emma into the fold."

Frankie breathes an audible sigh of relief that makes me scrutinize her closer.

"Don't look at me like that," she says, turning red.

"Like what?" I ask, genuinely unsure of what she means. I've long stopped giving her puppy-dog eyes. Equal parts because she's well and truly taken and because of whom she's taken *by*. I'd rather not get snapped in half by Julian anytime soon.

"Like I'm hiding something," she accuses me.

I raise an eyebrow at the guilt in her tone. "*Are* you hiding something?"

Frankie buries her face in her hands. "I'm pregnant again," she admits.

The shock only lasts a moment before I snort a laugh. "Of course you are. I mean, Lucia turns one tomorrow, yes? Considering she was conceived mere months after Nico came along, I'm honestly surprised it took so long."

Frankie drops her hands and gives me a mock-sour look. "So I'm fertile, sue me."

I try to hold back my amusement, but it's practically impossible. "And you two fuck like bunnies," I point out with a smirk.

Frankie rolls her eyes to the ceiling resignedly. "Yes, that we do ... but I think Julian plans this shit, honestly." Her gaze drops back down. "He loves being a dad and he's so damn happy. Which is great. I just don't know how we're going to keep all this —" She gives a sweeping gesture around the room that I take to mean the club and all of her other businesses "— going with three kids. Three fucking kids, Nils." She sighs and shakes her head.

I cross one leg over the other and give her a look. "You're not happy?"

A small smile tugs at her lips. "No, I'm happy. And Nonna is over the moon. I just … I'm overwhelmed, that's all."

"And worried."

She nods. "Is it that obvious?"

I huff a breath out of my nose. "You've only asked about Violent Mood Swings' private concert tonight … oh, I don't know … fifteen times today?" I tease.

She shrugs. "It's an important event."

I narrow my eyes at her. They're all important events, to the artists anyway. And the fans. And of course, our bottom line. But as I study her, I glean that's not what she means.

"You're sad because you're going to miss it," I deduce.

Her red lips pull into a grimace. "I am. But I'm old enough to know I can't stay up until three o'clock in the morning anymore and then wake up at six a.m. with my toddlers before a birthday party full of a million other toddlers hopped up on excitement and cake." She takes a deep breath and lets it out with a heavy sigh.

"Hey," I say firmly, concerned at how overwrought she is right now. Frankie looks up at me. "I have it on good authority that West is well and truly back on the wagon this time, and I have a feeling this is the first of many concerts for them. You'll get to see one of their performances. We'll make it happen. And in the meantime, I'll make sure all three clubs are doing well. So don't you worry about a damn thing, do you hear me?"

Frankie's eyes fill with tears, and she jumps out of her chair, rounding the desk to lean over and throw her arms around me. "Thank you," she whispers in my ear, hugging me tightly. Since she can't see me, I smile fondly. It's crazy how close we've gotten these last couple of years, especially considering our first year working together was such a rollercoaster.

"You're welcome. Now go *home*, woman. I have to help Ace get things ready."

Frankie straightens up, smiling as she wipes away the tears. "Yeah. You're right. I should go." She sniffs and wipes away her tears. "Stupid fucking pregnancy hormones."

2

ALEXSIS

"I can't do this."

I fight back a sigh and turn around to find Max stopped on the sidewalk. "You can totally do this," I reassure her. "You're a fucking badass rock journalist, girl."

She looks at me with pleading eyes. "You weren't there. West has got to be pissed at me, Alexsis. I can't distract him tonight. You go on, I'll just —"

I lean forward and put a hand over her mouth, cupping it carefully so I don't smudge her lipstick. "I did not just spend two hours doing your hair and makeup — making you look like a goddess — for you to back out now. So his apology tour has been heavy? We all knew it would be. But tonight is big for the band, so you're going in, you're going to act like everything is perfectly normal, and it'll all be just fine," I insist. "Besides, Jason will have your ass if you don't go."

Max pulls a face. "Yeah, okay, you're right."

I smirk at her. We both know our boss acts the softie when it suits him, but underneath he's all about the story. Like Max usually is, too, when she's not forced to follow her childhood rockstar crush around on his bid to

500

redeem himself after ripping his band apart years ago. I keep that thought to myself, though.

"Damn straight. Now come on. I'll prove to you that this is going to be no big deal. In fact, you might even have some fun," I persist airily.

She leans into me and groans, but allows me to pull her along and through the doors. I push her ahead of me when I hear West's voice, then another man's after him.

"Hey, Maxi," West greets her, running a hand through his dark hair while doing surprised elevator eyes over her. I smile smugly. He gestures to the guy standing beside him. "This is Nils, Baltia's manager."

My gaze bounces from West's face at the name and lands on the other man. *Nils?* No. It can't possibly be …

But it's that tall, lean body I remember. And I'd never forget that messy, sexy dark blond hair and those piercing blue eyes. My hands clap over my mouth.

"Oh my god, Nils Larssen?!" I flap my hands wildly, trying and failing to contain myself as West and Max both look at me like I'm nuts before exchanging a concerned look.

For his part, Nils looks at me like he's never seen me before. But then, I'm not surprised, considering.

"You don't remember me, do you?" I ask.

He studies my face for a moment before his ice-blue eyes meet mine. "I'm sorry, I don't," he replies. "You are …?"

"Alexsis Monaghan," I respond, then turn to Max since she's giving me the silent what-the-fuck-is-going-on-here vibe. "Nils was an exchange student who stayed with us … oh my gosh, what was it? Fifteen years ago?" My heart flutters at the memories of following him around for what was probably the best year of my young life.

"Holy shit." The words burst from his lips as his own memory clearly clicks into place. "Seventeen years ago," he corrects me in a hushed tone. "You were a baby. What, five years old? I'm surprised you even remember me. Now look at you."

And look at me he does. So intensely that my skin warms under his gaze. I may have been just a child, but he was the man who fueled my childish fantasies of falling in love for *years*.

"Are you kidding? You were my first crush," I reply honestly, batting my eyelashes at him coyly. Finally. *Finally*, after all these years, I can flirt with him in real life.

"Is that so?" he murmurs in a tone that sends a fresh wave of heat over my skin.

I nod, mesmerized, vaguely registering Max and West wordlessly wandering off together, but I'm too focused on Nils to acknowledge it. "I'm surprised you didn't know. My brothers teased me horribly about it for years," I admit.

"How are Asher and Aiden?" he asks, clearly as purposefully oblivious to our friends' departures.

"They're good," I respond. "Asher is a marketing director for Lexus and Aiden is an archivist at The Getty."

Nils takes a step forward. "Impressive. And you? What is it you do, Alexsis?" he purrs, sending shivers down my back.

God, he's flirting *back*. I half want to pinch myself to make sure I'm not dreaming.

"I'm a journalist at *Rock Scene* with Max," I respond. "I just finished college at the end of last year, though, so I'm still learning the ropes."

"Well, if you're looking for material, you're certainly in the right place. Baltia's seen it all."

What a perfect opening. I tip my head. "I bet you have, too, then."

He smiles vaguely. "I've only been in the industry just over five years. But yes, I suppose I have a few stories."

"Well, then I think I need a tour," I reply, gesturing around the club. I've been here dozens of times and I'm pretty familiar with its history, but like hell I'm going to pass up more time with him. Also, I can't help wondering how I never noticed him here all these years. Then again, I guess on some level I'd assumed the shy, Swedish boy who stole my heart had taken it back to his homeland with him.

He gives me a cryptic look but extends his arm. "Then come with me," he offers.

With a grin, I snake my arm through his and tuck in close against him. He smells like alcohol and leather. Two of my favorite things.

"Thank you," I reply. "You know, you don't even have an accent anymore."

Nils grimaces. Maybe a sore subject then. "Well, I have been in the States as long as I lived in Sweden," he points out.

I tilt my head as we step down into the stage pit. "You haven't gone back?"

"A few times, but never for long. Your family did a good job of helping me love my new home." He looks down at me and winks. I don't miss the subtle reminder that he was basically part of my family for a time.

I try to forget that fact as he politely escorts me around the club like he's giving a formal tour, sharing with me as much history of the club as he knows. I play the game, asking thoughtful questions and giving him a chance to see that I'm not a little girl anymore. That I'm on his level now. And I am, much more so than I'd ever even dreamed, as we clearly share a love for rock of all forms.

After the tour, we get drinks and watch Violent Mood Swings' private concert together from the VIP balcony. They're good. Really good. Maybe even better than they were before. Still, having Nils by my side in the dark, high-energy club is distracting, and I can't help sneaking glances at his tall, intimidating self. He always had presence, and it seems its lure has only grown with time. I also have to fight the grin that comes to my face every time I catch him staring at me out of the corner of my eye.

Who would ever have thought that a few side glances could be so damn hot? All new fantasies bloom in my mind that I'd never had the maturity to even consider back then. And despite his trying to reel things back to a respectfully polite distance, clearly I affect him. The thought makes me a little dizzy with glee.

After it's over, though, we head downstairs so I can meet up with Max.

"Where did you two sneak off to?" she whispers in my ear as Nils leads us backstage.

I elbow her and grin. "Wouldn't you like to know? But hey, good show, right?"

Max nods, her grin sliding up to megawatt status. "*So* good."

"Great show, West," I hear Nils say. I look up to find him patting West on the back. "Can't wait for the tour."

"You and me both, dude," West replies, looking well-pleased with himself.

Max joins the conversation, and the heated looks she and West are giving each other is all the cue I need to leave. I catch Nils's eye, and he tips his head back toward the club proper. I nod subtly and he splits off from the pair, who are now talking only to each other, so I follow.

"It was great running into you," I say as we emerge back into the now-bright club.

"You, too," he replies.

Butterflies from both happiness and nerves tumble inside me.

"We should get lunch or something sometime," I offer.

I can see the hesitation in his eyes. Even though I have a few guesses as to what's causing it, it makes me want to ask why. To hear it from his lips.

But I hold back for once.

"Yes. We should. I'll give you a call sometime," he finally says.

I deflate a little. Because everyone knows the phrase "I'll give you a call sometime" is the polite way to say, "you'll never see me naked." But I give him my phone number anyway. After all, as Aristotle said, hope is a waking dream.

Lord knows I've dreamed of this man many times. And now, here he is. Our chance meeting can't be for nothing. In fact, I refuse to believe it is. So, I dare to hope.

3

———

NILS

FOUR MONTHS LATER

J ust when I thought Violent Mood Swings was over after yet another embarrassingly messy public breakup, they pull an amazing new album out of their bag of tricks. I stand between the stairs to the stage and the entrance, listening to West and his band put it all on the line. They've got some big ones to try to win people back with a surprise album and concert, I'll give them that.

As I catalog the crowd, I don't miss that Max Marshall hangs in the back … but it takes me a moment to see that she's not alone. My chest tightens with anticipation as I catch a glimpse of Alexsis on Max's far side as she leans forward to talk to Max. I skirt forward, unconsciously trying to get a better look at her.

I can't help it. Even though I know I shouldn't, I feel myself pulled toward her. I stand at the railing to the side of the stairs and get my first full look at her in months as she sways to the music.

God, she's even more beautiful than I remembered. She's mesmerizing. Despite myself, I imagine where we'd be if I'd called her. Friends? Or

505

maybe more … and since it's all in my head, maybe more that involves touching her soft, supple skin, running my fingers through her cornsilk blond hair …

I'm so taken with my fantasy that I miss what's happening at the door until I hear shouting behind me. My skin prickles as I turn back just in time to see a swell of bodies push into the bouncers who usually keep things in check. But it quickly becomes obvious that there aren't enough to stem the tide.

And I know in an instant that all hell is about to break loose.

An hour later, the club has been cleared of the massive crowd that broke through the door, and West has gone off to find Max and win her heart back after winning the fans' back.

I drop into the chair across from Frankie's desk tiredly. She taps her bright red fingernails on the desk, clearly disconcerted.

"Well, that fucking sucked. What promised to be one of the most iconic nights in the history of owning this club has turned into an epic financial failure courtesy of a bunch of dickwads and the overzealous LAPD."

I smile tiredly in her direction. "It'll still be iconic."

She raises an eyebrow. "Yeah, I guess you're right." Then she looks at me in that way she does. The look I call the Frankie Detector. Not that I'd ever speak those words aloud. "Where were you when that shit was going down at the door?"

I raise a brow back. "What makes you think I wasn't at the door?"

The slant of her eyebrow steepens with disbelief, and it makes me chuckle.

"I was watching the crowd," I offer. And it's true. Even if it was just one member of the crowd.

"I have a feeling you're leaving something out," she presses.

There's The Detector. I suppress a sigh. "I was watching a woman, if you must know. I'm sorry, I should've been there to put a stop to it."

She waves a hand dismissively and leans back in her chair with a sigh. "If five bouncers and Julian couldn't, I doubt there would've been much you could've done to stop it." She examines me for a moment. "So, a woman, huh? This wouldn't be West's girl's blonde friend, would it?"

I shake my head and laugh. Francesca Greco doesn't miss a goddamn thing. I pity her children growing up with a mother that knows their every move before they even make it.

"Yes," I reply simply.

She nods slowly. "You like her."

I cut a sharp gaze at her. "Your point?"

"I think you know my point," she replies, her lips parting in a grin. "Not still carrying a torch for me, are you?" She winks at me.

I narrow my eyes, and my mouth tightens into a thin line. She knows I'll always want her on some level. But I've resigned myself to looking but never touching. Unfortunately, once you've fallen for someone like Frankie, it's hard to find other women as exciting.

And yet, I haven't stopped thinking about Alexsis since she popped back into my life. I know I shouldn't. It's why I haven't contacted her. She's young. Far too young. And it feels like an insult to the family who gave me footing here to turn around and lust after their baby girl. Even if our reunion left me with nightly dreams about her. I know I probably just need to get laid, but nobody else has been able to take my mind off of her. Not since she popped back into my life, then left an Alexsis-shaped hole in it.

That right there should've gotten my attention. There's something special about Alexsis that makes me want to set aside our twelve-year age difference and all the other reasons for not pursuing her.

"No," I murmur eventually. "No, I'm not. And I do know your point, but I can't have her. Same as I can't have you." I let the seriousness of my words hang in the air, but I don't look at her.

"Nils."

I sigh and raise my gaze to Frankie's.

"Quit being such a martyr and go get the goddamn girl."

"It's not that simple."

"What, does she bat for the other team or something?"

"No, she doesn't," I respond with a small smile. At least I know that much from the looks and touches she'd given me. Ones that didn't make my decision any easier.

"Is she into you?"

I roll my eyes to the ceiling. "I think so, yes." At least, she was months ago.

"Then I seriously don't know why we're having this conversation. Get off your reserved Swedish ass and do something about it."

I open my mouth to protest. To explain. But then … I realize maybe she's right. So Alexsis is young. So I stayed with her family ages ago. We're both adults now. And if her reappearance reminded me of anything, it's that I haven't stopped thinking about her. Why *am* I torturing myself like this?

There's something there. And if just the sight of her does things to me … well, I owe it to both of us to see why that is, don't I? I've certainly been with people, men and women, that I was less attracted to than Alexsis. And I'm rarely drawn to anyone the way I'm drawn to her.

Frankie is right. I was martyring myself over this. But maybe I don't need to. Maybe it would be okay to at least see if there might really be something between us before I go off the deep end.

I rise, giving a small shrug. "All right, if you insist." I turn and slide a hand into my pocket, strolling out the door casually to Frankie's laughter behind me.

"Atta boy. And don't come back until you've had a piece of that ass!" she calls after me.

I let the smile pull at my lips this time. Because as much as I'd enjoy doing exactly that, I have a feeling there's so much more to this thing between Alexsis and me.

4

ALEXSIS

I'm in the middle of a meeting when my phone pings with a text message.

Still up for lunch or something?

Just when I'd finally put Nils Larsson out of my mind. I stare down at my phone and shake my head in annoyance.

"What?" Max asks from across a table full of research ahead of our interview with Dermot Kennedy.

I was so jazzed a minute ago because interviewing him is monumental, not just because I'm a huge fan and this could be amazing for my career, but also for the magazine. Unfortunately, Nils's text has fully squashed that feeling, and I can't help the frown that pulls at my lips.

"It's nothing," I murmur.

Max smirks at me. "I know that look. That's the boy trouble look. Is it that guy that stood you up this weekend?"

I roll my eyes. "I already blocked him, so no." Another internet date flop I'd mentally dismissed. I worry my bottom lip between my teeth as I debate whether to say anything about Nils. Because Max was so insistent for weeks after running into each other that he was into me. I know anything I say will just restart that whole shtick.

Max just stares at me expectantly, one brow raised. And I cave because I can't not talk about this.

"Fine, it was Nils. He wants to know if I want to have lunch or something."

"And that's a bad thing?"

"No," I admit grudgingly. "I guess it's not."

"You're annoyed it took him so long," Max says. Not asks.

"Of course I am. But you know. He's a busy guy. I'm a busy gal. What-ever." I cringe internally at how obviously non-genuine that sounded.

Max folds her long fingers together under her chin. "Then I assume you're going to say yes?"

I scrunch my nose. Even though I never said it out loud, she knows what running into him again after all these years did to me. Even I could feel the stars in my eyes that day. Ugh, it's his fault for still being so damn handsome and charming and dangerously alluring. Even if I wanted to play hard to get, which I wouldn't anyway since I'm not that type, I already know I'm going to say yes. And so does Max. She just wants to hear me say it.

"Of course," I reply with exasperation. She claps her hands gleefully. "Even though it's almost insulting how long he waited to ask, if I said anything ..." I trail off, my eyes going wide.

"He'd know how into him you really are? It's okay, I already know. You can say it out loud." Max winks at me.

"Yeah okay, fine, I'm into him, all right? But it's just lunch *or some-thing*." I don't know why I say it sarcastically, since I'm pretty sure they were my words to begin with.

"Mm hmm," Max hums. "We'll see."

I stare at her across the table, torn between wanting to point out that someone who's into you doesn't wait this long to ask you out and ... well, hoping she's right.

Before I walk into the diner across from Baltia, I rub my sweaty palms on my pants. I may be dressed casually in a pink vee-neck tee, dark skinny jeans, and black low-top Chucks with my blond hair pulled up into a ponytail, but the pounding of my heart is anything but casual. I take a deep breath to steady myself and head inside.

I spot him immediately at a booth on the left side of the dingy little restaurant. His long, lithe frame is leaned back into the blue upholstered booth, his legs stretched out under the table. His shaggy blond hair falls over his forehead in the same reckless way it always has. But the short beard is new. And fucking hot.

I take another deep breath and slap a smile on my face as I approach.

"Nils," I call. "Hey!"

He looks up, then rises from the booth to meet me. I'm surprised when he leans down and kisses my cheek. Besides the soft press of his lips sending my insides tumbling, his amazing smell sets my head spinning.

So, when he pulls back and looks down at me with a smile, I stare blankly back up at him.

"It's good to see you." He gestures to the seat across from where he'd been sitting. "I'm glad you could join me."

I can feel the blush on my cheeks as I slide into the booth. "I'm glad you texted." He settles back into his seat. "Though I was a little surprised, honestly."

The corner of his mouth quirks up. "Oh? Why's that?"

"It had just been a while. I figured I wasn't going to hear from you." I pick up a menu from the holder against the wall, willing myself to stop saying every stupid thing that passes through my mind.

Nils taps his finger thoughtfully on the table in front of him. "Honestly," he says, clearly borrowing my use of the word, "I didn't think you were going to hear from me either." He leans forward, lacing his fingers together. "I didn't know if this sort of thing would be … appropriate."

I glance down at the menu, blushing again. Dammit. Since when do I blush?

"How so?" I ask, looking up at him from under my eyelashes.

His ice-blue eyes scan my face, making me blush even deeper. Jesus, his gaze has a way of wreaking havoc on me.

"Well, I *am* quite a bit older than you."

That gets my attention. My eyes open wide as I look back at him. *That's* what's bothering him about this? If he thinks age matters here, then …

"Nils, is this a date?"

The tilt of his lips deepens into the hint of a smile. "That's a very forward question."

I laugh. "Well, one of us has to be," I reply. "And you've always been quiet. So, I guess it's up to me."

Now Nils laughs, deep and throaty.

Ugh. Panties. Melted.

"Yes, I suppose some things will never change," he allows. His mirth melts into something more … puzzled.

"What?" I ask.

"Nothing," he responds quickly. I give him a look, and he relents. "I just didn't take you for the forward type."

I set the menu back in its holder, then lean toward him. "What type did you take me for?" I'll admit it; the knowledge that he may think we're more than friends has emboldened me.

He leans in closer, only inches away now across the small surface of the table. "The innocent, bashful type, I suppose," he murmurs.

And I can't help it. I burst into laughter. He draws back, watching me curiously.

I wave a hand as I calm myself. "I'm sorry," I say, catching my breath. "I may be younger than you, but I'm definitely not innocent."

And maybe I do blush a lot around him, but it's not because I'm bashful. But I don't say that part. Because the things being around this man makes me want to do are in no way innocent or bashful, and I don't want to scare him off just when he's come back around.

Nils tips his head. "Exactly how not innocent are we talking here?" he asks in a low voice.

I sink my teeth into my bottom lip. "I don't think that's the kind of thing we should talk about in public. Over lunch."

Nils swallows hard. My insides flutter. But I keep my expression neutral as we stare at each other across the table, the air between us thick with newly blossomed sexual tension.

This. This is exactly what I've craved for so long. That I've dreamed about. That I haven't found in so long. This longing. Attraction like sugar and spice that you can practically taste.

And the thought that he could be feeling it right now, too, is sending tremors of anticipation through my whole body.

The waitress chooses that moment to come over and take our orders, breaking the spell.

I use the opportunity to shift the conversation and ask Nils how he got into managing Francesca Greco's clubs, and if that's something he plans to stick with.

Clearly, he does. Listening to him talk about it, I can *feel* his passion for the job. I've never heard him talk so much, honestly. Though when he asks me why I chose journalism, it reverses the whole dynamic and I tell him how my passion for music, while completely lacking any talent myself, alongside a love of writing, naturally led me to the job.

It isn't until my phone vibrates in my purse that I realize my lunch hour is long since over.

"I'm sorry, I really have to get back to work," I admit sheepishly.

"No, I'm sorry, I should've remembered not everyone runs on nightclub hours," he offers, sliding out of the booth and holding out a hand.

I smile up at him, taking his hand. "Walk me to my car?" I look up into his eyes.

He stares down at me for a moment before nodding silently and tugging me toward the door. He keeps his large, warm hand wrapped around mine as we walk the half-block to where I'm parked.

"This is me," I say, tipping my head at my red Jetta.

He stops and turns toward me, studying my face for a moment. "Thank you for agreeing to see me today," he says.

I smirk up at him, fighting the urge to tease him for taking so damn long to ask. "Thank *you* for lunch. I had a great time," I respond instead.

He nods slowly and a lock of hair falls across his forehead. I fight the urge to reach up and tuck it back in with the rest of his glossy, dark-blond strands. Touching him would be a bad idea right now, because I really do need to get back to work.

"Can I take you to dinner tomorrow?" he asks.

My eyebrows jump in surprise. He's been unreadable until now, but I guess I wasn't the only one feeling this date.

"I'd love that," I admit softly. "Text me?" I squeeze his hand and open the car door.

"I will," he promises. "Goodbye, Alexsis."

My heart flutters at the sound of my name on his lips. "'Bye." I slide into the car and buckle in, fighting the urge to jump back out and into his arms. Instead, I flutter my fingers and blow a kiss at him as I pull away from the curb.

5

―――――

NILS

I couldn't get Alexsis out of my mind after our reunion, but now? I'm completely screwed. One hint at our lunch date as to how much there is I don't know about her, a few light touches, the unfulfilled desire to taste her lips, and she's practically turned into an obsession.

How did the adorable little girl of my memories turn into this smart, beautiful creature I can't stop thinking about? I thought perhaps lunch would cool me down; that the reality of her couldn't live up to the temptation that she presented when she appeared in my club. Looking like exactly the kind of woman I'd normally go after with her silky hair, big blue-grey eyes, lush lips, and perky tits accented by a red halter dress that hugged every curve of her delectable little body.

But there's nothing normal about what's going on between Alexsis and me, and as I approach her apartment door, I can only hope she's as mature as she seems. Because I still can't stop thinking that twenty-two … well, it's just so young. Then again, perhaps I'm only thinking of myself at that age, and not giving her enough credit.

I take a deep breath and knock. Even having seen her dressed up before, the sight of her opening the door in a slinky silver dress that ripples

515

over her curves like liquid metal … well, it leaves me speechless, to say the least.

"Hello," she says with a knowing smile. "Don't you look handsome?" Her eyes travel over my black blazer, black button-up open at the collar, and crisp black pants. I'm the night sky to her shining north star. Speechless, indeed.

I clear my throat. "Thank you," I finally manage. "You're absolutely stunning."

Her smile grows as she steps out and closes the door behind her, bringing the smell of jasmine, of sultry night-blooming desire, with her. "Shall we?"

I offer my arm, finally remembering myself. "I hope you're hungry," I murmur, looking down at her.

She stares back up at me, her eyes bright. A sly smile curves her lips. "Starved."

A shiver runs down my spine. Because something about the way she said it made me think she didn't mean for food.

FOOD, IN FACT, HAS BARELY CROSSED MY MIND, EVEN AS WE DINE AT ONE of the hottest restaurants in Los Angeles. The cozy, dark corner we're in has kept the tension going between us by sheer proximity as we eat and talk. And like yesterday, we talk easily and seemingly endlessly.

Unlike yesterday when we discussed our pasts, this time we talk about our lives now. Her career at *Rock Scene* and where she wants to be — a top writer with regular cover bylines. Mine with Baltia — confessing for the first time out loud that I've thought of offering to buy it from Frankie, make it mine completely. Her desire to travel — she surprises me when she shares that she's never traveled internationally. Which, naturally, reminds me of my own world travels and I can't help imagining revisiting my favorites, traveling with her, seeing it through her eyes.

The abruptness of the idea startles even me, so I say nothing. It would be too much, too fast. And yet, staring across the table at her, it feels almost … right.

But then, such is the spell she's weaved over me, leaning close to emphasize a point, reaching for my hand to show connection when I speak … by the end of the meal her body language alone has me so completely enthralled I don't realize that we've been sitting there for hours until the server taps the check presenter and says for the second time, "Whenever you're ready, no rush."

"I believe we've overstayed our welcome," I murmur to her, so he won't hear as he tends to a nearby table.

Alexsis checks her phone. "It is late. I should probably get home anyway," she allows. "Since I have to work tomorrow."

I nod, rising and offering her a hand. As she did yesterday, she takes it without hesitation, but this time I pull her against me as we leave the restaurant.

"As much as I love my job, it must be so nice being able to sleep in," Alexsis laments as I drive her home.

I laugh drily. "Every job has its downsides," I reply.

"What are the downsides for you?" she asks curiously.

I hesitate for a moment, realizing what I'm going to say may sound presumptuous. But then, it is what it is. "You work standard business hours and play on the weekends, right?" She dips her chin in agreement. I can't hide my disappointed frown, despite already knowing the answer. "Even though I'm usually there most of the week by choice, I *have* to be at the club Thursday through Sunday morning. Well, except for sleep, of course."

"Yeah, but you get to see all the performers, too, right?"

I tip my head back and forth as I pull into her apartment complex. "Yes, I guess I do," I accede.

"So, the downside is …?"

I pull into a guest spot in front of her building and turn to her. "I won't get to see you again until Sunday evening," I say more plainly.

I can see the moment she realizes how incompatible our schedules are, and her eyes search mine. "Walk me up?"

I give her a small smile. "Of course."

As we head up the stairs, she stays close, her fingers entwined with mine.

When we reach her door, she slides her hand up my arm. "So, was that you asking me out again for Sunday?" she teases, smoothing her hand over my lapel.

I reach up and thread my fingers with hers, lifting her hand to my mouth and placing a kiss on her palm. "Yes," I reply simply.

She nods slowly in answer. "Okay. Yes." Her chin tips up and the air is thick with anticipation.

I hesitate. Not because I don't want to kiss her. But because I want to savor this moment. The promise of it. The feeling. The desire.

Her pink lips. Her intoxicating smell. The way ever fiber of me responds to her.

Her mouth opens a fraction, and she sighs. It breaks my restraint, and I pull at her hand while wrapping my other arm around her and drawing her into me. She rises on her tiptoes and pushes her mouth into mine.

Her soft, warm lips open under mine, and I slip my tongue against hers, tasting the wine she had with dinner. I pull her in closer, tipping her head back to give me full access to her mouth as I hold nothing back. I let every desire that has flitted through my mouth play out in our kiss. Her hands slide around my neck and her body presses against mine as the intensity ratchets up.

With the touch of her breasts to my chest, my control slips further, and I ravage her mouth with mine while I run my hands down her lithe body. Our mouths break apart and come back together in a frantic dance of tongues and lips and teeth, and I know if it doesn't stop, I'm going to take her inside and, well, take her. I can't remember the last time I felt this way, and the tenuous grip I have on myself shocks me back to reality.

I slowly withdraw, nipping at her bottom lip gently before letting her go. She gives me a bewildered, lust-fogged look. "You have work in the morning," I explain.

She closes her eyes and sighs. "You're right. I do." She opens her eyes again and smiles. "Thank you for an amazing date, Nils."

I resist the urge to touch her again. To tell her that I hope it's the beginning of many more. I need to get used to the idea first. "Good night, Alexsis," I say instead.

And then, clearly before she can think better of it, she slips inside and closes the door. It takes all of my strength to walk away and get in my car.

THE LIMO PULLS UP AT THE CURB RIGHT ON TIME. I BREATHE A SIGH OF relief. As much as I love my job, it's been four days since I've seen Alexsis, and the anticipation has been killing me.

I open the back door, and she peers up at me. My pulse races as we lock eyes, and I extend a hand. She slides hers into mine and steps out.

Her silken sheaf of hair flows over one shoulder. Her lips are an attention-grabbing shade of pink. Her body is on full display in a simple tight, strapless black dress that ends just above her knee. And hot pink stilettos to match her gorgeous mouth. I swallow hard as she joins me, and the car pulls away.

"You sure know how to get a girl somewhere in style," she offers as a greeting.

"And the night has only just begun," I reply, lifting her hand to my mouth and placing a kiss on her palm.

The quick tuck of her lip into her mouth sends a shot of heat into places I can't think about yet.

I keep hold of her hand and lead her to the VIP entrance of Los Jardines.

"Well, aren't you special?" she teases as the bouncers make a path for us and she follows me in.

I pause just inside and smile down at her. "This is another of Frankie's clubs. I managed it for the first year. And while I love Latin music, I just missed Baltia too much. But tonight is Salsa night."

She peers around me, apprehension in her eyes. "Nils, I know I mentioned that I took Salsa classes in college, but that was years ago."

I slip a finger under her chin and draw her gaze up to meet mine. "Don't worry." I wink, then lead her further into the club.

I walk around the back of the crowd, toward the bar, letting her take it all in. What started as Salsa night to try to pull a crowd in on Sundays has now devolved into a night much the same as any for the club. Flashing strobe lights. A packed dance floor. Couples of all kinds grinding to the beat, though there are usually a few serious Salsa couples putting on a show that sets the tone of the evening. It's been a wild success, even if not in the way we intended.

What I'm hoping Alexsis will see is that this isn't some stuffy ballroom dance club for skilled dancers. It's a place to let go and *feel*. The music. The freedom. And hopefully, each other, since we're starting the night on the early side, for clubbing, anyway. I hoped it would take some of the time pressure off, at least.

I order a drink for us both, handing hers off wordlessly. Not that she could hear me now anyway. She looks up at me. Then down at her drink. And she slugs it back in one go.

I almost laugh. But instead, I master myself. Raising an eyebrow, I do the same and down mine, setting the empty glass on the bar behind me. And I offer my hand.

Alexsis takes it with a grin.

I lead her through the crowd, to the center, where the mass of bodies is thickest. It forces her into my arms immediately. She looks up at me, her hands resting on my chest. Before she has time to let her nerves get the better of her, I start to move.

She follows my steps flawlessly, despite her protests, her feet tracking mine, her hips moving seamlessly with the beat. I press back and spin her out, then draw her back sharply against my chest. Alexsis tips her head back and laughs, and seeing her enjoyment is everything.

Like a cord has been cut, her body loosens, starting to move more fluidly with mine. It's not long before she's turned, her back flush against my front, all notions of "proper" Salsa dancing a distant memory as her ass grinds into me. We move together for a while, getting closer, sweatier, dirtier. She's too sexy. Too enticing. And yet it's too much and not enough all at the same time. She drives me wild, and I'm ready to give in to it.

I skim my hands down her bare arms, wrapping them around her front, pulling her into me. My mouth drops to her ear, testing the waters with a light kiss. She arches, offering the slender column of her neck to me. If I was turned on before, I'm on fire now. But I don't want to make my move here. Like at her apartment before, I have a feeling once we really get started, I'm not going to be able to stop.

As we continue, though, she grinds against me in a way that becomes very hard to ignore. Hard being the operative word. And when she realizes that's exactly what I am, she turns toward me, her eyes locking on mine. It steals the breath from my chest. I can see in her gaze she's determined not to have to stop this time. My whole body tenses with delicious anticipation.

Her arms snake around my neck. Her frame molds to mine. The beat travels through our bodies as one.

I close the small distance between our faces, her breath now hot on my cheeks. I brush my lips lightly over hers. As eager as I am for her, I'm enjoying this.

She sighs, her mouth opening and tilting toward mine. I sink into her, our lips molding together as tightly as our bodies. Chills travel through me as our tongues find each other, as her hands sink into my hair, lightly scratching at my scalp. She tastes of tequila and sin and promise.

I slide my hands down her back, delving deep into her mouth with my tongue, pulling her into me as my fingers skate over the silky skin of her back. Something about it breaks my dam of restraint.

I need this woman. I need to know what she sounds like with my tongue between her thighs. I need to know if it feels as amazing as I imagine to sink into her. I need to know her inside and out, literally and figuratively. But right now? Literally.

When the kiss finally breaks, I lean my forehead against hers, dizzied by our connection. I'm so turned on it's all I can do not to take her right here, right now.

I suddenly understand the time Frankie and Julian practically fucked on the dance floor at Baltia, early in their relationship. Sometimes your need for someone is stronger than your sense of right and wrong.

And I'm ready to do some very wrong things to Alexsis.

I lean in and say loudly enough for her to hear, "Follow me."

And then, with a sharp tug on her hand, I'm leading her through the crowd. Down the hall toward the bathrooms. Then beyond through the employees-only door and toward the management office that I know lies empty beyond. It's probably as far as I can make it, but at least it's not the dance floor in a club owned by the woman I work for.

6

ALEXSIS

My head is still spinning from our kiss when Nils closes the door to the room we just entered and flicks on the lights. It's an office, with a steel desk and leather chair on one side, and a matched leather loveseat on the other.

But I barely have time to take it in before Nils shoves me against the back of the door, the impressive erection I'd felt on the dance floor pushing into my belly as he gazes down at me with lust written all over his face.

Everything in me swoons toward him. God, that kiss. It wasn't just pure fire; it was also filled with potential. Even more than our first. It was more than the lust he's staring at me with now. It was the fulfillment of every girlish fantasy I'd ever held about kissing him.

Though what I feel for him is already far beyond that. I want him so badly it hurts. But there are still things he needs to know before we go there.

"Stop." I say it softly, but he heeds right away, drawing back, brows bunching together.

"What's wrong?" he asks, cupping my cheek and looking earnestly into my eyes.

I swallow hard against a lump in my throat. "There's just so much we haven't talked about. So much we don't know about each other. I can't … *we* can't yet."

His expression darkens. "Who told you?" he asks somberly.

I look up at him quizzically. "Who told me what?"

He stares at me for a moment, his thumb stroking my cheek. "I'm sorry, I thought someone had … You're right. There's much we don't know about each other."

"What did you think someone told me?" I press.

He takes a deep breath in through his nose and slowly lets out a sigh. He steps away, settling down on the loveseat, gesturing for me to join him.

I sit down, now even more disconcerted.

He takes my hand, stroking it. "If it wasn't obvious, I like you Alexsis," he says plainly. "A lot. So, you're right. I think if we want to take this anywhere, I should be completely upfront about myself."

I raise an eyebrow. Because I thought he had been. Or at least more so than anyone I'd met in a long time. "What don't I know, Nils?"

He grimaces. "I didn't want to tell you and change the way you saw me. But I don't want you to feel like I'm holding back. So here it is. After school and before getting into the nightclub business, I was a fashion model. And since you've lived in L.A. your whole life, I'm sure you understand what that lifestyle comes with. Lots of traveling. Lots of partying. Lots of sex. But I promise you, that's all been behind me for years."

I can't help it; a smile breaks over my face. "You thought *that* would change things?" I'm not surprised in the least. He's insanely gorgeous, and I noticed he didn't talk much about what he did before his current job. But I'm no stranger to secrets, so I didn't press.

His expression remains calm, but I'm starting to know him well enough to sense the shift in his emotions. He suddenly seems … uncomfortable? Worried?

"Well, it was quite a lot of sex. I uh …" He clears his throat anxiously. "I had something of a reputation."

My smile turns into a full-on grin. "Well, that's saying something in this town. What for?"

And Nils actually *blushes*. I bite into my bottom lip, trying not to show how funny I find all of this.

"Orgies?" he says uncertainly. I'm sure he's not uncertain about whether that's what he did, more about telling me. Then he quickly follows it with, "But I'm not an idiot. It was always safe, so I never caught anything. It was just ... a lot of orgies." He shifts uncomfortably.

"Nils, you have nothing to worry about. That's not what I was talking about, but I'm glad you told me. More than you know," I admit.

His shoulders drop in relief. "Really?"

I nod. "Really."

"So, you're not scared off?" he asks, squeezing my hand and leaning forward.

"Not even a little. And I hope you're not either. Because I know you see me as young and innocent, but when I said there were things we didn't know about each other, I wasn't talking about you."

Nils's brows shoot up. "What don't *I* know, Alexsis?" he asks, the corner of his mouth tilting up.

And finally, I don't feel scared. Not after his admission.

"I've never told anyone this before," I hedge.

"Your secret is safe with me," he responds reassuringly.

My mouth feels suddenly dry, and I lick my lips, trying to regain enough composure to say out loud what I've never said to anyone.

"I did porn." I scrunch my nose, waiting for his reaction.

Nils stares at me blankly without responding.

After a minute, I swallow hard and clear my throat. "I was an adult film actress," I amend. "To pay for college. I enjoy sex, and I'm not ashamed of that. So, when I was approached to do some high-class videos for a porn site for women, I went for it. It was also all done safely. But yeah. Like I said before, I'm not exactly innocent either." I shrug self-consciously as he continues to stare. There's so much more, but I need to see how he reacts to this first.

And I thought after his admission he'd take it a little better. But his continued silence is unnerving. Guess I was wrong.

"If that's too weird for you, I understand." I slide my hand out from under the dead weight of his. "I'm not embarrassed by it. It's just not something I felt like anyone needed to know. Until now, anyway." I lift a shoulder.

And wait for him to say something. Anything. But he just stares at me.

"Please say something," I urge him.

His mouth opens. Then closes. He shakes his head.

Well, shit.

"Look. I get it, that's big. Maybe too big. I should just … go and give you some time to think about it." I stand up. "I'll … I'll talk to you later, then."

His eyes flick up to me, still clearly stunned. So, I do the only thing I can do in the absence of any sort of response from him. I turn around and leave.

I'm not sad. Just disappointed, I decide, as I reach for the door handle.

That is, until a hand closes over mine, turning me around.

7

———

NILS

I pull Alexsis to me, staring down at her, still in complete and utter disbelief.

"I'm sorry," I tell her. "I'm just in shock. Don't go."

She looks up at me warily. "It's understandable. Though I thought you might not be quite *so* shocked, considering."

I shake my head. "No, Alexsis," I correct her softly. "I'm shocked at what a fucking idiot I am. That I stayed away from you for months because I didn't want to taint you." I laugh at that thought. God, how wrong can one man be? "All that time wasted." I bring my eyes back to hers. And I see hope in her gaze.

"*That's* why you never called?" she asks incredulously.

I nod. "That's why I never called. I didn't want to corrupt the daughter of the family that took me in." I shake my head and chuckle. "Turns out, we're more well-suited for each other than I thought."

She smirks up at me. "I guess older doesn't mean wiser," she teases.

I lean in, my lips hovering over hers. "No, but it may mean just a touch more experience," I murmur.

I can feel her breathing pick up. "Show me what you've got, old man," she taunts, licking those perfect pink lips of hers.

An uncharacteristic grin spreads over my face as I put her back up against the door. Just where I had her before. But now I know she won't be scared off. That she'll appreciate every dirty thing I want to do to her.

I cage her in, putting my hands on the door on either side of her. I lay a light kiss on her lips.

"First, I think I'll play with your tits," I murmur, licking down the length of her neck and trailing my mouth down to one of her nipples that's protruding through her dress. I bite it none too gently and she gasps and arches into me. I do it to the other for good measure before grasping both breasts through the fabric and kneading them with my hands. Alexsis groans with approval.

"And then?" she asks, panting heavily.

"And then I'm going to eat you out until you come," I promise, dropping to my knees. I press my face into the warm center of her legs, breathing in her scent through the fabric. I feel her fingers lace into my hair, scraping against my scalp.

I lift one of her perfect legs up, her dress shifting just enough to reveal a nude thong soaked through with her arousal. I rest her leg over my shoulder, cupping the back of her leg and ass with one hand, pulling her toward me. I use the other to lift her dress fully so that I can taste her. I slip my tongue between her legs, along the base of the fabric, feeling the trembling heat of her pussy just within reach.

With a growl, I shove her panties aside and dive into her, my tongue pushing its way between her lips, tasting her, priming her, sending her head back, knocking against the door as she moans.

I let the hand holding her backside slip between her cheeks and stroke her ass, seeing how she responds. When she doesn't shy away, I rub a finger over her. Her pussy gets even more soaked, and I know she's ready.

I use the hand holding her to finger her ass while my tongue drives into and over her pussy. The leg she has on my shoulder starts to shake, her fingers grip my hair, and I know she's close. So, I fuck her harder from both sides. She comes, moaning my name more beautifully than I'd even imagined. And we're just getting started.

I let her leg down slowly and rise, pressing against her and kissing her fiercely. She grabs at my shirt, and I allow her to take it off. Her hands run over my chest as she presses her mouth back to mine, her fingers pinching at my nipples as her tongue laves against my bottom lip. My cock strains against my pants, yearning to be inside of her.

"Now what?" she pants against my lips.

I consider that for a moment. As tempting as it is to fuck her beautiful pink mouth, I can tell she needs me to show her I'm okay with everything she shared. That I'm not afraid. That I'm here for it. And fuck am I here for it.

So much so that I'm more vocal than I've ever been with a lover. Something about her brings it out in me.

"Now I'm going to lay you on that couch and suck every inch of your body until I figure out exactly which parts make you scream the loudest, then fuck you while I suck them," I promise, a thrill chasing through me.

And I do exactly that. Turns out there's a spot where her shoulder meets her neck that makes her so wet I have a hard time keeping it together.

I look down at her, now lying on the small couch as I crouch between her legs, her dress bunched around her waist, so her tits are on display and the small strip of hair over her pussy is visible with her panties pushed to the side. And I'm not sure how I haven't already come at the sight.

She looks up at me with glazed eyes, and it sends shivers through me. I let her watch as I unzip. As I pull out my cock. As I roll a condom on. As I tease her entrance. She tips her head up to watch.

"You like that? You like watching?" I ask.

She bites her lip and nods, breathing heavily but not looking away from where I'm rubbing the tip of my jacketed dick over her clit.

I slide in slowly, pressing a hand on her hip to keep her in place as I fill her.

Once I'm in deep, I lean in and kiss her softly, shifting as I pump slowly. "What's your pleasure, baby?"

"You," she breathes.

I tip my head back as my balls tighten at her answer. I look back down into her eyes.

"And you're mine," I assure her, bracing my arms next to her so I can continue to watch her as I slide slowly in, slowly out.

She writhes under me, her hands skimming my back, down to my ass, then back up again. Her touch sends jolts through me wholly unrelated to the amazing feeling of being inside of her. It spurs me on, and I ramp up my speed. When I start to feel my own orgasm build, I break my mouth from hers and move it to that spot on her shoulder. She groans and grinds against me.

I slide one hand down under her leg, lifting it so I can get to her ass as I fuck her. When I slide a finger into her other hole, she clenches hard.

"You like that?" I ask her.

She nods. "Yes," she breathes. "God, yes. More."

With a smile, I give her more. All of it. Everything. My mouth works her skin. My chest rubs her nipples. My hand rubs her ass. My cock takes her pussy, our joined centers creating friction over her clit. I give in to the tightening deep in my core, letting the building need drive the speed of my thrusts until I'm fucking her thoroughly and fast, the tip of my cock more sensitive with every motion until she clamps down, sending me reeling, my orgasm unfurling quickly in hot bursts as lights pop in my eyes. She holds me hard through her own orgasm until I'm empty, sated, and sure that she is, too.

And as I sink down onto her, our mouths melding and my heart pounding, the feeling of the absolute rightness of being wrapped in her settles over me. My doubts about age, experience, and how I "should" think of this woman are obliterated by the reality of what we are: Perfect for each other.

8

ALEXSIS

As the pounding of my heart subsides, the heat of Nils's body over me combines with the bliss from a record-setting orgasm to take me to a new level of relaxed and satiated.

"Nils?" I murmur.

He props himself back up on his arms so he can look down at me.

"Next time I get to suck every inch of your body until I figure out exactly which parts make you scream the loudest, then fuck you while I suck them," I promise.

As I expected it to, Nils's cock twitches inside of me and I tip my head back and laugh.

His mouth descends on the spot on my neck, and he swirls his tongue over it, causing me to take in a sharp breath.

"You're incredible," he moans into my skin. His mouth finds mine again, kissing me only briefly. "I'm looking forward to it. But first ..."

He pulls out, removes the condom, then wraps it in some tissue and bins it. As he tucks himself back into his pants, he drops to his knees between my legs. His head leans toward me and I suck in a breath. Is he really going to ...?

His tongue finds my pussy again and I moan. Yes, apparently, he is. This time he fingerfucks me while he laps at my clit and tweaks my nipple with his other hand. Even the expected is unexpected with Nils, as every lick, suck, and touch drives me wild in ways I can't say it ever has before.

Maybe it's knowing it's him that's doing it. Maybe it's because of the intense attraction I've always felt toward him, and the special magic that I knew we had the moment we reconnected. Or maybe it's just because he's that skilled. And damn if he isn't pretty much the best at what he's doing that I've ever had before, which is saying a lot.

Because when he goes for the shocker again … holy hell. I've never minded that kind of play before. But tonight is the first time I've understood why it's done. I knew it could make everything feel … *more* but god am I feeling it all, and then some. As a result, the next orgasm hits like a freight train. Hard, long, and it splits me into a million blissed-out pieces.

I watch Nils as he gently withdraws. He's so handsome it hurts. Though everything hurts so good right now. I pull my dress back down and scoot up so he can sit beside me. He loops an arm around me and pulls me into his lap.

"Okay, I have an odd question," he hedges.

I raise an eyebrow and give him a smirk. "I think we're past considering questions odd," I offer.

He chuckles. "Yes, perhaps."

I gesture for him to go on.

"What was your porn name?"

I suppress a smile. It's a question I should've expected. "Tessa Temptation," I tell him. "Why? Are you going to go watch my films?" I tease with a glint in my eye. I'm hoping he does because the idea is a surprisingly huge turn-on.

He cocks an eyebrow back at me. "Only if you watch them with me."

My eyes go wide. Oof. I was wrong. There's an even bigger turn-on. Holy hell.

"It won't bother you watching other people fuck me?" I ask slyly.

And I feel him shift in his pants under me. I burst out laughing again.

"Guess not," I follow up.

Nils cups my face and tilts my head so we've locked gazes. "Part of the orgy appeal was watching other people fuck, Alexsis. I have a feeling we're just getting started on finding all the amazing things we're going to do together. And I don't just mean in the bedroom."

I'm rendered speechless, but it's moot as his mouth finds mine for a soft kiss. It's tender and filled with promise. When I pull back, I'm struck hard by the feeling that he's right. Because a man that I'm this attracted to, that I find this fascinating, who not only accepts my past but is excited about what it means for us? He's my unicorn. The thought is overwhelming, to say the least.

I sigh heavily. "I have the biggest 'I told you so' of my life coming from Max," I murmur.

Nils huffs a laugh. "Oh? Why's that?"

"She told me you were into me. I didn't believe her."

Nils's lips tilt in a smile. "If it makes you feel better, I've got the same coming from Frankie."

"Sounds like we were both wrong."

"I've never been happier to be."

"Me neither." I pause. "Nils?"

"Hmmm?" he returns, sounding sleepy.

"How do you feel about bondage?"

His head snaps up. "I feel like if I were physically capable of it, I'd take you home and tie you up for even asking that question."

I grin widely. "Or I could tie you up."

He groans and tackles me into the couch, his mouth demanding on mine. When he pulls back and looks down at me, his gaze is so intense I can feel myself getting turned on again. Good lord, this man.

"I'm not wasting any more time with you, Alexsis. Whatever you want. I'm yours."

I reach up and stroke his beard. I've always been his on some level. He was my first crush, after all.

"Good to know," I reply, not wanting to give too much away. "But I think I need to recharge myself. How do you feel about pie?"

"If you're talking about the pie shop up the road, then I'm pretty much about to propose right now."

I laugh and he smiles widely. "You strike me as a black pepper cherry pie kind of guy. A spicy twist on a classic," I tease, ignoring the shock of his joking about proposing.

He raises an eyebrow. "Seriously. Marry me."

My breath catches. "Seriously?"

He grins, and it's something I've seen him do so rarely that it dazzles me. "Not really, no," he admits. He leans in and kisses me, then rises, extending a hand. "Ready?"

I look up at him. Am I ready? For pie, yes. For Nils … I know that ready or not, I'm in. I slide my hands into his with a smile.

"Ready."

9

———————

ALEXSIS

"I told you so," Max says with a smug grin.

I roll my eyes. "Yeah, yeah, yeah. You were right. Nils was totally into me. Happy?"

Max leans forward and rests a hand on my arm, giving me a pointed look. "Yes. But only because *you* are."

Despite my irritation, I don't even fight the smile that breaks over my face in answer. Because I am happy. At least, about my love life for once, anyway.

"Thanks," I murmur. "I am. He's …" I shudder and sigh, not knowing how to finish that sentence. I mean, I know how I want to finish that sentence, but there's so much about me Max doesn't know that would require explaining. And I love the girl, but she's also a colleague, so that's just not going to happen.

Max chuckles. "I know the feeling," she replies with her own satisfied sigh.

"I know you do," I tease. "Things good with you and West, then?"

"I mean … between *us*? So good," she responds. But something in her voice is off.

"But?" I prompt.

She chews on her lip nervously. "Honestly? The band is in some trouble with the record label. Something about not having the rights to use Violent Mood Swings' name to produce a record and hold a concert?" She shakes her head. "West and the rest of the band are all pretty upset."

"Shit," I curse. "I can see why they would be." The wheels in my head start to turn. "Are they even allowed to do that? Own the name, I mean?"

Max shrugs. "Who knows? They're a huge-ass record label. Maybe they are or maybe they aren't, but they'll probably get away with it either way." She growls in frustration. "God, I wish there was something I could do to help. I hate seeing him like this." I raise an eyebrow at her. "What?" she asks.

I give her a bland look. "Uh, you're a rock journalist?" I point out.

She narrows her eyes at me once she gets my meaning. "I can't write about this, Alexsis. *Total* conflict of interest."

Excitement rises in my chest. "But I can," I point out. "In fact, this might be just what I need to snag a byline."

Max arches an eyebrow. "That … could work. We'd just have to sell Jason on you covering it instead of someone more senior."

"Or maybe we just don't tell him I'm doing it," I suggest.

She fixes me with a look. "You know that's not how it goes around here."

I lift a shoulder. "Sometimes when the rules screw you, you have to say screw the rules."

Max snorts, then gives me an appraising look. "Still after that promotion, huh?"

I draw in a slow, deep breath and nod. "Not that I don't love being your assistant," I hedge. "But I'm ready for more."

Max taps a fingernail on her desk and twists her lips to the side. I already know what she's going to say, but I give her the "spit it out" look.

"It's just … you haven't even been here a year yet," she finally says.

This time I level her with a look because I know she didn't get promoted until she'd been here a couple years. "Do you think I don't have what it takes?" I ask plainly.

Max leans forward and looks me in the eye. "You know *I* think you have what it takes," she says quietly. "But we both know that's not the only thing you need to get ahead around here."

I scoff. "So, what, I need a penis to be taken seriously?"

Max gives me a wry smile. "Well, I can't honestly say that doesn't make a difference," she admits, her eyes darting around, making sure nobody is listening. "But you also know Jason values 'paying your dues.'"

I roll my eyes. "Whatever that means. Talent is talent. If I can bring him an article that sells mags, that should be all that matters."

Max leans back in her chair and sighs. "I mean … I can't say it won't work. But there's more to it than that." She pauses. "I think you just need to be patient."

I clench my jaw against a snarky retort. I know Max is just trying to help. But I didn't get a degree in journalism to be a gofer for years before getting my own byline.

I also don't throw it in her face that I did at least half of the legwork and writing for the piece on West's apology tour that brought record numbers of new subscribers. Mostly since it was such a difficult situation for her. And really, it was a great chance for me to prove myself. Except, I ended up getting so little credit that it made me realize doing anything as Max's assistant wasn't a recipe for long-term success. Or short-term success even, apparently.

"I hear you," I finally respond, nodding.

She eyes me warily. "Do you?" she asks. "Because I'd hate to see you go off and do something that blew up in your face and got you fired or something."

Reflexively, I give her a sharp look back. I wonder for a moment if she's worried about me or if she's really just worried about being upstaged. And then I feel a little like an asshole, because I know Max wouldn't begrudge me success. At least not consciously. But clearly, she's not behind my plan, so I decide keeping my mouth shut about it is probably for the best.

And then, of course, doing it anyway.

I give her a sweet smile. "You're right. I wouldn't want to risk that," I reply.

Do I respect Max for her talent and success? Absolutely. But we're very different people. She prefers to play by the rules. And I'm more the "no guts, no glory" type.

NILS TEXTS ME THAT FRANKIE'S ASKED HIM TO CHECK IN ON HER NEW CLUB and he wants me to join him. Given that our last club date involved some seriously sexy dancing followed by fantastic sex … well, how could I refuse?

Though he asked that I meet him there, he sent a car again at least. I sit in the backseat of said car as it winds through the streets of Hollywood. I run my hands over the buttery leather somewhat nervously. Mostly because I don't know exactly what this is. A date? Work, for Nils anyway? I guess I'll have to take my cues from him, I'm just used to knowing which version of myself I need to be. Or more accurately, whether I need to suppress my inner freak or not.

When we pull up to the club, I slide out to find Nils waiting for me, a hand extended to help me out of the car. I take it and look up at him with a smile as I adjust my purple minidress. His eyes slide over me approvingly and he lifts my hand to his mouth, placing a kiss on my knuckles.

And then he pulls me flush against him, ravishing my mouth. But it's over as abruptly as it began.

"I missed you," he says, nuzzling against my ear, his husky voice sending chills down my side.

I run my hand up his chest and lightly scratch my nails over the back of his neck. "I missed you, too," I murmur, looking up into his eyes.

He steps back, sliding his hand over mine and tugging me toward the VIP entrance. "Come with me," he commands.

I grin. "Yes, sir."

He looks over his shoulder at me and laughs, shaking his head.

Once we're in, I can't contain my curiosity any longer. "So, what are you checking on, exactly?" I shout into his ear, hoping he can hear me over the pounding EDM.

He shrugs and puts his mouth to my ear. "Everything." He leans back and gives me a wink before leading me to the bar.

He orders and hands me a drink a minute later. I give him a quizzical look at his not having one. He shakes his head in response. So, I guess he's not drinking? I shrug and take a sip of mine. Mint and citrus and sugar wrap around my tongue. A mojito. A pretty damn good one.

He points at the drink and raises an eyebrow in question. I give him a thumbs up and try not to smirk at the fact that he ordered a drink that bartenders notoriously hate making. Which he must know, given his line of work. So clearly, he's here to start some shit.

Next, he leads me on a lap around the club, observing the crowds, the DJ, and the atmosphere until we head up a flight of stairs. There's a bouncer at the top who Nils fist bumps. The dude then lets us into what is clearly the VIP area.

Just as we've barely cleared the entrance, a curvy blonde in black leather pants and a red halter approaches Nils.

I narrow my eyes as she leans into him and puts a hand to his chest while she speaks into his ear. When she pulls back, he nods and the blonde walks past us and down the stairs without even acknowledging my presence.

I turn and give Nils a sharp look. He chuckles and pulls me against him.

"That was Emma, the manager. It's her first week in the role, and

Frankie wanted me to check in on her." I flush a little in embarrassment and nod my understanding. Nils clearly doesn't miss a thing because he leans in again and whispers in my ear, "Were you jealous?"

I have to think about that for a moment. Not out of reluctance to admit it, but because I didn't even recognize that was the feeling her touching him had evoked. But yes, I realize it was. I look back up at him and nod.

His eyes bore into mine as his hand tightens on my backside. We stare at each other and the heat in his eyes matches the heat between my thighs. Apparently, feeling jealous is a bit of a turn on for me. And possibly for him, too.

He leans in slowly and nips gently at my lips before withdrawing and leading me to the railing. Back in observation mode, Nils's eyes scan the crowd for a few minutes. And while he watches them, I sneak furtive glances at him.

He finally catches me and one of his rare smiles nearly bowls me over. He snakes an arm around my waist and pulls me close. "Follow me," he murmurs into my ear.

He turns and heads deeper into the VIP section, down a dark hall. We pass restrooms, then a surveillance room, then round a corner.

"What, no dancing first?" I tease him as he comes to a door labeled "office."

He shoots me a wicked look over his shoulder as he opens the door and pulls me inside. "Later," he promises, leading me to the desk. He sits down on the edge and pulls me between his legs, nuzzling into my neck. "Your scent has been driving me crazy since you stepped out of the car." His tongue licks up the front of my throat and my fingers slide into his hair, tugging as the sensations he's causing in me curl through my body.

I take a step back, putting some space between us. "Oh really?" I tease, trailing a finger down his chest as I walk around the desk. I turn to face him from the opposite side. "What are you going to do about it?"

Nils braces on the desk, his hand gripping the edge and he *growls*. A sly grin spreads over my face at the possessive noise. I lean down over the desk, shaking my hips in invitation.

In a flash, he's rounded the desk and lifted the hem of my dress, sliding his hands over my sex. I lay my head down on the desk and look back at him, licking my lips.

"You gonna fuck me right here, you naughty boy?" I taunt him. He sucks in a sharp breath and hisses it back out. But his only response is to unbuckle his belt. My body tightens in anticipation. "That's right, no fore-play, baby. You know you need this pussy *right now*."

Nils rolls a condom on and again answers with his actions, slamming into me. I gasp as I slide up the desk, as he stretches and fills me. But he doesn't wait for me to adjust, he simply unleashes. I close my eyes to focus on the pleasure, groaning with each punishing thrust, unable to so much as move to meet him.

"Alexsis," he grits out. My eyes fly open to meet his. "Keep those eyes open while I fuck you, naughty girl."

I bite into my lip and nod, a fresh wave of arousal making me even slicker and tighter under his delicious assault.

"Use that pussy, baby," I encourage him.

"Yeah? You like it when I fuck that pussy hard enough to milk my cock?" he says, low and out of breath.

I try to arch, but all it does is push him deeper and I gasp.

God, the dirty talk. I've always been mouthy during sex, but hearing Nils do it? Unexpected. Thrilling. Ecstasy.

"I love it," I admit once I'm able to speak again. "I love you fucking me hard and deep. I love hearing you talk dirty while you use my hole. Let me hear you come because of my pussy, baby."

Nils's thrusts stutter at my words before picking up even harder and faster. "Touch yourself, Alexsis," he commands. "I need you to come and —"

"Oh shit!" someone exclaims.

My head snaps up to see the blonde — Emma — in the doorway. Apparently, we were fucking and dirty talking too loudly to hear the door.

She gapes at us for a moment while Nils slows … but doesn't stop. A feral grin spreads over my face.

"Sorry, you can't join in," I say, not sounding sorry at all. "But feel free to stay and watch."

Nils lets out a dark laugh and picks up his pace again.

"Are you fucking kidding me?" Emma demands. "You can't be … This is so … Stop it!"

I set my head back down on the desk, determined to ignore her. I reach down and finger my clit. I was so close anyway that even the slight brush sends me reeling and my walls clamp down on Nils's dick.

"Oh fuck, Alexsis," he groans, thickening inside of me as he comes. The sound and feel of his orgasm heightens my own and I groan with him.

Emma lets out a disgusted noise and flees the room, the sounds of our orgasms chasing after her.

Nils smacks me hard on the ass as he pulls out. "Well, that was interesting."

I rise, shimmying my dress back into place before turning and looking up at him. "That was fucking hot," I correct him.

Nils smirks down at me. "It was," he agrees. "Still, I think we should go to my place before Emma has another conniption."

"No dancing?" I pout teasingly.

He leans in, lust clear in his glazed eyes. "Not tonight. But don't worry. I'm far from done with you, naughty girl."

I shudder in anticipation. "Then lead the way."

Multiple orgasms later, Nils and I collapse together in his low, black satin-sheeted bed. I'm pleasantly sore *everywhere* and not sad at all that we didn't get to dance. In the club, anyway. There was plenty of dancing — and dirty talk — between the sheets.

"Had enough, naughty girl?" Nils murmurs, running his fingers down my back.

I snort and turn to look at him. "You're not seriously suggesting you can go again right now?"

He smiles vaguely. "I don't need an erection to fuck you."

My breath catches at his words, and I press my lips to his. "Even I need a break sometimes," I admit.

He chuckles lowly. "Mmm." He slides down, molding his body to mine. "I suppose I do, too. But something about you has made me … insatiable." He kisses my neck, and I tip my head back to give him better access, relishing in his touches, even if my libido is sated for the moment.

"It's been a long time since I've had a lover who could keep up," I admit. "I'm impressed."

Nils props his head up on his hand and looks down at me. "Be with me, Alexsis," he murmurs in a serious tone.

The abruptness of his comment has my eyes snapping open. "I *am* with you, Nils," I point out.

His brow furrows. "No, I mean, be with *just* me. I don't want to just claim your body."

Something inside me simultaneously melts and hardens. I realize it's the very thing he's asking for: my heart.

"Are you asking me to be your girlfriend?" I respond quietly.

"Something like that," he agrees.

I raise an eyebrow. "Something *like* that or *that*?" I press.

He lifts a shoulder. "I dislike that word but … yes, in essence."

I press my lips together. "Here's the thing …" I take a deep breath and close my eyes for a moment. When I reopen them, his eyes have tightened with concern. "I want to be honest with you, Nils. And that's big for me. Because I feel like there are two sides of me … the side I have to show to the world, and the real me. And those sides? Well, they have *very* different love lives."

Nils is silent for a minute before he finally says, "I don't know what that means."

I rub my lips together and sit up. He follows suit.

"It means, I've had boyfriends — men I've exclusively dated. But I've *never* promised sexual exclusivity. Ever. Romantic? Sure. I can do that. But sexual? I … I just need more. I have things I do that I love that I'd have to stop doing."

Nils leans back into the headboard, slinging one arm behind his head for support. I try not to stare at how it makes the lean muscles of his bicep pop.

"So, these boyfriends … you don't tell them about your other activities?" he asks thoughtfully.

"No," I admit. "But I don't lie about them either."

"Not telling *is* lying," he replies, clearly understanding what I'd meant.

I inhale deeply and let it out. "Yeah, I guess. But …" I trail off and shake my head. Nils tilts his to the side and fixes me with a questioning look. I let out another sigh and look up at the ceiling. Knowing I'm an asshole for what I'm about to say. "I've never wanted to be with someone enough to stop having sex with other people. I'm not sure I'm capable of it."

Nils rests a hand on my knee, stroking gently. The motion makes me look down at where his fingers brush my skin. What I don't say is that I thought Nils might be the one to break that mold … until he asked me to be with him. And only him.

"So, these other people … it's just sex?" he asks.

My eyes lift to meet his. "Yes."

He cocks an eyebrow. "And you have no intimate feelings beyond the physical with those lovers?" I let out an ironic laugh and his brows bunch together. "Why is that funny?"

"Would you be asking me that question if I were a man?" I point out.

Nils raises an eyebrow. "Yes, actually I would. I have."

Now my eyebrows fly up. "You've been in relationships with men?"

"Yes." His straightforward answer shouldn't surprise me, but for some reason, it does. "You haven't been in relationships with women?" he asks.

I shake my head. "Just sex," I say. "I'm pansexual, but no, I've never been in a romantic relationship with a woman." I shrug.

"Ah," he replies succinctly. "But you're still young." He looks down and I sense his mood shift. "It's only natural for you to want to continue exploring your sexual and romantic options."

I almost groan in frustration. "What do you identify as?" I parry back. Nils looks back at me in confusion. "Pan? Bi? Omni?"

"I've never labeled it," he responds thoughtfully. "But then, where I was raised, we don't have the kind of stigma attached to sexuality that exists here."

"Okay … my point was going to be that whatever you label it, age isn't prescriptive of sexual appetite. I have a high sex drive. I have since I hit puberty. I have no reason to believe that will change until and unless it actually does. So, I'm not writing off romance and relationships, just monogamy. In my opinion, it's the opposite of being young and immature to be one-hundred percent honest about that," I insist vehemently.

Nils looks like he's fighting a smile. "I suppose you're right."

I can't decide whether I should glare at him or kiss him. Either way, he's definitely got me all riled up. The thought deflates me a little. "I'm sorry. You asked a simple question, and I gave you a fairly complicated answer with more than a little snark."

Nils's fingers tug at my chin, drawing my gaze to his. "You gave me an honest answer and shared parts of you I know you don't share lightly," he replies. "Thank you."

I nuzzle my cheek into his palm, my face warming at his response. "You're welcome."

"So romantically monogamous, but not physically? Those are your terms?" he summarizes. I dip my chin in agreement and his eyes tighten. "Does that go both ways? Because you let me fuck you like a doll over that desk because you were jealous of Emma barely touching me."

My jaw drops at his blunt — and totally accurate — statement.

I think about his question deeply for a moment. He's not wrong — I was irrationally and uncharacteristically jealous.

But still, the thought of fucking other people with Nils ... a pleasant shudder runs through me.

"I didn't know what she was or wasn't to you," I finally respond, meeting his curious gaze. "And in the future, I'll try not to react before you can explain."

Nils surveys me carefully. "And I'll do the same. But any sex that's not just us will clearly merit careful discussion." He purses his lips, concern written all over his face.

Still, hope sparks in my chest that maybe, just maybe, I've finally found someone who understands. Who can meet my needs in a partner.

"Of course. And there'd be no sex outside of us without agreeing to it beforehand," I add. Nils's expression shifts and he withdraws his hand from my knee. "What?" I reach for his hand, unnerved. When he wraps his hand around mine, it settles me slightly.

"You said 'outside of us'" he points out. "Which I take to mean you plan to have sex with someone else without me there." He doesn't meet my eyes.

And the nerves return. Because normally? That's exactly how I'd play it with someone I'd just started dating. Take it at the pace it goes and get my immediate sexual needs fulfilled elsewhere until we were officially sexually exclusive — not that the latter happens often or lasts long.

But my relationship with Nils — because clearly that's what this is now — is new territory.

"I don't know," I admit. "I mean, usually, yes, that's how it'd go down. But this isn't normally how things play out." I press my lips together, knowing he needs reassurance right now that I'm into him, but not knowing how to give it. Because honestly, most guys just can't keep up. And while I hope Nils can, there's every chance it won't work out for that or other reasons. "Can't we just take this day by day?"

His gaze finally lifts to meet mine. I see concern there, but I also see heat. I crawl into his lap, straddling him. He inhales sharply and I rub my sex over his cock.

"Please?" I ask, mock pouting.

The corner of his mouth tilts up, and he pinches my bottom lip with his thumb.

"I think that's best," he finally agrees. And then seals it with a kiss. And an orgasm.

10

NILS

Frankie calls me into the club early on Saturday, forcing me out of bed long before I'd normally be up. So I'm already not in the best mood when I stroll into her office to find her, Julian, and Emma seated around the room.

I raise an eyebrow as I take the open seat next to Emma across from Frankie. Julian leans on the credenza behind her, his arms folded over his massive chest, his face unreadable, as usual.

Silence ripples through the room for a moment before Frankie leans back in her chair.

"Thanks for joining us," she opens.

I remain impassive, knowing Frankie either wants a report on Allure in front of Emma or … Emma tattled on me to Frankie after catching Alexsis and me fucking.

After another beat of silence, it's Julian who breaks first. "So, you gonna tell us what this is all about or what?" he asks, his eyes fixed on Emma.

Emma's chin tips up as she studiously avoids looking at me.

Ah. The latter. Though she hasn't tattled yet … but obviously she's about to.

I can't help the smirk that spreads over my lips, of which Frankie takes note, and lifts an eyebrow.

"Nils paid Allure a visit on Thursday," Emma opens, then pauses, shooting me a dirty look.

Frankie's raised eyebrow turns on Emma. "Which I asked him to do. I wanted a report on how you're doing."

Emma looks a little affronted at the idea of Frankie checking up on her, and my smirk deepens. Though I shouldn't be so smug; the tension that Emma has directed at me right now isn't going to make it easy for Frankie to navigate her loyalties.

"Fine, okay, I guess I get that," Emma finally allows. "But it's even worse that he was supposed to be working because I caught him balls deep in some skank on the desk in my office."

The corners of Frankie's mouth tighten, and I'd swear she was about to smile. "Well, that *is* a bit unprofessional," she replies tightly. Julian snickers behind her.

My eyes flick up to his and he smiles blithely at me. Because we all three know that Frankie and Julian fuck on this desk every Sunday after-noon. At least, that's the only regular time I've been able to pick out. There are still the occasional other times, but given their new penchant for routine, I've learned to listen at the door for a moment before I knock or, heaven forbid, walk in uninvited.

Not that it bothers me in the least. It's her desk. Her office. Her club. But I don't own Allure, nor is it my primary responsibility, so I can see in hindsight how it was a slight to Emma. Though it was hard to think about that in the moment.

"Am I missing something?" Emma asks, noting the look passing between Julian and me.

Frankie sighs and gives her friend a pitying look before turning her gaze to me. "Alexsis?" she asks. I nod. She presses her lips together. "I'm really trying to fight the urge to fist-bump you right now."

"Frankie!" Emma gasps in surprise. Julian chuckles.

Frankie turns back to Emma. "Look. I get it. I'm sure it was very shocking for you," she says soothingly, then turns her gaze at me. "And for the love of god, Nils, try to use a little discretion and fuck somewhere else next time?" I dip my chin in agreement as I fight a smile. She turns back to Emma. "But seriously, I thought you were going to accuse Nils of something way, way worse than that. I mean, that's not to say it wasn't inappropriate but I'm going to be honest with you, Emma. We've all fucked in every damn club I own. I don't know what to tell you. It's generally not a discipline-worthy event, so long as it's not on the clock or in public spaces. And it's definitely something you could have told me privately." *So as not to embarrass yourself like this* hangs in the air as Emma turns bright red.

"So, you're saying what he did was okay? What if another employee had caught them? God, what if a *patron* had caught them?" Emma insists.

"You know the offices are off-limits to everyone but management," Frankie points out.

"That's beside the point," Emma retorts.

Frankie taps her nails on the arm of her chair. "Fine. Will you please give us a moment alone with Nils?" Frankie replies.

"You're not just going to let him off the hook, are you?" she asks sharply.

"No, we're not going to let him off the hook," Julian assures her.

Emma scrutinizes both Julian and Frankie for a moment before deciding to accept that. Then, with a nod, she rises, shooting me an angry look on her way out.

As the door snicks shut behind her, I let out the breath I'd been holding and meet Frankie's amused stare.

"Truly, I'm sorry for upsetting Emma," I tell her sincerely, heading off whatever admonishment was coming.

Frankie snorts. "While I appreciate that, her making a mountain out of this molehill has more to do with her than you," she assures me. "But that being said, you still shouldn't have fucked someone in what's mostly her office."

I put on my best penitent expression. "I know. It's no excuse, but I wasn't exactly thinking clearly when it happened."

Julian smirks. "It isn't an excuse. But … we get it."

Frankie shoots him a suggestive look, and he winks at her. When she turns back to me, her cheeks are tinged pink. "Anyway, it was timely, because I'd already intended to share something with you that, coincidentally, will fix this particular problem," she continues as she opens a drawer, retrieves something, and tosses it over the desk to me.

I snatch it from the air and open my palm to find two small keys on a ring. I look up with a questioning look.

"I just finished moving the stuff from the storage room down the hall into an offsite unit," Julian explains.

"We're giving you your own office," Frankie adds in response to my bewildered look. "No more borrowing mine when I'm not here."

I look between them, shocked. Since I bounced between clubs so regularly, it had never bothered me to use the existing offices. But their doing this is a gesture I hadn't expected. One that goes deeper than four walls, a ceiling, and a floor. Frankie's eyes glow with the same appreciation I'm feeling right now.

"So, my punishment is —"

"From now on you are required to fuck in your office and your office only, young man," Frankie says mock-sternly with a teasing grin. "We're moving furniture in tomorrow after …" She trails off and bites her lip. But I know what she was going to say. After she and Julian fuck in *her* office.

I laugh and shake my head. "Thank you," I say simply, rising to leave.

"Nils?" I turn back at Frankie's call. "I'm happy for you."

My eyes bounce between her and Julian, and she gets my meaning. I'm happy for her, too. In a way I don't feel like I was ever fully capable of until now. Until Alexsis.

The first thing I do when I leave Frankie's office is text Alexsis that I want to see her tomorrow night. I have an office to christen, and just the idea already has me semi-hard.

But the next thing I do is take a deep breath and calm myself, then head into the club to find Emma and smooth things over.

11

———

ALEXSIS

"You know, Jim and Janie Roderick's son is here for the weekend," Dad says carefully casual, as we filter out of Sunday morning church service. "He's living out near you now."

I stifle a laugh. "Jonathan? Dad, he's three years younger than me," I remind him with a soft smile.

"Well, sure, but he's going to school out there for … something science-y," Dad returns with a shrug. "He's a real bright kid. I bet you two would have a lot in common, what with living in the same area now and all."

Asher snorts behind me and then covers it with a cough. My mother pats him on the back gently, oblivious to his attempts at hiding his laughter. Aiden smirks at me and I beam back in a way that makes it clear I'll take the heat for now, but they'll get theirs soon enough.

"Oh look, there they are now," Dad says happily as we exit the chapel.

"Just tell him you're seeing someone," Aiden mutters as Dad makes a beeline for the Rodericks.

I shoot him a swift look. "I will if you do," I taunt quietly under my breath.

554

Aiden's eyebrow ticks, but he says nothing. I give him another smug smile.

Which is promptly wiped off my face as Dad returns with Jonathan in tow, and I'm forced to make small talk under the intense late-morning sun.

It's awkward, and not just because I'm sweating in my long-sleeved blouse and full-length skirt. I remember Jonathan from high school, and he's every bit the geeky, enthusiastic kid he was the last time I saw him four years ago. Albeit a bit taller.

Thankfully, he turns down Dad's invitation to lunch, but not before we're coerced into exchanging phone numbers.

I breathe a sigh of relief as we head back to the van, and Aiden falls into place beside me again.

"So does that mean you're actually seeing someone?" he murmurs quietly, trying and failing not to look interested.

"Maybe," I reply airily. "How's Josh?"

"He's good. Now shush," he mutters, tensing a bit at the mention of his boyfriend. His eyes flick to Dad holding the van door open for Mom. We slide into the back wordlessly.

I feel a bit like an asshole for putting Aiden on edge because seeing my brothers is one of the main reasons I come here every Sunday. Even though they both live nearby, we all have jobs and lives. So normally I look forward to the visit, nagging from my parents to get married and start making babies aside.

Dad's attempt at setting me up was totally predictable. As was Aiden's teasing. But where I would normally laugh it off … well, I find I'm irritated, and it takes me until we've sat down for lunch to figure out why.

As Dad questions my brothers about their weeks — work, their love lives, their hobbies, their love lives, whether they prayed every day this week, their love lives — it hits me.

I'm so used to telling my parents nothing real about my life. How could I? It would break their hearts. And it would mean tearing apart our family.

It's why I've always looked for guys I could bring home to placate my parents with. And even with that intent, I never really found one. But now I've found someone I *am* excited to be with. And there's no way in hell I can say a word. It's the first time I've ever been disappointed with having to deceive them.

Like he hears my thoughts, Aiden's eyes flick to me. Until Asher clears his throat, and all eyes turn to him.

"So, I have something to tell everyone," he says, clearly nervous. He wrings his hands. "Katie and I are engaged."

In any other family, that news would've been met with cheers and congratulations. It's what I feel like doing. I've only met Katie twice, but I like her for Asher. Unfortunately, all eyes now move to Dad.

And Dad's eyes meet Mom's. I can see the disappointment on both of their faces and my heart breaks for my brother.

"Well, son," Dad finally manages. "That's … big news." He pauses and you could hear a pin drop in the room. "Are you sure though? No need to rush these things."

And there it is. No need to rush marrying someone they *don't* approve of, though by all means, rush to marry someone they *do*.

Asher noticeably deflates, and my chest aches with the desire to hug him.

"Yeah, Dad, I'm sure," he responds dully. "We've been dating for four years. I love her. Aren't you happy for me?"

Mom reaches out and squeezes Asher's hand with a reassuring smile. "Of course we're happy for you, dear."

Surprisingly, Dad doesn't contradict her, but he doesn't answer either. He simply goes back to eating, making his displeasure obvious to every-one. Because, while always polite, Dad has never made a secret of the fact that he expects Asher — all of us, really — to marry within our religion. Well, his religion. It's debatable whether any of his children claim it as theirs. Either way, Katie isn't Mormon. She's not even Christian, actually. And while it's not against our teachings to marry outside of the faith … well, Dad's old school.

So, when Asher ignores Dad and leans over to receive Mom's hug, I know he hadn't expected any better anyway.

I leap up and round the table to give Asher my own hug, finally.

"Congratulations," I murmur as I embrace him. "I'm so happy for you guys."

He gives me a half-hearted smile when he pulls away. "Thanks, Sis."

Aiden follows, and Mom starts asking questions about the wedding that make Dad draw further in. And what should've been happy news has cast a pall over the room until Dad finally can't take it anymore.

Aiden notices that Dad is about to start in on Asher again almost as soon as I do. "So, you guys won't believe who I heard from," he pipes up.

Asher gives him a relieved look. "Who?"

"Nils Larssen!" Aiden responds enthusiastically.

And my heart drops. "What?" I ask.

"I'm actually a little disappointed in you, Alexsis. He emailed me a couple of months ago and said he ran into you," he replies, clearly oblivious to my internal panic.

"Sorry, must've slipped my mind." The lie rolls easily off my tongue despite my brain trying to piece together what the hell is going on. "But if he emailed you two months ago, why didn't you say something sooner?"

Aiden shrugs. "It's an old email address I don't check often," he offers. "But cool, right? I can't believe you ran into him." He looks up. "Apparently, he's still living here and has been managing nightclubs in Hollywood."

"Wow, that's awesome," Asher says.

"Yes, isn't that something," Mom says with a smile. "I had no idea he was still in the States. How lovely. You should invite him to join us for lunch sometime soon."

Sheer panic overtakes me. I've worked so hard to keep so much from my family. And this thing with Nils is so new. I cannot let these worlds collide. Not yet. Probably not ever.

But I also can't say a damned word.

"Totally. It'll be just like old times," Aiden says with a grin. Then turns on me. "Remember how you used to have such a huge crush on him, Alexsis?"

My answering laugh is feeble and forced. "Yeah, that was hilarious," I reply tensely.

My family continues to reminisce about Nils, and bands of iron snake around my chest as everything spins out of my control.

12

NILS

I'm running a hand over my sleek new desk when Alexsis appears in the doorway. I jump up, surprised.

"Alexsis, I didn't expect you so soon," I offer, rounding the desk to embrace her. "How'd you get in?" I'd thought I was alone in the club and am suddenly concerned I'd forgotten to lock up.

"Frankie was on her way out and let me in," she replies.

I slide my arms around her and lean in to kiss her, but there's a tension in her expression, her body that stops me short. "Is everything okay?"

Her eyes bounce between mine as if she's debating what she wants to say.

"Fine," she finally says tightly. Clearly not fine. She gestures around. "So, what's all this?"

I study her face for a moment longer. "My new office. What do you think?" I step back and survey the half-placed furniture and boxes. "About its potential, I mean. I know it still needs some work."

She huffs a short laugh. "It's great. Congratulations."

I step back into her and cup her face in my hands. I'm unsure what to say since she's already denied anything being wrong. "I'd hoped you'd help me christen it," I finally murmur.

She closes her eyes and breathes deeply. When she reopens them, there's a clarity and fire in her gaze that wasn't there before. "That's exactly what I need," she breathes.

"Is it?" I question.

She pushes me around the desk until the backs of my legs hit the chair. "Yes. Now sit, bitch."

I raise an eyebrow and sink into the seat. "Yes, mistress," I tease, running my hands up her legs, lifting her skirt. I raise an eyebrow and meet her eyes. "No panties?"

She shakes her head and leans in to rub her hand over my cock through my pants. "No. Now take your cock out like a good boy."

It's a command I can't refuse. And once I do, we're fucking before I even know what's happening, her taking charge and riding me like her life depends on it.

It's simultaneously mind-blowing and worrisome. Because I've felt the need that has seized Alexsis right now; the need to take back control when something else in your life is spiraling away from you.

As we share a climax, I can only hope she'll also eventually share what's bothering her.

Before she's even caught her breath, she's looking down at me intensely. "There's somewhere I want to take you."

I raise an eyebrow. "Are you sure tonight is the best night?" I ask, alluding to her state of mind.

Her expression tightens. "If you don't want to, you can just say no," she says shortly, climbing off of me.

"It's hard to give an answer when I don't know what I'm agreeing to," I respond, watching her shimmy her skirt back down.

"It's where I go to get what I need. And it's something you should probably experience before you decide whether you're really in this or not."

My jaw clenches against the response that forms on my tongue. I'm not a fan of this aggressive and slightly combative version of her, but I bite that thought back as I pull off and discard the condom, then right my clothes. She watches me until I'm done. I rise and stand over her.

"You still haven't said where we're going," I point out evenly.

She runs her hands up my chest, lacing them around my neck and pressing herself into me. "It's a sex club, Nils," she says in a sultry voice, looking up at me from under her eyelashes. "Think you can handle that?"

I huff a laugh. "Yes."

We drive in silence, but I can tell some of the fight has drained out of her when she threads her fingers with mine as she gives me directions. I breathe a sigh of relief. If we're going to do this, I'd much rather it be with more positive feelings around the experience. Though I realize that I'd go, regardless. If she needs this to deal with whatever's on her mind … well, either way I plan to show her I can handle this side of her.

When we park, she goes to get out, but I stop her with a hand on her thigh. "What are we doing, Alexsis?" I ask quietly.

She sighs. "We're here to fuck, Nils," she says touchily.

The corner of my lips tugs up. "I figured that much," I reply, spearing her with a look. "I suppose I should've phrased that differently. What are we *not* doing?"

"Ah," she murmurs, nodding. "I hadn't thought that far ahead."

I give her a small, indulgent smile, sliding my hand between her legs and under her skirt. Lightly stroking her pussy. "Am I the only one fucking you tonight?" I murmur as her hips shift.

She shoots me a deeply frustrated look as I continue to lightly stroke her. "Do you want to watch someone fuck me?" she breathes.

A chuckle escapes me. "That depends on what I'm doing while you're being fucked. And by whom. Did you have someone in mind, naughty girl?" I circle my finger around her clit.

She sucks in a breath and groans. "There's a guy — Brody, the owner's son — he's almost always around," she breathes.

I nod slowly. "And he fucks you well?" I demand.

Her hand covers mine, and she pushes down until my fingers slide into her dripping-wet pussy before nodding. "Yes, but not as well as you." Her eyes are glazed when they meet mine.

"Anyone else you'd want to involve? Another man? Woman?"

Her eyes snap to mine, narrowed and full of fire. "No," she replies hotly. "No other women."

I curl my fingers inside of her with a smile. I may be more romantically possessive over Alexsis, but clearly she's more physically possessive over me. Interesting.

I pull her hand into my lap and over my thickening cock to show her how that makes me feel.

"Then let's go," I reply simply.

I follow Alexsis in and it's not my first visit to a sex club, so I'm not surprised by the low lights and naked, writhing bodies everywhere as soon as we get past the inner doors. But Alexsis leads us beyond all that, down a hall, past multiple doors, all in different colors.

I'm intrigued when she stops at a purple door and knocks four times.

When the door swings open, a naked, leggy brunette grins at Alexsis.

"Tessa," the brunette purrs at Alexsis, beckoning her forward. Then her dark eyes flick to me, wandering over my face, then down my body. "And you brought a friend." Her voice is filled with lustful approval. I remain impassive, waiting to see what else is in store beyond.

The room is lit with purple down lights, and matched plush benches lined along one wall with all manner of pillows. The far wall is covered with pegs and shelves that contain every sex toy imaginable. A large, purple satin-sheeted bed sits on the other side of the room. And on it is a naked young man, surrounded by three other naked women.

The guy is rolling a condom on as he watches the women play with each other; one eating out another, the third suckling at the breasts of the woman being serviced. Her moans bounce off the walls. The fourth woman rejoins them, positioning her ass toward the guy so he can fingerfuck her.

It's more debauchery and flesh and sex than I've seen at once in quite a while, and my cock aches behind my zipper. The smell of scented lube hangs in the air, and suddenly I feel ten years younger. Like my early-twenties self who fucked his way through half of Los Angeles.

Alexsis looks up at me like she knows, a smirk playing about her perfect mouth.

The young man, Brody, presumably, rises to his knees as we approach, sinking into the brunette with a groan. His eyes flick up to meet Alexsis's.

"Tessa," he says, echoing the brunette's greeting. "We've missed you. Why don't you introduce us to your friend and join us."

But Alexsis's gaze turns to me. I see her hesitation, and I instinctively know she's nervous that I'll want to touch these women. I place a hand on her back reassuringly. I lean in and murmur in her ear, "I'm here for you. Only you. He can fuck you while I watch, or I can fuck you while he watches. Whatever you want. But I'm not touching anyone except you." Her back arches slightly under my hand and she nods imperceptibly.

"Nils, this is Brody, Valentina, Riley, Gabbie, and Leah," Alexsis says. She gives a hard look at the women. "Nils is here for *me*." The brunette, Valentina, gives her a feline grin in return as Brody fucks her. The others barely look up.

"Welcome," Brody says with his own grin. "Refreshments are at the back. Feel free to do — or don't do — whomever you want."

Alexsis leads me toward the back, where she quickly removes her blouse and chucks it onto one of the padded benches. Her skirt follows before I've so much as caught up to her. I do, however, note the bottles of water, condoms, and tray of little blue pills on offer. I smirk. Figures fuck-boy would need Mycoxafloppin.

I'm just glad there wasn't anything harder sitting out. That's not saying they don't do that shit, but at least it's not so much part of the repertoire that they don't bother hiding it. Even in my day, a joint here or there was fine. Maybe some ecstasy from time to time. But I wasn't into a lot of the crap the other models did. Coke. Meth. Heroine. You name it. All were a big no thanks from me.

I go to start undressing and freeze for a moment when I realize I'd thought the words "in my day." If young and taut Brody with his surfer boy blond curls and lean, muscled body didn't make me feel a little old, that sure as fuck did.

"You okay?" Alexsis asks, removing her bra.

I shake the thoughts off and whip my shirt over my head. "Never better," I assure her, prowling forward and capturing her lips with mine.

She sinks against me with a sigh, opening her mouth to me and sliding her tongue along mine in invitation. The sounds of skin-on-skin behind me remind me — and my cock — what we're doing here. My hands trace down the soft skin of Alexsis's sides, and I lift her leg, then drop down and plunge my tongue into her pussy.

Her fingers curl into my hair, scratching along my scalp as I lick and suck at her clit. She tugs lightly and I rise, picking her up as I go. Her legs wrap around me, and I turn us toward the side of the bed facing us. I lay Alexsis down on the empty strip of mattress behind Brody, Valentina, and the trio of blondes fucking each other before filling my mouth with her delicious pussy once more. As tempting as the toys on the wall are, right now I need to feel her, taste her.

But Alexsis clearly has other ideas as her fingers tug at my hair again. I tilt my gaze up to meet hers, continuing to suck at her clit, her lips, her juices while her eyes beg me for more.

"Fuck me," she whimpers.

One of the blondes screams in orgasm.

I pause and take a deep breath before the erotic soundtrack ripping through the room has me shooting off too soon.

I pull back, extracting the condom I'd brought from my back pocket. I unbutton and let my stiff cock spring forth then roll it on. I can barely stand the moans and groans ripping through the room. I yank Alexsis's legs toward me and give her everything she asked for and more, plunging in so deep and hard she cries out, joining the pleasure chorus, then leaning onto my arms to piston myself rapidly and roughly into her.

But only for a minute until I back off to slow and shallow. And then when she's begging for more, I go full bore again. Another woman's orgasm shatters through the base noise of moans and skin slapping together and my balls tighten. I back off again and look up to find Brody watching us with a smirk.

Alexsis's head tips back to follow my gaze, and I see the moment she locks eyes with Brody. She reaches one slender hand out toward his now-free cock, wrapping her long fingers around it. He groans and rips his eyes from her to look at me. His considerable ab muscles tense as he holds back, waiting for my permission.

I give it in the form of a raised eyebrow and small smile. Without hesitation, he scoots toward us, his lithe muscles rippling under his skin. I feel a churning behind my cock, so I slow down further until I'm lazily dipping in and out of Alexsis's tight cunt.

I watch as he leans over her, letting her take him into her mouth. As he fills her, fucks her, uses her hole. Alexsis's legs tighten around me, and I didn't need the impetus to unleash once more.

In a frenzy of thrusts, I hold her down with one hand while I rub her clit with the other. Our rhythms sync until both Brody and I are fucking her hard and fast from both ends. A feminine hand reaches between our bodies, tweaking Alexsis's nipples. I look up into Valentina's face. She licks her lips at me. I let out a disbelieving huff of a laugh and shake my head. With a small shrug, she focuses on Alexsis, dropping her mouth to suckle at her breast.

Alexsis pops her mouth off Brody's cock and gasps, clearly hanging on the edge of orgasm. "Oh fuck," she cries. "Harder, Nils, harder."

I oblige, even though bright light is starting to push at the edges of my vision, my own orgasm threateningly close. Alexsis's hand grips Brody's cock, pumping it as she continues to pant and moan. Brody's breathing picks up just as Alexsis's pussy tightens around me, and I realize all three of us are about to come.

The thought alone has my cock emptying as Alexsis screams her pleasure and Brody's cum spurts all over her chest. Valentina licks it up, and the sight sends Alexsis and me reeling, jerking into each other, release continuing to tear through us as my cries meet hers.

Once we're spent, the feeling starts to fade, and some semblance of self returns. I sway on the spot, overtaken by the post-orgasmic feeling of blissful emptiness. It's all I can do not to collapse on top of Alexsis.

Instead, I withdraw my hand from her clit with one last gentle swipe that causes her inner walls to flutter around my spent cock.

"Fuck," I groan.

Brody chuckles and, still hard thanks to the Viagra, lays on his back. The blonde who'd been eating out her friend suits him up and straddles him, using his stiff cock to get herself off while the others touch and lick her all over. Valentina starts to move away as well.

But not before saying to Alexsis and me, "I'd love to fuck you two sometime." She pinches Alexsis's nipple and winks at me before joining the others.

Surprisingly, Alexsis giggles, throwing her hands over her face before running them down her body. "That was ..." She sighs with happiness. It's a different kind of happy than I've seen on her before.

I lean down and kiss the spot at the crook of her neck that she loves, driving my waning erection into her for a moment. She gasps and wriggles into me.

"That was unbelievable," I whisper into her ear. I press into her harder. "*You're* fucking unbelievable." Then I lean back and withdraw to deal with the condom.

When that's done, I grab a bottle of water and take a drink. Alexsis's hands slide around me from behind. I fold my hand over hers and turn toward her, offering her the rest of the bottle. She takes it, drinking deeply.

I run my hands lightly down her back. "So, what does round two look like?" I murmur.

She looks up at me contemplatively. "How about we go back to your place?"

I raise an eyebrow toward the bed where the sex toys have now been added to the mix and the women have paired up, kissing and biting and touching while riding double-ended dildos as Brody watches on.

"Unless you see something you like?" Alexsis asks sharply.

My eyes flick back to her, and I pull the water bottle from her hands, setting it back on the table. I pull her into my arms, my head dropping to lick her neck. "I'd be lying if I said I didn't want to fuck you as many ways as there are dildos in this room," I murmur against her skin. "But we can certainly do that at my place, too."

I pull back and Alexsis smirks up at me. "You have sex toys at your place?" she asks with a tone of disbelief.

I'm unable to fully suppress the wicked smile trying to break over my face. "Oh Alexsis, you have no idea," I reply, my tone laced with promise.

Her eyes go wide with excitement and her teeth sink into her lip. "On second thought, I may need one more orgasm before we leave," she admits.

I reach around her, wrapping my hand under her ass and feeling her pussy. My cock twitches between us at the wetness that coats my fingers. But he's not going to be of much use for a while yet, so I step back and gesture at the wall.

"Pick your pleasure, *Tessa*."

Her eyes glaze with lust and then flick to the wall.

"That one," she says, pointing to a triple-pronged pink dildo.

My eyebrows shoot up and my spent cock again jerks at the thought of all the screams and orgasms I'm going to pull out of her with that beast. And then I gladly get to work.

13

ALEXSIS

I'm utterly useless on Monday morning. Still boneless and mindless from orgasm after orgasm after orgasm. All the stress of yesterday's lunch gone.

Unfortunately, by the afternoon, the fact that I didn't tell Nils that he'd shortly be invited back to the Monaghan house sits heavy on my shoulders. I meant to last night. But taking Nils to the club … well, I thought it'd clear my mind enough to have that conversation. Turns out it distracted me completely. In a good way. But still, I know I need to talk to him about it soon.

Unfortunately, he calls me when I'm on my lunch break, well before I'm prepared to deal with it. Which would've been a welcome distraction but for the first words out of his mouth.

"Hey, beautiful. You'll never believe who I just heard from."

And suddenly I feel like I may lose my lunch. "Hey," I reply nervously. "Who'd you hear from?"

Please don't say Aiden, please don't say Aiden.

"Your brother, Aiden," he replies. *Well, fuck.* "Yeah, I'd emailed him after we ran into each other back in April but never heard back. Well, not until this morning anyway."

"Mmm, mmhm," I hum, waiting to see what Aiden actually said before I show my hand.

"He invited me to lunch with your family." And there it is. I should've prepared more for this, because I have no fucking clue what to say right now. After a minute of silence, Nils asks gently, "Is this what you were upset about last night?"

"No," I scoff indignantly. And then I crumple. I can't lie to Nils. Not now. Not about this. "Actually … yes. I'm sorry, I should've told you first. Aiden mentioned he'd found your email yesterday while I was having lunch at my family's house and my mom sort of suggested it."

Nils is quiet for a beat, and I try not to panic.

"And why did that upset you?" he finally asks in a reluctant tone.

I suck in a breath and my eyes dart around the office. "Can we talk about this later?" I respond. "I'm kind of at work right now, remember?"

"Of course," he replies immediately. "I'm sorry. Stop by the club when you're off work? We can grab a bite at the diner."

"I mean … I might be here late. I'm doing a bunch of research for this new article I'm going after," I hedge. While it's true, I can't deny — to myself anyway — that this is a conversation I really don't want to have.

"Another night then," he replies quietly.

My chest aches at the disappointment in his voice. "No, I didn't mean that. I'll just … I'll do my best, okay?"

"Okay," he agrees. "Because the conversation about your family aside … I can't stop thinking about last night, Alexsis. I've been hard since I woke up."

My inner muscles clench and heat spreads through me. "Boy, you sure know how to motivate a girl," I murmur.

"I thought that might help," he replies with a chuckle. "I'll see you later?"

"With bells on."

. . .

"I'M SHOCKED YOU CHOSE FOOD FIRST," NILS TEASES AS WE TAKE A SEAT in the familiar blue booths at the diner across from Baltia.

I narrow my eyes at him and pluck a menu from the holder against the wall. "Hey, food is important, too." I let out a sigh. "And I figured I might as well rip the band-aid off."

He raises an eyebrow and gestures for me to begin. Before I can, we're approached by a waitress, so I wait until we've ordered and she's out of earshot.

"You can't have lunch with my family," I blurt out.

Nils's brows pull together. "Why not?" he says simply, splaying his hands out on the table.

I chew at my lip and lean back into the booth, crossing my arms protectively over my chest.

"Do you remember anything about them at all?" I ask incredulously.

He tilts his head to the side, his eyes unfocused as he thinks about that. When they zero back in on mine, he leans forward. "I remember they were very nice people," he says carefully. "Much more authoritative than my own parents, but pleasant about it, nonetheless. Beyond that … well, I guess I mostly remember the time I spent with your brothers, Aiden in particular as we were the same age. Are the same age."

"You don't remember being dragged to church every Sunday?" I ask drily. Because lord if they didn't try their hardest to convert him.

"Vaguely?" he replies, his brow furrowing once more. "Why?"

I lean forward and rest my arms on the table. "They're Mormon, Nils. Like … old school LDS."

Nils raises an eyebrow. "I'm sorry, that doesn't mean anything to me," he replies, confused.

I let out an ironic laugh. "If you'd been anyone else, I'd be so fucking happy to hear you say that," I murmur, more to myself than him. Then distinctly to him, "You're so damn polite — and you're a man — so I can see how it didn't even register. But as a born and raised Mormon woman, as far as they're concerned anyway, well, their expectations of me are a little different."

"Different how?" he presses.

I scrunch my face and let out a sigh through my nose. "The short version is that there's no way in hell you can come to my family dinner. They simply can't know that we're dating," I reply, totally overwhelmed by the idea of explaining Mormonism to someone raised in one of the least religious countries in the world. And if I remember correctly, those in Sweden who are attend Lutheran churches; a *far* cry from LDS churches and all that entails, including the strict traditionalism, bizarre rules, and misogynistic attitudes, dress codes, and expectations.

"I'm going to need a little more than that," he prompts.

I let out another sigh. "My family — my father in particular — expect me to marry a Mormon man and pop out little Mormon babies for the rest of my life. The more the better. What they do *not* expect me to do is be with someone who is *not* Mormon, continue pursuing my own career, married or not, or — heaven forbid — not be totally sold on the idea of having kids at all."

Nils leans back with a contemplative expression. "I take it they don't know of your ah … previous career?"

I give him a wry smirk. "Definitely not."

"And your current job?"

I shift uncomfortably in my seat. "They know I write for a magazine," I hedge.

One of his eyebrows pops up. "But not what kind," he deduces.

"They know it's music?" I reply, heat creeping into my cheeks. "But no, they don't know it's a rock magazine."

"Can they not find out themselves by googling you?" he points out.

I laugh. "Oh please, give me some credit. I write under Alex M."

"Ah," he says quietly. "Your friend Max Marshall's suggestion?"

"She inspired it," I admit. "But Max doesn't know a damn thing about my … upbringing. Or the other stuff."

The waitress appears with our food, and while she sets it out, even when responding to her, Nils's eyes are fixed on me in a way that makes me nervous.

I pick up a fry as soon as I get my plate to avoid making eye contact.

"So, your family doesn't know about your work or personal life … and those in your work and personal life don't know about your family," he accurately infers after the waitress is gone.

My eyes flick up guiltily to meet his. "You say 'personal life' like that goes beyond you," I joke.

"It doesn't?" he asks bluntly.

I lift a shoulder and pop another fry in my mouth. "I mean, Max and I are friends. But like … mostly coworker friends?" I let out a sigh. "I had a couple of other female friends in college, but one had a boyfriend who recognized me as Tessa, and that was that. Both of them refused to have anything to do with me after that." I blink hard against the sting of tears at being slut shamed for bitch number one's boyfriend trying to fuck me at a frat party. I shouldn't feel sorry for myself. I knew what doing porn could mean for my friendships. Not to mention putting up with the awful behavior of many of the men who'd recognize me in public.

"Well, I'm hardly one to criticize. Work has been my life as well. Though now Frankie and Julian are more like family than anything," he muses.

Something stirs in my chest as I suspect Nils might be a lot like me … lonely in some senses. I watch him in silence for a few minutes as he eats.

"Maybe I was too hasty," I finally say, realizing that being so hard lined on his coming for lunch could have serious implications for our relationship. A relationship that, surprisingly, I want. Badly. "Maybe you *could* come for lunch … if we leave this —" I gesture between us "— out of it."

Nils smirks and finishes the bite of burger he'd eaten, his throat bobbing. "You mean pretend we're not together."

I inhale deeply. "Yes," I admit.

He wipes off his hands and leans back, slinging an arm over the back of the booth, putting those arm muscles of his that I love on display. I lick my lips and look back at him.

"Can you really do that?" he asks earnestly, his gaze roving over my face.

I stare back at him, letting his ice-blue eyes devour me, feeling it all the way to my core. Can I really pretend I don't know what he looks like naked? The heat in his eyes while he watched me suck another man's cock? How much he makes me feel, despite myself?

"Yes," I reply confidently. If nothing else, being an adult film actress honed my faking-it skills. "I think the better question is, can you?"

Nils lets out a throaty laugh. "Considering I pretended not to be in love with my boss for *months*? Yes, I think I can manage one lunch."

My eyebrows jump in surprise. "Wait … you're in love with Frankie Greco?" My throat constricts at the thought, my stomach tumbling. There's no way in hell I can compete with Frankie Greco.

Nils's brow furrows and he leans forward, snatching my hand from the table and squeezing it reassuringly. "I *was* in love with her. I haven't been in quite some time," he assures me. I take a deep, steadying breath and nod. He strokes his thumb over the back of my hand. "So, your brothers don't even know?"

I snort. "The golden boys? That'd be a big no."

"They're both married and pumping out the kids, then?" he returns skeptically as if he already knows they're not.

I bark an ironic laugh. "Oh no. They're men. While they're expected to obey our parents the same as me … well, let's say our father asks quite a lot less of them. They'll be required to do both eventually, but I'm already practically an old maid in my dad's eyes." I don't add that it's probably only thanks to them both moving to L.A. that my father even considered letting me. Lord knows a woman can't live without a man watching her every move, making sure she doesn't do something to dishonor the family.

Thank fuck neither of my brothers saw fit to actually follow through on Dad's directive to "keep an eye on" me.

Nils contemplates the information — and me — for a long moment. "What happens if they find out about us?"

My eyes go wide. "They can't, Nils. They'd disown me."

He frowns. "Is it wrong of me to say that I don't think that would be such a bad thing?"

I stare at him as I struggle to find my words. "Yes," I finally reply. "I mean, they're my parents."

Nils's frown deepens. "Your parents who not only don't accept and support you for who you are, but would actively shun you for it?" He shakes his head. "I'm afraid I don't understand. But then, I suppose ultimately, it's your decision."

I bristle at the judgment in his words. "Says the man who rarely goes back to his home country and family."

Nils pulls his hand away and gives me a sharp look. "I may not visit often, but I talk to my parents, my sister, regularly. It's because they support me that they don't expect me to leave the life I've built here — the life I love, that makes me happy."

I open my mouth to apologize, then close it out of embarrassment. Then open it again out of anger. "Forgive me if I can't shake a lifetime of programming that everything I want, everything I am, is considered shameful. If I can't just decide to live loud and proud at the expense of the only support system I've ever known," I snap, pulling back and wrapping my arms around myself.

"Well, that settles it," he says.

I give him a confused look. "Oh?"

His chin dips. "I'm going to lunch." I open my mouth, but he holds up a hand. "I promise I'll pretend like the last time I saw you was when we bumped into each other that first day. But I want to see what you see in them."

My whole body softens at his words. "If you're going for me … don't," I reply simply.

Nils shakes his head. "I'm sorry, Alexsis. But if these people are important to you, they're important to me, too. Hell, they *were* important to me once." He pauses. "I know that may not make sense to you, but I feel like I need to do this. Besides, I really would like to see Aiden again."

I take a shaky breath and decide against pointing out that he could see Aiden separately anytime. Because contrary to what he thinks, it does make sense. This is Nils wanting to be part of my support system in whatever way I'll let him.

While the thought terrifies and excites me in equal measure, I know this is one of those moments that's pivotal in a relationship. And if anyone is worth pushing through this terrifying ordeal for, it's Nils Larssen.

14

NILS

I've been sitting in front of Alexsis's parents' house for twenty minutes when an old van finally pulls into the driveway. I take a deep breath as it goes by before stepping out of the car and watching it disappear behind the garage door as it lowers.

I'm still unsure how I'm going to get through this. I'm torn between reuniting with the family I had such fond memories of and shoving down the less-than-charitable thoughts I have toward her parents at the possibility that they could truly disown their child for disobeying them. Their grown child. It seems simply too absurd, and I have to wonder if Alexsis might not be exaggerating because it's what she fears.

But the moment Aiden opens the door, my concerns take a backseat as seventeen years collapse into nothing. Aiden's face breaks into the same genuine smile I remember, and I can't help grinning back.

"Nils! Man, it's really you." He pulls me into a warm embrace that feels both foreign and familiar. When we break apart, he's shaking his head in disbelief. "You look exactly the same. Well, except for the beard."

I run a hand over my jaw self-consciously. "It's good to see you, Aiden. You haven't changed much either."

That's mostly true. His blond hair is shorter now, more conservative, and there are faint lines around his eyes that weren't there before. But the warmth in his expression, the easy way he carries himself — the kind of calm, collected self-assurance that you can't help but be drawn to — that's all achingly familiar.

"Mom! Dad! Nils is here," he calls over his shoulder before stepping aside. "Come in, come in."

I follow him inside and a strong wave of nostalgia hits me. The house smells exactly as I remember — lemon cleaning products mixed with something sugary baking in the oven. Mrs. Monaghan — Izzy, as she always insisted I call her but could never bring myself to — appears from the kitchen, wiping her hands on an apron. Her face lights up when she sees me.

"Oh, Nils!" She pulls me into a hug that's surprisingly strong for such a small woman. "Look at you! So handsome. We've missed you so much."

She presses me back and I'm able to take in her graying hair and age-worn features. A reminder of how much time has truly passed since I last was here. And I can't help the warm feelings I have toward her, toward them all, despite what Alexsis has told me. Though I suspect the feeling won't last long if what she shared about them is true.

"It's wonderful to see you again, Mrs. Monaghan," I reply, the formality feeling strange on my tongue after years of casual American greetings. But I can't start calling her Izzy now. It would be too strange. Far too strange.

"Like I've always told you, Nils, call me Izzy. It's been a long time, but we still consider you practically family." She pats my cheek in a gesture so maternal it makes my chest tight.

Mr. Monaghan — Ammon, who has *definitely* never invited me to call him that — appears behind her, extending his hand for a firm shake. His grip is exactly as I remember: testing, measuring. "Good to see you again, son."

"You, too, sir," I respond stoically.

And then I see her. Alexsis emerges from the kitchen doorway, and it takes every ounce of self-control I possess not to react. She's wearing a modest blue dress that makes her grey-blue eyes brighter and covers her from neck to knee, her hair pulled back in a simple style. She looks nothing like the woman who rides me in silver dresses and demands I fuck her harder. She looks younger, somehow. And like a version of herself that's … constrained.

Our eyes meet for a fraction of a second before she drops her gaze.

"Come on," Aiden says, clapping me on the shoulder. "Let's catch up while the ladies finish lunch."

I follow him and Asher into the living room, hyperaware of Alexsis disappearing back into the kitchen with her mother. The men settle into well-worn deep-brown leather furniture that hasn't changed since I lived here, save some additional creases and aging that only adds to their comfortability. Some of the tension in my shoulders eases at the familiarity of it.

"So, you're managing nightclubs," Aiden says, leaning forward with interest. "That must be exciting."

"It has its moments," I reply carefully. "Though it's more paperwork than most people imagine."

Aiden chuckles. "Isn't that always the way? I spend more time in meetings about archiving than actually preserving anything."

We fall into easy conversation about our careers, and I'm grateful for the distraction. Ammon sits silent in his recliner, observing but not participating. His presence is a weight in the room, just as it always was. Though it has a different tenor now. Perhaps because I'm older. Or because I can't help feeling that he's what's holding Alexsis back from reconciling the two halves of herself. The fact that he has a book in his lap that I can just make out the title of — The Book of Mormon — is an ironic underscore to his severe countenance.

"Lunch is ready," Izzy calls, snapping me out of my thoughts.

We rise as one and migrate to the dining room. The table is set with the good china, that I know they only brought out to impress guests, and I find myself a bit flattered. Then my eyes lift to the side-by-side portraits behind the head of the table, behind Mr. Monaghan's usual chair. I remember them well, though their significance was lost on me then. But I did my research after everything Alexsis told me. And the symbolism of Jesus and Joseph Smith flanking Ammon's seat, their austere gazes fixed on the family, isn't lost upon me.

Shaking off the somewhat creepy display of his power and authority as the head of the family, I take what I remember was my usual seat next to Aiden, directly across from Alexsis. I can't help recalling little Alexsis staring at me with big eyes across this very table all those years ago. Little did I know the already amorous thoughts she was having at such a tender age. I can't help the smirk that pulls at my lips. But this time, she keeps her eyes on her plate as we settle in. After Ammon says grace — another memory that hits unexpectedly hard, given what I know now — we begin eating in silence.

The pot roast is exactly as I remember, another familiarity that both soothes and chafes.

"This is delicious, Izzy. Just as good as I remembered," I offer.

She beams at the compliment. "Oh, you're too kind. I'm just so pleased you could join us. Tell us about your life, Nils. Aiden mentioned you manage nightclubs?"

"Yes, three of them, actually. All in Hollywood."

"My goodness. Hollywood. That sounds …" She frowns slightly while she clearly looks for a polite way to respond. "Well, that must keep you busy. What do you do when you're not working? Do you still attend church?"

I suppress a wry smile as the question lands exactly as she intended — pointed but polite.

"No, I don't," I respond succinctly.

"Oh." A pause as she likely considers her next attempt at staying on neutral topics. "Are you married? Any children?"

"Not yet … but maybe someday." I shrug nonchalantly to communicate how unimportant I find the conventions that seem to rule Americans' lives, then let my eyes slide over Alexsis as they move to Ammon on the other end of the table. Though he's diligently focused on his food, something tells me he's listening to every word.

Alas, I seem to have thwarted Mrs. Monaghan's attempts at pleasantries, and the silence that follows is suffocating. Alexsis shifts in her seat, and I catch the slight tightening around her eyes.

"Well," Izzy finally says, her tone forcefully bright, "it's just so wonderful to see you again. You know, we often talk about that year you stayed with us. You and Aiden were absolutely inseparable. He moped for months after you left."

"Mom," Aiden protests, pinkening around the ears. But he's smiling.

"It's true! Every day it was 'Nils this' and 'Nils that.'"

"We did keep in touch for a while," Aiden adds, shooting me a look that's almost apologetic. "But you know how it is. I got caught up with school, and then work …"

"Life happens," I say, letting him off the hook. "I'm just glad we reconnected now. It's really good to see you." I look around. "All of you."

Another stretch of silence. The clink of silverware on china sounds unnaturally loud.

"So, Asher," Izzy says, her voice taking on a particular quality I can't quite place. "Have you and Katie set a date yet?"

Asher's jaw tightens almost imperceptibly. "Not yet."

"Well, don't wait too long. You're not getting any younger." She says it airily, but with an undertone of impatience that I don't miss.

Unfortunately, next she turns her attention to Alexsis, and I see my girl — because that's what she is, whether her parents know it or not — brace herself. I wonder if they notice.

"Alexsis, dear, I forgot to mention. David will be meeting you here next Sunday after family time for your date. His eldest brother, Halden, will be chaperoning."

My brows pull together. "Chaperoning? I don't mean to intrude, but I'm not familiar with this word."

Izzy looks at me with surprise, as if she'd forgotten I wasn't part of their world anymore. "Oh! Well. It means … well, someone to go with them. It would be inappropriate for an unmarried woman to be alone with a man. Halden will accompany them to ensure Alexsis's reputation remains intact."

I set my fork down carefully, working to keep my voice neutral. "That's … an interesting custom." I try to say it diplomatically, but there's definitely a strain to my tone. "Is that usual even for adults?" My turn to ask pointed questions. And I give her a pointed look to match, in case it wasn't clear.

Apparently, it was, because the temperature in the room drops ten degrees. Ammon's voice cuts through the silence like a blade. "It absolutely is. No daughter of mine will be dishonored." He turns to Alexsis, and I watch her shrink under his gaze. "I expect you to start taking these suitors seriously, Alexsis. I want you married by next June."

The words hit me like a physical blow. "Why June specifically?" The words are out before I can stop them. I know as far as her parents are concerned that their daughter is none of my business. But I can't help it. I'm starting to see what she means, and my cool is slipping. Apparently along with my self control.

I expected Ammon to answer that it's none of my business, but it's Alexsis who offers, her voice barely above a whisper, "That's when I turn twenty-three."

As if that means something.

As if there's some … expiration date on unmarried Mormon women?

I don't know what.

But I must make some expression because Izzy's eyes narrow slightly as she watches me.

"Ah," I finally say, as if that settles everything.

Thankfully Asher jumps in to tell his father about a new marketing campaign he's spearheading and the rest of the meal passes in strained conversation.

When it's finally, mercifully over, I make my goodbyes as quickly as politeness allows. Ammon's handshake is perfunctory. Izzy's hug is a bit stiffer than before. Alexsis is nowhere to be found.

I kick myself internally for pushing like I did, hoping I didn't make things worse for her. For us.

Still, at least one good thing came out of it. I forgot how much I liked Aiden. How well we get along. So I'll cling to that bright spot, at least.

"Call me," I tell Aiden as we embrace. "We should get dinner sometime. Catch up properly."

"I'd like that," he says, and I think he means it.

Asher gets a quick hug, too, and it's then that Alexsis re-emerges from the kitchen.

"It was nice to see you, Nils," she says sedately, as if she truly couldn't care less.

I step forward to give her a hug, because it only makes sense after hugging almost everyone else.

The air between us crackles with everything we can't say. I have to force myself to keep it brief and casual, but my arms linger around her a moment too long. Right now she smells like vanilla and cinnamon, not jasmine, and somehow that makes it worse. Like she's truly a different person.

"Good to see you, too," I manage.

And then I'm outside, gulping in air that doesn't taste of propriety and expectations. I make it to my car on autopilot, my mind spinning as I absorb how true everything Alexsis told me really is. What that means for her. For us.

15

ALEXSIS

I can't get out of my parents' house fast enough. Married by June. I knew my father would run out of patience. But it wasn't until he laid down the law — in front of Nils, no less — that I remembered he once said that a respectable Mormon woman is married before she's twenty-three. I remember asking him why, and his justification was that if her parents had permitted her to go to college, twenty-two was reasonable to still be unmarried. But after college? Well, there would be no reason to get a job, because a *respectable* Mormon woman would want to start having babies, of course.

The lack of logic and respect for personal choice shouldn't surprise me. And I guess I'm not. Humiliated is more like it. I warned Nils, but even I didn't expect either of my parents to behave that way in front of a guest. Though, I suppose Nils is different, since he was once part of our household, if only for a time.

I shake my head as I slip into my car and start the engine. And the next thing I do before I get the fuck out of here is text Nils.

Meet me at the club?

I'm not even to the freeway when I hear my phone ping. Once I hit the red light before turning on, I check his response.

On my way.

I breathe a sigh of relief, then crank the radio loud to drown out the maelstrom of thoughts in my head.

Nils is already waiting when I pull up, leaning against his car in the same designer jeans and black tee he'd worn to lunch, with the addition of a smoking hot leather jacket he hadn't been. I pull in next to him and step out.

"Hey," he says quietly.

I step up to him and look into his eyes. I can see the pity there and it makes me even more disgusted with myself.

"You up for this?" I ask, hoping to dodge the conversation I sense coming.

He nods slowly. "But we need to talk first."

I can't help it; I roll my eyes and let out a long sigh. "Fine. You're probably right."

He reaches up and trails the back of his hand down my cheek.

"Are you really going on a date with this David?" he asks in a harsher tone than I'm used to hearing from him.

It makes my chest ache and pisses me off in equal measure. I shrug, wrapping my arms around myself. "I have to. It's part of keeping up the pretense of being the daughter they think I am."

"And what then? Are you going to marry him? Or someone like him? Keep up this charade forever?"

"Of course not," I snap. "Don't be silly."

"Then why?" He runs a hand through his hair, clearly frustrated. "You know this has to end, eventually. At the very least, you'll have to tell them you're not marrying a Mormon boy by next June."

"Don't ask me these questions." My voice cracks slightly. "I don't know, okay? You don't understand."

"You're right. I don't." He sounds so bitter and the ache in my chest expands. "I had a hard enough time pretending for one lunch. I can't imagine doing it for years, being someone I'm not."

I give him a sharp look. "Really? Because you did exactly that when you were in love with your boss and didn't tell her."

He staggers back as the intended blow lands. And though I meant the words to hurt, I instantly regret them.

"At least Frankie was just your boss," I continue, trying to soften the blow, to make him understand what I mean. How I feel. "It was just a job. These lies? They're to protect my relationship with the people who raised me, who love me, who support me."

"They may love you," he says quietly, "but they clearly don't support you. Not the real you."

Pain lances through me. It must show on my face as Nils holds his hands up in surrender.

"I'll let it go." He reaches out, touching my arm gently. "I know you came here to work off the stress from lunch. We should go inside."

Relief washes over me. The last thing I want to do is talk more about this. Think more about this.

"Thank you," I reply, placing my hands on his chest.

"What do you want to do in there?" he murmurs, stroking his thumb over the back of one hand.

I consider that for a moment. I breathe deeply. It has to be something special. Something that will make me forget everything else. That would make me feel like the center of *someone's* world, even if I'm not my parents.

"I want us to have a threesome with Brody," I say, then hold my breath as I tense for his rejection.

But to my surprise, he nods. "All right."

I bite into my bottom lip and go up on my toes to kiss him. I let all the anxiety and frustration out on his lips, writhing against him as I search for physical validation that our connection is still there.

He grips me to him and takes over, pressing my ass against my passenger door as his dick grows hard against my stomach. Finally, he breaks away, and we both pant as we lean our foreheads together.

"Come on," I say, tugging him gently toward the club.

He lets me lead him inside, to the purple room, where I can almost always count on Brody being.

And today is no exception, though it is exceptional that Brody is alone, wearing only a towel around his perfectly cut waist, wiping down surfaces and straightening pillows, either cleaning up from or preparing for a session. He looks up when we enter, his face breaking into a grin.

"Well, well, well. I was just about to head out, but I'm certainly glad I didn't." He tosses the cleaning cloth aside. "What can I do for my favorite couple tonight?"

With my fingers still twined in Nils's, I approach, getting right in Brody's space. I look up at him. "Up for a threesome?"

Brody's grin turns sly. "Oh, baby, you know I'm always up for *anything* that involves you." His eyes flick up to Nils. "I think the better question is, is lover boy?"

Nils's hand slides up my ass. "Anything to get this fucking dress off her."

I turn toward him, palming his semi-hard dick through his pants. "You don't like my dress?" I taunt.

Nils presses against me until my back is flush with Brody's front. "It's not you, love."

My breath catches at the endearment, and I tip my chin up. "Then take it off me," I breathe.

Nils obliges immediately, roughly yanking the gingham print dress over my head and throwing it across the room, exposing my tits to the cold air.

"Fuck me," Nils groans, leaning in to capture a nipple in his mouth. I feel Brody's hands slide over my hips and I lean my head back against his shoulder.

"Oh, you will," I promise, tilting my head. "But … would you fuck *him* first?" I slide my hand over Brody's very hard cock, yanking the towel until I feel the silken length against my backside. I slide my hand gently up and down as I watch Nils contemplate my request.

After a few beats, Brody chuckles behind me. "I don't think lover boy and I are … compatible," he murmurs in my ear loud enough for Nils to hear, too. Nils smirks as if in agreement.

My face scrunches in confusion. "How's that?"

Brody's hand slides to my sex, gently stroking as Nils rejoins, tugging at my nipples. "See, I know I'm a top. And I'm pretty sure he is, too."

I roll my eyes. Men. Always wanting to dominate. I pull Nils toward me, switching to stroking his cock now. "Is that true?" I ask, batting my eyelashes at him.

"It's true," he confirms. "But I'm more than happy to do whatever you want to this body." He slides his hand between us, thrusting his fingers abruptly into the heat between my legs.

I arch, sighing out my pleasure. "Fill all my holes," I say on a sigh. "Please, daddies."

And so, they do. Both totally focused on me, working in tandem. One fucking my mouth while the other fucks my pussy, then switching. It's everything … and yet somehow not enough. That is, until I'm riding Nils's cock and Brody decides to move from my mouth to behind me.

I've done double penetration, but it's not part of our usual repertoire, given that both Brody and I prefer a harem of women around us. But as he lightly runs the tip of his lubricated-condom-covered cock over my ass, waiting for permission, I realize it's exactly what I need. I did say "fill all my holes" after all.

"Yes, daddy," I groan. "Fuck my ass while he fucks my cunt."

Nils grows harder inside of me. I look down at him with a feline grin. "You like the dirty talk?" He nods. "You want him to fuck me while you do?" Nils lets out a strangled groan of agreement, so I swirl my hips over him before stilling for Brody. His hot, hard cock pushes in slowly, and a feeling of complete fullness and mind-numbing bliss washes over me. "God, yes, give me that cock. Fill me up," I encourage him. He keeps pushing until he's in to the hilt.

Sandwiched between them, I don't have to tell either what to do. They both start moving in turn, one in while the other pulls out, thrusting and fucking in a way no dildo could ever replicate.

And the pleasure … it's heaven.

A filthy diatribe of barely controlled thoughts spills from my mouth, encouraging them to take me, to fuck me, to use my holes, that I'm their little slut, that I want them to fuck me until they come. Then as the intensity builds, to spill all over my ass, in my cunt.

They get sweatier and harder and faster until I can't hold back the rising tide of pleasure and I come hard, speechless, mindless, lost to this, finally. Nils comes with me, his thrusts stuttering while Brody's stay true.

It's only when he stills that Brody pulls out, rips off his condom, and comes all over my ass. The hot, sticky cum drips down my side beautifully, and Brody collapses on top of us.

My mouth meets Nils' as Brody sucks at my neck.

"You're a fucking goddess, Tessa," Brody groans.

"My goddess," Nils whispers against my skin.

I grin, languishing in their attentions. Brody rolls off onto the bed next to us.

I wiggle over Nils, his flagging cock slipping out with a gush of his cum.

"That was …" I trail off, shivering.

Nils cocks an eyebrow. "Then you'll love what comes next." My eyebrows pop up as Nils lifts me as he sits up, setting me between Brody's legs. Brody scoots up onto his elbows with a questioning look at Nils. "Hold her up and fuck her ass while I eat her pussy?"

My whole body tightens at his words. "Yes, god, please, yes," I beg, whimpering.

Brody grins, suiting up and letting Nils lift me over Brody's supine form. I brace my hands as Brody's settle under my thighs, as his cock slowly settles back into my ass. He pumps slow and deep and spreads me open for Nils.

I look down as he positions himself between my legs. "You gonna lick all my juices and your cum off me?" I taunt him.

"You want that?" he murmurs, tracing a finger down my slit, causing me to spasm under their ministrations.

"Yes. Now, please," I beg.

Nils chuckles but then wastes no time. He uses only his tongue at first, licking me clean until I'm dripping wet again anyway, then adding fingers into the mix. Brody picks up his pace as Nils works, until I'm boneless and overwhelmed … and coming so hard I see stars.

Brody slides me down his body onto the bed where I lay, star-fish style, with a huge grin on my face.

Nils slides in next to me, tilting my head his way to place a claiming kiss on my lips. I curl into him, and Brody spoons me from behind.

"That was perfect," I murmur against Nils's chest. "Thank you, daddies."

Brody kisses my shoulder as Nils strokes my hair. I'm so relaxed I start to drift off.

I don't fall asleep, exactly, hovering somewhere between conscious and unconscious on a sea of sparkling bliss and contentment.

But they must *think* I'm asleep, because I'm fully aware when Nils asks Brody, "How often are you here?"

"Every day," Brody replies, his fingers brushing my hip possessively. "But I always look forward to the days Tessa drops by."

"Well, that's a shame she won't be coming by as often, then." Nils's tone is hard.

Brody laughs, the sound knowing. "We'll see."

"What's that supposed to mean?"

And I can almost hear the pity in Brody's voice when he responds, "I'm not worried about losing her, man. None of her boy toys stick around long. She always comes back to me. So, even if she's not around as much right now, she'll be back."

The challenge in his tone stirs me enough to bring me back to the moment. "Now, now, daddies," I grumble, stretching like a cat and running my claws down their chests. "We were having such a wonderful moment. Don't ruin it."

Brody slides out of bed, and one look at his face tells me he's more irked by Nils than I realized. "Nothing ruined," he says, his voice overly casual. "I have to go, anyway. Nice playing with you, Tessa. See you soon." And with that he grabs his towel, leaving without even wrapping it around his waist.

"Well," I say to Nils. "I know you didn't like him much, but clearly the feeling is mutual."

Nils grunts his agreement. "Clearly."

I run my nails over his nipple. "Funny, because you two fuck me so well together."

Nils's cock twitches between us and he leans in, kissing me long and sweetly. "That's all you. You're the magic here. Not that dickhead."

I laugh, scraping my nails over his stomach now. "He's not so bad. You're just both territorial."

Nils huffs. "He's in love with you, you know."

I snort. "Dogs fight over bitches in heat. That doesn't mean they love them." Nils gives me a skeptical look. I shake my head. "You don't know him like I do. He's definitely not in love with me."

Nils doesn't respond immediately. But eventually asks, "Are you sure about that?"

"Yes, I'm sure. Brody doesn't do feelings. Trust me." I sit up, over this conversation. It's letting the doubt and worry that is my life creep back in. "Let's not let that little pissing match ruin our night, okay?"

Nils sits up beside me, pulling me between his legs. "I'm here if you want to talk. About any of it, you know."

And I do know. I also know he doesn't mean Brody. He means my parents. And that I decidedly do *not* want to talk about. In fact, the less talking we do tonight, the better.

"I know. And I appreciate it. But what I really need right now is to go back to your place and test out some of these toys you say you have," I respond coyly, climbing fully into his lap, letting my breasts brush his chest.

His hands slide up my back and he sighs. "Go put that god awful dress back on. But only so I can take it off again as soon as possible."

I tip my head back and laugh. And I secretly love that he hates that disguise. That he doesn't want anything but the real me.

"Deal," I agree.

16

ALEXSIS

I t's with some very mixed feelings that I start the workweek. All the confusion of my father's latest demand-slash-deadline on top of everything getting deeper and more complicated with Nils and … well, I'm pretty damn happy to have work to distract me. Especially today. Because after weeks of preparation for the article idea that's been consuming me, things are getting real.

I did as much research as I could, then made a call, and now, after making a token appearance at the office, I've snuck out to take it to the next level. Which is why, at ten on the dot, I'm pulling up to a modest house in the Valley where James Kennedy, Violent Mood Swings' keyboardist, has his home studio.

This is it. This is the story that's going to change everything. You wouldn't expect that the small, ramshackle rancher houses one of our times' most famous musicians, but here we are. Walking up to the house, broken pavers litter the path, and toys are scattered all over the lawn.

I knock, my tummy a bundle of nerves. But when James opens the door, he's exactly what you'd expect from a dad-rocker with his kind eyes, slightly rumpled short-sleeved polo and flannel over well-worn jeans, and easy smile that probably still makes groupies swoon. It definitely puts me more at ease, anyway.

"Alexsis, right?"

I nod and smile. "That's right. I'm surprised you remember me."

"Really?" he asks with a laugh. "You were all over that apology tour."

I blush hard. "Yeah, but most guys in your position wouldn't notice one of the peons sent to follow them around," I reply honestly.

He steps back in invitation, so I cross the threshold. "Well, most musicians are assholes, I'll give you that." He laughs. "Anyway, come on in. The rest of the band is already here."

I follow him through a house that screams "family" – even more toys than outside scattered in corners, crayon drawings on the fridge, the faint smell of baby powder mixing with coffee. It's such a contrast to the rock star image that I have to hide my smile. He really isn't your typical famous musician.

When we finally get to his studio, the large space — which I think is a converted garage — is packed with instruments, a couch, and a few mismatched chairs. And, of course, the rest of the band.

West nods at me from where he's sitting backwards on a folding chair, his dark hair and leather jacket still screaming his bad boy image, even though I know he's left that behind. Ward is sprawled on a worn leather couch, all lanky arms and legs and shaggy blond hair, tattoos snaking down both lean, muscled arms. The newer members are the only ones behind their instruments —Michael being on the drum kit tapping out a quiet rhythm, and Nik cross-legged on the floor, bass in her lap. They all somehow look comfortable and pissed off at the same time. Rock stars.

"Thanks for agreeing to talk to me," I start, pulling out my recorder and notebook. I take a subtle deep breath to calm my nerves. It's not like I haven't done this before. Though that was almost always with — or for — Max. This is all me. No pressure.

"Are you kidding?" Ward says, leaning forward. "Someone actually wants to hear our side. We've been waiting for this." Everyone nods in agreement, and my nerves mellow a bit more. Enough to start down the list of questions I prepared, anyway.

Some of the answers are exactly what I expected. But many aren't and frankly make my blood boil. They tell me about signing their first contract when they were barely legal adults. How the label's lawyers sat them down and "explained" everything, assuring them they didn't need their own representation.

"They said it was standard," West says bitterly. "Said they were looking out for us."

"Standard my ass," Michael adds. "They own everything. Every song Violent Mood Swings has ever written under that contract. Every version of the band name. Hell, they probably own the air we breathed in their studios." Nik snorts.

Then Ward jumps in, explaining how they'd tried to release new music independently after getting back together, only to be hit with cease and desist letters, both facts I knew. "It just … it sucks. How can we not even use our own fucking name? I mean, we came up with it in my garage when we were teenagers."

"It's legalized theft at best," James says quietly. "But honestly? If it was just us … well, I guess we could figure out how to move on. But the worst part is, this is happening to bands everywhere. It's not a one-off. It's how the industry operates. Taking advantage of young kids who just want to make music by getting them locked into contracts that basically make them indentured servants." He shakes his head, and every member of the band makes their own noise of agreement.

They all have tidbits and examples to add, and by the time I leave, my notebook is full and my recorder has enough material for a whole *series* of articles. And I have so many ideas of who I could interview next to flesh this out.

I hadn't realized what pulling at this thread would unravel. Because this is huge. This could expose the whole industry's corrupt practices and help change how young musicians approach recording contracts. Or hell, whether they even go that route. Other options are opening up these days, after all.

The thought of being part of such a huge shift … well, I'm practically vibrating with excitement as I walk back into the *Rock Scene* office after lunch. I need to transcribe these interviews immediately, start organizing the story structure, schedule more interviews —

"Alexsis. My office. Now." Jason's voice cuts through my plans like a bucket of ice water. I follow him, noting the tense set of his shoulders. "Where were you this morning?" he asks as soon as the door closes.

I try to deflect by keeping it vague, knowing it won't fly. "Working on a story."

"What story?"

"Just … following up on some leads." Shit. Shit, shit, shit, shit. Pulling this off hinged on his not noticing. I should've been more careful. Come up with a better story if he did notice. As good as I am at lying to my parents, right now I can't think of a good enough story to give Jason that he'd actually buy.

His eyes narrow, as if he smells blood in the water. "Alexsis, I'm not going to ask again. And if you don't answer, we're going to have a disciplinary discussion about transparency and following proper channels."

Shit. I sink into the chair across from his desk. There's nothing to go with but the truth at this point. "I was interviewing Violent Mood Swings about their legal troubles with their former label."

The color drains from Jason's face. "You did what?"

"It's a great story, Jason. They're being completely screwed over —"

"Absolutely not." He's on his feet now, pacing behind his desk. "Do you have any idea what kind of legal shitstorm you could bring down on us? That label has deeper pockets than God. They could bury us in lawsuits just for fun. If they even got wind you talked to the band about the lawsuit, we could be in a world of hurt, Alexsis."

"But it's the truth! People deserve to know —"

"Not from us they don't." His tone brooks no argument. "You're not writing this. You're not pursuing this story. In fact, you're going to delete whatever notes and recordings you have."

I stand, too, anger flooding through me. "You can't be serious."

"Dead serious. This is non-negotiable, Alexsis. You have no idea what kind of power they have. We're a small magazine. We'd be a tiny bug on the windshield of their Bentleys, I promise you. Do you want us all to lose our jobs?" He shakes his head in disgust. "Get out of my sight." He waves me off angrily, sitting back down so hard his chair creaks in protest.

I storm out of his office, my hands shaking with rage. All that work. All that potential to actually make a difference. Gone because Jason is too scared of the big bad record label. What about the fact that it'd be a bad look to instantly crush a magazine that criticized you? Wouldn't that prove to everyone that we were right? I need to vent about this. Badly.

Thankfully, I find Max in her cubicle and collapse into her spare chair.

"Let me guess," she says after one look at my face. "Jason killed your story."

"How did you —"

"Because I warned you this might happen." Her tone is gentle, not gloating. "The magazine can't afford to take on that kind of fight. And even if we did anyway, it wouldn't change anything."

I look up at her. "What do you mean?" I ask.

Max sighs and leans forward. "Once you've been around a while, you start seeing the corruption. You get angry, at first. You want to expose it. But then you realize you can't expose something when the people you're after own the press, Alexsis. There is no world in which we win, in any way."

I shake my head, not wanting to believe her. But … the evidence is on my tape recorder. Well, until I'm forced to delete it, anyway.

"It's not fair," I mutter, knowing I sound like a petulant child but not caring.

"No, it's not." Max turns to face me fully. "But you know what? You're smart enough to find another angle. Another story. Something even better.

Something that you can bring to the public's attention that *can* make a difference in the industry."

"You really think so?"

"I know so. You're a talented writer and you have that fighting spirit, Alexsis. One setback isn't going to stop you."

Her faith in me is touching, even if it doesn't quite ease the sting of disappointment. I thank her and head out, needing air, needing space, needing ...

Nils.

I don't know why he's the person I want to see, but twenty minutes after I'm done at work, I'm walking into Baltia. It's early evening, so the club is just starting to come alive. I find him in his office, door open, bent over some paperwork.

"Hey," I say, knocking on the doorframe.

He looks up, and something warm flickers in those ice-blue eyes. "Alexsis. This is a pleasant surprise."

"Bad day," I admit, sinking into the chair across from him. "I thought maybe..."

I trail off as a rhythmic thumping starts from somewhere around us, accompanied by unmistakable moans. My eyes widen as I realize what we're hearing.

Nils sighs. "They must be in a good mood because usually it's only Sunday afternoons."

"Frankie and Julian?"

He nods, looking mildly exasperated. "I've learned to schedule my office time accordingly, but sometimes they can't resist."

An idea strikes me, bold and totally inappropriate, but my frustration needs an outlet. "We could make it a foursome."

Nils's head snaps back to me. "What?"

"You know, join them. Could be fun. Girls only touch girls, of course."

"Are you serious? No." His response comes out so sharply I blanch.

"Why not?" I challenge. "Still carrying a torch for the boss?"

He scoffs. "That's not — Alexsis, if I asked you to have a foursome with a couple where one of them was someone you used to be in love with — or was your boss … or fuck, *both* — how would you feel?"

"I'd be fine with it," I say stubbornly. "It's just sex. Funny how you can't separate sex and feelings, yet I can."

"I can separate them just fine most of the time," he says, his jaw tight.

"Good. Then maybe we could organize an orgy at the club instead."

"Would that include Brody?"

The question catches me off guard, even though it shouldn't. "Probably, why?"

"I'd rather he not be at every encounter we have."

Anger flares in my chest, mixing with all the frustration from earlier. "Are you seriously trying to tell me who I can and cannot fuck? Because that's not how this works, Nils."

I'm on my feet and heading for the door before he can respond, my emotions a tangled mess of professional disappointment and personal fury.

It's not until I'm home, after a long shower and half a bottle of wine, that I realize what I've done. I took all my anger about the article, about Jason shutting me down, about my career feeling stalled, and I dumped it on Nils.

He wasn't trying to control me. He was trying to tell me he wanted some encounters that didn't include Brody. And I threw it in his face because I was upset about something that had nothing to do with him. God, I suggested we waltz in on his boss, who he'd once been in love with, and ask if we can join them. What the hell is wrong with me? A lot, is the answer.

"Fuck," I mutter to my empty apartment.

I owe him an apology. And maybe more than that, I owe him some honesty about where I'm at. Why I really pushed too far, too hard today. And what I really want from whatever this thing between us is becoming.

Because the truth is, the thought of him with Frankie made me feel something I wasn't prepared for either, adding to the fuel of the dumpster fire that is my life right now. Not that it's an excuse for how I behaved tonight.

But that's tomorrow's problem. Right now, I'm going to wallow in my professional disappointment and try not to think about the hurt that flashed in Nils's eyes before I stormed out. It'll all get fixed. I hope.

Though why I bother hoping for anything these days is beyond me.

I sink my head back into the couch. It's official: I've fully devolved into a pity party. Get a grip on your life, Alexsis, before you ruin everything that's good about it.

It's the last thought I have before, drunker than I thought, I pass out.

NILS

I stare at the clock on my kitchen wall. Two in the afternoon. Normally, I'd be heading to Baltia right about now to catch up on paperwork, check the inventory, review the upcoming bookings. But today, the thought of going to my office — where just yesterday Alexsis suggested we interrupt Frankie and Julian's afternoon activities — makes my stomach turn.

Instead, I pour myself another cup of coffee and sink onto my couch. The silence of my apartment presses in on me, but it's better than the alternative. Better than running into Emma, who's still shooting me daggers every chance she gets. Better than potentially seeing Alexsis if she decides to show up again.

I'm overwhelmed. That's the word for this crushing weight on my chest. Alexsis is clearly spinning out of control, and I don't know how to help her. Hell, I don't even know if she wants my help. The way she stormed out yesterday ...

And underneath it all, there's this constant simmer of anger I have toward her parents and the impossible position they've put her in. The way they're forcing her to live this double life that's clearly tearing her apart.

Before I can think better of it, I pick up my phone and place a call. It's not too terribly late in Sweden, and I know they'd answer even if it were.

"Hej, son." My father's warm voice fills my ear, and immediately some of the tension leaves my shoulders.

"Hej, Pappa." I switch to Swedish without thinking, the familiar sounds of home wrapping around me like a blanket. "How are you and Mamma?"

"We're well. But you don't sound it. What's wrong?"

I lean back, closing my eyes. Trust my father to cut straight to the heart of things. "I'm ... dealing with a complicated situation."

"A woman?"

I huff a laugh. "How did you know?"

"Because you're my son, and I know that tone. Tell me about her."

So I do. Not everything — I leave out the more intimate details — but I tell him about Alexsis, about her family situation, about the pressure she's under. About how she's lashing out and I don't know how to help.

My father is quiet for a long moment after I finish. "This woman, she's important to you?"

"Yes," I admit to him and myself at the same time. "Very."

"Then be patient. She's carrying a heavy burden, trying to be two different people. That would break anyone. Give her time to figure out who she really wants to be."

"But what if she never figures it out? What if she just keeps doing things that push me away?"

"Then at least you'll know you tried. But Nils, from what you've told me, she sounds strong. She just needs someone to be steady while she finds her balance."

I absorb that for a moment. "When did you get so wise?"

He chuckles. "When you moved halfway around the world and I had to learn to give advice over the phone. Your mother wants to talk to you."

There's rustling, then my mother's voice. "Nils, darling. I was listening — well, to your father's end of the conversation, anyway."

"Of course you were," I say with a smile. "And what's your advice, Mamma?"

"My advice is to take your father's advice … but also, don't sit at home brooding. Go see friends. Distract yourself. It won't help her or you if you're sitting around overthinking everything."

I sigh heavily. "You're right. Thank you. I love you, Mamma."

"We love you, too. And Nils? Thank you for calling. Not all children would think to reach out to their parents when they're struggling."

The words hit differently after everything with Alexsis's family. "You and Pappa have always been there for me. Even when I moved here. Even when I chose a completely different life than you'd imagined for me. I'm grateful for that."

"Oh, darling." Her voice is thick with emotion. "We just want you to be happy."

"I miss you. All of you. Tell Astrid I love her, too."

"We miss you, too, and so does your sister. I'll tell her. Take care, hjärtat."

"Bye, Mamma."

I laugh, shaking my head once I've hung up. Only my mother can get away with calling me "sweetheart." But it's why I called them — they know me better than anyone. I'd be a fool not to listen to them.

I think about what they both said, my mother's advice in particular echoing in my head. Don't sit around brooding. Go see friends.

I scroll through my phone and stop at Aiden's number. We'd exchanged information after the lunch at his parents' house, but neither of us had reached out yet. Even though I invited him to, he's already done so once. Maybe now it's my turn.

He answers on the second ring. "Nils? Hey, man. I was actually going to call you this week."

"Yeah? What about?"

"That dinner we talked about. You free tonight?"

I glance around my empty apartment. "Actually, yes. That sounds perfect."

"Great. How about Musso & Frank's? Say, seven?"

"Sure, yeah, I love that place. See you there."

The rest of the afternoon passes more quickly with plans to look forward to. I shower, change into dark jeans and a burgundy button-down, and arrive at the historic Hollywood restaurant right on time.

Aiden's already there, seated in one of the iconic red leather booths. He stands when he sees me, and we embrace briefly before sitting across from each other.

"You sounded a little off on the phone," Aiden says after we've ordered drinks. "Everything okay?"

I fidget with my water glass. I can't tell him about Alexsis — not when I don't even know if she'd want her brother to know we're ... whatever we are. "Just work stress. Managing a nightclub isn't always glamorous."

"I bet." He leans back, studying me. "You know, it's still surreal seeing you after all these years. I never imagined when you left our house that you'd end up staying this long."

"Life has a way of surprising us."

"That it does." He pauses as our drinks arrive — scotch for him, a martini for me. "Speaking of surprises ... I'm seeing someone."

I raise an eyebrow, noting the careful way he says it. "That's great."

"His name is Josh." The words come out in a rush, like he's been holding them in too long. "We've been together for two years."

I smile. "He makes you happy?"

The relief on Aiden's face is palpable. "Yeah. He really does. My parents ... they don't know, obviously."

"Obviously," I echo, thinking of all the things Alexsis can't tell them either.

"God, it feels so good to tell someone." He smiles, clearly genuinely happy. "Actually, that reminds me." Aiden leans forward, lowering his voice. "You haven't told Alexsis our secret, have you?"

I freeze with my martini glass halfway to my mouth. "What? No. Why would you think I'd even be in a position where that would come up?"

"I don't know, just ... I know Alexsis said you guys just ran into each other at that concert the one time ... but at lunch, it seemed like there was something there. Chemistry. I thought maybe it was more than just that one meeting?"

He eyes me speculatively. And my discomfort must show on my face because Aiden's eyes widen slightly.

"I'm right, aren't I? You two are seeing each other."

I set down my martini carefully. "I'm not sure what to say to that."

A knowing smile spreads across his face. "You are. Holy shit. You're dating my sister."

"Aiden —"

"No, it's okay. I mean, it's weird, but it's okay." He pauses. "Look, I suspected you guys might be together and I just ... I didn't want ancient history to complicate things between you two if you were."

I grimace, thinking about how Alexsis has never told her brothers about her time as Tessa Temptation. How she'd probably be fine with the fact that her brother and I had brief but memorable encounters all those years ago. But I can't tell Aiden about her secrets any more than I can tell her about ours.

"It won't," I say finally. "We agreed to keep it between us back then. That hasn't changed."

"Good. Good." He takes a long drink. "God, the secrets we all keep from our parents. From each other. Sometimes I wonder if it's worth it."

"Yeah," I agree quietly, feeling the weight of all these lies and half-truths. "Me, too."

We manage to steer the conversation to safer topics after that — his work, my adjustment to American life becoming permanent, memories from when I lived with his family. But underneath it all, I can't shake the feeling that we're all trapped in an elaborate web of secrets that's going to collapse eventually.

It's late when I finally get home, and I'm getting ready for bed when my phone buzzes. Alexsis's name lights up the screen.

"Hey," I answer, confused and relieved to hear from her in equal measure.

"Hey. Can we talk?" Her voice is small, uncertain.

"Of course," I assure her.

"I'm sorry about yesterday. I was completely out of line."

I sink onto my bed. "I … appreciate you saying that. Because honestly you were. But that was out of character, even for you, Alexsis. What was that really about?"

Alexsis sighs heavily and starts back at that morning, about the article I know she'd been pursuing, sharing that she'd interviewed the band and was on cloud nine only to go back to work and get shut down hard by Jason. About how all that frustration and disappointment got channeled into jealousy when she heard Frankie and Julian, and knew it was something I regularly heard happening.

"I was already feeling like everything was out of control," she says. "And then hearing her, knowing you'd been in love with her, wondering if it brought up those feelings again ... I just lost it. It made me so fucking jealous. It was irrational and unfair, I know, and I'm so sorry."

"Alexsis." I keep my voice gentle. "I understand. You're under a lot of pressure."

"That's not an excuse for how I behaved."

"No, but it's an explanation. And I appreciate you telling me."

"Can you forgive me?"

"I already had. I know what you've been going through Alexsis. I mean … I may not *know* know, since I'm not in your position. But I get that this is all a lot. Fuck. I'm not saying this right at all. This is just … doing this over the phone … it's not enough. Can you come over?"

There's a pause. "Now?"

"Now."

"I'll be there in twenty minutes." I can hear the smile in her voice, and my own lips spread in a grin.

"Hurry," I urge her. A click is my only response.

I'm not waiting long — only fifteen minutes — before there's a knock on the door. When I open it, she looks smaller somehow, vulnerable in a way she rarely allows herself to be. I pull her into my arms without a word and close the door behind her.

"I'm sorry," she whispers against my chest.

"I know." I tilt her chin up. "We're okay."

When I kiss her, it's soft, careful. An acknowledgment of the fragility between us right now. She melts into me, running her hands over my chest.

I pull back and caress her face, slipping my hand gently around hers and leading her to my bedroom.

I undress her slowly, then myself. She lays down on the black sheets, sliding to the head of the bed, opening her legs invitingly. Still with that look of vulnerability about her.

I prowl slowly up the bed, placing a kiss at her ankle. Then her calf. Then her knee, then the inside of her thigh.

Her fingers slide into my hair as my tongue meets her sex, and she lets out a breathy sigh. I part her with two fingers and lick slowly, thoroughly until she's writhing under me. And then I rear up, gripping my hard length, stroking up and down. She licks her lips and whimpers. A small smile tugs at the corner of my mouth.

And then I enter her. Slowly. Sweetly. Until I'm as deep inside of her as I can be. Until her warmth wraps around me. Then I wrap myself around her and move. It's intense and quiet and simple. Sex like we've never had before.

No games, no power plays, just two people trying to find their way back to each other.

Her hands skim down my back, and my lips find hers again while I continue to piston my hips. She shudders against me, her walls fluttering around my cock.

"Yes," I whisper to her. "Come for me, Alexsis. Only me."

She nods, her chin tipping up as she tightens around me. The velvet grip she has on my cock pushes me into orgasm and I come so hard I sink into her neck, groaning my release.

Her hands find my face, pulling my lips to hers. She kisses me with a depth she never has before. It's apology and penance and a promise all at once.

And I know in this moment that I'll be whatever she needs for as long as she needs. So long as I get to be here, with her.

I pull away, running my nose down hers. "Be right back."

I go to the bathroom and do a quick clean-up, bringing back a warm, wet rag for Alexsis. She smiles when she sees me with it, spreading her legs, baring her sex to me. I sigh, settling down next to her and running a finger through her wet warmth, the evidence of our pleasure coating my fingertips. She wiggles against my hand, and I fight the urge to keep going. I want to hold her more right now. So I clean her up gently, though I'm unable to resist swirling the cloth over her clitoris a bit harder than necessary. She bites her lip and giggles when I do. With a smile, I toss the cloth into the laundry bin in the corner and settle next to her.

She curls against my side, tracing patterns on my chest.

"I'd love to spend all night making up, but I really should get home so I can get some actual sleep," she laments.

I huff out a dry laugh. "Don't worry, we can make up again another night," I tease.

"Sunday?" she asks hopefully.

"After church?"

She tenses slightly. "Actually ... I was thinking maybe we could skip the family lunch. Just spend the day together."

I press a kiss to her forehead. "Whatever you need."

"What I need," she says quietly, "is to figure out how to be myself. All the time. Not just when I'm with you."

"You'll get there," I promise, vowing silently to do whatever I can to make that happen. Even knowing it's really up to her.

I pull her against me. One last feel of her skin against mine. One last reminder of how well we fit together. Like she was the piece of me I'd been missing. Like maybe I'm one of the pieces *she's* been missing. Though I know there are more. Ones she needs to find for herself.

But for now, she's here in my arms, and that's enough. Right now, nothing else matters.

18

ALEXSIS

The next morning, I knock on Jason's office door with a determination I haven't felt in days. I may not be able to fix all of my problems, but I can fix this one.

When he calls me in, I sit on the edge of the chair opposite his desk, allowing my anxiety and chagrin to be on full display. An offering of my regret.

"I owe you an apology," I start before he can say anything.

His eyebrows rise, but he leans back in his chair, giving me space to continue.

"I pursued that story because I saw an opportunity. I wanted to be worthy of my own byline, and I thought this could be it. But I didn't look at the bigger picture for the magazine. I didn't consider the fallout." I take a breath. "I promise to come to you before pursuing something like that in the future. Though I'd also like you to be more willing to let me prove myself."

Jason is quiet for a long moment, studying me. "Thank you for the apology, Alexsis. I appreciate it. And you're right — I should give you more opportunities. I was only so angry because ..." He pauses, seeming to

609

choose his words carefully. "Because I think highly of you. Your talent. Your potential. I was disappointed by the lack of consideration, not the ambition."

The compliment catches me off guard, and I feel heat rise to my cheeks. "Thank you. That means a lot."

"Good. Now get back to work and find me a story that won't get us sued into oblivion."

I smile and nod, leaving his office with renewed energy.

He thinks highly of me. My talent. My potential.

And I'm going to find a story that proves him right.

The rest of the week flies by in a blur of productivity. I bounce idea after idea off Max, who praises each one enthusiastically.

"This one about the underground music scene in Koreatown? Brilliant," she says Wednesday.

"The profile on female drummers breaking barriers? Love it," she adds Thursday.

By Friday, when I suggest a piece on how streaming services are changing the way artists approach album creation, she actually claps.

I know she's probably just encouraging me to keep going after my setback, but I appreciate it anyway. Having someone in your corner makes all the difference.

By Sunday, I'm feeling good about life. Work is getting better, I don't have to deal with my parents this weekend, I cancelled that stupid date with David, and the new dress I bought yesterday — a barely-there metallic bronze number that clings to every curve — is definitely going to knock Nils's socks off.

And hopefully convince him to come to the orgy at Chained tonight. It's a club I've been to before but don't frequent. More importantly, that means Brody won't be there. Maybe that will help Nils relax into the experience.

I arrive at Baltia around six, early enough that the club isn't open yet but late enough that Nils should be done with his paperwork. The side door is unlocked, so I let myself in and head toward his office.

But as I approach, I hear voices. His door is closed, which is unusual, and I can hear a female voice inside. Emma, maybe? It's hard to tell, muffled as it is by the thick wood.

"Oh my god," the voice groans, loud and unrestrained enough to be clear as day. And my blood turns to ice.

That was too loud to be an argument. In my not inconsiderable experience, that level of volume only comes from one thing. Pleasure. The kind of pleasure I know Nils can give. The kind of "oh my god" I myself have screamed for him before.

I turn on my heel and stride back toward the exit, my heels clicking angrily on the floor. But halfway there, I stop. No. I'm not running away. If it's what I think is happening, I deserve to look him in the eye when I kick his ass to the curb.

I march back to his office and raise my fist to bang on the door — but it flies open before I can. Emma pushes past me, her hair disheveled, her face flushed. She doesn't even acknowledge me, just continues down the hallway.

I look into the office to find Nils sitting behind his desk, perfectly composed. Too composed. He rises when he sees me.

"Alexsis. You're early."

He moves to kiss me, but I step back. "What just happened?"

A pause. A purse of his lips. As if he's thinking up an excuse.

"Emma and I were having a private conversation."

"A conversation?" I can hear the skepticism in my own voice.

"Mostly fighting, actually. She's still upset about ... past incidents." He shrugs nonchalantly. He's either a really good actor ... or he's telling the truth.

"It sounded like there was something sexual going on," I say with the accusatory tone the words deserve.

His brows furrow. "There wasn't. Emma was upset about division of duties and got rather vocal about it."

"Her hair was a mess."

"She runs her hands through it when she's agitated." He tilts his head. "Are you jealous?"

The question hits too close to home. Because yes, I realize with a sinking feeling, I am jealous. Irrationally, possessively jealous. But I can't admit that. Not when I'm the one who keeps pushing for openness, for sexual freedom. Though that's supposed to come with the other's approval, and, by his request, their presence as well. Still, even the idea that he might be fucking her — or anyone else — brought out the worst in me.

"Of course not," I lie. "I just don't like being lied to."

Something flashes in his eyes — hurt, maybe. "I'm not lying to you."

The tension between us is palpable as we leave for dinner at the nearby Lemon Grove. Its rooftop views are spectacular, the city spreading out below us as the sun sets, but I can barely appreciate it. I keep replaying the scene in my mind. Emma's flushed face. The closed, *locked* door. That groan.

"The salmon is excellent here," Nils says, clearly trying to break through my mood.

"Mmm." I pretend to study the menu, but the words blur together.

"Alexsis." His hand covers mine on the table. "Nothing happened with Emma. I hope you can believe that."

I look up at him, wanting to believe. His ice-blue eyes are earnest, concerned. Maybe I'm being paranoid. Maybe the stress of everything is making me see things that aren't there.

"Okay," I say finally. "I believe you." And maybe I do. I want to, I realize.

The relief on his face makes me relax just a fraction. But my chest still feels tight with anxiety.

We manage to get through dinner with lighter conversation, but the earlier tension still hums beneath the surface.

As we leave the restaurant, Nils asks, "Would you like to see a movie? I'm in the mood for something relaxing."

"Does an orgy sound relaxing?" The words are out before I can stop them.

He chuckles, but it sounds forced. "Not particularly. But it's not out of the question."

"There's one tonight at a different club — Chained. Brody won't be there."

He considers this. "I'll go on one condition — we go to a movie another night. There's an independent film at the Nuart I'd really like to see."

"Deal." I smile, hoping it'll reassure him. I'm beyond relieved that he agreed to go to the orgy with me. Because I need it right now.

The ride to Chained is quiet. I fidget with the hem of my dress, second-guessing everything. Maybe this is a bad idea. Maybe we should just go home, talk things through. But it's the only way I know to move past the uncertainty … and then we're pulling up to the club, and it's too late to change course.

The moment we walk into the orgy room, I realize I forgot to tell Nils that it's a BDSM club … though he might have already picked up on it from the name. If he didn't, the deep red walls adorned with various restraints and implements, and the clientele dressed in leather and latex just clued him in.

"Interesting," Nils murmurs, taking it all in.

A glance down at the bulge in his pants tells me he's into it.

I reach out and run my hand over the hard length. "Can I tie you up?" I ask with a raised brow.

He smirks. "Only if I can peel that sinfully tempting dress off of you first," he murmurs, teasing the hem with his fingers.

A shiver rolls through me, and I nod.

He grips the shimmering fabric, slowly sliding his hand up my inner thigh, using his thumb to brush my sex as he goes. Then grazing a nipple as he passes. Then using it to pin my arms over my head, my eyes covered, my mouth exposed. He uses it like a mask, gripping it behind my head so I can't move, pressing me into the wall behind us.

"We didn't talk about our boundaries," Nils murmurs against my lips. "But I'm at least going to need your safe word, love."

I bite into my lip as a surge of heat flows through me. "Sluta," I respond, having already looked up the word in anticipation of surprising him.

He chuckles, low and dark. "Learning Swedish, are we?" He audibly draws in a breath. "You're killing me, you know."

I grin, flicking my tongue in what I think is his direction.

"Let me resurrect you, then."

He groans and his mouth is on mine, hot and hard and demanding. And then in one swift motion he pulls back and finishes removing my dress, revealing his naked body, his hard cock standing at attention.

I raise an impressed eyebrow. "You're sneaky, I'll give you that." I grab his cock and use it to force him against the wall, then clip him into the restraints and step back.

I tap my finger against my chin, turning to survey the room.

I lock eyes with a blonde taking it up the ass from a large, muscled and masked man while another works the clamps on her nipples. She licks her lips at me and winks. I beckon with a finger in response. At her signal, both men stop, and all three approach.

I hear Nils buck against the wall. "What are you going to do, Tessa?" he taunts.

I look over my shoulder and wiggle my ass at him. "I'm going to make you watch," I reply lightly.

Mr. Muscles fists his cock and grins. I pull the blonde to me by her nipple clamps and kiss her, our tongues mingling as both men place themselves behind us.

I pull away. "Ah ah ah." I wiggle a finger. "Spankings first."

Both men eagerly snatch the nearest paddles, and Blondie and I tongue fuck as they start to spank us. After a few good hits, my pussy is dripping wet and Nils is groaning, his cock weeping. I break away and step up to him, lightly scratching up his cock. He hisses as I lean down, purposely displaying my wet pussy to the trio while my mouth hovers at Nils's cock.

I'm so focused that I don't even know who it is approaching, but a massive cock shoves into me from behind, pushing me forward onto Nils's erection. The head of his cock hits the back of my throat and Nils curses. I groan purposefully, the vibration driving him to thrust wildly. The cock inside me thrusts just as wildly as a hand smacks my ass hard. As I'm fucked into oblivion. As I take Nils's cock down my throat.

Someone attaches clamps to my nipples, and I cry out, Nils's cock spilling from my mouth when I do. He gasps in protest.

"Don't stop," he pleads, breathless.

I look up at him as mind numbing pleasure and pain rip through me. As Blondie lays beside me, working my nipple clamps while the guy who was working hers fucks her until her tits shake. Which must mean Mr. Muscles is fucking me.

Fucking me so good. So deep. So hard. I'm so close to coming.

But he's not as good as Nils, who continues to beg for release.

"Give me that mouth, Tessa," he pleads. "I want to come in that mouth."

"I want to come in that mouth *please, Mistress Tessa*," I correct.

He bucks against his restraints, trying to shove his cock back into my mouth. He must be so turned on he can't think straight. The realization makes me even wetter.

"On second thought, I don't think you deserve to come yet, brat," I tell him.

I pull off the cock that was inside me, turning my ass to Nils and rubbing up and down him, then sinking my soaked pussy onto his cock. I gesture for Mr. Muscles to come forward.

"Now, Mistress Tessa wants you both to fuck me until I come. And then you can come inside me like good boys," I direct sternly.

"Yes, Mistress Tessa," they say in unison. I arch in pleasure as Nils starts to fuck me like a wild animal from behind while I'm simultaneously fucked in the mouth. It's not long before they both blow their loads, hot cum filling me up from both ends. I thrash and writhe and come so hard while their hot seed spills into and out of my holes. They disobeyed me, but fuck if I care right now. This is my church. This is my religion. I have a purpose, a calling, to bring and receive pleasure. And I've only just begun.

I right myself, cum dripping down my chin and inner thigh as I release Nils. He pounces, driving me to the floor and fucking me hard and fast with his waning erection.

"You're going to pay for that," he growls in my ear. "I'm *your* master now."

He hauls back up and reaches for the restraints built into the floor around us, handcuffing me down spread eagle. He walks a circle around me, surveying me as he eyes a rack of hard-core-looking sex toys. Chains. Whips. And humongous dildos. He grabs one of those and sprays it down before wiping it off and mounting it in a strap-on harness above his actual cock. He gestures Blondie and the guy she'd been fucking to join us.

"I want you to sit on her face and let her eat you out," he directs Blondie. "And you —" he pulls the man toward him "— can fuck me while she watches."

My pussy clenches at his dirty commands. "I thought you were a top?"

He smirks at me. "Normally I am, but you wanted to see me with a man, didn't you?" I bite my lip and nod eagerly. "Yes, please, master," he commands.

"Yes, please, master," I parrot breathlessly.

"Good girl," he praises me, dropping to his knees between my legs. "As a reward, I'll fuck you with this until I can take you properly."

"While he fucks you?"

Nils grins as he hauls my legs up by the knees, raising my hips to his and spearing me with the dildo. It's so huge I gasp at the intrusion. Thankfully, he supports my hips so I can have a moment to get used to it. Or so I think, until the guy lays down behind Nils, his massive, erect cock waiting. Nils lowers down enough to spear the waiting cock, groaning as it slides into his ass. And then he positions me carefully so every time he works over the cock in his ass, he pumps in and out of me on the dildo.

It's like nothing I've ever experienced. My entire body feels like it's on fire with need as I watch Nils fuck us both. I'm a wet, whimpering mess, climbing to peaks I never even knew existed before … and then Blondie's dripping pussy is in my face.

I groan, and let her ride my face, licking and sucking as I'm fucked, listening to the sounds of two sets of balls slapping, feeling the massive dildo stimulate the deep nerves of my G-spot.

The hedonistic symphony of flesh and moans, not just from us but the entire room — slapping and spanking and fucking and screaming — I come apart at the seams over and over again. Blondie with me as she finds her pleasure on my tongue.

Then Nils pulls out and lowers my hips.

"Come on her," I hear him say. And then the dildo slides back in as the guy who was fucking him comes into view, his cock red, aching, and ready to spill.

"On my tits," I beg.

He leans forward, rips off the condom he was wearing, and lets Blondie suck him almost to completion before pulling out of her mouth and coming all over both of our tits. And as he does, Nils fucks me hard and fast. And I come, shattering, spent, and utterly sated in a way I've never been before.

Blondie leans down and kisses me languidly before she and her man toy wander off to find their next pleasure.

Nils lifts me in his arms, leaning us against the wall. He offers me a water bottle I have no idea how he got but I drink greedily, nonetheless.

I give Nils a sex-soaked smile and wrap my legs around his middle, sitting up in his lap.

"That was — without exaggeration — the most insane, intense sexual experience of my entire life," I admit.

He kisses me softly on the lips. "After all the orgies I've been part of, I didn't think anything could surprise me," he responds. "But honestly, it was for me, too."

The way he looks at me takes my breath away. And I hear the words he doesn't say. The ones that I'm thinking. It's because of him. I've never experienced this before because I wasn't with him. With someone who understands me. Who is on my level. Who wants to please me. Tease me. Fuck me. And care for me. I'm not a hole to be filled. I'm not a plaything to discard. Somehow, even with all of the uncertainty in my life, our lives, we've managed to form a bond of trust.

My insides clench … this time in fear. Even though this is what I've been looking for all my life, now that I've found it … well, I know I can't keep it. I know I'll be forced to choose.

And I'll choose wrong.

It's what I do.

I chose porn to pay for college instead of simply admitting that my part time job wasn't cutting it and getting loans.

I choose to lie to my parents over and over. Going to church every Sunday, pretending to share their faith. Dating the never-ending parade of good Mormon boys they tried to entice me into marrying.

I choose to use sex to cover up the serious emotional damage of my childhood.

I'm just about to share that particular revelation when a familiar voice behind me says, "I thought I might find you here."

Nils and I freeze at the same time. There's anger in his eyes. And I'm sure there's fear in mine.

I turn to find Brody grinning at us.

"I thought you said he wouldn't be here," Nils says in a tone low enough for only me to hear.

"I thought he wouldn't." I rise and face Brody. "What are you doing here?"

His grin turns feline, and he steps forward, giving my nipple a cheeky pinch. "I'm here for the orgy, of course. Why else would I be here?" He looks to Nils. "I saw you topping as a bottom. Nice."

Nils huffs, rising and disengaging the strap-on harness, letting it drop to the floor. His hand wraps around me from behind, splaying possessively over my stomach.

And something about the gesture rubs me the wrong way. Like he's staking out his territory. Like I'm his property. I step away. Toward Brody.

"Mm," Brody murmurs. "Down to play after all, Tessa?" He steps forward to meet me.

"Tessa," Nils says tightly from behind me.

Brody grins and leans in. "You gonna let lover boy tell you who to fuck?" He reaches down and strokes me exactly the way he knows will make me wet for him. I arch mindlessly toward him.

Nils physically puts himself between Brody and me, pushing Brody backward.

"Are you really going to fuck him? Stop and think," he says firmly, his eyes full of angry fire. "He's practically stalking you. He's clearly obsessed with you. Isn't it obvious?"

"Maybe," I allow, stroking a hand down his chest. "Is it wrong that I'm incredibly turned on by your jealousy, though?"

Nils's lips set in a thin line. "You think I'm jealous of him?"

I step forward. "If you're telling me who I can and cannot fuck ... then yes, I'd say that makes you jealous."

He clenches his jaw so tight I see the muscle flutter. "I'm not telling you who you can fuck. I'm simply telling you what I see."

I tilt my head, already knowing I'm going to push. And hating myself for it. "So if I fucked him in front of you. Let him fill me up with his cum while you watched ... that wouldn't make you jealous?" My hand wraps around his cock and tugs. Unbelievably, he hardens at my touch. I look up at him from under my eyelashes. "You like watching someone fuck me, don't you, baby?"

His nostrils flare. "I like it better when I'm calling the shots. When I'm the reason you're coming, even if it's on someone else's cock."

I suck in a sharp breath as desire shoots through me. Why do I need to feel like I'm doing something wrong to get that rush?

"Then tell me how to fuck him."

Nils steps forward. And while he's usually so calm, there's a tension in him now that makes me take a step back. "Stop this. Anyone but him." He gestures around. "There's a room full of cocks, including mine. But that's not enough for you. Do you truly have to get off on the one you know will hurt me the most? Is that what gets you off? Controlling me? Hurting me?"

His words hit too close to home. Because on some level … I know he's right. But at the same time, it feels like he's wrong.

"Aren't you the one controlling me here?" I snap back. "I don't have feelings for him. It's just sex. Can't you trust that? Like I trust that you weren't fucking Emma?"

Nils gives a sharp, cutting laugh. "You're not going to back down on this, I can see that. Fine. I guess it's not fair to ask you to, considering this was the deal from the start. You were perfectly up front about the fact that you want to be able to fuck who you want, when you want. You go fuck Brody and I'll —"

"Go fuck another woman to make me jealous, too?" I resist the urge to clap a hand over my mouth once the words are out.

Nils's expression falls, the fire banking only to be replaced with disappointment. A look I know well. "No, Alexsis," he says quietly. "I would never do that to you. And I thought this thing between us, whatever it is, meant enough to you …" He trails off, shaking his head. "Never mind. Fuck him if that's what you really want. But I won't be staying to watch."

He turns and collects his clothes.

Before I know it, he's walking away.

I watch, my heart shattering with each step he takes. I instinctually move to follow him, but Brody's hand lands on my shoulder.

"Let him go," he says softly. "He can't give you what you need. But I can."

I turn to look at him, this man who's been a constant in my chaotic life. Who never judges, never asks for more than I can give. Who doesn't make me feel like I'm too much or not enough. Even if it's only flesh deep, I've always taken what he has to give, knowing I don't deserve more.

That's why I push Nils away. That's why I tested him. Because I know I don't deserve him. But Brody? He's as messed up as I am. Because Nils can not only give me what I need, he can also give me what I want. What I know I don't deserve. And Nils … he deserves better than me. So maybe it's better if I do let him go.

"Okay," I whisper, even as emptiness spreads through my chest.

He leads me to the wall, and I let him restrain me, touch me, move me, fill me. But it's mechanical now. My body responds out of habit, but my mind is elsewhere. On Nils walking away. On the hurt in his eyes. On the realization that I sabotaged the best thing in my life because I'm too broken to let go of my fear long enough to accept real intimacy.

When it's over, I slide back into my dress and turn to Brody.

"Why did you come here tonight?" I ask quietly. Hoping with Nils gone, he'll give me a real answer this time.

"I heard you might be here," he admits, rolling his eyes to play off the implications of that.

His answer should make me feel something. But I'm numb.

"From who?" I ask, mostly out of curiosity.

He doesn't answer, and I'm too tired to push. Too tired to do anything but wonder why I'm like this. Why I can't just be normal. Why I push away everyone who tries to really care about me.

"I should go," I say finally.

"Come on, Tessa, stay. All you need is a good spanking and you'll be right as rain," he says with a wink.

"No thanks. See you around, Brody."

I shake my head sadly as I leave. Because what I really need is to go home and figure out why I'm so broken. And how to fix it. How to fix what I have — had? — with Nils. If it can even be fixed at all.

When I get home, I take a long, hot shower. I may have let Brody fuck me, but it's Nils that I still smell all over me. And it's leaving me choking on regret. As I soap myself off and return to my own smell of jasmine-scented body wash, I reflect on the day. A day that started so promising. Things have been better at work —

I gasp as it hits me. Too many thoughts at once. I shave my legs as I untangle them.

I went after that record label article because I reacted emotionally. Max and West were upset, and the unfairness of it all seemed too great to let slide. But eventually I realized Jason was right; I needed to check myself. To focus on reality, even if it was hard to admit that I can't take on every fight and win. I mastered myself, apologized, and accepted what I needed to do to make things right. To pursue my goals in a way that wasn't self-sabotaging.

Which means I can do that with my personal life, too. I think. Maybe ... because my personal life is an emotional mess. A puzzle I clearly don't feel like I deserve to solve. To have the life I choose. To have love. Maybe that's because it's been denied to me by the people who were supposed to give it freely; my parents.

Maybe that's why I've been looking for validation in all the ways they told me were sinful to find it. My own career. Pleasures of the flesh. Love outside of marriage.

I've pursued them all trying to fill the hole the absence of their love left. The problem with that? Turns out it's more like a black hole, sucking up everything I throw into it and using it to grow.

Maybe I need to stop trying to fill that hole. Maybe I need to deal with it instead.

I fall asleep that night, tears staining my pillow, with no plan but at least with a deeper understanding of how I got here. And the desire to break this pattern of ignoring my pain and keeping people at arm's length with all of my secrets and lies. At least I've stopped lying to myself. It's a good first step in the right direction.

19

———

NILS

The morning light filtering through my bedroom window feels like an accusation. I've been staring at the ceiling for hours, replaying last night on an endless loop. The orgy. Brody. Walking away from Alexsis.

Did she fuck him?

The thought sends another wave of nausea through me, adding to the cocktail of regret that's been churning in my stomach since I left that club. I shouldn't have agreed to go. I should have seen it coming when she was already on edge about Emma. I should have stayed and fought for her instead of walking away like a coward.

But watching her step toward him, seeing that self-destructive glint in her eyes ... I couldn't do it. I couldn't stand there and watch her use sex with Brody as another way to push me away.

Did she fuck him?

I throw off the covers and head for the shower, cranking it as hot as it'll go. Maybe if I scald myself enough, I can burn away the image of her arching toward his touch. The memory of her asking if I'd fuck another woman to make her jealous, as if I could ever —

No. I'm not doing this. I have three clubs to run and dwelling on what may or may not have happened after I left isn't going to change anything.

By seven a.m., I'm at Baltia, a full three hours before I need to be. The empty club feels appropriate somehow — all that space meant for pounding music, sweating bodies, and visceral connection, echoing with nothing but my footsteps. I head straight for the stockroom and start doing inventory. Counting bottles is mindless enough that I can almost pretend my chest doesn't feel like it's been hollowed out.

I move on to checking the sound equipment, then reviewing the bar setup, then organizing the office supplies. Anything to keep my hands busy and my mind occupied. It works, mostly. Except for when I find one of Alexsis's hair ties behind my desk. Or when I catch a whiff of jasmine from god knows where — probably a figment of my masochistic imagination. Or when I realize I'm checking my phone every five minutes even though she hasn't texted.

Did she fuck him?

"You look like shit."

I glance up from the spreadsheet I've been staring at without seeing to find Frankie settling into the chair across from my desk. Julian looms behind her, arms crossed over his massive chest.

"Thanks," I mutter, turning back to my computer. "What are you doing here so early?"

"Emma called. Said you two had another blow-up yesterday, so I came to talk." Frankie leans back, studying me. "But now I'm more curious about why you look like someone killed your dog."

"I don't have a dog."

"Nils."

I sigh and save the spreadsheet before meeting her eyes. "Emma and I did have a fight. She's upset that I ordered supplies for Allure along with the other clubs. Apparently, I should be leaving her club alone and letting her run it as she sees fit."

Julian snorts. "Her club?"

"That's what I said. Well, more or less. I told her she may manage it, but she's still under my supervision." I run a hand through my hair. "Still, I apologized for overstepping, but she just kept yelling. Something about me undermining her authority."

"And?" Frankie prompts, because of course she knows there's more.

"And she's smart. She's capable. She's proven she can do the job. She just needs to stop trying to assert her authority in these aggressive bids to prove herself. There's no need for it."

"Interesting perspective," a voice says to my right.

I turn to find Emma standing in my doorway, and my stomach drops. "How long have you been there?"

"The whole time," Frankie says cheerfully. "I asked her to wait outside and listen. Figured it would be more honest this way."

I shoot Frankie a look that she completely ignores as Emma enters the office, closing the door behind her.

"I'm sorry," Emma says, and I can see she means it. "You're right. I have been trying too hard to prove myself. I've been taking business classes, learning everything I can, trying so hard to act like the boss that I forgot that being bossy isn't the same as being a leader."

"Exactly," Julian says, surprising all of us. He's usually content to let Frankie handle the talking. "Look at Nils. He's the most laid-back dude I've ever seen, and he runs everything perfectly. Three clubs, and barely a hiccup. You don't have to be a hard-ass to be in charge."

I stare at Julian, genuinely shocked by the praise. He's not exactly free with compliments.

He shrugs. "What? It's true."

Emma turns back to me. "Would you be willing to give me another shot? I promise to dial back the attitude and actually listen when you're trying to help."

"Of course," I say, meaning it. "We all have learning curves."

She moves toward me, arms opening for a hug, and I hold up a hand. She freezes, hurt flashing across her face.

"Under normal circumstances, I'd be happy to hug it out," I explain quickly. "But Alexsis already thinks we were fucking yesterday when we were actually fighting. I don't want to do anything that could be misconstrued."

Understanding dawns in Emma's eyes. "Oh god, is that why she — I wondered why she looked ready to murder me when I passed her in the hall." She winces. "Do you want me to talk to her? Explain that nothing happened?"

The offer is tempting, but I shake my head. "I appreciate it, but I wouldn't ask you to get in the middle of this."

Emma nods. "Well, if you change your mind ... I know we haven't exactly been besties lately, but I don't want to cause problems for you two."

I give her a vague smile in response and after an awkward pause, Frankie gestures for her to leave.

After she's gone, Frankie and Julian exchange a look.

"You want to talk about what's really going on?" Frankie asks gently.

"Not particularly."

"Too bad." She leans forward. "Spill."

I debate refusing, but the weight of last night is crushing me. "Alexsis and I went to an orgy last night. Everything was fine until Brody showed up."

"Brody?" Julian asks.

"Some fuck boy she has history with. He's obsessed with her, and she ..." I trail off, not sure how to explain the dynamic. "She wanted to fuck him. I didn't want her to. So, I walked away."

Frankie's eyebrows climb. "You just left?"

"What was I supposed to do? Stand there and watch her self-destruct? Watch her fuck him just to prove she could?" The words come out harsher than intended. "She accused me of being controlling, of being jealous."

"Are you jealous?" Frankie asks.

I consider lying, but what's the point? "Of course I am. But it's more than that. She uses sex like a weapon — against herself more than anyone. And Brody ... he enables it. He shows up wherever she is, he pushes her buttons, and she lets him because it's easier than dealing with whatever she's actually feeling."

"So, you walked away," Julian says. It's not a judgment, just a statement.

"I walked away." The admission sits heavy in the room. "And now I can't stop wondering if she actually went through with it."

"Does it matter?" Frankie asks.

I look at her sharply. "Of course it matters."

"Why? If she did fuck him, it's because she's spiraling. If she didn't, she's still spiraling. Either way, the question is what you're going to do about it."

I slump back in my chair. "Nothing. There's nothing to do. She made her choice."

"Did she? Or did she just do what she probably always does when someone gets too close?" Frankie's voice is gentle but pointed. "Look, I don't know Alexsis that well, but I know self-sabotage when I see it ... or hear it. You know what I mean. Anyway. What I also know is *you*. You don't give up on people you care about."

"Maybe I should start."

Julian laughs, a short bark of sound. "Right. Because that's worked so well for you in the past."

I glare at him, but he's unmoved.

"Come on, man. You carried a torch for Frankie for how long? And when that didn't work out, you threw yourself even deeper into this job, pretending like it never happened. Now you've finally found someone who actually wants you back, who's into all the same kinky shit you are, and you're going to give up because she's got issues?"

"We all have issues," Frankie adds. "The question is whether she's worth fighting through them."

Is she?

I think about Alexsis laughing at the diner, her eyes bright with mischief. The way she looks at me when we're alone, like I'm something precious. How right it feels when she's in my arms, even when everything else is chaos.

"She's worth it," I admit quietly. "But I can't be the only one fighting."

Frankie reaches across the desk and squeezes my hand. "Then give her a chance to fight, too. But first, maybe give both of you some time to cool off."

After they leave, I try to go back to work, but the spreadsheet might as well be hieroglyphics. I close my laptop and lean back, staring at the ceiling.

Did she fuck him?

I realize Frankie is right; it might not matter. What matters is that we're both hurting, both stuck in patterns we can't seem to break. Her with her self-destruction, me with my walking away.

Maybe Frankie's right. Maybe we both need time to figure out if we're willing to fight for this.

I pull out my phone and stare at our message thread. The last text from her was about meeting at the club yesterday. Before everything went to hell.

I don't type anything. Not yet. But for the first time since walking out of that club, I let myself hope that this isn't the end.

20

ALEXSIS

I'm in the conference room, elbow-deep in research on the underground music scene in Koreatown when someone clears their throat above me. I look up, expecting Max to have returned with lunch, but find Emma standing there instead. My stomach immediately clenches.

"Can we talk?" she asks, and there's something in her expression that stops me from telling her to fuck off.

"I guess," I say warily, gesturing to Max's empty chair.

Emma sits, smoothing her hands over her shorts. Gone is the leather-clad manager who caught Nils and me in her office. This Emma looks ... normal. Human, even in a knee-length jean cutoffs with a black tank top.

"I wanted to clear something up," she starts. "About yesterday, with Nils."

My jaw tightens. "I don't really want to hear —"

"Nothing happened." She says it firmly, meeting my eyes. "We were fighting about work stuff. I was being a bitch about him ordering supplies for my club. That's it."

I study her face, looking for the lie. "His door was locked."

"I did that. I didn't want anyone to walk in on us so I could give him a piece of my mind, uninterrupted. I was pissed off and combative, and it was dumb." She laughs, but it's self-deprecating. "Anyway. I'm actually seeing someone. Have been for a couple of months now. I assure you I have absolutely no interest in Nils, nor he in me, and there was definitely not anything sexual going on in that office. Unless he gets off on being told he's an idiot by a former hairdresser who's attempting to be a club manager. Doing a bang-up job, too, aren't I?" She rolls her eyes, clearly at herself.

She's so real, it's hard not to believe her. The knot in my chest loosens slightly, but I'm not ready to let my guard down completely. "Why did you feel the need to come here and tell me all this?"

Emma leans back, considering. "Because I've known Nils for a while now. I was there when he was hung up on Frankie." My eyebrows shoot up, and she nods. "Yeah, I knew. I kept my mouth shut because it wasn't my business. But my point is, I've never seen him like this before. The way he is with you."

"Like what?" The words come out smaller than I intended.

"Serious. Real. Completely fucking gone for you." She tilts her head to the side and gives me a small, pitying smile.

Nils is gone for me? I find it hard to believe, but … then, why else would he keep sticking around? She's right. He must be. And I didn't even realize it.

The tears come before I can stop them. Because that just makes it worse. Nils is incredible — patient, understanding, sexy as hell — and I'm the disaster who accused him of lying, who pushed him away, who chose to hurt him rather than deal with my own shit.

"Hey," Emma says softly, pulling tissues from her purse. "It's okay."

"It's not okay," I manage between sobs. "I'm horrible. The way I've treated him …"

Emma scoots her chair closer. "You want to talk about it?"

And for some reason — maybe because she's practically a stranger, maybe because I'm at rock bottom — I tell her everything. About my family, about the double life, about Brody and the sex clubs and how I use it all to keep people at a distance. About how I pushed Nils away because I don't know how to let anyone really love me, because deep down I think I don't deserve it.

Emma listens without judgment, occasionally making sympathetic noises. When I finally run out of words and tears, she hands me another tissue.

"You want my advice on how to fix it?" she asks.

I laugh, but it's watery. "I'm a sobbing mess, at *work* no less. So yeah, I'll take whatever I can get to get off this ride."

"Talk to him. Be honest. Tell him what you just told me." She shrugs. "He's a reasonable guy, and he obviously cares about you. Sometimes the simplest solution is the right one."

"You make it sound so easy."

"It's simple, yes, but not easy. It's worth it, though, don't you think?"

I nod, wiping my eyes. "It is. You're right. Thank you. For this. For coming here. You didn't have to."

"Yeah, well." Emma stands, looking slightly embarrassed by the emotional moment. "Us fuck-ups have to stick together, right?"

I surprise us both by standing and hugging her. She's stiff for a moment before returning it.

"Good luck," she says as she pulls away. "And Alexsis? Don't wait too long. Guys like Nils ... they don't come around often."

After she leaves, I sit back down and stare at my computer screen without seeing it. My phone buzzes — a text from Max explaining our order took longer than she thought it would and that she's finally headed back. I unlock my phone to text her back when I notice the missed call notification.

My parents.

With trembling fingers, I listen to the voicemail.

"Alexsis, this is your father." His voice is cold, clipped. "We've been waiting for you to call and explain yourself for missing lunch and canceling on David. A young man from a good family, and you couldn't even give him the courtesy of meeting him. Your mother is beside herself. We expect you to call back immediately."

I delete the voicemail and set my phone aside. Like that will make it go away. I know it won't, but I can't deal with them right now. Not when I have something more important to fix first.

Before I can lose my nerve, I pick up my phone again and call Nils.

He answers on the third ring. "Alexsis." Just my name, but I can hear the caution in his voice.

"Hey. I know I'm probably the last person you want to hear from right now, but … can we talk?" I ask. "In person? Please?"

A pause. "Yes, of course we can. When and where?"

"Tonight? You could come to my place?"

He sighs. "Okay. I'll be there at eight."

"Nils?" I say before he can hang up. "Thank you."

"Don't thank me yet," he says softly. "We've got a lot of shit to work through." And then he's gone.

AT SEVEN FORTY-FIVE, I'M PACING MY LIVING ROOM LIKE A CAGED animal. I've changed outfits three times before settling on jeans and a simple white scoop-neck tee — this isn't about seduction. It's about honesty.

When the knock comes at exactly eight, my heart lodges in my throat. I open the door to find Nils standing there in dark designer jeans and a grey henley that hugs his lean, toned torso, hands shoved in his pockets. He looks tired and wary, but still so beautiful it makes my chest ache.

"Come in," I say, stepping back.

He follows me to the couch but doesn't sit until I do, leaving careful space between us.

"I'm sorry," I start, because that's the most important thing. "For last night. For pushing you. For accusing you of lying about Emma. For ... all of it."

He's quiet, watching me with those ice-blue eyes that see too much.

"I talked to Emma," I continue. "She came to see me at work. She told me nothing happened between you two."

"I told you that." He sounds more exhausted than chastising. I just hope I haven't exhausted his ability to forgive. God knows he's had to do a lot of that where I'm concerned.

"I know. I should have believed you. I just ..." I take a shaky breath. "I've been doing a lot of thinking. About why I am the way I am. Why I push people away. Why I sabotage anything good in my life."

"And?"

That one syllable gives me hope. And the courage to keep going. Because at least he's not shutting me down. He's hearing me out. So, I meet his eyes.

"I think I've been trying to fill this hole inside me. The one my parents created with their conditional love, their expectations, their making me feel like who I am is shameful. And I've been filling it with sex and secrets and anything that lets me feel in control. But it just makes the hole bigger."

Nils shifts slightly closer. "Go on."

"You scare me," I admit. "Because you see me. The real me. And you don't run away. You don't try to fix me or change me. You just ... accept me. And I don't know how to handle that because I've never had it before."

"Alexsis —"

"I'm not done." I need to get this out before I lose my nerve. "I want to change. Not for you, but for me. Because I'm tired of being two different people. I'm tired of pushing away anyone who tries to care about me. I'm tired of being afraid."

My voice cracks on the last word, and suddenly Nils is pulling me into his arms. I bury my face in his chest, breathing in his familiar scent.

"I care about you," I whisper. "So much it terrifies me."

He pulls back enough to look at me. "I care about you, too. I'm falling for you, Alexsis. Hard."

"Even after everything?" I ask doubtfully.

"Because of everything." He cups my face in his hands. "You have such fire, such strength. You've been fighting this battle alone for so long, but you don't have to do it by yourself anymore. I'm here. If you'll let me be."

"I don't know how to do this," I admit. "How to be in a real relationship. How to be vulnerable."

He huffs out a dry laugh. "I can't exactly say I'm great at it either. But we'll figure it out together."

Together. The word splits my heart open, in the best way. I kiss him then, soft and sweet, trying to pour all the things I can't say yet into the contact. When we break apart, I rest my forehead against his.

"Can we just ... be normal for a while?" I ask. "Date like regular people? No sex clubs, no games, just us?"

A smile tugs at his lips. "I'd like that."

So we order takeout and watch a movie, curled together on my couch like any normal couple. And I invite him to stay the night. I let him undress me, lay me down on the bed. And he takes me, missionary style. Something I'd previously considered boring, vanilla. But with Nils? It could never be either. He arouses parts of me, physically and emotionally, that no one ever has. Every touch, every moan, every thrust is so much *more* than it's ever been. And when we come apart together, it's with an intimacy that doesn't need kinky positions, restraints, or lubricated toys; just the connection between us.

THE NEXT TWO WEEKS ARE THE HAPPIEST I CAN REMEMBER. WE SEE THAT indie film at the Nuart that Nils wanted to watch — a moody Swedish drama that I pretend to understand but mostly just enjoy observing his face as he watches. We go to an art gallery opening in Silver Lake where Nils surprises me with his knowledge of contemporary photography. We pack a picnic for a concert at the Hollywood Bowl, lying on a blanket under the stars while the LA Philharmonic plays.

It's all the wholesome dating I used to have to fake with the Mormon boys my parents threw at me, but with the crucial difference that I actually want to be here. That when Nils settles behind me and wraps me in his arms during the concert, my whole body sighs with contentment. That when we go back to his place or mine afterward, the sex is mind-blowing because it's real, it's us, and it's not about pushing boundaries, proving anything, or hiding from my emotions.

I don't miss the sex clubs. I don't miss Brody. I don't miss any of it, because what I have with Nils is so much better. He makes me laugh. He challenges me intellectually. He supports my career ambitions and listens to my article ideas with genuine interest. And the sex ... god, the sex is better than ever because there's trust there now. Real trust.

I'm in the middle of transcribing an interview on a Tuesday afternoon when my phone rings. The display shows a number I don't recognize, but something makes me answer anyway.

"Alexsis? It's Frankie Greco."

I straighten in my chair. "Oh, hi. Is everything okay? Is Nils —"

"He's fine," she says quickly. "But I am calling about him. It's his birthday tomorrow."

"What?" I practically shriek, then lower my voice when Max looks over. "He didn't tell me."

"Of course he didn't. He never makes a big deal about it. Which is why I forgot, too, what with the kids and the pregnancy — oh shit, you didn't know about that either. It's kind of still supposed to be a secret." She sighs.

"Congratulations," I say, laughing. "I promise I won't say anything."

"Thanks. Anyway, I want to throw him a surprise party at the club tomorrow night. Think you can keep him busy until we're ready?"

"Absolutely."

"Great. I'll text you when we're set up. Probably around nine?"

"Sounds good."

After we hang up, I immediately text Nils asking if he can meet me for dinner tomorrow night near my work — far enough from Baltia to keep him well away from the preparations — to discuss something important. He agrees, though I can read his concern in his texts. I smile, knowing for once it's going to be a *good* surprise.

WEDNESDAY EVENING, I'M A BUNDLE OF NERVES AS NILS WALKS INTO THE restaurant. He looks gorgeous in slim-fit tailored black slacks and a light blue button-down. But there's worry in his eyes as he slides into the booth across from me.

We order — pasta for me, steak for him — and make small talk until the food arrives. Finally, he can't take it anymore.

"What's this important thing you wanted to discuss?" he asks carefully. "Is everything okay?"

I put on my best stern face. "Actually, I'm very upset with you."

He pales slightly. "What did I do?"

"It's what you didn't do. You didn't tell me it was your birthday."

His shoulders relax, and he actually laughs. "How did you find out?"

Time for my acting skills. "I saw your driver's license when you pulled it out at the liquor store the other day."

"Ah." He looks sheepish. "Well, I don't really like making a big deal about it." He shrugs.

"Would it be making too big a deal to get a special dessert to celebrate?" I ask, letting my stern expression soften. "And then maybe I can be your dessert later?"

His eyes darken. "I'm definitely okay with that."

We return to normal chatter over dinner, then share a ridiculous chocolate lava cake that's more chocolate than cake for dessert. I'm licking fudge off my spoon in a way that has Nils shifting in his seat when my phone buzzes. I pull it out subtly to see a text from Frankie.

All ready!

I type back that we're almost done, and thirty seconds later, Nils's phone rings.

"Frankie?" He frowns. "What's wrong?"

I can hear her panicked voice from across the table. Something about missing equipment. Nils sighs and hangs up, giving me a wary look.

"Frankie needs me to stop by Baltia for a few minutes. Some crisis with equipment. I don't know what she's freaking out over, because there's nothing going on tonight at any of the clubs. But she says jump ..." I nod in understanding. "Do you mind?"

"Of course not," I say, fighting a smile. "Let's go. The sooner we get it over with, the sooner you get second dessert." I wink at him, and if I'm not mistaken, he moves just a bit faster.

It doesn't take long to get there and the club is suspiciously dark when we arrive. I have to bite my lip to keep from grinning as Nils uses his key to let us in.

"Frankie?" he calls. "Where —"

The lights flick on, revealing a good sized crowd of people who yell a chorus of "SURPRISE!"

Nils freezes, genuinely shocked as Frankie steps forward with a huge grin, Julian and Emma flanking her. Behind them, I spot Max with West and the rest of Violent Mood Swings setting up on stage, and, of course, the whole other crowd of people, none of whom I recognize. I'm impressed that she got this many people to be quiet.

"Happy birthday, you Swedish bastard," Frankie says, pulling him into a hug.

Nils looks at me over her shoulder, and I shrug innocently. "You really thought I was going to let your birthday pass without celebrating?"

He extracts himself from Frankie and pulls me against his side. "You were in on this."

"Guilty," I admit with a sly smile.

"Unfortunately," Frankie interrupts, "the equipment emergency wasn't entirely fake. We really can't find the backup sound board, and the main one isn't working."

Nils sighs, but he's smiling. "I'm pretty sure I know where it is."

For the next hour, I get a front-row seat to Nils in his element. Turns out it wasn't where it was supposed to be, so he systematically searches the club, checks inventory logs and makes calls to the other clubs to see if it was misplaced. I trail after him, genuinely fascinated.

"How do you keep track of all this?" I ask as he cross-references serial numbers on his phone.

"Practice," he says, but he looks pleased by my interest. "Each piece of equipment has a code. Once you know the system ..."

He explains the coding system, and then, as we continue to search, he fills me in on other aspects of the job like tracking maintenance schedules, creating employee schedules, handling vendor relationships, and all the other million moving parts that keep a club running. I had no idea how much went into it beyond booking acts and serving drinks. I say as much to him, which the band hears. Wade even adds in that a good club manager knows all the up-and-coming bands, as well as the big ones, so their shows are always stacked with talent, adding that Nils is particularly good at that. I'm in awe. It's like club managers have to be an office manager, equipment manager, finance expert, music industry guru, and too many other roles to count.

And my man does this for a living.

He is so getting extra laid tonight. As if he wasn't already. It is his birthday, after all.

"Found it," Emma calls from the basement storage. "Someone put it behind the Halloween decorations."

"From last year?" Nils asks, incredulous. "When I find out who —"

"Hey, don't worry about it. Problem solved," Frankie says. "It's your birthday. Kick asses tomorrow, party now." She turns to Ace, the stage manager. "Let's get the band playing so the birthday boy can actually enjoy his party?" Ace nods and scurries off to do just that.

Minutes later, the band launches into their set, and I pull Nils onto the dance floor. It's different from the sweaty, sexual dancing at Los Jardines or Allure. This is pure joy, celebration, us moving together to music that feels like possibility.

"Thank you," he says during a slower song, pulling me close. "For this. For everything."

"This was all Frankie," I hedge.

He shakes his head. "I meant thank you for being here. With me. For being you."

I smile up at him, my heart brimming with happiness. "Thank you for being born," I reply, and he laughs.

"I love you," he says suddenly, and my heart stops.

I look up at him, seeing the truth of it in his eyes. And I want to say it back. I can feel the words on my tongue. But …

"I'm getting there," I say softly, honestly. "I can feel it happening. But I can't say it yet. I need to really know I feel it before I do."

He kisses me softly. "I wouldn't want you to say it for any other reason."

"Take me home?" I ask. "I want to give you your real present."

We make our excuses to Frankie, who waggles her eyebrows suggestively, and head back to his place. And if I can't say the words yet, I show him with my body, with my mouth, with every touch how much he means to me. I worship him the way he's worshipped me, taking my time, taking him apart piece by piece until he's gasping my name like a prayer.

After, lying tangled in his sheets, as I fall asleep in his arms, I think about how different this feels from before. There's no urgency to fill a void, no desperate need to prove something. Just us, just this, just the quiet certainty that we're building something real.

"Best birthday ever," he murmurs sleepily.

I smile against his skin. "Wait until you see what I do for thirty-six."

He laughs loudly, honestly, and there goes my heart brimming with joy again. And maybe something more.

21

ALEXSIS

I'm still riding the high from Nils's birthday party when inspiration strikes Thursday morning. I'm at my desk, transcribing notes from the Korean underground music scene piece, when my mind keeps drifting back to watching Nils work. The way he'd handled the equipment crisis. Hearing about the complexities of all the many other tasks he handles. Wade's comment about how good managers know all the up-and-coming bands. How Frankie had pulled together that party on such short notice.

Club managers. The unseen architects of the rock world.

My fingers fly across the keyboard as I outline the article. How managers like Nils don't just book bands and count inventory — they shape careers. They give unknowns their first real stage. They create the environments where established acts can experiment. They're tastemakers, gatekeepers, and nurturers all rolled into one.

I'm so absorbed that I don't notice Jason approaching until he clears his throat.

"You look intense," he observes. "What's got you so focused?"

I spin my laptop toward him. "Article idea. The invisible influence of rock club managers. How they shape the industry from behind the scenes."

Jason's eyebrows rise as he scans my outline. "This is good. Really good. You have sources?"

"I can get them." I'm already mentally cataloging who to interview — Nils, obviously, but I'll need to be careful about bias. Frankie. Maybe some managers from The Roxy, The Viper Room, The Troubadour.

"Write it," Jason says. "If it's as good as this outline, it's your first byline."

My heart stops. "Really?"

"Really. Don't make me regret it."

I spend the week in a journalism fugue state. I barely see Nils — who is thankfully understanding and supportive of my need to focus, and also helps where he can — and I manage to interview eight different club managers, two booking agents, and a handful of musicians who credit specific venues with launching their careers. I'm careful to incorporate Nils's input objectively, just one voice among many, even though his insights are the most thoughtful, probably because he's comfortable being unguarded with me. Perks of the relationship, and I'm grateful for his help.

"It's about curation," he tells me during our formal interview, professional despite the fact that we'd been naked in his bed an hour earlier. "Anyone can book a band. But knowing which band to book on which night, how to build a lineup that creates energy, how to spot talent before they break — that's the art of it."

The article comes together like magic. I weave in stories of managers who championed acts that labels initially rejected, who created themed nights that became cultural movements, who turned struggling venues into institutions. By the time I submit it to Jason at the end of the week, I know it's good.

He calls me into his office the next Monday.

"Congratulations," he says, sliding a mockup across his desk. "Your first byline. It'll be on the cover and everything."

And there it is, in bold swirling letters next to the issue's cover photo: "The Puppet Masters: How Rock's Club Managers Shape the Sound of a

Generation." And on the inside mockup, the credit reads "by Alexsis Monaghan."

Not Alex M. Alexsis Monaghan.

I may actually cry.

Not here though.

"Thank you," I manage. "Thank you so much."

"You earned it. This is exactly the kind of piece I wanted from you — insightful, well-researched, a fresh angle on the industry." He leans back. "Keep this up and we'll talk about that promotion sooner rather than later."

I float out of his office. My first real byline. My name on a piece I'm genuinely proud of. Max stops me on the way to my desk to congratulate me and offers to take me out to lunch. I happily accept and head back to my desk. I'm reaching for my phone to text Nils when it buzzes with a voicemail notification.

My parents. Again.

The elation drains out of me as I listen to the voicemail.

"Alexsis Marie." My father's voice is steel. "Your behavior is absolutely unacceptable. Three weeks of silence. Ignoring our calls. Your mother is beside herself."

There's a shuffle, then my mother's voice, thick with tears. "What did we do wrong, sweetheart? Why are you punishing us like this? All we've ever done is love you, provide for you, try to guide you. And this is how you repay us? No contact, no explanation, no respect for everything we've sacrificed?"

Then, my father again: "Enough is enough. You will call us back today, or we're coming to check on you ourselves. We need to know you're safe, at the very least."

The voicemail ends. I stare at my phone, my professional triumph already fading under the familiar weight of guilt and obligation.

But something's different this time. I just got my first byline. I'm building something real with Nils. I'm finally starting to like who I am.

I'm strong enough for this.

Before I can lose my nerve, I call them back.

"Finally," my father answers. No hello, no concern. Just judgment. It fuels my resolve.

"I'm fine," I say, proud of how steady my voice is. "I've just had a lot going on."

"Too much to return your parents' calls? To show basic courtesy?"

I take a breath. What I don't say: I'm sorry. Because I'm not. Not anymore.

"I needed some space to figure things out."

"Figure what out? We've paved the way for a bright future for you, young lady, and all you needed to do was trust us." His voice hardens. "Speaking of which, do you have any idea how embarrassed we were when David showed up for your date and you weren't there?"

"I told you I was canceling —"

"The morning of! After we'd already arranged everything. We assumed you'd come to your senses! That young man comes from a good family, Alexsis. He would be a perfect husband. But you can't even give him the courtesy of meeting him."

"I don't want a perfect husband chosen by you," I say quietly. "I want to choose my own partner."

Silence. Then he says, "What does that mean?" His tone is hard and cold.

I take a deep breath. "I'm seeing someone."

"Who?" my mother asks, her voice sharp with interest. "What's his name? What ward is he in? What does he do?"

"He makes me happy. That's all you need to know."

"All we need to know?" My father's voice rises. "Young lady, you do not get to —"

"I'm twenty-two years old," I interrupt. "I'm an adult. I get to decide what information I share and when."

The silence that follows is deafening.

"If you're seeing someone seriously enough to refuse dates with appropriate suitors," my mother finally says, "then the least you can do is bring him to Sunday lunch so we can meet him."

I close my eyes. I knew this was coming. "Fine. We'll be there Sunday."

"We'll see you at noon," my father says coldly, and hangs up.

I immediately text Aiden.

Can you meet today? Need to talk.

His response is instant.

Everything okay? Coffee in an hour?

AN HOUR LATER, I'M SITTING ACROSS FROM MY BROTHER AT A HIPSTER coffee shop in WeHo, far from anywhere our parents would venture.

"You look stressed," he observes, sliding a lavender latte toward me.

"I just got off the phone with Mom and Dad."

He winces. "How bad was it?"

"Pretty bad. They were doing the whole guilt trip thing about me not calling, not coming to lunch, not pretending I give a shit about dating every Mormon boy they throw at me." I take a sip of the latte, letting the familiar comfort wash over me. "I told them I'm seeing someone."

Aiden's eyebrows rise. "Seriously?"

"They insisted I bring him to lunch Sunday."

"Him being ...?"

I meet his eyes. "Nils."

A slow smile spreads across his face. "I knew it. I mean, I strongly suspected after that lunch, but —"

"It was still new then," I clarify.

"Ah. So how long have you been dating?"

"A little over a month?" I estimate. Time feels fluid when it comes to Nils. Like we've been together forever and also like it's still brand new.

"And you're happy?"

The question catches me off guard with its simplicity. "Yeah. Really happy. He's ..." I search for words. "He sees me, you know? The real me. And he doesn't run away."

Aiden reaches across the table and squeezes my hand. "Good. You deserve that."

"Thanks." I squeeze back. "But Sunday's going to be rough. Bringing him as my actual boyfriend? They're going to have questions. Expectations."

"You want me to run interference?"

I shake my head. "I appreciate it, but you have your own secrets to protect. I don't want to put you in the position of defending me and potentially outing yourself."

His face softens. "Lex—"

"No." I hold up a hand. "I mean it. I know how hard it is, keeping parts of yourself hidden from them. I'm not going to make it harder."

He's quiet for a moment. "Josh and I are talking about getting married."

"Aiden!" I reach for his hand again. "That's amazing. I'm so happy for you."

"Thanks. But it means ..." He trails off.

"It means you'll have to tell them eventually."

"Or never see them again." The pain in his voice is evident. Pain I know well. But Aiden is so much stronger than I am. He's always been the quiet but steady and determined one.

"Hey." I wait until he meets my eyes. "Whatever you decide, whenever you decide it, I've got your back. Just like you've got mine."

He smiles, but it's sad. "How did we end up here? Hiding who we are from the people who supposedly love us most?"

"Because their love comes with conditions," I say simply. "Ones we could never meet."

We sit with that truth for a moment.

"So," Aiden finally says, "you need to tell Nils he's meeting the parents. As your boyfriend this time."

I groan. "I know. He was so good about it last time, pretending we barely knew each other. This is going to be so much worse."

"Maybe not. At least you don't have to pretend."

"No, just hide the fact that I'm a rock journalist who used to do porn and frequents sex clubs." I laugh, but it's hollow. "You know, totally normal dinner conversation."

Aiden's brows jump. "I'm sorry, you used to do what and you frequent where?"

I cover my laugh so I don't spit lavender latte all over him. I didn't mean to confess so nonchalantly. "You heard me," I say after I've swallowed.

Aiden leans back in his chair. "Wow. I mean … I got the impression you went a little wild after you left home, but I didn't realize it went *that* far."

I scrunch my nose. "Are you disappointed in me?"

Aiden reaches out and takes my hand. "God, no, Lex, I could never be disappointed in you. We all have to experience life before we figure out who we really are." He pauses. "So you're not still doing …" he lowers his voice to a whisper "… porn, are you?"

I bite into my bottom lip to keep from busting out laughing. "No. That was a phase. But I'm not going to pretend I still don't have kinks." I wink at him.

Now it's his turn to wrinkle his nose. "Ew. Didn't really need to know that about my sister, but okay. You do you. And yeah. So you may have to do *some* pretending at lunch after all."

I sigh. "Yeah. I mean, it's not like *those* things will come up. Really, the problem is, I'm tired of it. I'm tired of being two different people. I just want to be me."

"I know the feeling." He glances at his phone. "And I hate to say I have to cut the conversation here. I really have to head back to work. But Lex? I'm proud of you. For standing up to them. For going after what you want."

"Thanks." I stand and hug him tight. "Love you."

"Love you, too. Good luck with Nils."

I wave as he heads out, staying to finish my coffee before heading back to work myself.

I know I should text Nils now so we can meet up, but I also know he's holding a special event at Baltia tonight. Some sort of charity concert. So, he'll be busy. And I don't want to distract him from something so important.

I sigh as I chuck my now-empty coffee cup into the recycling. I'm still lying to myself. Because I'm already anxious about telling him what went down with my parents. And whether he'll even want to go with me. I should've asked him *before* I agreed he'd go. But I know him. He will because I said he would, and he wouldn't want to make things harder for me with my parents. But I feel like it's a lot to ask, after everything he's already given.

I have to stop myself from thinking I don't deserve that kind of love.

But then I realize, I do. And I'm going to show the people who never gave it to me, who wanted to arrange a future where I'd likely never have it, that I don't just deserve that kind of love, I have it. How they respond will decide whether I allow them in my life going forward. But I finally realize I don't need them anymore. In fact, I may be better off without them, just like Nils once said.

I know it's true, deep down. I probably even knew it then, I just needed to come to the realization on my own. Even though it makes me feel sad and strong in equal measure. It reminds me of that song that wonders if devotion is a gift or a thief ... I'm learning it can be either. You just have to be careful who you're devoted to.

22

———————

NILS

The charity concert is in full swing when I spot Emma weaving through the crowd. She's dressed to kill in a black minidress and heels, her blond hair loose around her shoulders. But what catches my attention is the tall guy trailing behind her — also blond, lean in the musician sort of way, with tattoos snaking down both arms.

Something about him seems familiar, but I can't place it in the dim lighting and chaos of the packed club.

I watch them find space on the dance floor, Emma grinding against him with an enthusiasm that makes me raise an eyebrow. Well, good for her. Maybe getting laid regularly will help with her attitude at work.

I'm about to turn my attention back to the sound levels when Marco, one of my bartenders, appears at my elbow.

"Boss, we got a problem. Customer says we overcharged his card by like two hundred bucks."

I sigh. "Show me."

The next twenty minutes are spent sorting out what turns out to be a simple case of the customer misreading his own receipt — he'd bought rounds for his entire group and forgotten. By the time I've smoothed things over with a complimentary drink, Emma and her mystery man have vanished from the dance floor.

The rest of the night passes in the usual controlled chaos of a successful event. The bands are tight, the crowd is generous with their donations, and we raise a decent amount for the local music education charity. By the time we're closing down, I'm exhausted but satisfied.

I head to my office to grab my things, already thinking about crawling into bed with Alexsis. The door is closed, which is odd — I'm sure I left it open. I push it open without thinking.

"Oh, for fuck's sake," I exclaim at the sight that greets me.

Emma is bent over my desk, her dress hiked up around her waist, while the blond guy pounds into her from behind. They both freeze at my voice.

"Seriously?" I ask, more amused than annoyed.

Emma looks my way, and instead of the mortification I expect, she grins. "Now we're even," she pants.

The blond guy pulls out and turns, and I finally recognize him. Ward from Violent Mood Swings, his face flushed and his impressive cock still hard.

I lean against the doorframe and raise an eyebrow. "How exactly does this make us even? Didn't you know? I *like* to watch."

Emma's face goes bright red as she realizes her revenge plan has back-fired. She scrambles to pull her dress down. "I — that's not — dammit!"

Ward, meanwhile, bursts out laughing. "Want to join us, mate? I don't mind sharing."

"Ward!" Emma smacks his arm. "Absolutely not. No way. We're leaving. Right now."

She grabs her purse and storms past me, her face still flaming. Ward follows more leisurely, not bothering to look embarrassed as he tucks himself back into his jeans.

I can't help but laugh as she stalks down the hallway.

"Good to see you, man," Ward says, pausing beside me. "Though I didn't expect you to see quite so much of me."

"Likewise," I reply drily. "Though I have to admit, Emma's revenge attempt was creative."

Ward grins. "She seemed to think giving you a taste of your own medicine would embarrass you." He shrugs. "Guess she doesn't know you very well."

"Guess not. Tell her to consider us even now." I pause. "I didn't know you two were dating."

"It's pretty new," Ward admits. "We've been seeing each other for a month or two. But I really like her. She's a firecracker."

"That's one word for it," I mutter.

Ward laughs. "She said you two have been butting heads at work."

"Bit of an understatement." I consider my words carefully. "We made peace, but apparently she still felt like we needed a level playing field." Ward smirks. "Look, she's smart and capable. She just needs to relax a little. Stop trying so hard to prove herself. I've told her this over and over, but maybe she'll listen if you tell her."

"I'll see what I can do," Ward says with a wink. "And maybe if I fuck her over her own desk a few more times, that'll help her mellow out."

"One can hope," I reply. "Just ... maybe lock the door next time?"

"Where's the fun in that?" He claps me on the shoulder. "See you around, Nils."

After he leaves, I survey my violated desk and shake my head. At least they didn't knock anything over. I'll have to sanitize the hell out of it tomorrow, though.

I check my phone and find texts from Alexsis from about an hour ago.

Can you come by after work?

I know it'll be late but I really need to see you

I check the time — nearly three a.m. But her last text was only twenty minutes ago. I send her one of my own.

Just closing up. It'll be closer to 4 by the time I get there. That okay?

Her response is immediate.

Yes please. I'll be in bed.

That last line makes me close up a little faster.

The drive to her place is quiet, the streets mostly empty except for other night shift workers and the occasional drunk stumbling home. I use the key she gave me for just these kinds of nights to let myself in, finding her curled up in bed in one of my T-shirts she'd stolen.

"Hey," she says softly, lifting the comforter and patting the empty spot next to her.

I lean down and kiss her on the forehead. "As inviting as that offer is, trust me — you really want me to shower before I get in there," I remind her.

She smiles sleepily and nods. I head into her bathroom for a quick rinse off and I slide on a fresh pair of boxer briefs before heading back.

Her eyes are closed, so I get into bed as carefully as I can, but her eyes instantly pop back open.

I smile and pull her into my arms. "Everything okay?"

She takes a deep breath. "My parents called. Well, left another voice-mail. I called them back."

I tense slightly, rubbing my thumb over her back. "And?"

"And I told them I'm seeing someone — I didn't tell them who. They want me to bring him — you — to lunch on Sunday."

I pull back to look at her face. "As your boyfriend this time."

"Yes." She searches my eyes. "Is that ... are you okay with that?"

"Of course I am," I say immediately. "But are you sure you want to do this? Last time was hard enough, and we were just pretending to be acquaintances."

"I know." She fidgets with the waistband of my underwear. "But I'm tired of lying to them. Tired of being two different people."

I study her face, seeing the determination there beneath the nervousness. "There might be a way to avoid a complete fallout," I offer carefully.

Her brows furrow. "What do you mean?"

"I've been thinking a lot about this. I could convert. Become Mormon. Maybe then they'd accept us."

Her eyes go wide. "You'd do that? For me?"

"If it meant you could have both — me and your family — then yes," I reply without hesitation.

She's quiet for a long moment, and when she speaks, her voice is thick with emotion. "They'd see right through it. My dad especially. And even if they didn't, they still wouldn't approve. You're not from the lifestyle, you're twelve years older than me, we've already been seeing each other unchaperoned ..." She shakes her head. "But the fact that you'd even consider it ..." She cups my face in her hands. "You matter to me, Nils. You matter so much. And I've always told myself that someday, when I found something that really mattered, I'd be honest with them."

My heart pounds as she continues.

"I love you," she says tenderly, looking deep into my eyes. "I love you, and I don't want to lie to my parents about that. I want to tell them we're together, that I'm not going to marry a good Mormon boy, even if it means losing them."

I pull her against me, overwhelmed at her declaration. "You love me?"

She nods against my chest. "I realized that maybe you were right. That losing them wouldn't be such a bad thing. It would hurt, but I'd be free. Free to be myself, to live authentically, without keeping secrets or telling lies. Free to love you without hiding in shame."

"Alexsis." I tilt her chin up. "I'm so proud of you. And I love you, too. So much."

She kisses me then, soft and deep, and I taste tears on her lips. When we break apart, I brush them away with my thumbs.

"We'll face them together," I promise. "Whatever happens."

"Together," she agrees, closing her eyes. "You have no idea how much I want that."

"You know what I want right now?" I ask huskily, sliding my hand under her shirt.

She arches against me and mewls. "Tell me," she breathes. "Or better — show me."

So, I do. I slip my hand lower, only to find she's not wearing panties. I groan as my fingers find her pussy slick and ready for me.

I don't waste it.

I roll onto my back, pulling her onto my stomach while I shimmy off my underwear. Then I slide her back onto my cock, impaling her without preamble. She gasps, leaning forward with her hands on my pecs. She rocks her hips over mine, adjusting. And as soon as she does, she sits up, whisks off her top and brings my hands to her breasts.

I knead and work them as she moves over me, chasing her pleasure. I watch her, fascinated, as her beautiful lips purse while my cock moves inside her.

"God, I love you," I breathe.

She pinches her eyes closed, fucking me harder. I pull at her nipples, helping her peak.

"I love you," I repeat, testing a theory. She breathes harder, goes faster.

She gets off on my declaration.

Fuck. I thicken inside her, getting just as turned on as she is.

We repeat the cycle over and over. Until our bodies are working in tandem to climb higher and higher.

This feels different from all the times before. She loves me. She's choosing me, choosing us, even knowing what it might cost her. And it's bringing an intensity to sex that we've never had.

The next time, it's her who whispers, "I love you," as she comes apart on top of me, her walls clamping down on my cock, bringing me right alongside her.

"I love you," I reply, following her over the edge.

She collapses onto my chest, and I stroke her back. We lay there silently. Me, basking in hearing her confess her love. But by the slight tension that's still in her shoulders, I'm pretty sure that brain of hers is still thinking too much.

"What is it?" I ask.

She leans up, resting her chin on my sternum. "Just ... thank you. For being willing to convert. Even if it wouldn't work, the fact that you'd even be willing to try ..."

"I'd do anything for you," I tell her honestly. "But I'm glad you want to do this on your terms. To be yourself."

"It's taken me long enough to figure out who that is," she says wryly.

"You're worth the wait," I assure her.

She slides off of me, not even caring when our combined come slides down our thighs. "Even if Sunday is a complete disaster? Even if they disown me?"

"Even then." I brush her hair back from her face. "We'll build our own family. You, me, Aiden, when he's ready. The friends who accept us as we are."

Fresh tears well in her eyes. "How did I get so lucky?"

"I'm the lucky one," I correct her, disentangling to grab a washcloth.

I wet and warm it, cleaning her, then myself, before sliding back into bed. She snuggles close to me, and I can feel her heart beating against my side. She idly plays with my cock, and I smile, closing my hand over hers.

"Let's get some sleep. We have a few days to prepare for Sunday."

She settles back against me, humming sleepily, and I feel her body gradually relax into sleep. But I lie awake for a while longer, thinking about what's coming. Her parents won't take this well — I knew that even before she dismissed the conversion idea. But she's ready to face them, to stand up for herself and what she wants.

I press a kiss to her hair. Whatever happens Sunday, we'll handle it together.

And maybe, just maybe, she'll finally be free.

23

ALEXSIS

My hands are shaking as Nils and I walk up to my parents' front door. He squeezes my fingers gently, and I look up at him. He's dressed conservatively in dark brown slacks and a cream-colored button-down, but there's no hiding what he is — gorgeous, confident, and decidedly not Mormon. Even my own outfit — snug jeans and a long-sleeved red top — is too fitted to be "appropriate" by my parents' definition.

"You ready for this?" he asks softly.

"No," I admit. "But I'm doing it anyway." He grins and squeezes my hand.

And the door opens before we can knock. My mother stands there, her face lighting up when she sees us.

"Nils! What a lovely surprise." She turns to me. "Alexsis, dear, come in. When will your gentleman friend be arriving?"

I take a deep breath. Here we go.

"Mom, Nils is the man I've been seeing."

The smile freezes on her face. Behind her, I see my father rise from his recliner, his expression darkening. I can see Aiden and Asher setting the dining table beyond where my dad sits, and both look like they'd rather be anywhere else.

"I'm sorry, what?" Mom's voice has gone up an octave.

"Nils is my boyfriend," I say clearly, stepping inside with him.

The silence that follows is deafening. My father's face has gone from red to purple, while my mother looks like I've slapped her.

"This is a joke," Dad finally says, staring me down, daring me to contradict him.

"It's not a joke," Nils says calmly. "I care very much for your daughter."

Dad's eyes snap to him, and if looks could kill, Nils would be ash. "You don't speak unless spoken to in my house."

"Dad!" I protest, but Aiden catches my eye and subtly shakes his head. Pick your battles, his expression says.

"Now, Ammon, let's … well, let's at least just go ahead and have lunch. We'll all be thinking more clearly on a full stomach," my mother says tensely.

So, we move to the dining room in the world's most awkward processional. As we sit, Aiden leans close.

"I told Asher the basics so he wouldn't be blindsided," he whispers. "Hope that's okay."

"Of course," I whisper back, reaching out and squeezing his hand to show him that I'm thankful for the support. I also give Asher a grateful smile.

Mom serves lunch with mechanical precision. Unfortunately, her famous pork loin roast tastes like cardboard in my mouth. I don't know if it's nerves or an actual failure on her part to live up to her own standards, given that she's apparently been beyond distressed by my behavior for weeks.

For a few minutes, we eat in silence that's broken only by the clink of silverware.

"So," Mom finally ventures, her voice artificially bright, "how long have you two been ... dating?"

"About six weeks," I answer.

"And have you had a proper chaperone for your outings?" she follows up.

I almost laugh. "No, Mom. We're adults. We don't need a chaperone."

Dad's fork clatters to his plate. "I'm disappointed in you, Nils. Deeply disappointed. We welcomed you into our home. Treated you like a son. And this is how you repay us? By taking advantage of an impressionable young woman?"

"With all due respect, sir," Nils says evenly, "Alexsis is twenty-two years old. A grown woman capable of making her own choices."

"How dare you —"

"And while I did have reservations at first because of our age difference," Nils continues as if Dad hadn't spoken, "Alexsis is one of the most mature, intelligent, wonderful women I've ever met. And I love her."

Dad looks like he's about to have a stroke. Mom quickly places a hand on his arm.

"Alexsis, sweetheart," she says in that tone that means she's about to be condescending, "this can't possibly be a real relationship. He's far too old for you. He's taking advantage of your naivety. And he's not even Mormon, so where could this possibly go?"

This is it. The moment of truth.

"I don't consider myself Mormon either," I say quietly but firmly.

Aiden, Asher, and my mother all suck in sharp breaths.

"What?" my mother demands.

"I haven't lived within the faith since I left home. I only come to church to make you happy, but it's not what I believe. It's not the life I want," I explain.

"Then what life do you want?" Dad's voice is dangerously low.

"One where I make my own choices. Where I can be with who I want to be with. Where I can pursue the career I want."

"You have a career," Mom says. "At that magazine."

"That music magazine," Dad adds with disgust.

"It's a rock music magazine," I clarify. "I'm a journalist at *Rock Scene*."

Both of their faces go white, then red.

"Rock music?" Mom gasps. "You told us it was reputable! Rock is … is … it's the *devil's* music!"

I have to resist rolling my eyes. "It is reputable. It's small, but still one of the best in the industry."

"You lied to us," Dad growls.

"Of course I lied to you!" The words explode out of me. "Because I couldn't bear to hurt your feelings. Because I knew it might mean losing you. But this is who I am, and I don't want to lie anymore." I stand, my whole body shaking. "You either love me enough to accept me for who I am, or you never really loved me at all."

"How dare you question our love!" Dad roars, rising to his feet. "We've given you everything! A pleasant home, strong values, a path to righteousness! And you throw it all away for what? For a satanic career and fornication with a man old enough to —"

"Stop." Everyone turns to stare at Aiden, who's also standing now. "Just stop, Dad," he says quietly. "You want to talk about lies? About disappointment? Fine. I'm gay."

The word hangs in the air with the stink of Dad's worst fear coming true.

"I've known since I was eight years old," Aiden continues, his voice gaining strength. "I haven't lived within the faith since I was a teenager, either. And I'm engaged to a man named Josh who I love more than anything in this world."

Mom makes a sound like a wounded animal. Dad's face has gone beyond purple to something approaching black.

"No son of mine —" Dad starts.

"Then I guess I'm not your son," Aiden cuts in simply.

"If you're disowning Aiden, then you should disown me, too," Asher suddenly announces. Everyone turns to him. "Katie and I have been living together for years. In sin, as you'd call it. And she's pregnant."

I gasp, then immediately cross to hug him. "Asher! Congratulations!"

He hugs me back, tears in his eyes. I turn and hug Aiden as well, all three of us standing together while our parents look on in horror.

"This is ... this can all be fixed," Mom says desperately. "We'll get counseling at church. Prayer. The bishop can —"

"Katie's Jewish," Asher interrupts. "She has no intention of converting. And neither do I, because I don't believe anymore either. I haven't for a long time."

"Then you're also no son of mine," Dad spits.

I laugh. I can't help it. The absurdity of it all just hits me.

"Seriously? That's all it takes? Asher living with his pregnant Jewish fiancée gets him disowned, but me dating Nils isn't enough?" I shake my head. "Well, let me make it easier for you. I also did porn to pay for college."

Mom stands abruptly. "Stop it. You're just saying that to scandalize us."

"Am I? How did you think I afforded a private university on a part-time internship? It's not like you could have helped, not with all your money going to the church."

"You ... you're a nymphomaniac! An abomination!" Dad sputters.

"The term is hypersexual," I correct him. "But that's not accurate either, in my case, anyway. My sexuality doesn't control my life. I'm perfectly productive. I just happen to enjoy kinky sex with strangers."

"Alexsis!" Mom shrieks.

"What? You wanted honesty, right? Fine. Here's some more honesty for you. I'm done hiding. I'm done pretending to be the perfect Mormon daughter you want me to be. And clearly, you're never going to accept that your children don't fit the obedient little mold your religion demands."

I move back to Nils, who rises and takes my hand.

"So here's the deal," I continue. "If you ever figure out what's really important in this world — your actual children, not the imaginary ones you wish you had — I'll be willing to accept your apology. For making me feel unloved and imperfect my whole life. For making all of us hide who we really are. But until then? You can fuck right off."

The profanity in their sacred dining room is the final straw. Mom sinks into her chair while Dad stands there, mouth opening and closing like a fish.

"We're leaving," I announce. Nils squeezes my hand in solidarity.

"Right behind you," Aiden says.

Asher hesitates for a second, looking at our parents. Then he shakes his head and follows us out without a word.

The moment we're outside, the adrenaline crashes, and I start laughing and crying at the same time. My brothers pull me into a group hug, and I feel Nils's hand on my back.

"Holy shit," Asher breathes. "We actually did it."

"Thank you," I manage through my tears. "Thank you both for standing with me."

"Are you kidding?" Aiden asks. "Thank *you*. I've wanted to do that for years."

"That was ..." Asher shakes his head. "Long overdue. All of it."

We stand there in our parents' driveway, outcasts who've finally found the courage to be ourselves.

"I have to go home and tell Josh about this, but we should meet up soon," Aiden says. "All of us. With Josh and Katie, too."

"Absolutely," I agree. "And if Mom and Dad come around ..."

"We'll deal with that if it happens," Asher says. "Though I doubt it will." We all nod in agreement, then exchange one more round of hugs, heading to our separate cars.

As Nils steps aside to say his goodbyes to Aiden, I look back at the house where I grew up. Where I learned to hide. Where I learned to lie.

Nils comes back to me, placing a hand on my back. "Are you okay?" he asks softly.

I turn to him, this man who loves me enough to face my parents, to offer to convert for me, to stand by me as I burned that bridge to ashes.

"Yeah," I say, and realize I mean it. "I am. I'm finally free."

He lifts our joined hands and kisses my knuckles. "Yes, you are."

As we drive away, I don't look back. There's nothing there for me anymore. My real family — the one that loves me as I am — is right here beside me.

And for the first time in my life, that's enough.

24

NILS

As Alexsis heads to the car, Aiden catches my arm.

"Hey, can I talk to you for a second?" he asks, looking nervous.

I glance at Alexsis, who nods. "Of course," I respond, following him a few paces away from his sister.

He shifts uncomfortably, then meets my eyes with determination. "I wanted to say … you should tell her everything. About us. I don't want to be another secret waiting to detonate."

My eyebrows rise. "Aiden —"

"I mean it," he interrupts. "You two are perfect for each other. And I don't want there to be anything hidden between you because of me. She deserves to know. She deserves a relationship where *no one* has to hide."

I study his face, seeing the sincerity there. "You're sure? It's not like we've discussed other past lovers."

"I'm sure. Because this is different, and I think you know it. Just ... maybe leave out the graphic details?" He manages a wry smile. "I don't need my sister knowing everything about my sex life from when I was seventeen."

I huff a laugh. "Fair enough. And you're right. I wouldn't want her to somehow learn about it another way. Thank you. For this. And for standing up in there. That took real courage."

"I think we all found our courage today." He glances back at the house. "Better late than never, right?"

We shake hands, then embrace briefly.

"Take care of her," he says as we part.

"Always," I promise.

In the car, Alexsis is practically vibrating with a mixture of emotions — relief, sadness, anger, and something that looks like joy.

"I can't believe we did that," she says as I pull away from the curb. "I can't believe they all stood with me. God, poor Aiden. And Asher! And oh my god, they're having a baby!" She puts her hands to her cheeks and shakes her head, clearly overwhelmed.

"Your brothers love you," I point out. "Of course they stood with you."

"I know, but still." She lets out a long, slow breath. "I feel like I should feel worse about this. About losing my parents. But mostly I just feel... free."

"You are free," I confirm. "Free to be yourself. All of yourself."

She's quiet for a moment. "Speaking of which, there's something I need to tell you."

My hands tighten on the wheel, remembering Aiden's words. "Actually, there's something I need to tell you first."

"Oh?" She turns in her seat to face me.

"About Aiden and me." I take a breath. "When I was living with your family, we ... we had a brief thing. Nothing serious, just two confused teenagers figuring things out. But I thought you should know."

There's a beat of silence, then Alexsis bursts out laughing.

"Are you serious right now?" she manages between giggles.

I glance at her, confused by her reaction. "Yes?"

"That's fucking awesome!" She's practically cackling now. "You've been part of the sexual awakening of two Monaghans. We should get you a plaque or a medal or something."

"I'm not sure that's the reaction I expected," I admit, a smile tugging at my lips.

"What, did you think I'd be upset? Jealous?" She shakes her head. "Nils, that's hilarious and kind of perfect. No wonder Aiden was so supportive from the start."

Relief washes through me. "He told me to tell you. He didn't want any secrets between us. And neither do I."

"You're both good men." She reaches over and takes my hand. "No secrets. Which brings me to what I wanted to say."

I squeeze her fingers. "I'm listening."

"I've been thinking a lot about us. About what we have." She pauses, seeming to gather her thoughts. "My whole adult life, I've been two people. Alexsis Monaghan, the good girl pretending for her parents. And Tessa Temptation, the sexual being who takes what she wants."

"And now?"

"Now I've found someone who accepts both. Who sees all of me and doesn't disown me." She turns our joined hands over, studying them. "I'd like to try something I've never been open to before."

My pulse quickens. "What's that?"

"Monogamy." The word hangs in the air between us. "True commitment. Setting aside sex with anyone else. Just us."

I pull over to the side of the road, needing to focus on this conversation fully. "Alexsis ..."

"I know what I said when this started," she rushes on. "About not being capable of it. But that was before I knew what it felt like to be truly seen. Truly loved."

I turn to face her fully. "I need you to understand something. I never needed you to change for me. I just wanted you to admit your feelings. To acknowledge that what we have is special enough to commit to."

"I know," she says softly. "And it is. God, it really is."

"And commitment doesn't mean we can't involve others sometimes," I continue carefully. "It just means it looks different. It's us together, choosing together. Not you seeking something I'm not giving you."

Her eyes brighten. "You mean like at the club? When we played together?"

"Exactly like that. If and when we both want it."

She unbuckles her seatbelt and slides across to straddle my lap, the steering wheel digging into her back. "I love you," she says, cupping my face. "I love you so much it scares me sometimes."

"I love you, too," I reply, pulling her down for a kiss. "And I promise, we'll figure this out together. What works for us. What we both need."

She kisses me deeply, and I lose myself in the taste of her, the feel of her. When we finally break apart, we're both breathing hard.

"Take me home," she whispers. "I want to celebrate our freedom. Our future. Us."

I help her back to her seat, my body already responding to the promise in her voice. The drive to my apartment is charged with anticipation.

The moment we're inside, she's on me, pushing me against the door and attacking the buttons of my shirt.

"Where are the rest of your sex toys?" she says against my throat. "I know the vibrators we've used can't be everything you've got."

I groan. "Bedroom closet. Top shelf."

She pulls back with a wicked grin. "Race you there."

She bolts toward the bedroom. I chuckle and head to the kitchen, grabbing a couple of glasses of water before leisurely joining her. I find her riffling through the bin, eyes wide, biting that luscious bottom lip of hers. She looks up as I set the glasses down on the nightstand.

"You've been holding out on me. This is quite the collection," she comments.

I raise a brow. "I didn't want to spring it on you all at once. I take it that means you approve?" I tease.

She grins. "Naturally." She holds up a set of silk restraint ties, complete with matching blindfold. "And I know exactly what I want you to do to me."

"You want me to blindfold you and tie you up?" I ask, my cock hardening even saying the words.

She nods slowly, setting the rest of the bin on the floor and tossing the silk bundle my way. And then she strips. Slowly. Tantalizingly. And crawls across the bed toward me, naked, her nipples hard, her pupils dilated. Needless to say, it makes me rock hard for her.

I lift the silk blindfold and run it down her chest, over her nipple.

"Are you sure about this?" I ask. "This will give me total control over you. I can touch you any way I want. Do whatever I want. I could keep you from coming for hours while I torture you."

"I trust you," she says, undoing the last few buttons of my shirt.

I wrap my hand around hers, and take both of her hands, guiding her to lay down on the bed.

"Close your eyes."

She complies and I kiss each eyelid before blindfolding her. And then I tie each wrist and ankle to the four corners of the bed frame. I step back, and suck in a sharp breath at the sight of her, spread out on my bed, her sex already glistening with her arousal. Her lips are parted, she's panting, and her hard nipples are peaked on her perfect breasts.

I grab a long feather from the bin and trace it slowly up her body, from toe … to knee … over her sex and all the way up to her chin. She arches beautifully as it tickles her face.

"You are a work of art," I tell her, placing a light kiss on her lips.

She squirms, clearly ready for more, and I chuckle, reaching down to pinch a nipple.

"Patience, my love," I say softly in her ear. "Don't worry. I'll give you what you need."

I return the feather to my stash in favor of a bullet vibrator. I turn it on, and she whimpers at the gentle humming noise. I likewise run it up her body, skipping her pussy this time, and running it around her nipples each in turn before settling it on her bottom lip. She licks it, but I only allow it for a moment before quickly dropping it to her clit, working it in gentle but firm circles.

"Yes," she hisses. And I remove it. She whimpers. And I touch it back to her sex.

I let it stimulate her until she's making the noises I know mean she's going to come … and I pull it away. She makes a deeper noise of frustration, and I chuckle.

I answer by undressing, making sure to audibly lower my zipper. That gets a sharp intake of breath from her. Once I'm naked, I loosen the ties on her ankles enough to put her knees up, then tighten them again.

I run a fingertip over the path the feather and vibrator had taken. One single digit. Goosebumps break out over her skin along the path that I touch.

"So sensitive," I murmur. When I get to her face, I climb on the bed, leaning in so my hard cock grazes her lips. "Suck it, Alexsis. Show me what a good girl you are, and I'll reward you."

Without hesitation, she takes me into her mouth, her tongue swirling around the head before she takes me to the back of her throat. I groan involuntarily at the wet warmth of her mouth, my balls tightening at the sudden shift.

"Brace yourself, älskling." I give her a mere moment before I move, fucking her mouth, holding nothing back.

She drools and gags but keeps bobbing on my cock in time with my thrusts. I get within a hair's edge of coming in her beautiful mouth before I pull back. I lean in, letting out my desire with my mouth on hers, tongue fucking her where my cock had just been doing the same. She returns in kind with the same desperation I feel to be inside her.

But not yet.

Instead, I drop between her legs, using only my tongue to lightly trace her nether lips. She gasps and stills, allowing me to slowly slip between her folds. To trace her entrance. To flick her clit. And again, with more pressure. Her hips buck. I add a finger, sliding it slowly into her dripping pussy before flexing it lightly as I flick her clit with my tongue. I keep going, slowly adding pressure and speed on both ends. Until I unleash, fucking her hard and fast from both directions and she comes instantly, gushing onto my waiting tongue.

"Fuck," she groans as I wring the last of her orgasm out of her with my finger. "I need more, Nils. I need your cock inside me."

"I need that, too," I promise as I untie her restraints. And then I give myself to her. I seat myself at her entrance and push in, smoothly and completely as her arms and legs wrap around me. I let go, slamming my cock into her over and over, tasting her with my tongue, feeling her with my hands over her skin.

We move together with an intensity we never have before. With a deep trust and newfound joy. It's freedom and connection and love all wrapped up in sweat-slicked skin and breathless moans.

I feel myself getting close, but I don't want it to end. So, holding her tightly to me, I roll and put her on top. She pushes up her blindfold and looks down at me with such love in her eyes that it makes my chest and cock ache at once. She watches me as she swirls her hips over me. At least, until the pleasure is too much. Then she leans forward, chasing her high. I pump into her from beneath, feeling her walls flutter.

"Give it to me, Alexsis," I beg. "Give me all of you. All of that pussy. I need it." She whimpers and twists her hips faster while I pound into her harder. "That's it, älskling. That's my good girl. Get yourself off on my cock."

She gasps — at my words, at the insane pleasure, or both — and her brows pinch together, her lips parting. So I go faster, knowing how close she is.

"Fuck, I'm going to come inside you," I grunt.

And that tips her over the edge. She comes with me, tightening around my emptying cock, wringing every last drop from me as she shatters, crying out.

Finally, exhausted and sated, we collapse together on the thoroughly destroyed bed.

"Holy fuck," Alexsis pants. "Why were we going to sex clubs when we could do this?"

I chuckle, letting her slide down and pulling her against my side. "You say that like we can't have both." I pause. "Don't you miss it? The club, I mean?"

She's quiet for a moment. "Sometimes," she admits. "But I don't want to complicate things. I'm happy with how we are right now." She pinches my nipple playfully. "Very happy."

"Me, too," I say, trailing my fingers down her spine. "But if I'm honest, *I* miss it sometimes."

She props herself up on an elbow. "You do?"

"The energy. The freedom. The way you look when you're in that space. I still dream about the way we fucked at Chained."

Alexsis arches against me. "That was ... something," she admits breathlessly.

I smirk down at her. "I did have an idea."

"Oh?" Her eyes light with interest

I roll toward her, kissing her lightly. "But I need to do some research before I share it."

She narrows her eyes. "Are you keeping secrets?"

I grin. "I promise it's one you'll like. And is it a secret if you know it's a secret?"

Her brows pull together. "That's ... I don't know," she admits. We both laugh. "Anyway, I trust you. Just ... don't wait too long to tell me or I might have to seduce it out of you."

I nip at her lips. "Still playing dirty, I see."

"Only the good kind of dirty now," she replies with a genuine smile. "No more secrets that make me live two lives. No more lies."

"No more hiding," I agree. "No more pretending. Just us, being exactly who we are."

She kisses me softly. "I love you," she says against my lips. "And I love that we can talk about this. Figure things out together."

As she settles back against me, I think about how far we've come. From that first meeting at Baltia to here, in my bed, planning a future neither of us could have imagined. It hasn't been easy, but the best things rarely are.

"What are you thinking about?" she asks sleepily.

"You," I answer honestly. "Us. How lucky I am."

"We both are," she corrects. "We found each other. Despite everything trying to keep us apart, even if it was me sometimes. We found our way to each other."

I press a kiss to her hair. "It wasn't just you. But yes, what matters is where we are now. And now that I have you, I'm never letting go."

She looks up sleepily. "I think I'd be okay with that," she replies with a self-satisfied smile.

I laugh and kiss her forehead. "Sleep, love."

She mumbles an incoherent response as she drifts off to sleep.

I lie awake a bit longer, planning. My secret project … our next adventure. Our future. A life where we can be exactly who we are, together.

No more secrets. No more lies. Just love, acceptance, and the freedom to be ourselves.

It's more than I ever dared hope for. And it's just the beginning.

EPILOGUE
ALEXSIS

Six months later

Six months. That's all it took to go from Nils's "I have an idea" to standing in the entrance of Temptation, our very own sex club.

The space is perfect — intimate but not cramped, luxurious but not intimidating. Deep purple walls, soft lighting, and rooms designed for every possible desire. The main play room has plush seating areas mixed with more adventurous equipment. There's a couples-only room, a voyeur room with one-way glass, and more, including my personal favorite — the girls-only room where I'll be spending most of tonight as Mistress Temptation.

"You ready for this?" Nils asks, adjusting his black button-down. He looks good enough to eat, and I make a mental note to do exactly that later.

"More than ready," I assure him, smoothing down my latex dress. It's deep red, hugging every curve, with strategic cutouts that leave little to the imagination. I deserved a killer outfit for my debut as a dominatrix.

"I still can't believe Frankie and Julian are some of our test subjects," I say, watching them enter through the VIP entrance. I tried to get Max to agree to it, too, but it was a little too risqué for her tastes. Her loss.

And Frankie looks like she was born for this. She's stunning in a black corset and leather pants, while Julian... well, Julian looks like he'd burn the place down if anyone other than his wife so much as breathed in his direction.

"They wanted to christen the toy room," Nils says with a shrug. "Who was I to deny our business partner?"

I laugh. "Just make sure they don't break anything expensive. Their Sunday fuck has gone next level since Frankie was cleared for sex after Bianca was born."

Nils grins at the reminder of our arrangement to use their erotic soundtrack to fuel our own simultaneous rendezvous. Our little secret.

He shrugs. "That's what insurance is for." He pulls me close for a quick kiss. "Now go. Your subjects await, Mistress."

The next few hours blur together in the best possible way. The girls-only room fills quickly with women eager to explore without male interference or pressure. As Mistress Temptation, I guide, encourage, and occasionally participate. It's empowering in a way I never expected — helping other women embrace their desires, their bodies, their pleasure.

By the time I surface to check on the rest of the club, I'm amazed to find we're at capacity.

"We had to close the doors after an hour," Nils tells me, looking slightly shell-shocked. "Most people are staying all night. I've had to turn away dozens more."

"On our first night?"

"Apparently there was more demand for this than we realized." He glances around at the full rooms, the satisfied faces, the couples reconnecting over shared experiences. "We did good, älskling."

Before I can respond, I realize I'm due back in the girls room, so I give him a quick kiss and make a mental note for later.

After closing time, when the last couple has reluctantly left and the cleaning crew has worked their magic, Nils leads me to his office.

"I believe we have some celebrating to do," he says, unlocking the door.

I step inside and laugh. "You weren't kidding about saving the best toys for yourself."

The office is professional enough — desk, chairs, the usual — but one wall is dedicated to the most impressive collection of high-end toys I've ever seen. And that's saying something.

"These were some of the premium samples the toy company sent over. Only the best for us," he says with a grin, already unbuttoning his shirt.

What follows is a thorough testing of several items from his wall of wonders. By the time we collapse on the wide leather couch he had the foresight to include, we're both thoroughly satisfied and slightly dazed.

"That was a perfect opening night," Nils murmurs, tracing lazy patterns on my bare hip.

"Mmm," I agree, remembering what I keep forgetting to mention. "It probably helped that my feature on the club got millions of views."

He props himself up on an elbow. "What?"

"The article I wrote for my magazine? About Temptation opening?" I grin at his stunned expression. "You didn't know?"

"Why didn't you tell me?"

"I keep getting distracted. We have been a little busy," I point out. "Between the final inspections, staff training, and making sure we had enough supplies ..."

"Millions of views?" He shakes his head in amazement. "No wonder we were slammed. Thank you."

"Thank my readers. Turns out there's a real hunger for shame-free discussions of female sexuality."

My online magazine, launched three months ago with backing from some very progressive investors, has exceeded every expectation. We cover everything from sex toy reviews to ethical porn recommendations, some of which are even available on the site, to honest discussions about desire and pleasure.

"I keep meaning to check out the videos section," Nils admits. "I'm curious what porn catered to women actually looks like."

I laugh. "I know what most people think, and no, it's not all videos of men vacuuming and doing dishes. Though, now that I think about it, that would be hot, too."

Nils chuckles. "Duly noted. So what is it?"

"Focus on female pleasure. Real pleasure, not performance. Multiple camera angles that actually show what's happening to her, not just close-ups of penetration. Actual foreplay. Men who know where the clitoris is." I trace a finger down his chest. "All orientations, too — straight, lesbian, threesomes, orgies. Whatever women want to watch."

His eyes darken. "Speaking of which, I've got some female-focused porn I'd like to film right now."

I raise an eyebrow. "Are you suggesting we make a sex tape?"

"I was joking. I just wanted to go down on you again." He pauses, considering. "But I wouldn't be totally opposed to that ..."

The idea sends a thrill through me. We've done so much together, pushed so many boundaries, but never this.

"Set up your phone," I tell him.

His eyes widen. "Really?"

"Really. But if it ends up online anywhere, I'll kill you."

"It's just for us," he promises, already reaching for his phone. "Our own private collection."

He props it on the desk, checking the angle, and I can't help but laugh at how serious he looks.

"Come here," I beckon. "Let's give us something good to watch later."

He joins me on the couch, and as his lips meet mine, I think about how far we've come. From secrets and lies to complete honesty. From hiding who we are to building a business, and a life, around it. From pushing each other away to being unable to imagine life apart.

"I love you," I whisper against his lips.

"I love you, too," he replies. "Ready?"

I glance at the phone, recording our next adventure, and smile. With Nils, I'm ready for anything. And thankfully, I already know my best angles.

"Always."

BONUS EPILOGUE
FRANKIE

Ten years later

The hostess at Katsuya doesn't even blink when I tell her we need a table for seven … without a reservation. Perks of being a regular, I suppose. Though "regular" is relative when you're juggling three kids who are in various stages of going through puberty and traveling the world with your husband after a well-earned two decades of working your ass off.

"Of course, Ms. Greco, right this way," she says, leading us to the private room in back.

Julian's hand finds the small of my back as we follow, and I lean into him slightly. Even after all these years, that simple touch still sends warmth through me.

"Kinda crazy we're even able to all get together tonight," he murmurs.

"It is. Though VIP tickets and backstage passes are hard to pass up."

We've only just sat down when we're joined by Nils and Alexsis. She's glowing in a way that has nothing to do with the low lighting, and when she hugs me, I catch him watching her with such naked adoration it makes my chest tight.

"You look incredible," I tell her. And she does — confident and settled in her skin in a way that took years to achieve after all the damage I know her family did to her sense of self.

"Says the woman who doesn't look a day over thirty," she returns.

Lie, the voice whispers. I suppress a smile because at least it's the good kind of lie. Generous and well-meaning.

"How's the new Copenhagen location?" I ask Nils as we settle into our seats.

"Thriving. Though I'm glad to be back home for a while." He squeezes Alexsis's hand. "Someone needs to film her content, after all."

Alexsis laughs, completely unbothered by the reference to her Only-Fans work. God, I love how comfortable they've become with themselves.

Max and West arrive next, apologizing for being late. Traffic from the label's office, apparently. West looks good — healthy in a way that still makes me grateful, even all these years after his recovery.

"Editor in chief," I say to Max, pulling her into a hug. "How does it feel?"

"Like I'm drowning in responsibility," she admits with a laugh. "But in the best way."

No lie there. Just honest satisfaction with the life she's built.

Emma practically sprints through the door ten minutes later, looking fantastic in red leather pants and a sparkly black halter. Bearing three children have somehow made her large chest and round ass even more luscious. Wish I could say the same.

"Sorry, sorry!" She collapses into a chair. "The twins' babysitter was late, and then Jackson decided he absolutely could not go to bed without his special dinosaur, which was naturally at the bottom of the toy chest —"

"Breathe," I interrupt, laughing. "You made it. That's what matters."

She does breathe, then immediately launches into, "Please tell me you're drinking tonight because if I have to be the only one, I'll feel like an alcoholic."

"When have I ever not had a drink?" I tease.

We order — probably too much food, but that's tradition at this point. As plates arrive and conversations flow, I find myself watching them all. My people. My chosen family, who I just don't get to see enough of these days.

"How are the clubs?" Max asks, gesturing between Julian and me with her chopsticks.

"Good. Really good." I glance at Emma. "Thanks to this one holding down the fort."

Emma preens. "Six locations and counting. Though I still say we should expand to Vegas."

"Over my dead body," Julian mutters, making everyone laugh.

"How's the label?" I ask West. "Ward's success must be bringing you tons of attention."

He nods, setting down his sake. "It's been crazy. Everyone wants us to rep them now that they see we actually treat our artists fairly. We're trying to focus on helping independent artists first, though. The ones who need it most."

"I'm so proud of you," Max says, and the love in her voice is so pure it makes me ache.

"Proud of you too," he returns. "Editor in chief is no joke."

She waves him off. "Please. I'm not nearly as successful as Alexsis with her whole empire."

"It's not an empire," Alexsis protests. "Just lucky timing with the sexual wellness boom."

Lie, whispers my voice. She worked her ass off for that success. But I'm cool with false modesty. She's got enough to brag about without taking that kind of bait.

"Actually," Alexsis continues, "I'm thinking of selling the site."

That gets everyone's attention.

"What?" Emma gapes. "Why?"

"To focus on my OnlyFans. It's more fun, more creative freedom." She grins. "Plus, Nils is getting really good with the camera."

"I'm getting good at many things," Nils says with such a straight face that it takes a moment before we all burst out laughing.

"God, you're all so lucky," Emma groans. "You can have careers and fuck whenever you want. Do you know the last time Ward and I had sex? Three weeks ago! Three weeks! Between the tour and the kids..."

"We offer VIP in-home childcare services now," Nils mentions casually. "For couples who want a night to themselves at the club."

Emma's jaw drops. "Are you serious?"

"Completely."

"Oh my god, we're absolutely taking you up on that. Once the tour's over. I'll tell him after the concert tonight that he'd better clear his calendar." She sighs. "I hope we can because fuck, getting away just for tonight was hard enough."

Julian and I laugh with her, knowing that pain, even though West, Max, Nils, and Alexsis sit there looking uncomfortably clueless with their child-free selves. Which just makes Emma and me laugh harder.

The conversation flows naturally after that — updates on businesses, gossip about people we know, shared memories that have us all cracking up. This is what I've missed during all our travels. Not the places or the adventures, amazing as they've been, but this. My people, together.

After dinner, we head to Staples Center for Ward's band's concert. Nightmare in My Jammies — ridiculous name, but they're actually brilliant. And I guess once you've already hit major rock star status with another band, nobody gives a shit what you name your next band.

In the VIP section, I watch Emma transform from harried mom to rock goddess, screaming along to every song.

"They're killing it! " West shouts over the music.

I nod, watching Ward command the stage. But then, he's always had presence. I can see what Emma sees in him, for sure, though tall, dark and brooding is definitely more my type. I look up at Julian doing exactly that, looking like a statue in the flashing stage lights. It makes me cackle to myself, causing him to look down with a smirk. I nuzzle up to him and kiss him. He slings an arm over my shoulder and we continue watching the show like that.

Backstage afterward is chaos in the best way. Emma immediately attacks Ward, and I politely look away from what's definitely going to leave marks.

"How are the kids?" West asks, approaching where I'm standing with Julian.

The question surprises me — West isn't usually one for kid talk. "They're good. Why?"

He shrugs. "Just wondering. They must be, what, twelve now?"

"Thirteen, twelve, and ten." I study him. "That's sweet of you to ask."

"Yeah, well." He looks uncomfortable, and my curiousity piques.

In all these years, Max and West never had kids. And I never asked why. Not something I usually would ask but we've all grown pretty close over the years.

"Can I ask you something?" I say quietly. He nods even though he gives me a wary look. "Why didn't you and Max ever have children?"

His discomfort deepens, and I immediately want to take it back. God, Frankie, read the room.

"I'm sorry," I rush to add. "That's none of my business —"

"No, it's okay." He glances at Max, who's deep in conversation with Alexsis about something that has them both gesturing wildly. "I guess with my childhood, what happened with my dad ... I was never sure I could be the dad type."

The honesty in his voice makes my chest tight. No whisper from my inner voice — he's telling the truth. The reminder of everything he went through, then had to go through again publicly ... god, I feel like a Grade A asshole for even broaching a subject I should've remembered was difficult for him.

"But we have a great life," he continues. "And Max is lukewarm on the kid thing too. It just ... never happened. But I couldn't be happier."

Still no whisper. He means every word.

I pull him into a hug, surprising us both. "I'm happy for you. For both of you."

When I return to Julian's side, he's talking to Ward and Emma about the tour. I open my mouth to ask where they're heading next when Ward cuts me off.

"You better not be about to ask when I'm making an honest woman out of Emma again."

Heat floods my cheeks. "I wasn't —"

"Yes, you were," Emma laughs. "You ask literally every time we see you."

"I was going to ask about the tour schedule!"

"Sure you were." But Emma's smiling as she says it. "Frankie, I love you, but I'm never getting married again. The one divorce was enough for a lifetime."

Ward nods. "Plus, marriage is so not rock and roll," he adds.

I snort. "Says the man whose band name contains the word 'jammies,'" I mutter, elbowing Ward playfully in the ribs.

Ward gives me joking stink eye and I blow him a kiss.

"After watching my parents' marriage, I was turned off the whole institution from a young age," Alexsis adds. "It doesn't always bring out the best in people." She glances around. "No offense to present company."

"None taken," I assure her. "We all know how important it is to choose for ourselves."

"There's no right or wrong choice," Max agrees.

I look at Emma, my best friend who has built an amazing life on her own terms. "Other people's choices are theirs. Even well-meaning loved ones can put undue pressure where it's not needed. I'm sorry if I'm one of those people sometimes. I just love you so fucking much, babe."

Emma's eyes soften. "Thanks, Frankie."

"I'm proud of all of you," I continue, meaning every word. "For following your hearts and doing what's right for each of you."

I don't know who starts it, but we end up in a group hug, me in the middle being squished to oblivion.

Julian pushes through to me, extracting me from the crushing bodies. "All right, all right, give my woman some space," he says loudly.

"Thanks, baby." I turn to everyone else. "Besides, we haven't had nearly enough alcohol to be this mushy yet."

Ward raises a plastic cup. "Then let's booze up this after party!" he hoots. The rest of the band hoots back as he goes to join them and their crowd of friends and fans.

We blend with the rest of the groupies, staying another few hours, drinking and reminiscing, before finally calling it a night.

In the car, instead of starting the engine, Julian leans in close.

"Good night?"

"The best." I trace patterns on his arm. "I'm proud of them. All of them."

"Me too." His hand slides under my shirt, resting just under my breasts. "Proud of us too."

"Yeah?" I grin up at him. "Because I'm pretty sure you just want to fuck in the car."

"You know me too well, baby."

And because we're us, and because some things never change no matter how many years pass, we do exactly that. In the back of our car, like teenagers who can't wait to get home. It's a celebration of being alive and in love and exactly where we're meant to be.

As Julian's hands map familiar territory, I think about my unconventional family. All of us choosing our own paths, defining love and success on our own terms. My gift tells me when people lie but tonight reminded me of a deeper truth — sometimes the most honest thing you can do is live exactly as you choose.

And I couldn't be fucking happier that we are all living and loving the lives we chose ... authentically ever after.

⟲

Thank you so much for reading! Please take a minute to leave a review on any retailer, goodreads, and/or BookBub. Even if it's just a couple of sentences, your opinion is important to potential readers and to me.
Thank you!

⟲

Want more? Check out *Last Kiss Under the Mistletoe: A Fated Love Psychic Suspense Romance* at:
https://melanieasmithauthor.com/books-last-kiss-under-the-mistletoe.html

⟲

Sign up for Melanie A. Smith's newsletter to get a FREE book plus all the latest news and more
https://melanieasmithauthor.com/newsletter.html

ACKNOWLEDGMENTS

Everybody Lies

First, always, a huge thank you to my husband for his support on every possible level. After being married nearly a decade, I know he didn't originally sign on for this, and I'll be nominating him for sainthood soon with his unending patience and bringing of the sugar and caffeine that fuel my marathon writing sessions. Not to mention distracting our mini-me, which is no small task.

Next, to the amazing and talented Jenny Gardner, editor, friend, and all-around woman extraordinaire. I love going through this journey with you, and you've been not only one of the best sources of support but also taught me so much through this process. Here's to almost twenty-one years of amazing friendship, may we have at least that many more!

A huge thanks to my fabulous beta readers, who are also both amazing authors — Lindsey Powell and Katie J. Douglas. Check out their books, y'all, you won't be disappointed!

Also, I don't know if I've ever included this in my acknowledgements before, but I must mention that I wouldn't be anywhere without the saving grace of God. Being a fairly private person, I'm not exactly vocal about my faith, but through writing this I've oddly felt His presence calming me through my less confident moments. Proof that you can write smut and still love Jesus. Just sayin'.

And, as always, a huge thank you to everyone who buys, reads, and/or reviews my books. It's my biggest goal and pleasure to share my stories with those who will enjoy them, and your support means the world to me!

Finding His Redemption

First thanks go to my gallbladder, for giving out and requiring removal. The scheduled surgery lit a fire under my butt to get this book done.

Seriously, though, it forced me to face this book, which I struggled with because it contains some themes that were tough for me personally (as I am sure they are for many). When I was a child, I had a stepfather who was a cocaine addict. It was, perhaps needless to say, extremely tough on our family. So there aren't enough thank yous to my mother for not only making sure we survived, but for being an example of bravery, grit, and setting difficult boundaries.

To my husband, thank you for endlessly discussing plots of books you have no desire to read and generally being ridiculously encouraging and supportive in the face of my frequent whining and exhaustion. Marriage is the best, y'all.

To my alpha reader, Erin, who is just one of the most wonderful human beings on the planet. I'm so thankful she chases after my introverted butt to make sure I know I'm cared for, supported, and appreciated. I appreciate you!

To Jenny, who isn't just my editor, she's a friend I miss dearly and will always wish I lived closer to but still somehow manages to make me feel like there's no distance between us whenever we talk. Love you, babe!

To the book community on social media, whether it be Instagram or Facebook or TikTok, I'm constantly amazed by the authors and readers who are all about support, kindness, and sharing.

To my readers, who finish the stories I start. Thank you. I hope you enjoyed this one.

Secrets, Lies, and Temptation

To my husband and son, for letting me disappear so often into fiction, and tolerating my stream-of-consciousness babble about characters and plots and all things writerly. I'm a verbal processor, and I am so grateful they put up with me.

To Erin. Where do I even begin? Friend, encourager, support, beta reader, fellow author, and amazing human being, I'm so damn grateful to have you in my life.

To Anne. Please don't arrest me for the level of smut in this book. XD Seriously, though, I couldn't do any of this without your support, advice, and shoulder to lean on. I appreciate you so much!

In writing this, I realize my acknowledgments have gotten shorter over the years as my community does. A mix of my personality, life, and the evolution of the author/book community have tightened my circle to those few who I know I can trust. The flip side is, it's made the support of readers like you even more important to me. And that, I think, is as it should be, because it's you, dear reader, that matters most. So I hope you enjoyed this super steamy departure from my more recent work. I simply went where the characters took me, and I appreciate you coming along on the journey.

L.A. Rock Scene Complete Series

This was a series I never expected to make, but readers (and my own) love for Frankie and Julian was real. So I had to find a way to keep checking in with them. I hope you enjoyed seeing them grow in the background of *Finding His Redemption*, and *Secrets, Lies, and Temptation*. I sure did. And while the series varies in subgenres and spice levels, I'm honestly so proud of all three of these sories. If you've come this far, thank you, from the bottom of my heart, for going on this journey with me.

All my love,

Melanie x

ABOUT THE AUTHOR

Melanie A. Smith is an award-winning, international best-selling author of steamy romance with smart, self-sufficient heroines and strong, swoony book boyfriends with hearts of gold. A former engineer turned stay-at-home mom and author, when Melanie is not lost in the world of books you'll find her spending time with her husband and son, crafting, or cross-stitching.

Connect with Melanie on:

MelanieASmithAuthor.com

BOOKS BY MELANIE A. SMITH

The Safeguarded Heart Series

The Safeguarded Heart

All of Me

Never Forget

Her Dirty Secret

Recipes from the Heart: A Companion to the Safeguarded Heart Series

The Safeguarded Heart Complete Series: All Five Books and Exclusive Bonus Material

Life Lessons

Never Date a Doctor

Bad Boys Don't Make Good Boyfriends

You Can't Buy Love

The Heart of Rutherford: The Complete Life Lessons Series

Alpine Ridge

Tough Love

Recklessly in Love

Unscripted Love

Elusive Love

TRUE Love: The Alpine Ridge Complete Series

L.A. Rock Scene

Everybody Lies

Finding His Redemption

Secrets, Lies, and Temptation

L.A. Rock Scene Complete Series

Stand-alones

Last Kiss Under the Mistletoe

Vegas Baby

Short Stories

Cruising for Love

Hot for Santa